The Scroll And The Sword

Book 2

Of The Warrior Series

By

Sandra J Yearman

1

Seraphim Publishing LLC

We Will Bring Light To All The Dark Places

Registered trademark-Sandra J Yearman

Seraphim Publishing
438 Water St
Cambridge, WI 53523
sandrajyearman@gmail.com

Produced in the United States of America

The Scroll And The Sword is a work of fiction. Names, characters, places and incidents are the product of the author's imagination or used fictitiously. Any resemblance to actual persons, living or dead, events or locale is entirely coincidental.

Library of Congress Catalog Number: 2014913973

ISBN: 978-0-9890263-0-7

First Edition

About The Author

Sandra J Yearman is a native of Wisconsin, where she currently resides. She graduated from the University of Wisconsin with a Bachelor of Arts degree in Journalism. Sandra was a member of the United States Army Reserves for over twenty years. She retired from the Dane County Sheriff's Office in Madison Wisconsin as a sergeant.

Sandra is a cancer survivor. And it is on this journey that she says she found her voice and began to write. She established Seraphim Publishing LLC in 2008. Sandra has spent decades supporting and working with rescued domestic animals.

Books written by Sandra:

Novels

Brother Kings
The Scroll And The Sword
Song Of The Second Son
The Faces Of The Damned
A Single Lion Roars
Stand Before The Children
Tyrants, Dictators And Kings

<u>Poetry</u>

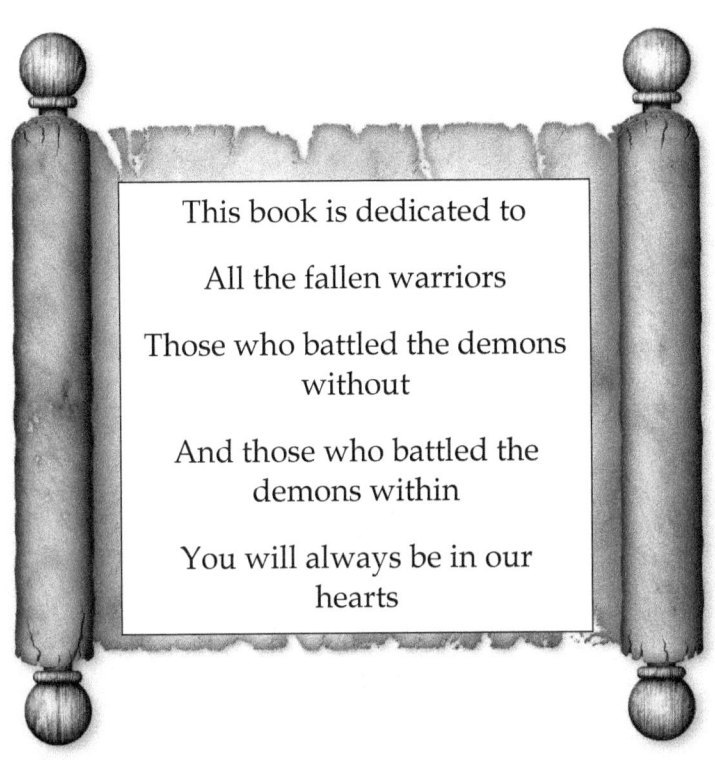

This book is dedicated to

All the fallen warriors

Those who battled the demons without

And those who battled the demons within

You will always be in our hearts

Contents

Contents

Contents

Chapter I
Ego of Darkness

Demetries screamed before the great fire as hundreds of naked Huta warriors danced in a large circle and paid homage to the demon in their midst. "Destroy the Sanuri," Demetries screamed into the darkness. "For the curse he has brought upon me and My Lord Sporos." At the mention of Sporos name, all of the warriors started to scream and wave their arms wildly.

"Lords of darkness," wailed the demon Demetries as he danced before the fire. "Help me to free my brother Sporos from his prison in The Abyss." The warriors danced faster and faster until they were completely taken over by the hatred and the rage of Demetries. The Huta warriors picked up their weapons and ran from the cave in a blind frenzy. Demetries smiled as he watched the warriors leave, knowing he had just unleashed a plague of destruction upon the Kingdom of Stordt.

"The Sanuri said he would return for the christenings," Queen Renya said to Laurel as they made preparations for the royal event.

It had been one year and one month since the Sanuri's last visit to the Royal Family of Wetpr. The time had passed quickly for all. Eight and one half months after the weddings, Raul and Vitomas gave birth to the first royal grandchild; a son they fittingly named Sudfad after the King.

Three weeks later Simon and Annabelle gave birth to twin boys. One was named Alexander after Annabelle's father and the second baby was named Anthony; which was the middle name of King Sudfad. It was a time of great joy for the entire family, especially Queen Renya who realized her prayers had been answered.

Petra, the heroic orphan boy who King Sudfad and Queen Renya adopted had adjusted well to his new loving family. The terror of his past no longer disturbed his dreams. Petra was receiving an education befitting a young prince and although he excelled at many lessons, especially swordsmanship; he had one gift that could only have been bestowed upon him by the Sanuri.

Petra, like the Sanuri, could communicate with many species of creatures.

King Sudfad spent long hours with his sons Raul and Simon preparing them for their new responsibilities as Keepers of The Holy Scrolls. The Princes were continually amazed as they learned of the many times their parents had fought to protect the holy objects; all the while keeping the secret and the dangers from the rest of the household.

Prince Matthew had returned to his home in the Kingdom of Lentz to aid his father King Mathas; who had been seriously injured in an attack orchestrated with black magics. Although Mathas and Matthew could not prove who sent the demons upon the King they strongly suspected Juleta, Matthew's older sister who had been banished from the kingdom and renounced as an heir to the throne.

As Juleta's hatred and anger grew, so did her powers as a dark lord. With all of the concerns that King Mathas had to face; little did he realize that his own beloved daughter would become the most severe threat to his family and to his kingdom.

Prince Matthew assumed the responsibilities of trying to maintain the fragile peace between the two largest tribes in the Kingdom of Lentz. Matthew was unaware that his own sister Juleta had already implemented plans to destroy the treaties.

The tribe of Valdore held lands in the northern most tip of the Kingdom of Lentz and was led by a sinister warlord named Usman. Under Usman's dictatorial reign, the Valdore Tribe isolated itself from all other peoples. Usman's long held hatred of the Royal Family as well as of Chief Sorren, who was the leader of the Nordes Tribe, made Usman a danger not to be ignored.

The Nordes Tribe controlled the lands that lay just north of the lands owned by the Royal Family of Lentz to the southern border of Snakes Crossing; which was a parcel of neutral ground which separated the two large tribes. The Nordes Tribe was led by a fierce chief named Sorren. Although a great warrior in battle, Sorren's age was tempering his ambitions. His thoughts now focused more on building a safe and prosperous home for his people than conquering other lands and overthrowing the government.

These two tribes had enjoyed a tempered peace for many years. But of late, factors far beyond the knowledge of either Usman or Sorren were igniting the long held hatreds between these two peoples. Factors that were influenced by pure darkness itself.

The Sanuri stopped his boca near the River Saz in the Kingdom of Gandt. He had visited the monastery at Myrea also in the Kingdom of Gandt for several weeks and now he was headed to the castle of King Sudfad for the christening of the King's grandchildren.

The Sanuri planned to follow the River Saz north until it intersected with the River Nebu in the Kingdom of Stordt. Then he would follow the River Nebu through the Kingdom of Stordt and into the Kingdom of Wetpr. This river would take the Sanuri to the City of Salar, home to Sudfad's family. The River Nebu would also take the Sanuri very close to the castle of King Roch, the notorious dictator and butcher of the Kingdom of Stordt.

The priests at the monastery at Myrea had been overrun with victims of Rogett attacks. These murderous creatures usually sought places of darkness and were well known for attacking miners and cave dwellers; but of late Rogetts were becoming more aggressive and attacking small villages in the light of day. This type of behavior was unheard of for the Rogetts; monsters who had so lost their humanity that their gnarled and deformed features belied their true species.

Mercy was not in the vocabulary of the Rogetts; their attacks were savage and brutal. They were cannibals who ate the people they killed. But driven by hunger the Rogetts would eat anything, even their own kind. The attacks of late, were not limited to one or two kingdoms but were being reported throughout the Continent of Opots.

The Sanuri went to Myrea to help the victims and to try and determine the reasons for the increased aggressiveness of the Rogetts and the change in their behavior. The Rogetts were not considered warriors by any culture because they never had the courage to fight one on one but attacked in packs and their victims were often defenseless.

The Rogetts were despised in every kingdom. They were a mutant race; once humans, they took to living in the bowels of the earth as a defense against attack. Over generations their bodies adapted to their living conditions until the average adult male Rogett was no larger than four feet tall. Their eyes grew so accustomed to the darkness that they rarely attacked above ground in the day light, as it was difficult for them to see.

It was said that the ears of the Rogetts grew larger as they developed a keen sense of hearing to adapt in the mines. Generation after generation of Rogetts changed in appearance until they barely resembled human beings in looks or nature. But the ancient legends say that the Rogetts became disfigured not from adaptation but from the darkness of their souls; for every Rogett boldly bears the Mark of Satan upon them, for all to see.

King Roch's collaboration with the demon Demetries proved profitable for Roch but horrifying and devastating for the towns and villages they raped. Roch, a man perpetually blinded by his greed and rage, failed to see the deceptions that Demetries played upon him. Demetries was being paid a great deal of money by the Insidiae to spy on Roch and to ensure his safety. The Insidiae, the ancient and clandestine organization that was responsible for bringing great darkness upon mankind, had plans for Roch that could not be deterred.

General Cerephus, Roch's second in command had long been working on plans to overthrow Roch and to seize the Kingdom of Stordt. Demetries' seemingly close association with King Roch filled Cerephus with both anger and jealously. Fearful that his plans would not come to fruition; Cerephus brought a powerful warlock from the Kingdom of Ryed to the Kingdom of Stordt.

Erebus was well known throughout Opots for his powers of black magic but he also had other qualities that Cerephus admired. Erebus was an exceptionally shrewd man with great abilities of strategizing; as well as possessing a keen sense of perception. Cerephus and Erebus had collaborated many times over the years and formed a strong friendship. Both of these men coveted power and wealth and overthrowing King Roch would fulfill their dreams and desires.

Sophie, a member of the Insidiae had been sent to Roch's castle over twenty years earlier to monitor his development into a vessel that could house the essence of a powerful demon. Sophie posed as Roch's cook, a job which gave her great access to the King. Although Sophie's older brother Meekos, a high priest who turned to darkness, was paying Demetries to keep Roch safe; Sophie did not trust Demetries.

Several times Sophie sent letters to Meekos stating that she feared the demon Demetries had private agendas that did not coincide with the plans of the Insidiae. Sophie never learned that Demetries had intercepted each of these letters and destroyed them.

Petra walked into the parlor where Renya and Laurel were both sitting and sewing clothing for the babies' christenings. He stood in the doorway looking at them without speaking.

"Petra dear, you are awfully quiet are you alright?" Renya asked as she put her sewing down on the table.

Without speaking Petra walked up to the women and handed each one a small box. Tears came to Renya's eyes as she saw how Petra had tried to decorate the boxes. Each box was childishly wrapped with paper that was decorated with colored drawings. Petra had a flower attached to the top of each box with string.

"What is this?" Renya asked.

"Open it," said Petra smiling.

Renya opened her box first. "Why Petra this is beautiful, where ever did you get it?" Renya asked as she held up an old and intricately decorated cameo brooch for Laurel to see.

"It belonged to my mother. I thought you should have it now."

Renya hugged Petra tightly as the tears ran down her face. "Petra, thank you I cannot tell you how much this means to me."

"Laurel open yours," said Petra with a huge smile on his face.

"I am already crying and I haven't even opened my gift yet," said Laurel smiling.

Opening her box, Laurel took out a golden chain that had a small oval golden locket linked to it. "Oh Petra, this is so beautiful." Laurel opened the locket and found a tiny lock of hair. "Is this your baby hair?" she asked.

Petra walked over and looked at the hair. "I don't know I didn't open the locket," he said.

"I will bet it is," said Laurel as she gave Petra a hug and a kiss on the cheek. "Thank you so much my dear."

Petra smiled as he watched both of the women put on their new gifts; then he turned and ran out of the parlor.

"I don't know why you keep trying to stop me," King Roch yelled angrily at Demetries.

"Because you are proposing a suicide mission," the demon yelled back. "Don't you think Sudfad and his sons expect you to attack their kingdom? You will be playing right into their hands."

"Demetries are you scared because of what the Sanuri did to you when you tried to attack that castle?" Roch asked sarcastically.

The tone of Roch's voice filled Demetries with rage, which he was trying desperately to control. "Roch you are a fool. You know Sudfad's army is greater than yours and that his family is protected by the Sanuri. I will always bear this curse that he has placed upon me. I do not fear the Sanuri; I now understand his powers and will be better prepared the next time."

"The next time?" Roch asked mockingly. "Are you going after him for what he has done to you?"

Demetries paused as he stared at Roch. "I plan to kill the Sanuri for many reasons. But unlike you I don't blindly charge into situations. You attack Sudfad now and you will lose but of course you are so arrogant you think you know everything; so Roch go ahead and attack your brother's kingdom. I will stay here and become King of Stordt when you are dead."

Roch was consumed with rage as he listened to the demon. "I suppose you have a better plan," yelled Roch sarcastically.

"Roch, you don't have a plan and that will be your downfall," Demetries yelled. He was taking great pleasure from knowing he was angering Roch. "I know you hate everyone but truly what is your main purpose for wanting to attack Sudfad's castle?"

"I don't understand your question," Roch replied angrily.

"It's not a difficult question," Demetries said tauntingly. "You say you want to kill Sudfad but you had not planned to attack him until you heard that Vitomas and Raul were married. Do you want to punish them for deceiving you or do you want Vitomas returned to you? Do you want to kill them or destroy them? Part of your problem Roch is that you lack imagination."

Roch listened intently to Demetries as he spoke, then a sadistic smile consumed Roch's face, "So what are you suggesting?"

"We have talked before about using Hutas or Rogetts to distract the Gants when you returned to the Caves of Muldun. But either of these groups could be used for quite a variety of tasks," Demetries said with a grin.

"Are you saying to attack Wetpr?" Roch did not complete his thoughts because suddenly Cerephus burst into the war room.

"Forgive me My Lord, but the city is under siege by Hutas."

"Take five hundred men to Taperia but leave the castle fortified," ordered Roch.

"Yes My Lord," said Cerephus as he turned to leave.

"Cerephus," said Roch with a smile. "This time take prisoners, I may have a use for them."

Before Cerephus and his men reached the City of Taperia they could see clouds of black smoke filling the sky and flames shooting into the air. An experienced general, Cerephus ordered his men to surround the city.

Huta warriors were a savage race that believed only the strongest of their kind should survive. They butchered any of their people who were sick, weak or somehow different. They prided themselves on courage and prowess in battle.

15

But it was not their savage appearances or their vicious actions that terrified other peoples. The Hutas were feared throughout all kingdoms because it was believed they obtained their powers from demons.

"The men are in place My Lord," said Titus, a lieutenant in the Taperian army.

"The King wants prisoners," growled Cerephus.

"Prisoners, My Lord," Titus said in utter disbelief. "Why everyone knows Hutas do not allow themselves to be taken prisoner."

"I know," Cerephus replied angrily. "Pick twenty men to watch the prisoners as we take them and put them in a place that we can fortify from the rest of the Hutas."

The City of Taperia had no walls around it for protection from invaders. As Cerephus led his men into the city, the horrified screams of the citizens and the war yelps of the Hutas blended into a deafening roar. The scene before Cerephus and his men was the chaos of war. People running for their lives. Buildings and bocas burning. Horses screamed as they tried to escape the madness. And the blood ran like water down the wooden sidewalks and dirt roads of the city. Cerephus and his men did not hesitate. Their attack on the Hutas was brutal.

The Sanuri made his camp next to the River Nebu. After dinner he sat and stared into the fire and smoked his pipe.

"Come out," called the Sanuri. "I could use the company. A Ruala warrior stepped into the firelight.

"Betu how nice to see you; please sit," said the Sanuri as he put another seat by the fire.

"I was not spying on you, I just wasn't sure if I should bother you," said Betu with embarrassment.

"I know," laughed the Sanuri and handed Betu a cup of hot coffee.

"I just wanted to warn you that the Hutas attacked Taperia again and you will be riding into their path," Betu said with concern.

"Why do you think they attacked that city so soon again?"

"Outside of Taperia under this very river are caves; we have seen Hutas and a demon with boils on his face enter there several times."

The Sanuri was quiet for a moment then he said, "I know of that demon and he is trying to free Sporos from The Abyss."

"He does not have the power to do that?" asked Betu in horror.

"No."

"But he knows you can?"

"Only The Great Ruler can release someone from The Abyss."

"But there is something that still bothers you."

"Sporos and that demon both know that too, yet they keep trying," said the Sanuri. "They are devising some evil; I just don't know what it is yet."

"Do you think it has anything to do with the Rogetts?"

"I wondered about that."

"King Roch has not returned to the Caves of Muldun for The Scroll of Imari."

"I know and I find that very curious. He has not gone after that treasure nor has he gone after Raul and Vitomas; I wonder what is stopping him."

Cerephus and his men drastically outnumbered the Hutas and took many prisoners. By sunrise the battle was over and the Huta prisoners were marched to the castle of King Roch and locked in the numerous dungeons. Cerephus himself supervised the imprisonment of the Hutas.

As the last of the Hutas were locked behind bars; Cerephus stared at the prisoners, "Something is not right here," he thought. Cerephus left the dungeons and marched to Roch's war room. When Cerephus entered he saw Demetries drinking with Roch; a common sight these many months.

"Cerephus have a drink," said Roch as he poured a large glass of whiskey. "We can toast the sunrise," Roch said and laughed loudly as he spilled his whiskey on the table top.

Cerephus took the drink and sat at the table across from Demetries. Cerephus could not stand to look upon Demetries or to smell him since the Sanuri destroyed the demon's ability to hide his true form. Cerephus did not trust Demetries and wondered what the demon's true agenda was. Like Roch, Cerephus was unaware of the Insidiae or their insidious plot.

"Many were killed in the city before we got there," Cerephus said. "And buildings are still burning."

Roch seemed unconcerned by Cerephus' report. "And the prisoners?" asked Roch.

"We have locked sixty Hutas in the dungeons," replied Cerephus.

"Good job my general," said Roch with pride.

"My Lord, have you ever heard of a single Huta allowing himself to be captured before, much less sixty?" asked Cerephus. Roch stared at Cerephus as he continued to speak. "Hutas will fight to the death; this seemed too easy," Cerephus said. "Something seems very wrong here."

"What are you saying?" asked Roch.

"We let them inside the gates," replied Cerephus.

"But they are locked in the dungeons," said Demetries with a grin.

"No Cerephus is right, this is most unusual," said Roch suspiciously.

"They are locked up; what are you afraid will happen?" asked Demetries.

"My Lord," Cerephus was talking to Roch but staring at Demetries. "Whose idea was it to capture the Hutas?" Roch could see the look of suspicion and hatred in Cerephus' eyes as he stared at Demetries.

"It was Demetries' idea," Roch replied and now he too stared at the demon. Even in Roch's drunken state he realized something seemed very wrong with this situation.

"My Lord, I know you have gotten rich working with this demon but don't you ever question his real purpose here?" Cerephus asked.

"Roch is too blinded by his greed and arrogance," Demetries said sarcastically. "But you Cerephus have agendas of your own."

"That I do," replied Cerephus without hesitation. "My agenda is to protect my King and to watch out for his interests. Tell me demon what is your agenda?"

Nica the leader of the Enrops flew through the open window of King Sudfad's study. Nica's morning visits were becoming a ritual.

"Nica," called out Sudfad. "Any sign of the Sanuri yet?"

"No but Hutas attacked Taperia again last night," replied Nica. "We saw the smoke and flew over the city."

"What happened?"

"About two hundred Hutas attacked the city until Roch's troops arrived; they battled and many Hutas were taken prisoners."

"Prisoners!" said Sudfad, "I have fought Hutas many times over the years and have never heard of them being taken alive."

"That is why I thought you should know."

"Thank you for the information," said Sudfad. "Also before you go, the people of Salar are completely enchanted with your tribe; are you being treated well?"

"Yes, we are very happy here."

After Nica left the study Sudfad called his sons into the room and told them the information he had just received from Nica. "What do you make of it Father?" asked Simon.

"I do not like it, something is not right," said Sudfad. "This is most unusual behavior for Hutas. Never before have they dared to attack this far north. And why are they continuously attacking Taperia? And another thing, all Hutas swear an oath to fight to the death. I will be glad when the Sanuri gets here, perhaps he can shed some light on all of this."

"There is more," said Raul. "This morning I was walking through the streets of Salar and overheard some travelers talking about Rogetts attacking villages in the light of day."

"Where are these attacks occurring?" asked Sudfad.

"From what these travelers said in the southern areas of the lower kingdoms, but they said there had been many attacks."

"Both the Hutas and the Rogetts are servants of the demons," Sudfad explained. "Now that you know of your responsibilities as Keepers of the Scrolls you need to be aware of such things. For two races to act so out of character simultaneously, something of great evil must be at work. Increase the patrols on our borders."

Both Roch and Cerephus were staring at Demetries waiting for him to answer Cerephus' question. As Demetries sat in silence, Cerephus continued. "Demetries, you are a powerful demon, why do you need Roch to help you rob villages? I would think you could handle that all by yourself. You can't tell me that you stay here because you enjoy our company because you treat all of us with loathing. So why are you really here?"

Demetries had seduced Roch with wealth and power. Roch was so caught up in the illusions that he never considered the questions that Cerephus now asked. Roch slowly pulled a dagger out of its sheath on his belt as he stared at Demetries.

Demetries stared across the table at these two humans who he despised. Demetries wanted so badly to kill them both but he had a job to do. Demetries knew that he could not yet reveal his true purpose for being at Roch's castle. "I am actually impressed Cerephus," Demetries replied with a sneer. "You really aren't as stupid as I thought." Cerephus started to lunge at Demetries but Roch grabbed him and pushed Cerephus back into his seat. "That's right Roch, keep your dog at bay," Demetries taunted.

"It wasn't you I was protecting," Roch growled. "Cerephus is right. What the hell do you really want Demetries?"

"Oh there are many things I want," the demon replied with a salacious grin. "I told you I wanted to do business with you and I do; I just have not yet revealed the nature of my business."

"My Lord be leery of his words," warned Cerephus.

Demetries sat back in his chair and stared at the two men arrogantly. "Roch I am about to tell you something that will change your life."

"Something is not right here," Prince Matthew said to Stephan as they looked down upon the Village of Arora. Stephan was Matthew's closest friend and a captain in the Army of Lentz.

"Don't hesitate, My Lord, attack these traitors," said Syrius, one of the three Bakken scouts who had led Matthew and his army to the tiny village that was located between the lands belonging to the Nordes Tribe and the Valdore Tribe.

"Stephan, I don't like this, all we see are women and children," Matthew said as his eyes searched the lands before him. "Where are the men?"

"They are probably lying in wait to attack you as they did your father," Syrius said. "I urge you My Lord do not hesitate, attack the village."

"Syrius you and your men came to us with the story that the men who tried to attack the King were hiding in this village, it is on your word that we are here," Stephan said with great authority in his voice.

"And now you keep urging us to attack women and children. I agree with Prince Matthew something is very wrong here."

Syrius started to sweat but pursued his urging of Matthew to attack the village. "Our men have been watching this village for many hours and all we have seen are women feeding their children and tending to animals," Matthew said with concern.

"My Lord kill them," screamed Syrius with frustration.

"Syrius for all I know you may be the traitors," Matthew said then turned to his soldiers. "Arrest these Bakken scouts." As the scouts were being pulled off from their horses, Syrius broke free and rode south at a full run. Stephan ordered four of the soldiers to go after Syrius.

"Stephan I am going down to that village, if I am attacked, well, you know what to do," said Matthew.

"You are not going down there alone," Stephan replied with a grin. "I promised your father long ago that I would watch out for you, I am coming along."

Children ran and hid as Matthew and Stephan rode into the small village. The women gathered together and walked up to the Prince. "My Lord," said an old woman as she bowed before Matthew and Stephan. "You honor us with your presence here."

"Please stand," said Matthew kindly. "We are tracking some men who attacked the King. Have you seen any strangers of late?"

"Why no My Lord," replied the woman with sincerity. "Only you."

"Where are your men?" Matthew asked. As he and Stephan looked for any sign of a trap.

"My Lord they are all hunting," replied the woman. "A large herd of Tangers was seen here and the River Shey, the men left three days ago."

"Good day," said Matthew and he and Stephan turned and rode out of the village.

"I believed her," said Stephan.

"I did too," replied Matthew. "We need to talk with those Bakkens."

Jaden, a sergeant, quickly rode up to Matthew and Stephan before they reached the rest of the troops. "My Lord, you will never believe what happened while you were gone."

"Jaden you look as if you saw a ghost, what is the matter?" asked Stephan.

"Truly I don't think I can explain it, you have to see for yourselves," Jaden replied and turned his horse around. The three men rode up to a group of soldiers who were staring at two large piles of black ash. The ropes that had been used to bind the hands of the Bakkens lay within the ash.

"My Lord one minute they were sitting here and the next they burst into flames," said a soldier in disbelief.

"Within seconds they were nothing but these piles before you, we did not even have time to help them," said another astonished soldier.

"What do you make of this?" asked Stephan.

"I think Juleta is behind this," said Matthew. "We need to return to the King at once."

"Roch there are riches in this world that you can't even imagine," Demetries said. "Things that contain power beyond your wildest dreams."

"I'm listening," said Roch as he pushed his dagger back into its sheath.

"The Great Ruler has given many treasures to the humans of this world but they are too stupid to know what to do with them," Demetries started to explain.

"Are you telling me there really is a Great Ruler?" Roch interrupted.

"Yes."

"A demon talking about The Great Ruler; this doesn't make sense," stated Cerephus.

"I know He exists, I'm just not on His team," Demetries said with a laugh. "Now are you going to let me tell you about these treasures or do you want to discuss the nature of the world?"

"Go on," Roch said as he stared skeptically at Demetries.

"As I said The Great Ruler has given many powerful treasures to the humans," Demetries continued. "So powerful that men have hidden them because they know the world isn't ready for such things."

"Why did The Great Ruler give men these treasures?" asked Cerephus.

"Who the hell knows," snapped Demetries. "And besides that is of no importance. What is important is that I know where some of them are."

"So why haven't you gone after them?" Roch asked as his eyes narrowed with suspicion.

"Well Roch; that is the part where I need you. A treasure from The Great Ruler is immersed in holiness and a demon cannot touch what is holy so I need you to help me get these treasures."

"And what is in it for me if I help you?" Roch asked.

"Oh you simple man you probably won't even understand when I tell you," Demetries said tauntingly. "Power beyond anything you can imagine, immortality and keys into other worlds."

Matthew was leading his men back towards his father's castle at a fast pace because he was afraid that the Bakkens were sent as a diversion; meaning that Mathas could be in danger. Matthew's troops had been travelling for less than half an hour when the four soldiers who had been chasing Syrius returned to them; leading Syrius' horse.

"My Lord, never will you believe what I am about to tell you," said a young soldier who appeared shaken.

"Oh, I bet I will," Matthew replied.

"While we were chasing Syrius, something spooked his horse and it reared up. Well, Syrius couldn't hold on and he fell but he got right up and was ready to fight us. By now we were up to him, so me and the others got off our horses and well, suddenly Syrius screamed and then he just burst into flames. It was like nothing I have ever seen before. Within seconds his entire body had burned up, bones and all."

Chapter II
Warrior Princess

Sophie served breakfast to Roch, Cerephus and Demetries in the war room, as Demetries explained the stories about the treasures of The Great Ruler. Sophie said nothing, but stared at Demetries disapprovingly as she listened to him talk.

"Will there be anything else My Lord?" Sophie asked of Roch.

"No, that will be all. No wait bring more bottles of whiskey."

"Yes, My Lord," Sophie turned to leave the room but saw a glint in Demetries' eyes that unnerved her. She turned back to Roch. "My Lord is it true that the dungeons are filled with Huta warriors?"

"Yes, how did you hear about it?"

"Why My Lord everyone is talking, it makes us uneasy to have them within the castle grounds."

"We were just talking about that," Roch said to Sophie but he was staring at Demetries. "As soon as Cerephus finishes his breakfast he will execute them all."

"My Lord we will all breathe much easier now," Sophie said and turning she smiled at Demetries. Sophie did not know what Demetries had been planning but the look of hatred that he gave her now, confirmed her suspicions.

"The Sanuri is here," screamed Petra as he ran down the front steps of the castle and jumped into the Sanuri's arms. "Did you miss me?" yelled Petra.

"I certainly did, now let's put you down so I can see how much you have grown," said the Sanuri happily. "Look at you Petra; I'll bet you have grown an inch."

Petra grabbed the Sanuri's hand and pulled him up the stairs. "Come in and see the babies," said Petra excitedly.

"What do you think about all these babies?"

"Oh, I really like them but they aren't big enough to really play yet."

Marie met them at the door. "Nice to see you Sanuri; they are all in the parlor waiting for you."

Queen Renya was waiting in the doorway of the parlor and hugged the Sanuri tightly. "Wait until you see all the grandbabies," she said with pride. King Sudfad shook the Sanuri's hand. "I have been thinking of you often as of late," said Sudfad seriously.

"Yes, and as usual there is much to discuss," said the Sanuri. "But first let me meet the grandchildren."

As the Sanuri entered the parlor he saw Simon and Annabelle sitting next to each other on a sofa, each holding a blonde haired, blue eyed baby boy. Vitomas was sitting in a large overstuffed chair on the far side of the sofa holding a baby boy with dark hair and large aqua eyes. Raul was sitting on the arm of the chair that Vitomas was seated in. All of the parents smiled proudly as the Sanuri entered the room. Petra was still holding onto the Sanuri's hand and now pulled him to the sofa to see the twins.

"Sanuri look at them, they look just alike," Petra said with continued amazement.

Annabelle handed the baby she was holding to the Sanuri. "This is Alexander and Simon has Anthony," explained Annabelle with a loving smile.

"Simon these boys are a mirror image of you," said the Sanuri. "And Annabelle they are such big babies, were they big when they were born?"

"Oh, yeah," said Simon. "I was scared to death she wasn't going to survive the delivery. But she did just fine."

"Actually Annabelle handled it all much better than Simon did," Raul said with a grin.

"Simon had to help me with almost everything that last couple of weeks; I couldn't even get out of bed by myself," Annabelle said with a laugh and hugged Simon's arm.

"And I didn't know this until the boys were born, but mother said there are twins on both sides of my parent's families."

"So you might have twins again," the Sanuri said as he cuddled the baby.

"I don't think Simon could live through that again," Raul joked and everyone laughed.

Still holding Alexander, the Sanuri walked over to Vitomas who was holding baby Sudfad. "Well hello little Raul," said the Sanuri with a joyful laugh.

"I know, the baby is just a smaller version of him," Vitomas said with pride.

As Vitomas spoke the Sanuri stared intently into her eyes for a few moments. "What is it, is something wrong?" asked Renya with concern.

"Raul would you please move here, next to me?" asked the Sanuri. Raul stood up from the arm of the chair and walked in front of Vitomas. "Would you give me your hand?" asked the Sanuri. Raul hesitated for a moment then extended his right hand to the Sanuri. The Sanuri took his hand and gently placed it against Vitomas' stomach. "Raul meet your new son; your wife is full of life."

"Really?" asked Raul excitedly.

"Really," replied the Sanuri. Raul grabbed Vitomas and hugged her tightly.

"I was wondering if I was pregnant, I just wasn't sure. I thought this might still be weight from little Sudfad," said Vitomas and kissed Raul. Everyone in the room was excited with the news.

"Marie," called out Sudfad.

"Yes My Lord," said Marie as she walked into the room. "Marie we are celebrating would you please bring some refreshments?" requested Sudfad. Vitomas walked up to Marie and hugged her. "Marie I am pregnant again," Vitomas said with tears of joy in her eyes.

Marie too, got tears in her eyes when she heard the news; she turned and hurried out of the parlor, trying to figure out a special treat she could make for the family.

The Sanuri sat down with baby Alexander in a large over-stuffed chair. Petra squeezed in the chair next to him.

"Sanuri, Sudfad and I were talking and since we feel that you are part of the family; we decided it was time you had your own chambers here; to call home," said Renya as she held Sudfad's hand. "We fixed up some rooms for you. Marie can take you to them later. But please let us know if they do not suit you or you find something is lacking."

"I'll take him to his chambers," offered Petra enthusiastically, causing everyone in the room to laugh.

"I thank you for your generosity it has been a long time since I had a place to call my own," the Sanuri said with great sincerity. "And I too feel as if we are all family." The Sanuri's heartfelt words caused everyone to pause for a moment, then Sudfad broke the silence.

"Renya has not allowed me to hire anyone to help with the grandchildren but since we have a fourth baby on the way I think the time is now, to get a nurse," said Sudfad as he gave Renya a serious look. Renya laughed and blushed. "Ok, now I will give my approval."

"You might want to hire two nurses," said the Sanuri and gave Simon and Annabelle a wink.

"Is Annabelle pregnant too?" asked Simon in astonishment.

"Not yet," said the Sanuri smiling. "But these old bones tell me it won't be too long."

Simon and Annabelle hugged each other at the news. The Sanuri looked around the room and asked, "Where is Matthew?"

"He left for Lentz shortly after you left here," said Sudfad. "One night he had a vision that his father was thrown by a horse because the ground was covered with snakes. He saw the frightened horse fall on top of Mathas."

"Matthew packed a few things and left that night. When Matthew got home, he found his father in bed with two broken legs and was told that everything in his vision had come true."

"Was he bitten by the snakes?" asked the Sanuri with great concern.

"No, fortunately for Mathas he was not riding alone, the other men fought the snakes off."

"Did Matthew say what the snakes looked like?" asked the Sanuri.

Sudfad paused for a moment, "Not that I remember." Then Sudfad looked around the room at his family, "Did he tell any of you?" No one replied.

"Do any of you write to Matthew?"

"I think mother and the girls write to him every week," Raul joked. "That guy always did get all the girls."

"In your next letter please ask him to describe the snakes."

"Sanuri, why is this so important?" asked Sudfad.

"Because they may not have been normal snakes, they may have been the tools of a dark lord." The Sanuri paused then said, "I hate to talk business so soon after my arrival here but there are some things we must discuss."

"Do you want us to leave?" asked Vitomas.

"No, these matters involve your entire family," the Sanuri said. "First, Juleta has moved into an old castle in the Kingdom of Zorta. It sits on the banks of the River Toba, across the water from the Village of Toman. It is said she is raising an army."

"Oh believe me we know," said Raul with disgust. "She hired a man named Thaos to gather her army. We found him talking to the girls in a store in Port Friada."

"Thaos, I have heard that name," the Sanuri said thoughtfully.

"He is a notorious mercenary," said Simon. "Raul and I were horrified when we found him with the girls."

"We feel badly that we were so duped by him," said Vitomas.

Annabelle looked at Vitomas, "At least you were suspicious of him. He kept asking me questions and I kept giving him the answers. I feel so embarrassed Sanuri but he was handsome and charming and polite and so well spoken, I would have never guessed he was a killer."

"Sometimes the most dangerous men are the ones who are disarming," said the Sanuri. "Their charm cloaks their darkness. Did he threaten you?"

"That was the interesting thing," Simon said. "It was obvious he let us find him with our wives so he could size us up. But then he tells us that Juleta has hired him and is building an army. He warned us that she hates us and especially the girls. And he said she was going after her father's throne. When I asked him why he gave us this information, he said it was a wedding gift and not to expect another."

"The Enrops saw him join a band of men outside of Port Friada but they did not try to attack us after we left that city. Of course we delayed our return trip a few days and changed our route," Raul said.

"It was my fault," Annabelle said apologetically. "I told him everything."

"Why do you think he warned you and didn't try to harm you?" the Sanuri asked.

"Oh, he seemed like he would enjoy a fight with Raul and me," Simon said. "So we were wondering the same thing. The only reason we could come up with is perhaps he was taken with the girls. He kept telling them over and over how beautiful and charming they were, perhaps he meant it."

"Marie always says that Vitomas and Annabelle could charm the devil himself," said Sudfad. "Perhaps this time they did."

"There are some other things we need to talk about," said the Sanuri. "First I want to say that you should never live your lives in fear. Fear feeds the darkness; but you do need to be careful. The news of the royal weddings has spread through all the kingdoms.

"Roch knows?" asked Raul.

"Yes and if he has not heard yet, he will soon hear of your sons and the christenings."

When Vitomas heard these words she gasped and held little Sudfad closer to her. Raul put his arm around Vitomas and said, "It will be alright Honey."

"Just so you know, it was not Roch who planned the attack on your wedding day," explained the Sanuri. "There were two separate groups from what I have been able to determine. I suspect the group led by Pravis was somehow connected with the Insidiae; the other group was led by one of the demons that the Hutas pray to. He walks in the body of a man but he is not a man," said the Sanuri. "I marked him so he would be recognizable to others."

"How did you mark him?" asked Sudfad.

"I simply let his darkness leak though the human mask. His body is covered with boils and open sores; he can no longer disguise himself. Now he often wears a hooded cloak," replied the Sanuri. "Because of your roles as Keepers of the Scrolls you are ever vigilant about attacks. But you are also men of great integrity, something your enemies do not possess. You must start thinking as they do."

Renya's voice became harsh and cold, "My children, the Sanuri is trying to warn us about the safety of the babies; to hurt them would cripple us."

"Sanuri do you know something that you are not telling us?" Sudfad asked.

"Just that I have had visions, like I did before the weddings. Only this time the eyes are watching your grandchildren."

"Marie," asked the Sanuri as she was bringing refreshments into the room. "Do you know of anyone who is good at taking care of babies?"

Marie gave the Sanuri a confused look at first, then replied, "Well, yes my little sisters, they do not have families of their own but they certainly have experience with children; what with all my nieces and nephews," said Marie. "And they are good girls and hard workers too." The Sanuri looked at Sudfad and Renya and nodded his head in approval.

"How old are they?" asked Renya.

"A couple of years younger than Vitomas and Annabelle," replied Marie.

"Would your parents allow them to work?" asked Sudfad.

"Oh my yes, My Lord," laughed Marie.

"Have them come here tomorrow morning so we can meet them," said Sudfad.

"Just one thing My Lord," said Marie. "They will be embarrassed that they do not have the proper clothes for an audience with you and Queen Renya."

"Tell them we understand and that is not important," said Renya warmly.

After Marie left the room Renya said to the Sanuri, "You really scared me when you started talking to Marie, I thought you meant she was a spy."

"Marie has a kind heart and she loves all of you as family. She would die for you, she is not a spy," said the Sanuri. "And you will be pleased with her sisters, they have a fine family. I apologize I do not want to put fear into your hearts but I do want to help you as much as possible while I am here," the Sanuri said then he turned to Simon and Raul. "Who are the people you see every day on the grounds but pay no attention to?"

"The stable hands?" asked Raul.

"And the men who make deliveries," Simon added.

"There are others also, if you do not mind I would like to accompany you on your duties tomorrow," said the Sanuri.

"So you are saying one of my people is acting as a spy now, as we speak?" asked Sudfad.

"I am saying that someone is spying on your family, I do not know yet if it is someone at the castle or someone from Salar but I will know him when I see him," said the Sanuri.

Like Sophie, Cerephus suspected that Demetries wanted the Hutas brought into the dungeons to attack the castle staff. The Hutas were powerful warriors by their own merits but Cerephus did not know what additional powers the demon Demetries may have bestowed upon them. Cerephus decided to act cautiously.

Each of the dungeon cells was packed with Huta warriors. Cerephus order his archers to shoot into the cells. Cerephus watched as the defenseless Hutas fell before him; the bodies were stacking on top of each other. When the last Huta warrior had fallen, Cerephus ordered his men to open one cell at a time and to pull out one body at a time. "If there is any life in them, cut their throats," growled Cerephus.

"Well?" demanded Roch as Cerephus entered the war room.

"They are all dead; I saw every one of those demons killed," Cerephus said as he took a seat at the table. "Where is Demetries?"

"I think he got mad that you were killing the Hutas," replied Roch with a sneer. "He stormed out of here right after you left."

"My Lord may I speak freely?"

Roch looked up from his map when he heard the sincerity of Cerephus' voice. "Yes, why don't you move your chair closer? Cerephus moved his chair so it was flush with Roch's desk then Cerephus leaned forward as he spoke, as if he was afraid that someone else would hear his words.

"My Lord, you know I have always had your best interests in the forefront. But I have been concerned ever since we discovered what Demetries was. I do not trust anything he says. And I have thought a great deal about what I would do if that demon did something to you. I mean, how do you really fight a demon?" Cerephus asked then paused.

"Go on, I know there is more to this."

"My Lord, I hope this does not anger you but I have a friend, well, I should say we have known each for years. He is a very powerful sorcerer and I asked him to come to Taperia; in case you would need his services."

Roch sat back in his chair and gave Cerephus one of those looks which was difficult to read. Cerephus thought that Roch was going to become enraged but instead Roch said, "Cerephus I like your idea. Just how powerful is this sorcerer?"

"He is one of the most powerful sorcerers in the Kingdom of Ryed and as you know that kingdom gives shelter to all who practice dark magics."

"And you believe him trustworthy?"

"Yes, but there is something I should tell you about him."

"Go on."

"He may anger you at times because he is outspoken and will tell you the truth whether you want to hear it or not. But when he says these things there is a purpose, not just to be rude."

"What is your friend's name?"

"Erebus."

"Bring him to me, perhaps he can tell us what Demetries is really up to."

"Do you see what I see?" Stephan asked as he and Matthew were on a morning ride on the grounds of the royal castle in Lentz. They both directed their horses west where they saw a person dressed in skins lurking around a thicket. The person disappeared into the trees as Stephan and Matthew approached.

"Come out of hiding," demanded Matthew as he and Stephan dismounted. "Tell me why you are trespassing." There was silence. Then Matthew spoke again, this time in a louder voice. "We saw you go into the thicket, come out of hiding."

Soon they heard a rustling in the brush then a female voice spoke. "I am not hiding," said the voice indignantly. "I am coming out." A girl, barely seventeen emerged from the bushes. She wore a dress made of tanned leather, it was short, exposing most of her legs, and sleeveless. Her skin was tanned from the sun; her frame was small but muscular.

The girl had long curly dark red hair that was decorated with beads and feathers. She wore sandals that had straps which tied just below her knees. A bow and quiver of arrows hung over her back. Her belt held three knife sheaths and a small battle ax. Both Matthew and Stephan were surprised at her appearance and at her beauty.

"Why did you hide from us?" asked Matthew as he walked towards the girl.

"I told you I wasn't hiding," said the girl angrily. "And do not come any closer; my father has warned me about the King's men."

"And what did your father say?" asked Matthew as he continued to approach her.

"Are you deaf My Lord? I will not warn you again; do not come any closer. My father told me what you do to women."

Matthew continued to walk towards the girl as he spoke, "First of all you are on royal grounds without an explanation; how do we know what your intent is. And secondly…"

Matthew did not finish speaking because the girl jumped into the air and punched him in the jaw with a right hook. She did what appeared to be a spin in mid-air and landed on her feet. Turning to her side she kicked Matthew in the stomach with her left leg. Then she quickly turned and kicked him again with her right leg.

The blows were painful but they did not take Matthew off his feet. Matthew started to grin at the thought of this girl attacking him. All the while he could hear Stephan's laughter roaring in the cold morning air. "I don't want to hurt you," said Matthew with a laugh. "Will you just stop for a minute?" As he uttered these words Matthew lunged at the girl intending to grab her arms; but she quickly side stepped his attack and grabbed Matthew's arm and threw him over her shoulder. He hit the ground hard.

Stephan was now bending over in fits of laughter. The girl turned to go back into the thicket. Matthew grabbed both of her ankles and pulled them from under her. She landed on her stomach with a thud; she quickly rolled onto her back but was not able to stand up before Matthew was on top of her. Matthew restrained her legs with his weight and pinned her arms above her head.

"I am sorry if that hurt you but I told you to stop," Matthew said.

"And I told you not to come any closer, now get off from me."

"Not until you tell me why you attacked me and why you are on our land," then Matthew grinned. "And who taught you to fight like that? I will say I did not see that coming."

"Then you are blind as well as stupid because I warned you," the girl said angrily. "My father taught me to fight."

"Oh yes, your father who tells lies about my men.

Matthew smiled as his words made the girl angrier. "My father is not a liar. I should kill you for those words."

"Well, he lied to you about my men. They act honorably and if they do not I demand to know about it." The girl stopped struggling and stared at Matthew.

"Who are you? Are you the King?"

"That is Prince Matthew that you attacked," Stephan said still laughing.

The girl stared deeply into Matthew's eyes as if searching for an answer. "Are you really Prince Matthew?"

"You mean you don't even know who you attack, girl?" Matthew asked mockingly.

"I am not a girl, now I will ask you again are you Prince Matthew?"

"Yes I am."

"Is it true that you refused to attack the Village of Arora even when your false guides were urging you to do so?"

"It might be."

"Well is it?" demanded the girl.

"Yes."

"Then you are a man of honor. I will not fight you anymore. You can let me up now."

"And how do I know you are telling me the truth?" asked Matthew who was thoroughly enjoying his encounter with this beautiful girl.

"I give you my word as a warrior princess."

Matthew pushed himself to a standing position pulling the girl up with him. "What is your name?"

"I am Angelina, daughter of Sorren, Chief of the Nordes Tribe," the girl said proudly.

"Angelina," repeated Matthew. "You sure don't dress or act much like an angel if you ask me."

"Oh and I suppose you would know a lot about angels," Angelina barked as she patted the dirt off from her dress.

"Well, you have me there," Matthew replied with a grin. "So why are you on our land and why did you attack me?"

"One of our horses was attacked by a panther. Our healer is taking care of the horse but her colt ran away. I tracked it to this thicket. I have been worried that the panther would get it." Matthew did not say anything. "It is our colt if you don't believe me come with me as I get it."

"Why did you attack me?"

"I already told you."

"Yeah that is right, all of our men are monsters," Matthew said sarcastically.

Angelina looked at Matthew and smiled. "Well perhaps not all of them," she said flirtatiously and turned and walked into the thicket. Matthew followed her. They both emerged from the trees a short time later with a spotted colt. Matthew held it as Angelina slipped a loosely tied rope around its neck.

"Angelina, the next time you need help you come to the castle, tell the soldiers I gave you permission," Matthew said as Angelina mounted her horse. Once Angelina was seated in the saddle she looked at Matthew, then her face lit up with a beautiful smile. "Perhaps I will my young prince," Angelina said and winked at him. Then Angelina turned her horse and rode north.

"You were a lot of help," Matthew said sarcastically as Stephan handed him the reigns to his horse.

"That little girl didn't look like she needed any help to me," Stephan said with a laugh as he mounted his horse. "Matthew the sight of that girl kicking your butt is the funniest thing I have ever seen."

Matthew started laughing, "I know, she was pretty good."

"You may have been too busy getting beaten up but did you notice how beautiful she was?"

"I did Stephan, yes I did." The two men rode in silence for a few minutes then Matthew said. "I wonder what she would look like in a regular dress."

"I thought she looked pretty damn good in that leather thing she was wearing," said Stephan.

"I did too," said Matthew with a grin.

"By the way, your lip is bleeding," Stephan said as he started to roar with laughter again.

"I am never going to hear the end of this, am I?" asked Matthew as he continued to laugh.

"Never, Matthew, never."

The next morning Marie entered the parlor and announced with pride, "My Lord and Lady my sisters have arrived."

"Please show them in," said Renya.

Marie turned to the door then turned back to the royal couple, "Please forgive them if they act like fools they are very nervous to meet you," said Marie with a smile and left the room. Marie's comment made both the King and Queen laugh but they fought to compose themselves when they heard voices in the hallway. Marie escorted her two sisters into the room, they appeared to be about fourteen and fifteen years of age and very nervous. Both girls were dressed in simple clothing but they were both clean and well groomed.

"King Sudfad and Queen Renya this is Gabriella," said Marie as she pointed to the older of the two girls. Gabriella curtsied and choked on her words as she tried to say, "Good morning." Gabriella was a pretty girl with chestnut brown curly hair that she wore in pigtails and large brown eyes. She resembled Marie in the eyes and the stocky build. Gabrielle looked and acted older than her fifteen years.

"And this is Abigail," Abigail also curtsied and blushed. Abigail did not resemble Marie physically except for the glint of mischief in her eyes. Abigail had a slender build with long straight black hair and blue eyes. At fourteen Abigail was not as reserved as her sister Gabriella; Abigail's spontaneous personality often got her into trouble.

"Marie tells us you have experience caring for children of all ages," said Sudfad smiling.

"Yes My Lord," replied both of the girls.

"Did Marie tell you we have three babies in the castle and a fourth on the way?" asked Sudfad.

"Yes," replied Gabriella nervously.

"Your positions would be to help us with the care of the children when needed, you would not be staying here at night," said Sudfad. "Do you think you could handle such work?"

Abigail piped up, "Oh yes My Lord; why our sister Sara has twelve children alone."

"Why doesn't Marie take you to meet the rest of the family and the babies and then we will discuss this matter further," Sudfad suggested to the girls; then he called out to Marie who was in the hallway.

"Marie, would you please escort your sisters to the hallway then return to the parlor."

After Marie reentered the parlor and closed the door she said, "I am afraid to ask what they might have said."

"They are fine but they certainly do not take after you," said Sudfad laughing.

"Oh My Lord, just wait until you get to know them better," said Marie with a laugh.

"They are precious but so nervous around us that we are not going to accompany them on the introductions," said Renya warmly. "Please take them to meet the rest of the family and let them play with the babies. Tonight we will discuss the matter during dinner."

"What is your name?" asked Petra of a girl with long straight red hair, who was sitting on the steps outside of the kitchen.

"Kyra, who are you?"

"My name is Petra, why are you sitting here?"

"My sisters are being talked to by the King."

"You're Marie's sister," said Petra smiling, "I like Marie she is funny." Then Petra took a step back and appeared to be examining Kyra's face. "You look like Marie." Kyra frowned. "What is the matter, don't you like looking like Marie?"

"She is old," Kyra said with a hint of annoyance.

"Well old or not, she is a great cook and a lot of fun," replied Petra as he defended his friend. Kyra didn't say anything. "Do you have to sit here all day or can you play?"

Kyra's face lit up. "I'll play," she said enthusiastically and jumped off from the steps.

Petra grabbed Kyra's hand, "You have got to meet our talking birds," he said as the two ran towards the barn.

Chapter III
When Demons Strike

"Have you ever seen such butchery?" cried Padre Bartholomew as he helped carry an injured woman inside of the monastery at Malga. The woman was covered in blood from multiple wounds.

"My children," she cried. "Have you seen my children?"

As the two priests laid the woman on a cot in the Great Hall, Padre Bartholomew leaned closer to the woman. "Tell me their names and I will find them," he said.

"Thomas and Rachel and bless you Father," the woman whispered.

Padre Bartholomew ran up to Padre Thomas who was opening the front gates for the victims of the Rogett attack. "I am looking for two children, their mother is seriously hurt," said Padre Bartholomew.

"I have not seen any children by themselves yet," replied Padre Thomas as he looked at the throngs of injured people entering the courtyard. Cries of fear and pain filled the normally serene gardens. Men and women with severe injuries carried in others who they deemed were more seriously injured. Voices of anguish rang out as people sought to locate lost loved ones. Everyone begged the priests for help. And the blood; later Padre Bartholomew would say the sight of so much blood haunted him the rest of his days.

The scene at the monastery was controlled chaos. The priests were everywhere. The Great Hall was turned into a massive hospital. The priests divided themselves into groups; some provided direct medical care. Others carried the patients with the most severe injuries into the Great Hall and found shelter and food for those few who managed to escape the demon attack with minor injuries. A third group of priests was bringing bedding, cloths, bandages and all other needs to the Great Hall.

And the fourth group were the priests who were especially gifted with making medicines. They were busy in the gardens and the kitchen; for the supply of medicines they had on hand was meager for such a devastation.

And all the priests; no matter where they were or what task they were assigned; prayed. They prayed for the healing of the victims; they prayed for an end to the violence and they prayed for the strength to face such horror and to do what they must. And they prayed.

The huge ancient bells of the monastery were ringing; their sounds could be heard for miles and served as a signal that some village was under attack and help was needed. Everyone at the monastery was yelling, for no one could hear over the ringing of those great bells. "Great Ruler please let King Tobias hear the distress call," prayed Padre Thomas. The fear that gripped the hearts of all in the monastery; was the knowledge that King Tobias only had one military outpost in the kingdom and it was located near his castle at Calix, which was a three day ride away.

By some miracle King Tobias of the Kingdom of Puntd heard the warning bells from the monastery at Malga. He dispatched five hundred soldiers to the monastery.

The soldiers were led by Banacus a general seasoned in the art of combat. Banacus had lost his left eye years earlier fighting with a Huta warrior, now he wears a patch made of spun gold to cover the injury. Some say Banacus cut out both of the eyes of the Huta in retaliation before he killed him.

Rarely did the priests ring the monastery bells and only under the most dire of circumstances. Banacus did not know what he was leading his men into but he had heard of recent Rogett attacks in neighboring kingdoms. Rogetts or Hutas it did not matter to him, Banacus loved to go to battle.

By noon the victims, from the attack at Afax, had stopped arriving at the monastery at Malga. The priests had originally put patients on the floor in the Great Hall but when there was no more room they started putting patients in the hallways. The bells continued to ring.

"Please Great Ruler help us to keep these poor people safe," prayed Padre Thomas.

The wall around the monastery was made of stone but the gates were made of heavy wood. Some priests were fortifying the gates while others were keeping watch in the towers and on the walkways that ran along the top of the stone walls. The priests knew it would be three days before the soldiers arrived, that was if the soldiers heard the bells ringing as an alarm.

It was well known that Rogetts' eyes were sensitive to light, which is why they usually attacked at night. The priests made huge wood piles around the interior of the stone wall to set on fire as soon as darkness fell. Armed with only their staffs and axes the priests prepared to do battle with the Rogetts.

"So from what you are saying, you all approve of Gabriella and Abigail, fine, I will hire them in the morning," said Sudfad as the entire family ate their supper in the dining room.

"Petra who was that little girl I saw you playing with?" asked Annabelle.

"Kyra, she is Marie's sister," said Petra without looking up from his food.

"You looked like you were having fun," Annabelle said.

"Yeah I like her, she has a toad named Grandor and she likes to fight," Petra said as he filled his mouth with mashed potatoes. This comment got the attention of everyone sitting at the table.

"What kind of fighting?" asked Raul.

"Well, I think any kind but today we were fighting with staffs."

"Do you know how to fight with a staff?" Raul asked with a grin.

"Yes, the priests at Malga were teaching me," replied Petra.

Raul looked across the table at the Sanuri, who nodded and said, "Yes, they said he was doing quite well."

"Where did you get the staffs?" asked Simon.

"Oh we didn't have real staffs, we were using sticks."

"Petra, you are a young prince now and it is fine to play with your friend but remember boys shouldn't beat up on girls," said Sudfad.

"I didn't beat her up, in fact I have a big bump on my leg where she walloped me with that stick," Petra said as he continued to put food into his mouth. "And why can't boys beat up on girls; I don't think Kyra would like it if I only pretended to fight with her."

Sudfad smiled and paused before answering the question, "Because boys are stronger and can hurt the girls."

"Oh I think she is a lot stronger than me, does that count?" asked Petra emphasizing the word stronger.

By this time the entire family was trying not to laugh. Simon and Raul just stared at their father with grins on their faces; they were not going to get involved in the discussion.

"Yes that counts," replied Sudfad as he was trying not to grin. "But I still don't want you hurting her."

"I didn't hit her I just stabbed her a couple of times with the stick," Petra said with frustration. "And maybe you should tell her she shouldn't hurt me."

Renya got a look on her face that usually meant someone was getting scolded. She looked at Petra for a moment then she turned to Raul and Simon. "Would one of you please teach Petra and his friend how to properly train with a staff so they do not hurt each other?" asked the Queen.

Simon looked at Petra and gave him a wink, "I will show you both the next time Kyra comes over."

Sudfad looked at his two grinning sons. "You know you both will be having this same talk with your children someday."

"We know Father," Raul replied while trying to hold back his laughter. Just then Marie entered the dining room and started to clear the dishes from the table.

"Marie, Petra was just telling us that he was playing with Kyra," said King Sudfad.

"Oh My Lord, I am sorry I did not know the girls were bringing her, she didn't come inside the castle," said Marie sincerely.

"No, it sounds like they were having fun with their toads and fighting," said Sudfad.

"I would not be surprised, Kyra is all tomboy, not really sure where she gets that from," said Marie.

"How old is she?" asked Renya.

"She is the same age as Petra, and another red head," replied Marie. "In fact with their red hair and freckles Petra and Kyra could pass for brother and sister."

At this comment Petra shot his head up. "Marie don't call her my sister!"

Before Marie could answer, Annabelle asked, "Petra does that upset you?"

"No," replied Petra slowly as he looked back down at his plate of food.

"Then why did you say it like that?"

"I don't want to tell you," Petra said with a pout.

"Petra answer Annabelle," said Sudfad.

Petra stared at Sudfad for a few moments, "Well, if I have to. I like her and everyone knows you can't like your sister." All of the adults in the room fought to control their urge to laugh. Sudfad had to look down at his plate to compose himself finally he looked up at Marie and said, "If the children want to play together Kyra is invited here any time."

Vitomas had just finished feeding little Sudfad and was putting the sleeping baby into his bed when Raul came up behind her. Moving Vitomas' long curly blonde hair to the side, Raul started to gently kiss her neck. Vitomas giggled at first but as Raul continued to run his lips down her neck and shoulder the giggles turned into moans.

Vitomas turned around and Raul leaned down and kissed her passionately on the lips; while pulling her body close to his. The thin silk nightgown Vitomas wore accented the curves of her slender body. Lost in the passion of their embrace, Vitomas didn't realize at first that Raul had picked her up and was carrying her to their bed. Vitomas kissed Raul's neck and chest as he carried her across the room. Raul lowered Vitomas onto the bed and sat beside her, just looking at her beautiful face and smiling.

"What are you smiling at my dear husband?" asked Vitomas softly.

"Every day I am so grateful for you and our son and now," said Raul as he placed his hand on her stomach. "We have a second son on the way; I never thought I could be this happy."

The tears ran down Vitomas' cheeks as she listened to Raul's heart speak. He wiped the tears from her face and they let their love consume them.

For a second morning the Sanuri accompanied Simon and Raul on their duties, which on this day included battle training with the soldiers and patrolling of the borders.

King Sudfad had been the first king in the Continent of Opots to build military outposts in various locations in his kingdom. The Kingdom of Wetpr covered such a vast area that King Sudfad felt his troops could not adequately protect his subjects if they were all garrisoned in Salar, the capital city and home of the Royal Family.

The farthest outpost was Fort Polta which was in western Wetpr located just east of the Tia forest. Fort Nir which stood just southeast of Lake Pejor was centrally located. In the remote northeastern corner of Wetpr; Fort Styls was located on the border between the kingdoms of Wetpr and Lentz and Fort Salar was located at Salar. A minimum of two hundred thousand soldiers were stationed at each fort. Three generals were assigned to each of the military outposts.

Simon and Raul had each been stationed at every military outpost during their careers. Because of the additional responsibilities Simon and Raul had as princes in the Royal Family; Sudfad had assigned them to Fort Salar as their permanent post. Sudfad, Raul and Simon were the three generals at Fort Salar. Sudfad would normally visit each outpost during the year; but because of the recent threats towards his family and The Holy Scrolls; Sudfad was not planning any trips this year.

The Sanuri did not take part in the battle training but sat on the side and observed. The training was intense and it was the first time the Sanuri had seen Raul and Simon fight as grown men. Watching not only their power and skill but their cunning on the battlefield reassured the Sanuri that they were perfectly chosen as Keepers of the Scrolls.

The Sanuri scrutinized every being he saw who had any contact with either Simon or Raul and did not feel the presence of darkness in them. But in all his many years the Sanuri had learned to trust the visions that The Great Ruler sent to him; there was a terrorist among the Royal Family, the Sanuri just had not found him yet.

The fears of the Royal Family dissolved as they prepared for the christenings and the advent of yet a fourth grandchild. As was the custom of King Sudfad and Queen Renya they planned to open their doors to their subjects for the grand celebrations.

The castle was a mixture of loving chaos and excitement. Sudfad greeted the Sanuri, Raul and Simon at the front door when they returned to the castle.

"I would suggest you come directly to my study," said Sudfad.

"Is something wrong?" asked Raul.

"No," said Sudfad laughing. "With one day before the christenings every woman in this house seems to be crazy."

When they entered the study they saw Alexander sitting in a chair drinking coffee. He looked up at the men and said, "I am hiding out," and laughed. Sudfad closed the door after everyone had entered the room.

"Is it really that bad?" asked Simon.

Sudfad and Alexander exchanged glances and smiled. "You just haven't been married long enough my son," said Alexander.

"Did you find the terrorist?" asked Sudfad.

"No," replied the Sanuri. "But, I was more than impressed with your sons; you have taught them well Sudfad." Sudfad smiled proudly at the compliment and poured each of the men a glass of whiskey.

As the men talked there was a small knock at the door, then Petra called, "Papa."

"Would you let him in?" Sudfad asked the Sanuri as the Sanuri was sitting next to the door.

When the Sanuri opened the door he saw Petra with a handful of papers and a tall woman standing behind him. "Papa my lessons are over," Petra said but before he could finish his statement the Sanuri grabbed Petra by the arm and quickly pulled him into the room. The woman and the Sanuri stared at each other for a moment before she ran out the front door of the castle. The Sanuri ran after her and Raul and Simon followed them both.

The woman ran towards the front gate of the wall surrounding the castle and pulled on the doors but could not open them. She quickly turned around and opened her short cropped jacket, pulling two daggers from small sheaths that were sewn inside of her jacket. The woman threw the first dagger at Simon as he was the closest to her. She threw it with power and with skill; Simon threw himself to the ground to avoid being hit in the heart.

The woman held the second dagger like one who had been trained in its use. She pointed the dagger menacingly at Raul who was closing in on her left side as Simon was on her right. The woman lunged at Raul with the dagger; he stepped to the side and grabbed her arm at the wrist and shoulder. Bringing his right knee up he slammed her wrist on his knee causing her to drop the dagger. Raul then pulled both of her arms behind her back. Laughing Raul looked at Simon and said, "Don't tell Petra I fought with a girl."

The Sanuri walked up to the woman without saying anything he just stared into her eyes. The woman screamed and spit at the Sanuri. Simon quickly moved her head to the side, so the spittle did not land on the Sanuri. Three soldiers ran up to the Princes. "Take her to the dungeons," Raul told the soldiers.

Simon picked up the daggers and noticed that the tips were blue. "These have been dipped in poison," Simon said.

"Petra," said the Sanuri and all three men hurried inside the castle. Sudfad had already checked Petra for injuries and had called the family and staff to his study.

"Petra is uninjured," Sudfad said as the three men ran into the study. "And apparently he is the only person to have contact with her today.

"Who is she?" asked the Sanuri.

"Petra's teacher, she has been working with him most of the year," replied Sudfad.

Simon squatted down so he could look Petra in the eyes, "Petra this is important, did she give you anything to eat or drink?"

"No, not today but sometimes she does," answered Petra with his voice shaking. "Was she a demon because she always seemed really nice?"

Simon hugged Petra, "No she is not a demon but she is not a nice person either. You are safe, we won't let anything happen to you." Simon picked Petra up and Petra wrapped his arms around Simon's neck.

When they were assured that no one was injured the Sanuri said, "I am going to the dungeons to speak with her."

"I will come with you; boys look after the others," said Sudfad.

A soldier led the King and the Sanuri down a long corridor that was lined with cells on both sides. When they reached the woman's cell they saw her hanging from a noose she had made with her jacket. The soldier quickly unlocked the cell door as Sudfad and the Sanuri ran into the cell and loosened the noose.

As Sudfad laid the woman's lifeless body onto the floor of the cell, a silver chain which she was wearing around her neck fell out of her blouse. The chain held a large ruby amulet that bore the same ancient symbols as the blood rings of Juleta, Pravis and Roch.

"Well, I guess we have our answer," the Sanuri said. "She is a member of the Insidiae."

"Why do you think she killed herself?"

"To prevent us from getting information from her."

"Sanuri this woman has walked freely in our castle for almost a year, think of the information she may have learned."

"I am actually more concerned with what she may have left behind."

"There, I saw a movement in the darkness," yelled a young priest who was standing guard on the top of the wall surrounding the monastery at Malga. "I see something too," said another priest fearfully who stood guard about one hundred yards away. The first priest yelled down to the priests below, "There is movement in the darkness, we don't know if it is Rogetts."

A large group of priests stood just inside of the wooden gates. They clutched their staffs and anything else they found to use as a weapon. They prayed as they prepared for the gates to fall and the monastery to be overrun with Rogetts. Two other groups of priests were hoisting large pots of boiling oil up to the priests who stood on top of the wall.

Another group of priests proceeded to light the many piles of wood that had been set up around the interior of the wall. The priests hoped the brightness of the fires would blind the Rogetts, and give the priests a little advantage in the battle.

Screams soon filled the air. Screams that would numb a man's soul; screams from the bowels of hell itself. As the Rogetts ran towards the monastery screaming; the demon Sporos screamed from his prison within The Abyss. The Rogetts heard his orders, they heard his commands; they understood what they had to do.

"We are surrounded," yelled a priest who was on top of the wall.

"Wait until they get closer," yelled Padre Thomas, his command was echoed around the wall. Soon an Enrop landed on Padre Thomas' shoulder then another landed on top of the wall. Enrop after Enrop landed until the top wall of the monastery was filled with the giant birds.

"After you pour the oil throw fire upon them," said Arca, the Enrop who was seated on Padre Thomas' shoulder.

"Quickly gather torches from the fires and throw them on the Rogetts after we have poured the oil," yelled Padre Thomas. The two groups of priests who had been hoisting up the pots of boiling oil now grabbed burning logs from the fires and carried them to the priests on top of the wall.

"Now," rang a cry around the wall as the Rogetts started to scale the ancient stone. Rogetts dwelled in caves and were accustomed to climbing rock walls with only their hands and feet. Hundreds of Rogetts swarmed the walls, the smell of fear spurring them on; their desire for human blood driving them and the demon Sporos commanding them.

The priests poured caldron after caldron of boiling oil on top of the invaders. Then they rained fire upon the Rogetts, who screamed and fell off from the wall landing onto their comrades and also igniting them. The monastery was ablaze with light but this did not deter the attack. Wave after wave of Rogetts tried to climb the walls but they were driven back by the oil and the fire.

"I fear we are running out of oil," Padre Thomas said to Arca.

"You are not alone here," replied the Enrop.

The priests started to gasp and to look around in the night sky. "That is not the moon, is that the sun coming up?" Padre Thomas asked.

"It is neither of those things," replied Arca.

Soon all the landscape was brilliantly lit up. A pure white light shown down from the heavens. A light that exposed the hordes of demons to the priests.

"The Great Ruler be with us," uttered one priest as he saw an army of Rogetts that must have counted into the thousands.

"No!" shrieked Sporos as his army burst into flames. "No!" screamed Sporos as the demons from hell were destroyed by the holiness of the light. "No," whispered Sporos as he felt his power fading with the destruction of his followers.

High Priests Meekos, Pravis and Tenebrae did not defend the walls of their monastery during this battle. They did not tend to the victims of the vicious Rogett attacks. They did not stand with their fellow priests against the darkness. Instead they were safely hidden in their underground chambers below the monastery at Malga.

They danced before a giant fire. The priests were naked, their faces painted with human blood. They were performing an ancient ritual meant to extend the power of a demon. These three high priests, so held in honor, were in fact, helping Sporos to control the Rogetts who were attacking their own monastery. Suddenly they saw the face of Sporos in the fire. The priests could hear Sporos screaming "No." Then darkness fell upon them.

Chapter IV
A Walk through Time

The sun shown warmly on the royal grounds as three future kings were christened. The Sanuri preformed the ceremony with the knowledge that these beautiful babies would leave their marks on the world. The Royal Family opened the ceremony to their subjects; but there was not the music and loud fanfare that had accompanied the royal weddings.

Two additional tables had to be erected to hold the many gifts that were brought for the babies. As was traditional for King Sudfad and Queen Renya they had tables upon tables set up with food and refreshments for all.

All three babies were dressed in white silk, trimmed with lace. Queen Renya and Laurel made the three almost identical outfits and the three matching blankets. King Sudfad had increased the number of soldiers guarding the ceremony, especially for the introductions of the babies to the public.

After the ceremony the royal couples, Prince Raul and Princess Vitomas and Prince Simon and Princess Annabelle, proudly and officially introduced their sons to their waiting subjects. Simon and Annabelle walked through the adoring crowds first, each holding one of their sons.

"On my, they are the spitting image of the Prince," a woman said loudly as others laughed. Anthony and Alexander were both large babies with bright blue eyes and blonde hair in contrast to Annabelle who was petite with long black curly hair and large hazel eyes.

Behind Simon and Annabelle walked Raul, who was holding baby Sudfad, and Vitomas at his side. Big like his father, baby Sudfad had Raul's black hair and aqua colored eyes.

"There isn't a bit of the Princess in him," exclaimed a woman looking at baby Sudfad; referring to Vitomas' long curly reddish blonde hair and green eyes.

The couples smiled as people kept saying how cute and beautiful the babies were. And to everyone's amazement none of the babies cried during either the ceremony or the introductions. The Sanuri stood with Sudfad and Renya as they watched the babies being paraded around the royal grounds.

"I hope those babies turn out just like their fathers," said the Sanuri. Renya reached over and squeezed the Sanuri's arm, for she had the same thoughts.

After the official introductions, the royal couples mingled with the people for about an hour before bringing the babies into the castle. The spectators were allowed to stay in the courtyard to eat and drink. Sudfad and the soldiers remained vigilant for an attack but none came. This day of joy and love was not marred by darkness.

Banacus and his men rode hard and long to get to the monastery at Malga. A well trained and experienced army; they feared the worse. The bells at the monastery rang every day for three days but they remained silent at night. Every morning Banacus felt relief when he heard the bells ringing for he knew at least one priest must still be alive.

The night of the third day brought a great feeling of apprehension to Banacus. He knew he was not the only one feeling the anxiety as his men were restless and on edge. Banacus woke his troops long before the sun rose and they resumed their journey to Malga.

When Banacus and his men arrived at the monastery; smoke from the night fires mingled with the morning fog to cast an eerie illusion over the grounds. The bells were still ringing so Banacus knew there must be some survivors.

Suddenly a voice called out, "They are here, the army is here." Within moments the massive wooden doors opened and Banacus and his men rode into the courtyard. The priests were overjoyed to see the arrival of the soldiers. As the most senior third level priest, Padre Thomas met with Banacus and gave him as much information as he could about the attacks.

"Padre let me see if I understand this correctly, you said you and the other priests battled hundreds of Rogetts and when you ran out of boiling oil; a bright light came from the sky and killed all of the Rogetts?" Banacus cleared his throat, "Padre I mean no disrespect but that is a pretty hard story to believe."

"Answers to prayers are always difficult to believe if you don't believe in miracles," Padre Thomas replied. "But don't take my word for it. Send your men around the exterior of the wall you will find burned bodies of Rogetts and many, many piles of ashes. The ashes are the remains of the Rogetts that were killed by the holy light." Banacus gave Padre Thomas a quizzical look. "No, really My Lord send your men out, and in the meantime I will take you to see the victims of the attack on Afax."

Banacus nodded at the soldiers standing nearest to him and they mounted their horses and rode outside of the massive wall that surrounded the monastery.

"As far as we know there was only one attack and it occurred in the early morning hours," said Padre Thomas. "But you have to see some of the victims; in all my years I have not seen such mutilations." Padre Thomas first took Banacus to an area in the rear courtyard where corpses were piled and covered with blankets. Banacus lifted the blanket on the corpse closest to him and saw the body of a man whose face had been eaten away." As he put the blanket down he asked, "Are they all this way?"

"Yes and many are far worse. From the accounts of the victims they awoke to a village filled with Rogetts; the monsters would start to feed on one person then move to the next."

"That does not sound like a normal Rogett attack," exclaimed Banacus. "Normally the Rogetts gang up on a few victims, kill them, feed and leave."

"Come speak with the villagers yourself; they all have the same story."

The smell of death filled their nostrils as Padre Thomas and Banacus entered the Great Hall. In many cases the priests could only try to keep their patients somewhat comfortable as they died.

The room was filled with the sounds of people moaning and crying. Banacus watched two priests as they tended to some of the villagers; the faces of the priests were strained and their eyes showed the damage that only horror can do to the soul.

As Padre Thomas and Banacus walked among the bodies of the dying, Banacus said with disgust, "I have seen enough Padre, we will hunt those monsters down." Banacus started to leave the Great Hall but he stopped and turned back to Padre Thomas.

"I will leave some of my men here for your protection and to help you bury the dead."

"Thank you My Lord," replied Padre Thomas gratefully.

As Banacus was turning back towards the door a soldier walked up to him. "My Lord we rode around the entire wall; and it is as the priests say."

"What!" exclaimed Banacus in utter disbelief.

"Just below the walls are bodies of Rogetts piled on top of each other. They are covered in oil and burned. But farther out, within yards of the monastery are thousands of piles of ash."

"Father can we talk?" asked Matthew as he peeked his head into Mathas' study.

"Certainly, Matthew come in."

"We can leave," said Fahron as he and Claudius started to stand up.

"No, please stay," said Matthew as he walked up to his father's desk. "You should hear this also."

"What is it my son?" Mathas asked as he saw that Matthew was holding an envelope.

"I received a letter from Vitomas, she says that the Sanuri wants to know the color of the snakes that scared your horse. I remember what I saw in my vision but I never asked you if the snakes were red."

Mathas stared at Matthew for a moment, "Why yes, they were red; and I remember thinking I had never seen red snakes with green eyes and yellow tongues before."

Matthew's face looked strained as he handed the letter to his father. A look of great sadness filled the King's face as he read the letter. Mathas handed the letter to Fahron when he was finished reading. "The Sanuri describes such snakes as the Mark of Satan and says they are often called forth by dark lords," uttered Mathas in a low whisper.

"Father I told you about those scouts that tried to talk me into attacking Arora. I cannot prove it but I believe Juleta is somehow behind the sudden problems between the Valdore and Nordes tribes. And there is something I should have told you long ago," continued Matthew. "But when I received the information you were still in very serious condition after your accident and I did not want to burden you more.

A few weeks after I came home I received a letter from Raul. He said that he, Simon, Vitomas and Annabelle were in Port Friada near the end of their trip. Raul said one day the girls were shopping and when he and Simon found them they were talking to a large man wearing an eye patch. The man said his name was Thaos."

"Thaos, I have heard that name," said Mathas thoughtfully.

"That is the name of the man we heard was raising an army in Zorta," Fahron said.

"Exactly; Raul said as soon as Thaos said his name they got between him and the girls. Raul and Simon felt Thaos deliberately set the situation up so he could see how they would react. Raul said that although Thaos taunted both him and Simon, Thaos told them that he was not their enemy but worked for one who was."

"Raul said that Thaos said Juleta had hired him to raise the army and that she hated Raul and Simon and particularly Vitomas and Annabelle. Raul said Thaos also said Juleta wanted your throne Father. When Simon asked Thaos why he warned them, Thaos replied it was a wedding gift and not to expect another."

Mathas sighed deeply but did not speak. Fahron handed the letter to Claudius and said, "I am more surprised that a man like Thaos would warn them than I am that Juleta is behind this." Then Fahron looked over at Mathas, "I know it breaks your heart but you know I speak the truth."

"I know," said Mathas sadly. Then Mathas slowly turned his head to his left and looked at Fahron, then to his right and looked at Claudius; Mathas moved as if there was a great weight upon him. "Claudius, Fahron, my two oldest and dearest friends. We have fought many battles together; we have saved each other's lives. We raised our children together and protect this kingdom together. I hope with all of my heart that you never feel such pain as this kind of betrayal of a child."

The room fell silent as no one had words to comfort the King. After several moments Claudius spoke, "Matthew did you tell Stephan about Raul's letter?"

"Not yet."

"Tell him, he too has encountered Thaos. It was several years ago in the Kingdom of Puntd. I sent him there with a message for King Tobias," Claudius said. "As you know Tobias is a distant cousin of our family. Before Stephan returned he stopped in a tavern in Calix. My son can tell the story better than I, but I will get the point across. Stephan said he was sitting at a table eating when six men walked into the tavern. Stephan said that directly across from him another man was sitting by himself, quietly eating his meal."

"Stephan said the six well-armed men surrounded the one man at the table. One of the group demanded to know the man's name. The man calmly replied 'Thaos'. The man who was speaking for the group said that they had orders to kill him. Stephan said Thaos calmly looked at the six men and asked who sent them. When Stephan heard them say that King Roch had sent them, Stephan decided that Thaos might need some help."

"The way Stephan describes it Thaos suddenly threw his table on the two men standing directly in front of him; then ran his sword through the man to his left as he dodged a blow from the man standing behind him. Stephan joined the fight and he and Thaos killed all six of Roch's men. Stephan said that Thaos was a fast and powerful fighter."

60

"I do remember Stephan telling me about that fight," said Matthew. "But I don't remember if he ever told me the name of the man he helped."

"Did anything else happen?" asked Mathas.

"After the fight, Stephan said he turned to Thaos and told him that King Roch was a dangerous enemy to have. Stephan said Thaos replied that he had many enemies but he would never count Stephan among them. He asked Stephan's name. Stephan told him that I was his father and that he was welcomed in the Kingdom of Lentz. Stephan said they shook hands and both rode out of Calix in different directions."

"So do you think he warned Raul and Simon out of some kind of debt he owes to Stephan?" Fahron asked.

"It is possible, he is a mercenary but that doesn't mean he is totally without honor," replied Claudius. "Or perhaps it is all part of some elaborate ruse."

"Did Thaos ever come here to visit Stephan?" asked Mathis.

"No," replied Claudius.

"According to Raul's letter, he and Simon wondered if Thaos decided to warn them because he seemed quite taken with Annabelle and Vitomas," Matthew said.

"Well, he will have to stand in line," Mathas said as he looked at Matthew with a grin.

Fahron laughed, "Matthew is it true you asked to be considered for the inheritance of both Raul's and Simon's wives?"

Mathas looked at Fahron, "They are truly beautiful girls."

"And just as sweet and smart as they are pretty," Matthew replied.

"Well son, your mother and I watched as Annabelle and Vitomas took care of you, Raul and Simon, after that last battle and we both thought that if someone did not know who they were married to, it would be hard to tell."

"What do you mean Father?"

"They seemed to treat you with the same affection they have for their husbands."

"Really?" replied Matthew in surprise.

"Matthew you would have to be blind not to see that both of those girls really care about you."

"Father I think they think of me as a brother."

"Son, I think perhaps that blow to your head was worse than I thought," said Mathas laughing. All the men in the room joined in the laughter.

"Matthew what about that girl who attacked you?" Claudius asked with a grin. "Stephan is still laughing about that."

"What girl attacked you?" asked Mathas.

"A couple of weeks ago Stephan and I were riding early in the morning when we found an intruder on our land. It was a girl and when I approached her she started punching and kicking me," Matthew said and started laughing.

"Why?" asked Mathas seriously.

"She said her father had told her that our soldiers would not treat women honorably."

"From what Stephan said she was a pretty good fighter," Claudius said grinning.

"Yes she was," Matthew said and winked.

"Stephan said she carried the weapons of a warrior and was dressed like a warrior but that she was very beautiful," Claudius added.

"That is all true," said Matthew.

"What was she doing on our land?" asked Mathas.

"A panther attacked one of their horses and she tracked the colt to that thicket of woods we have near the river. We did find the colt."

"Stephan said that after she found out Matthew was a prince she was still going to fight him unless he told her the story about Arora. When she found out that what she had heard was true," explained Claudius. "She said she would not fight a man of honor."

"Who is this girl?" Mathas asked.

"Chief Sorren's daughter, Angelina," Matthew replied.

Fahron threw his head back and roared with laughter. Mathias and Claudius also could not contain themselves.

"What is so funny?" asked Matthew with bewilderment.

"Oh, Matthew you are lucky that girl didn't kill you. The courage of a lion she has and smart too. She may have two younger brothers but she will end up being the leader of that tribe. And Sorren is as proud as he can be that she is such a fierce warrior," Fahron said as tears ran down his face from laughing.

"Mathas there is something you should know," Claudius said still chuckling. "According to Stephan, Sorren's daughter seemed quite taken with your Matthew."

"Son, seriously," said Mathas as he continued to laugh. "If you choose to get involved with this girl you have to think of the consequences. She is not like your other girlfriends. If you court her and it doesn't work out you could cause a civil war in this kingdom."

"Your father is right," advised Fahron. "If you an Angelina decide to become friends that could help to quell some of the unrest with her tribe. But this girl, do not take her to your bed unless you have feelings for her because your actions could strengthen our kingdom or divide it."

"They are both right," added Claudius. "We are laughing at the thought of her fighting with you, not because the seriousness of the situation escapes us."

"In fact I had this same conversation with Stephan. You might have some completion with this one Matthew."

Banacus and his soldiers rode into the desolated Village of Afax. The street was littered with mutilated bodies and blood seemed to be everywhere. The men rode down the middle of the main street of the village unaware of the eyes that peered from the darkness. Rogetts did not battle as warriors but they attacked the weak and unarmed in packs. Banacus did not see any sign of life in the village. He ordered his me to stop.

"Check for survivors," Banacus barked. "Though I doubt anyone could live through this."

After most of his men had dismounted, one of them yelled "Rogetts." Hundreds of Rogetts attacked the soldiers from every side. The soldiers were fighting the Rogetts on foot and on horseback. The Rogetts would attack each soldier in groups of four or five. Banacus rode through the Rogetts stabbing them and cutting off their heads with his sword; he deliberately trampled several Rogetts with his horse.

Banacus rode up to one of his soldiers who had been knocked onto his back by four Rogetts. Banacus jumped from his horse and stabbed each of the Rogetts in the back. These soldiers from Puntd were seasoned in battle but they were considerably outnumbered. The battle was bloody. When it ended hundreds of dead and dying Rogetts lined the streets.

Banacus ordered his men to round up the surviving Rogetts and to herd them into one of the buildings. Once the Rogetts were forced inside, the soldiers set the building on fire. The screams of the damned could be heard for some distance.

Banacus had his men pile up the bodies of the dead and wounded Rogetts and these too were set ablaze. Banacus gathered his wounded and his dead and they returned to the monastery at Malga.

"What are you doing?" giggled Annabelle.

"Now keep your eyes closed," said Simon as he led his wife through the gardens on the east side of the castle. Suddenly they stopped. "Ok, you can open your eyes now," Simon said.

Annabelle was overwhelmed when she looked before her. In the middle of the garden was a table with a white table cloth, candles and dinner settings for two. There were dozens of lit candles of various sizes spread around the garden illuminating their dining area.

"Oh Simon," Annabelle said as she reached up and kissed him. "What is the occasion?"

"We have not really been alone since the boys were born and we have not celebrated anything since our anniversary," Simon said as he lifted his wife into the air and kissed her.

"What about the babies?"

"Don't worry our mothers have them tonight."

"So, did they help you with all this?" asked Annabelle with a grin.

"No," replied Simon feigning indignation.

"So you did all of this by yourself?"

"Of course not," laughed Simon. "Marie helped me." Simon stood in front of Annabelle and bowed, "My Lady may I have this dance?"

"Of course My Lord," said Annabelle smiling. "But there is no music."

Simon held his wife and started to dance, "My dear there is always music," said Simon with a smile.

Annabelle looked up into her husband's radiant face, "That is what I love about you."

Cerephus entered Roch's war room first and announced, "My Lord, this is Erebus, Erebus this is King Roch."

Roch looked up from his desk and watched Erebus as he entered the room. Erebus was a tall with shoulder length brown hair and large, bushy eyebrows. He wore a red robe that was covered with symbols that were sewn into the fabric with black thread.

There was a power about Erebus that Roch could feel as soon as the warlock entered the room. And there was something else, yes now Roch realized that Erebus' eyes were as black as night. Erebus walked boldly up to Roch and the two men stared at each other across Roch's desk.

Sensing tension between Roch and Erebus, Cerephus spoke first. "My Lord, I did not tell Erebus why you were inquiring about his services."

"Do I know you?" Roch asked of Erebus.

"We have never met," Erebus said as he was trying to figure out the shadows he was seeing around Roch.

"Have a seat," Roch said then turned to Cerephus. "Pour us all some whiskey." Roch turned back to Erebus who had now pulled a chair up to the desk. "There is a demon here. He disguised himself as one of my men until the Sanuri put a curse on him and now he wears no disguise. He told me he wanted to do business together and over the past year we have made a great deal of money. But as Cerephus pointed out, the demon doesn't need my help to rob villages. So I am wondering why he is really here."

"Did you ask him?" Erebus asked.

"He said that he wanted me to help him steal treasures of The Great Ruler, which could be true. But he has done things that are untrustworthy."

Erebus laughed, "If he is truly a demon, everything he says and does is untrustworthy. But if you are doing business with him, why do you want my help?"

"I think he is up to something and I don't know how to fight a demon."

"I see," Erebus said as he sipped his whiskey. "What kind of demon is he?"

66

"How the hell would I know?" snapped Roch.

"You need to know," Erebus said in a voice that rang of authority. "There are many kinds of demons, some can be killed by humans, those are the lower level demons and others need someone with special powers to deal with them. But Roch you have already said several things which are very curious and make me wonder if something more is not going on here. First of all it is highly unusual for a demon to decide to accompany a human and secondly why didn't the Sanuri destroy the demon?"

Roch sat back in his chair and paused for a moment. "The Sanuri appeared here and was angry that I sent demons to him. Perhaps he isn't powerful enough to destroy Demetries."

"Roch, the Sanuri has been known to destroy entire armies of demons, yet he let this one return to your castle. That in and of itself makes me believe that Demetries is a threat to you. The Sanuri is just going to let him play out his role."

Roch's eyes grew wide as Erebus spoke. "What you say makes sense. But why would the demon say he wants to do business with me; why wouldn't he just attack me?"

"Perhaps he has been hired for another task," replied Erebus.

"Hired!"

"Of course demons can be hired," Erebus explained. "Usually by dark lords, or other demons. What you need to think about is why would a demon or dark lord hire another demon to virtually watch you and find out the workings of your castle?"

"Marie," called Renya as she saw Marie walk past the door. When Marie entered the parlor she saw Renya and Laurel sitting on the sofa together and each holding a sleeping baby.

"Marie how are things going out there?" asked Renya smiling.

"They are so cute," replied Marie with a grin. "They are laughing and dancing like there is music."

"They're dancing," repeated Renya with surprise.

"This was such a sweet idea," said Laurel looking at Renya.

"I had nothing to do with it until Simon asked us to watch the babies."

"It was his idea and I don't mind telling you My Lady, you could have knocked me over when he asked me to help," said Marie still smiling.

"Why? Simon is such a dear husband," Laurel asked.

Marie and Renya both looked at each other and smiled. Then Renya laughed and said, "Yes Marie you can say it."

"Those two were hellions, always into things, going off on adventures and fighting. When they couldn't find anyone else to fight with they would fight with each other, just for the sport of it," Marie said. "But they were never bad boys, just wild spirits. We never thought they would settle down." All three women laughed so loudly that baby Anthony started to wake.

"That first day you arrived at the castle, remember?" Renya asked Laurel. "Raul was so sick and on crutches and Simon was helping all of you out of the boca; then when everyone was out Simon stood next to Annabelle instead of his brother. I know it was a little thing but I saw the look on his face and I knew he had finally fallen in love."

"I think it was the same for Annabelle," said Laurel. "While we were traveling here, she and Raul would tease each other constantly and you know how headstrong she is; not to be outdone even by a prince."

"The day we arrived here, we were eating breakfast when Simon led a group of soldiers to our camp. When Raul and Simon saw each other you could easily see the love between them; after that Simon would not leave Raul. Simon sent the rest of the troops back to the castle and he never said anything but I think Simon was pretty worried about Raul, you know how bad he looked."

"I was so thankful to see Raul but it broke my heart to see the condition he was in," said Renya in almost a whisper.

"Well the only one you can thank that Raul lived, is Vitomas. She took so much mistreatment from King Roch."

68

"Oh Renya it would break your heart to know how badly he beat her sometimes."

"But Vitomas stood up for Raul over and over and devised that plan to get him out of the kingdom," said Laurel. "I am sure they told you this but Vitomas would not escape with us because she thought we had a better chance without her and she was right, but it tore Raul apart."

Renya looked at Marie then back at Laurel. "When Raul first told Sudfad and me that he was in love with Roch's Queen; we were appalled and worried. But then Raul told us how Vitomas found him and saved his life; actually saving him several times and then he started to cry. I had not seen Raul cry since he found Simon so injured that day and brought him home."

"It was obvious to us that Raul loved Vitomas but you have to understand also Laurel, when you first met Raul he was so badly injured and had been poisoned. But now you know him for the large and powerful man that he is. Raul and Simon have always been the ones who help and save others. Then this beautiful young girl saves him; well, Raul felt that he left her to die and he was so filled with guilt. I sometimes wonder if that is why he seems so overprotective of her now."

"Did they tell you that the man who kidnapped Vitomas was watching us leave then took her; which probably saved her life because Roch would most certainly have killed her if he knew Vitomas helped Raul escape, and we all knew that."

Tears came to Renya's eyes. Laurel reached over and grasped Renya's hand. "Oh my dear friend I do not mean to make you cry," Laurel said apologetically.

"No," said Renya. "I knew there was more than they would tell; no wonder they are all so close."

"Well, to make you smile again and to get back to Simon and Annabelle; when Simon walked into our camp that morning, Annabelle not only could not stop looking at him," said Laurel smiling. "She was so nervous she stopped talking; never had we seen Annabelle so quiet. And of course Raul picked up on it immediately. It was strange watching the three of them, because it was almost like Raul knew Simon and Annabelle would fall in love."

69

Cerephus, Roch and Erebus talked for hours in Roch's war room. Roch was feeling confident that Erebus was a man knowledgeable in many areas besides the black arts. "Erebus I would like to hire you as an advisor. I believe I could use a man with your talents. What is your price?" Cerephus felt his heart leap within his chest because this is exactly what he wanted, so he could proceed with his plans.

"Well, if you truly want me to work for you I will need more than pay."

"Go on."

"For me to do my work I will need a library of books and a work area with a hearth. I will need a variety of herbs, dishes and other things," Erebus explained. "I left all of my things behind when Cerephus contacted me to come and help his friend."

Roch was surprised that Erebus referenced him as Cerephus' friend. A choice of words that was well planned by Erebus.

"Of course, whatever you need. Cerephus can show you through the castle and you can choose your chambers."

"That is most generous of you," Erebus said. "As for pay, I think a small bag of gold coins every week is reasonable."

"As do I," replied Roch. No sooner had Roch uttered these words then there was a knock on the door.

"My Lord," a voice said.

"Sophie come in," Roch called. "I would like you to meet my new advisor Erebus, he will be staying at the castle."

Sophie stopped abruptly when she saw Erebus. The warlock quickly turned around in his chair and the two stared at each other in stunned silence.

"Do you two know each other?" Roch demanded.

"Yes, My Lord," Sophie stammered. "We met many years ago."

Once a week Annabelle and Vitomas would leave the children with Gabriella and Abigail and go shopping in Salar. They always took one of the small bocas which only required two horses and they would drive into the city. The two women loved to browse in the shops and to talk with the people.

The residents of Salar had always loved and admired King Sudfad and Queen Renya and they enjoyed the antics of the two young princes as they grew into men. But it was Princess Vitomas and Princess Annabelle who really stole the hearts of the people of Salar. The Princesses always remembered the names of anyone they spoke with and made even the humblest person feel special.

Annabelle and Vitomas tried to schedule their shopping trips on Tuesday mornings. In anticipation some of the shop keepers would have special items for them. But it was Myla the wife of the owner of the Dragon's Inn who would out do herself and make the finest pastries and treats for the Princesses.

As part of their routine Vitomas and Annabelle would stop at the Dragon's Inn for coffee and Myla's baking. Many times the other customers eating at the Dragon's Inn would gather around the two young princesses and they all would enjoy conversation and laughter.

"It was a trap, the Rogetts were waiting for us," spat Banacus with disgust. "They surrounded us and attacked; never have I heard of those creatures fighting like that before."

"This disturbs me greatly," said King Tobias. "You are sure the monastery is safe?"

"Yes My Lord, I left one hundred able bodied men at the monastery and twenty who were still healing from their injuries," replied Banacus.

"Send two hundred more, they can stay at the monastery and be closer to the villages if there are more attacks," said Tobias.

71

"If the priests do not like having their monastery turned into a temporary fort, please tell them it is the only way we can keep people safe."

"My Lord, after seeing the mutilated people the priests were treating I do not believe they will argue," said Banacus.

"Banacus one more thing, tomorrow morning I will give you messages that must be hand delivered to several other kings; I want to warn them of this drastic change in the behaviors of the Rogetts."

"I will choose my swiftest riders, My Lord."

"With all the Huta attacks a lone rider is not a good idea."

"Will you warn all the kingdoms?"

"No, I will only warn the kings that I am confident will not murder my men."

Chapter V
Snakes Crossing

"What is it Father?" asked Angelina as she brought her horse to a stop in the middle of her Village of Tyger. "Why did you sound the horn, are we under attack?"

"We aren't," replied Sorren with anger. "But Snakes Crossing was attacked by Valdore's men, follow me, we are meeting in the Great Hall. When Angelina and Sorren entered the Great Hall, which was nothing more than a large, one room wooden building, it was already filled with people. Angelina's gaze went immediately to two bloody villagers who were seated in the front of the room. Angelina followed her father as he walked up to these men.

"As we told the others, Sorren," said one of the injured villagers who appeared to be in pain. "We were tending our fields when suddenly they were upon us. They struck me and my brother Lorenzo as they rode past us; then they burned the village and injured many of the villagers."

"What is your name?" demanded Sorren in his normally deep and husky voice.

"Hamon, it is Hamon," replied the villager who had been speaking.

"Hamon, were any of the villagers killed?" asked Sorren.

"Three that I know of, a mother and her two children when they could not get out of their burning house."

"Did they take anything?"

"Sorren, not that I know of."

"And you are sure they were Valdore's men?"

"They wore the green and red sashes that his men wear," responded Hamon.

"Father I do not like this," said Angelina loudly. "Why would Usman's men burn the village and not steal their livestock or money. This looks more like an attempt to draw us into war. Father you know I will not back down from battle but after what happened at Arora, I think we should be wary."

"Who knows if that story about Arora is true," replied Sorren.

"I know it is true, I spoke to Prince Matthew myself."

"You did what! When?" yelled Sorren. "I told you to stay away from the King's soldiers."

"Father, I tracked the colt onto his land. Not only did Prince Matthew help me find the colt but he said that if we ever needed help to come to the castle and to tell the guards he had given us permission to be there. Father I found him to be an honorable man and I believed him about Arora."

Sorren stared at his only daughter for a while. "We have never received an invitation to the castle before, are you sure he did not give it because you are a beautiful woman?"

"Father I will take you to the Prince and you tell me yourself what you think of him," Angelina said defiantly.

A broad smile came across Sorren's face. One of the things that he loved about his daughter was that she was just as strong willed as he was. Although Angelina was young, Sorren had trained her well and knew Angelina was not easily influenced like other girls her age. "I have not spoken to our King since you were a baby, perhaps it is time to pay him a visit."

Sophie had avoided any contact with Erebus for over two days, now she was waiting for him outside of his chambers. Sophie felt like a nervous schoolgirl as the minutes ticked by. Suddenly Sophie heard steps and her heart leaped in her chest. Sophie was overwhelmed with a feeling to flee; just as she decided to leave, Sophie and Erebus saw each other in the hallway.

"Sophie!" said Erebus with a warm smile. "I have been wondering where you were." Sophie found herself frozen in place as Erebus walked towards her with his arms wide open.

Erebus hugged Sophie tightly but she did not hug him back. "What is the matter, aren't you glad to see me?" Sophie looked at Erebus as if she was going to cry. "Come let's go into my rooms," Erebus said and led Sophie inside.

"Erebus why are you here?" whispered Sophie once they had entered his chambers.

"A better question is why is a wealthy and powerful witch working as a cook for the most notorious king in the continent?" Erebus asked as he poured two glasses of red wine.

"Things are not as they appear here," Sophie said as she took the glass of wine.

"I would say that is a great understatement," Erebus said sarcastically. "Can you see those shadows that linger around Roch?"

"Shadows, why no."

"I have never seen anything like them. They appear to be talking."

"What! Erebus, tell me what else have you seen?"

"What, does this disturb you Sophie? You can't be attached to that monster?"

"Erebus you just have to trust me, I cannot tell you why I am here but you may be in great danger."

"Sophie I have always trusted you, even after you left me for another man."

"Erebus what are you talking about. You left me and you broke my heart. There has been no other since."

Erebus stared at the woman who was once the love of his life. "Sophie, Meekos told me you had agreed to marry another man."

"Meekos!"

Matthew knocked on the door to his father's study. "Father you summoned me?"

"Yes Matthew please come in," Mathas continued to speak as Matthew was opening the door. "We have company."

When Matthew walked into the room he first saw a huge man dressed in leather skins and wearing the trappings of a warrior, sitting in the chair across from his father's desk. The man had long curly red hair with a mustache and a long beard. Beads decorated both his hair and his beard.

"Son I would like you to meet Sorren Chief of the Nordes Tribe. Sorren this is my only son Matthew." Mathas made the introductions as Matthew walked across the room towards Sorren. Matthew extended his hand and Sorren stood up and shook the hand of the Prince, something he had never expected to do.

Mathas continued, "I believe you have already met his daughter Angelina." Mathew turned to his left and saw Angelina sitting in another chair across from Mathas. Once again she was wearing an outfit made of leather skins, but Matthew could not help but notice that the short dress she was wearing was decorated with small beads and exposed one shoulder.

Matthew walked up to Angelina, took her right hand and kissed the back of it. "My Lady." Angelina blushed but did not say a word.

"Matthew have a seat, Sorren has come to speak with both of us." Matthew took a seat to the side of his father so he could see the faces of all who were in the study.

"Mathas you and I have not spoken since our children were but babies. Time and family have tempered my ambitions and I want more for my people than constant bloodshed. I come to you now because my daughter said your son had offered us an invitation. She believes him to be an honorable man and I know that you are. Some things have been happening that I believe you and I should discuss."

"Sorren I am glad that you are here and I should have offered you an invitation before this but quite honestly I did not believe you would accept it," Mathas turned to Matthew. "Son, before we start would you pour us some whiskey?"

As Matthew stood up he looked at Angelina, "Do you drink whiskey?"

"I will have some wine," Angelina replied uncomfortably.

Matthew handed glasses of whiskey to Mathas and Sorren, then he set an entire bottle on the desk between them. Matthew returned to the group, handing a small glass of red wine to Angelina before taking his seat. Sorren noticed how quiet his daughter seemed around the young prince.

"Mathas I will get straight to the point. Angelina said that the stories we have heard about Bakken scouts trying to get your men to massacre a village of women and children are true. In the last few weeks we have had attacks on three of our northern villages. In each attack people are injured and buildings burned, but few are killed. The attackers all wear the sashes of Usman's men but we are not sure if they are who they appear to be."

"Why?" asked Mathas

Now Angelina spoke up with the voice of a warrior, "Because they take nothing from these villages, no valuables or livestock. They always attack in broad daylight so many can see them and they leave witnesses. This is not how Usman has attacked our people in the past."

Mathias looked at Angelina then at Sorren giving him a look of approval. "My daughter believes there are others who are trying to trick us into a war. This is why we have come here to speak with you," Sorren said then took a long drink from his glass of whiskey.

Mathas sat quietly for a few moments before he spoke. "Sorren, Matthew and I agree with Angelina. And we too have experienced some strange happenings that cause us to believe dark magics are at work here."

"What do you mean?" asked Sorren as he put his empty glass on the desk.

"Please help yourself," said Mathas as he pointed to the bottle of whiskey. "Matthew why don't you explain."

"As you probably heard my father was seriously injured in a riding accident," Matthew said. "The Bakken scouts came to us with information that only someone who was with my father could know. They told us they came by this information from some men who were hiding in Arora. Men they said, who had planned the accident. When I led our troops to Arora we watched the village for some time, seeing no men at all, only women and children."

"The scouts kept demanding that we attack the village. Stephan and I rode into the village and spoke with some of the women who said the men were all hunting. We returned to my soldiers and arrested the scouts, who suddenly burst into flames, within moments these men were nothing more than piles of ashes." Angelina watched her father as Matthew spoke.

"And there is more," continued Matthew. "My father was thrown from his horse because they came upon hundreds of snakes, which tried to attack Father once he was on the ground. The men who were with father prevented him from being bitten. These snakes were like none we have ever seen before. The Sanuri of Tabrul has told us that these particular snakes are a Mark of Satan and can only be called forth by a dark lord."

"A dark lord!" yelled Sorren. "Why would a dark lord be here?"

Matthew and Mathas looked at each other then Mathas started to speak. Matthew interrupted, "Father."

"It is alright son, Sorren has a right to know, especially if it could be affecting his people."

"What are you talking about?" asked Sorren gruffly.

"Sorren, as a father you may be able to understand the pain of what I am about to tell you," said Mathas sadly. "My oldest child, Juleta has been banned from the Kingdoms of Lentz and Wetpr for treason not only against me but the Royal Family of Wetpr. She wants my throne," Mathas paused for a moment. "And we have discovered that she is a dark lord."

"Mathas no," gasped Sorren.

"So you think Juleta is behind all of this?" asked Angelina.

"We don't know," replied Matthew. "But we strongly suspect that she is trying to cause a civil war so she somehow can take over the kingdom."

There were a few moments of silence, then Mathas spoke, "Sorren, if my daughter is behind the attacks on your villagers she will be dealt with as any other criminal. But if it is not Juleta do you have any idea who would try to trick the tribes into war?"

"It is no secret that Usman wants to control the kingdom but even he has been quiet for a long time. And Angelina is right; these new attacks do not have the earmarks of the Valdore Tribe. I can think of no others," Sorren said.

"Sorren, we have all lived in peace for some time. It is not to my advantage to attack the tribes or to start a civil war. I give you my word as King that my men are not behind any of these attacks and we will search for those who are," Mathas said as he extended his hand to Sorren.

Sorren shook the King's hand without hesitation. "I believe you Mathas and I am sorry to hear about your daughter being such a traitor."

"Sorren I have heard many good things about your daughter, she sounds like an able leader and a fierce warrior, you have done well." Sorren beamed with pride at Mathas' words. "And she has great courage; did she tell you she fought with Matthew and from the sounds of it, won?" Mathas asked with a grin.

"What!" yelled Sorren as he turned to Angelina. "You said he helped you find the colt."

"He did Father," said Angelina, suddenly feeling like a child. "But before that, well."

"Spit it out girl," said Sorren gruffly.

"Well, before that I attacked him."

"Why?" demanded Sorren.

"Because you said not to trust the soldiers."

79

"Did he do anything to make you not trust him?"

"No."

"Did you know he was the Prince?"

"His friend called out that I was attacking the Prince but that was after I had already started," Angelina said uncomfortably.

"Did you have the sense to stop then?"

"No Father," Angelina said after some hesitation.

"In her defense," said Matthew. "When she found out who I was she demanded to know if the stories about Arora were true. Then she stopped fighting and said she would not fight with an honorable man."

Sorren sat silent for a moment, trying to contain his anger, "So let me understand this, you were on the King's land. You attacked the King's son and then he helped you find the colt. You know you could have been put to death for treason. And then he invites us to the castle. I am sorry but I am confused," Sorren turned to Matthew, "Can you please explain this to me."

"In her defense two of us rode up to her. Angelina told me how you warned her about soldiers and I believe she was just trying to get the upper hand."

"Did she hurt you?"

"Only my pride," Matthew said with a laugh.

"Did he hurt you?"

"No Father, he didn't even try," said Angelina with embarrassment. "He kept telling me to stop."

"Why did you invite us here Matthew?"

"I don't know your people and I was so surprised and impressed at what a great fighter Angelina is; I wanted to meet the man who taught her." Angelina was very pleased with the words that Matthew was saying.

Sorren looked at Mathas. Both fathers smiled at each other knowingly. "Mathas my daughter was right about Matthew, he is a man of honor, you should be proud." Then Sorren turned back to Angelina and looked at her for a moment. "And you young lady are very lucky that the Prince is a man of honor. Now why don't the two of you leave us; so Mathas and I can talk." Matthew and Angelina were both confused and surprised that their fathers wanted them to leave the meeting.

"Do as he says," Mathas said. "Sorren and I have much to catch up on."

Matthew stood up and held out his hand to Angelina, who just stared at it. "Go!" barked Sorren. Angelina quickly stood up and grasped Matthew's outstretched hand and the two of them walked out of the study in silence.

As soon as the door closed Mathas turned to Sorren. "I think my son is attracted to your daughter," Mathas said with a warm smile.

Sorren too was smiling, "And I think my daughter is attracted to your son." Then he burst into laughter. "I hope they don't kill each other." Mathas also started laughing and filled both of their glasses with whiskey.

"Thank you for what you said," Angelina said shyly as she and Matthew walked in one of the castle gardens.

"It was the truth," said Matthew, who was still holding Angelina's hand. "But I must say I was surprised when I saw you and your father in the study."

"You said I should come if I needed help and I know it may sound strange but I just have a really bad feeling about these attacks on our people. I know I must sound crazy but several times when I have been hunting I feel like I am being watched. I don't know how to explain it; something is just not right," said Angelina who was looking at the ground as she and Matthew walked in the garden. "But after you told us about Juleta, I don't know, it somehow makes sense."

"Juleta has broken my father's heart," Matthew said sternly. "And she fills me with anger, not only is she threatening my family here but my family in Wetpr."

"You have another family in Wetpr?" Angelina asked hesitantly as she suddenly felt fear surge through her.

"Why did you ask it like that?"

"It really is none of my business but do you have a wife in Wetpr?" Matthew heard the fear in Angelina's voice as she spoke.

Matthew stopped walking and turned to face Angelina. He started to smile which made her blush. "No, I don't have a wife anywhere. My father's sister is the Queen of Wetpr. I have two cousins, Raul and Simon who are like brothers to me. They were both married a little over a year ago and now have sons. I wanted to go to the christenings but I couldn't leave here."

"You wanted to go to the christenings?" asked Angelina with surprise. "I guess I just have never heard a warrior say he wanted to go to a christening before."

Matthew laughed. "I am very close to that family, my cousin's wives write to me every week, King Sudfad adopted me as one of his sons and they built me my own quarters there."

"You mean you have your own room there?"

"No, it is more like a wing of the castle," said Mathew as he watched Angelina's eyes grow wide. "And you have to know Sudfad and my aunt Renya. They turn every family event into a big celebration for the entire city."

"It all sounds very nice there," said Angelina as she was going to start walking again. "I have never been to Wetpr." Angelina took but two steps before Matthew pulled her back in front of him again.

"What about you?"

"What do you mean?" asked Angelina as she looked up into Matthew's face. Angelina was not accustomed to feeling shy or awkward around men; she now found her feelings unsettling.

"Do you have a husband?"

Angelina turned red which made Matthew smile. "If I did, I don't think I would be holding hands with you, my young prince."

"Have you been promised to anyone?"

"No, my father said a warrior should be able to choose whoever they want to marry."

"I see," said Matthew with a grin.

"What does that mean?" asked Angelina with a coy smile.

"Do you have any suitors I should know about?"

Angelina started to laugh, "And why should you know about them?"

"I would like to see you again."

Angelina looked up into Matthew's eyes and said seriously, "And I would like to see you again, my prince." After a moment her demeanor changed.

"Angelina is something wrong?"

"There is a warrior in our village named Tobart. He has asked my father for me several times but my father has denied him.

"And still he keeps asking?"

"Yes and there is more," said Angelina hesitantly. "My father does not know this but Usman has confronted me a couple of times. The first time he asked me to marry him. He was very insulted when I said no. He told me he would make me his wife whether I was willing or not. Matthew he is older than my father and has several wives already."

"Angelina you haven't told your father any of this?"

"No, I didn't want to start a war."

"Angelina this may be the reason for the raids on your people. Come we are going to tell both our fathers right now."

When King Sudfad received word of a group of Rogetts ambushing Puntd soldiers he immediately alerted his military outposts. Sudfad also sent orders that the generals of the outposts should ensure the safety of the miners in their jurisdictions.

Fort Polta was located in the northwestern section of the kingdom. It backed up to the Tia Forest which in turn backed up to the Galeg Mountain range. This fort was situated between the River Neior and the Sea of Talmont. Three large gold mining sites were situated in that area. Each of these mining sites contained numerous mines which were worked by thousands of men. The mining sites were owned by several different families, all of whom greatly appreciated the protection of the soldiers.

The diamond mines as well as Fort Styls were located in far northeastern Wetpr, between the River Toba and the eastern border of the kingdom. These mines covered hundreds of miles of territory but in the middle of this vast range of mines was 'the beast'. Named by the miners who worked it, the beast was a mine of incredible proportions. As deep as it was wide the beast was the oldest of the mines yet it continually amazed the miners with its contents.

Fort Nir, which was located in the center of the kingdom and Fort Salar were not located near any mines, but they were still put on alert for Rogett attacks.

Sudfad sent messengers to each fort then he called his sons and the Sanuri into his study. The Sanuri read the letter then said, "Sudfad, I will be leaving for Malga this afternoon."

"I thought as much," replied Sudfad. "It sounds like they have a horrible situation on their hands. Please keep us informed of what is going on and let me know if you need anything." Then Sudfad turned to Simon and Raul. "Sons if this situation with the Rogetts threatens our people we will be going to battle, prepare your men."

Sorren pounded his large fist on top of Mathas' desk as Angelina told him of her encounters with Usman. Matthew stood next to Angelina and held her hand tightly as he could see she was scared to tell these things to her father.

"Angelina I have told you what a dangerous man Usman is. Why did you not tell me any of this before?"

"Because I did not want to anger you, Father."

"Anger me!" yelled Sorren. "Our enemy comes onto our lands and threatens my daughter and you don't want to anger me. Angelina he is not just a threat to you; he is a threat to all of our people. I taught you better than this." Sorren's voice kept rising as he yelled; his face was turning bright red and the veins in Sorren's neck were becoming visible.

"Yes Father."

"And you take a walk with this boy for a few minutes and you tell him of these things but you won't tell me, your father."

"Sorren I asked her if she had any suitors or if you had promised her to anyone," Matthew said calmly.

Sorren stopped yelling and stared into Matthew's eyes. Then he looked down and saw that Matthew and Angelina were holding hands. "Matthew why did you ask her these things?"

"Because I would like to see her again."

Sorren glanced over at Mathis then looked back at Matthew, "I see. You do know she scares most of her suitors away?" Sorren said with his demeanor relaxing considerably.

"Father!" said Angelina with embarrassment.

"How does she scare them away?" Matthew asked with a grin.

"Do you want to tell him?" Sorren asked as he looked at his daughter.

Angelina did not speak for a few moments then she let out a loud sigh, "I challenge them to fight with or without weapons and if I beat them I tell them to go," Angelina was looking at the floor as she spoke. Matthew and Mathas both started laughing.

Sorren was smiling, "So are you going to challenge Matthew to a fight?"

Angelina started to smile and looked at Matthew, "No, I already know I can't beat him."

"I see," said Sorren as he was desperately trying to hold back his laughter. "Would you like to see Matthew again?"

"Yes Father."

"Then I will give my approval but under one condition. If Usman or his men or anyone else threatens or bothers you that you tell me and Matthew."

"I promise Father."

As soon as the entire Royal Family of Wetpr was seated at the dining room table both Vitomas and Annabelle stood up.

"Before we eat Vitomas and I have a surprise for all of you," said Annabelle excitedly.

"Oh by The Great Ruler, Marie isn't trying to teach you to cook again?" asked Simon with a feigned sigh.

"No," replied Annabelle with a smile as she slapped Simon on the back of the head; at which the entire table burst into laughter. Marie put several dishes of food on the table and turned to leave the room. "Marie, please stay for this," said Annabelle as she turned and looked at Vitomas.

"I barely remember having a family and although Annabelle has Alexander and Laurel as you all know both of us were taken prisoners as children," said Vitomas. "Our lives were so vastly different from how they are now. We are both so happy now, sometimes I am afraid that I will wake up and find out this is all a dream."

Both Renya and Laurel started to cry at Vitomas' words. "All of you have done so much for us that Annabelle and I have been trying to find a way to pay you back."

"Which isn't easy because as the King and Queen you have so much which you have freely shared with my family," said Annabelle. "One of the reasons Vitomas and I have been going to Salar every week is because we have designed some gifts for you." As Annabelle spoke Vitomas walked around the table and placed a small box in front of each person.

"You can open them now," said Annabelle after everyone at the table had received a gift.

"Oh girls this is beautiful," said Renya with a gasp.

Laurel could barely say "Thank you," in between her tears.

"We took the two colors from the family crest for the center stones of the rings. All the men have the dark blue sapphires and all the women have the rubies. All of those smaller stones that are surrounding the large stones are the birth stones of each family member. Sudfad and Renya's are on top with Alexander's and Laurel's next. The rest belong to Raul, Simon, Matthew, Petra, Annabelle, all the grandbabies and me. In between the stones are small silver pieces which can be replaced with more birth stones as the family grows," said Vitomas as she patted her protruding stomach.

"These are wonderful," said King Sudfad as he slipped his ring onto his finger. "And it is a perfect fit."

"Fortunately for us Andrew, the jeweler in Salar, knows your sizes," said Annabelle. "But there is more."

"Marie you have cooked for this family since you were a girl, you helped to raise our husbands and you are helping to raise our children, so this is for you," said Vitomas as she walked up to Marie and handed her a long box. Marie opened the box and started to sob. Marie's hands were shaking so Vitomas helped her clasp the golden chain around her neck. At the end of the chain was a large golden locket decorated with the same birth stones as the rings.

Marie tried to talk but could not because she was crying so hard, so Annabelle and Vitomas each gave her a hug. Simon and Raul got up from the table and hugged and kissed their wives; then they too hugged Marie as they had never seen her cry in all the years she had served them. Soon the entire family was out of their seats and hugging Marie and the Princesses. Once they all realized that each golden ring was a slightly different design they were all looking at each other's rings and at Marie's locket.

"You gave us the perfect gifts," said Renya as she put her arm around Laurel who was still crying.

"Do you really like them, if not we can change them?" asked Vitomas.

"My dear daughters I do believe we all love our gifts just as they are," said Sudfad with a smile. "Except perhaps Petra who does seem more interested in the food."

"Petra we will get you a bigger ring when you grow," said Annabelle.

"Ok," replied Petra as he put a spoonful of mashed potatoes into his mouth.

"How did you girls pay for these? You never ask for money." asked Simon.

"Vitomas sold her jewels," replied Annabelle.

"What jewels?" asked Raul with amazement.

"Remember that earring I gave you at the cabin?" Vitomas asked Raul.

"Yes and I will never part with it," Raul said as he squeezed Vitomas' hand.

"I was wearing a matching necklace, a ring and a brooch; I gave them to the jeweler to make these rings."

"Oh my dear you did not have to sell your jewelry," Renya said disapprovingly.

"It would not have felt like a gift if we asked you for the money to pay for the rings and besides I do not want anything that reminds me of Roch," said Vitomas as Raul put his arm around her and kissed her on the lips.

Chapter VI
The Scroll and the Sword

Usually the first at the dinner table, tonight Petra was the last to be seated. Petra slid into his chair at the table without saying a word.

"How did you get that black eye Petra?" asked Simon with a grin. Petra shrank into his seat as now every eye at the table was upon him. He did not answer.

"We are waiting Petra," said Sudfad as he was trying to keep from smiling.

Petra looked down at his plate and said in a low voice, "Kyra."

"Kyra hit you?" asked Renya with astonishment.

Sudfad touched Renya's hand then asked, "Petra why did Kyra hit you?"

Petra quickly looked up from his plate and said with enthusiasm, "Because I told her that girls can't fight."

"So she punched you in the eye to prove that they can?" asked Raul, trying not to laugh out loud.

"Oh she did more than punch me in the eye."

"What did you do?" asked Sudfad.

"Nothing, I told her that you told me not to hit girls because I could hurt them; that made her madder and she wuped me." Everyone at the table was trying with great difficulty not to laugh.

"Did she hurt you?" asked Renya with concern.

"Not really, but I was mad that I couldn't hit her back."

"Well you did the right thing," said Sudfad.

"Who told you that girls can't fight?" asked Simon as he winked at Annabelle.

"Well everybody knows that," replied Petra.

"Well it sure looks like Kyra can fight and Annabelle can fight," said Simon.

"Annabelle?" asked Petra.

"Yes, I have been teaching her how to fight with a sword for a long time and she is very good," said Simon with pride. "In fact when we had that last Huta attack..."

Renya quickly spoke to change the subject; she looked at Simon and shook her head indicating to him not to talk about the attack. "How do you like your lessons?" Renya asked Annabelle.

"I really like them and Simon is a great teacher; Vitomas wants to learn too."

Raul looked at Vitomas with surprise, "I didn't know that."

"I was going to ask you to teach me after Samuel was born."

"So you picked the name?" asked Renya with excitement.

"Raul wants to name him after Simon so we chose Simon's middle name," said Vitomas happily. Both Vitomas and Raul looked at Simon who was smiling proudly.

"Very good," said Sudfad acknowledging that he was pleased with the name.

"So Raul are you going to teach Vitomas how to use a sword?" asked Simon, knowing what the answer would be.

Raul did not respond. "Don't you want me to learn how to protect myself?" asked Vitomas with surprise.

"No, it is not that."

"You don't think I can do it?" asked Vitomas with her voice lowering.

"No, I mean I know you can do it," said Raul.

"Then what is wrong?" asked Vitomas.

"I don't think I will be able to teach you because I would be too afraid of hurting you," said Raul softly. Vitomas smiled and kissed Raul on the cheek.

"Can Simon teach her?" asked Annabelle.

Raul looked at Vitomas then at Simon, both of whom were smiling at him. "That would be fine," said Raul although he was not convinced it was a good idea.

"Simon would you teach me after the baby is born?" asked Vitomas.

"I would be happy to," replied Simon with a grin.

"You summoned me My Lord," Erebus said as he entered Roch's war room.

"Yes, I have seen so little of you the last two days that I wanted to speak with you," Roch said. Cerephus was already seated at the table in the war room.

"My Lord, I have been kept busy obtaining the books and items that I need to work for you." Erebus responded nonchalantly.

"Yes, that is what Cerephus has told me. We have not seen Demetries since two days before your arrival. What do you make of this?"

"Why do you think he left?" Erebus asked.

"He left after he found out we killed the Huta prisoners," Cerephus replied.

"You know that the Hutas worship demons," Erebus said. "Have you considered that Demetries is the demon controlling the Hutas that have been attacking your castle and Taperia?" Both Roch and Cerephus got surprised looks on their faces but neither spoke. "I have spent most of the last two days in both Taperia and Cana trying to obtain the things that I need. I spent a great deal of time just talking with the people. I was told that Taperia has never been attacked by Hutas until this last year and there have been several attacks."

92

"Didn't Demetries appear about a year ago? And how do you explain the fact that Taperia keeps suffering attacks, yet not one Huta has even set foot in the Village of Cana? Roch I am going to tell you something which will anger you," Erebus continued. "But no matter how mad you get with me you must listen to my words."

"Go ahead," said Roch as he was already getting angry.

"Demons are very manipulative, all demons. Just from the things that you and Cerephus have told me I believe that Demetries knows exactly what will entice you and distract you from other things. Roch you are known as a man of cunning, yet these things I tell you about Demetries appear to come as a surprise to you. I believe this demon is trying to keep you in the dark about something; I just don't know what it is yet."

King Sudfad waited for the family to take their seats at the dinner table before he spoke. "I have something that I want us to discuss as a family. "Over the past few days I have found myself staring at this beautiful ring that Vitomas and Annabelle gave to me; as it pleases me greatly. Vitomas squeezed Raul's hand and smiled as the King spoke.

"In a few months we will be blessed with another child in this family and the rings will have to be taken into the jewelers for the addition of the new stone," said Sudfad. I am proposing that we make a small change to the rings; since all of the men's rings have such wide bands I would like to have a golden sword mounted on one side and a golden scroll on the other."

"My idea is to then declare these the official emblems of the Royal Family and they will not only represent family unity but the roles we play in this world. I would like to hear your thoughts on the matter." Sudfad looked at both Annabelle and Vitomas, "Now be honest with your answers girls because I do not want to ruin this gift for you."

"I don't know what to say; I feel honored," said Annabelle.

"As do I and I am so pleased you like them," said Vitomas.

"I like the idea Father," said Raul as Simon nodded in agreement.

"I love not only the rings but the thought and love that went into them but I have a suggestion," said Renya as she looked at Sudfad. "I think your idea is wonderful but is there a way the women's rings could also have the addition of the sword and scroll; perhaps if we make the bands a little wider?"

The entire family agreed on the changes to the rings. Then Sudfad led a toast, "May these beautiful rings represent, through all generations, our love of family, of our kingdom and of The Great Ruler."

"Miss me?" Demetries asked sarcastically as he walked into Roch's war room and poured himself a glass of whiskey.

"Actually I have been trying to figure out what you are up to," Roch said coldly.

"I was tracking down a rumor that I felt would be of great importance to you," Demetries said with a sadistic smile as he sat down at the table.

"I am listening," Roch said as he tried to maintain an emotional distance between himself and the demon.

"I just came from Salar," Demetries said as he tried to savor the moment. "Your brother's family had another huge celebration a little over a week ago. And as usual they invited the entire kingdom."

Roch's face was turning red. "Tell me."

"They christened three grandsons. Raul and Vitomas have a son named Sudfad. I heard he is the spitting image of Raul. And that little Annabelle had twin sons with Simon. Everyone was talking about what big babies they are and how they all look like their fathers."

Roch was squeezing his glass of whiskey with such force that it burst in his hand. In his rage, Roch did not realize he was bleeding. Demetries always enjoyed riling Roch up.

"Leave me," yelled Roch.

94

As soon as Demetries shut the door behind him, he heard something heavy hit it. Demetries stood in the hallway laughing as he listened to Roch breaking all of the furniture in the war room.

"That bitch never gave me a son!" Roch kept screaming over and over.

Almost a week had pasted before Matthew returned the visit to Sorren and Angelina. It was a hot and sunny afternoon when he rode into the Village of Tyger; home to Sorren's family. Tyger was a moderately sized village that lay just east of the River Shey, in the southwest corner of the lands belonging to the tribe of Nordes. The village was only a two hour ride to the King's castle.

As Matthew rode down the main street of the village he saw a large group of people gathered ahead of him; they appeared to be watching some kind of tournament. Matthew dismounted and walked up to Sorren, who's large and burly frame stood out in the crowd. Sorren greeted Matthew and the two men shook hands. Sorren then nodded towards the competition.

On one side of the street there was a line of people with bows and arrows. Directly across from them was a row of targets made of bags of straw. Each target had a face and heart drawn on it and was attached to a sturdy beam. The beams where attached to movable platforms. Matthew immediately noticed that all of the competitors were male except for Angelina, who was standing in the position closest to Sorren.

Matthew caught his breath when he saw Angelina. She was wearing a sleeveless leather camisole and a short leather skirt. The tough material did nothing to hide her extremely feminine curves. Angelina had a quiver of arrows slung over her back, two knife sheaths strapped to her waist and a third knife sheath strapped to her left thigh, which was easily visible because of her short skirt. Angelina's long red hair hung down her back and on this day was decorated with blue beads and blue feathers.

"The game is called Bozie," explained Sorren. "Each person must shoot three arrows into the heart then one knife must lodge in the throat and the second knife between the eyes."

"The contestant who completes these tasks with the most accuracy and the quickest time wins."

"Let me guess, Angelina usually wins," said Matthew.

"Yes, that is why she is standing in the winner's position. The game starts with many players and as they are eliminated the next player moves towards the winner's position."

"Would you mind?" asked Matthew as he picked up a bow and a quiver of arrows.

"Stop the game," bellowed Sorren's thunderous voice. "We have a new challenger." The eight players turned to look at Matthew as he walked towards them.

"Matthew you came!" exclaimed Angelina happily.

"You won't be sending me home if I lose," Matthew whispered into Angelina's ear before he continued to his place in line. Angelina smiled and blushed at his comment.

"Who is he?" demanded Tobart.

"He is Prince Matthew," replied Sorren without looking at Tobart.

"Why is he here?" Tobart asked angrily.

Sorren turned to look at Tobart, "Because I invited him. His father and I are old friends."

"So is that why the King's men are patrolling our northern border and not us?" Tobart asked with disgust.

"Tobart you are in no position to question my actions; nor will you ever be."

Tobart stared at Sorren angrily. Sorren could see that Tobart's body was tensing and that he was opening and closing his fists. Although a large man, Tobart knew he could not overpower Sorren in a fair fight. Without speaking Tobart walked to the other side of the crowd and watched the game.

Round after round Matthew outperformed the other players until he was standing next to Angelina, who was in the winner's position. "So tell me, did you wear that outfit to distract the other competitors?" Matthew asked with a grin.

Angelina laughed, "Does it distract you my prince?"

"Oh yes."

"Good."

Sorren was proud that his daughter was a fierce warrior and a strong leader. He had been training Angelina since she was very small. But now Sorren was taking delight in seeing his daughter act like a normal teenage girl. Sorren watched as Angelina and Matthew flirted and joked with each other. The flirtatious behavior was also noticed by the other villagers, especially Tobart.

Tobart was seething as he watched Angelina and Matthew. His head filled with thoughts of all the times Angelina had humiliated him by beating him in the games and competitions. Then she only added to his humiliation when Angelina repeatedly refused to be his bride. If Sorren would have been a weaker man, Tobart would have taken Angelina for his own. And now as he watched Angelina flirt with this young prince in front of the entire village; Tobart's anger was overwhelming him. "I will kill him," thought Tobart.

"Ready, Release," yelled Sorren. Each contestant shot their arrows perfectly into the hearts of the targets. Then with great speed and accuracy they both threw their knives which landed perfectly in their marks. "We have a tie, move the targets back ten feet," ordered Sorren.

After three more ties, Sorren walked up to Matthew and Angelina and grabbed both their arms, raising them into the air. "They are both winners. I am calling this game because it is clear we will be here all day and I am getting thirsty."

The crowd laughed and applauded. "Matthew come, we will have a drink," said Sorren then he turned to Angelina. "Will you retrieve Matthew's knives and bring them to the house?"

Matthew and Sorren walked about a block before they came to a large wooden house which was surrounded with gardens. As Matthew followed Sorren inside, he saw that the house was modest and exceptionally clean. "Shara we have company," Sorren called out. "We will be in the dining room."

Angelina's mother entered the room, a petite woman with long black hair. A difficult life left its marks on her once beautiful face. She was wearing a cloth skirt and blouse. Shara's apron was covered with flour and there were blotches of flour on her face. "Matthew this is my wife Shara," before Sorren could finish the introductions Shara started speaking.

"Oh my, I must be such a sight," said Shara as she tried to wipe the flour from her face. "Sorren why didn't you tell me the Prince was coming?"

"You look fine," Matthew said.

"Shara why don't you bring us some sausages and cheese," said Sorren as he took two glasses and a bottle of whiskey from a cupboard and placed them on the table. As Sorren filled the glasses he said, "I have two boys but they are off playing someplace."

The long dining room table had long wooden benches for seating on the sides and chairs at each end. Matthew took a seat on one of the benches. Angelina walked up to Matthew and handed him his knives. "You played well," she said with a flirtatious smile.

"You just aren't used to any real competition," Matthew replied with a laugh.

"Angelina why don't you help your mother in the kitchen," Sorren said then waited for Angelina to close the door behind her before he spoke again. "You made an enemy today."

"Was that the tall man with the black curly hair I saw you talking to?" Matthew asked as he took a drink of his whiskey.

"Yes, that is Tobart. He has desired Angelina since she was a small girl. She refuses to marry him, which I support, that man has no honor. Do not trust him."

98

"So he hates me because I won?" Matthew laughed.

"You have to understand, he has never been able to beat Angelina at any competition which greatly humiliates him and it angers him that the entire village knows she will not marry him. I saw the way he was watching the two of you. Matthew even a blind man could see the way you and Angelina look at each other; I am sure it angered Tobart that the villagers saw it too."

Before Matthew could reply, Angelina and her mother carried in plates of meat sausages, cheeses, fruits, freshly baked bread and honey. "Well, this looks like a fine meal," said Matthew as Angelina set plates, knives and forks before the two men.

"You may join us," Sorren said to his daughter.

"Thank you Father," Angelina said as she slid onto the bench next to Matthew.

Sorren sat back in his big chair at the head of the table and looked at them. "So the two of you never finished telling Mathas and me about the fight that you had; now I want to know exactly what happened."

Matthew started laughing and looked at Angelina who was bright red. "Do you want me to start?" Matthew asked as Angelina nodded with embarrassment.

"A friend and I were riding early one morning when we saw a person run into a thicket on our land. We could not make out if it was a man or woman and we thought the person ran when they saw us. When we got to the thicket I dismounted and called out for the person to come out of hiding. Imagine our surprise when we hear an angry girl's voice yelling that she was not hiding. Your daughter came out of the trees yelling at me and telling me how stupid I was." Angelina covered her face with her hands as Matthew spoke.

"I asked her twice why she was on our land and she would not tell me, I took a step forward and she came running at me, jumped into the air and punched me in the jaw. Then she did some sort of fancy twist in the air and when she landed she kicked me twice in the stomach. My friend was laughing so hard he doubled over."

Suddenly Angelina looked up, "Father I did warn him not to come towards me."

"That you did," Matthew said with laughter.

"What happened next?" asked Sorren while he was trying not to laugh.

"I tried to grab her arms and she threw me over her shoulder and onto the ground."

"Angelina said she found out she couldn't beat you, exactly how did you stop her?"

"When I was on the ground, I grabbed both of her ankles and pulled her feet from under her then I held her down until she promised to stop fighting."

"Father, Matthew kept telling me he didn't want to hurt me and to stop fighting."

"I see," Sorren said solemnly. Then he could no longer contain himself and he started to laugh. He laughed so hard his stomach shook. Finally Sorren said, "Daughter I hope you learned some things from this."

"You mean not to let anyone grab my ankles again?"

"Yes and that you should have told Matthew why you were on his land the first time he asked. Some people will kill trespassers on sight." Angelina looked at her father then at Matthew who nodded in agreement.

"Father why did you ask these questions."

"Because you told me he won but you did not tell me what he did. I am still a father."

"I am sorry Father. I was just so embarrassed because no one has ever been able to pin me before."

"You were lucky it was Matthew. You are a beautiful young girl who was with two strange men who had you pinned to the ground. My daughter some time you might get yourself in a situation you cannot fight your way out of."

"Your father is right; you should listen to him."

Angelina looked back and forth between Matthew and Sorren several times. She looked at them as if she was trying to read their thoughts. "Have you two realized how much you are alike?" Angelina asked in amazement.

"Erebus you know we can't be seen together," Sophie said as Erebus walked up behind her and put his arms around her waist, while Sophie was standing before the kitchen hearth.

"Sophie stop running away from me."

"Erebus I want you to leave Stordt."

"Because you don't want me here?" Erebus felt pain at her words.

"No because it is too dangerous for you to be here, please you have to trust me."

"Sophie I lost you once because of a lie; I am not leaving yet, at least not without knowing what is going on here."

"Erebus I told you, I cannot tell you."

"Sophie if you are in danger I want to help. Please come to my room later and we can talk."

Demetries waited several hours before returning to Roch's war room. "Are you still mad at me?" Demetries asked tauntingly as he entered the room, stepping over piles of broken furniture and glass. "Well, you could have left at least one chair," Demetries said with a laugh.

"It's not you I'm mad at," Roch growled. He was exhausted from his temper tantrum and quite drunk. Roch marched past Demetries and opened the door. "Get in here now!" Roch yelled. Two soldiers quickly entered the room. "Take all of this crap out of here and bring me some new furniture. And get Sophie!"

Sophie left Erebus in the kitchen when she heard Roch yelling her name. "Yes My Lord," Sophie said as she entered the room and saw the soldiers picking up armfuls of broken furniture.

"Sophie clean this mess up and bring me some more whiskey," Roch yelled.

"Perhaps you have had enough whiskey," Erebus said sternly as he entered the room. Sophie gave Erebus a warning look, which did not go unnoticed by Demetries.

"You two finally meet," Roch said with slurred speech. "Erebus this is the demon in our midst and Demetries this is Erebus my new advisor."

"Are you the warlock who lives in Ryed?" Demetries asked.

"Yes," replied Erebus as he stared boldly at the demon.

"I have heard about you," Demetries continued. "You are said to be a powerful warlock. What are you doing here?"

"Protecting the King's interests," Erebus replied as he walked towards Demetries.

"If you are protecting him from me, well, you aren't that powerful," Demetries said with a challenging sneer.

"What's going on here?" yelled Cerephus as he entered the room. "Have you been fighting?"

"No, I gave the King some news which must have upset him," Demetries said sarcastically.

"He's right," Roch said as he sat down on a chair that one of the soldiers brought into the room. "Vitomas and Raul have a son, and Annabelle and Simon have twin boys. And all of Salar has been celebrating."

"Is that where you have been?" Cerephus asked Demetries.

"Yes, mostly, why did you miss me?"

"My Lord, I have made some special treats for you," Sophie said loudly. "Why don't I serve you all dinner as soon as another table is brought in here?"

102

"That sounds fine," Roch said. "And bring more whiskey."

"Matthew's here," Angelina said with excitement as she ran to open the front door. Matthew took Angelina's hand when he entered the house and the two walked into the dining room and sat down at the table, joining the rest of the family. Matthew laughed, "You already have a place setting for me. Are you trying to tell me I am becoming a pest?"

"Never," said Shara. "We love having you here." Shara stood up from the table and walked into the kitchen, returning a moment later with two more platters of food.

"I don't know what you two have planned for today but I was thinking of taking Matthew to some of the other villages so he can meet our people. Of course you can come too," Sorren said with a laugh when he saw the look on Angelina's face.

"I would like that," Matthew said as he filled his plate with food. "We've been hearing more news about that army that Juleta is raising in Zorta. Sounds like its over two hundred well-trained men now."

"So where does your sister get the money to pay these men?" Sorren asked.

"That is a good question. Father gave her nothing but one small pouch of gold coins when he disinherited her."

"I would think that is something Mathias would want to look into," Sorren said. "Does he have any enemies who would pay Juleta to start a war?"

Roch, Cerephus, Erebus and Demetries ate their mid-day meal in the war room. There was a tension between all four of them that large quantities of whiskey were not easing. "Well Roch, I was going to wait until we were alone but I might as well bring it up now," Demetries said. "I think it is time we went after The Scroll of Imari. That is unless you are afraid to face the Gants again."

"I've been wanting to go after that for a year," Roch snapped. "What changed your mind?"

"In case you have forgotten, I just recently told you my real purpose for wanting to do business with you," Demetries said. "And I have a plan."

"Go on," said Roch suspiciously.

"Instead of taking the route you did before, we travel southwest until we reach the Tange Gold Mines. I will summon Rogetts from the mines and we will herd them north to the caves of Muldun. There, we use the Rogetts to distract the Gants. Oh yes, I may have forgotten to tell you that the real reason I was gone is I had to meet some, let's say acquaintances that I hired. They told me which cave the scroll is in," Demetries said with a satisfied smile; for now he had all of the men's attention.

"Can you summon and control the Rogetts?" Roch asked excitedly.

"Yes."

Roch looked at Erebus for his opinion. "I'm sure that Demetries can; the Rogetts all swear allegiance to Satan, which means they have given their free will over to demons."

"Which cave?" asked Roch as he hastily pulled his map from his shirt pocket.

"I'm not telling you until we get there," Demetries said. "I don't trust you any more than you trust me. This has to be a collaborative effort."

"Agreed," said Roch as he was overwhelmed with excitement. "When do you want to leave?"

"How soon can you get your men ready?" Demetries asked with a grin because he knew he had Roch back under his influence.

"We leave tomorrow," Roch announced. "Cerephus you are in-charge until I return."

As was becoming a routine, Matthew spent all day with Angelina and her family. After dinner Matthew asked Angelina to take a walk. The two walked hand in hand in the moonlight, both enjoying the presence of the other.

"You know Angelina; we have been spending all of our time together the past few weeks. And well, I've decided you are the only girl I want to spend time with." Angelina caught her breath as she listened to Matthew's words. "I was wondering how you felt." They stopped walking and now faced each other.

"Matthew I don't want to be with anyone else either. I've never felt about anyone like I feel for you."

"Good, then we are officially courting," Matthew said with a grin. Angelina stood on her toes, stretching to kiss him but Matthew turned back towards her home. "Let's tell your parents," he said.

Chapter VII
Illusions

"I am so glad to see you old friend," said Padre Bartholomew as the Sanuri stepped down from the boca.

"I came as soon as I heard," replied the Sanuri. "How bad is it?"

"Most of the villagers have died from their injuries and the ones who still survive are just holding on; and there are many who are unaccounted for," said Padre Bartholomew as he and the Sanuri walked towards the Great Hall.

"You look awful, when was the last time you slept?"

"I don't really know. We are all like this and it isn't so much the work and the lack of sleep; it is the condition of the victims that has worn us all down. Prepare yourself for a glimpse into hell," said Padre Bartholomew as he opened the door to the Great Hall.

The Sanuri saw cots and mattresses filling the floor of the huge room, with only small paths made between the patients. There were many priests and soldiers tending to the wounded, many of whom no longer resembled human beings. As the Sanuri looked around the room he realized the truth in Padre Bartholomew's words; the priests and even the soldiers looked like the walking dead, their spirits so traumatized by the horror before them.

"It is difficult to remember that the Rogetts are humans," said the Sanuri as they walked through rows of mutilated victims. Tears ran down the cheeks of the Sanuri as he saw once again the pain and suffering that humans can inflict upon their kind. The Sanuri prayed for the victims and the care givers and for all of mankind.

The Sanuri pulled a blanket over the face of another of the villagers who died. He said a prayer over the woman then turned to Padre Thomas. "I think Sporos is somehow behind all of this."

"But how is that possible? He is a prisoner in The Abyss."

"I do not know; but tomorrow I am going to Afax, perhaps I can find some clues there," said the Sanuri as he was deep in thought.

"You will have the soldiers accompany you?"

"I will be alright."

As Padre Thomas started to walk away, the Sanuri called after him. "Padre are there any soldiers here who took part in the battle at Afax?"

"My Lady, Master Thaos is here," said Selen as she entered the parlor.

"Finally," said Juleta angrily. "Please show him in before he disappears again."

Thaos was laughing when he entered the parlor. "Juleta did you miss me?" he asked tauntingly.

"Where have you been?" Juleta screamed as she spun around to look at Thaos.

Thaos stared at Juleta, a cold, sinister stare that made her stop talking. "First of all Juleta, I am not your slave and you will never speak to me like that again, do you understand?" Juleta stared at Thaos but did not respond. "Do you understand?" his voice was getting lower and harsher.

"I understand," Juleta replied without apologizing.

"Juleta you sit in this room all day and expect that things happen at the snap of your rich little fingers; while the rest of us work. You are paying me to do a job and I am doing it. You want an army I am raising an army and providing them with all they will need. You want information, I am sending out scouts and going out myself to find out the information you seek. You want the tribes of Lentz to start an uprising against your father. That has proven a little more difficult."

"Why?"

"I do not have all of the answers yet. From what I have heard your father and brother are well known for being intelligent, honorable and experienced warriors. If I had to guess I would say they aren't falling for your little magic tricks."

"Even if they don't the tribesmen should."

"Juleta you feel so superior that you always underestimate others. Usman and Sorren are not fools; they have been leaders of their tribes for decades."

"Let me think about this, I will have to try a different approach," said Juleta angrily. "Also Thaos I don't like the way you speak to me either."

"Then fire me," Thaos replied with a laugh. Juleta coldly stared at him. "Juleta you hired me because I am the best in my field, but you don't pay me enough to put up with your childish tantrums. If you don't like my work, just fire me." Juleta continued to stare at Thaos angrily then turned her back on him.

As Thaos was walking out of the room he said, "If you left this castle once in a while it might improve your mood." Juleta screamed and picked up a glass vase and threw it at Thaos but missed him. The vase hit the wall. Thaos laughed as he heard the glass shattering.

"We are going with you," said Padre Bartholomew and Padre Thomas as they climbed into the front seat of the boca.

"I don't think that is such a good idea," replied the Sanuri.

"You are looking for clues and perhaps two additional sets of eyes will be of help," said Padre Bartholomew smiling. The Sanuri did not respond.

"Let us feel that we are doing something to stop this madness," said Padre Thomas. The Sanuri looked at him for a moment then started the horses moving through the courtyard of the monastery. "We were thinking that perhaps we could bless that village and try to cleanse it from the evil that exists there."

"My dear friends, you may not be prepared to face that kind of evil," said the Sanuri solemnly as he drove the boca through the monastery gates.

"Oh, The Great Ruler be with us," gasped Padre Bartholomew as the lingering stench of burned flesh overwhelmed him. The Sanuri drove the boca past a huge pile of bones that were the remains of the Rogetts that Banacus and his men had killed.

As they traveled farther down the street they saw a building burned to the ground. "That is where Banacus had the Rogetts burned alive," explained Padre Thomas.

"A death of such horror belongs to no one, not even Rogetts," said the Sanuri solemnly. The Sanuri stopped the boca in the middle of the village and the three men surveyed the scene of terror and destruction.

"What exactly are we looking for?" asked Padre Bartholomew as he climbed off the boca.

"Anything out of the ordinary," said the Sanuri.

"Well, that is this entire village now," replied Padre Bartholomew.

"I am looking for any clue as to why the Rogetts acted as they did," said the Sanuri as he started to walk into the abandoned general store. He turned towards the priests, "You two stay together." The priests decided to look into the building next to the store which appeared to be a saddle shop. The three men searched building after building finding mutilated bodies of villagers. Blood seemed to have stained everything giving an unreal illusion to the grotesque scene. The smell was sickening, causing Padre Thomas to puke in one building.

The Sanuri walked out of the inn and onto the street, "I do not even know where they came from," thought the Sanuri as he could not see any tunnels or caves. The hot noonday sun burned on his back as the Sanuri walked down the street. The Sanuri heard one of his horses scream then he was knocked to the ground.

The Sanuri was flattened onto his stomach by great weight; he felt a sharp searing pain in his left shoulder. The Sanuri pushed himself up from the ground with all the force he had, knocking three of the Rogetts off from him. A fourth Rogett had his legs wrapped around the Sanuri and was biting him in the back of the neck.

The Sanuri reached behind him with both of his arms and pulled the Rogett over his head and threw him down onto the street. Before the Rogett hit the ground the Sanuri did a double forward roll and came up to a standing position now holding his staff which had been lying on the ground. In this new position all four of the Rogetts were facing the Sanuri.

One of the Rogetts lunged at the Sanuri who stepped forward and drove the end of the staff into the Rogetts stomach; instantly the Sanuri swung the backside of the staff to the right hitting another Rogett with the side of the staff. The Sanuri brought the staff up then thrust it down with great force over the head of the third Rogett. Then in a backward thrust the Sanuri drove the back end of the staff into the fourth Rogett that had moved behind him.

The first Rogett lay dead. The second Rogett lunged at the Sanuri again and in a sweeping motion with the staff the Sanuri knocked the Rogett off his feet. The Rogett fell onto his back and the Sanuri drove the end of the staff into his heart.

The Sanuri quickly swing around to face the other two Rogetts, one was still lying on the ground unconscious while the other was staring at the Sanuri and growling. The Rogett lunged and the Sanuri stepped forward into the attack. The Sanuri drove the end of his staff into the chest of the Rogett then swung the back of the staff and crushed the beast's skull.

"Bartholomew, Thomas," yelled the Sanuri, fearful for his friends. Both priests came running out of an abandoned home. The Sanuri was relieved to see they were unharmed. "Get some rope," yelled the Sanuri as he dragged the unconscious Rogett towards the walkway. It took a few minutes for the priests to return. The Sanuri bound the Rogett; then got some water from a nearby trough and poured it on the creature's face. The Rogett started to growl as soon as it regained consciousness.

"Both of you get into the boca, we may be leaving quickly," said the Sanuri. The priests did as they were told. After the priests left, the Sanuri pulled the Rogett onto its feet and stared closely into its small black eyes. The Sanuri spoke to the Rogett in its native tongue which surprised the creature but it did not respond. The Sanuri placed his right hand over the skull of the Rogett and slowly started to chant then he looked again into the creature's eyes.

This time the Sanuri saw hundreds of Rogetts coming from caves in the Safer Mountain Range and travelling above ground. He saw them surround and attack the Village of Afax; then The Sanuri saw the face of Sporos screaming from The Abyss. The image of Sporos in the Rogett's eyes was getting larger and larger and as the image grew the creature started to shake and to go into convulsions. The Rogett died before the Sanuri had his answers.

"Let Padre Bartholomew drive and let me look at those wounds," said Padre Thomas as he saw the blood seeping through the Sanuri's robe.

"When we get back to the monastery," said the Sanuri who was very disturbed by what he had just witnessed.

"What did that Rogett tell you?" asked Padre Bartholomew.

"He would not talk to me so I tried to read his thoughts," replied the Sanuri. "I saw great numbers of Rogetts coming from caves in the Safer Mountains and walking across land."

"Why, no one has ever seen Rogetts marching across land for any distance because they travel underground, do they not?" asked Padre Thomas.

"You are right and that was not the only disturbing thing I saw," said the Sanuri. "I saw the Rogetts attack Afax; it was like I was there, I could hear the screams and feel the terror." Padre Thomas and Padre Bartholomew both looked at each other without speaking. "Then I saw Sporos' face screaming from The Abyss, which is something I have seen before. But his face kept getting larger and larger and as it did the Rogett started to convulse and died."

"Does Sporos have power beyond The Abyss?" asked Padre Thomas incredulously.

"Can he be that powerful?" asked Padre Bartholomew.

"Somehow Sporos knew I was with that Rogett and killed him before I could get more information; I have no idea how he could have known," said the Sanuri.

"So Sporos must be behind the Rogett attacks," said Padre Thomas.

"I suspected as much," said the Sanuri who became lost in his thoughts for a moment before he spoke again. "There is another, a demon I marked named Demetries; he rides with Roch," said the Sanuri. "I know he has been calling to Sporos but I do not think he is powerful enough to help Sporos like this." The Sanuri grew quiet again. "I have to get to the Hall of Antiquities, there is something I am missing; there must be more demons at work here."

"Or something very powerful," said Padre Bartholomew.

"That is what bothers me," said the Sanuri. "How could there be a demon this powerful without me knowing of it?"

"Can I buy you a drink friend?" asked Thaos, as he stood in a tavern in the City of Langer, the capital city of the Kingdom of Lentz.

Tobart looked at Thaos suspiciously, but he would never turn down a free drink. "Yes but what do you want that you are buying me a drink?"

"I could not help but overhear you talking. You sound upset and it is too beautiful of a night for anyone to be upset," replied Thaos with a grin.

"Well I don't believe a word you just said but thank you for the drink," said Tobart as he grabbed the glass of whiskey and emptied it with one swallow.

Thaos motioned for the bartender to fill Tobart's glass again. Then Thaos told the bartender to leave the bottle with them. Thaos grabbed the bottle and his glass and nodded towards an empty table. Tobart grabbed his glass and the two men sat down.

"So what is it you really want?" asked Tobart skeptically.

"Information."

"What kind of information?"

"I am new to this area; have never been here before," said Thaos slyly. "And you sound like a man who is aware of everything that is going on around here. I am just curious about this place. It is a beautiful city I might stay here."

"Well you are an observant man," replied Tobart as he filled his glass again. "Where shall I begin?"

Thaos smiled as he leaned back in his chair and looked at Tobart. Thaos had been watching Tobart for several days and knew be belonged to the Nordes Tribe. Tobart was a man who preferred to spend more time in taverns than taking care of his home. Thaos was trying to determine Tobart's age. He knew Tobart had to be at least twenty years his senior; but long years of hard drinking took their toll on Tobart's appearance; a tall skinny man with a large stomach, a large nose and a permanently red face from the liquor.

Thaos doubted that Tobart has ever done a hard day's work or held his own in a fight. Thaos liked to study people; he believed that if he gave Tobart enough whiskey, Tobart would tell him anything. All Thaos had to do was to wait.

"You have some nasty wounds," said Padre Thomas as he was cleaning the bite marks the Sanuri had received from the Rogetts. "Will you hold still?"

"I am sorry, I just keep feeling like I am missing something that is right before my eyes," said the Sanuri with frustration.

"Have you had any visions as of late?" asked Padre Thomas. "This is going to sting," he added as he poured a brown liquid into the wounds.

"No and that of itself is unusual."

"Well, perhaps The Great Ruler already sent you the information you need; you just did not realize it."

The Sanuri turned and looked at Padre Thomas and smiled, "My friend you may be right. After you finish with me I am going to my room to mediate." The Sanuri stayed in his room, at the monastery, for three days and three nights without taking of food or drink. He was trying to remember even the littlest details of his visions. Day and night the Sanuri searched the corners of his consciousness for answers but none came.

The night of the third day the Sanuri had a new vision. He saw the image of The Lion. In the vision he followed The Lion as it walked through all of the kingdoms. The Sanuri saw places of great familiarity and places that he had never seen before and did not know if they existed in the Continent of Opots.

As they walked the Sanuri saw people calling to darkness again and again. He saw the faces of people but then the faces turned to masks and when the people removed the masks faces of demons were exposed. The Sanuri saw eyes watching from the darkness as he had seen in other visions. The Lion continued to walk without speaking for some time before it entered a cave. In the vision the Sanuri continued to follow The Lion as it followed passageways that took them deeper and deeper into the bowels of the world.

They were descending through tiers within the ground and each tier was identified by a sign with a number. When they reached the thirteen tier; the Sanuri saw that there were thirteen stairways all going downward. The Lion started to descend on the thirteenth stairway and the Sanuri followed him. At the bottom of the stairway was a small platform.

The Lion stopped on the platform and turned to the Sanuri and said, "You have been tested greatly my friend and you have pleased The Great Ruler; but there is a darkness more powerful than the limits of your mind can comprehend. If you choose to stand against such a force you will need to be tested again to undergo another transformation. You may freely choose not to endure more trials and The Great Ruler will bless you the same."

The Sanuri smiled, "My choice is to do whatever The Great Ruler would have me do."

"Then follow me," said The Lion and started to walk into another passageway.

"Old friend might I ask a favor?" asked the Sanuri.

"Of course," replied The Lion.

"While I am being tested would you protect those whom I protect?"

The atmosphere around The Lion illuminated and he smiled benevolently "Of course."

The Sanuri followed The Lion down a long dark corridor; soon they entered a chamber, cave-like in appearance. The chamber was round with thirteen doors. In the middle of the chamber was a bed, a table and a chair.

"So I take it I will be here for a while," said the Sanuri with a smile.

"As always that depends on you," replied The Lion. "Every human has their personal demons to conquer that is the holy test. But you my friend have chosen to carry the demons of others to lighten their loads, now you will understand some of their demons."

"The darkness is more aggressive and I fear many innocents may be lost while I am being tested," said the Sanuri.

"We have abandoned no one who asks for our help."

"And those who cannot ask?"

"They are the ones who you are helping with these tests; you will transform a little after each level you conquer," said The Lion. "And as always you will repeat a level until you can conquer it."

"And when I am done, I will have what I need to stop what is happening now?" the Sanuri called to The Lion who had left the chamber.

"You are always given what you need," The Lion's voice vibrated through the chamber.

The Sanuri sat in the chair waiting when he realized he no longer was having a vision but had been physically transported from his room in the monastery to the chamber. He had not even noticed the transition. "It must have occurred when The Lion left," thought the Sanuri.

After almost an hour's time had passed, the Sanuri got out of the chair and walked around the chamber trying to open each of the thirteen doors; but none of them would open. So he returned to his chair and saw that there was now food and wine on the table for him. The Sanuri ate the bread, cheese and fruit as he waited and waited and waited.

"Padre Thomas, Padre Thomas," called Padre Bartholomew as he hurried down the monastery hall. Padre Thomas stopped and waited for his friend to catch up to him.

"You will not believe this," huffed Padre Bartholomew as he tried to catch his breath. "I went to the Sanuri's room to check on him since he has not eaten in days and he is gone."

"Maybe he is in the Hall of Antiquities."

"That is what I thought but I have searched the entire monastery and no one has seen him; but his boca and horses are still here."

"I hope he did not get a bad infection from his wounds and wander off some place. I will help you and we will search again."

A click of a lock turning woke the Sanuri who was sleeping in the chair. He quickly looked around the chamber trying to determine which of the thirteen doors had unlocked. The Sanuri saw a door to his right slowly start to open. He stood up and waited but nothing came through the door so he walked across the chamber and opened the door wider. The Sanuri did not see or hear anything so he walked through the door into the darkness.

As the Sanuri walked through the blackness he suddenly had a sense of familiarity. "I have been here before," he thought. Suddenly the darkness turned into light as the Sanuri came upon a scene that he was not a part of. "This is like a vision but it is not mine," thought the Sanuri. It was as if the Sanuri was dead and not visible to the person before him.

The Sanuri saw an old man wearing a king's crown sitting at a desk. The face of the king would switch back and forth from a skeleton to the face of one who was living. The room the king was in was very dark but there was something familiar about it. The Sanuri kept looking at the king who was merely sitting at the table. "There must be some clues," thought the Sanuri as he strained his eyes to see into the darkness. Finally the Sanuri prayed, "Great Ruler give me light." And the scene before him was illuminated.

"I know that place," said the Sanuri out loud. When the Sanuri realized he was looking at the vault beneath the royal castle in Wetpr he started to worry. The Sanuri searched the scene before him detail after detail to try and figure out why he was being shown this image. "Who is that king, perhaps that is the clue," thought the Sanuri. "I cannot tell if this is the past or the future."

The Sanuri searched the scene with his eyes again, this time he spied a corner of a piece of paper on the king's desk. The Sanuri strained to see the writing; when he saw the words *King Sharonne*. "King Sharonne he was the great, great grandfather of Kings Sudfad and Roch. Why would he be in the vault; he was the King of Stordt?" thought the Sanuri.

The Sanuri could not see any of the other writing on the paper. Suddenly the scene went dark. The Sanuri waited in the dark for a while then returned to his chair in the chamber. This time the Sanuri found paper and pen on the table with more food. "This is a most curious test," thought the Sanuri as he sat down at the table.

The Sanuri worked long into the night trying to remember everything he could about King Sharonne and writing it down on the paper provided. Sharonne ruled over the Kingdom of Stordt for over eighty years. He was the father of Princess Annabar and Prince Micha; another child Prince Tresdore died at the age of three from an unknown illness.

Micha became King when Sharonne died. King Micha was the father of Prince Jaretta and Prince Alexandras. Jaretta became King of Stordt when Micha died.

Alexandras married Queen Sumona of Wetpr and became King of Wetpr. King Jaretta was the father of Prince Sudfad and Prince Roch. King Jaretta sent Sudfad to live with Alexandras and Sumona as he feared for his son's safety. Sudfad became King of Wetpr when Alexandras died and Roch became King of Stordt after he murdered his parents King Jaretta and Queen Lillian.

King Voltar and Queen Estral ruled over the Kingdom of Wetpr during the same time that King Sharonne and Queen Vinca ruled over the Kingdom of Stordt. King Voltar was the Keeper of the Scrolls during his reign. "Why would Sharonne be in the holy vault?" said the Sanuri out loud. "Only the Keepers of the Scrolls even know of its existence."

"I really don't understand why you are so interested in seeing our village," Tobart said with his words slurring.

"I am just a curious man," replied Thaos with a grin.

"Well don't make yourself known here because no one is supposed to be on our lands without the permission of Chief Sorren," Tobart was so drunk he could barely stay balanced on his horse as he spoke.

"Chief Sorren, is it not his daughter you desire so desperately?" asked Thaos with a mocking tone to his voice.

"I never said I was desperate."

"I see," replied Thaos with a laugh. "But do I understand correctly that you have taken no other wives and you are just waiting around for Sorren to give you permission to marry his daughter?"

Tobart stared at Thaos angrily, "I believe I have told you too much already, you should leave now."

"I am just kidding my good friend; don't take things so seriously."

"Well, I don't like you're kidding."

"Then I apologize, I will not kid you about the girl anymore."

"Be quiet; we will be at Sorren's house in just a moment."

Chapter VIII
When Children Cry

Once again the Sanuri was awakened by the sound of a lock clicking open. He sat up from his bed and looked at the thirteen doors. This time the door that started to open was behind the Sanuri and to his left. He walked over to the door and opened it but as soon as he walked through the door he was in a different world; he was not watching from the outside as with the first door.

The Sanuri found himself in a sunny garden with butterflies and rabbits. He could hear birds singing and smell the fragrances of the flowers. The Sanuri stood still at first trying to take in all the details of his surroundings. As he started to walk through the garden nothing seemed familiar to him or even extraordinary for a garden.

Suddenly the Sanuri heard a baby cry and he followed the sound until he came to a river. He saw a frightened woman who was standing near the water and holding a baby. The woman kept looking behind her as if she was being followed. The Sanuri spoke to the woman but she could neither see nor hear him. The frightened woman ran into the woods.

Soon the Sanuri saw soldiers wearing the uniforms of the Kingdom of Stordt riding through the woods. The Sanuri could see one of the soldiers pulling out his sword as he neared the running woman. The Sanuri ran to the woman but neither the soldiers nor the woman were aware of his presence. The soldier thrust his sword through the woman as she ran, then a second soldier dismounted and stabbed the baby.

"What is this; is this something that has happened in the past or something that is yet to come?" asked the Sanuri with anguish. "Am I being shown this so I can stop it?"

The soldiers left the two bodies in the forest; as they rode away the Sanuri could hear one of them speak. "The King will be pleased, he did not want a child that he fathered with a peasant to be heir to the throne."

The Sanuri walked up to the young mother and the baby, their bodies bleeding into the earth. "What is this?" asked the Sanuri again. He did not see anything on either body that would give him a clue as to who they were or which king had them killed. Frustrated the Sanuri continued to walk in the garden.

The Sanuri walked until he came to a well-worn road. He asked for guidance as to which direction to take but none came so he decided to follow the road to the right. The Sanuri came upon a small village of farmers. He watched the people for a while and saw nothing out of the ordinary until he started to leave the village. Suddenly the Sanuri realized that each of the small wooden homes had a talisman hanging over the doors. He walked closer and recognized one of the talismans as a type he had seen hundreds of years earlier.

This particular talisman was very ornate and usually made of colored stones and bird feathers; it was thought to dispel demons. "This scene must be in the past for I have not seen these in many years," thought the Sanuri. "But when they were in use they were seen throughout the entire continent." Suddenly the Sanuri found himself back at his table and chair in the middle of the chamber.

The Sanuri proceeded to write down the things he had seen through door number two. As he looked over his notes he became frustrated again. "I have no idea what these things mean and how they are related," thought the Sanuri. His frustration did not last long for as soon as he had finished writing, door number three started to open.

The Sanuri walked through the door and found himself on the outside of a scene as he was with the first door. To his great surprise he saw an image of himself as a young boy living at the monastery. "I remember that," said the Sanuri out loud as he watched himself being trained with a staff. There were several boys around the same age in the class, including Sporos.

"What was that?" asked the Sanuri as he realized he had seen something out of the corner of his left eye. Turning to the left the Sanuri saw a shadow in a doorway. He strained his eyes to figure out the shape of the shadow but he could not; then it moved again, ever so slightly.

The Sanuri looked over the scene again. "There are no trees or students in that area that could cast that shadow," thought the Sanuri. "This scene took place at the monastery at Avaide at least two hundred years before King Sharonne ruled; and this is a different kingdom." The Sanuri continued to watch the scene. As the boys left the class the shadow appeared to follow them. "Is The Great Ruler trying to show me that darkness stalked us?" thought the Sanuri.

Suddenly the scene changed to the inner chambers of the Hall of Antiquities at the monastery at Malga. All the Sanuri could see at first were the shelves upon shelves of scrolls and books. Then he saw a figure sitting at the table reading a scroll. The figure was wearing the robe of a priest but the hood was raised so that the Sanuri could not see the face. He heard the figure softly chanting; then the figure stopped and looked in the direction of the door.

Next the Sanuri saw both Padre Bartholomew and Padre Thomas walk into the Hall and sit at the table. The mysterious figure was no longer seated at the table and the Sanuri could not see him in the room. The Sanuri looked back at the priests, "Oh no," he groaned out loud as the Sanuri realized the priests looked exactly as they did when he last saw them.

"You never speak of Roch," said Raul as Vitomas was lying in his arm.

Vitomas quickly sat up in bed and stared into Raul's eyes, "Do you want me to?" she asked incredulously.

"I just think it is strange since you spent most of your life with him."

Vitomas was visibly tensing up. "Do you speak of your nightmares?"

Raul took her hand, "Vitomas I am not trying to start a fight; but you still have nightmares. Perhaps talking about them would help." Vitomas gave Raul a cold glance. "I am just repeating what mother used to tell us," said Raul as he was trying to force a smile.

Vitomas put her hands softly on Raul's face and kissed him on the mouth. "My dear husband I do not think you want to hear about my nightmares."

"Are the nightmares about Roch or Archetenus?"

"Archetenus scared me a great deal. I did not want to go with him but for the most part he treated me honorably," said Vitomas. "You know he really thought he was saving me from Roch." Vitomas looked Raul in the eyes, "Raul if I had never met you I might have gone with Archetenus, I do not know."

Raul did not utter a word. Vitomas stared at him. "Do you think I am hiding things from you because I do not talk about my life before you?" Raul looked embarrassed but still did not answer. "Raul I love you so much. I do not tell you because I do not want you to think differently of me," said Vitomas with tears in her eyes. "Has this been bothering you all this time?" Raul squeezed Vitomas' hand but still said nothing. "I will tell you if you want to know."

"I do," said Raul and kissed Vitomas on the forehead.

Vitomas moved so she was sitting across from Raul in the bed. "I am from the Village of Tadon and when I was Petra's age; Roch led his army into Tadon to destroy the monastery and to kill the priests; which they did in front of the villagers. Roch wanted the villagers to watch so they would know to fear him."

"He saw me in the crowd, hiding behind my mother. Roch grabbed me away from her and put me on his horse. When my mother begged him to give me back he threw three gold coins in the dirt, at her feet. He told me that if I ever tried to escape he would kill my family like he killed the priests." Vitomas paused because she was choking up. "He raped me that night in front of all his men, who stood around drinking and laughing."

"I was never the only woman Roch had in the castle; I was the one who could never leave." Raul noticed that Vitomas had grabbed the blanket and was wringing it in her hands. "Sometimes Roch would make us watch what he and the other men did to the women and girls they kidnapped from the villages. And sometimes they even raped and killed other men."

"You know he is a cruel man, I am sure you can imagine how he would scare me," said Vitomas. "But after a while something changed in him, I think in his own horrible way he loved me. Roch had gardens built for me and had beautiful chambers made; he started buying me beautiful dresses and jewels. As I got older I realized that if Roch was happy he was less cruel not only to me but to everyone else. I tried to love him and for a little while I thought I did, that was when I got a little older."

"Then when I was about fourteen I realized that I could use his affection for me to get him to do things sometimes." Vitomas quickly looked at Raul. "Not what you might be thinking. One day I got him to stop his men from killing a peasant because the man was too poor to pay his taxes. After that I realized perhaps some good could come out of my situation so I tried to use my position with Roch to help the people of Taperia."

Raul leaned over to pull Vitomas into his arms but she pushed him away and said, "No let me finish. Roch took Annabelle from her parents so I would have a companion. Annabelle was the only thing that really kept me alive. I would hide her when he was drunk; I never let him touch her." Vitomas put her face into her hands and started to cry.

Raul quickly moved across the bed and put both of his arms around Vitomas and hugged her tightly as she cried on his shoulder. Raul stroked Vitomas' hair and kissed her head, "I am sorry that was so painful for you; but you had to bring that out to the light."

Vitomas looked up at Raul through eyes filled with tears, "Do you still love me?"

"If it is possible I think I love you even more," Raul whispered into her ear.

"Father I have something to discuss with you and Simon and I do not want the others to hear," said Raul as he closed the door to his father's study. The three men sat down but no one spoke. Both Sudfad and Simon were looking at Raul who was visibly angry. Raul was clenching his fists and the veins were protruding from his neck.

"Raul what is it?" asked Sudfad.

124

When Raul finally spoke tears came to his eyes. "Vitomas has horrible nightmares always and she never talks about them. Last night I finally got her to tell me a little about her life with Roch. She told me I would not want to know and I fear she was right."

Raul looked at both his father and his brother, "I knew he was a monster but Vitomas told me things I could barely believe. Roch made her watch as he murdered the priests at Tadon then he raped her that same night as his men watched. She said Roch's men laughed at her and drank while he was raping her and she wasn't any older than Petra."

Raul turned to Simon, "Vitomas would hide Annabelle and protect her so Roch would not rape her too; those two girls kept each other alive through all those years of hell," Raul was having difficulty talking. Simon and Sudfad looked at each other, not knowing what to say. Raul composed himself, "Father the reason I am telling you this is I have decided to go to Stordt and kill Roch."

Sudfad moved closer to Raul, "Son I believe I am speaking for Simon too when I say all of us want to kill him and one day he will die at the hands of one of us. But you have a wife who clearly needs you and another baby that will be born in a few months; don't let Roch ruin her life again." Raul had been staring at the floor and now he looked up at his father as Sudfad continued speaking. "Vitomas needs your love right now, not your revenge."

"Father is right," said Simon through clenched teeth. "Annabelle rarely talks about their life at the castle but she has said that Vitomas suffered some awful things. I should try to get Annabelle to talk about it."

"It was not easy to get Vitomas to talk and it certainly wasn't easy to listen to what she said; I understand why she has nightmares now," said Raul in a whisper.

Sudfad looked at his sons and could see they were both consumed with anger. "Your wives are the most wonderful women I know other than my own dear wife. Do you not wonder how they could endure what they have and yet still be so kind and loving?" asked Sudfad. Simon and Raul looked at their father but neither spoke.

"They have learned a lesson that you two need to remember. If you let darkness grow in you it will consume you; your wives love you because you are not like Roch. You are good and honorable men, do not let that monster change you." said Sudfad.

"So Roch should go unpunished?" asked Raul angrily.

"It is just a matter of time before we deal with Roch; but neither of your wives will benefit from your anger," Sudfad said and then he sat back in his chair and smiled. "As your King I am giving you your assignments for today, take your wives into Salar."

"What?" asked Simon.

"A large herd of horses was brought to the arena last night for sale, you want to get Annabelle a horse and Vitomas loves horses; it might be good for all of you to get away for the day," said Sudfad smiling. "And leave the babies here."

Roch was leading three hundred men to the Caves of Muldun. This time Roch was better prepared for an encounter with the Gants as he brought more men, more weapons and Demetries. They had been travelling hard for four days, following the River Nebu.

"So you really think you can distract the Gants?" asked Roch.

"You keep asking me the same question over and over," replied Demetries with annoyance.

"That is because I do not trust your answer."

"Does it sound so impossible?"

"I don't know, does talking with a demon sound possible?" asked Roch angrily.

"You are so full of anger today," mocked Demetries. Roch did not respond so Demetries continued. "I do not know why you are angry with me, I am giving you the opportunity to fulfill your desires," added the demon with a grin.

"Well, for one you have been bossing me around and I do not take orders from anyone and you have yet to prove your worth," snarled Roch angrily.

"So what you are really saying is you want to know how powerful I am," said Demetries, who then stopped his horse and started to chant.

Roch stopped and stared at Demetries; suddenly the earth started to shake, a little at first then more and more as one hundred Rogetts charged out of the gold mines of Nora and ran towards Roch and his men.

"Rogetts," screamed Roch who led the charge into the oncoming mob. Roch and his men trampled many of the Rogetts with their horses as they ran through the mob over and over, swinging swords and clubs. The battle lasted but twenty minutes.

"Round up the survivors," ordered Roch as his men chased down the Rogetts who were trying to return to the safety of the mines. The soldiers herded the Rogetts against a stone wall.

"Archers ready!" ordered Roch. "Release!" As the soldiers rode away from the dead Rogetts, Roch rode up alongside of Demetries and said with a huge grin, "Now I am listening."

"Sudfad here you are," said Renya cheerfully, "I have been looking all over for you." When Renya entered Sudfad's study he was standing with his back to her, looking out the window. Sudfad turned and faced his wife. "Sudfad what is wrong, you look distressed?"

"Come in and close the door dear," said Sudfad as he sat down in the chair behind his desk.

"Where are the children?" asked Renya as she sat down in a chair near Sudfad's desk.

"I sent them all to Salar for the day. I told them to leave the babies with the nurses," said Sudfad seriously.

"Sudfad what is going on? You are worrying me."

"Last night Raul finally got Vitomas to talk about her nightmares; she told him a little about what Roch did to her and Annabelle," Sudfad paused for a second. "Our son has been through battles and seen butchery and yet he cried telling Simon and me just a few of the things that Vitomas said. He wants to kill Roch but I told them both to stay with their families." Sudfad looked across the desk at Renya, "It is time that this stopped; Roch killed my parents, raped my daughter and tried to kill my son, I am going to put an end to that monster."

"But Sudfad, you know what the Sanuri said."

"I know but perhaps he was wrong."

Nora was one of the wealthiest cities in the Kingdom of Stordt. The Endleson family owned most of the gold mines and much of the city. This family prided itself on civic duty and built a ballroom and a theater in Nora. The Endleson family also paid homage to King Roch; protection money is what Roch called it but it was protection from Roch and his men the Endleson's were paying for.

As Roch led his men down the main street of Nora they saw numerous people dressed in fine clothing who were entering the Nora Endleson Hotel. Roch turned to his men, "The night is yours but I expect every one of you back in the saddle and ready to move just after sunrise." With those words, Roch's soldiers were free to terrorize the city. Then Roch turned to Demetries and with a grin said, "I do believe I am going dancing."

Roch dismounted and grabbed a boy who was running down the street. "Take care of my horse," ordered Roch and watched as the boy took the horse to a stable. Then Roch entered the Nora Endleson Hotel. Off from the main lobby was a ballroom filled with people; Roch invited himself to the ball.

Roch's clothes were dusty and sweaty, in direct contrast to the fine clothing and jewels being worn by the other guests. Roch grabbed a drink out of the hand of a man who was walking past him; the man turned and started to yell at Roch, until he saw the look in Roch's eyes. That man decided to move himself and his wife to the opposite side of the ball room.

Roch pushed through the crowd in a challenging manner. Soon he spied Augustus Endleson standing with a small group of people. Roch walked up to the group and said sarcastically, "Hello Augustus." When Augustus turned and realized it was Roch speaking to him; his eyes filled with terror.

"My Lord, I did not realize you were here," said Augustus apologetically. Then Augustus yelled above the music, "My friends we are being honored with the presence of the King of Stordt himself." The music stopped and the people looked at Roch with looks of fear and disgust. Augustus started to clap and soon everyone in the ballroom was clapping for Roch.

"I was just passing through the area and thought I would pick up my payment in person," said Roch with a grin.

"Why certainly My Lord, I will have to run to my office to get it," said Augustus nervously.

"I expected as much," said Roch as he was looking over some of the women in the ballroom. "I will wait here."

As Roch surveyed the ballroom he saw a beautiful young girl with long blonde curly hair dancing with a young man. Roch walked across the dance floor, pushing people aside. When he reached the young couple Roch tapped the man on the back of the shoulder, when the man turned around Roch put his glass into the man's hand and said, "She will be dancing with me." Roch smiled at the girl and grabbed her hand and they finished the dance.

"What is your name?" Roch asked in a charming manner.

"Laurabelle Marcus," the little girl said politely. "And what is yours?"

"So you are Arthurs' daughter," Roch said with a smirk. "I am Roch, King of Stordt."

"Really?" Laurabelle said her eyes wide with excitement. "I've never met a king before."

"Well, Laurabelle you are very pretty, you remind me of someone I once knew," Roch said flirtatiously. "How old are you?"

"I'm going to be ten in two months, My Lord."

"Really, I love that age and Laurabelle you can call me Roch.

Roch danced several more dances with Laurabelle, who was obviously flattered that the King had asked her to dance. Arthur and Harriet Marcus stood near the dance floor watching in horror as Roch danced with their young daughter. "Arthur do something," Harriet pleaded as tears filled her eyes.

"Honey I don't like it either but they are just dancing," Arthur said as the sweat ran down his face.

Harriet then turned to Lloyd and his wife Edith who were standing behind them. Lloyd was one of the most prominent bankers in Nora, a thin man with thinning hair and spectacles. His appearance was in direct contrast to his close friend Augustus who was a large rotund man. "Lloyd please do something; get Laurabelle away from that monster." Lloyd stood frozen with fear.

Roch was taking great pleasure in the horror his presence was instilling in the people in the ballroom. Many of whom had stopped dancing and were watching Roch with Laurabelle; fear gripped their hearts but no one dared to say anything. Roch found the girl's innocence pleasing; she did not fear him because she did not know him.

When the music stopped after their fifth dance; Roch bowed to Laurabelle and kissed her hand, "I have some business to take care of then I will return, wait for me." The girl blushed and curtsied. Roch walked across the dance floor knowing all eyes were upon him.

Augustus Endleson was standing near the bar along with many other people. Roch stood next to Augustus and ordered a drink. Augustus handed a package of money to Roch and said, "Please, she is but a child do not hurt her." Roch took the package and put it in an inside shirt pocket. Then he gave Augustus a look that filled Augustus with fear. When Roch saw the terror in Augustus' eyes he sneered. Roch swallowed his drink in one gulp and put the glass on the bar, as he turned back to the dance floor he became filled with rage.

Roch walked up to a well dressed woman and grabbed the necklace she was wearing. "Where did you get this?" Roch yelled.

"My Lord," replied the terrified woman.

"Tell me where you got this necklace," Roch demanded as he started to twist the woman's arm.

The woman glanced pleadingly at her husband who was moving towards her through the crowd. "My husband, it was a gift from my husband," the woman stammered. "Please you are hurting me."

"Where did he get it?" demanded Roch loudly.

"I bought it in Salar a few weeks ago," said the man as he approached his wife and Roch.

"Where in Salar?"

"There is a jewelry store in the main shopping area it is run by a man named Andrew."

"Where did he get it?"

"I never thought to ask," replied the man in astonishment.

Roch stared at the man for a moment then he turned and marched across the dance floor. Roch roughly grabbed Laurabelle by the arm and dragged her across the floor.

"Laurabelle," screamed Harriet as she tried to push her way through the crowd.

"Mommy, Mommy," screamed the terrified little girl as she fought Roch's grasp.

Arthur grabbed Harriet and stopped her from going after their daughter. "Help her," a woman in the crowd screamed. "She is just a little girl." But all of the men stood motionless. Fear gripped their hearts as they watched the demon drag the girl to hell.

"I was impressed with your display yesterday," Roch said to Demetries as he led his men from Nora, in the early morning light. The smoke from burning buildings mingled with the morning fog. Although all of Roch's men were accounted for, they could still hear screams in the city.

"As I was with yours last night," replied Demetries as he and Roch looked at each other and smiled sadistically.

"So you claim you know which cave the scroll is in," Roch said. "But I have been in some of those caves and they cover miles. I don't know how long the Rogetts can distract the Gants. Do you have some magical way of locating the scroll once we are inside of the cave?"

"The scroll is not only protected by the Gants it is protected by holiness," said Demetries as he saw the confused look on Roch's face. "Think of it as an invisible wall which you can penetrate because you are a human but a demon cannot."

"So you plan to walk through the caves until you bump into an invisible wall?" asked Roch sarcastically.

Demetries smiled, "Something like that." Demetries paused and Roch noticed the demon got a most unusual look in his eyes. "Roch do you ever wonder why you are different from other men?"

"You mean superior?" snapped Roch.

Demetries laughed, "That was not the word I was thinking of but I won't argue."

Roch looked at Demetries with annoyance. "I do not know what you are talking about."

"Your capacity for cruelty; how the look of terror in someone's eyes makes your blood sing; you do realize most other men are not like you."

"You are always spinning webs Demetries if you are trying to tell me something just say it," barked Roch.

"I told you once you were born of darkness and you did not ask me what I meant; did you understand?"

"I find your constant talking exhausting; are all demons so annoying?"

Demetries smiled, "There are all kinds of demons."

"And I have to pair up with one who talks in riddles; what are you trying to say," yelled Roch.

"Nothing, I was just killing time," replied Demetries with a grin. Roch looked at Demetries with rage in his eyes which made Demetries burst into laughter. "When we rode out of Nora, why did you send some of your men back to the castle?" Demetries asked as he was enjoying how angry Roch was becoming.

"I didn't send them back to the castle."

"Are you going to tell me where they are going?"

"They are doing an errand for me," yelled Roch.

Chapter IX
The Sins of the Fathers

"Please Harriet," Arthur pleaded as he and Lloyd tried to pull her to a standing position. Harriet had been sitting in the middle of the street for hours, cradling Laurabelle's naked and bloody body and rocking back and forth.

"Leave me, both of you," Harriet shrieked hysterically. "You let him do this to our baby, you let him do this to our baby," Harriet repeated her words then started to sob again. Arthur let go of his wife's arm and stared at her. He felt dazed and everything seemed unreal. Arthur looked around at the city which was still in flames. People were carrying their dead and injured neighbors and family members to the offices of the physicians. Crying could be heard everywhere.

Dejectedly Arthur looked at Lloyd and said, "Lloyd I don't even know what to do."

"You're a member of the Insidiae," Lloyd growled. "Why didn't your damn demons save us from this?"

The Sanuri entered the fourth door that opened. He walked in darkness for some time before coming to a large chest that was illuminated. The chest appeared to be very old and heavy. The Sanuri looked at the chest for markings before he attempted to open it. Although he saw no lock the Sanuri could not open the lid to the chest. The Sanuri attempted to pick up the chest but this he could not do either. So he examined the chest a second time.

The Sanuri slowly ran his fingers over the top and sides of the chest. The chest had small round pieces of brass attached to it for decoration. When the Sanuri pushed on the thirteenth piece of brass a small compartment opened revealing a small scroll.

The Sanuri took the scroll from the chest and looked to see if there was anything else in the compartment; the scroll appeared to be the only treasure. The Sanuri slowly unrolled the scroll. A small red snake fell out of the scroll and disappeared as soon as it hit the ground.

The scroll was written in a language so old that even the Sanuri could not read it. But he did recognize the signature of King Sharonne. The Sanuri rolled the scroll up and put it into the pocket of his robe. He found himself back at his table and chair.

The Sanuri lost track of time in his chamber; he was so deep within the earth that he felt it altered his senses. The Sanuri thought he had been trying to translate the scroll for almost two days but he could not be sure. He was concerned about Padre Bartholomew and Padre Thomas, after seeing them in one of the images, as well as Sudfad's family.

"What am I not seeing?" asked the Sanuri out loud. "Roch's great, great grandfather had something to do with demons because of the snake that was with the scroll; but does that mean that he fought demons or worked with them?" thought the Sanuri. "And who was the baby that was killed in the forest, was that one of The Seven Sons?"

The Sanuri unrolled the scroll again. "Other than the language it is written in, nothing seems out of the ordinary," thought the Sanuri. "It certainly looks like it contains the official seal of King Sharonne; and the paper and ink could be from that time."

The Sanuri gently ran his finger over the entire scroll without feeling anything unusual, then he examined the back of the scroll again, thinking he might have missed something. It was when the Sanuri held the opened scroll up to the light of the candle that he found the clue he sought. Only when the candle light illuminated the paper could he see it; the image of a coiled snake.

Two days passed before Harriet would let the undertaker take Laurabelle's body. Harriet was not the only person who was crippled by her grief. Seventy four men, women and children were dead after Roch's men left Nora and many of the victims had been raped. The citizens of Nora incredibly outnumbered Roch and his men, yet almost no one stood up to the vigilantes or tried to stop them. The people of Nora stood by; as did Arthur, and watched Roch and his men brutalize and destroy their families and friends.

While many people were incapacitated by their grief, the entire city was crippled with its guilt. Wives no longer looked at their husbands with the same eyes, children despised their fathers. Although this was not the first time that Roch and his men had brutalized Nora; the damage done by this attack would mar the community for a very long time.

"I sent a message to Hannah," Arthur said as he tried to get Harriet to speak to him. "I told her what happened. She is coming home immediately."

Harriet was sitting in a rocking chair staring out of their bedroom window. She quickly swung around and glared at Arthur so intensely that he took a few steps back. "You told her what happened. Did you really Arthur?" Harriet screamed. "Did you tell her that you stood by and watched as Roch raped and murdered her baby sister? Did you tell her that you held me back when I tried to stop Roch? Arthur seriously what did you tell Hannah?" Arthur said nothing; he turned and walked out of the room.

Door number five opened while the Sanuri was studying the scroll. As soon as he went through the door the Sanuri was warmed by sunshine. The Sanuri found himself in a meadow; he could feel a warm breeze blowing against his face and blowing back his hair. The Sanuri looked at his surroundings without seeing anything familiar or unusual so he started to walk. Birds were singing and for just a moment he enjoyed the beauty of it all.

As the Sanuri walked he could hear the sounds of children laughing although he could not see them. The sounds of the children grew louder and louder, soon the Sanuri found himself outside of a castle. The castle he had seen before; it flew the flag of the Kingdom of Wetpr. Suddenly the iron gates opened by an unseen hand, allowing the Sanuri to walk into the royal courtyard. There were children running and playing; there were soldiers and staff in the area but none of them took notice of the Sanuri's presence.

The front door to the castle opened and the Sanuri walked inside. Immediately inside the entrance was a hallway with many closed doors; the Sanuri walked to the one door he heard opening. As soon as he walked into the room the Sanuri smiled as he saw his old friend King Voltar sitting behind the same desk that his great, great grandson Sudfad now uses. The Sanuri had always admired Voltar for his faith and his integrity. They had formed a close friendship while the King walked the earth.

Suddenly an image of the Sanuri, three generations younger, walked into King Voltar's study. "I have the scrolls," said the image of the Sanuri. "We need to put them into the vault."

"I am glad you came," said Voltar. "I have something of importance to tell you; in fact let us talk as we walk to the vault." King Voltar and the image of the Sanuri left the study through a concealed panel in the wall. As soon as they walked through the doorway they walked down seven flights of stone steps. At the bottom of the steps were six doors, the seventh, the door to the holy vault was concealed.

"A few days ago my men found two Taperian soldiers inside the castle gates; they were caught wandering around the back of the castle," said Voltar. "As you know the window to my study is at the back of the castle. When my soldiers stopped them, the two men acted like fools, they were babbling incoherently."

"Did you believe them to be afflicted?" asked the image of the Sanuri.

"I saw them myself and their eyes looked crazed; one of them was drooling. I had my men take them to the dungeons and try to find out what they were doing here," said Voltar.

"Did they say anything of significance?" asked the image of the Sanuri.

"That is what I must tell you as it disturbs me greatly," said the King as he opened the door to the holy vault. "Before we killed them, the only words they said that we could understand were 'vault' and 'lion'."

"How could I have forgotten that?" thought the Sanuri. "For those Taperian soldiers to have been present at the Castle of Wetpr, King Sharonne must have known about the vault."

137

The Sanuri suddenly found himself back at his table and chair. "But how can that be?" asked the Sanuri out loud. "Even the knowledge that the vault exists is a secret kept by the Holy Family of Wetpr." The Sanuri tried to remember King Voltar's family and staff all those generations ago. "If Sharonne planted a spy who would it have been?" thought the Sanuri. "And how would he even know to plant a spy in the castle of the Royal Family of Wetpr?"

The Sanuri proceeded to write down everything he could remember about the vision in door number five. He reviewed his notes. "It appears more and more that Sharonne was in allegiance with darkness; but did he call to darkness or was he forced? And who was the baby I saw murdered?" mused the Sanuri.

"We should reach Tanger tomorrow, I am planning to stay in the village overnight and go to the mines in the morning," said Roch as he and Demetries sat before an open fire. Demetries did not respond. "It is not like you to be quiet," said Roch sarcastically.

"I am just thinking over our plan."

"What now, are you going to tell me you can't do it?"

"I will get the Rogetts, do not worry," said Demetries smiling. "And I can control them."

"I am a little concerned about that," Roch admitted. "My men will watch them in shifts, although I doubt if any of them will sleep in the presence of those creatures."

"We should attack midmorning when the Gants will be sure to be sleeping."

"Depending on how long it takes us to herd the Rogetts, we will have to make the final camp far from the caves to avoid detection," said Roch. "And you are sure once you unleash the Rogetts they will attack the Gants and not my men?"

"That is what I promised. But you must remember that once the battle begins you have to stay with me; I can sense the location but I cannot go near the scroll."

"And after we have it, you can gather enough Rogetts to attack Wetpr?" Roch asked with a sinister grin.

Roch and his men rode into the small Village of Tanger late in the afternoon. "I don't know about you boys but I am thirsty," yelled Roch as he rode up to the only tavern on the main street. Roch dismounted and tied his horse to a railing. He started to walk into the tavern then turned and faced his men. "The village is yours boys; but everyone better be in the saddle by sun up."

Demetries stayed on his horse as Roch entered the tavern. Within moments a man was thrown out of the tavern and onto the sidewalk. Roch stood in the doorway and yelled, "I am King Roch and that is my horse. Take care of it and return it to this spot by sunup or I will kill your family."

"Yes sir," said the terrified man as he stood up and untied the reigns from the rail. Roch and his men laughed as they watched the man walk the horse to the stable.

A carriage stopped in front of the Marcus mansion. Hannah the eldest daughter of Arthur and Harriet stepped out of the carriage and looked around. Hannah had spent the last few years in the Kingdom of Wetpr studying to become a physician at the renowned Cicero College.

Barely twenty-one years of age; Hannah was a woman of not only exceptional beauty but great intellect. Like Laurabelle, Hannah had long curly blonde hair and large brown eyes. These attributes as well as her curvaceous figure brought her to the attention of many men while she attended college. But Hannah was very dedicated to her studies and her desire to help people.

Hannah had not been home in several years. Not because she did not miss her family; but because crossing the border of Stordt was very dangerous, especially for a woman alone.

"Miss Hannah!" called Gracie. "I can't believe it's you." The elderly cook ran out of the back kitchen door and hugged Hannah tightly. "Your parents will be so comforted to have you home."

"Gracie half of Nora is burned down, what has happened here?"

"Didn't your parents tell you?"

"No, Father said that Laurabelle died, he did not tell me how."

"Come, I will take you to your mother; she hasn't left her bedroom since..." Gracie started to cry and could not finish her sentence. Hannah put her arm around Gracie and the two women walked into the house.

Harriet was again sitting in her chair staring out the bedroom window and did not hear the women enter. "Miss Harriet," Gracie said sweetly. "Look who's here."

"Mother," Hannah said when Harriet did not turn around.

"Hannah," cried out Harriet. Hannah ran to her mother and the two hugged each other and cried. Within moments they heard a man's voice yelling.

"Where's Miss Harriet? Where's Miss Harriet?"

"Charles don't make such a commotion she is with Hannah," Gracie scolded the hired man.

"This is bad, real bad Gracie." Gracie led Charles into the bedroom where both Hannah and Harriet were already coming to the door.

"Charles what is it?" Harriet asked.

"It's Mr. Arthur he, well, he done hung himself in the barn."

"What!" shrieked Hannah who started to run from the room before she realized her mother was not moving. Hannah turned back to Harriet, "Mother please sit down, I will be right back."

To everyone's surprise Harriet looked at Hannah and said coldly, "He couldn't face you." Then Harriet returned to her chair by the window.

Chapter X
The Mark of Satan

The smell of burning buildings filled the air. Roch and his men laughed as they watched the villagers trying to put out the flames. The small Village of Tanger would never completely recover from Roch's terror. Their homes destroyed, their daughters raped, their husbands killed, the spirit of that village died that horrific night.

"You never cease to amuse me," said Demetries with a smile as Roch and his men mounted their horses, on the streets of Tanger; in the early morning hours.

"For a demon you don't really join in on the fun," said Roch with a grin.

"Actually you don't know what I do when I am not with you."

"That is true. Now let's round up some Rogetts."

The Tange mines were only an hour's ride north of the Village of Tanger and consisted of a dozen small shallow gold mines in a two mile area.

"We will position ourselves near the mines which are the farthest north," said Demetries. "Have your men remain mounted and position them in a semi-circle around the front of the mines."

"As you wish," said Roch and then gave the orders to his men. Demetries remained on his horse and placed himself in the middle of the semi-circle of soldiers. Demetries slowly raised his arms and started to chant in a language Roch had never heard before; soon the earth started to shake ever so slightly then more and more until Rogetts appeared; running out of the mines.

Almost two hundred Rogetts ran towards Demetries without looking at any of the soldiers. Just as the first Rogetts were about to reach him; Demetries yelled and there was a flash of light in his right hand, then it appeared that Demetries hurled something to the ground. The entire group of Rogetts stopped abruptly when they saw what Demetries had thrown on the ground. The Rogetts knelt down and bowed before the demon.

141

Roch moved his horse closer to Demetries so he could see what Demetries had thrown on the ground. Roch saw a large red snake posed to strike at the Rogetts. The snake had green eyes with red pupils and its tongue was bright yellow. "I have never seen a snake like that before," said Roch.

"Look at their tattoos," said Demetries with a grin. Roch realized every Rogett wore a tattoo with an identical image of the snake that was on the ground.

"What is it?"

"The Mark of Satan."

"It is as if they are in a trance," Roch said of the Rogetts his men were herding towards the Caves of Muldun.

"In a way they are," replied Demetries.

"It's really hard to believe they are humans," said Roch as he was looking at the almost rat-like appearance of the Rogetts. "What happened to them?"

"Fear, fear is a wonderful thing. You should know that, you feed off it."

"I will admit I have found people's fears to be more than useful; but look at these things," said Roch with disgust.

"They took to the underground centuries ago because they were afraid of everything around them; over time their bodies changed."

"So you are telling me that if I decided to live underground, in a few hundred years my descendants would look like those disgusting creatures?"

"What makes you think they aren't your descendants?" Demetries asked with a grin.

"Once again you are not making any sense," said Roch with frustration.

"You were born of darkness, so were the Rogetts; you both made the same choices" said Demetries. "Your tattoo is just harder to see."

Door number six opened with great noise. When the Sanuri walked through it he was in the middle of a battle scene. Taperian soldiers were fighting Huta warriors; two well trained and savage groups, the battle was horrendous. The Sanuri looked at the soldiers trying to determine when in time this battle took place.

The Taperian uniforms had not changed in centuries nor had the barbaric appearances of the Hutas. As the Sanuri watched the savage scene; he saw a slight movement on the left of the scenario. Soon he saw King Sharonne ride his white horse to the top of a hill. The King was dressed in full battle armor and he was leading more troops. The King ordered the men behind him to join their comrades on the battlefield. The additional troops turned the tide of the battle and the Hutas were quickly defeated.

The scene went black. The Sanuri turned to walk back to his chamber but door number six would not open, so he turned around and walked into the blackness. Soon another scene appeared. The Sanuri saw a room and heard muffled voices talking but could not make out what they were saying. The voices grew louder.

"For every gift I give to you, I need something in exchange. I do not give away favors," a man's voice said.

Suddenly the Sanuri saw the back of a man's head. The man had long wavy red hair and was dressed in full battle armor; when the man turned around the Sanuri saw King Sharonne's face, it appeared angry. "I got your message with the Huta attack," screamed Sharonne.

"As I told you I can make your life easier or considerably more difficult," said the first voice.

"What do you want from me," Sharonne yelled and hit his fist against the wall.

"You asked me for an alliance; you have expanded the borders of your kingdom, you have more wealth and power," said the voice calmly. "You have been able to fulfill your dirty little fantasies; now it is time for payment." The scene went black and soon the Sanuri found himself back at his table and chair in the chamber.

The Sanuri was reviewing the details of the scenes behind door number six in his head; again and again. The Sanuri was overwhelmed with a feeling that he had forgotten something very important. As he did after every journey through a door, the Sanuri wrote down all that he had seen and heard. He sat in his chair for hours hoping another door would open.

Finally the Sanuri lay down on his bed and closed his eyes and that is when he saw it. "The ring," said the Sanuri as he quickly sat up. The Sanuri went back to his table. "King Sharonne was wearing a ring on his right middle finger; a very large ruby in a silver setting; the same ring that King Roch wears, the same ring that Juleta said some of the Insidiae wear. Juleta said that the members of the Insidiae who wear this ring are loyal to the demon Omnibus. What exactly does that mean and why am I being shown it?" questioned the Sanuri.

"Padre Bartholomew, wake up," called Padre Thomas as he saw his friend with his head down on the table in the Hall of Antiquities. "Padre Bartholomew you fell asleep again."

"Padre Bartholomew," said Padre Thomas a third time as he gently shook the shoulder of the old priest. "Great Ruler be with us," gasped Padre Thomas as he saw blood on the back of Padre Bartholomew's head. "He is still breathing, thanks be to heaven," exclaimed Padre Thomas as he tried to lift Padre Bartholomew from the chair. The attempt was futile as Padre Bartholomew was almost twice the weight of Padre Thomas. "Great Ruler please watch over him until I return," prayed Padre Thomas as he ran out of the Hall of Antiquities looking for help.

"No one will sleep tonight," said Roch. "You seem to be controlling them but I still do not trust those creatures."

"You are safe to sleep Roch," said Demetries with a grin.

"You never did tell me what you were planning on doing with those Hutas we had in the dungeons."

"Yes I did, I thought we had agreed to use them to distract the Gants."

"Are you telling me you can control the Hutas like you control the Rogetts?"

"I have so far."

Roch was quiet for several minutes. "Demetries you said you took over Jonas' body when he died because of a Huta attack, you planned that didn't you?"

"You are finally starting to open your eyes Roch."

Roch stared at Demetries from across the camp fire. "So what, you were a demon in hell waiting to jump into someone's body?"

"Roch you are an arrogant man, you believe it is your thoughts and your actions that causes things to happen; you will realize you are but a pawn in a game of beings so powerful you cannot even imagine.

"Do you remember what happened to you?" asked Padre Thomas as Padre Bartholomew opened his eyes.

"How did I get here?" asked Padre Bartholomew groggily, then he winced with pain.

"I found you in the Hall of Antiquities and we brought you down here," replied Padre Thomas.

Padre Bartholomew looked around the Great Hall which was still set up as a medical area from the attack on Afax. "Well, I suppose it is good that I am the only patient," said Padre Bartholomew trying to force a smile. "What is wrong with me?" he asked.

"You have a deep cut on the back of your head just above your neck," said Padre Thomas. "I found you with your face down on the table; do you remember anything?"

Padre Bartholomew closed his eyes because the room was spinning; he tried to focus his thoughts.

"Padre Bartholomew."

"I am fine, I am just trying to think. I remember that I could not sleep so I got up and walked to the Hall of Antiquities, I thought I would get some research done before breakfast. I went to the thirteenth shelf, where you and I left off with the reading materials, and I grabbed the next two scrolls. I walked back to the table and unrolled a scroll and that is the last I remember."

Padre Thomas turned to the other priests who were standing around the bed, "Do any of you remember seeing scrolls on the table?" All the priests responded, "No." I will go back up there but I am sure there was nothing on that table except for your head," Padre Thomas said. "Do you remember hearing or seeing anyone in the room?"

"No but now that I think about it, the candles were already lit when I entered the room," Padre Bartholomew said. "I didn't even realize that to be unusual at the time."

"Do you remember which scrolls you had?"

"The first one I opened had the prophecy about The Seven Sons of Light."

Door number seven opened with great fanfare. The Sanuri was sitting at his table writing when he heard music coming through one of the doors. When he walked to the door he found it slightly open, he never heard the click as it unlocked. When the Sanuri walked through the door he saw a great celebration. There were cheering people in streets throwing flowers into the air. All the people were looking to the left as if they were waiting for someone to come from that direction.

The Sanuri saw men on horses riding down the street, led by King Sharonne. The cheering crowds started yelling 'Victory! Victory to Stordt!' The Sanuri noticed the same ruby ring on Sharonne's right hand. The Sanuri tried to take in every detail of Sharonne and his men then he searched the faces in the crowd.

The Sanuri saw three Enrops perched on a balcony railing; they appeared to be watching the crowd. He tried to see what the Enrops were looking at.

The Sanuri's eyes grew wide as he spat the word, "Sporos" with disgust. Sporos was wearing a green robe that indicated he was in training to be a priest. This revelation helped the Sanuri to try and determine a time frame for the illusion he was witnessing.

The Sanuri watched as Sporos turned and started to walk through the crowd in the same direction that Sharonne's army was coming from. It appeared that Sporos cast a large shadow but the shadow was not the same shape as Sporos and others near him were not casting shadows. The Sanuri quickly searched the scene before him and could not see anything that would cast that shadow.

There are no scrolls on or near the table," said Padre Thomas as he searched the area where Padre Bartholomew had been seated when he was attacked.

"The scroll with The Seven Sons prophesy isn't on the thirteenth shelf where Padre Bartholomew said he found it," said Padre Francis.

"Look at this," called Padre Stephens loudly as he held up a silver candle holder with blood on it.

The three priests walked the entire length of the Hall of Antiquities. "There is no one in here," said Padre Francis somewhat relieved.

"But how did the intruder get in?" asked Padre Thomas. "There are seven locks on each door and each lock has a different key and only the high priests and I have access to the keys."

"How did Padre Bartholomew get in?" asked Padre Francis.

"Why, I don't know," replied Padre Thomas. "The doors were locked when I arrived."

147

"What do you mean the doors were unlocked?" Padre Thomas asked.

"I guess I was so tired I really didn't think about it," Padre Bartholomew said. "I was all the way to the doors of the Hall of Antiquities when I realized I didn't get the keys from you. Just as I was about to turn and go back I saw that the door was slightly ajar. I was actually relieved and thought that perhaps we didn't close it properly the last time we were in there. I don't know what I was thinking I should have known something was wrong."

"Then we know the intruder entered through the front doors but all of the sets of keys are accounted for," Padre Thomas said.

"That makes no sense," said Padre Bartholomew as he winced with pain.

"I know," whispered Padre Thomas. "I fear something is greatly wrong here and until we can determine what it is, I think we should keep this to ourselves." Then Padre Thomas paused as he saw the color draining from Padre Bartholomew's face. "Are you alright?"

"Yes, still a bit dizzy," replied Padre Bartholomew as he grabbed his head.

"Do you want something for the pain?"

"No, with what is going on around here I want to have a clear head. I hate to even utter the words but if the keys and priests are accounted for; we may have a terrorist amongst us."

"I know and that leads to the question of why?" said Padre Thomas. "We still have to search the Hall of Antiquities to see if anything is missing."

"Yes, but that will take a very long time and if the terrorist is posing as a priest, what would stop him from putting the item back while you are taking the inventory?"

The Sanuri sat at his table reading his notes. "That is twice now that I have seen a shadow around Sporos. The first time the shadow appeared to be watching us, this second time it seemed to be following Sporos," thought the Sanuri.

"Sporos told me that he had sold his soul to the demons before he became a priest but I did not think that happened until we were tested in the desert. Sporos was much younger in that illusion."

"When did I really lose my friend?" the Sanuri asked himself sadly. "And how is Sporos connected to Sharonne?" As the Sanuri pondered these questions he heard a click as door number eight was unlocked.

As soon as the Sanuri walked through the door he heard a woman crying. "How could you?" she screamed. "I am your brother's wife." The woman's face was not visible to the Sanuri but he recognized the man standing over her. "If you tell him I will kill you both," growled King Sharonne. "I am your King and you live in the castle at my pleasure." Sharonne marched out of the room and the naked woman lay on the floor sobbing. "Roch certainly takes after Sharonne," thought the Sanuri with disgust. The scene went black.

"I do not remember Sharonne having a brother," thought the Sanuri. A new scene appeared before the Sanuri. Sporos was at a monastery speaking with a man wearing a priest's robe with the hood pulled over his face. Sporos' appearance was very similar to the last time the Sanuri saw him; when they had the great battle and Sporos was imprisoned in The Abyss for all eternity.

The Sanuri searched the scene for something that might tell him when this scene occurred. The Sanuri gasped in horror, when he saw an image of Petra coming out of the monastery and playing in the courtyard. The scene went black. "Please Great Ruler," prayed the Sanuri. "Do not let this be a sign that Petra is in danger, please protect him."

"So Sporos was at the monastery at Malga," thought the Sanuri. Then he remembered an earlier scene of a figure in the Hall of Antiquities wearing a priest's robe with the hood pulled up and Padres Thomas and Bartholomew entering the room. "Sporos has a spy at the monastery but how would he gain access to the Hall of Antiquities?" thought the Sanuri.

A third scene illuminated before the Sanuri. King Sharonne was arguing with another man who was shorter but similar in build and appearance to Sharonne and they both had the same distinctive red hair.

149

"My wife hung herself because you raped her," screamed the distraught man as he pulled his sword out of its sheath.

"Igor you are better off without her," yelled Sharonne. "You can have any woman you want."

"I loved her," screamed Igor. "You raped her." Igor lunged at Sharonne with his sword. Sharonne side stepped the assault; grabbed the back of his brother's shirt and threw him head first into the stone wall. Igor took two steps backwards, holding his head, then he fell to the ground. Sharonne picked up his brother's sword and thrust it into Igor's chest.

"Both Sharonne and Roch are rapists and murders," said the Sanuri out loud. "But I still do not see how all of this connects," he added with frustration.

The Sanuri had lost track of time in the chamber; perhaps a day had passed before door number nine was revealed. When he walked through the door he saw a woman in a room with a baby in a cradle. The head of the cradle had the crest of the Royal Family of Stordt carved into the wood. The Sanuri watched as the woman put a small talisman under the baby's blanket.

The woman was talking and as her voice grew louder the Sanuri realized she was praying, 'Great Ruler please forgive me I do not know what to do, first Tresdore suddenly dies as have so many others and now this baby died and has come back to life. Please Great Ruler protect us.' "I know that voice," said the Sanuri. "Of course." When Glenda turned around and the Sanuri saw her face the scene went black.

"Tresdore was Sharonne's first son who died at an early age, that baby must have been Micha his third child and second son," thought the Sanuri. "What did she mean that the child died and then came back to life?"

As the Sanuri stood in the darkness he could hear music, he walked down what he believed to be a dark corridor until he came upon the next scene. There appeared to be a great celebration, people were dancing in the streets. The Sanuri looked at the faces in the crowds and did not recognize anyone.

Soon there was a procession of soldiers on horseback and musicians then a boca pulled by six white horses. All the people cheered when they saw the boca. The scene suddenly changed to just the people who were sitting in the boca. "That is a young Prince Micha and his bride Berta," thought the Sanuri. The Sanuri noticed that Micha was not wearing the ruby ring in the silver setting. The scene went black.

"Padre Bartholomew are you awake?" whispered Padre Thomas.

"Yes," said Padre Bartholomew groggily and sat up on his cot.

"We have been taking inventory in the Hall of Antiquities and it seems that many scrolls are missing. Of course we are just starting to search in that huge room, but many scrolls are not in their assigned places."

"The scroll with the prophesy of The Seven Sons?"

"That cannot be located."

"What else is missing?"

"We have only started with the scrolls."

"I have been trying to remember what happened to me," said Padre Bartholomew as he leaned closer to his friend. "I remember sitting down at the table with the scrolls then there was a searing pain in my head and I think I blacked out for a moment. I remember hearing movement and I opened my eyes and saw a hand take the scrolls from the table. Padre Thomas I also saw the sleeve of whoever took the scrolls," said Padre Bartholomew in a whisper. "It was the sleeve of a priest's robe."

Chapter XI
A Glimpse of Horror

Like his men, Roch slept little with the Rogetts in the area. He sat by the fire thinking about his deal with Demetries. Roch did not want to give Demetries The Scroll of Imari. "If Demetries really can control the Rogetts and the Hutas then I can overthrow Wetpr and finally kill Sudfad," thought Roch. "But if I keep the scroll perhaps I can control the Rogetts and Hutas without him."

Roch kept looking over at the sleeping demon. Although Roch found Demetries annoying at times and repulsive to look at; he did find himself enjoying the demon's company. Roch never really trusted Demetries but Roch never trusted anyone. Roch realized that the one thing that irked him about Demetries was the fact that Demetries was more powerful than he was. Roch sat by the fire, scheming of how he could obtain such powers.

Just as Roch was starting to doze off he suddenly jumped; in the fire he saw the face of a lion. "That lion has haunted my dreams forever but never before have I seen it like this," thought Roch. The Lion appeared to be talking so Roch moved closer to the fire to try and understand what it was saying. Suddenly out of the flames jumped a full sized male lion. Roch thought he was dreaming as he watched The Lion walk around the camp looking at the sleeping men. The Lion lingered longer over Demetries then turned towards Roch.

Roch jumped up and grabbed his sword from its sheath and pointed it at The Lion. The Lion stopped and looked at Roch, suddenly the sword was on fire and Roch dropped it as it burned his hand. The Lion took two more steps toward Roch. "You feeble man," said The Lion. "You choose to be an errand boy for demons; you do not even understand the game much less how to play. You think of yourself as a mighty warrior but you will find out the meaning of errand boy in hell. You can still redeem yourself but do not take long to make your choice."

Roch looked around the camp and no one else seemed to be aware of The Lion's presence. Roch did not speak. "You have nothing to say mighty king," said The Lion mockingly.

"Who are you?" demanded Roch.

"I am a messenger and I am giving you the opportunity to save your soul."

"I think it is too late for that," sneered Roch.

"It is your choice. But know heaven sees all, your thoughts your deeds that black hole you call a heart."

"I am not afraid of heaven," said Roch.

"Your demon over there believes you to be a fool and I agree." The Lion started to walk away then stopped and again turned towards Roch. "If you ever make the right choice and want to be saved, call out to The Great Ruler."

"Damn The Great Ruler," said Roch angrily.

The Lion took a step closer to Roch and said, "Roch, you who have caused so much pain and misery in this world, I hold up a mirror so that all you have done will be brought back upon you." As The Lion walked out of camp Roch fell to the ground screaming in agony.

Taperian soldiers ran to Roch when they heard his screams. Roch was wildly throwing himself around on the ground as if he was on fire. The approaching soldiers stood and stared at him, finally one of the soldiers knelt down near Roch. "My Lord, what can I do for you?" asked the soldier. Roch had his face in the dirt and was yelling incoherently.

"I think he said to get Demetries," said one of the men.

A soldier walked to where Demetries was sleeping and all he saw was a blanket on the ground. The soldier picked up the blanket then jumped back when he saw a large red snake like the one Demetries had thrown at the Rogetts. The snake did not move so the soldier touched it with his sword.

"Demetries is gone," called the soldier. "There is just a dead snake here."

"The Rogetts," yelled another soldier. All the soldiers in camp grabbed their weapons and ran to where the Rogetts were being held. Roch was left by himself writhing in the dirt and screaming.

The Sanuri turned to walk back towards the chamber when another scene appeared before him. He saw a woman lying in a bed about to give birth. There were women standing around her including Glenda the healer from Cana, the great, great, grandmother of Gala. "Queen Vinca breathe," Glenda said. Suddenly the Sanuri saw a movement. There was a shadow in the room that was moving but nothing in the room appeared to be casting the shadow. The scene went black.

The Sanuri reached the door leading into the chamber but it would not open, so he turned and walked back down the long dark corridor. The Sanuri kept walking down the long dark corridor of door number nine. But no scenes presented themselves. "This in of itself must be a clue," thought The Sanuri. "I am in darkness without a sense of boundaries or time. Is the clue The Abyss?" asked the Sanuri out loud, then he heard the door click open.

"What is going on here?" whispered a soldier.

"This place is cursed, we should leave," said another.

"My Lord," said a soldier as they all gathered around Roch. "My Lord the Rogetts are gone."

Roch was still rolling around on the ground with his face in the dirt. "What do you mean they are gone?" Roch growled.

"Demetries and the Rogetts they just disappeared, all that is left is a bunch of dead snakes," said the soldier.

Roch slowly and painfully raised himself to his knees; he turned and faced the soldier who was speaking to him. "My Lord," gasped the soldier as he jumped away from Roch. The entire group of soldiers moved several steps back as they could see Roch's face in the firelight.

"He has leprosy," one soldier yelled. "This place is cursed!"

"My Lord what has happened to you?"

Roch looked at his hands and forearms and saw great lesions and boils. Then he put his hands up to his face and felt his cheeks. Roch raised his head towards the heavens and emitted a long piercing scream of rage.

The lock to door number ten clicked open as the Sanuri was pacing in his chamber. He eagerly walked into the mystery lying before him; instantaneously a scene appeared. The Sanuri saw a man crouching behind a large boulder. The man was wearing the clothing of a peasant and appeared very frightened. Suddenly five black horses appeared in the scene, each ridden by a person wearing the robe of a priest with the hood pulled up so the Sanuri could not see any of their faces.

The frightened man suddenly bolted from his hiding place and started to run in the forest. When the men in the robes saw him they took chase. The man ran as fast as he could, continually looking over his shoulder in fear. He tripped over tree roots and vines several times finally falling to the ground.

The men on horseback surrounded him. One man dismounted and walked over to the frightened man who was yelling, "I did not see anything, truly I did not see anything." The man who was standing pulled a large knife from under his robe and slit the throat of the peasant.

The murderer walked back to his horse; as he grabbed the saddle to hoist himself up his hands and forearms were exposed. The Sanuri did not see any markings on the man's arms. But the ring on the man's left hand stunned the Sanuri. It was the ring of the monastery of Malga, with four large diamonds which indicated a priest of very high standing. The scene went blank. The Sanuri stood staring into the dark space that had held the scene. "By The Great Ruler are there demons in the monastery?"

Roch screamed with rage as his men deserted him; filled they were with fear that the same plague would be set upon them. Roch screamed with rage that his plans for The Scroll of Imari had been foiled. Roch screamed with rage at the inflictions set upon him. Roch screamed with rage that he would never again lose to The Great Ruler.

The Sanuri was so disturbed by seeing the ring of a high priest on the murderer's hand that momentarily he had forgotten that High Priests Meekos, Pravis and Tenebrae all wore the blood rings of the Insidiae. Those three men always evaded the Sanuri when he visited the monastery at Malga, so he had never seen their hands; but he was sure their rank afforded them the privileges of wearing the highly honored diamond rings of that monastery.

Both anger and sadness filled the Sanuri as he thought of these men who professed to be servants of The Great Ruler yet they were filled with demons. The Lion had previously told the Sanuri to have High Priest Raphael of the Patronus investigate the three high priests. The Sanuri was writing a note to himself to share this new information with Raphael, when he realized that another scene had started.

King Sharonne was standing in front of a stone wall talking to someone the Sanuri could not see. "I killed the babies for you; I thought that paid my debt," growled Sharonne.

"You gave us a vessel for our seed, yes; but we have helped you in many ways and expect a payment for each deed," said the same man's voice that the Sanuri had heard in other scenes.

"You keep changing the rules," yelled Sharonne.

"Perhaps, do you want to give up what you have gained?"

"No."

"There has long been a legend that The Great Ruler has a protected place for things of great power, we want you to find it."

"And do you have any clues as to where this place might be or what it looks like?" asked Sharonne with frustration.

"That is for you to find out."

"Do you expect me to search the entire continent?" yelled Sharonne. "You are mad."

"Your army is now large enough and powerful enough for such a quest."

"Is that why you helped me?"

"We had many reasons for helping you."

"What exactly do you want?"

"We will tell you when we want you to get something in particular; for now find this protected place."

"How will I know it when I find it?"

"You will know."

"And if I do not succeed?" asked Sharonne contemptuously.

The person who the Sanuri could not see thrust his arm forward and placed his left hand on Sharonne's head as he said "Let me give you a glimpse of horror."

Sharonne started screaming and fell to the floor; the unknown man had to step out of the shadows to keep his hand on Sharonne's head. The man was wearing the robe of a priest with the hood pulled over his head. He wore the ring of the monastery of Malga on his hand; it had four large diamonds in it. When the man removed his hand from Sharonne's head; Sharonne was curled into a ball on the floor and weeping as a child. The Sanuri found himself back at his table and chair in the chamber.

Roch's men left him his horse and provisions; not as much out of kindness as fear. The night's events and the sight of Roch brought terror to even the hardest of hearts. The soldiers left the campsite so quickly that some of them left their belongings behind. When Roch finished his screaming tirade he walked over to Demetries blanket and saw the dead snake. Roch kicked the snake which caused him great pain as all of his bones felt as if they were on fire.

Roch walked around the camp, he was so angry he could hardly think. Then he grabbed a piece of burning wood from the fire and walked to the area where the Rogetts had been kept. His soldier's words rang true; all Roch saw were the dead red snakes.

157

Roch walked back to the campfire and sat down. He touched his shirt pocket, a habit he had of making sure the map was safe. "No," screamed Roch as he thrust his hand into all of his pockets. "Damn you!" screamed Roch. "Damn you!" Roch's precious map was gone. He ran around the campfire screaming with rage and pain. After several hours of insane behavior Roch raised his face to the heavens and screamed as loudly as he could, "Great Ruler you will pay for this!"

Door number eleven clicked open as the Sanuri sat at his table trying to put together all of the puzzle pieces he had seen so far. "How could all this have been going on, yet I did not know it?" thought the Sanuri as he walked to the door. The Sanuri saw a scene as soon as he passed through the doorway. He saw a Great Hall but he was not sure where it was located.

The room was filled with people and their faces were slowly coming into focus. The Sanuri's eyes grew wide as he started to recognize people, "That is Sudfad's sons' wedding," he said out loud. "That was when Sudfad moved all of the guests inside so they would not realize the castle was being attacked," thought the Sanuri. His heart smiled when he saw an image of little Petra dressed in a miniature military uniform trying to dance.

The Sanuri searched the crowd; he saw Renya and the brides, "Those girls were so beautiful," thought the Sanuri, but he did not see Sudfad or his sons. "The battle was still waging," said the Sanuri. The scene stayed on guests in the Great Hall who seem to be having a normal wedding celebration. "I must have missed something," thought the Sanuri.

The Sanuri slowly looked over every guest and that is when he saw it. The blood ring on the hand of someone putting a gift on one of the many tables set up for gifts. The body of the person was obscured by other guests. For just a moment the Sanuri started to feel anxious for the safety of the Royal Family; then he remembered that The Lion had agreed to protect those whom the Sanuri protected, during this test.

"High Priest Pravis was in the dungeons during the wedding," thought the Sanuri. "So who else would be wearing that ring?

And could that gift be dangerous to Sudfad's family?" The Sanuri felt the presence of another, turning he saw The Lion.

"I was just thinking about you," said the Sanuri.

"I know that is partially why I am here, let us walk to the chamber where you will be more comfortable," said The Lion as the lock on door number eleven clicked open. When they reached the chamber the Sanuri noticed there was more food and drink for him on the table.

"Tell me, that wedding gift that I was shown; is it a danger to Sudfad's family?"

"It was," replied The Lion. "But I destroyed the snake in that box when I destroyed the demons that were attacking the castle." The Sanuri sat silent for a moment. "Sanuri you have devoted your entire life to The Great Ruler and He is honored. But do not deprive yourself of the love of a family. Sudfad's family loves you as their own. You will see things that make you question if your presence in their home is a blessing or a curse; always remember it is a blessing."

"I don't understand what you are saying."

The Lion ignored the Sanuri's comment and continued, "The next two doors will go quickly. You have found this test to be very different from your previous experiences, do you like it?"

"Truthfully I find it annoying. I feel like I am wasting time between the doors; when I could be doing something more useful."

"Have you considered we could be testing your patience?"

"You make a point. But I have to tell you although I have learned a great deal, I have not solved this puzzle."

"That is what I am here to tell you; you will not solve it with the information we are giving you here but it will help you greatly when you are out of the chamber," The Lion said.

"When you have completed the last door you will find yourself back in your room at the monastery; some serious things have occurred there in your absence."

159

"You will be told of these events but do not stay there long. Before two days pass start your trip to Wetpr. King Sudfad will soon be in possession of some information he will need to share with you; it is more pieces to the puzzle you refer to. Plan to stay in Wetpr for a while; you will know when it is time to leave."

"Is everyone all right?"

"I have fulfilled my promise to you; but Padre Bartholomew has a good gash to his head."

"He was hurt, how?"

"You will find out the details, he would have been killed had a sound not startled his assailant."

"Would that sound have been a lion's roar?"

"It certainly may have been," replied The Lion. "Roch and Demetries led men to the Tange Mines to round up Rogetts, which Demetries was controlling. Their plan was to use the Rogetts to distract the Gants while Roch searched for The Scroll of Imari. Actually it was a pretty good plan which is why I paid them a visit."

The Sanuri smiled, "Please tell me the details of your visit."

"Since Demetries was trying to find a way to help his friend Sporos escape from The Abyss, I sent him and the Rogetts there. Roch was leaving a trail of destruction as he traveled. I gave him a choice and he made the wrong one. All the darkness he has sent out to this world has been returned to him. When his men saw him they abandoned him. Roch has learned nothing and has declared war against The Great Ruler. He is traveling to Taperia; Roch's efforts have been slowed but not yet stopped."

"It sickens me that we cannot stop him," said the Sanuri with disgust.

"Well we can stop him, The Great Ruler can do anything; but as you have figured out he is the second son of the second son of the second son and the Vessel of Darkness. He has a destiny, which we will only allow him to partially fulfill and when he fails the effects will be felt in all of the dark worlds," The Lion said.

160

"You have to be off soon; in just a moment door number twelve will open." As the last words were spoken The Lion was gone.

The pain that Roch was experiencing was intense and debilitating. He found several bottles of whiskey that his men had left behind and drank one straight down. The liquor caused Roch to pass out. The powerful King of Stordt lay in the dirt, writhing in pain as his evil nature was attacking his own body.

Roch had long been accustomed to having nightmares as beings more powerful than his mind could comprehend tried to communicate with him. But from this night forward Roch would be plagued with intense nightmares of a much different kind. Roch now would feel the terror and fear that he instilled in others.

Door number twelve opened almost immediately after The Lion left the chamber. As the Sanuri walked through this door he heard music. The scene had returned to the wedding celebrations of Raul and Vitomas and Simon and Annabelle. Now the scene changed to the royal courtyard outside of the castle of Wetpr. It appeared that two men were talking in the shadows. "My Lord, before she killed herself, she said the Sanuri was here again," said one voice.

"He spends a great deal of time with this Royal Family and I suspect there is more than friendship involved," said the second male voice.

"My Lord we have been watching him for a very long time; I feel confident that if there is a vault it is here in Wetpr," said the first voice.

"Thank you Demetries you have done well," replied the second male voice. "Continue to have the Sanuri watched; he will lead us to what we seek." The scene went black.

"So I am the clue to the vault and I have put everyone in danger," said the Sanuri out loud.

A new scene appeared before the Sanuri. He saw The Lion's face; then the scene changed back to the wedding reception.

161

The Sanuri saw Sudfad and his sons all leave the study as they were going to their assigned posts. Then a figure of a large richly dressed man walked down the hallway and stopped at the door to Sudfad's study. The man grabbed the doorknob to the study with his right hand, but the door was locked. The man hurried away as Marie came walking down the hallway. The scene went blank.

"It was all a diversion," thought the Sanuri. "Just as Roch must be a diversion. My old friend if you can hear me," the Sanuri called out. "Do you want the location of the vault changed?" The Sanuri waited but he neither heard nor saw anything so he walked back to the open door and returned to his table and chair.

The Sanuri had not finished writing down his notes before he heard the lock to door number thirteen open. He walked through the open door and saw nothing but darkness. The Sanuri kept walking up and down the dark corridor without seeing or hearing anything. "The darkness itself must be significant," thought the Sanuri as he paced. Suddenly it dawned on him, "The number thirteen must be the clue."

The Sanuri found himself back at his table and chair. He wrote down his notes and before the Sanuri could put his pen back into the ink well he found himself back in his bed at the monastery at Malga. The Sanuri quickly lit the candle next to his bed and searched for his tablet of notes from the chamber. He put the notes into a pocket of his robe and ran out of the bedroom and down the hallway. The Sanuri first knocked on Padre Bartholomew's door and was pleased when the priest answered.

"I need to speak with you and Padre Thomas," said the Sanuri quickly.

"Yes, yes of course; let me get dressed," said Padre Bartholomew as he turned from the door.

"Wait for me in my room," said the Sanuri and he left for Padre Thomas's room.

After both priests entered his room, the Sanuri looked down the hallway in both directions; before he closed the door.

"Where have you been?" asked Padre Bartholomew. "We have been so worried."

162

"I cannot tell you where I have been, only that I was being tested by The Great Ruler," said the Sanuri in a hushed voice. "I have much to tell you but first tell me what has happened here while I was gone."

The Sanuri talked with Padre Bartholomew and Padre Thomas for hours. They were all disturbed by the information that they shared. "I will be leaving for Wetpr soon," said the Sanuri.

"You don't mean now, it is the middle of the night," said Padre Thomas.

"Yes, The Lion told me that Sudfad will soon have something very important to tell me. I feel like I need to get to Wetpr immediately. But there are a few things I want to get from the Hall of Antiquities before I go," the Sanuri said.

"At least let me pack you some food," said Padre Bartholomew as he stood up.

"I will go with you to the Hall of Antiquities," said Padre Thomas.

The Sanuri searched through the hall for the scrolls and manuscripts he wanted to take with him. Padre Bartholomew had already shown him the list of missing items from the monastery.

"Some of these items will be safer with me," said the Sanuri as Padre Thomas helped him fill two large baskets which they loaded into the back of the boca. Padre Bartholomew met them with several baskets of food and drink, which they also put into the boca.

"Sanuri, if we truly have a terrorist here, should you not take more of the items, so you can protect them?" asked Padre Thomas.

"I agree," said Padre Bartholomew. And the three men returned to the Hall of Antiquities. They filled several more baskets with manuscripts, while Padre Thomas was careful to list all of the items that the Sanuri was taking so they could compare the list with the inventories. When the rest of the baskets had been loaded; the Sanuri climbed onto the front seat of the boca.

163

"The Great Ruler be with you my dear friends," said the Sanuri as he drove his team of horses towards the main gate of the monastery. Once he was through the gate the Sanuri prayed, "Great Ruler clear my path." And he sped off into the night. The two old priests watched their friend until the darkness of the night swallowed the image of the boca.

"It is a beautiful night," said Padre Thomas. "Do you want to take a walk in the gardens before we retire?"

Padre Bartholomew laughed, "Alright, but you do realize it will be sunup in a few hours?" as they turned towards the gardens, the two priests were not aware of the eyes that were watching them from the shadows.

Roch awoke late the next afternoon. His head hurt from the whiskey. Roch looked around the campsite, momentarily disorientated; he was trying to figure out where he was. Then he saw his hands and arms and he screamed loudly for he realized the events of the previous night were not just a nightmare. Roch grabbed a second bottle of whiskey and drank that straight down. The whiskey caused a numbing effect before Roch passed out again.

Roch would later find out that none of his men ever returned to his castle. They realized that if Roch survived, he would have them killed for abandoning him. Although they made no pacts or agreements, all of those Taperian soldiers left the Kingdom of Stordt, never to return.

Roch's pain only added to the ill temperament he was having from the effects of the whiskey. He started a fire and fixed himself dinner. As soon as Roch started to eat he immediately vomited. It was then that he realized he also had sores and boils inside of his mouth.

"I'll get the best physicians money can buy," growled Roch out loud as pus ran into his eyes from the open sores that covered his head. "He thinks he stopped me, me!" screamed Roch. "I will show him. The Great Ruler cannot stop me; He just started a war!"

Chapter XII
Terror in Her Eyes

Roch stayed at the campsite for several days, drinking and cursing The Great Ruler. Always an egotistical man, Roch was embarrassed by the thoughts of how he must look. His pain was so great that he did not walk with his normal swaggering stride, but walked as one much older than his years. Finally Roch decided it was time for him to return to his castle. He counted out the provisions his men had left behind. Roch wanted to avoid having to stop to buy food.

The sun was high in the sky as Roch started his journey home. The heat made Roch sweat, this in combination with the running pus from his sores, blinded him at times. Roch found himself constantly wiping his eyes. The movements of the horse only added to his pain. "I need more whiskey," thought Roch so he headed back to the Village of Tanger.

"Come in Matthew," said Mathas as his son was entering the study. "Your mother and I want to talk with you. Mathas was seated behind his desk, while Rosa was sitting in one of the chairs across from Mathas. Matthew chose a chair that was positioned so he could look at both of his parents.

"So Matthew tell me about Angelina," Rosa said with a coy smile.

"Is that why you called me in here?" Matthew asked and started grinning.

"Matthew we have hardly seen you for weeks because you are spending all of your time with Angelina and her family. I am curious to meet the girl who seems to be stealing your heart," Rosa said sincerely.

"Matthew your mother and I want to invite Sorren and his family here for dinner this week, how would you feel about that?"

"Fine, they are good people but they live modestly. It took a couple of weeks before Angelina's mother stopped getting embarrassed because I was there. I think Shara might feel a little overwhelmed by the castle."

"Well, we will do our best to make her feel welcomed," Rosa said. "Your father told me that Angelina is very beautiful and a warrior."

"Yes," Matthew with a warm smile. "I have never met anyone like her before. She is exciting and challenging. We have a great deal of fun together."

"By fun, I hope you remember what I said about sleeping with her," Mathas said.

"Father I haven't even kissed her yet. In fact I think she is starting to think something is wrong."

Mathas laughed, "Well son, I certainly didn't tell you that you couldn't kiss the girl."

"I know but I am afraid if I start I won't be able to stop."

"Is this our son talking?" Rosa teased.

"And besides my feelings for her, I really like Angelina's family, especially Sorren."

"Matthew there was something else I wanted to talk about and I hope you don't think I am interfering," Mathas said. "Quite honestly I have only seen you and Angelina together a couple of times for brief periods and well, the two of you look like you are in love. If that is the case, I think you should tell her about the inheritance. It is only fair for her to know that you could possibly have more wives someday. I fear that if you don't tell her she will feel betrayed."

"Father I have been thinking about that same thing for the last couple of weeks; I am not sure how to bring it up or when."

"I think you should sit down with Sorren and Angelina and tell them together. Angelina is young and Sorren told me you are her first love. She could react badly to what you have to say; but then at least Sorren would understand what the situation is. And unless I am mistaken their tribe also practices wife inheritance."

Roch waited until dark before he entered the remains of the Village of Tanger. The streets were dark and quiet. "I wonder where all the people are?" thought Roch. He stopped his horse in front of the tavern. "Fortunately we didn't burn this building down," he said to himself with a chuckle.

The doors to the tavern were locked and the room was dark. Roch kicked the doors open. He remembered where the bar was in the room and quickly walked behind it grabbing an armful of bottles of whiskey. Roch took three armfuls of bottles before his saddle bags were filled. "Well this should last me until I can get to Nora," Roch said out loud then laughed.

"This is so much fun," said Annabelle excitedly.

"I think Renya just enjoys throwing celebrations," said Vitomas as they worked on decorations.

"Celebrating all the babies' birthdays with one grand celebration is a wonderful idea."

"I am beginning to wonder if we will be celebrating Samuel's birth at the same time," said Vitomas as she tried to get comfortable in the chair.

"You are a lot bigger than you were with Sudfad," said Annabelle as she looked at Vitomas' stomach. "Wouldn't it be exciting if you had twins too?"

Vitomas laughed, "I did not tell Raul but I did think about it, or perhaps I am just farther along than I thought."

"Simon would never say anything but he is really proud that you are naming the baby after him."

"Actually I wanted to name the baby Simon but Raul said it would be too confusing especially since we already have two Sudfads; so he will be named Samuel Raul."

"I hope to get pregnant again soon. I would love to have a baby girl."

"Can you imagine how spoiled she would be," laughed Vitomas. "The only girl born into this family for a generation." Vitomas looked around as if someone could hear, "I never thought Raul and Simon would want to spend so much time with the babies; well, I guess I did not know what to expect."

Annabelle laughed, "Simon cannot wait until he can teach the boys to ride and hunt and do all those boy things."

"Every night," said Vitomas softly. "When I watch Raul playing with little Sudfad..." Vitomas did not finish her sentence.

"What, is something wrong?"

"Oh nothing," whispered Vitomas. "I just love Raul so much, that sometimes I feel like my heart could burst."

"Matthew I hate you," screamed Angelina as she ran outside, slamming the door behind her. Matthew started to stand up from the bench at the dining room table in Sorren's house.

"Matthew stay seated," said Sorren. "I will talk to her."

Angelina did not look up when she heard the door open or when her father sat on the ground next to her. "Angelina I know you are hurt but I taught you to think like a warrior and a leader. Don't you wonder why Matthew told you that he might inherit wives someday in the future?"

Angelina wiped the tears from her eyes and looked at her father. After a pause she asked, "Because he thinks I am going to be in his future?"

"I believe Matthew is planning to ask you to marry him which is why he is telling you these things and why our families are having dinner on Tuesday. He has come to know your life, now you must learn about his."

"Really Father?"

"Yes, now think about the stories he told us about Raul and Vitomas and the others. Both Raul and Simon are powerful warriors and wealthy men, yet they want Matthew to inherit their families. Ask yourself why."

"I'll tell you; it is because Matthew is a good man and he will provide for those families and protect those wives. I believe that says a lot about him."

"Oh Father you are right," Angelina said between sniffles.

"Now my daughter you must decide if you will lose Matthew because you are jealous over something that may never occur."

"I am so embarrassed," said Angelina as she wiped her face. "I feel like such a fool."

"Go in there and talk to that boy."

Angelina started to stand up, then quickly sat back down. "Father if Matthew asks me to marry him I will say yes."

"I know you will," Sorren said smiling.

"And you would approve, Father?"

"I feel like he is my son already."

Angelina gave her father a hug then ran into the house. Matthew stayed seated as Angelina entered the dining room and sat on the bench facing him. Her face was swollen and red from crying. Angelina grasped both of his hands. "Matthew I am sorry for the things I said and how I acted. I just couldn't stand the thought of sharing you with anyone. But I was wrong; it is a noble thing that you are doing."

Without speaking Matthew leaned down and kissed Angelina on the lips. Angelina kissed him back, then she put her arms around his neck and slid closer to Matthew. As they continued to kiss the electricity between them ignited and their love poured forth. As Sorren walked past the dining room he looked in and saw the two young lovers embrace. Sorren walked into the kitchen and hugged Shara. "I think we are going to have another son very soon," he said with pride.

"Hello Maggie," said Annabelle as she and Vitomas entered the General Store in Salar.

"We have a long list today," said Vitomas as she handed the list to the elderly woman. "We are preparing for the boys first birthday."

"I hope you girls brought a large boca today," said Maggie with a grin as she read the list. "A few of these things I will have to get from the back."

"Let me know if you need help," said Annabelle as she was looking at bolts of material.

"Oh look at the baby shoes," said Vitomas as she walked to the front of the store.

"Hello My Lady," said a man who approached Vitomas.

Vitomas looked up into his face, "Hello, do I know you?"

"King Roch would very much like to see you," said the man with a treacherous grin.

Vitomas stared at the man in terror for just a moment before he grabbed her arm and pulled her out of the store. "Annabelle!" screamed Vitomas.

Annabelle was at the rear of the store and quickly turned around when she heard the fear in Vitomas' voice. Annabelle saw Vitomas being dragged out of the store. Annabelle threw down the material she was holding and started to run after Vitomas. Annabelle was so focused on her friend that she did not see the two other men in the store.

Maggie came out of the back room when she heard Vitomas scream and saw two men attempting to control Annabelle's arms. Annabelle kicked the man to her right in the groin so hard that he doubled over and then she quickly turned to her left and bit the hand that was on her wrist.

Annabelle attempted to run towards the door but the man on the ground grabbed her ankle while the second man grabbed her arms. Maggie grabbed a large iron pot and hit the man over the head, who was holding Annabelle's arms; causing him to let go of Annabelle. Annabelle kicked the other man in the face and once again ran for the door.

The man on the floor got up and lunged at Annabelle, grabbing her long hair. Annabelle grabbed an unsheathed sword that was lying on a table and turning thrust it into the man's stomach. She quickly pulled the sword out of him as he stared at her in disbelief.

Annabelle turned to the right as the second man was coming towards her. Annabelle held the sword ready to strike; the man walked towards her, staring into Annabelle's eyes and smiling. Suddenly he picked up a basket from the counter and threw it at Annabelle. Annabelle leaned to the right, lowering herself as she swung and sliced the man's side with the sword.

Then Annabelle ran out of the store screaming, "Stop him, he is kidnapping the Princess." Annabelle could see a man had thrown Vitomas over the top of a horse and was riding quickly down the street.

Both men and women ran off the walkways to block the man's horse. The rider was kicking at people as they grabbed at him and Vitomas. Several men in the crowd pulled the rider off from the horse and proceeded to beat him. While some of the people were trying to keep the frightened horse still; two other men lowered Vitomas to the ground. She had been thrown over the horse so that she was lying on her stomach.

Simon and Raul were supervising training at Fort Salar when several Enrops flew around their heads in a frenzy. Raul batted at one of the birds as it almost hit him in the head.

"Your wives," yelled one of the Enrops.

"What?" called Raul.

"Your wives are in trouble, you need to come quickly," called the Enrop as the three birds turned towards Salar. Both Raul and Simon were already on horseback and followed the birds as fast as their horses could run. The sergeant leading the exercises told his men to mount up and they followed Raul and Simon into the city. When the two Princes reached Salar, people were running up to their horses and yelling.

"They are in the Dragon's Inn."

"Some men tried to take them."

Both Raul and Simon jumped off from their horses and ran into the Inn. When they entered, someone in the crowded room yelled, "They are here."

The crowd parted to let Raul and Simon get to the table where their wives were seated. Raul ran up to Vitomas, who was sitting in a chair, holding onto her stomach. As he kneeled down beside her he asked, "Are you alright?"

Vitomas looked at him through tear filled eyes and smiled, "Raul you look worse than I do."

Raul held Vitomas' hand, "Are you hurt?"

"I don't think so," said Vitomas as Raul hugged and kissed her.

Simon ran to Annabelle who was sitting across the table from Vitomas. He immediately grabbed Annabelle and hugged her, "Are you alright?"

"I think so," said Annabelle sounding dazed. "I think I killed them Simon."

Simon looked at his wife and realized she had blood on her dress, without saying a word she showed him the bloody sword she was still clutching with her right hand.

"Annabelle," gasped Simon.

"I fought just like you taught me," said Annabelle sounding stunned. "They almost got Vitomas."

Simon tried to take the sword out of Annabelle's hand but she would not let go of it. "Honey give me the sword," said Simon softly. Annabelle let Simon take the bloody sword and put it on the table. She looked at him and said, "We have to give that back to Maggie."

Simon hugged Annabelle tightly and kissed her on the head. Annabelle started to cry; Simon held her for a few moments when she suddenly pushed him away. "Simon those men are still in the store you should go and find out who they are; I am alright," said Annabelle looking and sounding more like herself.

"Are you sure?" asked Simon.

"Honey I am alright, they might still be alive," said Annabelle.

Simon looked at Raul then walked out of the Inn with several soldiers following him. Two men were pulling a bleeding man out of the General Store by his arms; they stopped when they saw Simon.

"This one is still alive, but hurt pretty bad," said one of the men. "That other one is dead."

Simon turned to the soldiers standing behind him. "Take him to the physician, I need him alive," ordered Simon. "And don't let him out of your sight; when the physician is done, take him to the dungeons." Simon walked into the store which was full of people looking at the dead man and talking with Maggie. Simon rolled the dead man onto his back and saw the wound. Simon did not recognize the man's face so Simon went through the man's pockets; other than money Simon found little.

Simon walked up to Maggie. "Are you alright," he asked.

"Yes and thank The Great Ruler those girls are too; you should be proud of your wife for such a little thing she sure can fight," said Maggie with a grin. Maggie proceeded to tell Simon and the other on-lookers detail by detail of Annabelle's fight with the two men and how she ran down the street screaming for help for Vitomas. As Simon listened to Maggie talk he was filled with horror.

Simon's heart felt like there was something tightening around it; as the thought that he could have lost Annabelle took hold. Maggie showed everyone the pot that she used to hit one of the men and showed them where the sword was lying that Annabelle grabbed. When Maggie finished talking Simon put a handful of gold coins on the counter. "This should cover the sword and any damages."

Maggie looked at Simon still grinning, "Yes that Annabelle is something, you must be so proud."

Simon managed to smile, a smile that hid the terror he felt. "I am always proud of her," said Simon.

As he turned to walk out of the store Simon heard Maggie calling behind him, "Thank you My Lord, this is more than generous."

After Simon left the store, three soldiers approached him; they were escorting a large man, whose arms were tied together. "We got another one," said one of the soldiers.

"Who sent you?" asked Simon angrily. The man just looked at Simon and smiled. "Take him to the dungeons," ordered Simon.

When Simon entered the Dragon's Inn the atmosphere seemed less tense. Annabelle smiled at him but remained seated with Vitomas. Simon thought both of the women looked better. Raul, who was standing next to Vitomas now walked up to Simon.

"Vitomas said that the man who grabbed her said that Roch wanted to see her," said Raul angrily.

"Annabelle killed one," said Simon in disbelief. "And seriously wounded another, I had soldiers take him to the physician with orders to take him to the dungeons if he lives. There is a third man, must be the one who grabbed Vitomas; the soldiers are taking him to the dungeons now."

"Let's get the girls home," said Raul who was visibly shaken.

Simon walked over to Annabelle and knelt down by her chair. "Maggie told me everything," said Simon then he put both of his arms around Annabelle and hugged her tightly. "I don't know what I would do if something happened to you," Simon said, then he kissed Annabelle on the head.

Annabelle put her arms around Simon's neck and kissed him on the lips, "Simon I am alright, really."

Simon looked at Annabelle, searching her face as he did not believe what she said. "Let's go home," said Simon as he stood up and looked at Raul and Vitomas.

Vitomas smiled. "I am fine," Vitomas said as she stood up from the chair. Suddenly Vitomas grabbed her stomach and called out, "Raul." Raul grabbed Vitomas as she lost consciousness.

Philip the Court Physician walked out of one of the guest bedrooms in the west wing. Vitomas and Annabelle customarily gave birth in the guest rooms so as not to soil the beds in the master bedrooms. Philip entered the parlor of the west wing where the Royal Family had gathered.

"You look worried," Renya said with a gasp.

"Well, I am not really sure what to say at this point. I gave her a powder so she is sleeping now."

"What do you mean you are not sure?" Raul asked with a mixture of fear and anger in his voice.

"Raul don't yell at him," Renya scolded.

"It's alright," said Philip. "Either she is carrying a large baby or she is farther along than we thought. And I am hoping she is farther along because I think this baby is going to come early."

"Will Vitomas and the baby be alright?" Raul asked in a hoarse whisper.

"Honestly I don't know yet," said Philip. "But I will tell you now; I don't want her getting out of that bed until after the baby is born."

"Raul if you don't mind I would like to stay with her for a while," said Annabelle. Raul smiled but did not respond.

Simon kissed Annabelle on the head and said, "You should get some rest too."

Annabelle squeezed Simon's hand and said, "Just a little while."

Simon smiled and walked up to Raul, "I will take little Sudfad home to sleep with the boys tonight." Raul just nodded. Sudfad motioned for Simon to come with him and the two left the room.

Raul and Annabelle both sat in silence for hours watching Vitomas sleep; everyone else had left. Annabelle looked over at Raul several times, the look of despair on his face made her want to cry. Annabelle started to fall asleep in the chair when the sound of Raul standing up woke her.

"Raul are you alright?" asked Annabelle as she saw a look in his eyes that scared her. Raul did not respond but walked past Annabelle and out of the room. "Raul," Annabelle called again as she quickly got out of her chair, but he kept walking.

"Open the cell door then leave," Raul ordered the soldiers who were guarding the prisoner. As he waited for the soldiers to get the keys Raul stared at the man who tried to kidnap Vitomas.

The man stood up; staring back at Raul. A large man, almost equal in size and weight to Raul, the man started to grin. "Well, if it isn't the man who won't die," said the prisoner with a sneer. "I thought we killed you."

The soldier was unlocking the cell door. "You could have killed my wife and child," said Raul as he fixated on the man.

"King Roch wants his property back," replied the prisoner grinning.

As soon as Raul heard the lock click he pushed the soldier out of his way with his left hand, while grabbing the cell door with his right. Raul rushed into the cell grabbing the prisoner and pinning him up against the wall. Raul hit the man in the stomach with his right fist; the blow was so powerful it doubled the man over.

Raul slammed the man's head against his left knee, then grabbed the prisoner's long hair with his left hand and pulled him back up to a standing position. Raul punched the man in the face three more times with his right fist before the prisoner was able to push Raul off from him.

As soon as the prisoner put some distance between them, he punched Raul in the face, somewhat knocking Raul backwards, then he hit Raul in the stomach with his left fist. The man swung another right punch at Raul's face, but Raul blocked it with his left forearm and punched the prisoner with an uppercut blow to the jaw.

The prisoner took a couple of steps backwards, Raul kept hitting the man who kept moving backwards until Raul had him pinned against the stone wall.

Raul was so filled with rage that he did not hear Simon yelling at him nor did he realize Simon was trying to pull him off from the prisoner.

"Raul stop!" yelled Simon over and over.

After a few moments Raul stopped hitting the prisoner but Raul still had him propped up against the stone wall. Raul looked at Simon. "He doesn't deserve to live," growled Raul.

"I know but Father wants him alive," said Simon.

"Why?"

"Because he has a plan."

Vitomas smiled when she awoke and saw Raul sleeping in the chair next to her bed. She lifted herself to a sitting position and reached over and gently touched his leg. "Raul wake up. Raul."

As soon as Raul awoke, he flew from the chair and sat beside Vitomas on the bed. "How are you feeling?" asked Raul as he took her hand in both of his and kissed it.

"I am fine."

"Philip wants you to stay in bed until the baby is born."

"Why is something wrong with the baby?" gasped Vitomas.

Raul did not want to worry Vitomas so he said, "He thinks everything is fine, he is just worried the baby might come early." Then Raul kissed Vitomas' hand again.

"Raul I cannot stay in bed."

"Of course you can," said Raul trying to smile. "Annabelle and Simon have little Sudfad and there are more than enough people here to help with things."

"Raul what happened to your hands?" asked Vitomas as she took his hands in hers and moved them so she could look at his swollen, cut and bruising knuckles. Raul did not respond.

"Raul there is blood on your face," said Vitomas as she softly touched a cut on the side of his mouth. "What happened?"

Raul looked down at the floor for a moment before looking Vitomas in the eyes; choking on his words Raul said, "I had a talk with the man who tried to kidnap you."

Vitomas looked into Raul's eyes and could see how upset he was. She softly kissed his injured knuckles then kissed the cut on Raul's face. "My love, you are and always will be my hero; you saved Annabelle and me from the real monsters in this world. Please do not let them fill you with their darkness."

Raul grabbed Vitomas and pulled her tightly against him. Raul buried his head on Vitomas' shoulder as he hugged her. Vitomas heard Raul's muffled voice say, "I could have lost you." Vitomas kissed his ear and said, "Come to bed my husband."

Chapter XIII
Family

"Mathas, Rosa this was a fine meal. Thank you, my family is honored," Sorren said with a broad smile on his face. Mathas and Sorren each sat at the ends of the table, which were positions of honor. Rosa and Shara sat across from each other as did Sorren's two young sons and Margarit. Matthew and Angelina sat next to each other.

"I am truly glad you came; it has been too long. We will do this again soon," Mathas said genuinely. Then he turned to Matthew and Angelina. "I don't know if Sorren told you but we were friends as young men but I guess life and families just pulled us apart." Sorren smiled at the King's words.

Suddenly a soldier walked up to the table. "My Lord I am sorry for the intrusion but an Enrop just flew in from Wetpr with this letter. He said the Prince must read it at once."

"Thank you," said Matthew as he quickly took the letter and read it. Everyone at the table watched as Matthew's face turned white. Without speaking Matthew handed the letter to his father.

"No Matthew, why don't you just tell us all what it says," Mathas said with concern.

Matthew looked visibly shaken as he spoke, "It is from Aunt Renya. She said some of Roch's men tried to kidnap Vitomas and Annabelle." Both Rosa and Angelina gasped when they heard his words. Matthew continued, "Annabelle killed one of the men and another is dying. But the third man got Vitomas. The citizens of Salar stopped him but Vitomas is hurt. At this point the physician doesn't know if Vitomas and the baby will make it through the delivery. Renya said Raul has fallen apart and she would like me there. Father I am going to leave immediately."

"Of course," Mathas said.

As Matthew stood up Angelina touched his arm. "Can I come with you?"

"That is up to your father," Matthew said as he looked at Sorren.

179

Sorren was quiet for a moment then said, "Yes."

"Oh thank you Father," Angelina said as she walked over to Sorren and hugged him.

"Angelina let me pack some food and a few things. I will be right back," Matthew said.

"Does Angelina need to pack anything?" Rosa asked.

"I will buy her whatever she needs," said Matthew as he walked out of the dining room.

As Angelina returned to her seat, she looked at Mathas. "Matthew is very upset; I will watch over him."

Mathas smiled warmly at Angelina, "I am sure you will my dear."

"Raul and Matthew are very close," said Rosa. "Raul is the big brother Matthew never had."

"Angelina," said Mathas. "When you meet the women in Wetpr they dress very differently than you do but I believe you will find you are all very much alike and you will like each other. My sister Renya is a great queen, a wonderful mother and a fierce warrior."

"Really," said Angelina with surprise.

"And the girls have not had the training you have but the last time the castle was under attack, those girls and Renya killed Huta warriors. And now it sounds like Annabelle has killed some of Roch's men."

Angelina did not speak. Sorren smiled at Mathas' because he knew Mathas was trying to make his daughter feel comfortable with Matthew's family. After a few moments Angelina said, "Matthew has told us stories and Roch sounds like a monster."

Suddenly Mathas' voice became stern. "Angelina I am speaking for Sorren as well as myself. You are well trained but you have no idea how evil that man is. And he is merciless to young girls. If you ever encounter him alone, you do not challenge him, you hide."

"Do as Mathas says," ordered Sorren.

"The horses are outside," Matthew said as he walked up to Angelina. Both Angelina and Matthew said goodbye to their parents. As they were prepared to leave the room, Matthew looked at Sorren and said, "Do not worry I will take good care of her."

"I know you will son." When Angelina and Matthew were almost to the door, Sorren called after them, "Wait. I know you are in a hurry but it is time."

"What do you mean Father?" asked Angelina.

"Angelina and Matthew, you are both children that make all of us in this room proud. Angelina after tonight you will no longer ask my permission to do things. It is time you and Matthew learned to work out your own decisions."

Matthew and Angelina rode late into the night. A full moon helped to guide their path. "A little further is a small pond, we will rest there for a few hours then start up again," Matthew said. Both Matthew and Angelina were exhausted as they cared for the horses and made camp. Matthew laid out both of their bedrolls, putting one on each side of the campfire. Then he crawled under his blankets.

"Matthew can I sleep with you?"

"Yes," Matthew said with a smile.

Angelina put her blankets over the top of Matthew's then she slid under them and cuddled close to Matthew, lying in his arm. "I am really glad you wanted to come along," Matthew said and kissed Angelina on the lips.

"I am glad Father permitted it. Matthew were you surprised by what he said?"

"You mean that he wasn't going to be making decisions for you anymore? Not really."

"Well I was," Angelina said then paused for a moment.

"Matthew, Father thinks a great deal of you; he told me he thinks of you as his son." This comment brought a smile to Matthew's face.

"I very much like and respect your father." Neither Matthew nor Angelina spoke for several minutes as their eyelids were getting heavy with fatigue.

"I love you Matthew," Angelina had wanted to tell Matthew her feelings for several weeks but her fears stopped her.

"I love you too," Matthew said and kissed Angelina on the lips, a kiss that said more than his words. The two young lovers fell asleep in each other's arms with smiles on their faces.

"Angelina wake up," whispered Matthew. She did not respond, so he kissed her on the lips. Without opening her eyes Angelina smiled and said, "Matthew I love waking up with you."

"Good," said Matthew and kissed her again. They continued to kiss as their passions grew. Suddenly Matthew stood up, pulling Angelina to her feet also. "Sorry but if we don't stop now; we won't for a very long time."

"What do you mean?" asked Angelina with a look of confusion.

Matthew looked down at her beautiful face, "Angelina have you ever made love to a man?"

"No," she replied hesitantly.

"Well, I guess you really did scare away all of your suitors," Matthew said with a laugh.

Angelina blushed then said shyly, "Matthew we can make love whenever you want."

Matthew pulled Angelina close to him and wrapped both of his arms around her. "Honey I have wanted to make love to you since that first morning I met you. But I want our first time to be special. Which means we are not going to make love in the dirt when we only have a few hours to sleep; is that alright with you?"

"Oh yes," Angelina replied nervously.

Matthew kissed Angelina on top of her head, "Why don't you start breakfast and I will tend to the horses."

As Angelina was making coffee she felt giddy. She found herself feeling both scared and excited that they were finally talking about making love.

"Father," said Raul as he and Simon entered Sudfad's study.

"Are you alright?" asked Sudfad as he saw Raul's swollen and bruised knuckles.

"Yes, nothing broken."

"Not on you," said Simon grinning.

"I understand you may be angry with me because I would not let you kill that monster," said Sudfad as he handed each of his son's a cup of coffee. "But I had my reasons. Now that you are Keepers of the Scrolls you will start to realize that many times we are asked to do things we do not understand."

"Asked by who?" asked Simon.

"We are protecting these holy objects because The Great Ruler wants us to, the Sanuri is not His only messenger," said Sudfad. "I will admit that during my life I have often been confused about things I have been asked to do because from my level at viewing this world it did not make sense. But later when I would see how my actions affected others, I understood why I was asked to do them. I know this sounds confusing but you will find yourselves in the same situations soon. You just have to have faith that The Great Ruler knows what He is doing."

"So you have had contacts with another messenger besides the Sanuri?" Simon asked.

"Yes," replied Sudfad.

"The Lion that the Sanuri said was protecting me; was he the messenger?" asked Raul.

"Yes, and I have had him come to me often in dreams," said Sudfad.

"How can you tell the difference between a messenger coming to you and a normal dream?" asked Simon.

"Trust me, you will know the difference when it happens. I am telling you this because I had such a dream. The night before the girls were attacked, The Lion came to me in a dream and told me not to have our prisoners killed. At the time I did not understand what he meant."

"Why would The Great Ruler protect such monsters?" asked Raul angrily.

"Well, I certainly cannot speak for The Great Ruler but in my dream I was told that the prisoners were a gift to us because they have information that can affect the safety of our entire kingdom," Sudfad continued. "Roch is in allegiance with a demon; that you already know from the Sanuri. It sounds like they are planning something of unthinkable proportions and those prisoners know what it is. So get that information from them."

"Father the prisoner that Annabelle stabbed is still being treated by the physician and well, the other one won't be talking for a while," said Simon as he glanced at Raul.

"Make sure they receive medical attention and food and water and when they are healthy enough get the information; you have to understand they may be our only source," said Sudfad. "And there is one more thing that we have to talk about my sons; that is Roch."

Both Raul and Simon tensed up at the mention of Roch's name. "There are many things in this world I do not understand, such as why a beast like Roch is allowed to exist. My heart hurts because I want to kill that monster so badly for what he has done to my family."

"Then let me," begged Raul.

Sudfad smiled, "The Sanuri and I have discussed this issue many times and I have been told not to go after him; at least not yet."

"But that does not make any sense Father; Roch is evil itself," said Simon with frustration.

"And I agree with you; but I will not go against the wishes of The Great Ruler and neither will my sons. I have been assured that Roch will pay for his sins and perhaps that will be at our hands, but not yet."

Vitomas unwillingly stayed in bed the next two days. She did not want to worry Raul, but she was having pains and did not feel well. Vitomas would only allow the horror of what happen to her surface when she was alone; then and only then Vitomas would start sobbing.

Vitomas knew Roch well. She knew how he carefully chose his punishments. And Vitomas knew what awaited her in Taperia if Roch captured her again. But it was the thought of what Roch would have done to her unborn baby and to Annabelle that made Vitomas momentarily revert back to that terrified child that Roch used to torture.

The third evening after the attack on Annabelle and Vitomas, Simon and Raul joined Sudfad in his study.

"What is the condition of the prisoners?" Sudfad asked as he handed each of his sons a glass of whiskey.

"The one that Annabelle stabbed has a fever now and the other one has broken bones in his face and will not be able to talk until the swelling goes down," explained Simon.

"I see," said Sudfad as he sat down behind his desk.

"Father..." Raul started to speak but stopped when Marie flew through the door. "My Lords I am so sorry but the Queen sent me to get all of you; she thinks the baby is coming."

All of the men stood up and quickly left the room. As they were heading towards the west wing Marie called after them, "She sent a soldier to get the Court Physician." Annabelle and Renya were with Vitomas when Raul, Simon and Sudfad entered the bedroom. Although Vitomas smiled when she saw them, Raul thought she looked very pale and weak.

"Where is Philip?" asked Raul angrily.

"He is coming," answered Renya. "You men will be more help if you wait outside." Renya pushed them out of the room and closed the door.

Minutes later Raul burst through the door; he was desperately trying to look calm. "The soldier returned. Philip was hurt in a riding accident; his leg is broken. I sent the soldier into Salar to find another physician."

Raul paced nervously in the parlor of the west wing, where the family had gathered. Suddenly they heard a familiar voice call out. Raul smiled when he saw Matthew and Angelina quickly enter the parlor.

"Marie told us the baby is coming. How is she?" Matthew asked with concern.

"I don't really know and the physician broke his leg today; so we are seeking another," Raul said fearfully.

"I can help," said Angelina to everyone's surprise. "My mother is a healer in our tribe and I have been helping her since I was a child." Both Raul and Matthew stared at Angelina as if they were not understanding the meaning of her words. "I have delivered many babies," Angelina said with a voice of authority. "Take me to her."

Raul grabbed Angelina's hand and took her into the bedroom. "Honey this is..." Raul stopped talking and turned to Angelina as he realized he did not know her name.

"It is Angelina," said Vitomas. "I would have recognized you anywhere; Matthew writes of you often."

"Vitomas don't let out all of my secrets," said Matthew as he tried to laugh and disguise his concern. Matthew was not prepared for how drained and weak Vitomas appeared.

Angelina quickly walked up to Vitomas, "My mother is a healer, I can help you." Angelina felt Vitomas' head, closely looked into her eyes, then felt her stomach. "Have you had any Tinchure water?" Angelina asked.

"I don't know what that is," Vitomas said.

Angelina looked at Raul and said, "Please send your cook in here." Then she turned to Vitomas and Annabelle. "It is a common herb, but my people have found that if it is boiled in water it greatly helps the pain without putting you to sleep."

"Marie is in the parlor," Raul said and turned to walk out the door.

"No, I will go," Angelina said and returned to the parlor. Once she found Marie, Angelina wrote down all of the things that she would need. When Angelina returned to Vitomas, she saw Raul, Simon, Matthew and Annabelle standing around the bed. "I need to examine her. I am sure at least some of you will want to leave the room." Angelina spoke with such authority and confidence that it gave Raul great relief.

As the men were walking out of the room, Vitomas called Matthew back to her. Matthew kneeled down at Vitomas' side and she grasped his hand. "Matthew I want you to make me a promise."

"Of course; what is it?"

"If I don't make it through this delivery; I want you to promise that you will watch over Raul."

"Of course I will dear; but you will be just fine." Matthew kissed Vitomas on her forehead. When he looked up he saw that both Annabelle and Angelina had tears in their eyes.

Three hours passed as the Royal Family of Wetpr waited for the birth of Vitomas' child. Marie brought refreshments into the parlor to comfort the family. A normally cheerful person, Marie showed signs of concern on her face.

"Was that a baby's cry?" asked Raul anxiously as he stood outside of the bedroom door. He grabbed the door handle but Simon stopped him.

"The girls will let us know when we should go in," Simon said as he put his hand on Raul's shoulder.

Suddenly a loud baby's cry could be heard. Moments later Annabelle peaked her head out of the door. "Mother and baby are fine. Give us a few minutes to clean up," she said smiling.

Annabelle quickly disappeared behind the door. Raul felt as if he could collapse; now that the weight of so much fear was leaving him. Ten minutes later Annabelle opened the door.

"Come in and meet your son," Vitomas said warmly when she saw Raul in the doorway.

Raul flew to Vitomas' side and kissed her; then he looked at the baby in her arms and kissed him on the forehead. "Simon he has blonde hair, he must have known we were naming him after you." Raul kidded as Vitomas put the baby into his arms.

The family all congregated in the doorway of the bedroom, where Raul met them with his infant son. "He is beautiful and so big," said Renya with tears in her eyes. Then she turned to Vitomas. "How are you feeling dear? You look so much better; you have your color back."

"I feel so much better. Whatever those tonics were that Angelina gave me really worked," Vitomas said as she looked at Angelina with a grateful smile. Matthew looked proudly at Angelina who was piling up soiled rags and bedding.

Annabelle grabbed Angelina's hand and started walking through the crowd in the doorway. "We both are very soiled and need to clean up, please excuse us," said Annabelle with a laugh. "We will be back." Suddenly Raul grabbed Angelina's shoulder and gently turned her around.

"Thank you so much," Raul said and kissed Angelina on her forehead.

"Matthew," called out Annabelle with a huge smile as she and Angelina returned to the parlor in the west wing of the castle. Matthew and Simon were standing together talking and they both turned around. Matthew's mouth fell open and his eyes grew wide when he saw Angelina.

Angelina was wearing one of Annabelle's dresses. The green of the dress accented Angelina's dark red hair. The design of the dress accented her tiny waist and the plunging neckline exposed her womanly breasts. Angelina was wearing a delicate necklace of pearls and emeralds with matching earrings.

Annabelle had replaced the beads and feathers in Angelina's hair with jeweled combs.

"Well Matthew say something," said Annabelle with a proud laugh.

The look on Matthew's face made Angelina blush. "Forgive me you just look so incredibly beautiful you took my breath away," Matthew said and leaned down and kissed Angelina on the cheek. "Are you wearing perfume?"

"Yes, do you like it?"

"Very much," replied Matthew who kept staring at her.

"I am having a little problem walking in these shoes," said Angelina. "But this is fun, I feel like a princess."

Simon was laughing, "Angelina you do look beautiful and I am laughing because I have never seen Matthew at a loss for words before."

"A physician arrived from Salar. He is in with Vitomas now and would like to speak with you," Matthew said to Angelina and took her hand in his. As they walked into Vitomas' bedroom, Simon leaned down and kissed Annabelle on the cheek. Suddenly she got a glint in her eyes. "Simon, make sure Matthew and Angelina don't leave this area for about a half hour."

"What are you up to?" Simon asked with a laugh.

"I will tell you later, just keep them here."

"Matthew you have to see the children, they are so cute," Angelina said after the meeting with the physician. "They are mirrors of their fathers." Angelina turned to Simon. "Can I show him the children?"

"I'll go with you," Simon said as he led them to a room down the hallway where they found Abigail and Gabriella sitting on the floor of the room playing with the three boys. Matthew picked up the child closest to him. "Which one is this?" Matthew asked as he looked at the identical twins.

Simon stepped forward and looked behind the child's ear, "Anthony has a small birth mark behind his ear; that is the only way we can tell them apart. You have Alexander." Simon said as he picked up Anthony. Angelina was already holding baby Sudfad. Simon started to laugh when he saw the way Matthew was watching Angelina play with the baby.

Angelina looked up at Matthew, "Is something wrong you are looking at me so strangely?"

"No," said Matthew with a smile.

"Simon, I cannot believe how big these boys are for their ages," Angelina said as she held Sudfad up in the air.

Simon put his hand on Angelina's shoulder, "I have to warn you this is what your babies are going to look like if you become part of this family." Angelina looked at Matthew and blushed.

"There you are," said Annabelle as she entered the room. "Matthew I think you should show Angelina your chambers now."

"What have you been up too?" asked Matthew with a grin. "You certainly have a mischievous look on your face."

"Well I guess you will just have to go to your chambers to find out," Annabelle said smiling. "Here give me the baby."

As Angelina handed baby Sudfad to Abigail, Annabelle said, "Angelina I put some more outfits for you in Matthew's chambers, if you don't like them I can always find you something else."

Angelina hugged Annabelle and said, "You have been so wonderful to me, thank you."

Matthew bent down and kissed Annabelle on the cheek then whispered into her ear, "Thank you dear."

"Oh this is so beautiful," said Angelina as she and Matthew entered his chambers.

"There must be two hundred candles in here," said Matthew as they saw lit candles of every size and proportion forming a walkway to the master bedroom.

"I can't believe she did all of this," said Angelina in awe as they entered the master bedroom which was decorated with candles and bouquets of freshly cut flowers. On one end of the huge bedroom a small table was set up with wine, whiskey and a variety of food.

"Matthew look," said Angelina as she held up a beautiful silk and lace nightgown that was lying on the bed.

Matthew did not speak as he poured two glasses of wine. When he handed one to Angelina he asked, "You told her didn't you?"

"You mean that you wanted our first time to be special? Yes, are you angry?"

"Why would I be angry? I am in a romantic room with the most beautiful girl in the world." Matthew said and leaned down and kissed Angelina on the lips. "Let's walk in the garden," Matthew said and took Angelina's hand and led her outside to the patio.

"Matthew I have to confess something," Angelina said shyly. "I had pictured Annabelle and Vitomas to be so different and I was jealous still of the idea of you inheriting them as your wives. But just the little time that we have been here, well this family seems so wonderful and loving. And Annabelle and Vitomas treat me like their sister. I feel guilty for the thoughts I had."

Matthew smiled and squeezed Angelina's hand. "I think your thoughts were quite normal; you have nothing to feel guilty about."

"Perhaps. I know you told me about these people, this family of yours. But still I did not expect. Oh I don't know how to say it Matthew. I like your father and mother very much; but here, it almost seems like this is your real family. Do you understand what I am trying to say?"

Matthew stopped walking and turned and faced Angelina. He smiled and moved a strand of her hair from her eyes. "I know exactly what you are saying and although I would never admit it to my parents I feel the same way."

"Aunt Renya and the girls send me letters every week. And I will admit I look forward to them. I only wish I would have gotten to know them all sooner."

"What do you mean?"

"Well, I met them a few times as a boy but it wasn't until a couple of years ago when Raul came to visit us that I really got to know him and well, it was like he instantly was my older brother. Then I got to know the rest of the family when I came here for the weddings."

"You mean you have only known them for two years?"

"Actually less than that," Matthew said. "But the moment I entered the castle it seemed like I was home. Sudfad adopted me and Raul and Simon built me this beautiful home. I enjoy it here very much. I hope that you will also."

"Matthew I already love it here and I think your home is wonderful."

"Good, because I hope that you will be staying with me here from now on." Angelina's eyes grew wide but she did not speak. Matthew took both of their glasses of wine and set them on the table that was in the middle of the stone patio. Then he picked Angelina up and carried her to their bed.

"We missed you at breakfast," Simon said jokingly as Matthew and Angelina entered the parlor of Raul and Vitomas' home. They were walking hand in hand and Angelina blushed deeply at Simon's comment. When Simon saw how red Angelina was he decided to continue. "Well, from the smiles on your faces I assume you both enjoyed the gift that Annabelle gave you," Simon said then started to laugh.

"Yes we did," replied Matthew who also laughed when he saw how red Angelina was. "In fact we enjoyed it all night and again this morning." Angelina turned and pressed her face against Matthew's chest so the others could not see how badly she was blushing.

"I can't believe you said that," Angelina said with a laugh.

"You are part of the family now, we all tease each other," Matthew said smiling. Angelina looked up into Matthew's face and smiled, wondering what he meant by his comment. But before she could say anything they heard a baby cry.

"How is Vitomas?" Matthew asked.

"She seems to be just fine," said Laurel. "And so is little Samuel. We were all so worried."

Renya and Sudfad had been watching Matthew and Angelina. "Matthew were you ever planning on introducing your friend to the family?" asked Renya with a warm smile. Now it was Matthew's turn to be embarrassed.

"I am sorry, I don't know how I could have forgotten that," said Matthew as he and Angelina walked up to Sudfad and Renya who were sitting at a table drinking coffee. "This is King Sudfad and Queen Renya and this is Angelina a princess of the warrior tribe Nordes." A panicked look filled Angelina's face as she suddenly didn't know how to address the King and Queen.

Angelina started to curtsey when Renya said, "My dear we are all family now, just give us a hug."

Matthew introduced Angelina to Laurel and Alexander then they returned to Renya and Sudfad.

"So you are a warrior and a healer; that is very impressive especially for one so young," Renya said.

"Matthew's father says that you also are a fierce warrior," Angelina said with obvious respect in her voice.

Renya was surprised by Angelina's statement and asked, "He did?"

"Yes King Mathas said you were a great queen, a wonderful mother and a fierce warrior. Mathas said that you and Vitomas and Annabelle killed Huta warriors when the castle was attacked. And he told me I would like all of you very much and he was right."

"Well we like you also," said Sudfad. "And we owe you a great debt for helping Vitomas and Samuel."

"Thank you but you do not owe me anything; I was pleased to help. But there are some more herbs I would like to give Vitomas to help her heal but you do not have them in your kitchen." Then Angelina turned to Matthew. "Would you take me to a store where we can buy some?"

"You don't have to buy the herbs," Renya said.

"Yes we can," said Matthew. "I was planning on taking her into Salar this morning to go shopping anyways." Then Matthew walked over to Simon and they whispered together. As Matthew and Angelina walked out of the parlor, Matthew said sarcastically to Simon, "I am not making the same mistake you and Raul did."

"What did he mean?" asked Renya after the couple had left.

"He is going to buy her an engagement ring today," Simon said with a large grin. "I told him to take her to Andrew's shop."

Sudfad looked at Renya and said, "Well my dear I believe you have a celebration to plan."

"I want to sleep in our bed tonight," said Vitomas as she was feeding baby Samuel. Raul was sitting in the chair next to her bed.

"I will carry you then, because the physician said he didn't want you to walk for a couple of days."

"I feel fine Raul, just a little tired."

"When I took your tray to the kitchen, mother said that Angelina and Matthew were in Salar buying some herbs that Angelina said would help you heal faster."

"And Simon said that Matthew is going to buy her an engagement ring today," Raul said with a smile.

"Oh Raul," Vitomas said happily. "I am so happy for them. Did you see the way they look at each other; they are so much in love."

"Actually Honey, all I could think of was you and the baby."

"Matthew why are you buying me so many things?" asked Angelina as they were sorting through clothing in the store where Raul and Simon bought their wives' clothing.

"Honey if you like something get a couple of them, one to keep in our home in Wetpr and one to take back to Lentz," said Matthew as he pulled a beautiful dress off a rack. "Here try this on."

"Matthew you said our home."

"Yes I did, now try this on we have a lot to do today."

Angelina was looking at Matthew and her eyes were smiling as happily as her face. "Matthew are you...?"

He interrupted her. "No questions now," Matthew said with a grin. "As I said we have a lot to do today."

"Oh Matthew look at this dress," said Angelina on her way to the fitting room.

"Don't you think that is too big for you?" asked Matthew who did not particularly like the dress.

"Oh not for me; mother would just love this."

"Do you think that would fit her?"

"Yes."

"Then put it on the counter and if we are buying a gift for your mother we should get the entire family some things."

Angelina ran back to Matthew and threw her arms around his neck, kissing him on the lips, "Matthew I love you so much."

"A jeweler's, why are we going in here?" asked Angelina with a shy smile.

"Because I am told it is custom for a man to give a woman a ring when he asks her to marry him," Matthew said smiling.

"Oh Matthew," cried Angelina as she jumped up and kissed him.

"Now don't get so excited, I haven't asked you yet," Matthew teased. He put his arm around Angelina's shoulders as they entered the store.

"Hello my name is Jeremy can I help you find something?" asked the friendly man behind the counter.

"Yes, we are getting married and need some rings," said Matthew with a large smile. "Please show us the finest that you have."

As they sorted through the rings, Matthew found an extremely large diamond ring with a golden band. "I like this one, try it on."

"Oh Matthew this must be so expensive," said Angelina hesitantly.

"You are marrying a prince, please try on the ring," Matthew whispered into her ear.

"Oh Matthew this is so incredibly beautiful but I cannot wear this."

"Why not?"

"I cannot wear something this large in the competitions or when I fight."

Matthew laughed loudly, "You had me worried there for a minute. I guess you will just have to wear a wedding band at those times."

They chose matching golden wedding bands with diamonds. "Mine fits fine but you will have to make the bands smaller on her rings."

"Yes My Lord," said Jeremy as he measured Angelina's finger. "It will take a couple of days. My cousin Andrew, who owns this shop, was attacked by those men who tried to kidnap the Princesses; so I am a little behind in the work."

"Do you know why they attacked him?" asked Matthew, his entire demeanor changing.

"No, but they hurt him badly."

"The Princesses are my cousins," said Matthew. "I am going to tell Simon and Raul what you said. Do they know where Andrew lives?"

"Why he lives above this shop, My Lord."

"Where are Raul and Simon?" asked Matthew as he and Angelina entered the castle.

"They are in the King's study," said Marie with concern as she heard the seriousness in Matthew's voice.

"Come in," called out Sudfad when he heard a knock at the door. "Matthew what is it?" Sudfad asked when he saw the look on Matthew's face.

"We are sorry to interrupt but we came back as quickly as we could," Matthew explained. "While we were at your jeweler's we were told that the owner of the shop, a man named Andrew had been beaten very badly by the three men who tried to kidnap the girls. His cousin, who told us, did not know why Andrew was beaten. I was going to question Andrew myself then thought you would rather be there." Both Raul and Simon stood up to leave.

"Stay here with the family," Matthew said to Angelina and kissed her on the cheek.

Three of The Seven Sons rode into Salar.

Chapter IV
The Image in the Mirror

"My Lords!" exclaimed Andrew's wife when she opened the door and saw three princes standing on her porch.

"We are sorry to bother you but we heard that Andrew was injured by the same men who tried to kidnap our wives," Simon said. "May we speak with him?"

"Of course My Lords, but please forgive how my house looks; what with nine children and now that Andrew is hurt I have not had much time for cleaning," the woman apologized as she led the Princes to the parlor.

Sensing the woman's embarrassment Matthew said with his flirtatious smile, "My Lady your home is lovely."

"Andrew you have company," his wife said as the Princes entered the room.

"Andrew please don't try to stand," said Raul as he quickly moved to Andrew's side and helped him back into a chair. Andrew had bruises and cuts covering his face and arms. Both of his hands appeared very swollen and were wrapped with bandages. "Andrew we came because we heard that you were attacked by the same men who tried to kidnap Vitomas and Annabelle," Raul explained.

"I was attacked," Andrew said. "And later when I heard about the men who tried to take the Princesses, well, they fit the same descriptions."

"Andrew what can you remember about the attack?" asked Raul.

"I was just closing the shop when three men walked in," said Andrew. "There wasn't anyone else in the store. One man stood by the door and the other two grabbed me. I thought it was a robbery at first."

Andrew's wife brought a tray of biscuits and coffee into the parlor. "I am sorry I do not have more, we were not expecting company," the woman said apologetically.

"This looks very good, thank you," said Matthew.

Simon waited for Andrew's wife to leave the room then he asked, "What did they say to you?"

"They wanted to know about the jewelry that Princes Vitomas sold me," said Andrew. "From what they said they knew both the Princesses lived at the castle."

"What exactly did they say?" asked Raul.

"They said, 'How did you come by the jewelry of Princess Vitomas?' I told them I bought it, that it was not stolen. Then one of the men hit me and said 'who did you buy it from?' I am sorry but I told them I bought it from the Princess."

"Did they say why they wanted to know who sold you the jewelry?" Raul asked.

"This is why I feel so bad; after I told them they beat me and when they were done beating me two of them held my hands on the floor so that the third man could stomp on them," Andrew said. "The last thing I remember is hearing them talking; one of the men said, 'When Roch finds out she sold his jewels he is going to kill her.' Then they all walked out of my shop and I think I must have passed out."

"I did not find him until later that night and he was unconscious for three days," said Andrew's wife who reentered the room.

"When I got better, I heard three men tried to kidnap both of the Princesses," said Andrew. "I would have warned you if I could."

Raul put his hand on Andrew's shoulder, "Andrew I know you would have and I am so sorry they did this to you."

"There is something else but I am not sure if I heard it or dreamt it," said Andrew. "But I think one of them said that others would be coming,"

"Do you remember their exact words?" Simon asked.

"Now mind you My Lord, I am not clear on this but I think one of them said, 'If we don't get her this time we will when the rest come.' But My Lord, they were already walking out of the shop, I could have heard it wrong."

Raul placed a large bag of gold coins on the table in front of Andrew and his wife. "One of us will check in on you and bring you money every week until you are back on your feet Andrew. Again, I am so sorry this happened to you."

"My Lord, you are more than generous, thank you," said Andrew as tears welled up in his eyes.

"Bless you, bless all of you," said Andrew's wife as she walked them to the door.

"Did you miss me?" asked Thaos mockingly as he walked into Juleta's parlor. "I saw your boyfriend as he was leaving, that man must be one hundred years old, can't you do better?" Thaos flopped down in a chair and laughed.

"George is a kind man and very wealthy," replied Juleta as she poured Thaos a glass of whiskey.

"So what, you do him little favors for money?" Thaos asked with a smirk.

"How I raise the money to pay you is none of your business," snapped Juleta as she handed Thaos the drink.

"Oh, so you are sleeping with that old man just to pay me, how thoughtful you are Juleta."

"Thaos why must it always be this cat and mouse game when we are together?" asked Juleta with great frustration.

"Because it is fun," replied Thaos. "But I do have some news you may find interesting. I have been spending my time in Lentz, getting to know some of the people. The gossip is that your brother is romancing the Princess of the Nordes Tribe; apparently they are in love."

"Do you know her name?" asked Juleta with great interest.

"Angelina, she is said to be very beautiful and a fierce warrior; I was looking forward to meeting her but I heard that Matthew and Angelina are in Wetpr."

"Why are they in Wetpr?"

"I do not know."

"Did you find out anything else?"

"I am becoming friends with a drunken traitor of the Nordes Tribe, he will prove useful."

"Did you find out why the Nordes Tribe did not attack the Valdore Tribe after our men did those scattered attacks?"

"Well, according to my new friend Tobart, Chief Sorren, that is Angelina's father is an old friend of your father. I was told that the King's troops now patrol the border between the two tribes. I suspect Sorren and your father suspected something was wrong and did not play into your little game."

"Why do you say that?"

"From what I have heard about Sorren he is a fierce warrior and strong leader. He does not back down from anything."

"This could be bad if the Nordes Tribe and my father have an alliance." Juleta said then paused thoughtfully. "You have done well Thaos. Go back to Lentz and find out everything you can about Angelina and Matthew. If they are in love, the chaos of a royal wedding might be the perfect time for an attack."

"Can't imagine why your family kicked you out of the kingdom," Thaos said with an amused smirk.

"Thaos why are you always insulting me?"

"Because I don't like you," replied Thaos as he stared coldly into Juleta's eyes. "But you are paying me to do a job."

Juleta stared at Thaos, she was trying to control her anger but her face was turning red and the veins were protruding in her neck. The sight of her made Thaos laugh loudly.

"So Thaos are you planning on completing the job I am paying you for?" Juleta asked as her eyes narrowed with anger.

"I told you I would."

"You can leave now," said Juleta with a condescending tone.

Thaos stood up, "Oh I forgot to tell you; a few months back I introduced myself to the Princesses of Wetpr. I can see why you are so jealous of them. I don't know if I have ever seen two more beautiful women in my life. I watched them for quite a while before I spoke with them. They seem to be just as sweet as they are beautiful."

Juleta was filled with rage as she glared at Thaos. "You can be replaced."

"So fire me," said Thaos as he walked out of the parlor.

"It is so nice to have you join us Angelina," Renya said as the family were taking their seats at the dinner table.

Before Angelina could speak Laurel gasped and asked, "Vitomas should you be out of bed?" Everyone turned and watched as Raul was walking with Vitomas towards the table.

"She insisted on getting out of bed," said Raul as he held his new son in one arm and supported his wife with the other.

Once everyone was seated Sudfad said, "We have much to celebrate this night. First let's have a toast for the arrival of baby Samuel and the health of both Vitomas and the baby." After the toast Sudfad turned to Matthew, "Do you have an announcement to make?"

Surprised, Matthew said, "I haven't formally asked Angelina to marry me yet but we bought our wedding rings today. Everyone at the table applauded; then Sudfad proposed a second toast in honor of the pending marriage.

"I am already planning a celebration for you two," said Renya cheerfully.

"You are planning on staying long enough for the boy's birthday celebration, aren't you?" asked Annabelle.

Matthew looked at Angelina, "Is there any reason you need to get back right away?"

"No," Angelina answered with a warm smile.

"I think we could say for a few weeks, but I will have to send a message to Father so he knows we are alright," said Matthew then he turned to Renya. "Aunt Renya perhaps you and the girls could take Angelina shopping so she can furnish our home here."

"Oh, I would love to," replied Renya. "Girls we will have so much fun."

"Matthew how do you want me to decorate because I have never done that before?" asked Angelina hesitantly. "I think we have what we need in those chambers."

"Once you are married your needs change Angelina," Renya explained. "Besides your household needs; you two will be King and Queen someday and will be entertaining. I can help you get the things you will need."

No sooner had Renya spoken these words when Angelina gasped loudly, "Queen! Matthew is that true?" Angelina asked with fear in her voice.

"Well yes dear, I am the only Prince," Matthew said with a laugh.

"I never realized I might be the Queen someday. I don't know how to be a queen and I don't know how to entertain," said Angelina frantically. Everyone at the table was smiling at her.

"That is how Vitomas and I felt too," said Annabelle soothingly. "Talk to Renya, she is great; she makes it all look so easy."

Matthew put his arm around Angelina and pulled her close to him. He kissed her on the forehead and said, "Honey I have never seen you afraid of anything before."

"I know," cried Angelina. "I don't know why all of this scares me so."

"Well, at least I know you aren't marrying me for my position," Matthew said with a laugh.

"Padre Bartholomew, you should be in bed," said Padre Francis.

"I have been in bed for days; I cannot lay there any longer," said Padre Bartholomew. "I thought I would help with the inventory."

"It is not good," said Padre Francis in a lowered voice. "We seem to be missing many things."

"What things?"

"That is the list over there," said Padre Francis as he pointed to a small stack of papers sitting at the end of a table. Padre Bartholomew sat down at the table and started to read the long list.

Roch rode into Nora late at night; he waited until the cover of darkness would mask his appearance. He climbed the staircase to the physician's door and beat on it until someone opened it. "I need to see the physician," demanded Roch.

"That would be me," said the tired man. "Come in, let me get the lights."

Roch walked into the office, "Are there any other patients here?"

"No, just us," said the physician as he was lighting the candles. "So what is the nature of your problem?" asked the physician as he was turning around to face Roch. "By The Great Ruler what happened to you?" asked the astonished man.

"I am not sure, I was camping and woke up in pain," replied Roch.

"Sit down; let me look at you," said the physician as he picked up Roch's right arm. "Did you get bit by anything?"

"I don't know."

"I have never seen anything like this in a living person," said the physician as he looked at Roch's face.

"What do you mean?"

"All of your skin tissue looks and smells like it is dead; take off your shirt, are you like this all over?"

"I don't know," replied Roch fearfully.

"Have you seen what you look like?"

"No."

The physician walked into the next room and brought out a large mirror, which he held up for Roch to look in. Roch screamed with rage. He did not recognize the monster he saw in the mirror. His skin was bloated and discolored; he was covered with boils and sores with running pus. Roch tore open his shirt, his chest and back had the same affliction. "Cursed, I have been cursed!" screamed Roch.

"Sir, I can give you medicine for the pain and to clean those sores; but I do not know of a cure for something like this," said the physician apologetically.

"Give me all the pain medicine you have," demanded Roch. "Do you know any physicians who might be able to help me?"

"I am the only physician still in Nora, the others left after King Roch and his men attacked the city. Perhaps you could find a physician in Taperia," offered the physician. "Also there are many priests and healers who have been trained in the old medicine who could possibly help."

The physician handed Roch a bag of medicines and bandages. "As a trained physician I should never utter these words but if you do believe your condition is the result of a curse, it is probably not a physician you need."

Roch handed the physician some gold coins and walked out into the night. He made camp just a few miles out of Nora. Roch sat before his campfire drinking a bottle of the pain killer the physician had given him. The medicine was not stopping his pain, so Roch kept drinking more.

205

"He's right I do look like a corpse," said Roch out loud. "And he was probably right about the curse too," Roch continued to talk out loud. "Who can lift a curse?" Although the pain killer was not stopping Roch's pain it was making him stupefied. "A demon, perhaps a demon could lift a curse; well, then wait a minute then why didn't Demetries cure himself?" As Roch talked to himself, his voice grew louder, "Demetries, I actually wish you were here." Then Roch started to sob, "I look worse than Demetries."

"Padre Thomas," called Padre Bartholomew as he knocked on the door to the priest's room. "I am sorry to wake you," said Padre Bartholomew as Padre Thomas opened the door.

"Come in. What is wrong?"

"I could not sleep so I went to the Hall of Antiquities to help with the inventory. I read the list of missing items which is very long, especially so early into the inventory and I noticed something very disturbing." Padre Bartholomew looked around as if he thought someone could here, then he whispered, "Many of the scrolls and texts that are missing deal with the subject of The Abyss."

"Do you think someone is trying to help Sporos escape from The Abyss?"

"The idea has entered my mind. And for so many items to be missing, the person must be entering the Hall of Antiquities often."

Both priests were lost in thought for a few moments. "So are you thinking that whoever is taking these items is someone who we would not be suspicious to find in there?" asked Padre Thomas.

"I am considering that but then why would they hit me over the head?"

"I will tell you, that I suspect that High Priests Meekos, Tenebrae and Pravis have something to do with this," said Padre Thomas in a whisper.

"But they have been gone for weeks. Besides why would they attack me? It would not be suspicious to see them in the Hall of Antiquities."

Roch sat in front of his camp fire, drinking and cursing The Great Ruler; a ritual that was becoming nightly for him. He threw an empty whiskey bottle, smashing it against a tree. Then Roch grabbed a full bottle from his saddlebag. Roch found that great quantities of whiskey seemed to numb his pain a little.

"I will show him," mumbled Roch to himself. "He can't get away with doing this to me."

Suddenly Roch sniffed the air. "There must be a dead animal near here," he thought. Roch grabbed a burning log to use as a torch and searched a wide area around his campsite. Finding nothing he returned to the fire and his bottle of whiskey. "That smell is so strong I must have missed something," said Roch out loud; when suddenly he realized the stench of death was coming from him. "No!" Roch screamed into the darkness.

"Sorren, Shara we are so glad you could come," said Mathas cheerfully. "The children have sent us a letter." Sorren and Shara took seats in the parlor with Rosa and Mathas. Mathas poured everyone a glass of wine, "This is our finest wine, we have much to celebrate tonight. Sorren would you like to read the letter out loud?"

Sorren took the letter and read, *"This letter is for both of our dear families. First of all we arrived safely at Wetpr. But immediately upon our arrival we were told that Vitomas was ready to give birth and there was no physician. When Angelina and I walked into the bedroom I was not prepared for the condition that Vitomas was in, she herself did not think she would live through the delivery.*

But unknown to me; Angelina's mother is a healer. Angelina performed miracles, I am so proud to say. The tonics that Angelina made restored Vitomas and Angelina delivered a healthy baby boy that they named Samuel. The entire family feels in Angelina's debt for they all feared that Vitomas and the baby would die.

Now for our news, Angelina and I are engaged to be married. We have bought our wedding rings and are fixing up our home here in Wetpr. We plan to stay here for a couple of weeks because Renya is having a large birthday celebration for all of the children. Aunt Renya told us that she is also planning a celebration for our engagement but she has told us little else. You know how she loves to plan celebrations. I would expect that you will receive invitations soon, if you have not already.

Now that Angelina and are spending all of our time together we cannot bear the thought of being separated during the long months it will take to plan a royal wedding. So we want to have a small wedding with just the family upon our arrival home; then as families we can plan all of the big celebrations that are to follow. We hope our decision does not cause any of you distress. And we will need to discuss our living quarters with you.

The family here has fallen in love with Angelina, as I expected they would. And she with them. Angelina said she feels like Vitomas and Annabelle are her sisters.

Sorren, Angelina says she cannot believe you kept such a secret from her all those weeks.

With all our love

Matthew and Angelina.

"What secret is he talking about?" asked Rosa.

"Matthew asked me for her hand in marriage a couple of weeks before they left for Wetpr."

"My Lord is that you?" asked Sophie as she entered Roch's war room. Roch was standing behind his desk with his back to the door; he turned around and Sophie screamed.

"Sophie it is alright, it's me, Roch."

"Oh Master Roch did you get the same disease that Demetries had?"

"Yes, Sophie I did, would you summons Cerephus for me?" asked Roch. "Also I am starving; bring me some food and another bottle of whiskey."

Cerephus entered Roch's war room and stared at Roch. "How do I know you are King Roch?"

Roch smiled, "Ask me anything."

Cerephus thought for a moment, "King Roch had an unusual visitor one night a few months ago, who was it?"

"Do you mean the Sanuri or the demon Demetries?" replied Roch with a smile. "Very good, I like it that you are always protecting my interests."

"My Lord what happened to you and where are the others?"

"I have much to tell you Cerephus but first I want you to send your men out to bring all the physicians and healers to me that they can find in Stordt."

"Did the Court Physician see you?"

"Yes but he told me little more than the physician I saw in Nora; and bring Erebus here, perhaps he can reverse this curse," said Roch as he drank another glass of whiskey.

"And your name?" demanded Roch.

"Gala, My Lord, my name is Gala."

"My men tell me you are a well-known healer in Cana," said Roch. "I have a proposition for you Gala; if you can heal my affliction I will give you whatever you desire."

Gala curtsied before the King as soon as she entered the war room; she had remained in that position with her face looking downward.

Gala was trembling with fear for she thought King Roch had called her to the castle because he found out that she had helped Vitomas, Raul and the others escape from the kingdom.

Roch's words shocked Gala and now she raised her eyes to look at him. Gala's eyes grew wide as she saw his rotting flesh.

"You have seen this affliction before," said Roch. "I can tell from your expression."

"Yes My Lord," said Gala softly.

"Woman come closer so I can hear you," barked Roch.

"You have seen this before, tell me all you know," demanded Roch, who could see that Gala was extremely frightened. "I will not hurt you for telling me the truth."

"My Lord I fear you will not like what I tell you."

"I demand that you tell me all you know about this affliction," growled Roch as he was losing his patience with Gala.

"Years ago a traveler came to our village; he bore the same marks that you bear. He said he had come across some dead Hutas, who bore the same marks as you My Lord. The traveler stole all of their belongings; which included a golden chalice with jewels and a set of Holy Scrolls. The man said he planned to take these items to Port Friada and to sell them. The traveler said that after he stole these things he started having nightmares of a great lion that was telling him to return the items to a monastery."

Gala continued, "He said after three such nights he thought he had a vision of the lion coming into his camp. In his vision he cursed the lion and refused to take the holy objects to a monastery. The man said when he awoke the next morning he had the affliction." Gala saw the look on Roch's face as she spoke. "My Lord have you also seen The Lion?"

"Yes. What happened to that traveler?"

"He told me that he was so frightened that he buried the chalice and scrolls in a cave in the Kingdom of Puntd. Then he tried to find a cure for his affliction."

"Gala, tell me did this man have great pain in his joints and bones?"

"My Lord he never mentioned it, just the pain of his flesh. He said he had the affliction for over a year before he came to me."

"Could you help him?"

"No, My Lord I will tell you the same thing I told that traveler. In the old religion of The Great Ruler; The Lion was known as a holy messenger. If you received this affliction from a holy messenger there is no cure of man that will help you. You will need to find someone of great holiness and ask for their assistance." Roch did not say anything.

"My Lord I can give you some tonics for the pain and salves for your skin."

"Gala, I have had many physicians brought before me and you are the first person who has told me something that I believe. Yes I will take your medicines and reward you for your information; what would you like?"

Suddenly Gala heard the words coming out of her mouth, "My Lord, my mother is very ill, she lives just on the other side of the border into Wetpr; might I have permission to visit her before she dies?"

"Your request is granted," said Roch as he reached into his desk drawer and pulled out a small scroll. "Show this to the border guards and they will let you pass," said Roch as he handed the scroll to Gala.

"Thank you My Lord," said Gala gratefully. "I will go to my home and get the medicines and return this afternoon."

Gala started to cry as she left the castle, her fears now overwhelming her. Gala had always feared Roch but to know he offended the messenger of The Great Ruler terrified her. "Why did I tell him I needed to see my mother; she is no longer living?" thought Gala as she walked through the forest back towards her home.

Suddenly Gala realized she was consumed with a feeling to flee Stordt. Gala was trying to calm herself and to get control of her emotions. Many thoughts filled Gala's mind as she walked back to Cana.

Gala was so distracted she was not paying attention to her route. Suddenly Gala stopped as a great lion stood before her. Gala stood motionless and looked at the giant cat.

"Gala do not fear," said The Lion. Upon hearing his words Gala instantly fell to the ground and bowed before the great beast. "Gala I am not The Great Ruler; you do not bow before me, please stand."

"Are you here to punish me for what I told King Roch?" asked Gala.

"Not at all, I am here to help you," said The Lion. "Gala you have always been a faithful follower of The Great Ruler and you told Roch what he needed to hear but soon your words will turn into anger inside of him and he will order your death. You have that scroll, go home now, take but a few belongings and be in Wetpr by the end of this day. Go straight to the castle of King Sudfad, you have friends there and tell them all you have seen and heard this day. Gala it is important that you tell them."

"Yes My Lord," said Gala, not really knowing what to call The Lion. "And thank you."

"Gala there is one more thing, in the bottom of that chest in your bedroom is an old box that belonged to your great, great grandmother give it to King Sudfad, and tell him I told you to do so."

"My Lord, I will not be returning will I?" asked Gala.

"No and you must hurry now."

Chapter XV
Coming Together

A week to the day after Matthew bought the wedding rings; he proposed to Angelina. The proposal was simple but he asked her to marry him as they sat at a candlelit table in the middle of one of the rose gardens at the castle. Angelina said 'yes' before Matthew barely got the words out. They laughed and they cried and they danced to music that they heard only in their hearts.

"I thought this was going to be for just the family," said Sudfad as he buttoned the back of Renya's gown.

"Sudfad, they will be King and Queen someday and it does them well to know prominent people," Renya said as she turned around and kissed Sudfad on the lips. "I just invited some of the business families, the physicians and the priests from the monastery," said Renya as she quickly moved past Sudfad to grab a pair of earrings that were lying on a dresser. "Oh, I may have invited a few others also," Renya said with a smile. "I am ready now, what do you think?"

Sudfad looked at Renya who was wearing a form-fitting sapphire blue silk gown with sapphire and diamond earrings. "I always say you still look like you did when we first met," he said with a grin. "And you look absolutely beautiful," Sudfad added as he kissed Renya on the cheek. The King and Queen walked hand in hand to the Great Hall, which was filled with guests.

"There the children are," pointed out Renya as they saw Matthew and Angelina standing near a table talking with Raul. "My, doesn't she look beautiful," said Renya of Angelina who was wearing a light blue silk gown that draped across one shoulder. Angelina was wearing her hair up with long ringlets dangling on one side and she wore pearl earrings and a pearl necklace as well as pearls in her hair.

Sudfad walked to the front of the Great Hall, and stood in front of the musicians who stopped playing. One of the soldiers in the hall yelled out, "Attention, King Sudfad is about to speak."

Sudfad motioned for Renya to join him and he waited until she was at his side before he spoke. "My family would like to thank all of you for coming this evening to help us celebrate the engagement of our son Matthew and Angelina, Princess of the Nordes Tribe from the Kingdom of Lentz."

Sudfad motioned for Matthew and Angelina to join them in front of the guests. "Now some of you may be a little confused by my introduction. Matthew is the son of King Mathas of Lentz, and is my nephew. But he has become such a beloved member of our family that Renya and I have also adopted him as our son." Loud applause filled the Great Hall.

Sudfad turned to Matthew and Angelina, "It is only fitting that you lead us in the first dance." Angelina got a panicked look on her face as Matthew took her hand and put his arm around her waist. "It is just like we practiced," he whispered into her ear. "Just follow my lead." Renya and Sudfad were the second couple to dance. Raul and Simon stood near a table as their wives had not yet arrived.

"I am sorry we are late, I had to feed Samuel and Annabelle waited for me," said Vitomas.

"You still take my breath away," said Raul as he bent down and kissed Vitomas on the cheek. Vitomas was wearing a lavender gown with tiny straps. She wore gold and amethyst jewelry.

Annabelle was wearing a light blue strapless gown that accented her curves. Simon kissed her on the lips, "I am not going to be able to concentrate on anything with you wearing that dress," he said and kissed Annabelle again. As the two couples danced around the ballroom they saw a soldier come up to Sudfad; after talking for a few moments Sudfad left the Great Hall.

"My Lord there is a woman who asks to see you, she might be crazy, she told me she had a message for you from a lion," said the soldier.

"Please show her to my study," said Sudfad, who entered his study just moments before the woman arrived.

Gala walked into the study and curtsied before Sudfad, "Thank you for seeing me My Lord."

"Please take a seat," said Sudfad.

"My Lord I am truly sorry to disturb you when you have guests," said Gala hesitantly. "And I know that soldier believes me to be crazy. My name is Gala; I am a healer from Cana. Queen Vitomas brought me to Roch's castle to help your son Raul, then I cared for him when we hid him in a cabin near the Lake of the Pors. I helped Raul, Annabelle, Alexander and Laurel to escape and come here; please they will tell you I am not crazy. I am just very scared."

"Gala, do not be afraid of me; I have heard them speak of you," said Sudfad. "And I owe you a great debt."

"My Lord, I do not mean to be rude but The Lion told me that it was very important that I tell you some things and well, I have never spoken with a holy messenger before and forgive me if I am still a bit shaken."

"Gala, would you like something to drink?"

"My Lord a glass of water would be fine, I have not eaten or drank anything in two days."

Sudfad got up from his desk and walked into the hallway. He returned a few minutes later. "Gala I am having some food and drink brought here and I have summoned my sons they should hear what you have to say; so we will wait until they come."

"Yes My Lord. How is Simon, I had not heard since I tended to his wounds after they found Vitomas."

"He is just fine. You know that he and Annabelle married and have twin boys," Sudfad said proudly. "And Raul and Vitomas just had their second son. They are all very happy and truthfully they have spoken of you often."

Gala turned around when she heard the door open. "Gala, what are you doing here?" asked Raul happily. Gala stood up and hugged both of the young princes. "Did you take my offer to move here?" asked Raul.

"Raul it is more than that, I have something very important to tell all of you," said Gala as she looked on the verge of tears.

Marie knocked on the door. "My Lord, I have a tray."

"Thank you Marie, it is for Gala," said Sudfad. "Gala has been so diligent about getting a message to us she has not eaten in two days."

Gala waited for Marie to close the door. "My Lord I hardly know where to begin. Two days ago King Roch sent his soldiers to bring me to the castle. I thought he had found out that I helped Raul but instead he wanted my help. He had the mark of death upon him and he wanted to be healed."

"What do you mean the mark of death?" asked Raul.

"I told him once before I saw a man in his condition. I am sorry there is no short way for me to explain this and The Lion told me to tell you everything. When I saw Roch I did not recognize him. His skin is rotting on his body; he is bloated and has the smell of death. He has boils and open sores with pus running from them. He said he had summoned many physicians to the castle but no one could help him. He demanded I tell him everything I knew about the affliction."

"I told him about a traveler who came to me for help years ago; he had the same affliction." Gala started to cough and took a drink of water. "I am so sorry My Lord," said Gala as she apologized for coughing. "The traveler told me he had come upon some dead Hutas with the same affliction as King Roch. The traveler said he stole all of the Hutas' belongings and found a set of Holy Scrolls and a golden chalice with jewels embedded in it. The man said he planned to sell the scrolls and chalice in Port Friada."

"The man said for three nights he had dreams of a lion telling him to take the holy items to a monastery. Then he said he thought he had a vision where the lion came into his camp and told him the same thing. The man told me he cursed the lion and refused to take the scrolls and chalice to a monastery; he said when he awoke in the morning he had the affliction. The man said he was so scared that he hid the scrolls and chalice in a cave in the Kingdom of Puntd then started searching for a cure," said Gala.

"I found those scrolls," said Raul in amazement.

"Did you find the chalice?" asked Gala.

"No, I was in the cave and a part of a wall collapsed and I saw the pouch with the scrolls."

"We will have to go back for the chalice," said Sudfad. "But we can discuss that later; Gala please continue."

"Roch asked me if the traveler had great pain in his joints and muscles and I said the man did not complain of any. Roch did look like he was in pain," said Gala. "But it was the look in his eyes, as I told the story that scared me. I asked him if he had seen The Lion and Roch said 'Yes'. I told Roch that in the old religion of The Great Ruler The Lion was a holy messenger and if his affliction was from a holy messenger no medicine of man would help him. I told him he would have to find someone very holy and ask for help."

"I bet he goes after the Sanuri," said Sudfad.

"I did not mean to put the Sanuri in danger," said Gala apologetically.

"You know the Sanuri?" asked Sudfad as he had forgotten that he had been told that information when Laurel and Alexander brought Raul back to the castle.

"Yes we are old friends and I am a student of The Holy Scrolls," said Gala. "But there is much more to tell you and I am afraid I will forget something. Roch said I was the only person who was brought to him who told him something that he believed; so he offered to pay for the information. I do not even know why the words came out of my mouth but I told him a lie. I told him that my mother was dying and I asked for permission to cross the border to come to Wetpr. He gave me a scroll, like the one Vitomas gave you," Gala said as she looked at Raul.

"It surprises me that he paid you for information," said Sudfad.

"My Lord he was almost nice to me when he spoke. I told him I would return with some medicine for his pain. I was scared when I left the castle and I was walking in the woods and all of a sudden there was a great lion standing in front of me."

217

"I was terrified. Then it spoke to me and I thought The Great Ruler had sent it to punish me because of what I told Roch. The Lion said he had come to help me. He said Roch would soon become angry and order my death. The Lion told me to go home and take a few belongings and to come to you and tell you everything of what I saw and heard that day. He told me it was very important that I tell you every detail."

Gala opened a bag she had been carrying and handed a small box to King Sudfad. "The Lion told me that in the bottom of a chest in my bedroom was a small box that had belonged to my great, great grandmother and that I should give it to you. I do not know if it makes any difference but I think the only thing I forgot to tell you is that The Lion told me to be in Wetpr before the day ended."

"Gala you are shaking, please eat your food," said Sudfad as he looked at the box. "Do you know what is in here?"

"No, that chest belonged to my great, great grandmother and I never really looked through it. My Lord I did not even know the box was in the chest until The Lion told me and then I was too scared to open it. I will leave the room so you can open it."

"Gala perhaps you should leave the room, as I do not know what we will find," said Sudfad.

Gala stood up. "Wait Gala," said Raul. "Did you bring any belongings from your home?"

"Hardly anything; and The Lion told me to leave right away and he said I would not be going back."

"Gala you will stay with Vitomas and me until we can get you settled," said Raul.

"Bless you," said Gala.

Simon opened the door and called for Marie, "Marie, this is Gala she is an old friend of Annabelle's and Vitomas; would you take her to the kitchen to finish her meal and would you tell our wives they have a guest?"

After the women left the room, Raul looked at Sudfad, "Father, Gala put her safety at risk many times to help this family, I would believe what she says."

"I have no doubt she is telling the truth," said Sudfad. "But she kept saying The Lion told her to tell us every detail which makes me think there is some kind of message in what she said."

"Gone, what do you mean she is gone?" screamed Roch.

"Everything appears to be in her house; her neighbors said they have not seen her for days," replied the soldier.

"So you are telling me that woman just disappeared between here and Cana?" asked Roch sarcastically. "Look harder, I want that woman brought before me," growled Roch.

Sudfad examined the box before he opened it. The box was of modest design and had the remnants of hand painted flowers on it. The box appeared very old but was in good condition. Sudfad opened the box while both Simon and Raul stood at his desk. Inside the box were the type of items someone might keep for memories. There was a dried rose, a golden ring, three ornate keys, a small blue ribbon, as one might put on a baby, a small talisman, and a small leather bound book.

The leather and the binding of the book were very worn. Sudfad opened the book and saw that its pages were filled with writing. Sudfad was looking over the book itself, while Simon, who was standing behind Sudfad and looking over Sudfad's shoulder, read the last page.

"Father read this," said Simon pointing to a worn page.

Sudfad read the page out loud so Raul could also hear: *This is the diary of Glenda, healer to the royal family of Stordt. Let not these words come to light unless by the desire of The Great Ruler himself. Lest some of these words contain the same evil which I have witnessed to. Great Ruler protect us from the darkness that is upon us.*

"Sons, I am going to read this diary now, you do not have to stay here," said Sudfad. "Enjoy the celebration, you can read it later."

Simon and Raul looked at each other, then Raul spoke, "I believe we both would like to know what it says this night."

"Very well my sons, why don't one of you pour us drinks and I will read it out loud," said Sudfad.

I am compelled to write down these words although by doing so my life has no value. I have been a healer to the royal family of Stordt all my thirty four years, as my mother before me and her mother before her. I came to the castle when King Sharonne was but a boy. But I will not go into that as it is only the last few years that brings terror to my heart.

Five years ago King Sharonne changed greatly, an evil came over him that could not be explained. It is as if he is a different man. At first I thought it was due to the stress of battle. King Sharonne has sought to greatly expand his kingdom and has launched attack after attack on his neighbors. It seems the only king he cannot conquer is King Voltar of Wetpr.

Sudfad put down the book for a moment, "Do you remember who Sharonne was?"

"He is our great, great, great grandfather, is he not?" asked Raul.

"That is correct," replied Sudfad then he picked up the book and continued to read. *I realized it was not stress from battle when the madness began. The Great Ruler forgive me for the words I am about to write. Sharonne took his own daughter Princess Annabar to his bed, she bore him a son which Sharonne ordered one of his soldiers to kill. Every night he has women and girls brought to the castle from the villages; their screams fill the walls of the castle. My heart goes out to Queen Vinca who now lives in terror of the man she once loved.*

Sudfad stopped reading, "This woman appears to put a small star by each new entry, I do not know if that is of importance, but I will tell you when I come across one. If you notice some kind of pattern please say so. New entry."

The Great Ruler be with us Prince Tresdore died today. He was Sharonne's oldest son by Queen Vinca and was only three years old. I examined the body myself and am greatly confused as to the cause of death. But what terrifies me the most is the King himself. While the rest of the family mourns; the King's own indifference seems greatly unnatural. It seems the desires of his heart have greatly changed. Fear fills the castle always, nothing is the same; there is a sense of great evil here. Sudfad stopped reading.

"Father many of the things this woman writes of sound like the same things Vitomas told me about Roch," Raul said.

"I was thinking the same thing," said Simon. "Can this kind of evil be handed down in families?"

"That would be a question for the Sanuri," Sudfad responded, then returned to the diary.

"New entry," said Sudfad. *Many evil looking men have been coming to the castle as of late. The King often meets with them in the lowest level of the castle which is unusual since his war room is on the first floor. I was told that one of the peasant girls the King had brought to the castle bore him a son and he had his soldiers kill her and the baby.*

"New entry," Sudfad said. *A most unusual thing has happened as of late; King Sharonne has been meeting with priests. Sharonne does not believe in The Great Ruler, I do not know what he believes in but it must be darkness.*

"New entry." *Queen Vinca will give birth soon, this is her third child. She says that she is greatly afraid and she does not know why. I went into Taperia today to purchase supplies. To my horror I was told about two more young women who bore Sharonne sons and were murdered by the soldiers. That is five sons he has murdered, may The Great Ruler bless their souls.*

"New entry," said Sudfad. *My heart is fearful as I write these words. Queen Vinca gave birth to a son yesterday, Micha, the birth was normal but thirteen hours later Micha died. By the time I got to his room he was blue and cold, I could see no signs of injury or cause of death.*

221

That made six sons of Sharonne that died. Suddenly the King himself walked into the room and took the dead baby from his crib; he walked to the lower level of the castle.

Within the hour King Sharonne returned and Micha was alive. He said the baby suddenly started to breathe. I do not believe him but I do not understand what has happened either. I put a small talisman under Micha's blanket and I am praying to The Great Ruler to protect him but I fear it is too late. After Micha died Queen Vinca was hysterical, she kept saying 'he said the price was six'. I asked her what she was saying and she said that Sharonne said the 'price was six'.

King Sudfad put the book on the desk and looked at his son's. "I think Glenda is saying that Sharonne made a pact with darkness and he had to pay with the lives of six innocent children."

"I have heard of such things in my travels but I thought them just stories," said Raul.

"I think of our children; who I would die for, how could a father make such a deal?" asked Simon.

"New entry." *Prince Micha appears to be growing into a normal child; I truly hope that is so. Queen Vinca is slipping into madness, the poor creature. I believe the King to somehow be responsible. I have not heard of the deaths of anymore babies which makes me fearful of the Queen's words, 'the price is six'.*

"New entry." *A new horror is upon us. Last night Princess Mata, the wife of Sharonne's younger brother Igor hung herself in her bedroom. Igor found her and a letter she left for him. Later I saw the letter, Princes Mata said she killed herself because Sharonne had taken her to his bed and she could not live with the shame. Igor confronted Sharonne and now Igor is dead. The priests that meet with Sharonne have not offered comfort to any of the royal family during all of these difficulties. The Great Ruler be with me but I question if they are truly priests.*

"Father listening to you read these words it is as if Sharonne and Roch are the same person," said Raul.

"I know," said Sudfad. "So we come from a line of rapists and murderers."

"New entry." *King Sharonne has won another battle and taken the land from the Tange Mines east to the River Cheban from the Kingdom of Ryed. The more he acquires the more he wants. He has locked Queen Vinca in the eastern tower of the castle. I tend to her often; she seems rather relieved to be separated from the King.*

He is forcing his only daughter Annabar to marry one of the men he has secret meetings with; the poor child is terrified. Hopefully she will have a better life than she has here. I have been fortunate, The Great Ruler is watching over me. Sharonne has not been kind to me but he has not been cruel either; sometimes it is as if he does not realize I am here. I have noticed that he seems preoccupied and he talks to himself often.

"Before I start the next entry I have to admit this woman seems very perceptive," said King Sudfad. "Next entry." *I was in the lower level of the castle collecting mushrooms when I overheard voices. I hid in a small room, afraid of being seen. I could hear King Sharonne yelling at someone. He was saying 'What else do you want from me?' A man's voice I did not recognized told the King he had helped him in battles and expected payment. I did not even breathe for fear they would find me. The men walked past the room I was hiding in. I could not see the face of the man with Sharonne but he was wearing a priest's robe.*

As frightened as I was I decided to see what Sharonne kept in the lower level. I crept through the hallways opening the doors that were not locked. I smelled candles burning and followed the scent until I came to a room at the furthest end of a hallway. The door was half open so I peaked inside and The Great Ruler be with me I wish I never would have looked through that door. At first I did not understand what I was seeing; then the horror was upon me when I realized I was looking at an unholy altar.

There were many, many lit candles and bowls of blood. There were bones and human skulls in various stages of decay. There was a great painting on the wall of a red snake with green eyes and red pupils. The snake had a bright yellow tongue and was coiled to strike. I heard a movement and fear gripped my soul. Then I realized there were snakes moving on the floor of the room. I ran as fast as I could and I never returned.

"That sounds like the same mark all Rogetts carry, they say it is the Mark of Satan," Simon said.

"It is," replied Sudfad. "So Sharonne worshipped Satan or some other demon and made some kind of deal with darkness; I do not yet understand a connection to Roch."

"Next entry." *Annabar is dead; her husband beat her to death on their wedding night. That leaves just Micha, the King's second son. The King shows no sadness for the loss of his daughter. Queen Vinca has not yet been told.*

"Next entry." *King Sharonne is attacking Wetpr again, he seems fixated on King Voltar.*

"This is the last entry" said Sudfad. *King Sharonne lost his battle to King Voltar again. Sharonne's anger is overwhelming; he has kicked everyone out of the castle including me. I praise The Great Ruler for my freedom but I worry about Queen Vinca and Micha. But my last day at the castle should be noted for the madness of the King. When Sharonne returned from his battle against Wetpr he acted as a mad man. The King was screaming that Voltar and stopped him from paying his debt and this seemed to terrify Sharonne. In all my many years at the castle I had never seen King Sharonne act scared of anything.*

"Do you think Sharonne was trying to get to the vault?" Raul asked.

"If those really were priests visiting Sharonne, could they have known of the vault?" asked Simon.

"I think we need to show this to the Sanuri and ask him those questions," said Sudfad. "The Great Ruler wants us to have this information, I am not sure what to do with it yet. But there was a passage that disturbed me. The one about the second son; there is something familiar about that phrase."

"There is that song," said Simon.

"What song?" asked Sudfad.

"It's more of a kid's song," said Simon. "I do not remember all of the words but it goes; *the second son of the second son of the second son wants to be praised but beware he will bring darkness all his days.*"

"What is it Father?" asked Raul.

"Micha was the second son of Sharonne. My father King Jaretta was the second son of Micha and Roch is the second son of Jaretta," said Sudfad as they all stared at each other in disbelief.

"You do not think that song was a prophecy, do you?" asked Raul.

"It might be interesting to find out where that song came from," said Sudfad. "Let's bring Gala back in here, perhaps she knows what these keys unlock."

Raul walked into the main kitchen to get Gala. He opened the door to a burst of laughter. Seated at the table were Renya, Gala, Laurel, Vitomas and Annabelle. Marie was standing next to the table taking part in the conversation. When Vitomas saw Raul her face lit up, "Raul, Renya is giving Gala one of the cottages to live in, isn't that wonderful?"

"Your mother is more than generous," said Gala humbly.

"The children have told us that you risked your life several times to help them, this is the least that Sudfad and I can do. Besides it will be nice to have a healer so close."

Annabelle was starting to tell Gala that Angelina was a healer when Raul interrupted her. "I am sorry but Father wants to speak with Gala now, perhaps you can finish telling her about Angelina later," Raul said.

"Of course," said Gala and followed Raul to Sudfad's study.

No sooner had Raul and Gala taken seats when Renya walked into the study, "Sudfad they are here, you must come."

"Darling I will be delayed, please apologize for me. I will be with you as soon as I am done here. Sons why don't you go with your mother."

As the door closed Sudfad said, "Gala I would like you to examine the items we found in the box and tell me any information you can about them, no matter how insignificant you may think it to be."

"Raul since your father is busy you should make the announcement," said Renya cheerfully.

Raul walked to the platform that held the musicians and asked them to stop playing. When all eyes were upon him; Raul said, "Matthew and Angelina will you please come up here. Unfortunately Father is tied up with business now, but he and mother have a surprise for the both of you." Matthew and Angelina walked up to the platform and stood next to Raul.

"I am so nervous," Angelina whispered into Matthew's ear as she squeezed his hand.

As soon as Raul stopped speaking four soldiers dressed in the uniform of the Wetpr Honor Guard walked towards them. The crowd moved to make a pathway. Behind the honor guard were three soldiers with trumpets whose music announced the arrival of the Royal Family of Lentz and guests and the family of Chief Sorren and guests. As the thirty new guests filed into the Great Hall, Matthew and Angelina were filled with joy and walked down the pathway to great their families and friends.

"Mother I have never seen you look so beautiful," Angelina cried as she hugged her mother and her father. "And Father you look so handsome."

"Well it is not every day our only daughter celebrates her engagement," said Sorren with a grin. "And child there aren't words to say how beautiful you look this night."

As introductions were being made, Stephan walked up to Angelina and Matthew. "My Lady," Stephan said with a grin and kissed Angelina's hand.

Angelina turned dark red when she realized who Stephan was. "You were with Matthew that first morning that I met him, weren't you?"

"I certainly was and the image of you kicking his butt will stay with me forever," Stephan replied with a grin.

Angelina was too embarrassed to respond, so Matthew changed the subject. "Stephan we want a small wedding as soon as we get back and then we can have the large formal wedding celebrations later. Would you do me the honor of standing up for me at the wedding?"

"This is horrible," said Gala after she finished reading Glenda's diary. I am sorry My Lord but neither this diary nor any of those objects have meaning for me."

"And you have no idea what these keys are for?" asked Sudfad as he held them up for her to look at a second time.

"No My Lord," said Gala then she hesitated. "My Lord I live in the same house that Glenda did and I sleep in the same bedroom. I left her things untouched. That is why I didn't even know of this box until The Lion told me. Perhaps there are other things in her room that would be of importance to you."

"You certainly cannot go back there Gala; Roch would show no mercy. Let me think about this for a while. In the meantime we are celebrating the engagement of one of my adopted sons; you are welcome to join the festivities."

"Oh thank you My Lord," said Gala wearily. "I do not mean to be ungrateful but I had neither slept nor eaten from the time I saw The Lion until I arrived here. I am very exhausted."

"I understand, I will have Vitomas show you to your chambers but first I have what may sound like a strange request."

Sudfad joined the celebration about an hour after the guests from Lentz arrived. Renya took his hand and personally made all of the introductions. The Great Hall was filled with music and laughter late into the night. The only guests who were staying at the castle were the families and friends from Lentz.

"Well it is your choice, Matthew," said Renya. "But I already have guest quarters set up for all of the guests in the center wing."

Matthew looked at his father and Sorren. "Son, you and Angelina don't need your parents staying with you on the night of your engagement. I think we should all stay in the guest rooms tonight," said Sorren with a grin.

"Very well, but tomorrow you are all visiting our home here," said Matthew with a proud smile. "Where is Stephan?"

Mathas chuckled, "The last time I saw him he was heading out to the gardens with a very pretty girl."

The last light had just been extinguished in the castle when there was a knock on Sudfad's bedroom door. "I am sorry to disturb you My Lord but the Sanuri just arrived and said he must speak with you at once," said a soldier.

"Meekos, while you were gone, one of our men watched as the Sanuri loaded baskets of items into his boca," said Tenebrae.

"What!" screamed Meekos. "And he did not stop him?"

"Meekos, he did not know what was in the baskets, it could have been provisions. Padres Thomas and Bartholomew were helping him."

"Really," replied Meekos with an evil smile. "I want those two watched night and day, do you understand me?"

"Of course."

"And Tenebrae when I am not here I do expect you and Pravis to handle things, not just wait to tell me about them when I return," Meekos said angrily.

Tenebrae now was angered. "Meekos, you yourself said that the Sanuri is a powerful being and that we should use the upmost caution when observing him. How would we have explained taking away baskets of food without drawing suspicion on us and giving away the fact that they are all being watched?"

Meekos was silent for a few moments, "Perhaps you are right Tenebrae. For now let's increase the number of men that we have watching those two old fools; perhaps we will get a better idea of what is going on."

"So was your mission successful?" Tenebrae asked as he deliberately changed the subject.

"That remains to be seen. You know how the Old Ones are; they do not give you much information," said Meekos. "At this point they want to see if we can resurrect Omnibus from The Abyss and if that plan works they will help us with Sporos."

"But Meekos, to raise Omnibus, well, that plan has been in the works for generations and Sporos was an integral part of that plan. Without Sporos we may not be able to raise Omnibus," Tenebrae gasped fearfully.

"Tenebrae, control yourself. As for me I certainly do not plan on letting the Old Ones collect on the debt. We need to be more creative in our thinking. We have to find a way to increase Sporos' power beyond The Abyss," Meekos said thoughtfully. "By the way when was the last time you heard from Demetries?"

The sun was starting to shine through the window in Sudfad's study, when the Sanuri finished reading Glenda's diary. "Sudfad this is most unusual, everything written here was shown to me in visions while I was being tested; but the diary helps me to understand what it was I saw."

"The Great Ruler usually does not send me the exact same information twice, so the mysteries contained here must be very important." The Sanuri held up the diary as he spoke. "I knew Glenda; she was a faithful follower of The Great Ruler as is Gala. We can trust the words that she wrote."

"Sanuri, I am going to tell you again, you cannot feel guilty that the dark lords suspect the vault is here because of your presence. You look so depressed."

"I cannot help but to feel guilt."

"Well don't you think The Great Ruler would have sent you a message before this if He wanted you to change your actions? Instead He sends you back here again. Perhaps this is all part of a plan."

"You are right Sudfad."

"Sanuri you look exhausted so I don't want to keep you long but have you ever heard of a song about the Second Son?"

"Yes, but it is more than a song. There is an ancient prophesy about a great evil that will rise from a second son. The prophesy does not state what the evil will be only that it will be devastating to all worlds."

"Does the prophesy say how many generations of second sons are involved? Because that diary just listed three generations of second sons," Sudfad said.

The Sanuri's eyes widened, "You are right Sudfad. May I take this diary to my room; I brought many scrolls and manuscripts from the monastery I would very much like to compare writings."

"Of course, my friend."

The Sanuri stood up, "I am very tired and need to rest."

"We have a house filled with guests now. Matthew has fallen in love with a warrior princess of the Nordes Tribe from Lentz. We celebrated their engagement last night. Both of their families are staying with us. Would you like to meet them before you retire?"

The Sanuri looked at Sudfad skeptically. "So then who is guarding that kingdom?"

"Well this is certainly a late hour for you to be sneaking in here," said Matthew with a laugh. "The sun is coming up."

"It wasn't so long ago you were keeping these hours my friend," laughed Stephan as Matthew handed him a cup of coffee. "Actually I am surprised that you and your beautiful bride are up this early."

Matthew sat down at the kitchen table with Stephan, "Well usually we aren't but both of our fathers get up with the sun and we thought we might have company."

"I don't think either of them want to walk in on the two of you in bed," Stephan said with a grin. "I will say Angelina took my breath away last night. It is hard to believe that she looks even more beautiful in that gown then her little leather dress."

"And speaking of beautiful, I met Raul's and Simon's wives; I now understand why you requested to be considered for the inheritance."

"Well, Angelina and I had a surprise for you but you had to go off carousing last night," Matthew said as he took a sip of his coffee.

Stephan stared at Matthew suspiciously. "What are you saying?"

"Raul and Simon are also going to be standing up for me in the wedding and their wives will be standing up for Angelina. So we needed another woman to stand up with you."

"Yes go on," said Stephan with a laugh."

Matthew turned his face towards the open door to the garden and called out, "Angelina will you bring Ingr in here to meet Stephan?" Within moments they heard the two girls laughing. Angelina walked into the castle holding hands with a girl of exceptional beauty.

Ingr was close to Angelina's age and a childhood friend. Also a warrior of the Nordes Tribe, Ingr wore a short leather skirt and a leather camisole; which exposed her tanned, muscular body and her womanly curves. Ingr's long blonde hair was almost white and very straight. Her bright blue eyes glistened.

Matthew watched Stephan's face as the two girls walked up to them. "Breathe," Matthew said jokingly to Stephan. When the two girls reached the table, Stephan stood up and kissed Ingr's hand. "My Lady, I apologize for staring but you are incredibly beautiful."

"Thank you," said Ingr as she blushed. Ingr had never been outside of her village before and was both excited and overwhelmed by the castle and the people she was meeting.

"You will be my best man at the wedding and Ingr is Angelina's maid of honor," said Matthew with a grin as both Stephan and Ingr were staring at each other and not listening to him. "Ingr is staying with us in these quarters we thought you would be also."

"I certainly am now," said Stephan as he pulled chairs out for both Ingr and Angelina. As Angelina was about to sit down she whispered into Stephan's ear, "And Ingr can kick your butt too."

Stephan laughed loudly and kissed Angelina on top of her head. "Matthew these women are dangerous."

"I know," said Matthew as he put his arm around Angelina.

Stephan sat across the table from Ingr and kept staring at her so intently that she would become embarrassed and look away. Ingr tried to pay attention to what Angelina and Matthew were saying but the excitement that was surging through her made it difficult to concentrate on anything besides Stephan. He was the most handsome man Ingr had ever seen.

Stephan had short black hair and a black beard and mustache. His beard and mustache were cut very short so they accented his face without hiding it. Stephan's gray eyes were penetrating. He was large and muscular like Matthew and Ingr thought perhaps the same age. Stephan had a gentle smile yet he carried himself with the confidence of an experienced warrior.

"Ingr did you hear anything I said?" Angelina asked then laughed.

Ingr blushed. "I am sorry Angelina what did you say?"

"I don't think either of these two are listening to us," Matthew said with a grin. "They are too absorbed with staring at each other."

"Matthew," Ingr said and blushed a deeper shade of red. Stephan grinned at Matthew's comment and continued to stare at Ingr.

"Stephan," Angelina said loudly. "Matthew and I were wondering if you wanted to join us and Ingr in some friendly competitions."

"Sure," Stephan said and turned towards Angelina. "What kind of competitions?"

"Have you ever heard of the game Bozie?" Angelina asked with a smile.

Later that morning, Sudfad and Renya introduced the Sanuri to all of their guests including Angelina. The Sanuri stared at Angelina for a few moments then looked at Matthew and nodded. Matthew smiled with relief that Angelina was the wife The Great Ruler meant for him. Sorren continued to stare at the Sanuri long after their introductions. The Sanuri walked back up to Sorren and said with a smile, "You look as if you have seen a spirit."

"I have heard stories about you since I was a small child," said Sorren skeptically. "I did not believe you existed."

"Do you believe in The Great Ruler?" asked the Sanuri.

"Of course."

"I am merely an emissary on His behalf; nothing more."

"I beg to differ," said Sorren. "From the stories I have heard I believe you are much more."

"So my friend, do you have any news for me?" asked Thaos as he poured a glass of whiskey for Tobart, who looked at Thaos then nodded his head towards an empty table in the tavern. Thaos picked up the bottle and the two men sat at the table. Tobart looked around the room nervously before he spoke. He leaned closer to Thaos and said, "Sorren, his family and some of the villagers are gone; it is being said that they have joined King Mathas and his family in Wetpr."

"Do you believe this to be true?"

"I don't know it is gossip," said Tobart. "But I can tell you that Sorren and his family are gone, even the children, so he did not go to battle."

"Why would they go to Wetpr?"

Tobart's face grew red as he said angrily, "The only thing I can think of is it has something to do with Angelina and that Prince."

"When are they to return?"

"That I do not know."

"Tobart do you know Usman, the leader of the Valdore Tribe?"

"Yes but not well. He is a vicious man."

"Can you set up a meeting with him?"

"Why?" Tobart asked fearfully.

"Because I have an idea that might solve both of our problems," Thaos said as he sipped his drink.

The next few days were filled with great activities as Sudfad's family became friends with all of their guests. Sudfad, Raul and Simon took the male guests to the fort and showed them their military exercises. Later Sorren and members of his tribe gave demonstrations of their unique fighting styles and training games; Angelina and Ingr both participated and impressed all observers.

Shara and Angelina became close friends with Gala as they shared many of their secret recipes and stories as healers. Petra was thrilled to have Margarit and Sorren's two sons Nathanial and Peter to play with. But Petra was confused by the behaviors of Margarit, who was almost two years older than him and Kyra, who became jealous at Margarit's attention to Petra.

Nathanial was nine years old and Peter seven years old. Both boys were overwhelmed by all the pets and toy's Petra had. Renya took the women on shopping trips and everyone seemed to want to hold all of the babies.

The second evening after the engagement celebration, all of the families were in the Great Hall, as the formal dining room was too small to seat so many guests. Musicians played as dinner was served and everyone danced after the meal. "I have never seen my father and mother dance before they came here," Angelina whispered to Matthew as they glided around the dance floor.

Matthew looked into Angelina's large green eyes and said, "I think it is time for an announcement."

"But Matthew they might get mad."

"Well then I guess we will see," said Matthew as he stopped dancing, took Angelina's hand and walked to the platform where the musicians were standing. The music stopped and all eyes were upon the young couple. "Angelina and I are both so happy that all of you are here with us. And now that the Sanuri has joined us also; we were thinking of having the small family wedding here, in one of the gardens. It can be very informal then we will have the large celebrations when we return home." There was silence in the room.

"Would anyone be opposed to that?" Matthew asked as he was rather surprised by the silence. Suddenly Sorren and Mathas started to laugh.

"Sorren and I had a bet on whether you would marry here or in Lentz. I believe I owe Sorren a case of wine," Mathas said happily.

"Actually we all thought of that," said Renya smiling. "Shara, Rosa and I have already made some preparations."

"What sort of preparations?" asked Matthew.

"Well, we just happened to find the most beautiful dresses that we bought all of the girls, including Angelina and we may have purchased just a few other things too."

"Really," gasped Angelina happily.

"Now Matthew, Laurel is a great seamstress and she may have to adjust some of the dresses and we have a few other things to do so we will need at least two days to prepare," Renya said happily.

Matthew whispered into Angelina's ear, then she nodded in agreement. "How about Saturday morning that would give you three days?" asked Matthew.

Tobart had warned Thaos that Usman hated everyone, especially strangers. Tobart felt that if he took Thaos with him into Valdore territory that Usman would kill them both. So Tobart agreed to bring Usman to some caves by the River Shey, just south of the border of the Valdore lands.

The caves were well sheltered and not only afforded Thaos a quantity of places to hide but also a great observation post to view anyone who was approaching the area.

Two days passed. Thaos waited but knew that the longer it took for Tobart to return was a sign of trouble. The evening of the third day, Thaos mounted his horse and rode along the southern border of the Valdore lands without crossing into Valdore territory. Thaos saw three vultures circling in the air about a mile ahead of him. He carefully approached the area, ever mindful of it being a trap.

"Well, I guess the old drunk was right," Thaos said out loud as he looked at pieces of Tobart's dismembered body lying in a heap on the ground. Thaos turned and headed towards Langer.

The excitement and joy in Sudfad's castle rose as preparations for the pending wedding were underway.

"So you and Ingr have been spending a great deal of time together," Matthew said with a grin.

"Yes we have," said Stephan smiling. "Now I understand what you meant when you said being with Angelina was challenging and exciting. The other day we were shooting arrows at targets while on horseback; Ingr never missed her mark. She is such a skilled warrior and yet so feminine and beautiful at the same time..." Stephan stopped speaking in mid-sentence.

"Yes, go on," Matthew said with a grin.

"Matthew she just drives me crazy," Stephan said.

"I do have to warn you that Sorren promised her parents that he would personally watch over her while she was here."

"Don't worry, Angelina already told me that about twenty minutes after I met the girl," Stephan said with a laugh. "Besides I am aware of the political ramifications; I won't try to seduce her. But I certainly enjoy her company."

Matthew laughed loudly, "Stephan you sound just like me when I met Angelina."

The wedding of Matthew and Angelina was held in the same garden where Raul and Simon married their wives. Once again the Sanuri was proud to stand under the archway of flowers as the wedding and guests assembled before him. Renya, Shara and Rosa had chosen gowns for the girls that were more befitting a garden wedding. Rosa had already hired several seamstresses to design the dresses for the formal wedding that would be held in Lentz.

Matthew and Stephan wore the dress uniforms of the Military of Lentz, which Mathas and Rosa just happened to bring with them; while Raul and Simon wore the dress uniforms of the Military of Wetpr. The black and scarlet uniforms of the Wetprian Military made a stunning contrast to the dark blue and golden colors of the uniforms of the Military of Lentz.

Musicians were playing flutes, harps and violins in the garden as the guests took their seats. Renya, Shara, Rosa and Laurel all wore different gowns but they were all in various shades of purple and complimented each other. As they waited for the music to change, the Sanuri found himself watching the sky and landscape for any sign of danger.

Soon Ingr was walking down the pathway towards the Sanuri. All of the bridesmaids wore identical silk dresses that were lilac in color and decorated with small pearls. The silk formed to the different body types of each girl, and complimented them considerably. Ingr smiled and blushed as she took her place across from Stephan; who could not stop staring at her. Vitomas was next to walk down the pathway. Tears started to fill her eyes as she thought of her own wedding ceremony in this garden.

Annabelle was the last bridesmaid and instead of holding a bouquet of roses like the others, she carried a basket of long stemmed roses. Before Annabelle took her place across from Simon, she stopped and handed Shara, Rosa, Renya and Laurel each a rose, as this was a wedding custom of the Nordes Tribe.

All of the bridesmaid dresses had small puffy sleeves which covered little more than the shoulders of the women. Angelina's white silk dress was a very similar design as that of the bridesmaids; although her dress had a fuller skirt. Pearls decorated both the wedding dress and the long veil. Angelina and Matthew both smiled when they saw each other and for them; nothing else existed in that moment.

The Sanuri blessed the young couple, then blessed all who were in attendance. Then he turned around and lit three large white candles. "This wedding ceremony will combine traditions of all the cultures represented here. In the tradition of the Nordes Tribe Matthew and Angelina will first make their promises to each other."

Matthew took both of Angelina's hands in his, "Angelina I promise to love you, care for you and protect you as long as we shall live."

Tears were running down Angelina's cheeks at hearing Matthew's words. "Matthew, my dear husband I promise to love you, care for you and protect you as long as we shall live." Both Matthew and Angelina turned and knelt before the Sanuri.

"Matthew and Angelina do you promise to honor this gift of marriage that The Great Ruler is giving you?"

"Yes we do," Matthew and Angelina said in unison.

"Matthew and Angelina do you promise to follow whatever path that The Great Ruler puts before you, especially when you do not know where it leads?"

"Yes we do."

"Then stand up and face your guests as man and wife."

Chapter XVI
Alliances

"Thank you for coming," said the Sanuri as the men took seats in Sudfad's study. "Matthew I know this is your wedding night and I promise not to keep you from your beautiful bride for very long. But I do need to speak with all of you together."

"For those of you who do not know me very well, I must explain that I often receive visions from The Great Ruler. This is one means by which He sends me information. Now you must know that sometimes these visions seem as riddles and I am left with many questions after seeing them. Since my return to Sudfad's castle I have received multiple visions regarding all of you."

Every man in the room listened intently to the words that the Sanuri was speaking. "Sudfad, Mathis and Sorren when I look at you I see commonalities that make me proud. You are all good and faithful men, strong and wise leaders, fierce warriors and you all care about the people you lead and your families."

"And the next generation that is represented in this room, Raul, Simon, Matthew and Stephan you have all inherited these same traits. Stephan I know your father stayed behind to guard the kingdom while Mathas came here. But you have been a second son to Mathas and a brother to Matthew; you are strongly connected to their family."

"In my visions I have seen images of the many enemies of darkness that surround all of you. Some enemies you share in common as Juleta. Mathas I know it breaks your heart but know she is dangerous and would kill your entire family to take the crown. Juleta has not yet come to her full powers as a dark lord and will not for some time; but she is none the less a very dangerous person."

"The Valdore Tribe is a rising threat to your kingdom. King Roch casts an ever present shadow of darkness over the family of Wetpr. But understand I am naming powerful enemies that you are already aware of."

"There are others, whose identities have not yet been revealed to me. Understand your enemies know how powerful you are and will try to turn you against each other. I would ask that this night you form an alliance. You promise to work together against your enemies and you do not allow them to separate you by any means."

"Sudfad do you promise to work with the men in this room to fight the forces of darkness and to do the will of The Great Ruler?"

Without hesitation Sudfad answered, "I do."

The Sanuri asked each man in the room the same question and they all gave the same answer.

Stephan took Ingr's hand and opened a door leading to one of the castle gardens. A surge of excitement filled her being as this was the first time in all these weeks that Stephan had held her hand. "Ingr I wanted to speak with you alone," said Stephan as they walked through the moonlit garden. "Ingr we will be leaving for Lentz in a few days and well, I would like to continue to see you." Ingr did not speak as the two found a bench in the garden and sat down. "Sorren told me that I must ask your father permission to see you again but before I do; I would like to know if you wish to see me also."

Ingr looked up into Stephan's face and tears started to run down her cheeks, "Yes, Stephan I would very much like to see you again but, but it just isn't that simple."

"Ingr what is wrong?"

Ingr suddenly put both of her hands over her face and began to sob. Ingr was crying so hard that her body was shaking. At first Stephan just looked at her, not really knowing what to do. Then he put both of his arms around Ingr, "I don't understand why you are crying, did I say something wrong?"

"No, I am sorry," said Ingr as she tried to compose herself. "Stephan you have done nothing wrong."

"Then will you tell me why you are crying?"

"Stephan I have so enjoyed the time we have spent together these last few weeks. You make me have feelings I never thought I had. I think you are absolutely wonderful..." Ingr did not finish her sentence because she started to cry again.

Stephan held Ingr and stroked her silky hair until she could compose herself again. "Some way for a warrior to act, isn't it?" Ingr asked as she sat up and looked into Stephan's eyes. "Just before we left to come here a man made an offer for me and my father is working out a price."

"What! Are you telling me that your own father is selling you?" Stephan asked loudly.

"Yes," whispered Ingr.

"Do you even know the man he is selling you to?"

Ingr shook her head and said, "No."

"Ingr tell me what you want," Stephan said with great intensity. Ingr was looking at the ground, so Stephan gently lifted her chin so he could look into her eyes. "Tell me what you want to do."

"I don't want to go with that man. I wish I could just stay here in Wetpr with you."

"Ingr I am returning to Lentz."

"I know," Ingr said sadly.

Stephan suddenly stood up, pulling Ingr to her feet also, "We are going to talk with Sorren."

"Sorren I need to talk to you," said Stephan angrily when he found Sorren in the study with Sudfad. Stephan was holding Ingr's hand but she was standing behind him.

"I will leave you here to talk," said Sudfad as he stood up and started to walk out of the room.

"Ingr go with Sudfad," said Sorren. "I believe I know why Stephan is here."

Sorren and Stephan stared at each other. Then Stephan turned to Ingr and said softly, "Go with him." When the door closed. Stephan yelled, "You know her father is selling her like she is an animal. Sorren is this the custom of your tribe?"

Sorren turned his back on Stephan as he poured each of them a small glass of whiskey. "You are so upset Stephan, do you have feelings for the girl?"

Stephan was surprised by the question. "Yes, but even if I didn't this is just plain wrong. She is just a young innocent girl. She doesn't even know the man who is buying her."

Sorren turned around and handed Stephan the drink, "Tell me Stephan do you love her?"

"Why are you asking me these questions?" yelled Stephan angrily.

"Please just answer them."

"I don't know. We have only known each other for a few weeks. I guess I haven't thought about it."

"Matthew and Angelina knew they were in love after a few weeks."

"Sorren, honestly I don't know. Will you tell me how I can help her?"

"What are you willing to do?"

"What do you mean?"

"Ingr's father Thaddies is a poor man. He is selling his daughter because she is the only thing he has of value to sell."

"Well he certainly can't love her."

"Stephan you don't know that. He has other children to feed also."

"So are you condoning this?"

"I am simply explaining the facts to you. If you want to help Ingr you will have to buy her from her father."

242

"The idea of buying another human being is disgusting. What if I challenge the other man to a fight?"

"You will win and her father will just sell her to someone else."

"What if I buy her and set her free?"

"Where will she go?" asked Sorren. "This is the very first time she has even been out of our village. Ingr will stay with her family and her father will sell her the next time he needs money."

Stephan sat down in one of the overstuffed chairs. He suddenly felt defeated. "Sorren, I don't know if I am ready for a wife and I don't believe in slaves. What would I do with the girl?"

"That Stephan is a decision only you can make. I have learned a great deal about you tonight and you are a good man. I know Ingr well; she is like a daughter to me. She is a sweet, innocent young girl who needs help. You need to decide what you are going to do."

Thaos became a regular in the taverns in Langer. He listened to people talk and bought drinks to loosen their tongues. One hot evening Thaos was standing at the bar of a tavern called Nates watching five men sitting around a table playing cards. Suddenly one of the men pulled a large knife out of a sheath and rammed it into the middle of the table. "You have been cheating us all night. Now I want my money back."

The man he was accusing of cheating was considerably smaller. This man stood up and pounded the table with his fist. "Do you know who I am? I work for Usman and if you hurt me he will have you killed." The larger man grabbed his knife from the table top and held it menacingly at the smaller man.

"Come, come," said Thaos as he walked up to the table. "Let me buy you all a drink."

"Mind your business," yelled the larger man who suddenly lunged at the smaller man.

Thaos grabbed the arm of the larger man and twisted it behind his back, while putting his left arm tightly around the man's neck. "Just leave," said Thaos. The man tried to struggle against Thaos' hold so Thaos twisted his arm harder. "Ok, I'll go," said the man. "But this isn't over," he said to the smaller man as he walked out of the tavern. Thaos walked back to the bar. Within moments the smaller man walked up to him, as Thaos knew he would.

"Let me buy you a drink friend," said the man. "What is your name?"

"Thaos and yours?"

"Kadin."

"So, Kadin is it true you work for Usman?'

Kadin looked at Thaos skeptically. "Why?"

"Well do you?"

"I am from his tribe; I never worked for him."

"Well, I work for someone who would like to do business with Usman but he is a hard man to find. Do you think you could set up a meeting?"

When Stephan entered Matthew's and Angelina's chambers it appeared that everyone was sleeping. Stephan walked into his room, took off his clothes and slid under the blankets. He was very disturbed by Sorren's words and lay in bed with too many thoughts racing through his head. Stephan was lying on his side with his back to the door; when he saw the reflection of a flickering light on the wall across from him. Stephan rolled over and saw Ingr standing next to his bed, holding a plate with a candle on it. She was dressed only in a thin white nightgown.

"Ingr is something wrong?"

"Stephan I am sorry to wake you, but I can't sleep. Please tell me what Sorren said."

Stephan sat up and moved over so Ingr could sit on the bed but to his surprise she put the candle on the table next to his bed and crawled under the blankets with him. "Ingr what are you doing?"

"I don't know," Ingr said and started to cry. "What did Sorren say?"

Stephan didn't know what to tell Ingr, so he put both of his arms around her and hugged Ingr as she cried.

"He said I have to go through with it, didn't he?"

"He and I talked about different things but no decisions were made. I will speak with him again tomorrow."

"Thank you for trying to help me. You must think I am awful but I know Father needs the money."

Stephan pulled away from Ingr so he could look her in the eyes. "Ingr no one has the right to sell another person; I don't care how badly he needs the money." Ingr started to cry again. Stephan held her until she cried herself to sleep. When Stephan was sure Ingr was sleeping he lowered her down on the bed and covered her with a blanket then left the room.

Pravis and Tenebrae joined Meekos in his chambers at the monastery in Malga. Meekos' chambers were lavish and befitting a king. The three sat in front of a large fireplace in Meekos' parlor. "I have been thinking very carefully about our situation," Meekos said. "We may not be able to raise Omnibus from The Abyss without the help of Sporos. So as I see it. We either have to find a way to help Sporos extend his power from The Abyss; more than we are now. Or we need to find another powerful demon to help us."

"What of Demetries?" asked Pravis.

"Demetries is not strong enough and I have not heard from him in weeks," replied Meekos.

"You are right," said Tenebrae. "But every demon that we align with demands such high payments."

"You know what the payment will be if we fail to raise Omnibus," warned Meekos.

Stephan knocked on Matthew's bedroom door. "Is something wrong?" Matthew asked sleepily.

"Can we talk?"

The two men walked into the kitchen and Stephan poured a couple of small glasses of whiskey. "Ingr cried herself to sleep in my bed."

"What did you do?" Matthew asked, as he was quickly waking up.

"No, nothing like that," replied Stephan. "I learned tonight that her father is selling her to a man she doesn't even know because he needs money. I talked with Sorren and according to him my only option to help Ingr is to buy her. Can you believe that her own father is selling her like she is an animal? It just makes me so angry."

"Are you going to marry her?"

"Matthew I don't really know how I feel about her yet and I don't think I am ready to have a wife; but someone has to help that poor little thing. She is so sweet and innocent."

"Why don't you buy her then set her free?"

"I already thought about that but Sorren said she would stay with her family and her father would just try to sell her again."

"Then I will buy her and she can live in the castle with us."

"You shouldn't have to buy her. It should be me."

"Stephan if you buy her she may think you want her for a wife. If I buy her, it will just be helping Angelina's friend."

"Well, let me think about who is going to buy her, but I am grateful you will allow her to live in the castle."

Stephan returned to his room and tried to crawl into bed without waking Ingr. "Stephan where have you been?" she asked sleepily.

"I have some great news Ingr. Are you awake enough to hear it?" Stephan asked. Ingr sat up in bed and looked at Stephan. "I will buy you from your father and set you free. Matthew said that you can live with him and Angelina in the castle."

"Really? Stephan, really?" Ingr threw her arms around Stephan's neck; kissing his face and neck over and over in between saying "thank you." After a few moments Stephan took Ingr into his arms and kissed her on the lips. A slow passionate kiss that stirred deeply within them both.

They stopped kissing and stared at each other for a moment as they were both surprised by their feelings. Stephan pulled Ingr close to him and kissed her again. As one, they both laid down while they were kissing. Ingr was surrendering to her passion and to Stephan. Suddenly Stephan stopped kissing her. Breathless and sweating Stephan said, "You need to go back to your room now."

"Why? Have I done something to make you mad?"

"No, but if you don't go now I am afraid we will make love."

Ingr was quiet for a moment, "Perhaps that is how I can pay you back for helping me."

Stephan quickly sat up in bed. "No," he said angrily. "I am not buying you to have sex with me."

"Stephan I am sorry I made you angry."

"Ingr do you understand what I am trying to say to you?"

"I think so," Ingr said with her lower lip trembling.

"I just want to help you; you do not owe me anything. Now go to your room."

Ingr sat up in bed and looked at Stephan. "No," she said defiantly.

247

"What!" Stephan could not believe what he was hearing.

"Stephan I am staying here with you. If you want me to go you will have to force me."

Stephan stared at Ingr in disbelief. She was not angry or crying she simply refused to leave. Then Stephan started to laugh. "Ok stay but keep your nightgown on." Ingr smiled and cuddled close to Stephan. "You really aren't going to make this easy are you?" Stephan asked.

"Stephan what do you mean?"

Stephan propped his head up on his hand and looked into Ingr's eyes. "I mean when I am with you I want to make love to you." Ingr started to speak but Stephan interrupted her. "We aren't going to make love, not yet."

"Stephan I am really confused."

"I know," Stephan said and put his arms around Ingr.

"Lazo you have done well for me," Juleta said as she handed him a glass of whiskey.

Lazo was flattered by Juleta's flirtatious attention. Lazo was a man of medium height and very skinny. His unkempt brownish hair and scraggly brownish gray whiskers had never enamored him to women. Lazo was a cunning man with high ambitions and a soul as dark as hell. "Thank ya My Lady," Lazo said with a large grin that exposed his rotted teeth.

"Thaos is gone so much, I need a strong man who I can count on around here," Juleta said as she took a seat across from Lazo in her parlor.

"What do ya need My Lady?"

"I need a great deal more money to raise the size of army that I desire," Juleta said with a coy smile. "I want you to gather a group of our men and ride across the border into the Kingdom of Ganz. I have heard that every week shipments of gold ore are taken from the mines to Hadne."

"I want you to find out as much information as you can about these mines and the shipments for me."

"Ya just want the information?"

"At this point, yes. And when you have gotten the information I have another little job for you to do in Lentz."

"And how will I be paid for this work?" Lazo asked with a sly grin.

When Ingr and Stephan walked out of his bedroom the next morning, Matthew and Angelia were sitting at the kitchen table within view of the bedroom door. Stephan looked at Angelina and said, "Before you start yelling at me, this isn't what it looks like."

Angelina walked up to them and said, "I know exactly what it is and I think you are wonderful for helping my friend." Then Angelina stretched upwards and kissed Stephan on the cheek. "Why didn't you tell me?" Angelina asked as she looked at Ingr.

"Because I was too ashamed," Ingr said and started to cry. Angelina put her arm around Ingr and the two women walked into the garden.

Stephan sat down at the kitchen table with Matthew and poured himself a cup of coffee. "Don't look at me like that, nothing happened."

"Really?"

"And it wasn't easy. First of all she says that she can pay me back by making love. Then she refuses to leave my bed. Ingr said I would have to force her if I wanted her to leave. I'll bet she doesn't even know how to make love," Stephan said as he sipped his coffee.

"Probably not, Angelina didn't."

"This sounds awful to say but I will bet her father is getting a higher price for her because she is so innocent."

"So why didn't you make love to her?"

249

"I don't know. I certainly wanted to. It just seems like there is no one who cares enough to stand up for her; I just don't want to take advantage of her too. Matthew why are you giving me that look?"

"Because I think you care about her more than you realize."

"Now you sound just like Sorren."

Later that morning, Stephan and Matthew found Sorren in Sudfad's study, along with Mathas and Sudfad.

"I hope it is alright that I told Mathas and Sudfad about Ingr?" Sorren asked but before Stephan could answer Sorren continued. "Did you make any decisions Stephan?"

"Yes, I am going to buy Ingr and set her free. Matthew said she can live with him and Angelina."

Sorren looked at Mathas and Sudfad with a proud look on his face. "That is an excellent plan; you both have done well."

"In case there is trouble; I am going with Stephan when he meets her father," Matthew said.

"As am I," said Sorren. "I said I knew Thaddies, not that I liked him. Now Stephan, when you haggle over the price you must tell him that you want her for your wife. I fear that if Thaddies knows Ingr is free he will try to make money off her in some other way."

"Do I have to say that?" Stephan asked.

"Why, is there a problem?"

"I just don't want Ingr to get the wrong idea."

"Why would she get the wrong idea?" Sorren asked.

"Last night Ingr climbed into bed with me and refused to leave." All the men in the room looked at Stephan and smiled. Stephan threw both of his hands into the air and said with frustration, "I did not touch her."

"I see," said Sorren with a knowing look on his face.

"Sorren now you are giving me that same look that Matthew did."

"The physician said that Taperian soldier is finally able to speak to us," Simon said as he was walking into Sudfad's study.

Raul jumped out of his seat and started towards the door. "Now you two just wait a moment," yelled Sudfad. Both Simon and Raul were taken by surprise since they rarely ever heard their father yell. "You two may be exactly the wrong people to talk to him, now please sit down. Both of you are so angry and fearful for your families that you want to kill this man; I do understand," said Sudfad as Simon and Raul reluctantly sat down.

"But I am afraid these things may blind you to the fact that a messenger from The Great Ruler told us we needed to get information from him. Raul you said the man was deliberately antagonizing you; what makes you think he will not react in the same manner a second time? After we get our information you may do as you wish with him, but I have a plan," said Sudfad.

Both Raul and Simon stared angrily at Sudfad, after a few moments Raul said, "You are right Father I would beat him again under the same circumstances; what is your plan?"

"Your story about Gala concocting a tonic to make you appear dead intrigued me; at my request she has been working on a tonic that will make this man tell us the truth," said Sudfad. "It took a few days for me to get her all the ingredients she needed; the tonic may be ready now, I have not spoken to Gala yet this morning."

"Is there such a tonic or is she experimenting?" asked Simon.

"Years ago I heard about this tonic from an old healer. That was why I was interested in knowing Gala's history. Fortunately she has kept the recipes of her family through the generations. She has made it before and swears it works."

"Why would she have made this before?" asked Raul.

"Gala said the recipe is very old and she made it to test if it worked," Sudfad replied.

"I want to send Gala to the prisoner as a healer. She will tell him she is working with the Royal Physician and give him the tonic; after it has taken effect we all will interview him."

"You Father?" asked Raul.

"Yes, you both are brilliant men; but I fear your emotions will take control. We have been told this prisoner is a gift to us. We cannot lose sight of the fact that we must obtain information from him. This may be our only chance and since we do not know the specifics about the information, we will need to ask many questions."

"I will go to Gala's cottage now," said Simon. "And find out if the tonic is ready for use."

"One more thing," said Sudfad. "We need to take the prisoner to a place where others will not hear our conversation, I do not care where."

"Yes Father," said Simon as he and Raul left the study.

"Simon, two of these cottages are empty and it is secluded back here," Raul said as they dismounted in front of Gala's cottage. "We will bring the prisoner here."

Gala came to the door when she heard the horses. "Are you here for the tonic?"

"Is it ready?" asked Simon.

"I finished it this morning," said Gala as they walked inside the cottage. She handed them two small bottles. "I made two in case one is broken," said Gala. "It will take about thirty minutes for this to take effect; you will know because he will act as if he is drunk. Are you ready for me now?"

"Yes but Gala this man is dangerous please be careful," said Raul.

"Won't the guards be near when I go into the cell?" asked Gala.

"Yes but still be careful," Raul said.

"I thought that after I gave him the tonic I would act as if I was seeing other prisoners, that way I can keep an eye on him," said Gala as she grabbed her medicine basket and shawl.

Thaos was not surprised when he found the dismembered body of Kadin thrown in a heap just over the border from the Valdore lands. Thaos believed Usman was depositing the bodies near the border as a warning to strangers.

In order for Thaos to get from Langer to the border of the Valdore lands he had to travel through the lands belonging to the Nordes Tribe and near the castle of King Mathas. Thaos found the roads on his route to be flanked by small farms and tiny villages.

Thaos often came upon other travelers and enjoyed engaging them in conversation. Thaos' handsome looks and disarming smile often masked his true intentions. People seemed to enjoy Thaos' friendly demeanor and often invited him into their homes. It was just such a friendly act that led Thaos to meet Jeb.

Jeb was the grandfather of Ryan, a young man who Thaos met as he traveled back towards Langer. Both Ryan and Jeb were fishermen who lived in the large Village of Minges, which was on the shores of the Sea of Grevtd in the lands belonging to the Nordes Tribe.

"I brought a traveler home for dinner," Ryan said as he and Thaos entered the small wooden house.

"Well I hope he likes fish stew," Jeb said as he turned from the kettle he was stirring on the hearth and faced Thaos and Ryan.

There was a great familiarity about Jeb that Thaos could not place. He stared at the old man whose frame was bent from age. Jeb's white hair and dark tan face were set alive by his brilliant blue eyes. Jeb had eyes that danced and glistened.

"Ryan where are your manners, offer the man a drink. I am sure he is thirsty if he has been traveling," said Jeb. "It is just me and my grandson here, nothing fancy but you are welcome to a hot meal and a bed for the night."

"I thank you for your kindness," Thaos said genuinely. "Can I help you with anything?"

"No, you are our guest please take a seat," Jeb said as he put a loaf of hot bread on the table. "Ryan set another place for; I am sorry I did not get your name."

"Thaos, my name is Thaos."

"I am glad to meet you Thaos. That is an unusual name but I believe I have heard it before. Let me try and remember," said Jeb as he put a large kettle of thick fish stew on the table.

"This might be the best fish stew I have ever tasted," said Thaos as he ate hungrily.

"Grandfather is a good cook," Ryan said. "Can't say I take after him with that," Ryan added and laughed.

"He may not be the best cook but he is a good boy. I've been raising him since he was a child. His parents were killed in a massacre; it is amazing the child survived."

"What massacre?" asked Thaos.

"Hutas, those demons attacked Hafsfat and killed my son Leven and his wife Sophine. Ryan was just a baby and Sophine managed to hide him under the bed before they killed her. Thank The Great Ruler those devils didn't burn the house down."

"Hafsfat, you mean the Hafsfat that is in the Kingdom of Ganz?" Thaos asked.

"Yes, you know of it?" Jeb asked.

"That is where I was born, my family was also killed in that massacre," Thaos said as he stared at Jeb. "There is something familiar about you Jeb, have we met before?"

"I used to own the General Store in Hafsfat."

Suddenly a broad smile came across Thaos' face. "And you had large jars of candy on a table across from the counter. And you always let me have some candy even though my parents were too poor to pay for it."

"Who were your parents, boy?"

"Torance and Melina, they owned a small farm outside of Hafsfat."

"I remember your family. You had three sisters didn't you?"

"Yes and they were all raped and butchered by the Hutas," Thaos said with anger in his voice. "I was fishing that day. When I came home I found them all."

"How old were you, son?"

"I was nine," Thaos answered.

Chapter XVII
Answers

The families of Mathas and Sorren returned to the Kingdom of Lentz together. But Stephan, Mathew and Sorren decided to speak with Ingr's father before returning to their homes. Angelina and Ingr joined them and the five rode up to Ingr's home, which was little more than a shack. Several dirty children ran out of the house to greet them.

They could hear a man's voice bellowing before they saw Thaddies in the doorway. He smiled and walked towards them. Thaddies' gait was unsteady and as he got closer they all noticed that he reeked of alcohol. Thaddies was filthy and his hair looked like it had not been tended to in a very long time.

"Well baby girl, come on here," said Thaddies with a salacious grin.

Without turning Stephan said, "Ingr stay on your horse."

From the tone of Stephan's voice, Sorren decided he should intervene. "Thaddies, this is Prince Matthew, my son-in-law and his close friend Stephan. Stephan is a captain in the King's military. While we were all in Wetpr for the wedding of Matthew and Angelina; Stephan and Ingr fell in love and want to be married."

Thaddies started to scratch the stubble on his chin, "Well, I already sold her. In fact he has been waiting for her to come home."

"I will pay you much more, what is your price," demanded Stephan in an angry voice.

Thaddies started to smile, then he tilted to the left and caught himself before he fell. "Well let me see." Thaddies pretended to be deep in thought. "You see the problem is that I already spent the money he gave me, so I will have to pay him back and make a profit."

Matthew could see Stephan tensing up. Without turning Stephan said, "Angelina why don't you go in the house with Ingr and get her things. And take the children with you."

No one spoke until the door to the house was closed. Stephan slid off from his horse and walked up to Thaddies. In his drunken state Thaddies did not realize how angry Stephan was until Stephan grabbed him by the shirt.

"I will give you a bag of gold coins and you will take it. I don't care about your profit. You disgust me, what kind of a man sells his own children. After we leave here you will never come near Ingr again, do you understand me?"

"Yes," Thaddies stuttered as Stephan pushed him to the ground.

"If I hear of you selling any of your other children I will be back and believe me it will be the last disgusting act you ever do," Stephan almost snarled when he said the words.

Thaddies lay on the ground looking up at Stephan, "Sorren are you going to let him talk to me like that?"

"Thaddies, not only do I agree with him but if he returns I will help him."

Angelina and Ingr walked out of the house each carrying a small basket of items. They stopped when they saw Thaddies on the ground and Stephan angrily standing over him. "Girls get on your horses; we are leaving," Stephan said as he threw a leather bag of gold coins at Thaddies and growled, "Remember what I said."

The small group was quiet for several minutes after they rode away from Thaddies, then Matthew started to laugh and Sorren joined him. "I like it when you get angry," Matthew said to Stephan.

The soldiers tied the prisoner to a chair in the empty cottage then went outside as they were ordered.

"Well, he certainly is acting like he is drunk," said Simon.

"I wonder how long that tonic lasts." Raul said.

"We always have the second bottle if we need more," said Simon as they waited for Sudfad to arrive.

Sudfad walked into the cottage; glad to see the prisoner was still alive. "What is your name?" asked Sudfad

"Thatus," replied the prisoner groggily.

"Who do you work for?" Sudfad asked.

"King Roch."

"Did Roch send you to Wetpr?"

"Yeah."

"How many were with you?"

"Four."

Both Simon and Raul looked at each other after Thatus gave this answer.

"Where is the fourth man?" Sudfad asked.

"Probably back in Taperia, he left when he saw the people pulling me from my horse."

"What was your mission here?"

"Roch saw a necklace that he gave the Queen on the neck of a woman in Nora; he sent us to Wetpr to find out who sold the necklace."

"Why would that matter?"

"If Roch finds out Vitomas sold it; he will punish her."

"Did he know she was in Wetpr?"

"Yes, the demon Demetries told him."

"How did Demetries know this information?"

"He led the attack on your castle at the wedding."

"Did Roch order that attack on my castle?"

258

"I don't think he knew anything about it until the demon told him later."

"So the demon decided to attack the castle at our weddings?" asked Raul.

"From what I heard, yes."

"You said Roch will punish Vitomas, how will he get to her?" asked Sudfad.

"He and Demetries are planning to attack Wetpr."

"When?"

"I don't know. Roch has to get something for Demetries before the demon will summon up the Rogetts and the Hutas."

"Does Demetries have the power to summon the Rogetts and Hutas?"

"I don't know about the Hutas but I saw with my own eyes, him summon a hundred Rogetts from the Nora mines."

"What happened when he did that?"

"We killed them; it was to prove a point that he had the power to do it."

"Why were you in Nora?"

"Roch let us lose on the city as a gift," Thatus sneered as he said this.

"Why would Roch give you this gift?"

"Because the next morning we were leaving for the Tange Mines to capture Rogetts."

"What is Roch going to do with the Rogetts?'

"Use them to distract the Gants in the Caves of Muldun."

"Why is he going to the Caves of Muldun?"

"The thing that Demetries wants is in those caves."

259

Sudfad gave a worried look to his sons. "Was Roch successful?"

"I don't know; he sent us here from Nora."

"Has Roch sent his men to Salar before?"

"Yeah."

"Why?"

"Just to watch, he wants to kill your family," said Thatus with a laugh. "And he wants his woman back; that's why I grabbed her when I saw her go into a shop."

Raul stepped towards Thatus but Sudfad help up his hand. "Tell us about Roch wanting Vitomas and Annabelle," said Sudfad.

"Roch will not tolerate people stealing from him that is why he will kill your sons himself; but I think he loves her. He has us bring him girls from the villages and cities; the ones he wants all look like her," said Thatus.

"And Annabelle?"

"I don't know his thoughts about Annabelle," suddenly Thatus smiled. "But if he wants to punish Vitomas he will hurt Annabelle."

"When does Roch plan to kill my sons?"

"When he attacks."

"Do you know his plans for the attack?"

"If Roch finalized them he did not tell us; but I know he was going to have the Rogetts, Hutas and us all attack Wetpr at the same time but in different areas."

"Do you know what areas?"

"No, I think he was still planning that."

"Does he know how strong my army is?"

Thatus laughed loudly. "Yes that is why he has waited until he had the help of the demon; he has been planning on attacking Wetpr since I started to work for him."

"How long have you worked for Roch?"

"Fifteen years."

"If Roch wants Vitomas so badly why did he stop looking for her?" asked Raul.

"Vitomas left, while Roch was gone; when he returned he and Jonas were both injured from fighting Hutas. Then he went to the Caves of Muldun and lost all his men. And this is hard to explain but at some time the demon took over Jonas' body and he seemed to be telling Roch what to do."

"When did Roch find out Vitomas and Annabelle were in Wetpr?" asked Simon.

"When the demon told him about the wedding; we all thought Archetenus had taken her because he returned to the castle while Roch was gone then disappeared again."

"Why has Roch wanted to attack Wetpr for over fifteen years?" Sudfad asked.

"Because he hates his brother," Then Thatus paused. "But I think there might be something else too."

"You mean something besides Vitomas?" asked Sudfad.

"Yeah."

"Do you have any idea what that is?"

"No."

"Why does he hate his brother?" asked Raul.

"I think jealousy; but Roch hates many things." Thatus started laughing loudly again. "I think he even hates himself."

"Do you know anything else about Roch's plans to attack Wetpr or its Royal Family?"

"Nope."

"Do you have anything else to tell me that I might value?" asked Sudfad.

Thatus thought for a few moments, "Nope."

Sudfad looked at Simon and Raul, "Do either of you have any more questions?"

"No," both Simon and Raul said in unison.

"He is yours," said Sudfad. "When you are done, return to my study." Sudfad started to walk out of the door then turned around. "Your mother will be mad if you get blood all over this cottage."

After Sudfad finished interrogating the Taperian solider he went straight to the Sanuri's chambers. "I am sorry, I was so involved in my studies that I did not hear you knock," apologized the Sanuri as Sudfad entered the chambers. Sudfad sat in one of the overstuffed chairs and proceeded to tell the Sanuri about the interrogation word for word.

"I did know that Roch was trying to get The Scroll of Imari but I did not know he intended to give it to the demon," said the Sanuri. "By the way, The Lion sent that demon and all of the Rogetts they had gathered to The Abyss. We will not be hearing from them again." Suddenly the Sanuri's eyes grew wide, "By The Great Ruler."

"What?"

"That demon Demetries has been trying to raise Sporos from The Abyss. I have been trying to figure out how all of these things are connected. I had been concentrating on Roch and Sporos trying to use The Scroll of Imari with The Box of Itifer to control the minds of men. But if The Scroll of Imari is used in conjunction with The Chalice of Ascension the combined powers might be strong enough to raise Sporos. I should have seen this before, what with all of the items missing from the Hall of Antiquities."

"What are you saying and where is The Chalice of Ascension?"

"Padre Bartholomew was attacked in the Hall of Antiquities. The scrolls that he was reading at the time of the attack went missing. So several priests decided to do an inventory of the Hall and found many items were missing. They had not completed the inventory when I was there but I saw the list of items, which included many manuscripts about The Abyss," the Sanuri explained as he quickly walked to his desk and wrote a few words on a piece of paper.

The Sanuri then stood in front of a window silently calling to the Enrops; soon several appeared. He gave one of the great birds the piece of paper, "Please give this to either Padre Thomas or Padre Bartholomew at the monastery in Malga and tell them it is of the upmost importance." The Sanuri turned back to Sudfad, "The Chalice of Ascension is hidden in the Hall of Antiquities. We need to bring it here."

"I agree," said Sudfad. "I will leave you to your studies." Sudfad stood up and started towards the door, then he turned back to the Sanuri. "There has been something I have been thinking about since Matthew's wedding."

"What concerns you?"

"Is it possible that either Sorren or Stephan could be the seventh son?"

"That has not been revealed to me yet," said the Sanuri. "But The Lion said we would know him because he would be bearing scars from his battles with the demons."

"So are you avoiding me or Ingr?" asked Matthew as he and Stephan inspected the troops.

"I am not avoiding anyone," Stephan replied coldly.

"You haven't been to the castle in weeks; in fact since we returned from Wetpr."

"I have been busy," Stephan said without looking at Matthew.

"Well, the King and Queen are wondering where their second son is; so I told them you would be coming over for dinner tonight," said Matthew with a grin.

"I know what you are trying to do," Stephan said with anger in his voice.

"Stephan I am telling you the truth, Mother, Father and Angelina have been asking about you. Angelina is wondering if you are staying away because we got married."

"No, it has nothing to do with Angelina."

"Great, we will see you at seven," Matthew said.

"Is he dead?" asked Sudfad as Raul and Simon walked into the study.

"Yes," said Simon.

"Father, Simon and I have been talking and you were right all along," said Raul. "We never would have gotten as much information from him because we were so angry. We are sorry that we doubted you."

"Thank you sons," said Sudfad. "But I wanted you to learn something from this too. You are excellent military generals but now you have a new role also as Keepers of the Scrolls and that is the priority. Both of you always question how events affect the security of our kingdom now you must also question how they could be related to the holy items we protect."

"So the attack by the demon had to have been related to The Holy Scrolls," said Simon.

"Do you think that demon knows the vault is here?" asked Raul.

"I think that if the demons were certain of the vault's location we would have suffered many more attacks," Sudfad said. "But I also believe that the attack was somehow related to the vault. And I believe that is why the Sanuri made sure he was here; sometimes our weapons are not effective on creatures from other worlds, such as demons," said Sudfad.

"And how do you know this?" asked Raul.

"Stories for another time," said Sudfad with a grin. "Remember the Sanuri told us that Roch would keep trying to find The Scroll of Imari in the Caves of Muldun. Well, today the Sanuri told me that many holy objects and manuscripts are missing from the Hall of Antiquities at the monastery in Malga. Every gift from The Great Ruler has mysteries and powers that are not yet revealed to mankind. When some of these gifts are used in combination with others their combined powers are inconceivable. We need to be concerned whenever holy objects disappear."

"What would you have us do Father?" asked Raul.

"The Sanuri will tell us what needs to be done about the holy objects. Fortunately for us, the demon that Roch was working with has been banished to The Abyss; but there is nothing to prevent Roch from calling to other demons. I want the two of you to work on battle strategies. We must be prepared if we should be attacked by Rogetts, Hutas and Roch's men simultaneously."

"Well it is about time," said Mathas with a laugh as he handed Stephan a glass of whiskey.

"We've missed you," said Rosa as Stephan bent down and kissed her on the cheek.

"I am sorry, I have been busy."

"Well, remember to make time for your family," Rosa said with a sweet smile.

"Did Matthew tell you about the remodeling we are doing?" Mathas asked.

"No."

"We want him and Angelina to live here so we are remodeling one of the wings; like Sudfad and Renya did for their children. After dinner I will show you," said Mathas.

"Where is Matthew?" asked Rosa.

"Did I hear my name?" asked Matthew with a smile as he escorted both Angelina and Ingr into the parlor. Angelina was wearing a pink sleeveless gown with tiny straps and Ingr was wearing a light blue gown with only one strap that fit over her left shoulder. Stephan was in the process of taking a drink when they walked into the room; but instead he stood with the glass to his lips, staring at Ingr.

Ingr's heart leaped when she saw Stephan; she wanted to run up to him, but remained at Matthew's side.

"You both look beautiful," said Mathas. "Don't you agree Stephan?"

"Yes," Stephan said all the while staring at Ingr.

"Let's have a drink before dinner," Mathas suggested.

Matthew walked up to them and deliberately positioned the girls so that Ingr was standing next to Stephan; an act that did not go unnoticed by Stephan. Ingr looked up at Stephan and smiled shyly, his large muscular frame seemed to dwarf her. Ingr became very nervous and did not know what to say to him. As the others in the room talked, Ingr found herself just being conscious of Stephan's presence near her. Suddenly Stephan leaned down and whispered into Ingr's ear, "Do you want to take a walk?"

"We will be back," Stephan said as he led Ingr to the garden.

"They make such a handsome couple," Rosa said.

Stephan held Ingr's hand as they walked in the garden. "How have you been doing?"

"Well, they are very good to me here; but I do miss my mother and brothers and sisters."

"Ingr you can't go back home, at least not by yourself."

"Matthew told me what you said to my father."

"Are you angry?"

"No, I worried that he would try to sell the others too."

They stopped walking and faced each other. Stephan was overwhelmed with Ingr's beauty and passionately kissed her on the lips. Ingr put her arms around Stephan's neck and they held an embrace for several minutes, when he abruptly pushed her away.

"We have to talk," Stephan said gruffly. "Just because Matthew and Angelina knew they wanted to marry after a couple of weeks does not mean it is the same for us. Do you understand what I am trying to say?"

"I don't know," Ingr said hesitantly; her heart starting to sink within her chest.

"Ingr I don't know when I will be ready for marriage. Maybe I never will be."

"But Stephan we have never talked about marriage," Ingr said softly.

"I don't want you waiting around for me; it is not fair to you."

"What do you mean?" asked Ingr with tears starting to well in her eyes.

"We are not courting."

"I see," Ingr said with her voice trembling. She suddenly wanted to flee from Stephan. "Perhaps we should go back in." They walked back into the parlor without speaking. The tension between them was noticed by all in the room.

"Let's take our seats at the table," Rosa said, trying to be cheerful.

Mathas and Rosa each sat at opposite ends of the dining room table. Matthew and Angelina sat together and Rosa told Stephan and Ingr to sit together on the opposite side of the table. Barely had they taken their seats when Ingr looked at Mathas, "I am not feeling well may I be excused?"

"Of course dear."

Angelina saw that her friend looked like she was going to cry. "May I also be excused?" asked Angelina.

Mathas nodded and the two girls walked out of the dining room. All eyes were on Stephan and he felt compelled to explain why Ingr left. "I care about her, she is a sweet and beautiful girl; but Mathas I don't think I am ready to get married and I told her that."

"Has she talked to you about marriage?" Mathas asked.

"No, but I can tell by the way she looks at me."

"Stephan, you are a grown man, whether you marry that girl or not is your decision. But she is young and naïve. The entire time we were in Wetpr you never left her side, you didn't let her talk to other men. You swept her off her feet; then you saved her and now you want nothing to do with her. She is very confused. You at least owe it to her to try and explain what is happening," Mathas scolded.

"Actually I am not sure that I understand," Stephan said apologetically. "But you are right, which is her room?"

"The fourth door on the left at the top of the stairs," Matthew said.

Stephan stood before the door to Ingr's bedroom for several moments before he knocked. He could hear her crying. "Ingr, it is me, Stephan."

There was silence, then Ingr called through the door, "Please go away." Stephan waited for a few moments then he turned and started to walk towards the staircase. Ingr suddenly opened her door, "No, please wait."

Stephan turned around, "Is Angelina with you?"

"No, I sent her away. Do you want to come in?"

The two were standing in her doorway trying to decide what to say to each other, when Stephan saw a movement at Ingr's window. He grabbed Ingr and quickly moved her behind him and into the hallway. "Matthew we have intruders!" yelled Stephan as he grabbed his sword and ran towards the six creatures that were coming through the window.

The intruders wore the robes of priests but they were bright red. Their hoods were up and their faces where covered with white clay masks. The faces of the masks where contorted to look as monsters.

Ingr ran back into her room and grabbed her sword that was lying on a table along with her other weapons. She saw that Stephan was fighting with two of the intruders, the others looked at her. Ingr grabbed one of her knives and threw it, hitting one creature in the throat. The second knife landed between the eyes of one of the other monsters. Ingr saw that a third creature was behind Stephan and prepared to stab him in the back. Ingr flew across the bed and plunged her sword into the creature's back before he could stab Stephan.

Stephan killed the two creatures he was fighting with and he saw another starting to come through the window. Stephan thrust his sword through the neck of this creature and as it fell backwards Stephan looked out of the window and saw that more of these hideous beings were climbing up a long wooden ladder. Stephan pushed the ladder away from the castle wall. The ladder as well as the beings fell into the courtyard.

Stephan turned to his right and saw Ingr struggling with one of the creatures. She had dropped her sword; the creature had Ingr by the throat, choking the life from her. Ingr was hitting and kicking the monster but she could not break his hold on her. Stephan stabbed the creature in the back with his sword, then he threw it to the ground. "Are you alright?" Stephan asked fearfully when he saw blood on Ingr's torn gown.

"It is not my blood."

Stephan grabbed Ingr's hand and started to lead her out of the room. "Wait, my sword." Ingr retrieved her sword and the two started for the hallway. Matthew and Angelina were running up the stairs with swords.

"Mathas and Rosa?" asked Stephan.

"They are alright. The soldiers captured the ones who were on the ladder. Do you know who they are?" Matthew asked. The four walked back into Ingr's bedroom, which was covered in blood.

Stephan pulled a mask off one of the creatures, exposing a gnarled and disfigured face. "Are these human?" Stephan asked.

"I don't know, I have never seen anything like them," said Matthew as he pulled a mask off another of the dead bodies. I will send a description to the Sanuri, perhaps he can tell us?"

Stephan looked at Ingr and said, "Pack up some of your things; you will sleep in my room tonight."

It had taken Thaos almost a week before he found another man who had a connection to Usman. Tito was an arrogant young man who was consumed with proving that he was someone to be taken seriously. Night after night Tito would frequent the various taverns in Langer bragging about every fight he had ever been in and every woman he had ever had.

Thaos had found in his experiences that the kind of men who had to keep telling everyone they were fierce, usually weren't. Thaos often found these types of men to be insecure about themselves or just plain cowards; so he did not pay much attention to Tito at first. Then one night, Thaos overheard Tito bragging about how he helped Usman tear a traitor apart. This got Thaos' attention. Thaos had been sitting at a table and now walked up to the bar and stood next to Tito.

"I couldn't help but overhear you, I am curious how did you tear the traitor apart?" Thaos asked as he handed Tito a glass of whiskey.

"The way we do it in Usman's camp," Tito said arrogantly. "Is we tie each limb to a horse then start all of the horses running in different directions. Of course you don't want to be standing too close or you will get covered in blood and guts," Tito said with a laugh.

"So what did this man do that made him a traitor?"

"Why he told outsiders about Usman's camp."

"You mean like you are doing now," Thaos asked while giving Tito a cold stare.

Fear filled Tito's eyes. "Do you work for Usman?"

"No but I work for someone who wants to do business with Usman. Now you take a message to him or I will send him a message that you have been shooting off your mouth in every tavern in the city."

"But he might kill me if I give him a message," Tito said anxiously.

"Well, he will certainly kill you if you don't."

After the soldiers searched the grounds and the castle, the Royal Family of Lentz slowly gathered in the parlor. Six soldiers had stayed with Rosa and Margarit while the rest of the family joined in the search. "Are you alright my dear?" Mathas asked as he put his arm around Rosa.

"Yes dear, who attacked us?" Rosa asked.

"I saw them but I don't know what they are," Mathas said. "I don't even know if they are human."

"Matthew and Angelina are you alright?" Rosa asked fearfully when the two entered the room.

"Yes, they were all coming in through Ingr's window. The soldiers only found one ladder," Matthew said.

"Where are Ingr and Stephan?" Mathas asked apprehensively.

"They should be here soon," said Matthew. "Everything in her room is covered in blood; Stephan was helping her pack a few things."

"Do you think they were after Ingr?" Angelina asked.

"I don't know why they would be, but I am certainly glad the two of you girls were not in there alone," Matthew said as he put his arm around Angelina.

"So am I," said Stephan as he and Ingr entered the room.

"Ingr are you alright?" gasped Rosa when she saw Ingr's bloody and torn dress.

"Yes and I am sorry about the dress, it was so beautiful," said Ingr apologetically.

"My dear it is not the dress we are worried about," Mathas said. "And what is on your neck?"

Stephan gently examined Ingr's neck. "One of those creatures was choking her," Stephan explained. "I am afraid you are showing bruises," he said to Ingr. "She fought well," Stephan said with pride as he looked at Mathas and Matthew. "She saved my life."

"We saved each other," Ingr said humbly.

"We will get you a different room dear," Rosa said.

Stephan put his arm around Ingr, which surprised everyone. "She is staying in my room tonight. I don't want her to be alone if there is another attack."

"Father the soldiers tried getting information from those creatures but all of them have had their tongues cut out; so they can't speak," said Matthew.

"What!" exclaimed Mathas, then his voice was filled with sadness. "I suspect Juleta is behind this."

"Annabelle," called Simon as he walked into their living quarters. No one answered so he walked into the dining room. Simon smiled when he saw the table set for two with lit candles everywhere. He looked up as Annabelle walked into the room holding a glass of wine. She was wearing a low cut light pink dress with a high waste and small puff sleeves; small pink ribbons adorned her long curly black hair.

"Honey you look beautiful," said Simon.

Annabelle walked up to Simon smiling and handed him the glass of wine. "Laurel and Renya took the boys tonight."

"So we are alone," said Simon with a grin. He bent down and kissed Annabelle passionately on the lips. As they kissed Simon picked her up and started walking towards their bedroom.

272

"Simon there is more," said Annabelle excitedly. "Put me down for a moment."

When Simon set Annabelle on her feet she took his right hand and placed the palm against her stomach. "You are going to be a father again, my dear." Simon put both of his arms around Annabelle; hugging her tightly and kissed her on the lips. "Are you pleased?" asked Annabelle as she gazed up into his eyes.

"Do you remember the first time we made love?" asked Simon. "I told you that I wanted to grow old with you and have lots of babies, and I meant it. Yes I am very pleased."

Annabelle threw her arms around Simon's neck and they kissed in a long embrace. As they were kissing Simon rubbed her stomach with his hand. "How far along are you?"

"Well I am not really sure."

"What," Simon said in a kidding manner.

Annabelle tilted her head to the side and said, "Simon."

"What?" he asked laughing.

"We make love all the time how can I figure out which day," said Annabelle.

Simon laughed loudly, "What is your best guess?"

"Four months," replied Annabelle smiling.

Simon took Annabelle's hand. "Let's tell the family then we will come back here," he said with a proud grin. They walked hand in hand to the main dining room. The Royal Family had already started to eat their evening meal. "Sorry to interrupt," said Simon with a smile so big his face could barely contain it. "But we wanted to tell you our news. We are going to have another baby."

Everyone at the table was very pleased with the news and got out of their seats to hug Annabelle and Simon. "How far along are you dear?" asked Renya.

Annabelle gave Simon a look, as he started to laugh, "I think about four months; I am really hoping for a girl this time, said Annabelle excitedly.

As Renya hugged Annabelle; Sudfad asked, "And how about you son?"

"Oh, I don't care if it is a boy or a girl, I am just happy we are having another baby."

When everyone was done congratulating the young couple; Simon and Annabelle started to walk out of the dining room hand in hand. "So did Marie help you with the meal?" asked Simon smiling, as he was always kidding Annabelle about her cooking skills.

"Yes dear, I don't want to kill you," Annabelle said sweetly.

Ingr was surprised when she entered Stephan's room. It was sparsely furnished. There were many weapons on the walls and lying on the two tables in the room. "This looks like the room of a warrior," she thought. There was a large bed in the middle of the room, three chairs and a dresser.

"Where should I put this?" Ingr asked shyly. She was carrying a large basket which held many of the things from her room.

"You can just put it on a chair," Stephan said. "Would you like a glass of wine?"

"Yes, thank you. But first I really want to get out of this dress. Where can I change?"

Stephan pointed at a door, "There is a closet but you will have to keep the door ajar so you can see. Give me the knives in your basket and I will clean your weapons."

Ingr took her basket into the closet. She felt like crying but she didn't want to cry in front of Stephan. In fact Ingr wasn't sure she even wanted to be with Stephan; she felt very sad and confused. After struggling with the buttons on the back of her dress for several minutes Ingr called out, "Stephan would you help me, I can't get these buttons?"

When Ingr walked out of the closet she saw that Stephan was wearing only his trousers, he had removed his shirt and boots. Stephan put down the sword he was cleaning and walked up to her. Ingr turned her back to him and moved her long hair to the side. "You are awfully quiet; are you upset about the attack?"

"A little, I am more upset about our talk."

"I thought so," Stephan said as he worked on the many small buttons on the back of her dress. "After you change we will talk again."

Ingr was quiet for a few moments. Part of her was afraid of what Stephan was going to say. "Are we going back down stairs?" Ingr asked shyly.

"No, not unless you want to."

"I just didn't know if I should change into another dress or a nightgown," Ingr said uncomfortably.

"Put on a night gown," Stephan said as he struggled with the many tiny buttons on her dress. "How did you get into this dress?" he asked with a laugh.

"Angelina helped me. Stephan I didn't know you had a room here. You haven't been here in weeks. Have you not been coming home because I am here?" Ingr asked fearfully.

"I don't stay here all the time; my family has a home not far away." When Stephan finished unbuttoning Ingr's dress he opened the back of it, which exposed her bare back. Stephan gently ran his fingers down Ingr's spine, she trembled at his touch. Stephan put his hands inside of Ingr's dress and grasped her tiny waist as he kissed her shoulders, "Why don't you change now."

Ingr walked out of the closet wearing a beautiful light pink silk night gown with a plunging neckline. She felt so uncomfortable that part of her just wanted to run away. Stephan walked up to Ingr and handed her a glass of wine. Ingr took a sip then decided to drink most of the glass hoping it would give her the courage to say the words of her heart. Stephan laughed when he saw Ingr drinking the entire glass of wine. "Do you want another?" Stephan asked as he put Ingr's empty glass on the table.

275

"You have so many scars are they all from battle?" Ingr asked as she gently ran her fingers along a large scar on Stephan's chest, which was barely visible under his dark hair.

"Yes," Stephan said as he was leaning down to kiss Ingr but she suddenly backed up and started to cry. Ingr's words burst out of her. "Stephan, I don't know what I did to make you not want me anymore but I am really sorry and I won't do it again if you will but tell me."

"Honey, you didn't do anything wrong."

"Well, then I am even more confused. You kiss me and look at me like you care about me but then you push me away and say you don't want me, Stephan I just don't understand any of this. You told me not to wait for you but Stephan, Stephan I love you and I don't ever want to be with anyone else." The tears were running down Ingr's face. She stopped talking because she was starting to cry harder.

Stephan cradled Ingr's face in both of his hands. "Honey don't cry. I never said I didn't want you."

"That's what it sounded like."

"Ingr I love you too. I just didn't realize it until tonight when I saw that creature trying to kill you. The thought that I might lose you filled me with horror. I am sorry that I hurt you." Stephan leaned down and kissed Ingr softly on the lips. Ingr's lips quivered as she tried not to return Stephan's kiss. But he kissed her again and again until her passion for him overwhelmed her and she returned his kisses; pouring her heart into them.

They were both trembling and sweating when Stephan stopped kissing Ingr and stared into her eyes. "Ingr as much as I love you; I still don't think I am ready to get married."

"Stephan we don't have to get married, I just want to be with you," she whispered.

"So let's agree to take it slow," Stephan said as he gently kissed the side of Ingr's neck.

Ingr moaned as Stephan was kissing her neck, then her shoulder. "Yes," she said breathlessly. Suddenly Ingr felt like she was floating as Stephan picked her up and carried her to his bed.

After Simon and Annabelle left the dining room, Vitomas leaned over and whispered into Raul's ear. A large smile took over Raul's face. "Are you sure you want to get pregnant again so soon; Samuel is not very old?" Raul asked.

Vitomas blushed slightly as she looked around the table realizing everyone was now listening to their conversation. "I know it may sound a little crazy but Annabelle is convinced she is going to have a girl this time and well, we have been talking, one little girl and four boys; we want to have daughters together." Vitomas gave Raul an especially sweet smile, "So what do you think?" she asked.

"I think I will be coming home during the days," said Raul with a smile, then he leaned over and kissed Vitomas on the lips. Renya squeezed Sudfad's hand as they listen to the young couple talk.

Matthew got a mischievous grin on his face as he watched Stephan and Ingr walk into the dining room for breakfast, the morning after the attack. "We didn't think you were going to make it," Matthew said.

"Are we late?" Ingr asked with concern.

"No," said Stephan with a grin as he pulled Ingr's chair out for her. Mathas, Rosa, Margarit, Angelina and Matthew were all sitting in the same places they had sat the night before at dinner.

Matthew kept staring at Stephan and Ingr. "Ingr why are you blushing; I haven't even said anything yet."

"Matthew you don't have to," Ingr replied with an embarrassed smile.

"I was just going to say the two of you look like you've made up since last night," Matthew joked.

"Matthew," Rosa said in a scolding voice.

277

"Mother he deserves every bit of it," Matthew said. "So what happened?" Matthew asked as he looked at Stephan.

"Honestly I guess I didn't realize how much I cared about Ingr until I saw that creature trying to kill her," as Stephan said these words he squeezed Ingr's hand. "We talked last night and decided to take our relationship slowly."

"I see," said Matthew as he was looking at the smiles on their faces. "But there is a relationship?"

"Yes, Matthew not everyone gets married after knowing someone for two weeks," Stephan said sarcastically.

Angelina leaned over and kissed Matthew on the cheek, "Was it only two weeks dear?" she kidded.

Stephan turned to Mathas and Rosa, "We are going to move the rest of Ingr's things into my room, permanently."

Matthew started to choke on the coffee he was trying to swallow, "I thought you said you were taking it slow. Stephan you are just plain crazy when you are in love." Everyone laughed at Matthew's comment.

"Stephan your room is too small for both of you to live in," Rosa said. Then she turned to Mathas, "Mathas don't you think so?"

"Yes, after breakfast you two go upstairs and choose one of the larger living chambers, then I want you and Matthew to join us in the study for the morning meeting. We need to discuss the attack last night. I already sent a message to the Sanuri describing the creatures we have in the dungeons."

Since his return to Sudfad's castle the Sanuri had kept to his room, studying the manuscripts he brought from the monastery, his notes from his test and Glenda's diary. The Sanuri was feeling frustrated because the more he read the more questions he had. He was trying to figure out how Sporos could have power beyond The Abyss; this had never been heard of before. One thing the Sanuri had learned as an emissary of The Great Ruler; is that there are no coincidences. Sporos, the items missing from the Hall of Antiquities, the test and the diary they all had to be connected somehow; but he just couldn't see it.

"Sanuri," called Marie as she knocked on his door. "There is a soldier here with a message for you."

When the Sanuri walked into the hallway he saw Marie standing with a young soldier who was dressed in the uniform of the Military of Lentz. "My Lord, I was ordered by King Mathas to personally hand this to you."

"Thank you," said the Sanuri as he took the note and read it.

"My Lord, would you like me to take a note to the King?" asked the soldier.

"Just tell him that I am on my way."

Chapter XVIII
Demons in the Night

Claudius and Fahron had already joined Mathas in the King's study when Matthew, Stephan and Ingr entered the room.

"Father I would like you to meet Ingr," Stephan said as he held her hand. "Ingr this is my father Claudius."

Ingr curtsied and said, "It is nice to meet you My Lord."

"Ingr this is Fahron, he and my father are both chief advisors to the King."

Ingr also curtsied before Fahron, "It is nice to meet you also, My Lord."

Claudius was watching Stephan intently but he spoke to Ingr, "Ingr since you and my son are holding hands I will assume you are close friends. So in the future you don't have to be so formal with me or Fahron, a hug will do." Then Claudius laughed loudly when he saw the looks on both Stephan's and Ingr's faces. "Tell me are you the girl who was attacked by those monsters last night?"

"Yes."

"Why don't you sit down with us for a few minutes and you and Stephan tell us exactly what happened."

Stephan spoke first. "Ingr and I were standing in the open doorway of her room. She was facing the hallway and I was facing the window in her bedroom. We were in the doorway less than a minute when I saw three of those creatures climbing in through her window. I pushed her into the hallway and yelled to Matthew that there were intruders. By the time I got to the window three more creatures had entered the room. I started to fight with two of them and had my back to Ingr who ran back into the room and grabbed her weapons."

"Her weapons?" Fahron asked with surprise.

"Yes she is a warrior of the Nordes Tribe and a close friend of Angelina's," Matthew said proudly.

Stephan turned to Ingr, "Why don't you tell what you did."

"I had my weapons lying on a table next to my bed. When I ran into the room two of the creatures started to come towards me. I grabbed a knife and struck one in the throat and then the second between the eyes with my other knife. Then I saw one of the creatures about to stab Stephan in the back; so I ran across the bed and ran my sword through him."

"As soon as I pulled my sword out, one of them hit me in the back of the head. I couldn't see for a moment but I could feel him grabbing at my sword. We fought but he knocked my sword out of my hand and hit me a couple of times then he started to choke me. I kept hitting and kicking him but he would have killed me had not Stephan stabbed him."

"Show them your bruises," Stephan said. Ingr pulled the collar of her blouse down about an inch and exposed black and purple hand prints on her neck.

"Just after Ingr killed the creature that was going to stab me in the back, I killed the two I was fighting with. Another was coming through the window and I stabbed him in the neck. When I looked out the window I saw a ladder propped up against the side of the castle and maybe four more creatures climbing it. I pushed the ladder away from the wall and it fell to the courtyard, then I turned and saw that thing trying to kill Ingr."

"Stephan I know you are a great fighter but I must say I am impressed with how Ingr fought also," said Fahron.

"I think we all are," said Matthew.

"Do you think they were after Ingr?" Claudius asked.

"We don't know why they attacked," said Mathas.

"Ingr were you in your room before the attack and did you have candles lit?" Claudius asked. "I am just trying to figure out if they were watching you or if they just happened to enter a room with people in it."

"I was alone in my room with candles lit until Stephan knocked at the door."

"Did you hear or see anything unusual, try to remember?" Claudius asked.

Ingr looked at Stephan, then said "No."

"Father I had said some things to Ingr that I shouldn't have. She was in her room crying when I knocked at the door."

"I was lying on my bed crying, in fact I had my back to the window," said Ingr. "If they made any sounds I didn't hear them."

"Well I hope things are better between the two of you now," Claudius said. "Because you were both damn lucky you were together and you owe each other your lives." Claudius turned to Mathas and Fahron, "Do either of you have any more questions for Ingr?"

Mathas said, "No."

But Fahron asked, "I know you were in the midst of battle but did those creatures act like they were looking for anything?"

"No, once we all saw each other we just fought," Ingr replied.

"Ingr thank you and it was nice to meet you," Claudius said.

Stephan was sitting next to Ingr, "Why don't you and Angelina move our things and I will join you later."

After Ingr left the room Claudius turned to Stephan, "Is she the reason you have been acting like a madman since you returned from Wetpr?"

"Tell him," said Matthew with a grin. "Or I will. In fact let me tell it so your father really understands." Matthew faced Claudius, "Ingr and Stephan stood up for us in our wedding. From the moment Stephan met her, Stephan was with Ingr constantly. He wouldn't even let another man talk to Ingr. But and you may not believe this, Stephan was a perfect gentlemen. And I know this because they stayed with Angelina and me."

"Then just before we are coming home she crawls into his bed crying and tells him she doesn't want to return to Lentz because her father sold her to a man she didn't know. Stephan, Sorren and I went to her father and Stephan bought her and scared the hell out of the old drunk."

"You bought her?" Claudius asked loudly.

"Sorren said it was the only way I could free her," Stephan said. "Matthew said Ingr could live with them, so that was the plan."

"Then we come home and Stephan won't come near any of us for weeks. Ingr is so in love with him that she could barely eat or sleep because she thought something might have happened to him. Then I tricked Stephan into coming here for dinner last night and within minutes he has her in tears."

"Stephan is this all true?" Claudius asked.

"Yes Father."

"You have been angry and moody ever since you returned and that is not like you at all. What has been going on?"

"I am not really sure I understand Father," Stephan said seriously. "I wanted her but I didn't want to settle down."

"Stephan you are a fool," Fahron said. "You do know most men would cut their arm off to have a girl like that love them."

"Believe me, I know. It wasn't until I saw that creature trying to kill Ingr that I realized how much I cared about her. So last night was the first time we made love and we are going to be staying together. Mathas just let us move into one of the larger chambers."

"You are going to be living with this girl and I am just meeting her now," Claudius said sternly. "You had better bring her home soon to meet your mother or neither of us will ever hear the end of this. In fact, bring her home for dinner tomorrow night. And we will move you to larger quarters for when you stay with us. Are you planning on marrying her?"

"I don't know yet. We agreed to take it slow."

"I see," said Claudius. "Actually I don't but we have discussed this matter enough for now. Mathas back to the attack. You said you sent a message to the Sanuri?"

"Yes, I thought he might be able to tell us what those creatures are. I think we are all thinking the same thing that Juleta sent them," said Mathas.

"But why would she send them after Ingr?" Matthew asked.

"Perhaps they really did just happen to enter a window where people were in the room," said Fahron. "They may have been coming here to kill all of you. Or perhaps Juleta has heard about Angelina; who would be your queen. If this is the case, Juleta could have sent them after Angelina but they got the wrong girl."

"Lazo, I hope you have good news for me," said Juleta.

"Well yes and no," Lazo replied as he took a seat in the parlor. "We have everything in place to attack the next gold shipment to Hadne next week."

"And what else," asked Juleta after Lazo paused.

"The attack on Stephan and the girl failed. My men said that all of the Demalogs were either killed or captured. The next morning Stephan and the girl were seen at your father's castle."

Lazo was shocked when Juleta screamed with rage and knocked over a chair. Then she grabbed a vase of flowers and threw it against the wall. "I want them dead, do you hear me? Dead!" Juleta screamed.

"Can I ask what is so important about Stephan and that girl, they aren't standing in your way for the throne?"

"I don't pay you to ask questions," Juleta screamed as she continued with her tantrum.

Lazo stood up and started walking towards the door. "Lazo, Stephan has rooms at both his father's castle and at my father's castle. I want him and his wife watched. I want to know where they are living."

Lazo left the room without speaking. "She is insane," he thought as he walked out of the castle.

"Stephan I am so nervous, what if your parents don't like me?" Ingr asked as they rode their horses to the castle of Stephan's parents. The castle of Claudius was almost a two hour ride west of the castle of King Mathas. The castle of Stephan's parents was located on the eastern shore of the River Shey and almost ten miles south of Tyger, home to Chief Sorren.

"Ingr don't worry they will love you; now we are going to be there in a few minutes, you will see it as we top this hill.

"Stephan that is your home?" Ingr asked as they looked down on a large castle. "You didn't tell me you lived in a castle. Now I am even more embarrassed that you saw my home."

"Ingr I don't care what kind of home you lived in. You saw the room I had at Matthew's; it was like a barracks and that is what my room here is like also."

Within minutes they were riding through the large wooden gate of the massive stone wall that surrounded the castle.

"My Lord, I can take your horses," said a soldier as soon as Stephan and Ingr stopped in front of the main door.

"Wait, I will help you," Stephan said to Ingr.

"I can get down myself; I ride all of the time."

"Not in those shoes and that dress," Stephan said as he lifted Ingr off her horse. "As soon as he set Ingr on her feet, Stephan kissed her on the lips, "Now don't worry so much; just enjoy yourself."

"I didn't know you had soldiers here," Ingr said as they were walking through the front door.

"Yes, most of the soldiers have barracks at Fort Langer, but there are also barracks at Matthew's, here and at Fahron's castle. We probably have close to one thousand men here."

285

"Stephan we are in here," Claudius called out; as he heard Stephan and Ingr talking in the entrance way.

Stephan and Ingr turned and entered a massive room. It had two large hearths. The room was filled with overstuffed chairs, sofas and tables all with ornately carved wood. Huge round iron candelabras hung from the ceilings. Claudius and a woman, who Ingr assumed was Stephan's mother, were seated in front of one of the hearths.

"You are early, good!" said Claudius as he stood up and walked towards them. "A hug Ingr," Claudius said with a laugh. After he hugged her, Claudius put his arm around Stephan's shoulder. "I haven't told your mother that you are living together. That will be up to you my son," Claudius said these words in a lower voice. Claudius was a massive man; large, muscular and rugged looking. He had gray curly hair and a large battle scar that ran the length of the left side of his face. He walked with the confidence of a great warrior.

"Ingr I would like you to meet my beautiful wife and Stephan's mother Bella."

Ingr curtsied before Bella, who stood up and said, "Nonsense just give me a hug." When Bella stood up she towered over Ingr although she was shorter than Claudius and Stephan. Bella had a large bone structure which seemed inconsistent with the soft features of her face. A beautiful woman she had the same raven black hair and gray eyes as Stephan.

"Stephan, she is such a tiny little thing and Claudius said she saved your life," Bella said in astonishment. Claudius handed everyone a glass of wine and they all sat around one of the great hearths.

"Yes Ingr is a warrior from the Nordes Tribe, as is Matthew's wife. They are very well trained," Stephan said with a proud smile.

"You finally bring a girl home, I should have guessed she would be a warrior," Bella said warmly.

By the time they sat for dinner, Ingr's fears and nervousness had subsided and she was sharing stories of the Nordes Tribe with Stephan's parents. Ingr wasn't sure how Stephan would act in front of his parents but he too seemed to become more comfortable as the night went on. Ingr found Stephan's parents charming. They both seemed sincere and loving and both Bella and Claudius loved to laugh. After dinner they returned to the large sitting room and talked and laughed late into the night.

Thaos felt no remorse when he found the remains of Tito's dismembered body dumped like the others. Thaos had not liked Tito from the beginning. "Three is enough," thought Thaos as he started to ride to Minges. "The witch will have to use her magic if she wants a meeting with Usman."

Thaos visited Jeb and Ryan almost daily. It had been a long time since Thaos had met anyone from his past and it gave him comfort to spend time with Jeb and Ryan. Thaos was very fond of Jeb; Thaos felt that Jeb had more life in him than most men half his age. Jeb enjoyed Thaos' company and soon started to think of him as another grandson. Ryan looked at Thaos as the big brother he never had.

On his own since the age of nine, Thaos had learned to shut down his feelings in order to survive. Thaos buried his entire family by himself. Thaos buried everyone he had ever cared about. And to survive that nine year old boy buried his emotions that same day. Thaos was good at his job because he never cared about anyone. Thaos was good at his job because he had nothing to live for.

"It is getting late, why don't the two of you just stay here tonight?" Bella offered. "I will get a room ready for Ingr."

Stephan paused for a moment then said, "Mother that is alright, she will stay in my room."

"I see," replied Bella hesitantly.

Stephan decided it was time to speak with his mother so he turned to Ingr, "My room is just down the hallway, I will show you." They walked just a short distance down a hallway that led off the front entrance. Stephan opened the door and lit several candles. "I will be right back; I want to talk to mother. Why don't you get ready for bed?" Stephan kissed Ingr on the cheek and left the room, closing the door behind him.

Ingr looked around at the weapons and shields that decorated all of the walls. Like his room at Mathas' castle; this room was also sparsely decorated. There were three tables that all contained neatly displayed weapons. There were two simple chairs and a dresser. The large bed near the wall was unmade with blankets piled on it. Ingr walked to the bed and sat on the edge. As she started to remove one shoe she felt movement in the bed.

Ingr stood up and walked to the closest table and picked up a sword. She stood near the table for several moments watching something move under the blankets. Ingr walked quietly to the bed and lifted an end of the blanket with the tip of her sword. Suddenly Ingr heard hissing and she jumped back as a huge red snake lunged at her. Ingr swung her sword and sliced the head off the snake as it was coming at her. She ran to the door, opening it and yelled, "Stephan, Stephan come quickly."

Stephan and Claudius both jumped out of their chairs and ran down the hallway with Stephan in the lead. Bella walked quickly behind them. Stephan instinctively grabbed Ingr and pulled her behind him. "Are you alright?" Stephan asked as he and Claudius stared at the eight foot snake in his room. Stephan walked over to the head of the snake which was lying on the floor and oozing a black sticky substance. The rest of the snake's body was draped across his bed.

"Stephan it was under your blankets," Ingr said. "That is the same snake that Matthew described as trying to attack his father. He said the snake was created by dark magics."

"Ingr is right, I was with Mathas that day," Claudius said as he walked around Stephan's room.

Suddenly they heard a gasp in the hallway. Claudius quickly walked out of the room and put his arm around Bella. "Why don't you go back to the sitting room dear? We will take care of this." Bella turned and walked back down the hallway.

Stephan took the sword out of Ingr's hand and examined the black tar-like substance on it, "Do you think this is blood?"

"I have my suspicions about what is going on here," Claudius said solemnly.

"Father what do you think it is?"

Claudius glanced at Ingr and said, "We will discuss this matter at the meeting tomorrow morning. But for tonight I want you and Ingr to stay in one of the rooms in the center of the castle; those rooms do not have windows. I will put a guard outside of the door. And I don't want either of you left alone for any reason. Do you understand?"

Ingr nodded and Stephan asked, "Father do you think that is really necessary?"

"If my suspicions are true, it may be."

"Stephan, I didn't bring any of my weapons," Ingr said as she walked to the tables in his room.

Claudius and Stephan smiled as they watched Ingr carefully choose three knives, a dagger and a sword. "I like this girl," Claudius whispered to Stephan.

"Stephan can I take these?"

"Yes," he replied with a grin.

Outside the walls of Claudius' castle; hidden in the darkness of the night, two beasts from hell chanted in an ancient language, rarely heard in the world of man.

Chapter XIX
Conspiring

After breakfast the next morning, Claudius, Stephan and Ingr rode to Mathas' castle. They joined Mathas, Fahron and Matthew in the King's study, where they met every morning. Claudius turned to Ingr, "Find Angelina and stay with her. I don't want either of you girls to leave this castle until after this meeting; then your husbands will tell you what you should do?"

"Are the girls in danger?" Matthew asked quickly.

"There was another attack last night," Claudius said then he turned back to Ingr. "You did well last night, I am proud of you but do not let your guard down; now go and find Angelina and tell her what happened."

"Yes Claudius," Ingr said as she turned towards the door. But Stephan stopped Ingr and kissed her before she left the room.

After the door closed Claudius turned to the others. "Last night Ingr was alone in Stephan's bedroom. She discovered a giant red snake under his blankets and killed it as it lunged at her. I will say that girl has fast reflexes. But Mathas it was the same type of snake that tried to attack you."

"So Juleta sent it," Matthew said with disgust.

"But why is she targeting Stephan and Ingr and not Mathas?" Fahron asked.

"Well, I have been thinking about that," Claudius said as he poured himself a cup of coffee. "Remember how we all used to tease Stephan because Juleta had a crush on him? I believe she has spies here and has found out that Stephan has taken a wife."

"You think she is jealous?" Stephan asked incredulously.

"I think she is furious," replied Claudius. "And if she knows about Ingr she probably knows about Angelina. Didn't you say that Juleta said she would never let anyone else be the Queen but her?"

"Stephan I have to ask," Fahron said. "Did you ever, well, spend time with Juleta?"

Stephan looked at Mathas and Matthew, "I do not want to hurt or anger either of you. But Matthew already knows how I feel about Juleta. Although she is a handsome woman, her temperament has always been so hateful that I never wanted anything to do with her."

"Sadly you speak the truth, son," said Mathas.

"Stephan the only place I have heard Ingr referred to as your wife, other than Claudius now saying it, was when you bought her. Sorren told Ingr's father you wanted her for your wife. I wonder if there are spies in Sorren's tribe. We should speak with him," Matthew said.

"I would not be surprised, if Juleta did not have all sorts of spies in this kingdom," Claudius said. "She is a very smart woman and now we are realizing how cunning she is."

"Fahron, so far your family has not been attacked but Juleta knows she has to kill all of us to get the throne. You too will need to take precautions," said Mathas. "And I am so sorry my dear friends that my child is putting your families in danger."

"So you are saying that you failed," Juleta said angrily.

"What I said was that three men were murdered trying to get your message to Usman. I think it is time you used some of your hocus pocus crap and get the message to him yourself."

"Don't mock me. I pay you good money."

"You don't pay me enough to have my limbs ripped out by running horses, which is how Usman greets strangers. Besides Usman has a small army, which will be of little use now that your father and the Nordes Tribe are united."

Juleta had been standing by the window with her back to Thaos; she quickly turned around, "What are you talking about?"

"Your brother married Sorren's daughter in Wetpr."

"What and you are just telling me now!" screamed Juleta.

"First of all I told you not to speak to me like I am your servant and secondly I told Lazo to tell you a couple of weeks ago."

"Lazo?"

"Yes, you know, the guy you are grooming to take my job," Thaos said sarcastically. "Well speak of the devil or should I say another devil," Thaos said with a grin as Lazo appeared in the doorway of the parlor.

"Lazo is it true that Thaos told you to tell me my brother had married the Princess of the Nordes Tribe?"

"Yes, I did tell ya but ya are so focused on Stephan; ya probably forgot."

"I would not forget something like that," Juleta snapped. "Why are you here anyways?"

"Bad news, the second attack did not work either."

"Are you sure?"

"Yes my men watched Stephan and the girl ride with his father to the King's castle the next morning."

"What are you talking about?" Thaos demanded.

"Stephan, the friend of Matthew has taken a wife and we have tried twice to kill them with dark magics," Lazo explained to Thaos. "But the magics don't seem to work so well," he added with a sneer.

"This Stephan is he the son of Claudius, one of your father's advisors?"

"Yes, why do you know him?" Juleta asked with surprise.

"I met him once. He seemed like a good man. So why are you trying to kill him?" Thaos asked.

Lazo started to laugh, "Because she is jealous that he took a wife. And a beauty she is too."

"Jealous, Juleta if you try to kill every man that turned you down, you would probably kill the whole damn kingdom," Thaos said with a laugh. Lazo laughed loudly at Thaos' comment.

Juleta was enraged that her two hired men were laughing at her. "I will not be talked to like that, you are both fired," she screamed and threw a glass at them. Both men continued to laugh as the glass flew past them and hit the floor.

"Fine," said Thaos. "Pay us and we will be gone."

Juleta marched out of the room, slamming the door behind her. "That woman is just crazy," Lazo said as he poured himself a drink. "And to think I was interested in her, why it just makes me shudder."

"Lazo, you were interested in the witch? Don't you know better?"

"What can I say," Lazo said with a loud laugh. "I am a lonely man."

"Juleta returned to the parlor and handed each man a large pouch of gold coins. "Count it," she said indignantly.

"Oh we will," Lazo said with a grin.

After the two men counted their money and finished their drinks they both stood up and started to walk out of the room.

"Wait, where are you going?" asked Juleta as she was starting to calm down.

"You just fired us, we are going to get our things and leave," Thaos said with disgust and walked out of the castle.

"So what is going on between you and Ingr," Matthew asked as he and Stephan rode to the lands of the Nordes Tribe.

"Honestly Matthew I don't understand it myself," Stephan said. "When I am with her, I can't keep my hands off from her. I find myself wanting to take care of her and to protect her. And I haven't said anything to Ingr yet, but I have actually found myself thinking about children."

"Then when I am not with her; it is like I have this voice screaming in my head, 'What are you doing?'"

Matthew listened intently to his friend. "Stephan I can't say that I really understand what you are going through because I knew I wanted Angelina to be my wife almost from the beginning. But you have to know that Ingr is perfect for you."

"I know, I think that is what scares me."

"Well I hope you decide what you want soon," Matthew said with a grin. "Angelina and I are working on a baby and you know it is going to need a playmate." Both men laughed as they entered the lands of the Nordes Tribe.

"Well, I was just thinking about you," Sorren said happily as Matthew and Stephan dismounted in front of his house. Sorren clasped hands with the two young men.

"First father wants to know if you and the family can have dinner at the castle on Sunday," Matthew said as he looked at the faces of the people who were gathering around them.

"Certainly, what time?" Sorren said as he noticed how Matthew and Stephan were looking around.

"He said about seven."

"Come on in boys, Shara will be glad to see you."

The three men entered Sorren's house and took seats at the dining room table. "You are acting strangely, what is going on?" Sorren asked.

"Before we get into that I wanted to tell you not to be a stranger," Matthew said. "You, Shara and the boys are welcome at the castle anytime. Angelina misses her family and well, I may not let her ride here by herself for a while."

"Matthew what is this about?" Sorren asked.

Shara brought coffee and biscuits to the men as Matthew and Stephan told Sorren about the two attacks. "So you think there is a spy here, among us?" Sorren asked.

"Our fathers think there are many spies throughout the kingdom," Stephan answered. "But the only time Ingr was referred to as my wife was the day we spoke with Thaddies. And my father thinks the attacks have been aimed at me and Ingr because Juleta is jealous that Ingr and I are together."

"Why would she be jealous?"

"Juleta has had feelings for Stephan since they were children," Matthew explained. "I used to tease him about her."

"And there has never been anything between you and Juleta?" Sorren asked.

"No, I can't stand the woman," Stephan said. "No disrespect Matthew," he added with a grin.

"I can't stand her either and she is my sister," Matthew said seriously. "Sorren, we believe Juleta has been trying to start conflict between the tribes and the King. She may become very angry if she learns our peoples have been united through our marriage. I cannot say that Juleta may not try to attack your tribe as well."

Cerephus walked into Roch's war room. "My Lord, Tendas has returned from Wetpr."

"Only Tendas?" asked Roch. "Bring him in."

Cerephus walked into the hallway then returned with a soldier whose appearance was unkempt and his clothing was torn. "My Lord," said Tendas with shock at Roch's horrid appearance.

"Tell me what happened," demanded Roch. "And why have you been gone so long?"

"We found the jeweler; I stood watch on the street while the others worked him over," Tendas said. "He said that Vitomas sold him the necklace. Afterwards we went to a place to eat and heard a woman talking about the pastries she was making for the Princesses. As we listened we heard that the Princesses go into Salar every Tuesday morning to go shopping. So we stayed in town until the next Tuesday." Tendas looked at Roch fearfully.

"Go on," ordered Roch.

"Sure enough, Tuesday morning we see Annabelle and Vitomas riding into Salar in a small boca. Thatus told me to hold the horses and he and the others followed the girls into the General Store. Pretty soon Thatus comes running out with Vitomas. He throws her over the top of his horse and yells at me to ride.

We were riding out of town when I heard yelling; I turned around and saw a mob of people pulling Thatus off his horse. I did not see the others. I turned and rode towards Thatus and some guys pulled me off my horse and beat the hell out of me. When I regained consciousness, I found my horse and stayed near Salar to find the others."

"Tendas why are you acting so strangely?" asked Roch.

Tendas hesitated for a moment then said. "I watched Thatus as he threw Vitomas over his horse and she was very much pregnant."

Roch did not say anything for a moment. "Continue," he said through clenched teeth.

"Everyone in the city was talking about what had happened for days," said Tendas. "You are never going to believe this. When Thatus grabbed Vitomas, Annabelle was left in the store with Zacks and Thomas. Everyone was talking about how Annabelle grabbed a sword and killed both of them."

"What?" screamed Roch. "Are you sure, little Annabelle?"

"They said her husband, Prince Simon, taught her how to use a sword. After Annabelle killed those two, she ran into the street screaming, that is when the people grabbed Thatus."

"Where is Thatus?" asked Cerephus.

"I stayed in Salar trying to find him. I heard that Sudfad's sons had taken him to the dungeons at Fort Salar."

"Did you hear anything else?" asked Roch.

"Only the people talking about Vitomas and Annabelle."

"Tell me what they said," Roch demanded.

"The people in Salar love those girls. I heard that Annabelle has twin boys about a year old and that Vitomas has a son about the same age and they all live in Sudfad's castle." Roch did not say anything for Demetries had already given him this information. But the anger rose in Roch every time he thought about Vitomas giving Raul a son.

"My Lord, one thing that might interest you, every time the family has any type of celebration, they open the celebrations up to the people of Salar," said Tendas.

"What kind of celebrations?" asked Roch.

"The weddings, the christenings, people were preparing for the kids birthdays."

"Really," said Roch with amazement.

"So why did it take you so long to get back here?" asked Cerephus.

"I could not figure out how to help Thatus so I started a fight and the soldiers threw me into the dungeons," Tendas said. "But I never did find him."

"That will be all Tendas."

"Yes My Lord."

As Tendas was leaving the room Roch called out. "Tendas if you remember anything else; come and tell me."

"Yes My Lord."

"It is inconceivable that Annabelle could be that good with a sword," said Cerephus in disbelief.

"Or our men that bad," replied Roch. Roch was quiet for a few moments. "Raul and Simon will have killed Thatus by now."

"Are you sure?" asked Cerephus.

"Wouldn't you if someone tried to take your wife?"

"Thatus would not have told them anything, My Lord."

"I know," said Roch. "Thatus was a good man."

Sorren decided to accompany Matthew and Stephan back to Mathas' castle. "Do you think Thaddies could be a spy?" Matthew asked.

"He is not smart enough," Sorren said sarcastically. "But he would tell anything or do anything for the price of a drink."

"Sorren the girls will be glad to see you; I think they both miss their tribe," Matthew said.

"Shara and I both have noticed how quiet it is with Angelina gone."

"Not to change the subject, but how much of a threat is Usman and the Valdore Tribe," Stephan asked.

"Usman is my age now but time has not tempered his hatred or his ambitions," Sorren said. "At one time Usman tried to overthrow the King and take the throne."

"I didn't know that," Matthew said.

"Yes but his warriors were no match for the King's army. After the last big battle they fought, Usman and his men retreated to their lands and for the most part have stayed there. Usman is an evil, dangerous man. He kills all strangers who come onto his land. I have even heard that he kills his own people if they talk about the tribe to outsiders," Sorren said.

"So then no one really knows the size of the army he has now?" Stephan asked.

"That is right," Sorren said as the three men dismounted in front of Mathas' castle. When they walked into Mathas' study they found the Sanuri had joined Mathas, Claudius and Fahron.

"Come in," said Mathas. "The Sanuri decided to pay us a visit. He was just about to explain what those creatures are that attacked the castle."

298

"From your description they sound like Demalogs. They are considered an inferior species of demons. They have low intelligence and are used by other demons and dark lords, much in the same way that you might use a guard dog or attack dog. I want to see them after this meeting. I know they have no tongues but I might still be able to communicate with them."

"So you are saying they were sent here by a demon or dark lord?" Mathas asked.

"Yes and the Demalogs aren't smart enough to devise their own plans so it was likely you had other visitors outside of your castle that night."

"Do you think Juleta was here?" Fahron asked.

"She probably sent some of her men to handle the Demalogs," the Sanuri replied.

Roch poured himself another glass of whiskey after Cerephus and Tendas left his war room. Roch was drinking more and more but nothing would dull his pain. He threw his glass against the wall, breaking it; then he poured himself another drink.

"If Demetries could control the Rogetts and Hutas, then there have to be other demons that can do the same thing," thought Roch as he paced in his war room. "I have to find another demon." Roch started to laugh loudly at his own thoughts. "I have to find another demon," he said out loud. Roch stopped laughing and became filled with rage.

"How I hate that family," Roch screamed and overturned the table. Roch picked up a chair and threw it against the wall. "Damn her, all those years and she never gave me a damn son," screamed Roch.

Thaos was in his room packing and changing his clothes when he heard his door open. Before Juleta entered the room, Thaos had a knife to her throat. When he realized who the intruder was, Thaos lowered his knife and walked back to his bed, where he was putting clothing into his saddlebags. Thaos ignored Juleta, who stood silent for several minutes.

Thaos was not wearing a shirt. Juleta watched him as he was packing. She admired his muscular build. "Where did you get all of those scars?" Juleta asked.

"That is none of your business," Thaos replied calmly. "Now either tell me what you want or leave."

"I want you to stay; I changed my mind about you and Lazo; I want you both to stay." Thaos did not respond; he kept packing. "So what is your answer?"

"I am thinking about it," Thaos said without turning around.

"Ok what do you want?" Juleta asked impatiently. "Do you want more money?"

"Yes," said Thaos as he turned and faced Juleta.

"Very well, you will get an extra pouch of gold coins every week," Juleta said as she turned to leave.

"I am not done," Thaos said. "I want to be apprised of all the missions you have going."

"That is not your business," Juleta said resentfully.

"You are an amateur and amateurs get people killed. It may be more dangerous to work with you than against you."

"I still don't think you need to know everything."

"You hired me because I am very good at what I do. Tell me Juleta have any of the attacks you planned been successful?"

"Very well," she said angrily and turned to leave.

"One more thing Juleta, don't ever come into my room again." Juleta slammed the door behind her.

Cerephus walked up to Sophie as she was carrying a large basket of broken glass out of Roch's war room. "Did something happen?" Cerephus asked.

Sophie looked around to make sure no one was listening before she spoke, "My Lord I am so worried about King Roch. He drinks so much now. Why he was talking to himself when I took his food in to him. He never leaves his war room anymore. He even sleeps in there now."

"Did he break all of these things?"

"Yes, My Lord, but..." Sophie did not finish her sentence.

"But what Sophie?"

"I thought he was just throwing things at the walls because he was angry. But, well, listen to him yourself. I think he is throwing things at imaginary people."

All the men who were in Mathas' study accompanied the Sanuri to the dungeons after the meeting. Two soldiers met them at the front gate and escorted the group to the four small cells that contained the Demalogs. Each demon was alone in a cell. One of the Demalogs flew against the bars and made a hissing sound when the group approached. But when the Sanuri walked up to the bars the demon backed away and sat down in a corner.

The Sanuri studied all four of the demons for several moments. Then he told the soldiers to open one of the doors. The Sanuri walked into the cell and told the soldier to lock the door behind him. The demon lunged at the Sanuri, who knocked it to the ground. The demon stared at the Sanuri for a few seconds then started to crawl backwards to get away from him.

"The demon acts like it is afraid of the Sanuri," Sorren said with disbelief.

The Sanuri reached down and effortlessly pulled the demon to its feet. Then the Sanuri placed both of his hands tightly on the demon's head and stared into its eyes. The demon tried to struggle but appeared powerless in the Sanuri's hands. The Sanuri saw flames and heard cries but did not understand exactly what he was seeing. Then the Sanuri saw an image of Juleta surrounded by the faces of demons. He recognized the faces of Sporos and Stolas but did not know the other demons. Suddenly the images were gone and the Demalog slumped to the floor.

"Is he dead?" asked Claudius.

"Yes," said the Sanuri who was very disturbed. "And I don't know why."

"You mean you didn't kill it?" Fahron asked.

"No but a powerful demon might have to prevent me from getting more information," said the Sanuri. "Guard, please open the door and let me into the next cell."

When the Sanuri walked into the second cell, the demon crouched on his hands and knees like an animal. It watched the Sanuri carefully, then it struck. Just as the Demalog was about to grasp the Sanuri's neck, he grabbed it in mid-air. The Sanuri held the monster with one hand and placed this other hand over the creature's head; after a moment it acted as if in a trance.

The Sanuri then set the demon on the ground and put both of his hands on the Demalog's head. Once again the Sanuri saw flames shooting into a black sky and heard cries. Then he saw images of Ingr and Stephan walking together in a garden. She was wearing a blue dress that only had one strap. This image faded into darkness. The Sanuri readjusted his hands on the creatures head before he realized that the demon was dead.

When the Sanuri walked into the next two cells he found both of the Demalogs dead. "What sort of madness is this?" asked Sorren.

"Something was stopping me," the Sanuri said. "Mathas we should return to your study."

"Vitomas," called Raul as he entered their living quarters.

"You could make it home," said Vitomas happily as she met Raul at the door. "Abigail is here helping with the boys. Why are you smiling like that?"

"I have something for you," said Raul as he handed her a box.

"What is this for?" asked Vitomas with surprise.

"I don't think you know how much I love you," said Raul as he put his arms around Vitomas.

"Honey you show me all the time," said Vitomas as she kissed Raul on the lips.

"Open it."

"Raul," said Vitomas as tears came to her eyes. "This is so beautiful."

"If you don't like it I can get something else."

"I love it, I don't want anything else, said Vitomas as she held up a golden chain that held a very large tear shaped diamond pendant. "Help me put it on," said Vitomas as she handed Raul the necklace. Vitomas used both hands to hold up her long hair as Raul clasped the necklace around her neck. Then she ran to a mirror in the parlor.

"It is so beautiful, I am never taking it off," said Vitomas.

"You told me once you did not like large necklaces," said Raul as he smiled.

"I cannot believe you remembered that," said Vitomas thoughtfully. "Didn't I tell you that the first day I talked with you, after you were injured?"

"Yes," said Raul as he pulled her close to him. "I did not remember you finding me lying in that ditch. I woke up in Roch's castle and did not have any idea where I was or how I had gotten there. Then you walked into the room with fresh water and towels and I thought 'If she is not an angel she is the most beautiful woman I have ever seen.'"

"I remember that, I was so excited that you were awake," said Vitomas. "Honey you were so badly injured, I was so scared for you."

"We talked for hours that day," said Raul. "I remember thinking you were the most charming creature I had ever met."

"I was so fascinated by the stories about your travels," said Vitomas. "I don't think I ever told you how attracted I was to you from the beginning. And all of those days and nights of caring for you and bathing you because your fever was so high; well, my feelings for you grew stronger even though I had hardly spoken to you, I know that sounds crazy. Then when your fever broke and you could carry on a conversation I was afraid you would be able to tell how attracted I was to you," Vitomas said with a coy smile.

"You were wearing a blue and purple dress and you had on lots of jewelry, I commented about it because I had no idea if you were a servant or a queen. And you told me you hated the jewelry because it was so large and consuming that it was pompous. And I asked you why you wore it if you hated it and you did not answer."

"I still feel badly for how you found out about Roch," said Vitomas. Every time I would go into your room I planned to tell you but I just could not; I was so afraid of what you would think of me."

"I will tell you that day Sophie told me you were Roch's Queen; my heart broke," said Raul as he hugged Vitomas. "Looking back I think I fell in love with you that first day we talked."

"I was so afraid that Roch would be able to tell that we had feelings for each other and I was afraid he would kill you. When Roch said he was leaving for a trip, I was so relieved. I should have guessed he would have someone else kill you. I just did not think he would have the physician poison you until you got so sick again," said Vitomas with tears in her eyes.

"Honey it's alright, look how wonderfully everything has turned out," said Raul as he cradled her in his arms.

Vitomas smiled, then looking up into Raul's face she asked, "So could you tell how attracted I was to you?"

"Oh yeah," said Raul with a laugh. Then he picked Vitomas up and carried her into their bedroom.

304

After Juleta left Thaos' room he put on a shirt and walked out of the door. All of Juleta's hired men lived on the castle grounds; they stayed in the buildings that had been used as guest quarters or servant's quarters by the former owner. The men had turned the largest room into a makeshift tavern, where they drank and played cards. They named the room *The Witches Den* as a joke about Juleta, who was unaware of the name.

Thaos found Lazo sitting at a table in The Witches Den and watching four other men play cards. Thaos bought a bottle of whiskey and grabbed two glasses; then he slid into the seat next to Lazo. "Can you believe her?" Thaos asked as he filled the two glasses with whiskey. Thaos did not like Lazo or trust him but he wanted information. As the day wore on, Thaos kept filling Lazo's glass while pretending to drink from his own.

Their conversation stopped when Lazo passed out from the whiskey. Lazo's head dropped and hit the wooden table hard. Thaos left The Witches Den and walked back to his room. "Lazo is really going to have a headache tomorrow," Thaos thought to himself with a laugh.

After the Sanuri told the men of the things that he had seen in the minds of the Demalogs, they walked into the main dining room of Mathas' castle for a late lunch. Rosa, Margarit, Angelina and Ingr were already seated at the table.

"Father," said Angelina happily as she got up and gave Sorren a hug. "Sit here, next to me," she said with delight.

"I told you she missed you Sorren," Matthew said with a smile as he sat on the other side of his wife.

Stephan walked over to Ingr and kissed her on the head before he sat down. She leaned over and kissed him on the lips, without saying anything. Claudius watched his son and Ingr.

"Sorren, I must say I am impressed with the way you have trained these girls, Ingr has fought bravely and skillfully during these attacks," Claudius said.

"All the children start the training usually when they are about ten. But Angelina here started at the age of seven. I couldn't keep her away from the games and training fields," Sorren said with pride. "When the children start to train they work in teams, Ingr and Angelina always made sure they were on the same team."

"Yes, we got great pleasure out of beating the boys," Angelina said with a laugh. "I would like to start training our children when they are young, if Matthew allows it," Angelina said as she smiled at her husband.

"That sounds like a great idea to me," said Matthew as he put several lamb chops on his plate.

"Stephan how about you and Ingr?" Claudius asked as he turned to his son.

Stephan smiled, "Well Father, Ingr and I have only been living together for a few days now; we really haven't talked about children yet. But if we do have children I would approve of them going through Sorren's training."

"Excellent," said Sorren with a huge grin. "I guess I hadn't really thought about grandchildren until now."

"Sanuri, we have not yet set a date for the big wedding ceremonies," Matthew said. "We would like you to perform the marriage again. But also, with everything that is going on, do you have any thoughts about the matter?"

"I think it would be the perfect time for Juleta to launch an attack," replied the Sanuri then he turned to Stephen. "Stephen I don't mean to meddle but are you and Ingr going to marry anytime soon?"

Stephan was surprised at the Sanuri's question. "We haven't discussed it, why?"

"Perhaps a double wedding ceremony, like Raul and Simon had would be enough to drive Juleta out of hiding. Instead of waiting around for her to kill off your families, I suggest you consider a trap. And I will be here to assist you if that is your plan," the Sanuri said to everyone at the table then he turned back to Stephan.

"Now if you and Ingr do not want to marry we can make it appear to be a wedding ceremony. It would seem that Juleta's jealousy over Ingr is causing her to take her eye off from Mathas' throne momentarily. We could use that to our advantage."

"Sanuri I have never thought of you as a warrior," Claudius said with a smile. "I like your idea."

"As do I," said Fahron.

"I am not so sure I want to put the girls in anymore danger than they already are," Matthew said.

"Honey we cannot live our lives in fear, I agree with the Sanuri," Angelina said.

Stephan turned to Ingr, "What do you think?"

Ingr smiled lovingly at Stephan then turned to the Sanuri, "How quickly can we do this?"

"You are too good to us," Jeb said as Thaos handed him a small bag of gold coins. "But I can't take this."

"Let's just say it is payment for all of the candy you used to give me," Thaos said with a smile. "Where is Ryan?"

"He is still fishing. Can you stay for dinner?"

"Yes, I was looking forward to it," Thaos said as he sat down at the table. "Jeb you are the best cook in the kingdom," Thaos added with a laugh.

"Now boy, I have something for you," said Jeb as he walked into a back bedroom.

Thaos could hear Jeb rustling through things. "Do you need some help?" Thaos called.

"No, I found them. I forgot to give them to you the last time you were here. Its hell to get old and forget things all of the time," Jeb said with a chuckle. "These belonged to your father. He didn't have money for seed one year and he paid me with these." Jeb handed Thaos two simple golden rings.

"Were these my parent's wedding rings?" Thaos could barely choke the words out.

"Yes My Lord, you summoned me?" asked Cerephus.

"Cerephus take a seat, would you like a drink," offered Roch as he handed a glass of whiskey to Cerephus. Cerephus was reluctant to drink the whiskey since it was only sunrise; but he would not say no to Roch. "Cerephus I have been thinking, just because Demetries is gone, does not mean I want to give up my plans to attack Wetpr," said Roch as he paced back and forth in the war room. "Other than the Hutas, do you know of anyone who communicates with demons?"

"Well I suppose we could capture a Huta," said Cerephus. "My Lord may I speak freely?"

"Yes Cerephus."

"I know that Demetries offered you a lot, but I never believed he had your best interest at heart; are you sure you want to get involved with another demon?"

"Cerephus, above all you have always shown me your loyalty," said Roch. "But do not worry, I can control the demons," he said arrogantly.

"Thaos you've been gone for a week, do you have a woman stashed some place?" Juleta asked angrily.

"Well if I did, I certainly wouldn't tell you, you would probably try to have her killed," Thaos replied sarcastically. "Before we start fighting why don't you offer me a drink and I will tell you what information I have." Thaos' words got Juleta's interest. She poured Thaos a glass of whiskey and handed it to him with a smile.

"First of all Juleta, I don't torture people to get information. I have found I can get more accurate information by being friendly and talking with people, which by the way is something you should try once in a while." Thaos smiled and took a sip of his drink. "All of Langer is a buzz, can you guess why?"

"Matthew's public wedding ceremonies?"

"Oh better than that?"

"Tell me Thaos."

"First of all whoever told you that Stephan was married gave you the wrong information. They are living together but not yet married."

"How do you know this?"

"I have my sources," Thaos said. "The gossip among all of the shopkeepers in Langer is that Matthew and Stephan are going to have a double wedding ceremony like the Princes of Wetpr did."

"Do you know when?"

"From what I am hearing there is no set date yet because it is going to be on such a grand scale that the preparations may take a while. So Juleta are you happy about this because you look rather sad."

"Not that it is any of your business," Juleta said angrily. "I don't know how I feel."

Thaos leaned forward and stared into her eyes. "Juleta take it from me, you can never get your family back once they are gone. You might want to think twice about murdering yours."

"You almost seem sincere," Juleta said with surprise.

"I am."

Chapter XX
Revelations

"Where are you two?" Matthew called out.

"We are in the bedroom but you can't come in," Angelina yelled.

Matthew stood outside the door, "Why not?"

"We are trying on wedding dresses and it is bad luck for you to see me."

"Honey I think that only matters with the first wedding," Matthew said laughing and walked into the room. White dresses were draped over the bed and all of the chairs. Both Angelina and Ingr were standing in front of mirrors wearing wedding dresses.

"Rosa had the seamstresses bring us all these dresses because we have no idea what we like. What do you think?" Angelina said as she twirled around.

"I liked the one you wore for our garden wedding better."

"Matthew will you help us?" Ingr asked with frustration.

"I don't know," said Matthew with a laugh.

"If you do I will show you the hidden weapons sheaths I made," Ingr said with a coy smile.

Matthew walked over to the bed and examined dresses, then to the chairs and back to the bed. He chose two dresses, handing one to each girl, then he turned his back. Several minutes later Angelina told Matthew to turn around. Angelina and Ingr stared at each other and then at themselves in the mirror.

"You both look beautiful, those are the dresses you should wear," Matthew said.

"Matthew how did you do that, we have been in here for an hour and you picked out the perfect dresses right away?" Angelina asked in awe.

"Guess I spend more time looking at your bodies," he said with a grin.

Angelina was wearing a strapless dress with a full lace skirt. It was made of silk and covered with embroidery and pearls. Ingr's dress had tiny straps that were off the shoulder. It also was silk but considerably more form fitting with a narrow skirt. This dress too, was decorated with pearls and lace.

"Ingr you don't look very happy, you don't have to wear that dress," Matthew said.

"Oh Matthew the dress is beautiful, it's just, well, I wish I was really getting married," Ingr said sadly. "I mean I know that Angelina and I must be decoys to stop all of these attacks and I am fine with that."

"How are things with you and Stephan?" Matthew asked.

"Matthew, he is so good to me. And I love him so much," Ingr hesitated before continuing. "It's just that sometimes he seems so happy and content and other times he seems scared about us being together. And I am just so afraid he will disappear again."

"Have you talked to him about this?"

"No, I am afraid to. I mean we don't have to get married. I just want to be with him."

Matthew moved a pile of dresses and sat down on the bed. "Stephan and I have talked a little and you are right, he does get scared of the idea of settling down sometimes and he doesn't understand why. But he does care about you. I have never seen him act around another woman the way he acts with you. I think you just need to give him some time."

"I just don't want him to leave me again."

"I don't think you have to worry about that, but you should talk to him."

"Talk to him about what?" asked Stephan as he walked into the bedroom.

311

"Stephan get out, you can't see her in her wedding dress," Angelina scolded.

"Honey they aren't really getting married so it doesn't matter," Matthew said.

Ingr turned around and Stephan stopped and stared at her. "Matthew picked out the dress. Do you like it?"

"Turn around, while I catch my breath," Stephan said. "You look incredible." He walked up behind Ingr and slid his hands down the sides of her body. "And you feel great in this too," Stephan said before he kissed Ingr's neck.

"Ok, now show us what you made," Matthew said with a broad grin.

Both girls looked at each other and grinned, then they pulled their skirts up exposing their thighs. They both had leather straps fastened to each of their thighs. The straps held knife sheaths in place; so each girl was wearing two knives under her wedding dress. Both Matthew and Stephan laughed loudly. "I told you these women were dangerous," Stephan said.

"Thaos, son, you can't keep giving us money," Jeb said. "Why are you doing this?"

"I travel a lot for my job and I just want to be sure you will be alright if I have to leave."

"You know you never did tell us what kind of work you do," Jeb said.

"You might say that I am a jack of all trades," Thaos said with a laugh. Thaos was sitting at the kitchen table facing a window. He saw the slightest movement in darkness. "I will be right back," Thaos said and he walked out into the night. Thaos saw a man leaning against a tree near the house. As Thaos got closer he recognized the man as one of Juleta's hired fighters. "What are you doing here?" Thaos asked suspiciously as he looked around.

"It is just me," said Stiller. "Juleta wanted me to follow you and report back to her where you have been. I don't think it is any of her damn business which is why I am warning you."

"Are you the only one she has sent to spy on me?"

"As far as I know, but I know she sent Larson to follow Lazo and Larson told Lazo as I am telling you."

"Do you know why she is having us followed?"

"She didn't say, but she is plain crazy. The way I figure it she either doesn't trust you two or she is interested in you, either way you lose," Stiller said jokingly.

"Thanks for the warning," Thaos said as he handed Stiller some gold coins.

"Don't insult me, I don't want your money," Stiller said seriously. "But I think you should know what has been going on when you are gone. I think she is trying to hide some things from you, because she waits until you leave."

"Waits to do what?"

"She's had some of the men working on a room in the basement of the castle. She told them to build all kinds of strange things. Well, once things started coming together a couple of the men said it looked like a torture chamber. But what really got them was the altar she had them build."

"An altar?"

"Yes, but not the kind you will find in any monastery or temple."

"A witches' altar!"

"Do you think all that crap she keeps telling us about being a dark lord is true?"

"If it is she can't be a very good one because she fails at everything she does," Thaos said with disgust.

"There's more, she has been meeting with some strange men. I have seen the one there twice now. He is big; actually he kind of looks like you but with darker skin and without the eye patch."

"Thaos some of the boys and I have been talking. I know I promised you I would hire on but I don't like the witch and I don't want to get involved in any of her dark magics. There is about eight of us who are thinking of leaving."

"Can't say that I blame you, I have been thinking the same thing myself. Don't stay because of any promises you made to me."

"Thaos, me and the guys have been talking. We are wondering if she is bringing in new bosses to replace you and Lazo. If so, we think you are in danger because you know so much about her plans."

"I was just thinking the same thing. When you get back, tell her you followed me to Nates tavern. But wait a couple of hours before you go back," Thaos said seriously. "And Stiller you don't really know who you can trust there, be careful who you talk to. Don't tell anyone that you and Larson warned us."

At the Sanuri's request, Mathas invited the families of Fahron and Claudius to dinner on Sunday along with Sorren's family. Everyone was in the parlor before the meal was served. Mathas was taking the Sanuri around the room for introductions.

"Sanuri, this is my wife Isadore and my three children Timothy, Chaez and Tabeth," Fahron said as he proudly introduced his family. The Sanuri stopped and stared at Timothy which made Timothy very uneasy.

"What are you staring at?" Timothy snapped.

"Timothy don't be so disrespectful," Fahron said angrily. "The Sanuri is a holy man."

"Well look at the way he is looking at me," Timothy said defensively. "He is..."

Timothy did not finish his sentence because the Sanuri interrupted him. "Timothy there is a darkness to your soul that will bring shame upon this kingdom. Your family has no idea of your dark desires. You must change the path you are on."

Everyone in the room fell silent and stared at Timothy until he left the room. Matthew and Stephan did not like nor did they trust Timothy; now the Sanuri's words deepened their suspicions of Fahron's oldest son. After several moments Claudius spoke. "Sanuri this is my beautiful wife Bella," Claudius said.

"I am so very honored to meet you," Bella said humbly.

The Sanuri squeezed Bella's hands then he walked over to one of the open windows in the parlor and stood for a moment looking outside. "May I have everyone's attention please?" asked the Sanuri as he turned and faced the group again. "First I would like to say it is a pleasure to meet all of you and I am so glad you could come on such short notice. Now I would like to introduce you to some friends that I have invited." Four Enrops landed on the large window sill behind the Sanuri; he turned and introduced each bird by name, "This is Jatu, Napo, Jama and Arca."

"It is nice to meet you," Arca said to the amazement of everyone in the room but Matthew.

"These lovely creatures are called Enrops. They are often used as messengers by The Great Ruler. King Sudfad has given his kingdom as a sanctuary to this tribe; in return they are the eyes where mere men cannot see. They are highly intelligent beings and can speak in a variety of languages. Arca, Jama, Napo and Jatu have each led a flock of Enrops here. Each flock will be watching over one of your families."

"Arca this is King Mathas, you will watch over him and his family. I believe you already know Matthew and Angelina. Napo this is Claudius you will watch over his family, Jatu this is Fahron you will watch over his family and Jama this is Chief Sorren you will watch over his family. Please treat these Enrops as you would any warrior. If they give you information or a warning listen to them, do not discard their words."

"Matthew told us how these birds not only spied the terrorists at Raul's and Simon's weddings but the Enrops also saved the Princes by attacking the intruders," Mathas explained to the group as he was walking towards the birds that were sitting on the windowsill.

"I am proud to finally meet your kind," Mathas said genuinely to the Enrops. "Your tribe will always have sanctuary in the Kingdom of Lentz."

Cerephus knocked on the door to Roch's war room. "It is Cerephus."

"Come in," yelled Roch. When Cerephus entered the room he saw the table overturned and all of the chairs that usually surrounded the table were broken. There were small piles of broken glass on the floor as well as papers scattered around.

"Do you want a drink?" asked Roch.

"Thank you," replied Cerephus.

"Sorry, I guess there isn't any place to sit," said Roch and started to laugh. "I have run out of pain medications so I have to drink more. Not that any of it really helps." Roch started to get angry again. He threw his glass of whiskey against the wall then picked up another glass and filled it.

"My Lord what can I do to help you?"

"Find your friend Erebus. Where the hell does he go all of the time? I am not paying for him to travel."

"The reason he is travelling is because he is trying to find a cure for your affliction My Lord. He has been meeting with other sorcerers and witches. He has not abandoned you."

Roch appeared to visibly calm down as he listened to Cerephus speak. "I didn't know that, he never said anything to me. Cerephus if Erebus needs anything at all you let me know."

Mathas had asked all of his dinner guests to spend the night in the castle. As Rosa took everyone to their rooms, Claudius motioned for Stephan to come to him. "Son, I would like to talk with you, why don't you send Ingr to your chambers."

As he did every night, Stephan searched their chambers for any signs of intruders. "Honey father wants to speak with me, I don't know how long I will be," Stephan said and kissed Ingr.

"Do you want me to wait up for you?"

"That is up to you, but it is not necessary."

Stephan joined his father in the dining room. "Let's take a walk in the garden," Claudius said. "We will get a little air before we retire." The two men walked for several minutes before Claudius spoke, "Mathas told me that you offered to pay for half of the wedding preparations. I am your father I was planning on paying for it."

"But we aren't really getting married; this is just a ruse to get Juleta out in the open."

"Son do you know why your mother was so upset that first night that you brought Ingr home?"

"You mean besides the snake?"

"You know what I am talking about. Stephan you have been fiercely independent since you were a small child. Your mother and I learned that we just had to let you go on your own. Which doesn't mean we did not want to be more involved in your life. You finally bring a girl home to meet us then tell us you are already living as man and wife. You have to understand how your mother felt. Her only child and you excluded her from such an important part of your life. Things like weddings mean a lot to women."

"I didn't mean to hurt anyone; I guess I just didn't think, I am sorry Father."

"It is your mother that you should apologize to. You know son I do understand what you are going through and the things that I am about to tell you, go no further than us." Stephan looked at his father in surprise since they rarely talked about personal things.

"Your mother and I had a great deal of fun when we were courting. She loves to dance and we would attend many parties and celebrations."

"As you know Mathas, Fahron and I all got married around the same time. We had great celebrations. Shortly after our marriages we went to battle. The Hutas attacked from the south. Usman and his men took advantage of the situation and attacked from the north."

"Then after we won those battles we were attacked by those horrid creatures from across the Sea of Grevtd. You were born within the first year of our marriage. I was always gone and Bella was home alone raising a baby. That is why your mother, Rosa and Isadore are so close. They were all raising their children without husbands. I have never told your mother this but after months on the battlefield, I did not want to come home and handle the concerns of a household. I was young and certainly felt imprisoned at times."

"And your mother never said anything but I believe she felt imprisoned also, being left alone in a big castle with a baby. Those first years were difficult times for all the families here tonight. But ask Fahron or Mathas we would do it all again. Stephan you have always enjoyed the wild freedom of a warrior. But there is a completeness and a happiness that can only be found in a good marriage. It is normal to feel afraid when you are making changes to your life."

"Father I am surprised; we never talk of such things."

"Perhaps if we had sooner, you would not feel so conflicted about Ingr."

"You think I should marry her."

"I think you both love each other very much. I think she is an excellent wife for you. And I think that as long as we are paying for the wedding preparations you might as well take advantage of them. But my son you already know all of these things. You have to make your own decisions."

When Stephan returned to his chambers, he saw that Ingr had fallen asleep in her nightgown, in one of the chairs in the parlor. Stephan picked Ingr up and carried her to their bed. Ingr woke up as Stephan was carrying her and started to kiss his neck and chest.

Stephan laid Ingr on the bed, then he sat down next to her and began removing his boots. Ingr sat up and started kissing the back of Stephan's neck.

"So what was Matthew talking about this morning when he said that you should talk to me?" Ingr stopped kissing Stephan and moved away from him without saying anything. "Well this does not look good," Stephan said as he turned and looked at her.

"Stephan I don't want to talk about it."

"You talked about it with Matthew."

"I shouldn't have," Ingr said softly.

"Honey what is it?"

"Please don't get mad at me Stephan."

"Ingr just tell me."

"Stephan I am so happy with you but I am always afraid that you are going to leave me and disappear again."

Stephan stared at Ingr; of all the things he thought she might say, this was not one of them. Tears started to run down Ingr's cheeks as the two looked at each other in silence. Then Stephan put his arms around her. "Honey I am not going to leave you again."

"Stephan do you promise?"

Thaos returned to Juleta's castle but did not go to his room. He spent the next two days in the forest surrounding most of her castle. Juleta's castle was hidden deep within a thick old forest; only the west side of the castle was exposed and that was because it was on the bank of the River Toba.

Thaos was an experienced woodsman. He found several places where he could watch the castle without being seen. He also found two excellent hiding places.

The morning of the third day Thaos was going to return to the castle when he heard men's voices. Thaos followed the sound and saw six men riding towards the castle. And in the lead was a man who somewhat resembled Thaos. The men entered Juleta's castle and left about an hour later.

Thaos followed them to Sendra a village fifteen miles north of Juleta's castle. He watched as the men entered a small tavern on the main street of the village. Thaos checked their horses for markings then walked inside of the tavern and sat at a table in the corner of the room. He sat with his back against the wall, so he could not be attacked from behind and watched the men who were all standing at the bar, laughing and talking.

Not wanting to be conspicuous, Thaos ordered breakfast. The advantage to being in a small tavern during the morning hours was that although there were a lot of men eating, they were not loud and boisterous; so Thaos could easily hear the men at the bar. The six men looked exactly like the kind of men he would have hired for Juleta, hired fighters. The man who resembled Thaos was buying the drinks, finally he heard one of the men call his name, Hector. Thaos had not heard his name before.

As Thaos watched the men he found it curious that the leader did resemble him. Knowing Juleta, Thaos knew that was not a coincidence. He could only think of two reasons she would hire someone who could be his double; she was going to frame him for some act or perhaps she was attracted to men who looked like him. Both of these ideas were odious to Thaos.

Thaos listened as the men joked and bragged. He decided they were amateurs because they spoke too freely in front of others. Thaos knew if he listen long enough he would hear something of importance. Then, Hector said it; the statement that Thaos had been waiting for. Thaos left the tavern and rode out of Sendra.

"You know you are going to have to buy her a ring," Matthew said as he and Stephan were heading towards Langer for the morning inspection of the troops.

"A ring, I hadn't thought about that," Stephan said.

"If you want to make the wedding look real you will need an engagement ring and bands for each of you for the ceremony."

"Trust me if Juleta is in the crowd she will be looking at Ingr's hand to see what you bought her for a ring."

"Really?"

"Yes, and if you really want to make Juleta angry, buy Ingr a large beautiful stone," Matthew said with a laugh.

"Did you pick out the rings?"

"No, Angelina and I went shopping together in Wetpr and picked out the ones we liked." Stephan was silent for several moments. "Stephan if it concerns you, you only have to wear them for a day."

"You mean I should give Ingr a ring then tell her not to wear it, that doesn't sound like a good idea to me."

"What if she wears it, what will it hurt? I mean you are living together as man and wife."

"You are right."

"Stephan, Ingr will kill me if she knows I told you this, but she got really sad when she was trying on wedding dresses."

"Because she wants the wedding to be real?"

"Yes and I only told you because she might get that way when you give her the ring."

"I suppose that if we really want Juleta to believe this, I should give her an engagement ring soon so people can see it."

After everyone was seated at the dining room table, Renya asked, "Raul, Vitomas have you made any decisions about when you want Samuel christened?"

"He is still so little, I would like to wait another month or two," Vitomas said. "But we really haven't talked about it."

"Whatever you want is alright by me," Raul said.

"Raul that is because you are never involved with the planning," Renya said with a laugh. "I have an idea and tell me what you think. Petra will be ten in two months; I was thinking that perhaps we could have another big celebration for both events."

Petra's face lit up when he heard this. "Petra, would you mind sharing your birthday celebration with Samuel?" Sudfad asked.

"No," Petra said with excitement. "But he is too little to play with anything." Everyone at the table laughed at Petra's comment.

Raul looked at Vitomas who nodded. "That is fine with us," Raul said with a grin. "Mother I am beginning to think having grandchildren is just an excuse for you to throw celebrations."

Renya laughed, "I do love planning them." Then she turned to Sudfad. "Do you know when the Sanuri will return?"

"No, I think he is planning on staying with Mathas for a while because of the attacks."

After the morning inspection was completed Stephan and Matthew returned to Mathas' castle. They found Angelina and Ingr walking in one of the gardens. Angelina sweetly kissed Matthew then she complained. "We don't like feeling like prisoners here, we want to go riding."

"Well I was going to take Ingr riding now," Stephan said as he put his arm around her waist.

"Oh, Matthew can we go with them?"

"I think they need to go on their ride alone," Matthew said with a grin. "But I will take you someplace for a surprise."

Stephan did not tell Ingr why they were riding to Langer. They took their horses to a stable and walked hand in hand down the streets of Langer stopping in various stores and buying things. "Stephan this is so much fun, thank you," Ingr said and kissed him on the cheek.

"I am glad you are enjoying this. We will have to come here more often," Stephan said sincerely. "But we aren't done yet." They walked past a few more shops when Stephan stopped in front of a jeweler's. Ingr did not say anything as they walked into the shop.

The store was large and contained may items besides jewelry. "Why don't you look around, I will be right back," Stephan said then walked to the far end of the store. Ingr had never been in a jewelry store before. She was amazed at the different designs of the jewelry and the colors of the stones. Ingr was so engrossed in what she was looking at that she did not hear Stephan come up behind her.

"What do you think?" Stephan asked smiling.

"Stephan I have never seen such things before," Ingr said in awe.

"Come in the back room, I have something to show you," Stephan said as he took Ingr's hand and led her through some heavy black drapes that hung behind one of the counters. They entered a small parlor. There was a table in the middle of the room with a man sitting behind it. On top of the table were boxes of all varieties of jewels. Ingr and Stephan sat at the two chairs in front of the table.

"Stephan what are you doing?" Ingr asked hesitantly.

"We are picking out your engagement ring and the wedding rings."

Ingr searched Stephan's face but got no indications as to whether the rings were just for the diversion or if he really might ask her to marry him. She felt both happy and incredibly sad at the same time.

"What kind of stones do you like?" asked the man behind the table.

"I don't really know," Ingr said in a whisper.

The jeweler proceeded to show Ingr a variety of rings but she was so flooded with emotions and so overwhelmed that she wasn't really seeing them.

"I just don't know," Ingr said hesitantly. "Stephan what do you think?"

Stephan could clearly see that Ingr was overwhelmed. He picked up three rings and placed them in front of her. "These are my favorites but you need to pick out what you want to wear," he said.

Ingr looked at the three rings which all had large diamonds in the centers with different stones in designs around the diamonds. Stephan was watching Ingr's face closely and saw her eyes light up when she looked at a diamond ring that had small rubies on the sides of the large stone. "Try this on," Stephan said as he slipped the diamond and ruby ring onto her finger. Ingr's hands were trembling.

"Stephan it is so beautiful but..."

"But what?" he interrupted her. "Do you like it?"

"Oh yes."

"Do you want it?" Stephan asked with a smile.

Tears came to Ingr's eyes but she did not answer. Stephan turned to the smiling jeweler, "It is a little big; can you make this smaller?"

"Yes My Lord," the man said as he measured Ingr's finger.

"So we should probably have rubies and diamonds in the wedding bands," Stephan said.

"I will be right back with the wedding bands My Lord and in the meantime I will have one of my men work on this ring," the jeweler said and left Stephan and Ingr alone in the room.

"Are you alright?" Stephan asked.

"I don't know," Ingr said in a voice that was barely audible. "I guess I don't understand what we are doing here."

"Lazo have you seen Thaos lately?" Juleta asked angrily.

This was the first time that Lazo had been in the castle since Larson warned him that Juleta was having him followed. Larson had told Lazo that she was having Thaos followed also. "Can't say that I have," Lazo replied warily. "Is that why ya called me here?"

"No, there will be a shipment of gold ore from the mines in Ganz to Hadne tomorrow morning. The wagon is scheduled to leave the mines just after sunrise. They usually have six men accompany the shipments. I want you to take as many men as you want and steal that gold for me. Steal the entire wagon and bring it back here," Juleta said. "Do you have any questions?"

Lazo stared at Juleta as he did not trust her, "And ya are sure it will be only six men?"

"That is what they have had in the past but as I said take as many men for the job as you want. Just get me that gold, I need to have it now."

"Then I will have to choose the men and leave tonight," Lazo said skeptically.

"That would sound wise," Juleta replied.

Lazo walked out of the parlor with a sense of doom filling his being. He was not a superstitious man but he did trust his gut instincts. Lazo retrieved his items from his room and rode away from Juleta's castle, heading south to Port Friada.

Claudius sat in his study listening to the thunder and pouring rain. He didn't know why but he always liked storms. This night Claudius was enjoying a glass of fine whiskey and a pipe of good tobacco as he finished his paperwork, a job Claudius found tedious. An ambitious man, Claudius was often dismayed with how much paperwork replaced his sword as he rose in the ranks.

Claudius and Fahron were the King's main advisors; which meant they shared many of the King's responsibilities. Mathas did this deliberately so that both Claudius and Fahron would have a working knowledge of all the affairs of the kingdom in case he was killed. Claudius and Fahron would run the kingdom until Matthew became King.

It was Mathas' wish that if both he and Matthew were killed that Claudius would succeed him as King and if Claudius was killed Fahron would become King.

"My Lord, there is a man here to see you and Stephan, he says it is of the utmost importance," said a young soldier.

"Thank you and show him in then wake Stephan and have him join us."

The young soldier returned to the study with a large man who was wearing a rain poncho and a wide brimmed hat. "Thank you for seeing me at such a late hour," the man said as he removed his poncho. "I assure you that what I have to tell you is worth any inconvenience my visit may cause."

"Would you like a drink?" Claudius offered as he stood up and walked to the table which contained bottles of wine and whiskey and empty glasses.

"Thank you," the man said as he took a seat.

Claudius handed the man a glass of whiskey, "That soldier is waking Stephan, he will join us soon. What is your name?"

"Thaos."

"Thaos," Claudius said with surprise. "Aren't you the one who is working for Juleta?"

"I was. The reason I am here is that Stephan saved my life once. That is not something one forgets. I am here tonight to pay back the debt."

Both Claudius and Thaos stared at each other, trying to read the others face. "Interesting," Claudius said as he returned to his seat.

Thaos laughed. "You did not expect a hired fighter to have a sense of responsibilities?" Thaos asked as he took a sip of his whiskey.

Claudius smiled, he did not trust Thaos but there was something about the young man that Claudius liked. "I guess I didn't know what to expect son."

"The storm is too severe for any of Juleta's spies to have seen me come into your castle. You have no spies working for you on the inside."

Before Claudius could respond Stephan entered the room. "Son, you have a friend visiting. He said he came to pay back a debt he owes you."

Thaos turned in his chair so he could face Stephan. "Thaos," Stephan said with surprise.

"Stephan close the door and join us," Claudius said as he poured Stephan a drink.

"First, I know you don't trust me and I would feel the same way if the roles were reversed but you must hear what I have to say," Thaos explained. "About a year ago I was in Port Friada when I was approached by a man who said he was an advisor for King Fahra of Zorta. This man said he knew someone who was greatly in need of my services and he gave me a pouch of gold coins and said I would be paid well if I returned with him to Zorta. The man really is an advisor for the King, but it was Juleta's castle that he took me to."

"Why? Is he working for Juleta?" Stephan asked.

"No he is a very old and rich man who Juleta has sex with so he will give her money. Juleta told me she had many enemies and needed protection. She asked me to hire a small army for her. Then she wanted me to gather information and set up meetings for her. The people who hire me usually want me to fight for them against war lords or criminals. But Juleta made me suspicious from the beginning so I started to look up some of the people she calls enemies; like the Princesses of Wetpr."

"We heard of your encounter with them in Port Friada," Claudius said. "Raul and Simon said you warned them."

"I have killed more men than I can remember," Thaos said. "But I don't kill women and children; although I might make an exception for Juleta. I was getting information for her and when I returned to her castle I heard of the attacks against Stephan and his wife." Thaos turned to Stephan, "Juleta is trying to kill you because she is jealous. That woman is insane."

"Juleta recently started to have me and another of her hired men followed. I found out she has hired some other men and one of them looks remarkably like me. Which makes me suspicious; she may be crazy but she is cunning. I followed these men to a tavern in Sendra and listened to them talk. They said they were paid greatly to grab a girl. I don't know which girl they are talking about but it is most likely your wife."

"Did they say when they were going to do this?" Stephan asked.

"When I left Sendra to come here, they were still in the tavern so they will be close behind me."

The three men talked for about an hour before Claudius said. "I think we should gather everyone for a meeting and discuss this. I don't want to take a chance of any spies seeing Thaos so I will send soldiers to bring everyone here." As Claudius stood up he asked, "Thaos are you hungry?"

"I could eat."

"I will have the cook start an early breakfast." Claudius opened the door to his study and gave instructions to one of the soldiers.

"Father I am going to wake Ingr and have her join us," Stephan said with concern.

Chapter XXI
Laughter In the Darkness

Mathias, Matthew, Angelina and the Sanuri rode through the brutal storm to the castle of Claudius in the predawn hours. When they entered the front door, the housekeeper directed them to the dining room. "Something smells good," the Sanuri said as they walked into a banquet prepared for them.

"I am sorry to get you out on a night like this so I thought I should feed you," Claudius said with a laugh. "Please help yourselves, Fahron has not yet arrived." As they removed their rain ponchos and milled around the table, Stephan and Thaos walked into the dining room. "This is Thaos he is the man who has brought us information," Claudius said.

"But how can we trust him?" Mathas asked.

"You are the Sanuri are you not?" Thaos asked as he looked at the holy man.

The Sanuri smiled. "Yes."

"If even half of what I have heard about you is true, I believe you would be able to tell if I was lying. I heard a story once about you placing your hands on a Huta and getting information from him," Thaos said.

"That story is true and if you would permit me to place my hands on your head I would be able to tell if you are telling us the truth," the Sanuri said. "It will not hurt you."

Thaos walked up to the Sanuri with a grin and said, "I'm all yours." Just as the Sanuri placed his hands on Thaos head, Fahron walked into the dining room. Fahron started to speak but Mathas motioned for him to be quiet. Thaos and the Sanuri were about the same height; the Sanuri stared into Thaos' eyes seeing his life events.

After several minutes the Sanuri stepped away from Thaos. "This man speaks the truth, he is not our enemy. But what does concern me is what I saw in Juleta's castle through his eyes. She is trying to contact powerful demons."

329

"Let us all sit down and Thaos can relate his information," Claudius said.

"Ingr will be here in a minute Father," Stephan said. No sooner had he spoken the words when Ingr appeared in the doorway of the dining room wearing a leather dress. "This is much easier to fight in," Ingr said when she saw the look on Stephan's face.

"Ingr please come here," the Sanuri asked. Ingr walked up to the Sanuri and he gently touched her chin to tilt her face upwards so he could look into her eyes. After a few moments his face lit up with a smile. "Stephan congratulations you are going to be the father of a son," the Sanuri said.

"Is she pregnant?" Stephan asked with excitement in his voice.

"It is very early in his life, but yes."

"What!" gasped Ingr. "Are you sure? I cannot be. It's impossible," she blurted out in a panic. Then Ingr looked at Stephan who was walking up to her. "Stephan it is impossible!"

"Honey no it isn't," Stephan said as he stroked her hair. Stephan was smiling at the shocked look on Ingr's face.

"But we have only been together for, oh I can't think, I just can't think, Stephan I think it has been weeks."

"And we have made love a great deal," Stephan said warmly.

"Oh my," Ingr said and started to sit down but there was no chair; Stephan grabbed Ingr's arm while Thaos quickly put a chair under her, although Ingr was oblivious to the gesture. "I just don't know if I am ready for this," Ingr said.

Everyone in the room was looking at Ingr and grinning. "Now I would have expected Stephan to be the one to act like that," Matthew said with a laugh.

"I am happy about it," Stephan said with a proud smile.

"You are?" Ingr asked in dazed amazement.

"I am happy too," said Claudius jubilantly.

"Sanuri will you stay long enough to marry us?" Stephan asked.

"Of course."

"What, we are getting married now?" Ingr asked still sounding stunned.

"Stephan perhaps you should take Ingr in the other room and talk," Claudius suggested.

"No, no Claudius, I will be alright," Ingr said. "I have to focus on the matter at hand."

"Look at this," gasped Padre Bartholomew as he handed the list of items missing from the Hall of Antiquities to Padre Thomas.

"The Chalice of Ascension is missing," said Padre Thomas as he read the list with horror.

"Do you think the Sanuri took it and forgot to tell us?"

"No he only took scrolls and manuscripts. I wrote them down on a list."

"We will have to send him word that it is missing," said a very worried Padre Bartholomew.

"I think that perhaps we should wait until we find out more about the chalice and any other items that may be needed for ceremonies," said Padre Thomas. "That way the Sanuri will have a better idea of what he is up against."

The two priests searched the shelves for all that was written about The Chalice of Ascension and piled the scrolls and texts on a table. "It looks like we have our work cut out for us," said Padre Bartholomew as he grabbed a scroll and sat down at the table.

The sun was rising in the sky when Thaos finished telling the ruling families of Lentz about Juleta, her plans and her fortress. It was still raining but the powerful storm that had battered the landscape all night had subsided.

"Juleta is more cunning than I gave her credit for," Fahron said. "She is guarded about the information she gives out. That is a smart move on her part."

"Thaos did you ever see any men wearing priest's robes with Juleta or around her castle?" asked the Sanuri.

"No, she actually is pretty much of a recluse," Thaos said. "Juleta has few visitors and she rarely leaves the castle. In fact I have only ever seen her in one room of the castle and that is the parlor."

"Then that must be the room I saw through your eyes," said the Sanuri thoughtfully. "She had many objects of dark magic displayed in that room. I will bet her altar and torture room are directly under that parlor."

Angelina and Ingr looked at each other and both stood up simultaneously. "It is time for Ingr and me to address you," Angelina said with both authority and sincerity. "Before I start I want to tell you how much we both love all of you for taking us into your families of warriors; that is why these words must be said. Ingr and I do not have the attachment to Juleta as the rest of you. We were not raised with her, or love her as a sister or a daughter; to us she is a demon who is trying to hurt everyone we care about."

"As I look around this table every man here is honorable. Would any of you be able to kill a woman even if your life depended on it? You know I speak the truth when I say that if a man performed the same acts and made the same threats as Juleta, you would take them as a declaration of war. But instead you hide your wives and we meet in darkness."

"We are all warriors; we do not hide in the shadows. Mathas and Matthew both of your hearts are broken and neither of you could order an attack against your own blood. So we have a proposition. Ingr and I have trained our entire lives for battle; let me go to my father and take some of our tribe and we will stop Juleta."

"You have been so good to us," Ingr said. "Let us do this for you; let us give your families peace again." Stephan grasped Ingr's hand and was about to speak when she looked at him and said, "Angelina and I have much to learn about being wives but we are warriors and all of the beautiful dresses in the kingdom will not change that. Stephan, Juleta has tried to kill you twice; if she does kill you I have no reason to live and Angelina feels the same way about Matthew."

Everyone sat motionless, staring at Angelina and Ingr for what seemed like minutes before the Sanuri spoke, "Angelina, Ingr when you were in Wetpr I saw the blushing brides, but now I see the women and the warriors. I hope everyone at this table realizes their words are acts of love not disrespect. Angelina I agree with what you have said except for one thing; even your tribe is not prepared to stop a dark lord; that is why I am here."

Fahron cleared his throat then said, "Angelina it is obvious Sorren raised you to be the leader of your people; I only wish he could have been seated at this table tonight."

Mathas was clearly emotional when he spoke, "Girls I am not offended by your words but you must understand it is me and me alone who has been crippled by this. Claudius and Fahron have not acted out of respect for me. But you are right it is time for me to turn this matter over to more capable hands. Claudius you prepare an offensive and Fahron you take charge of our defenses. And I am so sorry that my child as put so many people in danger." Then Mathas looked at Matthew and said sadly, "Son you do not have to be involved with this."

"Father the girls are right. But neither Stephan or I are going to let our wives fight our battles for us." Then Matthew turned to Angelina and took her hand, "We were hiding you to protect you not do dishonor you."

"We know," Angelina said and kissed Matthew on the cheek.

"It was not my place to speak until Mathas spoke," Claudius said. "I am so proud of you two little girls my heart could burst. We all know you want to protect your families. As do I. Mathas, I am sorry but I lost my attachment to Juleta when she tried to kill you. She has sent her monsters into our homes to kill our children; I too see her as a demon and will have no problem going to war against her."

Mathas turned to the Sanuri, "We would welcome your help with this."

Both Angelina and Ingr sat down at the table and kissed their husbands. Thaos had been listening to everything with a grin on his face. "I have just one question," Thaos asked. "Are all the Nordes women like you two?"

Both Angelina and Ingr laughed. "They are not all warriors," Angelina said. "They have a choice but most of them are."

"I need to visit your tribe," Thaos said with a laugh and was about to make another statement when a soldier ran into the dining room.

"My Lord," the soldier said addressing Mathas. "You must come quickly Margarit is missing."

"What?" screamed Mathas as everyone jumped up from the table.

"The Queen went to her room this morning and could not find her and there are muddy boot prints on her floor and windowsill."

"Mathas I will get the men ready and we will meet you at the castle," Claudius said then he turned to Thaos, "How many men does she have at the castle?"

"One hundred and fifty that I know of," Thaos said as he was putting on his rain poncho.

"Stephan, prepare three hundred men and provisions," Claudius ordered as everyone left for Mathas' castle except for Thaos, Stephan and Ingr.

"Ingr go to our room and get weapons," Stephan said as he was leaving the room.

"What do you want me to do?" Thaos asked.

"Draw me a map," Claudius said.

Rosa was crying hysterically when Mathas found her lying on the floor of Margarit's bedroom. "Who would take our baby?" she cried as Mathas put his arms around her.

"I fear it was Juleta but we now know where Juleta's castle is, that was why I was gone. We will get her back," Mathas said as tears filled his eyes.

Matthew, Angelina and the Sanuri were examining the ground below Margarit's second floor window. "There is no sign of a ladder and the rain has washed away any prints," Matthew said as he continued searching the ground anxiously.

"Here," called the Sanuri as he held up a rope he found behind a bush. There was a large metal prong fastened to one end. "They must have hooked this over the windowsill and climbed up." Matthew grabbed the robe and threw it against the wall.

"Honey we will find her," Angelina said as she touched Matthew's hand.

"I am going to see if Claudius is here yet," Matthew said as he walked around the building. Fear gripped his heart at the thought of Juleta hurting Margarit. "I will kill her myself," Matthew said under his breath.

The Sanuri started to follow Matthew when Angelina grabbed his arm. "I have heard that dark lords sacrifice children," Angelina said. "Is that true?"

"Sometimes."

Lazo jumped up; something had awakened him. Lazo strained his eyes to see in the dark cave he had taken shelter in from the storm. Lazo listened intently then he heard something move. He grabbed his sword with his right hand and slowly stood up. If there was a bear or lion in the cave Lazo did not want to alarm it. Lazo was not a fearful man but he had felt paranoid ever since he left Juleta's castle. Lazo decided he would rather be out in the storm. He quickly walked out of the cave, leaving his blankets on the ground.

As Lazo was mounting his horse, something grabbed him from behind. Lazo turned around and thrust his sword into a creature wearing a red priest's robe with an odious clay mask. Lazo pulled his sword out of the creature and tried to mount his horse a second time, when another Demalog jumped on his back pulling Lazo backwards. Lazo backed up and rammed the creature against the rock wall that housed the cave. Two, three more times Lazo rammed the Demalog against the rock wall before it loosened its grip on him. Lazo turned around to face the creature and ran his sword through the creature's stomach.

Lazo looked around but did not see any other creatures, so he ran to his horse, mounted it and started to ride south. As he was riding around the rocky hill that contained the cave, another Demalog jumped down onto the back of Lazo's horse. But the horse was moving fast causing the creature to lose its grip and fall under the horse's hooves.

Claudius and Thaos led the troops southward towards Juleta's castle. Six soldiers rode ahead of the troops looking for signs of an ambush. Matthew had great difficulty talking his father into staying home. But even Mathas realized this kidnapping was probably a trap to kill him. The Sanuri, Matthew, Stephan, Angelina and Ingr all rode in silence praying that they would find Margarit alive.

Fahron quickly set up perimeters of soldiers around each of the three castles, in case the kidnapping was a diversion for an attack on the ruling families. Fahron had his wife and children and Bella brought to Mathas' castle so he could watch over all of the families. Isadore and Bella tried to comfort Rosa and Mathas but their despair was too great.

"Fahron, should I have killed one daughter to save the other? No father should have to make that decision," Mathas asked in anguish.

"Mathas no one can answer a question like that," Fahron said as he put his arm around Mathas' shoulders. They will find Margarit and bring her home." Fahron's heart was breaking to see his friend in such despair.

Mathas was lost in his sorrow for several moments then he said, "We should send a messenger to Sorren."

"I already have, my friend. Take care of your wife during this nightmare and I will take care of the kingdom."

Lazo was well into the Kingdom of Ganz when he was attacked. As Lazo rode he wondered why those creatures had waited so long to attack him.

Once his heart stopped racing and his body was calming down, Lazo realized he felt a searing pain in his right shoulder. Touching his shoulder Lazo felt warm sticky blood.

Lazo was not going to stop to tend to his wound. He knew he was past the Village of Hafsfat and Port Friada was still a two day ride away. Lazo decided to head to the monastery at Leven to get help. So he turned his horse southeast and rode as fast as his horse could carry him.

Claudius and his troops made camp late into the night. They had ridden hard all day with little rest. Angelina was preparing food while Matthew took care of the horses. It broke her heart to see how much pain he was in. Angelina knew how close Matthew was to Margarit. Matthew sat down next to Angelina by the fire without saying a word.

"Matthew you know we had to take a break, the horses and men need to rest." Matthew did not respond. "Honey we will find her." Matthew suddenly grabbed Angelina and hugged her tightly but he could not speak because his sorrow was overwhelming.

After Stephan took care of his and Ingr's horses he met with his father, Thaos and the Sanuri. Ingr made their camp and prepared food and waited for Stephan to return. When he returned Stephan sat near the fire and started to eat without speaking to her.

"Stephan, you have barely spoken to me since last night, are you angry with me?"

Stephan looked at Ingr for a few moments as if he was choosing his words carefully, "Yes, but I am also proud. You and Angelina said the words that Mathas needed to hear; the words that we could not say to him. Ingr I understand that you are a warrior and I admire that in you. But you are going to be my wife soon and you are carrying our baby. You asked permission of the King to go to battle without saying anything to me. That will not happen again, I would not do that to you," Stephan said sternly.

"Stephan you are right and it will never happen again. But Juleta needs to be stopped and I knew you would not allow me to try and stop her. I would rather have you alive and mad at me then dead."

"But I am your husband, I will take care of this family," Stephan said angrily. He paused for a few moments trying to contain his anger. "Ingr I love you, I don't want anything to happen to you or the baby."

"Stephan are you really happy about this baby?" Ingr asked hesitantly.

"Yes, aren't you?"

"I was fearful when the Sanuri told us about the baby because I thought it would scare you even more than our relationship. You were not sure you were ready for the responsibilities of marriage but there are more responsibilities with being a father. Are you mad at me for being pregnant?"

Stephan stared at Ingr with disbelief, then he set his plate down and reached over and took her hand. "I can't believe you asked me that," Steven said softly. "I am sorry I have made it so difficult for you; I know I have hurt you a great deal. But somehow when the Sanuri said we were having a son it was like all of the conflict I was feeling just went away. I want us to be married and to have a family. And the fact that you are pregnant does make me very happy."

Ingr moved closer to Stephan and put her arms around his neck. "I am so happy to hear you say these words; I wasn't sure what I would do if you said you didn't want the baby," Ingr kissed Stephan on the lips. "I hope our son turns out just like you."

"Honey you have to promise me that you will be careful, stay near me when we get to Juleta's."

Thaos drew several maps for Claudius; one of the inside of the castle, another of the buildings where the hired men stayed and a third map of the hiding and observation spots he had found in the woods surrounding the castle.

"She will most likely have ravens watching from the skies for intruders," said the Sanuri. "Let me take care of them. I did not want to speak in front of Matthew but there is a chance that Juleta wants to sacrifice her sister on that altar. Once the fighting starts I have to get to that altar quickly. Thaos would you allow me to look into your mind again? The first time I was trying to read what kind of man you are; now I am looking for clues as to Juleta's intentions."

"Go ahead," Thaos said with a laugh. "But you may not like some of what you see."

"Thaos I saw that you have had a very difficult and sorrowful life. And as anyone you have made some poor choices. But through it all you have maintained your honor and integrity and that says a lot about you." The Sanuri looked at both Claudius and Stephan as he spoke. "I also saw that the family you have been taking care of will need you soon, you should consider staying in Lentz for a while."

"Has Juleta found them?" Thaos asked with great concern.

"I could not see the reason."

"Thaos you are welcomed to stay at the castle with us until you decide what you want to do, we have plenty of rooms," Claudius offered.

Thaos was touched by Claudius' offer but did not speak; he merely nodded then walked closer to the Sanuri. The Sanuri placed his hands on Thaos' head and asked that the dark secrets of Juleta be revealed.

Claudius and his troops slept but a few hours and resumed their journey to Juleta's castle. The things that the Sanuri saw when he looked into the mind of Thaos concerned him considerably. Before the troops left their campsites, the Sanuri had called to the Enrops for help.

The flock was divided up into several groups, one to watch for Margarit and her abductors, one to try and see inside of Juleta's castle and the rest to watch over all the lands surrounding the castle. The Sanuri did not speak of what he saw in Thaos' mind but he feared that Margarit would become a sacrifice to a demon.

The Sanuri predicted correctly; Juleta had huge flocks of ravens guarding her grounds. As the flocks of Enrops infiltrated the lands of the dark lord these great birds; the birds that represented darkness and the birds that represented light went to battle. High above the ground they fought for the rulers they served. Juleta's hired men below were oblivious to the battle that was taking place overhead. Another battle in the ancient war between good and evil.

About midday Lazo rode up to the gates of the monastery outside of the small Village of Leven in the southern part of the Kingdom of Ganz. The hot sun beat down on his hatless head; that combined with the loss of blood made Lazo light headed and dizzy. Lazo sat unsteadily on his horse looking at the great walls that loomed before him. He was trying to see if there were guards or priests that he could call to open the gates.

Suddenly Lazo fell to the ground. He landed on his stomach. He tried to lift himself up but could not. Lazo managed to roll onto his back. Everything was spinning and his vision was bleary. As Lazo was losing consciousness he thought he heard voices.

"You have done well Hector," Juleta said. "I will reward you greatly."

"Where do you want her?" Hector asked. It was apparent to Juleta that he was pleased by her praise.

"Bring her in here," Juleta ordered.

Two of Hector's men walked into the parlor, one was carrying Margarit over his shoulder. He stood the little girl up in front of Juleta. "Juleta," gasped Margarit in amazement. "Did you have me taken?"

"Yes," said Juleta coldly.

"Juleta I have missed you; why don't you ever come home anymore?"

"Because Father has banned me," Juleta said angrily.

"I don't think that is true," Margarit said innocently. "I know he misses you and is sad that you are gone. In fact I heard him say he 'is sad that he lost his daughter.' I asked him where you got lost but he didn't answer me. And I know Matthew misses you too. Why don't you come home Juleta?"

Juleta stared at her little sister in silence as Juleta was fighting the emotions that were rising within her. "Hector take her to the first room on the right at the top of the stairs and post a guard outside of her door."

Hector returned to the parlor a few minutes later. "You are sure your father will follow?"

"Of course he will," Juleta responded sharply. "Wouldn't you if someone stole your child? Nothing has changed to our plans; prepare your men."

A seasoned warrior, Claudius had never been defeated in battle. He was a shrewd strategist but this was the first time he had led his own children into battle. Claudius had always thought of Matthew as another son and the girls made him proud, yet he worried about them. Claudius knew that this kidnapping was likely a maneuver to draw his children into Juleta's sights. Without his children knowing it; Claudius told some of his soldiers to specifically guard Stephan, Matthew and their wives during the battle.

By early afternoon they were near the lands of Juleta. The Sanuri told them to stop as he called to the Enrops. A lone Enrop answered his call.

"Bali why are you alone?" the Sanuri asked.

"Because the others are still battling the ravens."

"Have you been able to watch the castle?"

"No we are greatly outnumbered by ravens."

The Sanuri closed his eyes for a moment. "You have the help now that you need. After the battle I need to find out what kind of trap she has planned for us."

341

When Bali returned to the castle he saw the skies filled with huge blue eagles. The eagles seemed to be impervious to the raven's attacks. The eagles were crushing the ravens with their beaks and talons. Soon the ground was littered with the bodies of hundreds of dead ravens. When the ravens were defeated the eagles flew to the trees surrounding the castle.

"I know you are impatient but we must wait for the Enrops to return," the Sanuri said.

"I have never depended on creatures to dictate my attacks," Claudius said angrily.

"And you have never fought against sorcery before. Claudius the hired men will be the least of your problems." No sooner had the Sanuri spoken those words when Bali and several other Enrops landed near him.

"You are right it is a trap," Bali said. "About two hundred yards before her castle gate is a large ditch that surrounds the castle, it is filled with large red serpents. There are archers all along the wall that surrounds the castle and many armed men inside of wall."

"We saw creatures on chains inside of the wall also; they look to be half wolf and half panther. They are large and lunge at anything that comes near them. The child is alive and in a room on the second floor, but there are bars on her window. And there is more, there are four towers on the castle inside each is a Talmuth. There may be more creatures inside that we have not seen."

"Thank you Bali, did you see her altar?"

"No, we looked in the windows above ground and did not see it."

"What are these creatures they are talking about?" asked Claudius in amazement.

"They are all beasts of hell that only demons and dark lords can call to. The Talmuth are a type of dragon that bears the symbol of Satan. You are familiar with the serpents. The creatures that look to be half wolf and half panther are Telgras, they are vicious and powerful. They secrete a poison that goes into their victims when they bite them. They are chained now but Juleta will release them during battle. Claudius gather your men."

The Sanuri explained the monsters waiting for them at Juleta's castle. "Claudius this is what I am proposing, as we speak this forest is filling with giant blue eagles; they are an ancient species that are only found near the Ice Caves of Mordv in Mount Petrov. They are called Hengers. Juleta is prepared for a ground attack but not an attack from the air. The Hengers are large enough for a man to ride on. The Hengers can fly your men over the snakes and over the castle walls."

"Your archers can shoot the men on the walls and grounds and the rest of your soldiers can land behind the wall. The archers should kill the Telgras before your men land. The Hengers will fight the Talmuth. Regardless of what you decide Claudius, I will be riding a Henger to get to the castle, if Juleta gets that child to the altar I may be the only one who can stop her. Claudius the decision is yours."

"Can't the snakes escape that ditch they are hiding in?" Claudius asked.

"I was going to ask for fire to rain down on them after your men have passed," the Sanuri replied.

"Who among you are willing to ride on the Hengers?" Claudius asked.

Matthew and Angelina stood up immediately. Ingr and Stephan stood up, then Thaos and one by one each soldier stood up. "Excellent," said Claudius with a smile. "Never in my days did I think I would ride a great eagle. Matthew, Angelina, Ingr and Stephan I do not have to tell you that this trap is to kill you. You must be careful Juleta may try to lure you away from the others."

Then Claudius spoke to the rest of his men, "The Sanuri said that the Enrops will be fighting with us, they are our allies do not harm them." Claudius divided his archers into three groups Matthew and Angelina would lead the first group, Stephan and Ingr the second and Thaos the third. Each group of archers would attack from a different direction. After the archers had destroyed the Telgras the rest of the soldiers would be flown over the wall to fight with Juleta's men.

Chapter XXII
Proelium

"I am proud of the strategies you boys have developed," Sudfad said as he reviewed the maps and drawings that Raul and Simon had given him. "These ideas are very clever. I will send dispatches to the generals of each fort telling them your plans and advising them the materials they need to get. But you boys will have to go to the forts and oversee the building of these weapons. And you will need to inspect our borders; we have not done that in a while."

Although proud of their father's praise neither Simon nor Raul relished the idea of visiting every fort because of the time it would take them away from their families. Sudfad saw the looks on his son's faces. "Believe me I understand that you don't want to leave your families but this has to be done. If Roch enlists the aid of demons and attacks us on multiple fronts with Rogetts, Hutas and his men as he has planned, our kingdom will be in grave danger. This is the only way you can really keep your families safe."

"When do you want us to leave Father?" Raul asked.

"Oversee the projects at this fort first, that will give the generals time to procure the materials that you need. You might want to send them the drawings and dimensions of the weapons and tell them to start construction before you get there; hopefully that will lessen the amount of time you have to spend at each fort," Sudfad advised. "We must make haste incase the demons attack."

In less than an hour the Sanuri had called enough Hengers for everyone to ride. "How do we let them know where we want to go?" Matthew asked.

"Just tell them," said the Sanuri. "They cannot speak with you as the Enrops do but they will understand your directions. They are also an ancient bird of war, they come alive in the midst of battle, they will also take you where you need to go."

"They are going to take you high into the air at first, so hopefully the men standing guard on the walls do not see you. Then when you are close to your enemies the Hengers will fly down so you can shoot them. "

"How do you know this?" asked Stephan.

"I have gone to war with them before," the Sanuri replied.

The plan was for Matthew to lead men from the north, Stephan from the south and Thaos from the east. They decided against attacking from the west because Thaos said that Juleta spent all of her time looking out her parlor window which faced the west. Claudius was going to lead the men who would fight on the ground. And the Sanuri was going straight to the castle to find Margarit.

"If you have to fight with any of the Talmuth shoot for their throats, hearts and eyes. They are covered in hard scales that will resist penetration of an arrow," the Sanuri advised.

Once all of the men were in place the Sanuri's voice could be heard by only the leaders. "Attack," was all he said and the battle against darkness began. As the Sanuri predicted the men on the walls were concentrating on a ground attack and did not look up to the heavens. The sun was up and the sky was clear, the soldiers of Lentz could easily see their targets as the great birds descended.

Angelina was thrilled at the ride and had to contain herself from yelling a war cry. The three groups attacked simultaneously and took the men on the wall by surprise. All of the archers aimed first at the men on the wall. As the Hengers continued to fly across the courtyard the archers of Lentz aimed at the men on the ground and at the Telgras. The Hengers would turn around giving the archers a second chance to cover their area. Each group was able to make several passes over the castle before the Talmuth realized there were enemies among them.

Thaos was surprised when he saw the number of men that Juleta had as fighters; there were at least three times the number he knew of. "I wonder what else the witch hid from me," he thought. Suddenly the Henger Thaos was riding bolted upwards.

Thaos clung tightly to the bird as it charged a Talmuth which was hovering over them. The great bird was flying upwards so quickly that Thaos could not shoot his bow; he had all he could do to stay on the Henger's back.

The Henger came underneath the Talmuth tearing at the dragon's stomach and throat. The dragon screamed in pain and tried to free itself from the Henger's grasp. Now Thaos was hanging onto the bird for his life as the two ancient creatures battled high over the castle. The Henger maintained its grip on the Talmuth as it tore at the dragon's throat with its massive beak. The Talmuth fell from the sky but as it fell it hit Thaos with its wing knocking him off the Henger.

As Thaos fell through the air, the sights around him seemed surreal. He saw Hengers and Talmuth battling in the skies as well as men fighting on the ground. Thaos saw huge flames of fire leaping in the air from the ditches that contained the serpents. As fear started to consume him, Thaos' body jerked upwards and he realized he was in the claws of a Henger.

He tried to figure out if there was a way he could climb up the bird and get onto its back but he decided it was impossible. The Henger deposited Thaos on the ground in the midst of the bloody combat and returned to the sky to fight with the Talmuth.

Thaos heard screams and saw a Talmuth fall from the skies, striking the wall surrounding the castle. The dead Talmuth hit with such force that it knocked part of the wall down and crushed the men who were on it. Thaos looked for Claudius and saw him fighting with two of Juleta's men. Thaos moved quickly to Claudius' side and stabbed one of the men.

The air was filled with smoke from the great fires that were burning the serpents of Satan. Thaos looked into the air and saw there were still archers attacking from the backs of the Hengers. A hideous scream was heard as a Telgra broke free from its chain and lunged at the combatants. The hell beast did not distinguish Juleta's men from the rest and sought to attack any creature within its reach.

Suddenly two Hengers swooped down from the sky and Stephan and Ingr shot multiple arrows into the head and neck of the Telgra. The great beast screamed with rage, dropping the remains of a man it held in its teeth. The Telgra looked upwards and lunged at the Henger that Ingr was riding. Stephan's first arrow struck the Telgra in the throat and the second impaled the beasts' heart.

Another Talmuth fell, striking one of the towers of the castle. The tower collapsed and huge boulders struck the ground, crushing everything in their path. The screams of the men and the beasts filled the air; the sounds were deafening. The ground was so covered in blood that men were sliding in it as they fought. The horror of war was upon them.

Juleta was in the cellar of the castle when the attack began. She had cut Margarit's arm and drained some of the child's blood into a bowl which she had placed on the altar. Juleta was lighting candles around the altar. She stripped all of her clothing off and put on only a black hooded robe. Juleta approached the altar and dipped her fingers into the bowl of blood. With two fingers she drew bloody symbols on her face.

After the completion of each symbol Juleta praised the demon Stolas. Her altar was built below ground so no one could hear the screams of her victims. But the depth of the chamber prevented Juleta from hearing the battle. Suddenly the earth shook tremendously as a tower of the castle was destroyed by a falling Talmuth; Juleta grabbed a dagger and quickly ran up the stone steps.

An Enrop flew ahead of the Henger that the Sanuri was riding; it took the Sanuri to the window of the room where Margarit was being held captive. The Henger grabbed the metal bars on the window with its powerful claws. Within moments it tore the metal bars out of the stone wall and threw them on the ground. "Thank you old friend," said the Sanuri as he climbed into the window.

There was a rich purple carpet on the floor with fresh blood stains on it. The Sanuri quickly searched the room even looking under the bed but he did not find the child. He ran out of the room and into the hallway. The Sanuri heard voices. When he found the parlor, Matthew, Angelina and Thaos were in the room searching for a hidden doorway.

Matthew was becoming frantic as he saw fresh blood stains on the carpet in the parlor. The Sanuri started to examine the items of dark magic that were displayed in the room, thinking one of them might be a key. He picked up a statue of the demon Stolas and they all heard movement in the room. A large bookcase moved across the floor exposing a large wooden door. Matthew was the first through the door and down the stone steps.

When they reached the cellar they saw the instruments of torture and the altar but they did not find Juleta or Margarit. The Sanuri found the small bowl of fresh blood and knew it had to be Margarit's. Matthew, Angelina and Thaos stared at the Sanuri as he was destroying the altar. Smoke started to rise as the Sanuri broke the foundation of the altar and crushed the bones that were placed in symbolic messages.

"Where is that smoke coming from?" Angelina asked.

"I don't know," Thaos said as he looked around the room.

The Sanuri picked up the small bowl of blood and held it into the air, "Stolas you will not have this victim," shouted the Sanuri in a commanding voice. "You have no power here, leave this place." And with these words the Sanuri threw the bowl of blood on the floor, smashing it. As soon as the bowl broke the room filled with smoke. And from the smoke came an angry voice screaming from hell. Suddenly spirit-like creatures appeared in the room.

"Do not be afraid, they cannot hurt you," said the Sanuri. "Demons feed off from fear, do not feed him."

Matthew grabbed Angelina and pushed her behind him. Thaos moved next to Matthew as they faced the apparitions. The Sanuri started to chant and the apparitions disappeared. Stolas was enraged. "I curse you Sanuri!" Stolas screamed and suddenly objects in the cellar started to fly through the air.

The Sanuri held up his hands and the objects fell to the floor. "Demon be gone, you have no power here," ordered the Sanuri. They all heard Stolas scream although they could not see his image. Suddenly the room burst into flames. The Sanuri motioned for them to leave. The four ran upstairs and started searching the castle for Juleta and Margarit.

"Let the child go," ordered Stephan as he and Ingr walked towards Juleta. She was running out of the castle when they saw her. Now Juleta stood with her back to the burning ditch, holding Margarit in front of her with a dagger to the child's throat.

"Is this the whore that you married Stephan?" screamed Juleta angrily.

"This is my wife who you have tried to murder," Stephan responded as he walked towards her. Juleta had her eyes on Stephan. Ingr pulled one of her knives from its sheath. Stephan saw the movement out of the corner of his eye. "Juleta I don't know why you would think I could ever want you, you disgust me." Stephan continued to walk towards Juleta trying to keep her attention on him. "Thaos told me how all of your men laugh at you and call you the witch behind your back."

"You lie," screamed Juleta and raised her arm to throw the dagger at Stephan. Ingr threw her knife and it lodged in Juleta's shoulder causing her to drop the dagger.

"Run!" screamed Stephan as he ran towards Margarit who was hysterically running towards him. Ingr threw a second knife striking Juleta in her other shoulder. Ingr pulled a third knife from its sheath and walked towards Juleta; as Ingr threw the knife Juleta jumped backwards and fell into the burning ditch of serpents.

Stephan hugged Margarit tightly, then tore off part of his shirt and tied it around the cut on her arm. Stephan picked up the terrified child. Margarit put her arms around Stephan's neck and cried. Stephan put his arm around Ingr's shoulders and they walked back to the castle.

The battle was over. Thaos went to his room to retrieve his belongings. He found the bodies of Stiller and Larson, hanging from nooses in the main room of the building. Both bodies looked as if they had been tortured. Thaos cut them down and put blankets over them. He knew they had been killed because they warned him and Lazo about Juleta. When Thaos walked out of the building to put his things into his saddle bags; he found Stephan waiting for him.

"So what are you going to do now?" Stephan asked.

"Not really sure. I have some friends in Lentz and the Sanuri said they would need my help soon. I thought I would pay them a visit when we get back," Thaos said as he mounted his horse.

"Father said you should stay at the castle with us."

"I know."

"He meant it but just so you know nothing is free with my father, he will put you to work," Stephan said with a grin.

Thaos laughed loudly as the two men rode towards Claudius and the others. The Hengers returned to their home on Mount Petrov. The Enrops flew over the soldiers as they rode towards home. Margarit rode with Matthew and the two could not stop hugging each other. As they rode the Sanuri heard the voice of Stolas laughing.

As Claudius and his men rode towards Lentz, they left Juleta's castle in flames. The towers had all been toppled by the battle between the Hengers and the Talmuth. Bodies of creatures and men littered the grounds. The bodies of the soldiers from Lentz were tied over their horses so they could be buried in the kingdom they defended. Claudius showed mercy to the men they conquered and let them go after the battle was done.

Back at the castle, Juleta was climbing out of the fiery ditch. She pulled herself along the ground as she winced in pain from the burns and the knife wounds. Every movement brought Juleta great agony. As she crawled along the ground Juleta kept repeating one phrase, "I curse thee, I curse thee, I curse thee."

Chapter XXIII
Redemption

That night after the troops made camp; Claudius called a meeting. As the leader, his campsite was separate from that of the other soldiers; the meeting was to take place at his campsite. When Stephan and Ingr arrived, arm in arm; Thaos was already with Claudius. The two men were sitting near the campfire drinking whiskey.

"I assume things are alright between the two of you now," Claudius said as he watched Stephan and Ingr take seats near the fire.

"Yes," Stephan said with a smile.

"After all of this, I have come to realize that in some ways you and Ingr are very much alike," Claudius said with a grin. "And that may be what causes you conflict." Both Stephan and Ingr looked at each other as they had never thought about the things that Claudius said. Soon the Sanuri sat down at the fire.

"We are just waiting for Matthew and Angelina," Claudius said as he handed everyone but Ingr cups of whiskey. Within moments Angelina walked up to the fire. "Where is Matthew?" Claudius asked.

"Poor Margarit is still so terrified she won't let go of him and he does not want her to hear the things we will discuss," Angelina said. "I will tell him about the meeting after she falls asleep."

"In all my years this was the most amazing battle I have ever been in," Claudius said. "I brought you here so we could discuss the different aspects that we witnessed and to determine if this threat has truly ceased. Before we start I do want to tell you that the Sanuri sent some Enrops ahead to tell Mathas and Rosa that we have Margarit and that she is unharmed."

Starting with Claudius, every one told of the specific details of their parts in the actual battle. Then Angelina, Thaos and the Sanuri told of their experiences inside of the castle with the demon Stolas.

"So she really was going to sacrifice her own baby sister to a demon," Claudius said in disbelief. "As difficult as this will be we must tell Mathas the complete truth; he needs to know it, not only as a father but as our King."

Stephan and Ingr told of their part in confronting Juleta and saving Margarit. "You both did very well," Claudius said. "But I have just one question. Ingr why did you throw the second knife at her other shoulder?"

Ingr looked at the faces around the fire, "You will think I am awful but I wanted her to suffer a little before I killed her."

"I think we all wanted her to suffer," Stephan said.

Thaos told the group about finding the two men who had warned him and Lazo, tortured and hung in the bunkhouse. "This concerns me not only because of the reason and manner in which they died but as tortured as they were I am sure they gave up the location of my friends in Minges."

"You have friends who live on the lands of our tribe," Angelina said in surprise.

Thaos looked at the Sanuri then spoke, "They are not from your tribe. It is an old man and his grandson. When I was a boy my family lived on a small farm outside of Hafsfat. The Hutas massacred that village and the surrounding farms. These people are the only other survivors that I have met. They are good people. The old man used to run the General Store in Hafsfat, he was always good to me as a boy. I am trying to pay him back for his kindness."

No one said anything for a few minutes then Ingr spoke, "Thaos you don't have to answer this question, but how did you survive that attack?"

"I was fishing, didn't even know there was an attack until I came home and found my home in flames. They raped my mother and three sisters before they killed them. I am not sure if my father was dead before they started to butcher him. After I buried them all I left Hafsfat and still have not returned." Thaos could feel the emotions rising within him as he had not spoken about this to anyone other than Jeb, since he was a child.

"How old were you?" Angelina asked.

"I was nine."

The group was silent after listening to Thaos' story. Finally the Sanuri spoke. "I have one more thing to say," he said solemnly. "As we rode away from the castle I heard the voice of Stolas laughing; which leads me to believe this is not over."

"Then Jeb and Ryan could be in great danger," Thaos said as he started to stand up. "I need to leave."

"Thaos you can relax, not all of the Hengers returned to Mount Petrov," said the Sanuri. "There are a couple standing watch over that small fishing cottage."

"Raul how long will you be gone?" asked Vitomas as tears started to fill her eyes. She was lying in his arm. Raul kissed Vitomas gently on the lips and started to stroke her hair. "Likely six months, if there are problems maybe longer."

"Raul I wanted to wait until I was sure but I think I am pregnant," Vitomas said with her voice shaking. "I hope you return before the baby is born."

Raul was ecstatic at the news and hugged and kissed Vitomas again and again. "Honey I am so sorry to leave you now but you understand the threats we are facing."

"I know," Vitomas whispered. Then suddenly her eyes grew wide. "Oh no, Annabelle's baby is due before you can come home, it will be horrible for her to go through that without Simon."

"Honey we can't help it. We don't want to leave either but I told you about Roch's plans. If he attacked today our kingdom and all of you would be in great danger."

"I know; I hate him so. Not as much for what he did to me but for what he has put our family through," Vitomas said with a sigh. "Raul, what about Samuel? Should we wait with the christening until you return?"

"Yes, the Sanuri is still helping Mathas, who knows when he will return."

The next afternoon was a time of great joy as Claudius and his men rode up to Mathas' castle. Bella and Fahron's family were still staying with Mathas and Rosa and were ecstatic to see the families come home safely. Both Mathas and Rosa were crying as they hugged their young daughter. "I am so sorry," Mathas kept repeating.

"Sorry for what papa?"

"I am sorry I did not stop your sister before she had a chance to hurt you." Mathas handed Margarit to Rosa and walked up to Claudius. "Is she dead?"

"We think so, but we have much to discuss. Perhaps we should have a meeting tonight?" suggested Claudius.

"No, you and Fahron have shielded me enough," replied Mathas with determination. "Everyone is here, let's have the meeting now and I will have lunch prepared for all of you." As the warriors gathered in the King's study they all dreaded telling Mathas about the battle; because no one wanted to bring him more pain.

"Honey please stop crying," Simon said as he held Annabelle in his arms. "I feel bad enough already."

"I am sorry, I can't help it; I miss you already."

"You know we have to do this."

"I know," Annabelle sobbed. "It is just that we have hardly been apart since we met and you won't be here when the baby is born."

"I know," Simon said and hugged Annabelle tightly.

Suddenly Annabelle looked up at him. "Simon we need to pick out baby names before you go. And we should probably pick out two of each in case we have twins again."

"I have been thinking about that. If we have a girl I would like to name her after mother."

"You want to call her Renya?"

"No, I was thinking of mother's middle name which is Arianna."

"Oh, I like that very much," Annabelle said as she wiped the tears from her eyes.

"And for a boy I like the names Timothy and David. I thought we could have middle names of Raul and Matthew. Have you picked out any names?"

"No."

"Well think about what you like; we have plenty of time yet. We will be able to write to each other."

"The Chalice of Ascension is more powerful than I ever realized," said Padre Bartholomew as he finished reading a stack of old scrolls.

"I just do not like this," said Padre Thomas. "The more I read the more I am convinced that only someone educated in these materials would steal the chalice."

"From what I have read so far; the chalice has great power and can be used in several ways but additional instruments are needed to unleash and focus the powers."

"We need to make a list of all the additional instruments and determine if any of them are missing from here also."

"I may sound paranoid but with all that has happened; I think we need to find a place to hide our notes. If someone has access to the keys to enter the Hall of Antiquities, they certainly can gain entrance to our rooms," said Padre Bartholomew.

The fear of losing Margarit to the insanity of Juleta changed Mathas' perceptions. He now realized that the little girl who used to sit on his lap was gone, never to return. Mathas realized that to protect his family and his kingdom he had to view Juleta as the enemy she was. As the meeting continued his friends and family were reluctant to tell Mathas all of the details of the battle; but eventually the entire story unfolded. Ingr asked Mathas to forgive her before she told him what she did to Juleta.

"My dear, you did what had to be done, and you, all of you saved Margarit. I could not ask for more. I now see my daughter for the monster that she is. I will let her cripple me no more. But you all do know that if she did not die on that battlefield she will come back with a vengeance." Then Mathas turned to Claudius who sat on his right and then to Fahron who sat on his left. "My dearest friends you have done your jobs exceptionally well and will be rewarded. But like any great warrior a man must understand his strengths and his weaknesses."

"I now understand that Juleta is my weakness. And all though I see her differently today, as I see her the way all of you do; I cannot guarantee that I will always have such clarity of mind. As the Sanuri said this war may not be over; so Claudius I would like you to continue in your position of preparing our offensive against Juleta and her demons. And Fahron I would like you to continue to be in charge of our inner defenses. That way if I am not strong enough to stop my daughter I can trust that the two of you will."

The room remained quiet for several moments before Claudius spoke. "Mathas you just showed us what a great King you are. Your decisions are wise and in the best interest of your kingdom. But do not be so hard on yourself. Fahron and I do not know if we would act the same way if it was one of our children working with the demons."

"Your words are kind Claudius," Mathas said. "Tomorrow night we will have a feast to celebrate your victory and all of you will be rewarded for the roles you played. And now Claudius I will let you tell them the rest."

Claudius started to laugh, "Matthew and Stephan when you have been married as long as the three of us have; you learn that you should leave your wives with something to think about other than your possible deaths on the battlefield. Son, I hope you aren't angry with me but I told your mother about the baby and the wedding before we left. And according to Fahron all of our wives are already working on things for both the events. You and Ingr should probably speak with your mother if you want to have any say at all about your wedding."

"They are already making baby clothes," Fahron said with a laugh. "But actually it was what they needed to get their minds off from the horror of the situation."

"That is fine with me," Stephan said. Then he turned to Matthew. "You do know we expect you and Angelina to stand up for us?"

Matthew started to laugh, "I would have been hurt if you didn't want us."

Stephan turned to Ingr, "Honey why don't you and Angelina meet with mother after this meeting; I have a little trip to take. Whatever you decide on for the wedding is alright with me."

"Where are you going?" Ingr asked with surprise.

"Well Thaos doesn't know it yet but I was going to ride with him when he went to check on his friends."

"Really," said Thaos with a grin.

"Hengers or not you don't know what you are riding into," Stephan said.

"Actually I thought I would tag along too," Matthew said.

"I was waiting until we were alone to talk about the baby," Angelina said seriously. "I was going to congratulate you the other night but I wasn't really sure if you were happy about it."

"I know I sound crazy but I have been so focused on Stephan and trying to figure out what is going on with him that I, well I did think about us having children someday; but I guess I just never thought it would be so soon. And when the Sanuri told us, I felt scared because I really thought Stephan would be angry," Ingr said.

"Why would you think he would be angry?"

"He has been so conflicted about us being together and a baby is so much responsibility, I just don't know what I thought."

"So have you talked with him about it?"

"Yes and he said that when the Sanuri told us about the baby that all of the conflict he was feeling left him, can you believe that? He really wants the baby and to get married now."

"Ingr how do you feel about this?"

"Oh, I am happy about the baby and what Stephan said, it's just that he has been so unpredictable I am half expecting him to change again, and that scares me."

It was late into the night when Stephan slid into bed next to Ingr. She was sleeping on her side when he whispered into her ear, "Are you awake?" and started to kiss her neck.

Ingr smiled and rolled over and kissed Stephan on the lips. "It is so late, I was starting to worry."

"We moved Thaos' friends to Matthew's castle. Thaos was right it was an old man and a boy, who has never been trained in fighting; they are no match for anyone who Juleta might send."

"So you think she is still alive?" Ingr asked as she sat up in bed.

"I really don't know what to think; especially after hearing Matthew and Thaos talk about what happened in that cellar."

"Oh, Stephan I know I should have thrown that knife at her throat instead of her shoulder," Ingr cried.

"Honey don't look back on that; you did well. Besides maybe you couldn't kill her."

"What do you mean Stephan?"

"Well Matthew, Thaos and I were talking about it as we rode. The Sanuri told Matthew that a person can become a demon, which is why he was so concerned about the items he saw in Juleta's parlor. Apparently the process does not happen quickly, but if Juleta is a demon or part demon only the Sanuri would have been able to destroy her."

The villagers of Minges slept peacefully, unaware of the monsters that walked their streets this night. Four Demalogs moved silently in the shadows until they came upon a small fishing cottage on the shores of the Sea of Grevtd. They circled the tiny structure looking for any sign of movement. They peeked through the windows into the dark and silent home.

The four hell beasts climbed through the windows. Anger filled them as they realized their prey was gone. They searched the house a second time looking for hidden passageways. Then they walked around outside until they could pick up the scents that filled the house. They followed the trail southward.

The following night the ruling families of Lentz, Thaos and the Sanuri were among many who gathered in the King's castle for a celebration. Angelina was overjoyed when she saw her family in the Great Hall mingling with the other guests. "Father, Mother," Angelina called and ran up to them, giving them each a big hug."

"I was just telling Sorren how proud he should be of both you and Ingr, just for your words alone, much less your skills and courage in battle," Fahron said. Sorren smiled proudly as Fahron spoke. "You did well Sorren," Fahron added.

Bella and Claudius were already in the Great Hall when Stephan and Ingr arrived. Bella ran up to Stephan and kissed him. "Son, I haven't seen you to congratulate you. I am so happy and excited."

Stephan put his arm around his mother. "About what the wedding or the baby?" he asked with a laugh.

"Both," Bella said happily then hugged Ingr.

All of the guests were dressed for such a royal event; most of the men wore the military uniform of the Army of Lentz and the women wore gowns. Thaos and the Sanuri were standing together. "Guess I don't own the right kind of clothes," Thaos said with a grin.

"That matters to no one here; you did a great service to the King," the Sanuri replied.

When Mathas was informed that all of the guests had arrived, he took Rosa's hand and the two of them stood in the front of the room facing their guests.

"The King is about to speak," Claudius bellowed and the room became silent.

"Tonight we celebrate the safe return of my daughter, Margarit, and to honor those of you who bravely risked your lives to save her; a debt I can never truly repay. Tonight before we dine, I want to bestow gifts upon the people who selflessly served this kingdom and its king so well. As I call your name I would like you to come up here with Rosa and me so the rest of the guests can see who these heroes are."

"Claudius and Fahron please come forward." As the two men walked toward the King and Queen, Mathas continued to speak to the audience. "Claudius led the troops who engaged in a great battle to save my daughter and Fahron put into place strategies that safeguarded the kingdom during this act of war."

Mathas handed each man a scroll. "I have greatly increased your land holdings in this kingdom; I believe you will be pleased." As the guests clapped Claudius and Fahron walked back to their wives.

"Thaos would you come up here?" Mathas asked, then continued to address his guests. "This young man came to us with the necessary information that we needed to save Margarit. Then instead of leaving, as he certainly could have, he chose to join the battle to save her."

Mathas turned to Thaos. "Claudius tells me that you will be staying in his home until you decide your next move. First I want to tell you that you will always be welcomed in our home also for as long as you choose." The guests loudly applauded this young stranger.

Mathas handed Thaos a large pouch of gold coins. "This does little to repay you for your services. Claudius, Matthew and Stephan have all told me of your skill and bravery in battle. I am offering you the rank of captain in our army with the hope that you will decide to make your home in Lentz."

The guests applauded as Thaos stood speechless. "Say yes," yelled Stephan from the crowd. Thaos extended his hand to shake the King's. "I would be honored," Thaos said in a hoarse voice.

"Excellent," said Mathas. "Of course that means you will be working with Matthew and Stephan every day," he said and winked.

"Now for the Sanuri," Mathas said warmly. As the Sanuri walked to the front of the room, Mathas said. "For those of you who may not be familiar with the Sanuri he is an emissary of The Great Ruler, not only is he a powerful priest but also a fierce warrior and a truly great man." People were pushing through the crowd to get a better look at the Sanuri. Now Mathas turned to the Sanuri who was standing next to him.

"My old friend; over the years I have learned that you set little value to the riches of this world. So I am going to offer you the same gift that the King and Queen of Wetpr have. You will always have a home in this castle. Tomorrow you can choose your chambers and we will tailor them to your desires. And tomorrow morning you and I will visit my personal stables and you will choose of my best stallions."

People whispered and applauded as the Sanuri joined the rest of the guests. Mathas motioned for Claudius, Fahron and Sorren to join him and Rosa in the front of the room. "First I would like Angelina and Ingr to step forward then I will call their husbands forward." Both women walked to the front of the room in silence as they were very embarrassed.

Mathas addressed the crowd. "I want to introduce you to these two beautiful girls because they are warriors in their own right. Most of you may not know them because we are still preparing for the grand public ceremonies; but this is Angelina, wife of my son Matthew and daughter of Chief Sorren of the Nordes Tribe." Mathas turned to Ingr, "And this is Ingr who will soon marry Stephan, the son of Claudius. Ingr is also of the Nordes Tribe."

"Sorren trains his warriors from a very early age and their skills are truly impressive," Mathas continued. "But Angelina and Ingr did a service to this kingdom that others could not. They held a mirror up to an old man and made him see the truth. Then much to the dismay of their husbands they offered to save Margarit, in an effort to protect the rest of our families. Angelina and Ingr tomorrow morning you will accompany the Sanuri and me to my stables and choose horses for yourselves." Both Angelina and Ingr smiled with excitement. Once again there was applause which embarrassed the women.

"Matthew and Stephan would you please join us?" Mathas asked. Both men walked to the front of the room and stood next to their wives. "I too heard of the skills and bravery that all four of you displayed in the rescue of my daughter. Stephan and Matthew, you are both being promoted to the rank of general; Fahron and Claudius will pin the new rank on your uniforms." The room was quiet until Fahron and Claudius had finished, then everyone applauded. Stephan and Ingr started to walk towards the guests when Mathas stopped them.

"Stay right where you are, we are not finished. Tomorrow morning I want both Matthew and Stephan to report here. You will give bonuses to the soldiers who accompanied you to battle. And you will make arrangements for the care of the families who lost their husbands and sons in that battle."

"Now Angelina it has not gone unnoticed by anyone how much you miss your family. So in the living quarters that Rosa and I are redesigning for your home, there will be separate chambers for your family." Then Mathis turned to Sorren and said, "You and your family are welcomed here always." Sorren smiled proudly and grasped Mathas' hand.

"Mathas turned again to Stephan and Ingr. Your father and I argued about this one, so as a compromise I will pay for the home he is having built for you in his castle and he will pay for your wedding. But should you or Matthew ever decide you want homes outside of the castles, here are deeds to your own lands."

As all the guests in the Great Hall of the castle of King Mathas were being seated; a lone Enrop flew through the window and landed on the Sanuri's shoulder. The bird said, "There are four Demalogs trying to enter the back of this castle, the flock is attacking them."

The Sanuri quickly stood up, "Stephan, Thaos take some men and follow this Enrop; you have Demalogs trying to get into the castle, I will be close behind. Matthew and Angelina go to Margarit." The Sanuri turned to Mathas, "So far the Enrops have only seen four of the beasts and the flock is attacking them." With these words the Sanuri ran from the banquet hall.

Claudius followed the Sanuri as Fahron and Sorren took troops to search the castle. Mathas called for more troops to come into the castle; when Mathas felt he had a sufficient number of soldiers to protect the families in the Great Hall, he ran to Margarit's room.

Stephan and Thaos were running in the lead of their men, when they came upon the Demalogs they stopped in amazement because the Enrops had literally torn the demons apart. Suddenly Ingr joined them; she had stopped to grab a sword.

"What are you doing here?" Stephan asked.

"My place is with you," Ingr said then took a step forward so she could see the remains of the Demalogs. "Did the Enrops do that?"

Thaos charged forward as he realized who the demons were after. He ran into the room where Jeb and Ryan were spending the night. With relief Thaos saw that both men were sleeping when he entered their room but they both awoke at the sound of the door. "Jeb, Ryan get dressed you need to move to a different room for the night."

"Why, what is going on son?" Jeb asked.

"There has been an attack on the castle and some of the intruders were outside of your window."

Stephan walked into the room, "Are they alright?"

"Yes but we need to move them."

"I will show you some rooms upstairs," Stephan said and led the men up a back staircase to the third floor of the castle.

Ingr and the Sanuri waited for Stephan and Thaos near the bodies of the intruders. "How did they know Jeb and Ryan were here?" Thaos asked as he walked up to the Sanuri.

"My guess is they went to their home to attack them and tracked Jeb and Ryan here," replied the Sanuri.

"This means Juleta is still alive," Stephan said as he put his arm around Ingr's shoulders.

When they returned to the Great Hall they were told there had been no other attacks or sightings of the Demalogs; but the ruling families knew this was a sign that the nightmare was not over.

Claudius and his family were the last to leave the celebration. Thaos felt obligated to stay with them since he was temporarily living in their castle. Shortly after they returned home; Bella, Stephan and Ingr each walked to their chambers, Claudius looked at Thaos. "Have a drink with me son," he said and walked into the study.

"You were kind of in a bad position there when Mathas made you that offer in front of all those people," Claudius said as he handed Thaos a glass of whiskey. "I saw you hesitate, you don't have to take the position in the military if you don't want to." Claudius sat down across from Thaos, who seemed deep in thought.

"Actually I was very surprised at the King's generosity," Thaos said. "I did not help because I expected to get paid."

"We all know that son," Claudius said. "You risked your life to help complete strangers; of course the King is going to reward you and if he didn't I was going to. But you do realize he also gave you the chance to start over, a new beginning."

"I know," Thaos said softly.

"What is bothering you Thaos?"

Thaos hesitated for a few moments then he said, "It was when he said he hoped I would make my home here. I have not had a home for a very long time."

Chapter XXIV
Beginnings

Both Raul and Simon rode in silence as they led their troops north from Fort Salar to Fort Styles. Fort Styles was in the northeastern corner of the kingdom, near the border of the Kingdom of Lentz. Both the Kingdom of Wetpr and the Kingdom of Lentz had large diamond mines in that area; mines that could conceal armies of Rogetts.

The mission of the two young princes was to ensure that the generals in charge of each fort increased security details, implemented new combat strategies and built the weapons that Raul and Simon had designed. Before leaving for Lentz, the Sanuri had given Simon and Raul some suggestions with their designs and important information for battling the dark lords.

Raul and Simon had always thrived on the challenges and adventures they found in the military. They had both volunteered to be stationed at each fort as they were working their way up the ranks. Never had they given a second thought to leaving home before. But now their hearts were saddened as they struggled with their duties to their kingdom and their desires to stay home with their families. Both Princes were leaving babies and pregnant wives behind.

Although Vitomas and Annabelle tried to be strong for their husbands, their sorrow could not be contained as they helped Raul and Simon prepare for their mission. Each wife had given her husband a small package with instructions that they not be opened until their first night away from home.

"My, don't you look handsome," Bella said. "Ingr don't you think he looks handsome?"

"You do," Ingr said to Thaos as they saw him in his military uniform for the first time. Stephan and Thaos had entered the dining room in Claudius' castle to join the family for lunch.

Stephan could see that Thaos felt uncomfortable so he slapped Thaos on the back and said with a laugh, "Don't let them embarrass you, have a seat." Stephan kissed Ingr before sitting down next to her.

"Ingr start your story from the beginning so the boys can hear it," Claudius said.

"After you left me off with Mathas and Angelina, the Sanuri joined us and we all walked to one of the royal stables. Stephan there were the most beautiful horses there. Mathas took us in the back where there were several corrals of different sizes; he said we should choose our horses from those corrals. Angelina and I walked around in wonder, Stephan those horses are all still wild."

"As we were looking at the animals, Mathas came up and tapped Angelina's shoulder and pointed to the Sanuri. We just stood there and watched him; it was the most amazing thing. The Sanuri walked into the middle of the largest corral and appeared to be talking to the horses. They were all very calm around him, some even nuzzling him. When suddenly this incredible black stallion walked up to the Sanuri and stood still, while the Sanuri mounted him bareback. Then the horse started to run and it jumped over the railings of the corral and the Sanuri rode him all morning."

"And you saw all of this?" Stephan asked.

"Yes we were standing close to that corral when the Sanuri went in."

"Your wife picked out a fine horse herself," Claudius said with a grin. "She plans to start breaking it tomorrow."

"What!" Stephan said as he quickly turned towards Ingr. "Honey you can't do that while you are pregnant." Ingr did not say anything but looked like she might cry. "I will break the horse for you," Stephan said. Ingr's face broke into a big smile and she kissed Stephan on the cheek.

"He's beautiful Stephan, he is a huge white stallion," Ingr said with pride.

"Stephan, what day would you like for your wedding?" Bella asked.

Stephan looked at Ingr and smiled, "I don't know, as soon as possible mother."

"Good," said Bella with authority. "The wedding will be Saturday morning; that will give you a week to prepare." Then she turned to Thaos. "You are in the wedding too, so Stephan will have to help you get a dress uniform."

After Raul and Simon had eaten dinner and checked on the soldiers who were standing guard; they returned to their campsite and sat by the fire. Raul poured them each a cup of whiskey.

"Well, should we open them now?" Simon asked.

In silence both men took the gifts their wives had given them out of their pockets. Simon was going to make a joke but then decided not to. There was a small note attached to each gift. The notes were identical and read only, B*ecause we can't be with you.*

Raul and Simon both slowly unwrapped the gifts which exposed a large golden locket for each of them. Inscribed on the outside of the lockets were the words *We love you.* Inside of the lockets were tiny locks of hair each fastened together by the tiniest of bows. The children's hair had blue bows and Annabelle's and Vitomas' hair were fastened with pink bows. Both men sat in silence holding their gifts.

"Bella please join me in the study," Claudius said after dinner. The two walked into the study and Claudius closed the door, then he opened a bottle of fine wine and poured two glasses.

"What is the occasion?" Bella asked.

"Well, we haven't been alone much lately," Claudius said and kissed Bella on the cheek. "And we have much to celebrate; we have a new daughter and a grandson on the way. And I was waiting until we were alone to look at the gift Mathas gave us." They both sat down in front of the large hearth.

"Rosa said Mathas tried to make your gifts equal in value," Bella said as she took a sip of her wine.

Claudius unrolled the scroll. The castle of Claudius was built on the eastern shore of the River Shey. Mathas' and Fahron's castles both were to the east of Claudius' and were built on the western shore of the Sea of Grevtd. The locations of the three castles formed a triangle, with Fort Langer in the middle of them. The castles were but a few hours ride away from each other.

"Bella, he extended our land westward through the Langa woods to the western border of the kingdom. We now have water rights to the River Shey." As Claudius read the deeds, a broad smile came across his face. "And we now own part of the diamond mines."

"He has made us very wealthy with this gift," Bella said in amazement.

"Mathas is a generous man," Claudius said of his dear friend.

"Claudius I think we should share our good fortune."

"What do you mean Bella?"

"Well, I was so disturbed by the story you told me about Thaos and his family. He seems like such a fine boy, well, I know he is a grown man but he still seems like a boy to me. I overheard him talking to Stephan and he is thinking of moving into the barracks with the other soldiers. Would you consider asking him to live here with us, as part of the family?"

Claudius reached over and hugged Bella tightly. "I very much like your idea dear."

"You are not going to break that horse, and that is final," Matthew said.

"Matthew!" Angelina yelled angrily.

Matthew grabbed Angelina and pulled her against him, then he kissed her passionately. "Do you want to wrestle to see who wins this fight?" he asked with a grin. "I will break the horse for you." Matthew said and kissed Angelina again. "I have something for you, wait here," Matthew said as he walked into his study.

"Matthew, before I forget; mother and father are coming to speak with the workmen about their new chambers here. They are very excited. Your father is so good to us."

"My father is a good man," Matthew said as he returned to the kitchen and walked up to Angelina with his hands behind his back. "I bought you a new saddle for your new horse but then I didn't think that was very romantic so I got you this," Matthew was smiling as he handed Angelina a box.

"But why?"

"The other night when you and I were both sitting up with Margarit; I realized you have always been there for me when I needed you; and that means a lot."

"Oh Matthew," Angelina started to get tears in her eyes and reached up and kissed him on the lips.

"Open it."

Angelina carefully opened the box that had red ribbons wrapped around it. "Matthew they are beautiful, I don't know what to say, I love them," said Angelina as she looked at a necklace that had a golden chain with tiny tear drop rubies around it and matching earrings."

Matthew picked Angelina up and walked to their bedroom, "How much time do we have before your parents get here?" he asked as Angelina laughed.

That night Sorren and Shara joined Mathas' family for dinner. "We are so honored that you gave us a home here in the castle," Sorren said. "This way we can be closer when the grandchildren arrive."

"Well don't wait until then," Mathas said with a laugh. "Let me know if you have any problems with the workmen."

"Before we eat," Matthew said as he stood up. "I have a little surprise for you." He left the table and walked into the main kitchen. When Matthew returned he had an old man and a teenage boy with him, "These are Thaos' friends," Matthew introduced. "This is Jeb and his grandson Ryan."

371

"It is an honor to meet you My Lord," Jeb said humbly.

"Why are you all coming out of the kitchen?" Rosa asked.

"Well that is the surprise; Jeb cooked your meal tonight. And if it is only half as good as the meal he made for us at his cottage; you will love it. And Father, Ryan would like to enlist in our army."

Mathas smiled, "Ryan how old are you?"

"Eighteen, My Lord."

"Have you spoken with your grandfather about this?"

"Oh yes, My Lord."

"You know it will be a lot of hard work."

"My Lord, I am not afraid of hard work."

"Very well, if it is alright with your grandfather it is alright with me. Matthew can take care of it."

One of the female servants served the different courses that Jeb prepared. All the adults at the table were delighted by the new delicacies they were trying. The children had their favorites but they were completely won over by the desserts.

"Father if you like Jeb's cooking I would suggest you hire him now, because Stephan is going to tell Claudius to hire him."

At the end of the meal, Mathas called Jeb to the table. "Everything you prepared was wonderful. Would you consider running our kitchen?"

Jeb was speechless; he looked over at Matthew who winked at him. "My Lord, I would be honored. I am sorry I wasn't expecting this I don't know what to say."

Mathas and Rosa smiled. "I am sure Matthew will work out a fair wage and living quarters for you," Mathas said.

Vitomas was almost asleep when a sound made her jump up in bed. She quickly got out of bed and checked on babies Sudfad and Samuel, both were sound asleep. As Vitomas walked back to her bed she heard another sound. All of Raul's weapons were in his study, which was down the hallway. Vitomas could not think of anything in their bedroom she could use as a weapon. She decided to try and get to the study. As Vitomas walked down the hallway she heard movement again.

"Vitomas."

"Annabelle is that you?"

"Yes, can you light a candle I am trying to carry both of the boys."

Vitomas turned and quickly lit a candle and ran down the hallway where she saw Annabelle standing in a nightgown, holding the twins who were dressed for bed. Vitomas quickly took one of the boys. "What is wrong?" Vitomas asked.

Annabelle started laughing, "I can't stand to be over there without Simon, can we spend the night with you?"

Vitomas laughed, "You fool I was going to the study to get a sword."

"You don't know how to use one anyway," Annabelle joked.

"Yes you can spend the night, honestly I would enjoy the company," said Vitomas. "I really miss Raul and it is only the first night."

"I know, I wonder how many months they will be gone," said Annabelle sadly.

The week before Stephan's and Ingr's wedding was chaotic. Even though they wanted a simple garden ceremony like Matthew and Angelina had, Bella would not hear of it. Bella said 'This might be her only chance to plan a wedding and she was going to enjoy it.' Bella planned an engagement celebration the night before the wedding. Since Bella had so little time to organize all of the celebrations both Rosa and Isadore were more than glad to help her.

As Stephan and Matthew entered the Great Hall where the engagement celebration was being held, they looked at the crowded room. "I don't even know some of these people," Stephan said with a laugh. "Here come the girls." Both Angelina and Ingr were walking towards them. Both women were dressed in elegant gowns that Bella had bought for them. Ingr was wearing an emerald green gown and Angelina a light pink gown.

"You two are the most beautiful women in this room," Matthew said as he kissed Angelina on the lips.

"Well, speaking of girls, where is Thaos?" Angelina asked with a big smile.

"Why?" asked Stephan suspiciously.

"Because Ingr and I told a few of our friends about him and they are coming to meet him," Angelina said with a giggle.

"Does he know this?" Stephan asked.

"No, it will be a surprise," Ingr said with a grin. Then she looked towards the entrance to the Great Hall, "Angelina here they are now. Stephan please find Thaos."

"Actually," said Angelina with a mischievous grin. "Let us introduce him to the girls first. Then give us a couple of minutes and the two of you join us."

"Listen to you," Matthew said laughing. "Why do you want us to wait to meet your friends?"

"Honey because you two are so handsome the girls won't look at anyone else," Angelina said and kissed Matthew on the cheek.

"Why do I have a feeling like we have just been had?" Matthew asked. "Ok, we will find him for you."

Stephan knocked on the door to Thaos' room. "It's Stephan are you coming to the...?" Stephan didn't finish his sentence before Thaos called through the closed door.

"Come in I am getting dressed."

"When Stephan opened the door he saw Thaos standing with his back to the door, putting on a shirt. Stephan saw that Thaos' back was covered with scars.

"Sorry to bother you but the girls are looking for you," Stephan said with a laugh.

"What girls?" asked Thaos as he turned around.

"Ingr and Angelina."

"Why?"

"They have a surprise for you."

"And why does that scare me?" Thaos said and laughed.

"Actually I think you are going to like it," Stephan said as the two men walked towards the celebration. Ingr and Angelina had been watching for them; so before Stephan and Thaos entered the room, both Angelina and Ingr walked up to Thaos' and they each took one of his arms.

"We have some friends who want to meet you," Angelina said sweetly.

Thaos looked at both Matthew and Stephan, who were laughing. Then he said to Ingr and Angelina, "You two make me nervous."

"It will be alright," Ingr said soothingly. "And if you don't like any of these girls we have a lot more friends."

Sorren walked up to Matthew and Stephan as they watched Thaos being introduced to four very pretty girls. "He really looks uncomfortable," Stephan and laughed.

"Look at the one with the black curly hair," Matthew said with a grin. "She is already flirting with him. Ok, do you two want to place a small wager on this?"

"What are we betting on?" Sorren asked.

"Which one he chooses," Matthew said. "I kind of think it might be that little redhead."

"That's because you like redheads," Stephan joked. "Oh look at that blonde she is pushing ahead of the rest."

"I think we need to make two bets, one on who he chooses and the other on whether they all fight over him," Matthew said with a grin.

"I'm in," said Sorren and his loud laugh bellowed through the room.

"I'm putting my money on the one who just walked in," Stephan said.

"She is beautiful but she isn't paying any attention to him," Matthew said.

"Exactly, I think Thaos is the kind of guy who likes a challenge."

"Thaos we would like you to meet some of our friends," Angelina said. "This is Isla." Angelina introduced him to a pretty girl with blonde curly hair and brown eyes. Isla was not subtle about pushing past her friends to get closer to Thaos.

"And this is Lana," Angelina said. Lana too, had blonde hair but it hung straight down her back. She was very pretty with green eyes. Lana was considerably shyer than her friends.

Next Angelina introduced Thaos to a pretty girl with long curly red hair and large brown eyes, "This is Lillian."

"And this is Elexas," Angelina said. Elexas had long black curly hair and blue eyes. It was obvious to everyone present that she and Isla were competing for Thaos' attention.

As soon as Angelina had finished introducing their four friends to Thaos, Ingr asked them, "Where is Nikki?"

"With her horse," replied Isla. "He started limping on the way here."

"There you are," Ingr said as a slender girl with long straight black hair and large brown eyes walked up to her. All of the girls from the Nordes Tribe were wearing the leather outfits befitting their status as warriors. Angelina motioned for Matthew and Stephan to join them.

"Ingr I heard what your father did to you, is that why you never come home?" Nikki asked.

Ingr hesitated, "Stephan is afraid to have me return to the tribe without him."

"Is this Stephan?" Nikki asked as she looked at Thaos.

"No, this is Thaos; you are standing up with him in the wedding," Ingr said, then she turned to Stephan. "This is Stephan."

Nikki looked at Stephan earnestly and asked, "Stephan would you please help me with my horse?"

"Sure," Stephan replied apprehensively. "Thaos why don't you join us?"

As soon as the three were outside, Nikki turned to Stephan, "I am sorry but I need to speak with you, it is about Ingr's father. Can we speak in front of him?"

"Yes, Thaos can hear," said Stephan. "What is wrong?"

"I don't know if Sorren really told you what a horrible man Thaddies is. Did you know that Sorren and Shara took Ingr in so her father would not touch her as a husband?"

"No," said Stephan angrily.

Nikki looked at Thaos, "Thaddies sold Ingr to a stranger for money to buy whiskey but Stephan saved her and the whole village talks about it. We know you threatened to kill Thaddies if he hurt any of his children. Stephan I think he is trying to have you killed. Thaddies won't speak of you on our lands because he is afraid of Sorren; but he drinks often at taverns in Langer. Some of the men of our tribe said Thaddies has been telling men that he would give Ingr to anyone who could take her away from you."

"What!" Stephan was enraged.

"There is more, one of the men from our village stopped me a couple of miles back and said Thaddies is in a tavern called Nates and he is saying those things again."

Stephan grasped Nikki's hand and said, "Thank you and please do not say anything to Ingr; I will tell her after the wedding."

"Stephan, you should have killed him; that family would be better off," Nikki said as Stephan walked back into the castle.

"Do you really have a problem with your horse?" Thaos asked.

"Yes."

"I will look at it when we return," Thaos said and walked into the castle. When he returned to the celebration Thaos saw Stephan, Matthew and Angelina talking with Sorren. Thaos walked up to the group and stood near Stephan.

"No," Sorren said gruffly. "Thaddies is a monster but he is still her father. Even as angry as you are, you must realize it is not a good idea to kill your wife's father the night before your wedding. You stay here at your celebration and I will take care of him."

"We will take care of him," Thaos said with a coldness to his voice that Stephan had not heard before. "Think of it as a wedding gift," Thaos said then turned to Sorren. "I am familiar with Nates; some of Usman's men drink there every night. I have a plan, let me just get one thing from my room and we can leave."

Thaos and Matthew walked through the open door into Nates Tavern. As soon as they set foot inside Thaos said, "Far corner." Matthew saw four tough looking men sitting at the corner table. Matthew walked over and sat at an empty table near the four men; while Thaos went to the bar and got a bottle of whiskey and three glasses. Both Matthew and Thaos positioned themselves at the table so they could see the bar and the four men sitting near them.

A few minutes later Sorren walked into the tavern and looked around until he saw Thaddies standing at the bar. Sorren walked boldly up to Thaddies and stood very close to him.

"Sorren what are you doing here?" Thaddies asked. Thaddies was slurring his words and steadying himself by hanging onto the bar.

"I have a proposition for you," Sorren said gruffly. "Leave my tribe and never return."

"Why should I?" Thaddies asked with a grin.

"Because I might kill you if you don't." Sorren was staring intently into Thaddies eyes.

"But where would I go Sorren?"

"I was thinking about that," Sorren pulled a small pouch of gold coins out of his pocket and slid it in front of Thaddies. "Actually I don't care where you go. You can stay in this tavern for all I care; but as of tonight you do not return to our lands."

Thaddies opened the pouch and poured the gold coins onto the bar, they clanged as they hit the wood. "Why thank you Sorren," Thaddies said with a grin.

Sorren left Thaddies and joined Matthew and Thaos at the table. As Sorren poured himself a drink, Matthew said loud enough for the four men to hear, "What did you pay that old drunk for?"

"Information." Then Sorren leaned forward as if he only wanted Matthew and Thaos to hear what he was saying. "Thaddies gives me information about Usman's men and I give him money for whiskey." The three men sat in silence and drank their whiskey as the four men at the next table stood up and walked over to Thaddies.

"What's going on?" Thaddies yelled as the four men dragged him out of the tavern.

"I know where they dump the bodies; tomorrow we can check for his," Thaos said solemnly.

When the three men returned to the celebration, Stephan immediately walked up to them, "Did you find him?"

379

"Yes and Thaos' plan worked," Sorren said with a laugh.

"If Thaddies is still alive when they get him to Usman; he will be torn apart by horses tonight. I know where Usman dumps the bodies and will check for his tomorrow."

"I owe you all a great debt," Stephan said sincerely. "I have been so angry I didn't even want to go near Ingr."

"Son, this is your engagement celebration, go and enjoy it," Sorren said.

Matthew turned to Thaos and said with a laugh, "And you need to go back to Angelina's friends because we have bets riding on you."

Thaos started laughing, "What are you betting on?"

"Well we have two bets going, "Matthew explained with a grin. "The first is which girl you choose and the second is to see if all those girls just plain fight over you."

Thaos laughed loudly, "Well I guess I better try to earn someone some money." As soon as Thaos stepped away from Matthew both Elexas and Isla ran up to him.

"Thaos would you like to dance?" Elexas asked.

"I would like to dance with you too," Isla said with a flirtatious smile.

Thaos was flattered by the attention of these two very attractive women. "Sure but later," Thaos said as he looked around the room. "Where is Nikki?"

"Nikki!" Elexas said with a huff. "Thaos, Nikki didn't even come here to meet you."

"I told her I would help her with her horse," Thaos said as he searched the room with his eyes. Finally Thaos saw Nikki and Ingr talking at the far end of the Great Hall. Nikki was just a little taller than Ingr. Both girls wore their hair long and loose and they both had bangs. As Thaos looked at them he noticed other similarities. Both Ingr and Nikki had long legs, firm muscular bodies and deep tans.

Ingr was wearing a beautiful gown; in contrast, Nikki was wearing the short leather skirt and sleeveless leather camisole of the female Nordes warriors; these outfits provided them freedom of movement when fighting. Thaos stood for just a moment admiring Nikki's figure, although she was slender she had large full breasts which were greatly accentuated by her camisole. Thaos started to walk towards Nikki then turned back to Elexas and Isla, who both got hopeful looks on their faces. "Is the reason she didn't come here to meet me because she has a man?"

Neither girl responded immediately, then Isla said, "No, Nikki doesn't have a husband or a boyfriend."

Both Ingr and Nikki smiled when Thaos approached them. "Do you still need help with your horse?" he asked.

"Yes, but I don't want to take you away from your admirers," Nikki said with a smile that lit up her face. Thaos smiled and held out his hand to her. This act surprised Nikki and she stared at him for a moment.

"I don't bite," Thaos joked. Nikki continued to look at Thaos without moving. "Nikki are you afraid of me?"

"No," Nikki said as she blushed. Nikki looked at Ingr who had a confused look on her face.

"Nikki, Thaos is really nice and a fierce warrior," Ingr said as she was surprised at how her close friend was acting.

Nikki took Thaos' hand without saying a word and they proceeded to walk through the crowded room. Nikki was as confused by her own actions as Ingr was. A proud and courageous warrior, Nikki was not used to feeling nervous or intimidated and she didn't understand why she felt both of these emotions as she walked with this handsome man.

"You seem uncomfortable," Thaos remarked as they walked across the crowded room. "What is the matter?" Before Nikki could answer Thaos asked another question. "Is there a man here that you are afraid will get jealous?"

"There is no other man and I don't know you and I usually don't hold hands with someone I don't know."

381

Thaos laughed, "Well maybe we should get to know each other."

"You are really bold."

"Does that offend you?"

Nikki didn't immediately answer. "No, I just wasn't expecting, well, Thaos I don't want to hurt your feelings but I didn't come here to find a husband."

"I didn't ask you to marry me. I offered to help you with your horse," Thaos said with a grin as he held the door open so Nikki could walk outside.

As soon as they were away from the celebration, Nikki asked in a whisper, "So what happened with Thaddies?"

"He won't be a threat to them anymore."

After a few moments of silence Nikki asked, "Is that all you are going to say?"

"Yep."

"Well did you kill him?" Nikki asked with frustration.

"Which is your horse?" Thaos asked as they approached a railing that had two horses tied to it.

"The paint, it's his front left leg. He started limping but I couldn't see a reason." Nikki watched as Thaos carefully examined her horses' leg and hoof. Then he examined the horse's right leg and then the left leg again.

"Why won't you tell me if Thaddies is dead?" Nikki asked as Thaos was examining her horse.

"Look here, his leg is starting to swell," Thaos said as he took Nikki's hand and rubbed it against the area of the horse's leg that was becoming puffy. "I think something stung him. Let's go to the kitchen, I am sure we can find what we need to make a poultice." Thaos took Nikki's hand but she did not move.

"Why aren't you answering my questions that is very rude of you?" Nikki asked with frustration. "Are you playing some kind of game?"

Thaos walked closer to Nikki and looked deeply into her eyes. "I will answer your questions if you answer mine. And I am not playing games with you." Nikki suddenly felt overwhelmed; she was both attracted to Thaos and wanted to flee from him at the same time. Nikki didn't understand why she was having these feelings.

Instead of saying what she was thinking Nikki asked, "Thaos are you making fun of me?"

"I don't even know why you asked me that, no I am not. Nikki are you afraid to answer my questions?"

"I am a warrior, I am not afraid of your questions," Nikki responded with indignation. Although for some reason that Nikki didn't understand she was afraid to answer Thaos' questions.

"Nikki I am going to ask you again, are you afraid of me?"

"No, why do you keep asking me that?"

"If you are a close friend of Ingr's and Angelina's I assume you are a fierce warrior and yet you are acting so strangely around me. Have I done something to offend you or have you heard something about me that scares you?"

"No you have done nothing wrong except that you won't answer my questions."

"It is only fair that you tell me why you are acting so strangely around me and I will tell you about Thaddies."

"Don't laugh at me if I tell you."

"I won't laugh."

"You make me nervous and I don't understand why and I don't understand why I am acting strangely. I can't give you more of an answer."

Thaos smiled because now he understood. "Some of Usman's men drink at Nates every night. Without going into a lot of detail, we made Usman's men believe that Thaddies was selling information about their tribe. The last I saw Thaddies, four of Usman's men were dragging him out of the tavern. I suspect Thaddies will be killed tonight. I know where Usman dumps his bodies and I will look for Thaddies' body tomorrow."

Nikki was silent for a few moments then all she said was, "Good, he didn't deserve to live."

"Are you staying at the castle tonight?"

"Why?" Nikki asked suspiciously.

"See there you go again," Thaos said. "I asked because I am going to put your horse into the barn. Once we put the poultice on him you shouldn't ride him for a day."

Thaos took Nikki's hand again and they walked to the kitchen. "You are very irritating," Nikki said angrily. "Besides I don't know why you care about what I think, you have plenty of girls in that celebration who want to be with you."

"I am very attracted to you and you are to me although I don't think you realize it," Thaos said as they walked around the castle to the back door of the kitchen.

"Thaos wouldn't I know if I was attracted to you?" Nikki asked with both irritation and fear in her voice.

"We'll continue this conversation later," Thaos said as they entered the kitchen which was filled with staff.

With the distraction of making the poultice, Nikki relaxed. She and Thaos laughed as they worked together on the concoction.

"How old are you?" Thaos asked as soon as they left the kitchen.

"Why?"

"Nikki do you always try to turn everything into a battle or are you just scared of the questions I am asking?"

384

"I'm not scared, I told you. And I am almost eighteen. How old are you?" Nikki's tone of voice was defensive.

"I'm twenty-six," Thaos replied. "You haven't had many boyfriends have you?" Nikki's mouth fell open and a look of shock overtook her face but she did not answer him. "Nikki, I am making a new life here but in my former line of work, my life depended on my ability to read people and I am pretty good at it. Do you want to hear what I think?"

"Not really but I know you are going to tell me," Nikki said in a whisper.

"I think you are a fierce warrior and a woman of integrity like Ingr and Angelina; I admire both of your friends very much. I think you have devoted your life to being a warrior and now when you are around a man you are attracted to you feel uncomfortable and a loss of control. So am I right?" Nikki stared at Thaos, her eyes wide with amazement.

"Did Ingr and Angelina tell you that?"

"No," Thaos said. "I told you I am good at reading people. And judging by your reaction I assume I am correct. Now what I find curious is why you don't have a husband or boyfriend. Nikki you are an intoxicatingly beautiful woman."

"You think I am beautiful?"

"Don't you?"

Nikki did not answer Thaos' question as they untied her horse from the railing and put it into a stall in the barn. Thaos started to apply the poultice to the horse's leg as Nikki sat near Thaos and watched him.

"My father died in a hunting accident three years ago. I am the eldest and I take care of the family. My mother is not a warrior, she plants gardens but she does not know how to hunt or fish."

"See I was right, you are a woman of integrity. How many brothers and sisters do you have?"

"I have five, three brothers and two sisters."

385

Thaos wiped the poultice off his hands and onto a towel he had brought from the kitchen. "So is it that you have never met anyone you were interested in before or did you swear off men altogether so you can care for your family?"

"I don't believe how bold you are," Nikki said angrily.

"You think I am bold because my questions are hitting a nerve. You haven't yet told me I was wrong about anything I have said. So what is your answer?"

"Both I guess," Nikki said in a whisper.

"Nikki, you know you aren't betraying your family by having your own life too. I would doubt that your family expects that kind of sacrifice from you."

"My mother is a wonderful woman, she never asks me to do the things I do, it's just that she needs so much help."

"Are there people in your village who could help her?"

"Yes but mother can't afford to pay them and she has her pride too."

Thaos stood up; as he did he grasped both of Nikki's hands and gently pulled her to her feet. They were standing close to each other and looking into the other's eyes. "Nikki I would like you to attend that celebration with me."

"But what about those other girls? They came here just to meet you."

"I have chosen you." Both excitement and fear surged through Nikki as Thaos said these words.

"Thaos I don't know how to dance," Nikki said shyly.

"Well then we are both in luck, because I do and I can teach you."

Nikki and Thaos returned to the celebration holding hands only now Nikki was not reluctant about holding Thaos' hand. Thaos walked directly to the dance floor.

"I am going to hold you tight so you can feel the movement of my body," Thaos explained. "Just relax and let me lead."

"I'm so sorry," Nikki apologized after she stepped on Thaos' foot.

"Nikki, look up at me and not at your feet, you are trying too hard. Just follow the movement of my body." Thaos' pulled Nikki closer to him.

Within minutes Nikki was surprised at herself that she was dancing. "I don't believe this," she said with a smile. "I didn't realize it would be so easy."

"You have a beautiful smile," Thaos said as they glided across the floor. "Are you feeling more relaxed with me?"

"Yes," Nikki hesitated. "Thaos you were right about everything you said. I do find you attractive; I just was not expecting this."

"Expecting what?"

Nikki didn't answer for a moment, "You. I really didn't come here to meet a man."

"I know and that was one of the things I found attractive about you."

Now Nikki looked up into Thaos' face as if searching for answers. "Thaos I don't understand why you choose me. All of those girls are beautiful and they want you."

"I too did not come to this celebration looking for a wife. I didn't know that Angelina and Ingr had asked their friends here until moments before I was being introduced. You are right, every one of those women is beautiful but Nikki you greatly stand out from the rest. Not only are you beautiful but you came here to protect your friends instead of acting like a silly school girl. You are a woman of honor and integrity. I have dated women like Elexas and I want more than fun for one night."

Nikki didn't say a word but moved closer to Thaos and laid her head on his chest. They continued to dance in this close embrace; after a few minutes Thaos asked. "What are you thinking?"

"I was thinking about how nice this feels."

"Funny, so was I," Thaos said and kissed Nikki on top of her head.

Chapter XXV
Unaware

"Nikki," Ingr said as she walked up to Thaos and Nikki who were dancing slowly on the ballroom floor. "Nikki, Bella wants us all to have one last fitting with the seamstress." Both Thaos and Nikki were so lost in their thoughts and emotions that neither of them were aware of Ingr's presence at first. Then Ingr started to laugh.

"Oh Ingr, I am sorry," Nikki said with embarrassment. "What did you say?"

"I said the seamstress just arrived and Bella wants us to have one more fitting," Ingr looked back and forth between Nikki and Thaos. "You two really look cute together."

"Ingr," Nikki said and blushed. Then Nikki looked up at Thaos. "Where will I find you afterwards?"

Thaos smiled warmly at Nikki's words. "Come back to the ballroom, I will find you," Thaos said and kissed Nikki on the cheek.

"Well, it looks like you owe me some money," Stephan said with a smirk as he walked up to Matthew who was standing near one of the tables of refreshments.

"I'm not paying anything yet," Matthew said with a grin. "Look at the faces of the girls he isn't dancing with. There just might be a fight yet."

Thaos walked up to Stephan and Matthew. "You are going to make me a rich man," Stephan kidded.

"You bet on Nikki? She didn't even come here to meet me," Thaos said and laughed.

"Exactly, she looked like a challenge," Stephan said.

Matthew handed both Stephan and Thaos glasses of whiskey. "Thaos don't let him pull your leg. Ingr and Angelina have talked a lot about their friends and Nikki sounds like a really nice girl. We just weren't sure that is what you were looking for."

"I'm used to spending time with girls like Elexas," Thaos said. "Oh she is beautiful but two minutes after I leave her bed another guy will take my place."

"Thaos are you telling us you are looking to settle down?" Matthew asked with a grin.

"Why, did you bet on that too?" Thaos asked and laughed again.

"Sort of," Stephan said grinning. "Mother has become very attached to you Thaos and she keeps saying that she can see you settling down and starting a family here."

"What?" asked Thaos with surprise.

"Thaos you have to understand," Matthew explained. "Bella and Claudius always wanted lots of children and all they had was this vagabond son who never came home," Matthew kidded. "So I am considered one of her kids and Bella is starting to look at you the same way."

"Don't let it scare you," Stephan joked.

"Actually I think it's a compliment," Thaos said with more feeling than he was letting Matthew and Stephan see.

"Your admirers just realized that Nikki is not with you," Stephan said with a grin as he watched Elexas and Isla walking towards them.

Thaos started to laugh, "I wanted to talk to Sorren anyway. Do you know where he is?"

"The last time I saw him he was on the back patio," Matthew said.

As Thaos was walking off the dance floor he heard Stephan laughing, "Thaos you're breaking hearts tonight," Stephan called after him.

"So what did you want to talk to me about?" Sorren asked as he shut the door to Claudius' study. Only Thaos and Sorren were in the room.

"I just had some questions about the customs of your tribe?"

"Really?" Sorren asked as he filled both of their glasses with whiskey. "These questions wouldn't have anything to do with Nikki would they?"

Thaos grinned, "Nothing gets past you does it Sorren? Actually the questions are more about her family."

"Go on," said Sorren as he sat down in one of the large overstuffed chairs in the study.

"Nikki told me that her father was killed in a hunting accident three years ago and that she has been taking care of her family since."

"Yes that is true."

"She told me that she has not had a man in her life so she can take care of her family." Sorren's smile was growing wider as Thaos spoke. "So if I wanted Nikki to spend time with me here, I would need to find ways to take care of her family. Are there men in your village who I could hire to help Nikki's family?"

"These are some pretty serious questions for meeting a girl just hours ago," Sorren said. "I know Nikki has no idea you are asking me these things or she would be in here yelling at both of us. Let me tell you a little about her and her family. Nikki was one of my students who started training before the required age of ten. Angelina, Nikki and Ingr were together constantly and since Angelina and Ingr lived under my roof, Nikki stayed with us always."

"She is a good girl but proud and has a temper. Nikki worshipped her father, Duran. He was a warrior and spent a great deal of time with Nikki. Three years ago he was hunting and wounded a bear. The animal tore Duran apart. Nikki and her mother Gladys both fell apart for months after his death." Sorren paused for a few moments.

"I saw the two of you dancing it was hard not to notice. You need to know that Nikki doesn't have much romantic experience with men. The girls that Ingr and Angelina invited here to meet you have very different personalities. If you are looking for a girl just to have fun with for a while, I would suggest you turn your interest to the two who have been following you throughout the celebration."

Thaos smiled at Sorren's comments. "You still haven't answered my question."

"Yes," Sorren said with a grin. "There are men and women in the village that you could hire to help Gladys and the children and I would be happy to assist you with that."

"Sorren I will take you up on the offer," Thaos said. "But can you explain to me how a girl of Nikki's beauty has no suitors?"

"Oh there are plenty of men who would have her for their wife but as I told you; Nikki worshipped her father and I don't think she will consider any man unless he can measure up to Duran." Thaos was quiet for several moments. "Son," Sorren continued. "I have known the girl her entire life and I have never seen her act around anyone like she is acting with you."

"Is this where you live?" Nikki asked as she and Thaos entered his chambers later that night. The chambers consisted of three rooms of ornately decorated furniture and fine drapes. There was a fire in the hearth and candles lit in all of the rooms.

"Yes, Claudius and Bella have been very good to me. Would you like a glass of wine?" Thaos asked.

"Yes," said Nikki as she was walking around the parlor admiring the decorations. "This is very nice. Ingr said that I have a room here but I haven't seen it yet."

Nikki turned around and saw that Thaos was sitting on the sofa in front of the hearth. Nikki walked over to the sofa and sat so close to Thaos that their knees were touching.

"Do I still make you nervous?" Thaos asked as he handed Nikki her wine.

"Yes," Nikki said then started to giggle. "But I am getting used to it."

"Nikki I really do want to talk to you about some things but I have to admit that I have wanted to kiss you all night. If I kiss you are you going to run out of this room?" Thaos asked with a grin.

"No," Nikki said with indignation. "Thaos you keep saying that I..." Nikki didn't finish her sentence because Thaos kissed her on the lips. Without hesitation Nikki put her arms around his neck and slid closer to Thaos as she kissed him back. Both Nikki and Thaos were moaning and starting to sweat when he whispered, "Why don't you take your weapons off."

Nikki started laughing, "I will if you will."

They both stood up and started removing sheaths and weapons. "Well, if I take my shirt and boots off, will you take yours off?" Thaos asked with a grin.

Nikki looked at Thaos and started giggling, "I will take my sandals off." Nikki's sandals laced up to her knees and as she was removing them she watched Thaos take his shirt off. He had a broad chest and large muscular arms, the sight of which sent a surge of excitement through her. "You have so many scars, are they all from battle?" Nikki asked as she walked up to Thaos.

"Most of them," Thaos said as he lifted Nikki up. She wrapped her long legs around his waist and the two kissed with such passion that neither of them heard the knocking at the door for several moments.

"Thaos someone is here," Nikki said breathlessly.

Thaos set Nikki on her feet. "Don't go away," he said with a suggestive smile and walked to the door of his chambers.

"Elexas," Thaos said with surprise when he opened the door.

"I thought you would like some company," Elexas said and walked into his chambers. Thaos left the door open.

"I have company," Thaos replied loud enough for Nikki to hear.

Elexas was staring at Thaos' chest. "You have a beautiful body," she said flirtatiously.

"Elexas I have company."

"Really? Who?" Elexas asked. Nikki walked out of the parlor wearing Thaos' shirt. She walked up to Thaos and put her arms around his waist. Thaos looked at Nikki and smiled and put his arm around her shoulder. "Nikki I must say I am surprised," Elexas said sarcastically.

"Why?" Nikki asked.

"Honestly I didn't know if you liked men." Thaos could feel Nikki stiffening up as she listened to the tone of Elexas' voice.

"Elexas you should go now," Thaos said.

"The evening isn't lost," Elexas said smugly. "The three of us could have some fun."

"You really need to go now," Thaos said. Elexas hesitated then walked out of the door. Thaos closed and bolted the door behind her. Then he turned to Nikki. "Do you have anything on under my shirt?" Thaos asked with a grin.

"No," Nikki said with a coy smile.

"Good," Thaos said and took her hand.

As they were walking to his bed Nikki asked, "What was Elexas talking about?"

"I'll explain later."

The engagement celebration went late into the night and the wedding ceremony was early the next morning. Many of the guests from the engagement celebration stayed the night at Claudius' castle. The wedding was being held in one of the large flower gardens as Ingr and Stephan had requested. Bella had an archway made of white roses for the couple and the Sanuri to stand under. Rows upon rows of chairs were set in uniform lines in the yard. Tables of refreshments were set up in the yard and the castle. And there were flowers everywhere.

When Ingr awoke that morning she found Stephan watching her and smiling. "Stephan what is it?" she asked groggily. "I have something I want you to wear with your wedding dress," he said and handed her a box.

"Wait," Ingr said with a smile and jumped out of bed and ran into the parlor. She returned with a box for him.

"Open mine first," Stephan said warmly.

"Stephan, this is so beautiful," Ingr said excitedly. She held up a necklace made of gold with light blue sapphire stones and pearls. There were matching earrings in the box. "I have never seen anything so beautiful in my life. Thank you so much," Ingr said and kissed Stephan on the lips.

"The blue matches your eyes," Stephan said as he admired the necklace against her neck.

"I hope you like my gift, I wasn't sure what to get you," Ingr said apologetically. "You seem to have everything. So Matthew helped me." Ingr handed Stephan a long box.

"This is beautiful," Stephan said as he admired a dagger that was in a golden sheath. Both the sheath and the handle of the dagger had rubies and diamonds set deep inside the gold.

"Matthew had it made for me. It is very well balanced," Ingr said.

"Honey how on earth did you pay for this?"

"Claudius offered to pay for anything I wanted to get you for a gift."

395

"I love it, thank you," Stephan said and kissed Ingr passionately.

Thaos and Nikki got little sleep that night. They passionately made love as these two lonely warriors surrendered to their hungers and their needs. During the brief periods in between their love making they talked, not frivolous conversation but the kind of conversation that is opened up by love making. Both Nikki and Thaos were the kind of private people who were guarded about their emotions and their lives. But as they became one, their walls became smaller.

Towards dawn, Thaos moved off from Nikki and lay on his side facing her with his head propped up in his hand. Nikki too, rolled onto her side so she could face him. Thaos reached over and started to stroke her hair. "Are you going home right after the wedding?" he asked.

"I left four days' worth of meat with the family, so I can stay that long."

"While you are here at the castle I would like you to stay with me," Thaos said softly. "What do you think?"

"Really," Nikki said with obvious excitement. "I would like that."

"Good," Thaos said and kissed Nikki on the lips. "Do you do all the hunting for your family?"

"Yes, since Father died."

"When you go back to your village I will come with you and help you hunt."

"Thaos my village is small; you will meet my mother if you come home with me."

"Is that a problem?"

"No but do you think she will be able to tell that we have made love?"

Thaos laughed, "I don't know." He leaned forward and kissed Nikki again, when they heard a knock at his door and Angelina's voice.

"Thaos is Nikki in there?"

Thaos got out of bed and put only his trousers on. When he opened the door, Angelina just grinned at him. "Nikki's getting dressed; come in," Thaos said with a smile.

Angelina leaned close to Thaos and whispered as she did not want Nikki to hear her words. "Thaos my friend has little experience with men, don't break her heart."

"I wasn't planning to," Thaos said warmly.

"What are you two whispering about?" Nikki asked with a smile. Then she abruptly stopped. "Angelina you didn't hear us did you?" Nikki asked as a look of horror crossed her face.

"I don't know what you are talking about," Angelina said.

"Nikki got a little loud last night," Thaos said with a grin.

Angelina laughed then said, "We need to get ready."

Nikki walked up to Thaos and kissed him on the lips. Angelina waited as their kiss seemed to go on forever. Finally Angelina grabbed Nikki's arm. "You two have plenty of time for that later," Angelina said with a laugh as she pulled Nikki out the door. After they heard Thaos close his door Angelina leaned over to Nikki and asked, "So how was it?"

"I never imagined it could be so wonderful," Nikki gushed.

"That's exactly what Ingr and I said too."

Thirty minutes later Angelina knocked on the door to Stephan and Ingr's chambers. "It's Angelina and Nikki," she called out three times before Stephan opened the door; wearing only his trousers.

"Stephan you aren't dressed yet? What have you been doing?" Angelina asked in a scolding tone.

Stephan grinned at her. Angelina rolled her eyes, "Stephan you have the rest of your lives for that; you are going to be late for your own wedding. Now take your things and go get ready with Matthew; Nikki and I are here to help Ingr.

Stephan laughed as he turned back to the bedroom to get his clothes. You two look very nice," he called over his shoulder.

Excitement filled the castle as the guests started to arrive. Claudius and Bella had arranged a variety of activities to keep their guests occupied between the wedding and the evening ball. Rooms of all sizes were prepared for guests to spend the night. And each room was stocked with fine wines, whiskies, fruits and sweets of all types. Bella had hired several groups of musicians but in the garden she wanted only harps to be played for the wedding.

At the stroke of nine the Sanuri took his place beneath the rose arbor. Stephan, Matthew and Thaos all took their places in front of the arbor. They wore the dress uniform of the Army of Lentz which was dark blue with gold stripes running down the sides of the pants and a golden sash worn across the chest. Bella started to cry when she saw Stephan at the arbor. Claudius put his arm around her and smiled.

Mathas and Rosa and Fahron and Isadore sat on the groom's side of the aisle; while Sorren and Shara were to sit on the bride's side of the aisle since Ingr's parents were not attending the wedding. Many members of the Nordes Tribe were in attendance wearing the traditional outfits of the warriors.

Margarit walked down the aisle first, with a basket of yellow rose petals which she threw on the carpet before the bridesmaids. Margarit was dressed in a light yellow dress with a full lace skirt. The excitement over being in the wedding helped Margarit to overcome some of the trauma of her kidnapping. Angelina followed Margarit and carried a bouquet of white and yellow roses.

Nikki walked behind Angelina carrying a basket of long stemmed yellow roses which she handed out to the families of the wedding party, as was the tradition of the Nordes Tribe. Both bridesmaids wore pale yellow silk dresses that were the same design as Ingr's dress. The dresses were simple and formfitting with narrow skirts and tiny off the shoulder straps; they were decorated with lace and pearls.

Sorren walked Ingr down the aisle and smiled proudly. Ingr had a bouquet of white and yellow roses and wore the necklace and earrings Stephan had given her that morning. Although Stephan had seen Ingr in the dress before, he felt his heart leap in his chest as he watched Ingr walk down the aisle. The Sanuri smiled warmly as Ingr walked towards him; then he looked at the skies for any sign of attack. Enrops and Hengers sat in the trees surrounding Claudius' castle.

The Sanuri turned around and lit three white candles, he held the middle one up to the heavens and prayed then he set it back in its holder. He walked over to Stephan and Ingr and as he raised his hands over them, the ground began to shake.

"Stephan and Ingr do you promise to cherish this gift of marriage that The Great Ruler has blessed you with?"

"We do."

The ground was shaking more violently.

"Stephan and Ingr do you promise to always follow the path of The Great Ruler especially when you cannot see where it goes?"

"We do."

A great shadow was cast over the wedding. The shadow was made by thousands of ravens but before the ravens could attack the Enrops and Hengers took to the skies. The Sanuri looked at Margarit. "Child go over to your father," he said. Margarit ran to Mathas and sat on his lap.

"You might want to make this short," Stephan said to the Sanuri.

"Do you promise to love, care for and protect each other for the rest of your lives?"

"We do."

"At this time I am going to ask all of the guests to go inside of the castle quickly," the Sanuri said.

Ingr lifted her skirt and grabbed one of the knives she had sheathed to her thighs. Angelina and Nikki followed suit. The soldiers and the warriors remained outside.

"What is making the ground shake like that?" Stephan asked. And then he saw them; hundreds of running Demalogs. "Go inside," Stephan screamed to Ingr. She and Angelina both ran inside but it was to get more weapons not to escape the attack. Hengers and Enrops started to attack the demons that were fighting with the soldiers and the guests.

Thaos grabbed Nikki who was standing near him and threw her behind him so violently that she fell to the ground; as two Demalogs hit Thaos with such force that they knocked him on his back. Nikki ran to Thaos and plunged her dagger into the back of one Demalog and grabbed the second demon by the hair and slit its throat. Thaos jumped up but before he could speak, Nikki was screaming at him, "Don't you ever do that to me again, I am a warrior too." Then Nikki turned and joined the battle.

A second wave of Demalogs was running towards the battle. The Sanuri raised his hands and spoke in an ancient tongue and the ground underneath those demons opened up. Hundreds of Demalogs screamed as they fell into blackness and the ground closed over them. The demons and the humans were fighting hand to hand. The Enrops and Hengers had defeated the ravens and now focused on the demons.

The Sanuri joined the fight, every demon he touched turned into a pile of ashes. Ingr and Angelina ran outside with swords and their bows and arrows. Sorren was fighting with three Demalogs and the girls ran to help him. After they killed the three demons, Ingr screamed, "Where is Stephan?"

Angelina and Ingr ran through the chaos trying to find their husbands, who were fighting back to back because they were surrounded by a large pack of Demalogs. The girls each quickly shot three arrows, as they were trained. Each arrow hit its mark, not only killing six demons but turning the attention of the demons away from Stephan and Matthew.

The Demalogs advanced towards Ingr and Angelina who stood their ground and continued to shoot their arrows into the hell beasts. Matthew and Stephan were both injured but savagely attacked the Demalogs that were now advancing on their wives. Soon Sorren ran to his daughter with several warriors from his tribe, who killed the remaining demons.

Both Stephan and Matthew were bleeding from multiple wounds as their wives ran up to them. "Father help us," Angelina cried as she tried to help Matthew walk towards the castle. The battle was finished. The wounded were being carried into the castle where Bella and Isadore were preparing the Great Hall for the injured.

"I'm getting blood on your dress," Stephan said as Ingr was helping him into the castle. Tears were streaming down her face. "Our fathers?" Stephan asked.

"They are alright, I saw them moments ago," Sorren said.

"Where is Thaos?" Stephan asked.

"I don't know," whispered Ingr who could barely talk as her husband's blood was soaking into her wedding dress.

Claudius and Mathas came running to help their injured sons. "They were attacked by a large group of demons," Angelina cried. Mathas and Sorren helped Matthew walk. Claudius was a giant of a man and he picked his son up and carried him into the castle.

Bella had soldiers carrying mattresses and chairs to the room designated for the wounded. Isadore was getting bandages, water and medical supplies. These two women had spent their lives married to warriors; this was a sad routine for them. Several of the wedding guests were physicians. Shara and Angelina were healers. All of the members of the Nordes Tribe and many of the soldiers had some knowledge of wound care. Anyone who was not put on guard duty was helping the wounded.

Matthew and Stephan were laid on mattresses that were near to each other. Shara and Angelina were attending to Matthew as one of the physicians was trying to stop the bleeding from Stephan's wounds. Both men were conscious. "Mother have you seen Thaos yet?" Stephan asked Bella who was kneeling next to him.

Bella stood up and looked around the room after a few moments she said happily, "I see him, but who is he carrying?"

Thaos walked up to them with tears in his eyes, "Would you look at him?" Thaos asked as he held Jeb's lifeless body in his arms.

"Son, you know he is dead," Sorren said softly as he tried to take Jeb's body from Thaos.

"No," Thaos said and walked back outside with Jeb.

Mathas gave Stephan and Matthew each a bottle of whiskey, "Drink these, you are going to need it, we will have to burn those wounds."

"I am sorry I didn't kill her Stephan," Ingr said as she cried and held his hand. "Stephan, Stephan," Ingr screamed with terror seizing her heart.

"He is alive, he has just passed out," the physician said.

Somewhere in the room, a girl screamed then started to cry. The room was filled with chaos as the wounded were being tended to. Cries, screams and the smell of burning flesh filled the air. The Sanuri walked into the castle carrying the last of the wounded soldiers off from the battlefield. As he looked around, despair filled his heart for these people. "It is time," he said to himself.

After the Sanuri placed the wounded soldier on a mattress, he walked over to Stephan and Matthew, both of whom were now unconscious and laying side by side. Without saying a word the Sanuri placed the palm of each of his hands on the foreheads of the young men. Their families watched as the Sanuri appeared to go into a trance.

"What is he doing?" whispered Sorren.

Mathas just shook his head as he did not understand. After a few minutes, the Sanuri smiled. "They will be alright," he said and started to walk towards other wounded victims.

"Sanuri what did you do?" Sorren asked.

402

"I gave to them of my grace," replied the Sanuri and walked away.

Thaos carried Jeb to one of the gardens that surrounded the castle. He laid the body gently on the ground and began to weep. Not since he buried his family at the age of nine, had Thaos cried. Suddenly Thaos' head jerked up. "Nikki," he said out loud and ran back into the castle. Sorren was standing close to the door. "Sorren where is Nikki?" Thaos asked fearfully.

"Thaos she is alright, she's over there," Sorren said sadly and nodded his head towards a group of Nordes warriors, many of whom were crying. Thaos ran to the group which was standing in a circle around a body. When Thaos reached Nikki he saw her standing over Isla, who was dead.

"Are you alright?" Thaos whispered into Nikki's ear. She quickly turned around and buried her head in his chest.

"Look at what they did to her," Nikki cried. Now Thaos realized that parts of Isla's face and legs had been eaten away.

Thaos had his arms around Nikki. "Come," is all he said as he walked her away from Isla's body. They reached Stephan and Matthew just as soldiers were moving the two injured men from the Great Hall. Thaos and Nikki followed the soldiers, who entered Stephan's and Ingr's chambers.

Bella, Ingr and Angelina were preparing beds in two different rooms. Stephan was put into his own bed while Matthew was put into the next bedroom. Thaos and Nikki walked up to Claudius who was standing in the parlor watching the two young men being put into bed. "How bad are they?" Thaos asked.

"The wounds are bad but the Sanuri did something to help them heal," Claudius said. "I am not really sure what he did but he said the boys would be alright."

Thaos saw Angelina trying to move some furniture around in the bedroom that Matthew was in. "Honey you stay with Claudius," Thaos said to Nikki and kissed her on the head. Then he walked up to Angelina. "What do you need me to do?"

"I want to get that table and a couple of chairs near his bed," Angelina said with tears running down her cheeks. As Thaos was moving the furniture, Angelina asked. "Thaos would you and Nikki stay here tonight in case we need help? There is another bedroom."

"Of course," Thaos said then he walked into Stephan's room. Ingr was sitting next to the bed holding Stephan's hand and crying. Bella was also sitting in a chair on the opposite side of the bed and crying. "Is there anything I can do?" Thaos asked.

"No but thank you," Bella said.

"Nikki and I will stay in that other bedroom tonight so we can help you."

"Good," Ingr said as she wiped the tears from her face. "Stephan and Matthew are too big for us to move by ourselves."

When Thaos returned to the parlor he found Nikki sitting on the sofa, she was no longer crying although her face was red and swollen. Nikki stood up when she saw Thaos. "Nikki, Ingr and Angelina want us to stay here and help them. They said there is another bedroom here." Nikki put her arms around Thaos' chest and back and hugged him tightly.

"I am so glad you weren't hurt," Nikki whispered then she looked into Thaos' face. "I'm so upset I almost forgot that Claudius and King Mathas want you to join them in Claudius' study."

"Will you be alright?" Thaos asked.

"Yes, do you want me to move some of your things over here while you are gone?"

"Yes, that would be nice," Thaos said and kissed Nikki. "But I really don't have much to move."

Thaos knocked on the door to Claudius' study; when Thaos entered only Claudius was in the room. But the maps that Thaos had made of Juleta's castle and grounds were spread out on the table.

Claudius poured two large glasses of whiskey and handed one to Thaos. "We are waiting for Mathas to return with the Sanuri. Have a seat son," Claudius said. "Bella and I had planned on meeting with you tonight because there was something we wanted to discuss. But with all of this going on, well, I might as well take this opportunity."

Claudius sat down in a chair across from Thaos. "Bella and I have been talking and we would like you to live here, in the castle with us as family," Claudius said. "I know we really haven't known each other that long but both Bella and I are very fond of you. In some ways you and Stephan are so much alike it's like having two sons."

Thaos was taken by surprise by Claudius' words. "I will admit I don't really know what to say," Thaos was choking up as he spoke.

"Well say yes," Claudius said and smiled.

"Yes and thank you." Thaos cleared his throat. "I have become very fond of all of you also. You are good people and I would be honored."

"Now are you going to need bigger chambers?" Claudius asked.

"No, my chambers are more than generous."

"Son, I saw you and Nikki together, if you decide you need more room just let Bella know."

"Nikki and I have just started to see each other."

"Son, I met Bella at a ball. Couldn't take my eyes off from her. The woman loves to dance and had a line of men vying for her attention. Once I got her to dance with me, I didn't let her go; we danced and laughed all night. By the end of that week I asked her to marry me."

"Well it might be a little different with me and Nikki," Thaos said. "She says she doesn't want to be domesticated like Ingr and Angelina."

"Oh hell Thaos, a blind man could see she is falling in love with you. The question is what are you going to do about it. Because you look at her the same way."

"You think Nikki is in love with me?" Thaos asked seriously.

"Yes and she is a beautiful woman. You two make a handsome couple; Bella said so too, when we were watching you dance last night. I hope you aren't like Stephan and all conflicted over the idea of settling down. Take my advice and don't let that little girl go."

"You know in my line of work I couldn't afford the luxury of falling in love or settling down. It was just too dangerous. You and Bella are giving me the first home I have had since my family was killed. The idea of settling down and raising a family sounds pretty damn good to me."

As Thaos was speaking Mathas walked into the room. "The Sanuri will be here momentarily he is still helping the wounded," Mathas said and poured himself a drink.

Twenty minutes later the Sanuri entered Claudius' study. He found Claudius, Mathas and Thaos looking at maps and strategizing an attack on Juleta's castle.

"No," the Sanuri said with a voice of authority.

"No! What do you mean no?" yelled Claudius, who was consumed with rage.

"There are some things that must be played out by the children of The Great Ruler. Things which I cannot interfere with; but it is time now," said the Sanuri. "You cannot come where I need to go. There has been enough bloodshed this day; take care of your families they need you. I will administer justice for these dark acts." Then the Sanuri turned to Mathas and put his hand on the King's shoulder. "You do understand that the daughter you once knew; exists no more."

Mathas was filled with despair and rage; he only nodded his head and said, "Sanuri where did I go wrong?"

"Mathas you gave her a life filled with love, you could do no more. We are all responsible for our own choices; that is the test. Juleta chose darkness. There is nothing you could have done to prevent that," said the Sanuri softly. "But, now I must stop her because the killing will not stop. Juleta is being empowered by the fear and chaos she is creating in this world."

Chapter XXVI
Screaming into the Darkness

As the Sanuri flew to Juleta's castle on the back of a Henger he prayed. Then he talked to The Lion. The Sanuri knew that time and space had no limitations on communications with the heavens.

"Old friend, you warned me that Juleta would hurt many if I did not stop her. Somehow I know that the time is now. If I am wrong please correct me and if I am right I could use some help down here."

As the Henger flew over the lands that once belonged to Juleta, the Sanuri could plainly see the destruction from the last battle. The large ditch that had held the serpents formed a huge black circle around the remains of the castle. The fight between the Hengers and Talmuth had destroyed all of the castle's towers and parts of the roof. The fire that Stolas started destroyed the rest.

The Sanuri saw little signs of life as he circled over the castle. The Henger landed on the remains of the third floor. As the Sanuri dismounted, he could feel the ominous presence of evil. After searching the third floor the Sanuri found some old stone steps to descend to the second floor as the wooden steps had been destroyed in the fire. The Sanuri searched the second floor then took the stone stairway down to the first floor, but before he reached the bottom the Sanuri could hear Stolas laughing.

The Sanuri walked directly to the remains of the parlor and that is when he saw her. Juleta was on her hands and knees like an animal. Her clothes were torn, bloody and burned. When Juleta raised her head the Sanuri could see the scars on her face from the fire. He looked into Juleta's eyes and saw that there was no humanity left in her.

"You dare to come here alone?" the voice of Stolas thundered through the room. Stolas was speaking through Juleta.

"Release her!" the Sanuri commanded.

"You still want to save her even though you know it is far too late; you holy men are all the same," Stolas said in a mocking tone. "But I am not yet done with her. You know how these humans are; they always think that they are in control. Well, my little pet here; still has some lessons to learn."

"How are you teaching her lessons?"

"Put your hands on her head and see for yourself," Stolas said with a sneer.

Juleta snarled at the Sanuri then jumped to attack him. But he knocked her to the floor and placed his hands on either side of her head. What consciousness that was left of Juleta was being tortured inside of her body, which now was her prison cell.

The Sanuri stood up, "Did you or Juleta attack the wedding?" he demanded.

"Well, that is a little complicated," Stolas said as he started to laugh loudly. "She promised me great things in exchange for the attack. But she has not yet fulfilled her promises.

"Then why are you torturing her?"

"To show her who is in charge," Stolas yelled. "Her arrogance angered even me."

"You know why I am here," the Sanuri said. "Are you going to hide behind Juleta or are you going to face me?" Stolas laughed. "You are full of grand talk but you always hide. Are you the demon of fear Stolas?" the Sanuri asked mockingly.

There was silence; then a black mist appeared in the room. The mist became thicker and thicker, forming into a dark cloud. The cloud grew larger and took form until the image of Stolas loomed over the Sanuri.

The Sanuri smiled as he watched the form of Stolas take shape." You always had a flair for the parlor tricks," the Sanuri said sarcastically.

The form of Stolas changed faces multiple times. He showed the Sanuri the many faces of demons, the masks the humans wear. Juleta began to yelp and whine like an animal as she watched Stolas appear in the room. Juleta seemed to be afraid of him. Stolas continued to show the Sanuri faces of monsters and faces of humans then he showed the face of Sporos.

"It was I who stalked you and Sporos when you were young priests. It was I who corrupted your dear friend," Stolas boasted as he was trying to make the Sanuri angry.

"I would have thought it would have taken more than you to corrupt a young priest," the Sanuri replied calmly.

"Oh, I did not work alone," Stolas taunted. "I was just better than the rest."

"Stolas your time in this world has ended. You no longer have power here," the Sanuri said in a commanding voice.

Stolas laughed loudly. "And you human; think you have the power to stop me?"

"I have the power to stop you," roared The Lion as it appeared in the parlor.

Stolas had been wearing the face of Sporos to taunt the Sanuri but the shock of seeing The Lion brought Stolas' own face forward. The Sanuri watched as Stolas' face reverted to its natural hideous and distorted form. Marked by lesions and boils, his face somewhat resembled that of a Rogett only considerably more gruesome.

"There is a special place in hell for holy men who call to demons and for the demons that corrupt them," The Lion said with disgust. Stolas made his image grow larger in an attempt to intimidate The Lion and the Sanuri.

"Only the weak feel the need to prove their power," The Lion said. "The Great Ruler has all power." And with these words The Lion attacked Stolas causing the two immortal beings to hurl through dimensions and worlds that Stolas was not even aware of. They sped through space and time as the ancient demon fought to release himself from the grasp of the holy messenger.

"Stolas you will spend all of eternity being a victim of your own hand." As soon as The Lion said these words, Stolas found himself in a darkness that scared even him. Suddenly Stolas was surrounded with images of himself, who were inflicting the same torment and pain on him as he had onto others. Stolas' screams were heard beyond the dimension he was imprisoned in.

When The Lion hurled Stolas out of that dimension, Juleta was freed from Stolas' punishment. She quickly jumped to her feet, "You!" Juleta screamed and lunged at the Sanuri.

The Sanuri pushed Juleta back to the floor. "Demon," he spat.

Juleta looked at the Sanuri and smiled, "Yes, although you delayed my plans with your constant interference."

"This is what you worked for," the Sanuri said with disgust. "To be the face of horror."

"Well no one seemed to like my face before," Juleta said angrily.

"Your father and mother and brother and sister did; the ones you have been torturing and trying to kill. You blame everyone for your own weakness and failures but yourself. I saw what is in your mind. You seek to punish the men you wanted because they turned you away. Stephan and Thaos saw the monster in you and that is why they did not want you; so what do you do, you turn yourself into more of a monster. So now are you going to blame the world for not treating you the way you wanted; when all the time your choices drove the actions of others?" the Sanuri spoke in a commanding voice.

"I do not have to listen to you," Juleta responded angrily. "I am stronger than you now, you are only a human."

"That I am, but I swore allegiance to one who is not."

"As did I," Juleta replied with a condescending tone. With these words she breathed fire at the Sanuri. He quickly jumped to his left, causing the fire to miss him but to consume the remnants of a chair.

As the Sanuri quickly stood back up, he raised both of his arms and the floor beneath Juleta's feet began to shake violently.

411

"You have nothing," Juleta spat and with a wave of her right arm the things that were left in the parlor started to rise into the air. Juleta waved her arm a second time and these pieces of broken objects hurled through the air at the Sanuri.

The Sanuri put up his hands and all of the items fell to the floor. Juleta screamed with rage and breathed fire at the Sanuri a second time. Her focus on the Sanuri prevented Juleta from realizing that the floor beneath her was cracking. The Sanuri once again evaded the fireball, this time by throwing himself to his right.

"It is not too late for you to give up the darkness," the Sanuri yelled as he rolled forward on the floor to elude another fireball.

"Never, I have worked too hard for this," Juleta screamed.

"And what has it gotten you, look at yourself and your castle. You gave up all that is good to live like this; then you are insane. And you have no one to blame but yourself."

"Why do you keep saying these things; you bore me." Juleta yelled as she hurled another fireball at the Sanuri.

"So that you will ponder them the rest of your days, in the darkness you so desire," the Sanuri's voice grew increasingly louder as he spoke. As his voice grew louder the cracks in the floor grew wider. Suddenly the floor beneath Juleta's feet divided, creating a great chasm. Her screams permeated the dark worlds as she fell to her prison. The Sanuri waited for the chasm to close over her before he left the remnants of Juleta's castle.

"My Lord, Erebus has returned and wants to speak with you," said Cerephus as he walked into the war room. Once again there was broken furniture and glass thrown throughout the room.

"Bring him in," replied Roch.

"My Lord are you alright?" Cerephus asked.

"Of course I am alright, what do you mean?" Cerephus pointed at all the damage in the war room.

"Guess I had too much to drink last night," Roch replied with a laugh. "Bring Erebus in here."

When Erebus entered the war room he too, first noticed the damage. "Was there a fight in here?" he asked.

"No" growled Roch. "Sit and have a drink. Cerephus tells me you have been on a journey to find information for me. Tell me what you have learned."

"I do not yet have the answers that you seek," Erebus said as he stared at Roch. "But I have much to tell you. And I have many questions of you. I have visited some of the most powerful witches and dark lords in this continent and none of them know how to reverse the affliction put upon you by a holy messenger." Roch started to speak but Erebus held up his hand for Roch to remain silent. "Roch before you have a tantrum you must listen to me. This affliction is truly not the worst of your problems."

Roch stared angrily at Erebus for a moment then said, "Go on."

"With every dark lord and witch that I visited we tried to combine our powers to contact other worlds for the answers you seek. In each and every case we were either threatened by powerful demons to stop asking questions or physically attacked. Roch you have to understand these things that I am telling you are unheard of for those who practice dark magics." Erebus looked over at Cerephus with a look of concern and now Cerephus realized that his friend was not just concocting a story for Roch, but Erebus was telling the truth.

"Roch I don't know how much you know about demons but there are all different types and class systems just like with humans in this world. The most powerful demons are the original demons that came to this world; they are called the Old Ones. Their powers are beyond the comprehensions of mankind."

"Then there are hundreds of types of demons that are lower classes than the Old Ones," Erebus continued to explain. "The demons that are the product of demons and humans breeding are the easiest for humans to kill. Your friend Demetries could not be killed by a human, yet as powerful as he was he was still considered very low in the hierarchy of demons." Erebus was surprised that Roch was quiet and listening intently.

413

"So Roch I need to just give you an example before I can explain the rest. Let's pretend that you as king of the second largest kingdom in this continent were as powerful as one of the Old Ones. You share your plans and agendas with few; even though you have many who work for you. Also as king you have your own agendas and rivalries as with your brother."

"What I have found out is that there are Old Ones who pay great attention to you and are somehow interfering with your life. Now you have to understand that at the level that the Old Ones are at, they pay little attention to specific humans because the humans are considered so far beneath them. Roch, I know that you pride yourself on being an evil man. But to have the attention of the Old Ones is not good and should scare you greatly."

Roch did not speak for several moments and when he did it was in a hoarse whisper, "Demetries told me that I was a pawn in a game of beings whose power was beyond my understanding. I dismissed his words because he was always talking in riddles."

"Roch I have been doing a great deal of research," Erebus continued. "I would like to try some new spells that I believe are more powerful. But to do them I will need some samples of your blood and hair."

"Take what you need," Roch said. He did not want to admit to Erebus or Cerephus how disturbed he was by Erebus' words. Nor was Roch ready to tell Erebus about his nightmares or his encounter with the demon that broke his ankle.

After Erebus took his samples, he left the war room and headed towards his chambers. Cerephus followed Erebus and when the two men believed they were alone, they spoke in whispers. "Was that garbage or the truth you were telling him?" Cerephus asked.

"It was the truth and I think we have to tread very carefully Cerephus. We cannot afford to draw the wrath of the Old Ones. I need to find out what is really going on with Roch and until I do we cannot move forward with your plans."

Neither Erebus nor Cerephus were aware of the group Insidiae or that group's plans for Roch. And although Sophie and Erebus were slowly renewing the love affair of their youth; Sophie had not confided to Erebus that she was a member of the Insidiae and a spy. Neither of these treacherous men realized what they were walking into.

Stephan and Matthew were in and out of consciousness the rest of that day and into the evening. Thaos stayed up with Ingr and Angelina so he could help them give their husbands the evening doses of medication. It was late when Thaos walked into the bedroom in Stephan's chambers that he and Nikki were temporarily staying in. Thaos smiled when he walked into the room. The fire in the hearth was roaring and just a few candles were lit. Nikki was sitting up in bed wearing a beautiful pink silk and lace nightgown. She had pen and paper in hand.

"This is nice, seeing you in bed waiting for me," Thaos said as he started to remove his weapon's belt and his bloodstained clothing. "What are you working on?"

"I am writing down what I should say at Isla's funeral," Nikki said as she put the paper and pen on a table next to the bed. "Thaos I was so upset about Isla that I didn't even realize your friend was killed. I am sorry." Thaos did not respond and Nikki knew it was because of the sadness in his heart. She got out of bed and walked up to Thaos and kissed him. "I will help you with whatever arrangements you need to make for Jeb." Thaos pulled Nikki close to him and hugged her tightly but he still did not speak.

"Let me pour you a glass of whiskey," Nikki said and walked over to a table that contained some bottles and glasses.

"You look so beautiful," Thaos said.

"Ingr let me wear one of her nightgowns. I cannot believe how much clothes she has now. She said Stephan keeps giving her money and telling her to buy clothes," Nikki laughed as she said this and handed Thaos his glass of whiskey. As Thaos took the glass he kissed Nikki's hand. Thaos sat down on the bed and stared at Nikki, who then sat down beside him. "You look like you have a lot on your mind," she said.

"I want to talk to you about some things and I am not sure if what I want to say will make you happy or really upset you." As Thaos said these words he could see Nikki stiffening up.

"Say them," Nikki said as if she was preparing to hear something awful.

"Claudius and Bella have asked me to live here as part of their family and I said yes. They are wonderful people."

"Thaos that is good news why would that upset me?"

"They said they have been watching the way you and I look at each other and offered to move me to larger chambers if you wanted to live here with me." Thaos was half expecting Nikki to run out of the room as he spoke but instead she only stared at him.

"What did you tell them?" Nikki asked.

"I said that we have just started to spend time together and that you are scared of getting into a serious relationship."

"So Bella and Claudius would like to see us together?"

"Yes."

"But what are your thoughts Thaos?"

Thaos set his glass down and turned on the bed so he was completely facing Nikki. "I care about you very much and I want to have you with me. I can see us making a home together and having a family. I know you feel responsible for your mother and brothers and sisters and I can help you take care of them." Thaos could see the fear in Nikki's eyes as he spoke. "I can see how scared you are. We could just try and live together for a while and see how things work out."

Nikki sat on the bed looking at Thaos. She was fighting her conflicting feelings of throwing her arms around him or running out of the room. "Nikki tell me what you are thinking," Thaos said softly.

"Thaos in the little time that we have been together, you know me so well. A part of me wants to run out of this room and the other part wants to hug you and live with you. I have very strong feelings for you. And being with you not only seems natural but somehow seems right. I know I will regret it if I run out of here. But know too that I am really scared."

A huge smile engulfed Thaos' face. "So are you saying you will move in here with me?"

"Yes but let's take things one step at a time as I try to calm my fears."

Thaos put his arms around Nikki and kissed her hard on the lips. She put her arms around his neck and pulled herself closer to him. They kissed for several moments then Nikki started to giggle. "What are you laughing about?" Thaos asked.

"You were serious about what you said and not just trying to help Stephan win his bet?" Thaos roared with laughter.

Erebus took the blood of Roch and slowly dripped some of it into the boiling herbs. He added three chicken bones, a raven's feather, an eye of a snake and a lock of Roch's hair. The mixture started to boil harder and harder as each ingredient was added. Soon it started to boil over, out of the pan and into the fire causing great clouds of black smoke to rise. As the room began to fill with smoke, Erebus called forth a messenger from the darkness.

"I need answers; I seek to speak with one who can help me." Erebus repeated these words over and over, each time raising his voice a little more until he was screaming into the darkness. Suddenly the black smoke turned red and screams could be heard coming from it. As Erebus listened, the screams sounded like someone was in great pain. Then the screams stopped.

The smoke cleared and there was silence. "I have performed this ritual many times," thought Erebus. "And this has never happened; I must have done something wrong." Erebus grabbed another pot to make the potion again.

When Erebus turned to get some herbs from the table behind him; he stopped and stared at the wall before him. Written in large bloody letters was a single word *Leave*.

Stephan woke up before the first rays of dawn broke through the night sky. The room was well lit with many candles as well as the fire in the hearth. Immediately Stephan reached for Ingr who usually slept on his left. When he did not feel her he turned to his right and saw her in a chair next to the bed. Ingr was asleep but leaning forward with her head resting on the bed. Stephan stroked her hair. "Ingr, Honey come to bed."

Instantly Ingr jumped up, her heart pounding wildly. "Stephan, oh Stephan I have been so worried about you. How are you feeling?"

"Better than I should, considering."

"The Sanuri did something to you and Matthew and said you would heal just fine," Ingr said as tears, again, ran down her cheeks. "Are you in pain?"

"Yes."

"Let me get Thaos, he's sleeping in the next room."

"Why is he here?"

"To help Angelina and me sit you and Matthew up so we can give you medicine. Matthew and Angelina are in the third bedroom. I'll be right back," Ingr said and literally ran out of the room and into the bedroom where Thaos and Nikki were sleeping. "Thaos," Ingr whispered.

Thaos jumped, "Ingr is he alright?"

"Stephan's in pain and I need you to help me sit him up so I can give him some Tincture water."

Thaos started to get out of bed then stopped as he saw Ingr was still standing next to the bed watching him. "Ingr I'm naked, I mean I don't care if you don't."

"Oh, I am sorry, I am just so upset about Stephan," Ingr said and left the room to return to Stephan's side.

Thaos walked into Stephan's room wearing only his trousers. "So are you a nurse now?" Stephan asked and tried to laugh.

"I'm a man of many talents," Thaos said with a grin. "And I will say you sure look a lot better than you did yesterday. This might hurt a little." Thaos lifted Stephan to a sitting position while Ingr piled pillows behind Stephan's back.

"Drink this entire glass down," said Ingr as she handed Stephan a glass of Tincture water.

"So Ingr just told me I won the bet," Stephan kidded. Stephan was trying to make jokes because he didn't want Ingr to know how much pain he was in.

"Yes and Nikki just agreed to move in here with me," Thaos said with a smile.

"What!" Stephan said. "And I though Ingr and I moved fast."

"Nikki is moving in here? Oh good!" Ingr said excitedly. "I have missed her."

"Stephan you look like you need to sleep," Thaos said. "I will be back later; I am going to check on Matthew now."

Erebus left his chambers and ran to Cerephus' cottage. Cerephus was already up and drinking coffee when Erebus knocked at his door. "You have to come quickly, there is something I must show you," Erebus said anxiously. The two men returned to the castle without delay.

"What is that awful smell?" Cerephus asked as he entered Erebus' chambers.

"That smell is the potion I was making. I have made it many times before but this time some strange things happened, like this," Erebus said as he pointed to the bloody writing on the wall.

"Who did this?"

"Something from the dark worlds. Before I saw the writing the room filled with red smoke and I could hear screaming, like someone was in pain. When the smoke cleared I saw the writing. None of these things have ever happened before."

"What do you think it means?"

"Cerephus something like this is highly unusual," Erebus said as he was still shaken by the events. "I need you to tell me everything you can remember that Demetries said to Roch or about him."

It was almost ten in the morning, when Thaos and Nikki walked out of the bedroom hand in hand. To Nikki's embarrassment Claudius, Bella, Mathas, Rosa and Margarit were in the chambers visiting Stephan and Matthew.

"I should go," Nikki said as she blushed deeply.

"Wait until I get done with the funeral preparations for Jeb," Thaos said quietly. "Then I will ride back to your village with you."

"I am really embarrassed Thaos."

"I know but I don't think any of them really care about what we have been doing," he said with a smile. "It will be alright."

When Thaos and Nikki walked into Stephan's bedroom, Claudius immediately saw that they were holding hands. "Why Nikki I didn't know you were still here." Claudius said. "Mathas and Rosa are going to join us for dinner tonight; why don't you stay and have dinner with us also?"

"Claudius, Nikki and I have talked and she will be living with me here in the castle," Thaos said with a broad smile.

"Excellent!" said Claudius. "When you two are ready, talk with Bella and she will find you larger chambers." Claudius turned and winked at Bella as he spoke.

"We are going to Nikki's village to speak with her mother this morning." Thaos continued then looked at Stephan. "And I have some business with Sorren. Claudius can I speak with you in the parlor for a moment?" The two men talked for several minutes about Jeb's funeral. To Thaos' surprise Claudius had already made arrangements for Jeb to be buried in their family cemetery.

Claudius also told Thaos that an Enrop had brought a message from the Sanuri, telling them that Juleta was gone and he would be returning that night and would explain everything. "I was going to ask the Sanuri to say a few words over the dead before we buried them," Claudius added.

"Thank you for doing this but please let me pay for the coffin and any expenses," Thaos said.

"Perhaps your money would be better spent with his grandson."

Thaos' eyes grew wide, "Ryan I cannot believe I forgot about him."

The Sanuri returned to the castle of Claudius earlier than expected; he met with Mathas and Claudius as soon as he arrived. The Sanuri told them everything that he had seen and heard. He thought Mathas should understand that Juleta, the human, was no more.

"It is with a heavy heart that I tell you these things, Mathas. My purpose is not to hurt you but to protect you," the Sanuri said.

"Protect me from what?" Mathas asked as the grief of losing his daughter became real to him. "It is over now."

"That is what concerns me," the Sanuri said. "And that is why I did not want to speak with you in front of your families."

"Sanuri I don't understand," Mathas said.

"When Stolas told me to look inside of Juleta's head; I don't think he realized all that I would see. I saw a great deal about Juleta's involvement with the conspirators called the Insidiae and I must return to Wetpr to speak with Sudfad about what I saw. But I also saw other things and it breaks my heart to tell you."

The Sanuri hesitated. "Stolas was not the only demon that Juleta bartered with, to attack your family. But what I could not see was how she would pay for their services. If there is something she left behind in this world that could be a payment, the attacks may not be finished."

"What!" yelled Claudius.

"Claudius is Thaos still here?" asked the Sanuri.

"Bella and I asked him to live here as family and he has accepted our offer."

"Juleta not only had feelings for Stephan but for Thaos as well and she is filled with anger because she feels they both rejected her. I fear that both of your families as well as Sudfad's are still in danger from Juleta's wrath."

"Vessel of Darkness, are you absolutely sure those are the words that Demetries said?" Erebus asked.

"It is what Roch told me," Cerephus said. "That was before Roch became a drunk, so he made more sense in those days. He would get very frustrated with Demetries because he said the demon was always talking in riddles."

"Cerephus I promised you that I would help you with your plans but I think we need to take it slow and find out what is really going on with Roch. I don't like the sounds of that term, 'Vessel of Darkness'. It makes me think there are some plans in progress..."

Cerephus interrupted Erebus, "What kind of plans?"

"That's what I need to find out. Cerephus this could be very dangerous for us. If any demons, especially the Old Ones feel that we are interfering with their plans, well, their punishments are unthinkable."

That night after dinner, the Sanuri, Mathas and Claudius returned to the living quarters of Stephan and Ingr. They asked Thaos and Nikki to join them. Ingr and Angelina were taking their meals in these quarters with their husbands so they had not been a part of the dinner conversation.

The bedrooms that Stephan and Matthew occupied were next to each other and both had a similar limited view of the parlor. It was in this small viewing space that was shared by the two rooms; that King Mathas, Claudius and the Sanuri stood to address the group. Thaos and Nikki took seats in the parlor.

The Sanuri repeated all that he had previously told Mathas and Claudius. And to everyone's surprise it was Ingr who flew into a rage. "I am so sick of that woman and what she has done to everyone," Ingr screamed. "Sanuri why is it that we can kill some demons and not others?"

"That is an excellent question," he replied. "It depends on how much power the demons have. There are many different hierarchies of demons. The Demalogs that attacked your wedding are considered pets to other demons. Although vicious they are a lower level of demon, with low intelligence and that is why you can kill them."

"Sanuri can you teach us how to kill all different demons or at least how to stop them?" Angelina asked. "Because it sounds like Juleta is going to keep sending them after us."

"A human does not possess the power to destroy a powerful demon without the help of The Great Ruler. Your training as warriors is sufficient to kill the lower level demons and monsters. And of course I will always come to help you."

"But how do you kill the demons?" Angelina asked.

"That is a little complicated. I gave myself to The Great Ruler many hundreds of years ago. I work on His behalf; so He assists me with destroying the demons because I do not possess that power on my own."

"And you know He is always going to help you?" asked Ingr.

"I have faith," the Sanuri said. "That may be the most powerful weapon against darkness there is."

423

"But look at all of the attacks that have happened and we are going to have a baby," Ingr said with frustration. "There has to be something more that we can do."

"Well, you can always ask The Great Ruler to help you; that is what I would suggest first," the Sanuri said. "After the funerals tomorrow I will be returning to Wetpr briefly then I am going to the monastery in Malga to study. Let me see if I can find you some answers."

After the Sanuri left the room, Thaos took Nikki's hand and they walked into their bedroom. "You heard what the Sanuri said, you can change your mind about living with me," Thaos said.

"Thaos I can't believe you are even saying this," Nikki said angrily. Thaos smiled as Nikki put her hands on her hips and tilted her head as she talked in a scolding manner. "I am not running from that demon or witch or whatever she is and I am certainly not losing you because I am afraid something might happen. We are warriors; we will fight her together until this is over."

Chapter XXVII
Journeys

Every morning Bella, Claudius, Mathas, Rosa and Margarit visited Stephan and Matthew. Claudius and Mathas would leave for periods of time to tend to business but the mothers stayed the entire day.

"Maybe I should stay," Ingr said with concern.

"Nonsense," Bella said. "We were taking care of our sons long before you girls were born. Everything will be alright. Besides you two could use a few hours away even if it is for such a solemn event."

"I am sorry," Ingr said. "I didn't mean for it to sound like that."

"I know, you are just worried," said Bella warmly.

Stephan was sitting up in bed listening to the two women in his life with a smile on his face. "Listen to Mother," he said. "And you two stay with Thaos."

"My father probably won't even attend the funerals," Ingr said before she kissed Stephan.

"I don't care, there might still be demons roaming around. "Please do as I say," Stephan said.

A similar conversation was taking place in Matthew's bedroom. "We aren't children," Angelina said as she kissed Matthew.

"I know but please stay with Thaos and do what he says." Angelina gave Matthew a look of disapproval as he said these words.

Margarit was sitting on Matthew's bed singing him a song. She stopped and looked at Angelina with a coy smile. "Angelina the last time that Matthew got hurt Annabelle and Vitomas took care of him."

Angelina smiled at the little girl, "I know, Matthew told me."

"Well they would make us cookies," Margarit said. Everyone in the room started to laugh.

"Would you like me to make you some cookies?" Angelina asked.

Margarit's eyes grew wide and a big smile came on her face, "Yes."

"I will bake you some when Ingr and I return."

"You can cook?" Matthew teased.

"Honey I wasn't the one who grew up with servants," Angelina said with a smile. "In fact, when we get back home I should fix a dinner for all of you with the dishes of my people."

"We would like that," said Mathas.

Thaos and Nikki walked into the parlor to get Ingr and Angelina. "Thaos," Angelina said sarcastically. "We were told to stay with you and to do everything you say. Of course you know we aren't going to do that."

Thaos grinned. "This may be harder than I thought," he said as they were walking out of the room.

As soon as the door closed, Stephen turned to Bella and said seriously, "I need you to bring Father here now; I have to talk to both of you about something."

Thaos, Angelina, Ingr and Nikki had no sooner ridden through the castle gates when the Sanuri rode up to them. "Mind if I join you?" he asked. "I thought I would attend the funerals."

"Glad to have you," Thaos said although he wasn't really sure why the Sanuri was joining them. Thaos wondered if the Sanuri feared they were in danger.

As they rode towards The Village of Tyger, Angelina, Ingr and Nikki told the Sanuri about their tribe and their customs. "Sanuri, my father will be proud that you came to our village. Do not be surprised if he asks you to stay for dinner," Angelina said.

"Would the rest of you be staying for dinner?" the Sanuri asked.

"I need to speak with my mother," said Nikki. "I need to see if she needs anything."

"Will Gladys be at the funeral?" Thaos asked

"You know Gladys?" Ingr asked with surprise.

"I met her family yesterday," Thaos said; noticing the grins on the faces of Ingr and Angelina. "We told her mother that Nikki will be living in the castle with me."

"What did Gladys say?" asked Ingr. "Was she mad?"

"It was all so very strange," Nikki said with a proud smile. "Mother and Thaos talked for a while before we told her. She seems to really like him and did not disapprove at all. Then he gives her a bag of gold coins and tells her that he will be providing for the family." Nikki had a proud look on her face as she said these words. Both Ingr and Angelina looked at Thaos with a combination of warmth and surprise. The conversation ended because they were riding into the village.

"Well, this is Tyger," Angelina said as they rode down the main street. "The cemetery is on the opposite end of the village."

The Sanuri was surprised at how friendly the villagers were, as everyone they passed spoke to them. They could see the crowd of people seated at the cemetery long before they could hear their voices and cries. The three warriors who died in the battle with the Demalogs were being buried at the same time.

Sorren was standing in front of the crowd with his back to the caskets that were lined up side by side. Each casket was covered with flowers and a bow and quiver of arrows had been carefully placed on top of each flower arrangement. Sorren smiled and walked through the crowd to greet his daughter and her friends.

"Sanuri we are honored by your presence here," Sorren said. "Would you consider saying a few words over the dead?"

"I would be honored," the Sanuri said as he followed Sorren to the front of the crowd.

Thaos sat between Nikki and Ingr as the four took seats in the rear of the crowd. All three of the girls started to cry as soon as they sat down. Thaos wasn't sure what to do, so he put his arms around Nikki and Ingr in an effort to comfort them. He watched Angelina try to be strong and not cry.

Thaos looked around at the large crowd and thought of Jeb's funeral which had been earlier that morning. Ryan, Nikki and Thaos were the only people in attendance. Thaos was saddened that such a good man as Jeb would have such little recognition at his funeral. Thaos only half listened to the words that Sorren and the Sanuri were saying as his eyes continuously searched the landscape for any sign of attack.

Claudius and Bella sat silently as Stephan told them about Thaddies and his attempts to have Ingr taken from him. "And you are sure he is dead?" Claudius asked.

"Thaos and Sorren found the remains of his body yesterday," Stephan replied.

"That man sounds like a monster," Bella said with disgust.

"You are lucky you have such good friends," said Claudius. "Sorren was right; Thaddies should not have died at your hands."

"Do you think I should tell Ingr?"

"Honey, you are going to have to," Bella said. "So many people already know about it that she may find out; then she will feel like you deceived her."

"Your mother is right," Claudius said. "Besides the girl has a right to know."

After the three warriors of the Nordes Tribe were lowered into the ground, the mourners started to disburse. As Angelina had predicted, Sorren invited the Sanuri to dinner; to decline would have been a great insult to the Chief of the Nordes Tribe. Ingr and Angelina mingled with villagers, many of whom they had not seen for some time. Nikki walked to her home to speak with her mother. Thaos stood by himself in the crowd trying to watch all three women who had scattered in different directions.

Suddenly Elexas ran up to Thaos and threw her arms around him. Thaos was a tall man so her arms surrounded his chest. She appeared to be crying. "Oh, I never thought I would see you here Thaos," Elexas said. "I am so glad you came." Both Angelina and Ingr saw Elexas run up to Thaos and decided to watch them; the two women walked towards the couple and stopped when they were about a hundred yards away.

Thaos thought that Elexas was a very beautiful woman but there was something about her that he did not trust. Elexas reminded Thaos of the type of women he would meet in taverns. Elexas knew she was beautiful and seemed to use her looks to manipulate people and it was obvious that attention from men fed her ego.

Both Angelina and Ingr found themselves getting irritated as they watched Elexas' exaggerated movements and expressions as she flirted with Thaos. While Elexas had never been shy about her appreciation of male attention; Angelina, Ingr and Nikki had always been more serious about their training.

Like any small community, gossip travels quickly among its members; and the Nordes Tribe was no exception. Elexas knew that Thaos had met Nikki's family and that she had been spending time at the castle. But for a competitive spirit like Elexas this was nothing short of a challenge; Elexas had never lost the attention of a man she desired.

"At least he doesn't seem to be falling for it," Angelina said disapprovingly.

"I think we should go over there before Nikki sees them," Ingr said and started to move towards the couple when Angelina grabbed her arm, stopping her. "It is too late for that," Angelina said as they now watched Nikki walk up to Thaos and Elexas.

Because of Thaos' size, Nikki did not see Elexas until she was almost next to him. Nikki could not help but focus on Elexas' behavior. Nikki stopped suddenly and was overwhelmed with an unfamiliar feeling; she had no idea of what to do.

"There you are," Thaos said as he realized Nikki was near him. He reached out and put his arm around Nikki's shoulders pulling her towards him.

"Do you think they will fight?" Ingr asked as she and Angelina watched the faces and movements of their friends.

Thaos saw the looks on the faces of Nikki and Elexas and although it caused him some amusement he decided to try and calm the tensions. "Does Gladys need anything?" he asked.

Nikki looked at Thaos, "Yes I will have to go hunting tomorrow."

"I will go with you," Thaos said.

Nikki gave Thaos a quizzical look, "That is not necessary."

"What, do you think you are the only one who knows how to hunt?" Thaos asked sarcastically. Both of the girls laughed at his comment.

"Thaos I will see you later," Elexas said sweetly as she fluttered her eyelashes at him. Then she turned and walked away.

"Elexas," Nikki said as she was trying to maintain her composure. Elexas turned around. "Did Thaos tell you we are living together now?"

"Yes he did," Elexas said with a coy smile. "I am happy for you and I will admit a bit jealous."

Nikki knew that Elexas would never stop pursuing any man who she was attracted to until she caught him. And Nikki found herself very jealous of Elexas' attention to Thaos. "Did he also tell you that we are trying to start a family?"

A look of shock came across Elexas' face because even for her this changed the game. "No he didn't," Elexas said and turned and walked away.

Nikki looked up at Thaos, wondering if he would be mad at the story she just fabricated. To Nikki's surprise Thaos was grinning at her. "I can't believe that came out of your mouth," he said.

"Thaos I am sorry but she just makes me so mad, the way she acts around you. And you don't know Elexas like I do; she never stops chasing any man."

430

"Nikki are you telling me that you are jealous?" Thaos asked as his grin widened.

Nikki did not want to admit that she was jealous, so she paused for a few moments then she rolled her eyes and said with annoyance, "Yes Thaos and there are more girls than just Elexas who want you. And I know you're going to tell me that is not how a warrior should act but I can't help it; I've never had feelings for anyone before like I do for you. Everything is just so different now."

"How are things different?"

"They just are," Nikki said and did not want to be forced to say the words in her heart.

"Nikki, I really need you to tell me how you feel."

Nikki looked at Thaos for a few moments, "I think I am falling in love with you. Actually I know I am falling in love with you. I have just never felt like this before. You are all I can think about. I can't concentrate on anything else. I feel so alive when I am with you."

Thaos put both of his arms around Nikki and pulled her close to him. "Nikki you are just full of surprises today. You have been acting so afraid of a committed relationship that you make me feel afraid to tell you my feelings because I don't want to scare you off. I am going to be honest with you now. I want to marry you and have a family and I want to start a family right away. I have been alone for a long time and you are the first girl that I have met that I want a family with. I very much hope you were telling Elexas the truth."

It took a week for Raul and Simon to travel from Fort Salar north to Fort Styls. It took another two weeks for General Loftus, the senior general at Fort Styls; to obtain all of the items needed to make the weapons that Simon and Raul had designed. As generals Raul and Simon did not stay in the barracks with their men; they had private quarters assigned to them.

These quarters were actually small rooms that each contained a bed, a writing desk, a couple of chairs and small side tables. Raul had a large table moved into his room so they could spread out their maps and drawings. According to General Loftus, the men at Fort Styls had dealt with little that was out of the ordinary for months.

Raul and Simon received letters from home almost daily, but they did not write as frequently because they felt they had little to say. "This one is for both of us," said Simon as he walked into Raul's room with a large envelope. "Look at how thick this is."

"Read it out loud," Raul said as he poured two glasses of whiskey.

"Well, there is just a short note from Annabelle and Vitomas saying how much they miss us," then Simon laughed. "And apparently my wife and children have moved into your home permanently. Annabelle said she can't stand being in the east wing without me."

"It probably is better for the both of them to stay together," Raul said as he sat across the table from Simon.

"Yes," Simon said sadly. "They said Mother is taking them on a big shopping trip next week to buy baby things. And that the rest of this letter is actually a letter they got from Matthew. They said Sudfad thought we should read it. His letter is ten pages long," Simon said in amazement.

Simon read Matthew's letter out loud that told of the Demalog and snake attacks. Matthew told of Margarit's abduction and the battle to save his little sister. He wrote about the incredible creatures that took part in the battle on both sides of the conflict and he told of their contact with the demon Stolas in the cellar of Juleta's castle. The letter told of the marriage of Ingr and Stephan and the fact that they were expecting a baby.

"Of all the things he wrote about," Raul said. "I think the thing that surprised me the most was Thaos."

"I don't know if I am that surprised," Simon said. "He actually did us a service in Port Friada."

"Renya, this is the third shopping trip you have taken us on," Annabelle said. "We have had so much fun, thank you." Renya and Laurel sat next to each other in the Queen's specially made carriage, while Annabelle and Vitomas sat across from them.

"I remember how lonely I would get when Sudfad was gone," Renya said. "We had Raul the first year of our marriage and I had just moved here from the Kingdom of Lentz. I really didn't know anyone and that was a time of great wars for both Wetpr and Lentz. You girls know how busy a baby can keep you but you can't have a conversation with it. I would cry myself to sleep every night because I was so homesick and lonely. Things did get better as Raul grew and then when Simon came to live with us. That is why I am so grateful to have all of you here now. I finally have the big family I always wanted."

Both Annabelle and Vitomas felt surprised and empathetic towards Renya as she spoke. "Renya, I was going to wait and let Simon tell you but he may not be back in time. But if the baby is a girl we are going to name her Arianna after you," Annabelle said. Renya smiled warmly at the news. "That is Renya's middle name," Annabelle said to Laurel

"Laurel what is your middle name?" Vitomas asked.

"Ariel."

"Ariel, I like that very much," Vitomas said. "Let me ask Raul what he thinks. We haven't discussed any names for our baby yet."

Several weeks passed as Stephan and Matthew healed from their wounds. As soon as Matthew was well enough, his family moved him back to their castle. Thaos had moved out of Stephan's quarters and back to his own, which he now shared with Nikki. Stephan deliberately waited until some of the chaos and emotional stress from the Demalog attack had passed before he told Ingr about her father.

To Stephan's surprise, Ingr never questioned a word that he said; for Ingr always knew the man her father was, even though she did not want to admit it.

Ingr's emotions alternated between anger, humiliation and fear for what could have happened if their friends would not have stopped Thaddies. In the weeks that would follow, Ingr would thank Nikki, Thaos, Sorren and Matthew for the parts they played in saving her and Stephan from a possibly devastating situation.

Simon and Raul stayed six weeks longer at Fort Styls than they had planned. Sudfad had them leave Salar before they had a chance to build prototypes of the weapons they had designed. At Fort Styls they discovered some flaws in their designs and had to find ways to correct them. To avoid the same mistakes they sent copies of the corrected designs to Fort Nir and Fort Polta. They also sent copies to Sudfad, who was going to have the weapons constructed in the absence of the young princes.

Word had come to them at Fort Styles that some victims of Rogett attacks had been taken to the monastery at Philiste. This was the first news of Rogett attacks in the Kingdom of Wetpr for many years. The monastery at Philiste lay south of the Forest of Tobar and southeast of Fort Nir. Raul and Simon had originally planned to travel from Fort Styls westward along the northernmost boundary of Wetpr then turn south to Fort Nir. But with the news of a Rogett attack they changed their route. They planned to travel west until they reached the Dulag Tar Pits then turn south and travel through the Forest of Tobar.

Legends said the Forest of Tobar was enchanted; that people entered, never to be seen again. It was said that people who lived in the Villages of Prohec and Mener, two small villages that bordered this forest, refused to enter the Forest of Tobar for any reason. Stories were told about a great drought that had brought famine to that area, yet these villagers would not go into the forest to hunt; their fears of the unknown were stronger than their fears of starvation. Raul and Simon had never traveled into this forest before.

"Erebus we have to be careful," Sophie said as he came up behind her and started to kiss her neck. Although Sophie was scolding Erebus she enjoyed the affection and turned around and kissed him on the lips. "I have hardly seen you, where have you been?" Sophie asked.

"I have been working on spells to try and get information about Roch's condition but Sophie I have never seen such things. Something from the dark worlds is blocking my spells and even threatening me if I don't stop. Come to my room tonight and I will tell you more."

Sophie's eyes grew wide as she listened to him speak. "Erebus please do not do anymore spells it is too dangerous, you must trust me I know what I am talking about."

"Sophie I know you have been keeping secrets from me. But I am beginning to realize you are somehow involved in this thing with Roch, aren't you?"

"Erebus we cannot talk here. Do a protection spell in your chambers so that nothing can listen to our conversation and I will be up after nine."

Raul, Simon and their men had been traveling for four days before they crossed the River Toba. They were just a few miles from where the long stretch of the Dulag Tar pits started. "Let's go straight to the tar pits," Raul said. "Some of the men may never have seen them."

"Remember how intrigued we were with them when we were kids?" Simon asked. "I loved watching that hot tar bubbling up out of the earth. We will have to bring the girls up here some time so they can see them."

Raul was quiet for a few moments, "Remember how much fun we used to have going on these missions? Now all I can think about is Vitomas and the boys. I never thought I would miss them so much."

"I know," Simon said. "Just the other night I was thinking about how much we have changed. We used to have a girl in every village; I haven't looked at another girl since that day I met Annabelle."

"Yes, we used to laugh at the guys who act like we do now," Raul said with a grin.

Many of the soldiers that Raul and Simon were leading, had never seen the huge bubbling hot tar pits and were intrigued by the natural wonders. The two Princes decided to camp early near the pits to give their men a chance to explore the area. That night as Simon and Raul sat around their fire they wrote to their wives about the tar pits and promised to bring the families to see them.

"There is so little to write," Simon complained. "So I just keep telling Annabelle how much I miss her."

"I know," Raul said. "This trip has certainly been uneventful."

"Well Meekos was right," the demon Tapster said to Tarig, a Huta lieutenant. "They changed their route when they heard about the Rogett attack. He wants us to wait until they enter the forest. We will just keep watching them tonight."

"Padre Thomas, Padre Thomas," screamed Padre Bartholomew as he pounded on the door to Padre Thomas' room.

"What is it?" Padre Thomas asked with concern as he opened the door. "What has happened?"

"Did you not hear?"

"Hear what? I don't know what you are talking about," said Padre Thomas as he moved to the side to allow Padre Bartholomew to enter the room.

"There was a fire in the Hall of Antiquities," Padre Bartholomew said as he motioned for Padre Thomas to close the door. "Padre Francis said the doors to the hall were locked when he entered and none of the candles were lit. He said he smelled smoke and found a fire had been started in the very back of the room. He ran for help and several priests put the fire out but not before many things were destroyed. Padre Francis is trying to figure out what items were lost in the fire." Padre Bartholomew lowered his voice as if others might hear him speak. "Padre Francis said the fire had to have been intentionally set."

The demon Tapster waited in the Forest of Tobar with his small army of Huta warriors. They had orders to wait for Raul and Simon to lead their men into the darkness of the old forest before they attacked. In the early morning hours Raul and Simon did just as Meekos had predicted; they led their men through the forest instead of riding around it. The thick canopy made by the huge ancient trees blocked out much of the sunlight, only a few scattered rays of light worked their way through the enormous branches.

"It is too quiet in here," Simon said as he realized the birds had stopped singing and the other forest sounds had ceased.

"I did notice that," Raul said as he thrust his left fist into the air as a signal for his men to stop. Raul then opened his left hand twice, each time extending his fingers; this was a signal for the troops to be alert to an attack. Raul was the senior general; when he and Simon worked together Raul was in charge. But their troops were divided under each of their commands. Each general now raised their hands and motioned for their men to follow them as they split up. Raul led his men to the right while Simon led his to the left.

Simultaneously Enrops landed on the shoulders of Raul and Simon. Both of the Princes were given the same message, "There are about forty Hutas and a demon waiting to ambush you. They are in two groups, apparently to surround you as you passed them. They lay in wait about five hundred yards ahead."

"Thank you," Raul said to the Enrop. "Please tell my brother it is time to tryout the new weapons."

The men following Raul and Simon were not just on horseback; some were driving bocas and others were driving teams of horses that were pulling adaptations of trebuchets. Trebuchets were wooden machines designed to catapult objects. They had been used in battle for hundreds of years and could be made in various sizes and widths.

Simon and Raul had redesigned the standard trebuchet into several variations. The trebuchets were not their new weapons; it was the items they designed to be hurled by the trebuchets that were the Princes' creations.

Each general ordered tobisks to be loaded into the buckets of the trebuchets. Tobisks were sphere-shaped, metal and hollow inside. The Sanuri, Gala, Raul and Simon created several different mixtures to be put inside of the tobisks. These objects were designed to explode on impact.

The tobisks that Raul and Simon were about to launch were called Oran's; they were the size of a melon and contained ramni oil, buruto powder and meno salts. These ingredients would burst into flames upon impact. Both Raul and Simon gave the same order, as soon as the dark landscape was lit up by the exploding tobisks; the archers were to shoot at any Hutas they saw.

Tapster was starting to get suspicious. He knew the Princes of Wetpr had entered the forest because he too had noticed the sudden silence of all living things. "They should be here by now," Tapster thought to himself; so he sent four Huta warriors from the ambush site to find the men of Wetpr. Hutas had refined the art of guerrilla warfare. Their hatred of all other beings and their feelings of racial superiority propelled them to constant combat.

But the Hutas were a unique group from all other beings. Most cultures grew and advanced overtime but after the Huta race decided to sell their souls to the demons they worshipped, their race started to degenerate. Unlike The Great Ruler, darkness obliterates man's free will; partially by destroying man's intellect. Although vicious, driven killers, this once proud race was becoming nothing more than the hand puppets of the demons and the dark lords.

The four Huta warriors spread out and moved silently through the underbrush. Their eyes had become accustomed to the darkness of the forest. As they moved towards the area where the warriors of Wetpr had entered the forest, their senses heightened. Something was very wrong; there was no sign of the soldiers.

The darkness of the forest charitably concealed the men of Wetpr as it had done the Hutas. Raul watched the four Huta warriors as they had watched his camp the night before. On Raul's command, arrows dipped in the poison of the Atha serpent hurled through the trees and struck the Hutas.

The venom of the Atha serpent contained elements that caused instant paralysis. The warriors did not scream out. Raul did not realize the irony of his choice of poison as it was the venom of the Atha serpent that the Hutas had used when they tried to eradicate the Shettee race.

Experienced in battle, Raul and Simon had no intentions of walking into the lair of the Hutas; instead the Huta's would come to them. Less than twenty minutes passed before both Simon and Raul watched more Huta warriors sneak through the forest. As with the first four; poison tipped arrows stopped the Hutas in their tracks. The poison took such immediate control that some of the Hutas died before they realized they had been shot.

When the second group of Hutas did not return, Tapster knew the ambush would not go as planned. He unleashed his small army of Hutas and followed them to observe the battle. The Huta warriors walked with the stealth of experienced woodsmen. Silently they moved through the great forest looking for their prey. Suddenly the sky lit up as dozens of tobisks were hurled through the trees from different directions.

The tobisks had two purposes, one to light up the area they were thrown into and the second to burn whatever they hit. Huta war cries rang throughout the forest as the barbarians charged the soldiers of Wetpr. The light created by the exploding tobisks affected the night sight of the Hutas, so they could not see the arrows propelling towards them, nor could they see their enemy. Screams were heard as the hot ramni oil burned the skin of the Huta warriors. Tapster realized the battle was lost; he had his orders, he disappeared into the darkness of the forest.

Simon and Raul had their men walk through the battlefield to ensure the Hutas were dead. Fortunately for them all, the forest experienced almost daily rain showers, so the brush was not dry. The soldiers of Wetpr easily put out any tiny fires caused by the tobisks.

"The demon has not been found," Simon said as he rode up to Raul. "Well our ideas worked," Raul said solemnly. "Not one of our men was hurt and we stopped the attack. Although I am pleased; there is a sadness inside of me. If we can create weapons to kill as these; what will others create?"

Chapter XXVIII
Secrets

Erebus heard a knock on the door to his chambers, opening the door he saw Sophie standing in the hallway. Erebus did not move to let her enter his room. "A little late aren't you?" he asked sarcastically.

"Erebus please let me in before anyone sees us."

Erebus moved to the side and closed the door behind Sophie before he started yelling. "Sophie you were supposed to come here three days ago, every night I have been waiting for you. What the hell is going on?"

"You haven't done any more spells to learn about Roch have you?"

"First of all quit changing the subject and secondly of course I have."

"But I warned you."

"You also told me you would visit me three days ago," Erebus said angrily.

"Did you put a protection spell on your chambers?" Sophie asked.

"Yes, three days ago."

"Do another spell. We have much to talk about and no one can hear."

By the time Raul, Simon and their men reached the monastery at Philiste the last of the victims of the Rogett attack had died. There were no witnesses to the gruesome massacre. Simon and Raul were both aware of the direct correlation between the Rogett attack and their changing their route to ride into an ambush. What troubled them is that someone knew the plans of their route.

When they wrote to Sudfad about the ambush he informed them that he had sent the information of their plans and routes to the commanding generals of each fort. Now the Royal Family of Wetpr questioned whether they had a spy among their soldiers. The Princes changed their routes and sent the information only to Sudfad.

Once Matthew was healthy enough, he resumed writing his weekly letters to Sudfad's family. After Raul and Simon read about the Demalog attack at Stephan and Ingr's wedding; they started to send letters directly to Matthew with any information about possible threats to their kingdoms. A growing concern of them all was that Roch was indeed working with demons to implement his plans of attack on the Kingdom of Wetpr.

Philiste was but a two day ride to Fort Nir. Raul and Simon had originally planned on arriving at Fort Nir from the north, now they would be riding from the east. And whoever was behind the Rogett attack and the ambush would know that.

Sophie nervously drank a glass of wine while Erebus was performing a spell that would prevent demons and dark lords from eavesdropping on their conversation. As his anger was subsiding, Erebus became aware of how nervous and frightened Sophie was acting. When Erebus was done with the spell he poured more wine into Sophie's glass and poured himself a glass; then he sat next to her on the sofa.

"Sophie I don't know if I have ever seen you look frightened before. What is going on?"

"Erebus you have put me in an awful situation. If I tell you about Roch I am putting us both in great danger and if I don't you will probably be killed. I have sworn an oath of secrecy and I am prepared to defy it to save you; but you may wish I had never answered your questions."

"Sophie you are an incredibly powerful witch and my powers have grown immensely over the years."

"Erebus, we are dealing with the Old Ones. Do you still want me to answer your questions?"

Before the Sanuri left the Kingdom of Lentz he promised Matthew that he would return and explain to Angelina her new role as a wife of a Keeper of the Scrolls. The Sanuri left Lentz and drove directly to the castle of Sudfad. Upon his arrival, the Sanuri and Sudfad met in the King's study to discuss the many things which had occurred since their last meeting.

"When I looked into Juleta's mind I saw some very disturbing things," the Sanuri explained. "Now you have to understand it was rather like looking at pieces of different puzzles. It appears that the covert group the Insidiae is very large but it is fractured into small secretive groups of which Juleta was a member of one. She belonged to a group that called itself the Recupero Sect, which means to regain or recover; but this we already suspected.

"As we have already learned, only the members of Recupero Sect wear the ruby rings that we have seen. I thought the rings were used merely to identify members of the sect but I now know that these rings will somehow signify to the group when their plans are unfolding. I was prevented from seeing anything else about the group or the rings. I sensed that it was a demon much more powerful than Stolas that was blocking my sight. I also saw images of Raul and Simon and this castle, as if I was looking through the eyes of another."

"What do you think that means?" Sudfad asked with concern.

"I am not sure but I would like to go to the vault," the Sanuri said. "I have a feeling I am missing something."

Sudfad led the Sanuri to the vault hidden underneath his study. "Are you looking for anything in particular?"

"No. I just feel like there is something down here which I need to find."

The two men searched the shelves of scrolls, texts and other holy items together. Sudfad would pick up items and show them to the Sanuri, who would shake his head and continue searching.

"As many times as I have been down here I really do not remember this," Sudfad said with surprise as he picked up a small dust covered metal box. "And it is locked."

"Let me see," said the Sanuri as he turned around. He took the box over to a candle so he could better examine it. "Sudfad I think I saw this in my test," said the Sanuri. "I believe it was on a shelf behind the image of Sharonne." The box was modest with no decoration, and it appeared quite old. Both the Sanuri and Sudfad searched for a key without success.

"There were three keys in the box with Glenda's diary," said Sudfad. "They are sure not to work but might as well give them a try." Sudfad went to his study and returned with the box Gala had given to him. As Sudfad was trying to fit the keys into the lock of the small metal box, the Sanuri looked through the box of Glenda's things. He picked up the small talisman that was under the diary. "I saw Glenda put this under Micha's baby blanket during my test," said the Sanuri as he turned it over in his hand.

"You are not going to believe this," said Sudfad. "One of the keys fits." Sudfad lifted the top of the box and pulled out a small envelope which he handed to the Sanuri. "There is nothing else in here."

The Sanuri looked at the envelope, which appeared to once have been white; it had yellowed with age and had a brown stain on it. The envelope was not sealed; the Sanuri opened it and took out a hand written letter which he read out loud to Sudfad.

My Dearest Igor,

I want you to always remember how much I loved you. I will be dead by time you read these words and I do not want you to always wonder why I would leave the man I love so dearly. Please leave this horrid castle and find happiness again; only death and darkness fills the halls here. It is very difficult for me to even write these words. After your brother Sharonne sent you out of the castle he came to our bedroom and raped me, again and again.

My mind is crazy thinking I must have done something to provoke such an attack; but my love, I can think of nothing. He is a savage and cursed man; promise me you will leave this castle. He threatened to kill us both if I told you. But my dear the worst is yet to come.

Think me not crazy, but as he attacked me Sharonne changed. It was as if one moment I saw his face and the next I saw the face of a demon. Terror so gripped my heart I could hardly breathe. So intent was his attack on me that I do not know if he realized what was happening.

My dear the shame he has brought upon me weighs heavily upon my soul and the fear that it will happen again overwhelms me. I know the question that will linger in your heart long after I am gone is-- why, why did she do it? He wanted to impregnate me and I will not give birth to a demon child lest I spend eternity burning in hell.

Remember me

Your loving wife

Mata.

"Glenda spoke about this letter in her diary," said Sudfad.

"Yes but how did it get inside this vault? Sudfad you said that Gala was so frightened that she only took from her house some food and the box she gave to you?"

"That is what she told me and she had nothing with her but the clothes on her back."

"I think I need to take her back to her house; there will be more of Glenda's things there, if Roch has not destroyed them."

"She may be too frightened to return."

"She will have to trust that I can protect her. When is Petra's celebration?"

"In five days time."

"We will return before then," said the Sanuri and walked out of the vault.

Erebus sat back on the sofa and stared at Sophie. He was trying to take in everything she had told him about being a member of the Insidiae and Roch being the Vessel of Darkness. Suddenly Erebus' eyes grew wide. "Sophie, Roch is in the condition he is because of his encounter with a holy messenger. If he has been touched by holiness he can no longer be a vessel for Omnibus can he? Is there another who can fill his place? Is Omnibus going to think you failed and punish you?"

"I don't know," Sophie cried. "I have been thinking about all of those questions and more. I keep sending messages to Meekos asking him what I should do about Roch but he has not sent me any answers and that is not like him. I usually hear from him at least once a week and it has been many weeks now."

"Do you think something has happened to him?"

"I don't know, I love my brother and I'm really worried," Sophie paused for a moment before continuing. "Erebus I don't want anything to happen to you and I am afraid that it is the Old Ones that are blocking your spells and threatening you."

"A few nights before we left, Annabelle asked me how many girlfriends I had before her," Simon said with a smile as he and Raul rode next to each other. The two generals were leading their men towards Fort Nir.

"Did you tell her?" asked Raul grinning.

"Are you kidding Brother, that girl knows how to use a sword now," Simon said with a laugh. "And I do not plan on telling her."

"Vitomas never asks but she has said several times that she can tell I have slept with other women."

"Yes, that is about the same circumstances for Annabelle's question. Do you tell her?"

"No, if she asked I might. But I think she is afraid that if she asks me about my past relationships that I will ask her more about Roch."

"Is she still having nightmares?"

445

"She has not had one for some time, I think talking about some of her experiences has helped. Vitomas said it is not because of shame that she will not tell me everything but she thinks if I find out I will go crazy."

"Vitomas is probably right. I have asked Annabelle several times and she always changes the subject and pretends that life never happened."

"Simon, should we be trying to get them to tell us?"

"I don't know," said Simon. Then he laughed, "I am still trying to figure out what I should be saying half the time as it is."

"You want to know one thing she did tell me about Roch?" asked Raul with disgust. "He does not just rape little girls and women."

Simon looked at Raul and asked, "He rapes little boys too?"

"And grown men."

"Sanuri please do not be offended but I do have to admit I am scared," said Gala as they rode towards Cana in the boca.

"Gala we have known each other for years; have I ever disappointed you?" asked the Sanuri smiling.

Gala laughed. "It is just, if you could have seen what a monster Roch looks like now."

"Roch has always been a monster; now his mask has been removed," said the Sanuri. He looked over at Gala who was seated next to him in the front seat of the boca. "Gala, when we get to your home, bring back whatever belongings you like, there is plenty of room in this boca."

"Oh thank you, there are things I would like to have," said Gala happily.

"I also need a favor from you."

"Of course, what is it?"

"Help me figure out what to get Petra for his birthday," said the Sanuri with a laugh.

"Actually that is pretty easy," said Gala smiling. "That boy talks about you all of the time; he even told me he wants to travel with you when he gets older. Give the boy something of yours so he can feel closer to you."

Sophie had stayed late into the night with Erebus. That night they did not make love but talked seriously for hours. After Sophie left, Erebus sat up until dawn trying to figure out what to do. He did not confide in Sophie that Cerephus was planning on killing Roch and taking control of the kingdom. But after listening to Sophie, Erebus realized that if it was even possible for him and Cerephus to kill Roch, they would bring the wrath of the Insidiae and the Old Ones upon them.

Erebus was also very worried about Sophie; he wanted to take care of her and to protect her. And he knew he dare not share her secrets with Cerephus. Sophie and Erebus had been passionate lovers in their youth. Neither of them discovered the truth about their break up until Erebus arrived at Roch's castle.

Meekos, Sophie's older brother had lied to both of them and manipulated a situation where both Sophie and Erebus believed the other had left them for another person. Meekos committed this treacherous act not out of love for his sister or because he disliked Erebus but because he was jealous; Meekos wanted all Sophie's attention.

Of all the things Sophie told Erebus, the most disturbing to him was her reasoning for joining the Insidiae. In her youth, Sophie was a vibrant, beautiful woman who loved life. Erebus could not conceive of the fact that she would help Omnibus escape his prison. Erebus knew the history of this infamous demon.

The Great Ruler cast Omnibus into The Abyss to protect all worlds from him. And to think that Sophie would unleash such a monster into any world was beyond Erebus' comprehension. Erebus' heart broke when Sophie told him that she was so lost after they broke up; that all their love was replaced by hatred and rage. Sophie said she hadn't cared about anyone for so long that she just wanted everyone else to hurt as much as she did.

The land between the Village of Philiste and Fort Nir consisted of small farms and their fields. There were no caves or mines for enemies to hide in. There were no forests or mountains to conceal the dark ones. The road to Fort Nir was open and spacious, yet Raul and Simon were ever alert.

"I just don't like this," Raul said to his brother. "I feel like we are walking into another trap."

"Let's make camp early so we can thoroughly examine the area we will be spending the night in," Simon said. "And we should double the guards."

As became their morning routine, Thaos would wake Nikki so they could make love before he left for the fort. Nikki smiled as she felt Thaos' hand caressing her body. "Are you going to stay at the castle today?" Thaos asked.

Nikki had been sleeping with her head on Thaos' chest, now she looked into his face. "I could, why?"

"I thought I would come home over lunch and we could work on that baby," Thaos said with a grin.

Nikki rose up and looked at him but did not speak. Thaos sat up and said, "You have a strange look on your face. Did you change your mind about having a baby?"

"Thaos it isn't that I don't want a baby, it is just, why is everything going so fast?" Nikki asked with concern in her voice. "Is there something you haven't told me? Like you are expecting something awful to happen or you are dying?"

Thaos laughed, "Why would you even think something like that?"

"Because you never tell me anything. Thaos I love you but in some ways you are a complete stranger to me. Is there a reason you never tell me about your life before I met you?"

"Yes," Thaos said as he looked into Nikki's eyes. "Because I don't think you are going to like what you hear." Nikki stared at Thaos with tears filling her eyes. He held her hand. "I told you I was on my own since the age of nine. Well, I had to make a living and I made some pretty bad choices at times. I have done some things that I am not proud of Nikki," Thaos paused. "I learned I could make a living fighting."

"You mean like the Gefrey Games?"

"Yes, I have fought for sport but I became a hired fighter."

"I don't understand."

"People would hire me to fix their problems."

"Do you mean like when you got rid Thaddies?"

"Exactly."

"If you got rid of people like Thaddies then I think you did good things," Nikki said with a warm smile.

Thaos kissed Nikki on the tip of her nose, "I am sorry that I am pushing you into things before you are ready. Once I make up my mind about something I have always jumped in with both boots on. I have never been in a position before where I have had to consider someone else's feelings and I guess I am not very good at it."

"Are you saying I am your first girlfriend?"

"I am saying you are the first girl I have wanted to have a committed relationship with. And now that I am starting a new life I am finally free to consider a serious relationship and a family. Nikki do you want to have a family with me?"

Nikki moved closer to Thaos and put her arms around his neck, "So what time were you planning on coming home to work on that baby?" Nikki asked and slowly kissed Thaos' neck and chest.

The Sanuri and Gala entered her house by the back door during the early morning hours. "I am surprised your house is still intact," said the Sanuri.

"My neighbors are wonderful people they would never steal my things."

"Not your neighbors, Roch's men," said the Sanuri.

"The trunks belonging to Glenda and other family members are in that room," said Gala as she pointed at a closed door. "I am going to start packing."

"Gala, you do not have to hurry so, we will be alright," said the Sanuri reassuringly. "Why don't you put on a pot of coffee?"

Although Gala trusted the Sanuri she could not quell the fear that rose within her when she thought about King Roch. Gala hurriedly filled baskets with medicines, herbs and dry food. The Sanuri came out of the back bedroom as Gala was packing dishes. "Gala is there any other place that your mother or grandmothers might hide things?"

Gala filled the Sanuri's cup with coffee and said, "They always feared the Kings, they may have secret hiding places that I do not know about; I will help you search."

"No, you just keep packing and Gala; we do have room for some furniture also."

The Sanuri walked back into the bedroom and looked over the room, "If I was afraid of King Sharonne where would I hide something," thought the Sanuri. He looked over at a small shelf of manuscripts near the bed. The Sanuri looked through two manuscripts and put them aside for Gala as they were books on herbs and medicines. He picked up a Bible and a piece of paper fell to the floor. The Sanuri unfolded the paper and saw it was a drawing. He flipped through the pages of the Bible and found several more drawings.

Six drawings in all; the Sanuri laid them out on the bed. Each appeared to be a charcoal drawing by an untrained hand. Every drawing contained the face of one man, except for one that showed Sharonne with another man. "I think Glenda is trying to tell me who Sharonne's visitors were," thought the Sanuri. He folded the pictures and put them into a pocket of his robe, then he continued to search the room.

Gala took a picture off from the wall and heard something drop; she bent down and saw a key lying on the floor. "Sanuri, come into the dining room." Gala held up the key, "It fell out of the back of this picture." The Sanuri examined the picture and the frame and did not find anything unusual. "I have no idea what it goes to," said Gala.

"I think it is a good thing you are packing the house. I feel we may find more." The Sanuri started to load some of Gala's belongings into the boca to clear space for their search. The sun was now up. As the Sanuri was walking to the boca he spied a couple of old buildings behind Gala's house and decided to investigate.

The Sanuri entered a barn behind Gala's house; it was old but surprisingly clean. He slowly checked the walls for any sign of hidden compartments. He searched the bins and the hay loft without finding anything unusual. Just as he was about to walk into the second building he heard Gala calling him.

"Sanuri," she said excitedly "Come you have to see this," Gala turned and ran back into the house. "I was trying to move this cupboard to see if it was too heavy for you and me to carry to the boca and look what I found." Gala pointed to a door in the kitchen wall.

The Sanuri opened the door; the hinges squeaked loudly. The doorway was filled with spider webs. Gala handed him a lit candle. "There are stairs back here," said the Sanuri. He propped the door open and started to walk down the steps; Gala followed behind with another lit candle. They kept hitting spider webs out of the way, as they descended the steps.

"This appears to be a storage cellar," said the Sanuri as he saw shelves of canned goods.

"But that makes no sense that there would be a cupboard hiding the door as there is plenty of room in that kitchen for the cupboard."

The Sanuri looked at Gala and smiled, "Then we search."

451

The Sanuri and Gala searched in the cellar for hours without success. Gala brought down many more candles to illuminate the old stone cellar. "There has to be something down here," said Gala with frustration. "Sanuri would you like me to fix something to eat?"

"Very much so," replied the Sanuri. "I will keep working until it is ready." The Sanuri was slowly going around the walls running his hand over the cold stones. When some grains of grout fell into his hand. He carefully checked each stone on that wall and smiled when he found one that was loose. The Sanuri gently pulled the stone out of the wall and held the candle up to look into the hole. "Well hello there," he said with a grin as he pulled a small box out of the wall. He extinguished the candles and walked up stairs.

"Sanuri," whispered Gala, "There are Taperian soldiers outside."

"Hide, let me talk with them," said the Sanuri as he hid the box in a bowl of flour; then walked outside.

"You there," yelled one of the guards. "Where is the healer?"

The Sanuri walked up to the soldiers who were on horseback, "What healer?"

"The woman who lives in this house."

"My wife and I were told this house was abandoned, we are moving in," the Sanuri replied. "Are we on someone's property?"

"We do not care about the house; just the healer," said the soldier.

"Then is it alright for us to move in?"

"It does not matter to us if you move in here."

"If this healer returns, who should I tell her is looking for her?"

"She has been summoned to the castle by King Roch," said the soldier and they turned and rode away.

The Sanuri watched the soldiers leave then went into the house. "Will they return?" asked Gala fearfully.

"Yes but not for a while."

"How can you be so sure?"

"Because in a few minutes they will be attacked by a flock of Enrops," replied the Sanuri. "Let's get your things inside the boca. Gala was madly running around the house grabbing things. "Gala we cannot leave too quickly or they will see us on the road." An hour later they were heading north towards Wetpr.

"I will feel better when we cross the border," Gala said as she opened a basket and handed the Sanuri an apple. "I am sorry, I did not get a chance to make anything; all I have is cheese, apples and jerky," she said apologetically.

"That sounds like a fine meal."

"Did you open that box?" asked Gala.

"No."

"So what all did you find?"

"Six drawings, a key and that box."

"I put some baskets of things in the back that I had not opened, perhaps we will find more," said Gala.

Chapter XXIX
The Cries of Demons

The Sanuri and Gala only took breaks to care for the horses. "We will make camp as soon as we cross the border," said the Sanuri.

"Thank you," said Gala. "I would not be able to relax one moment in this dark place."

"Gala if you do not mind me asking; I find it curious that you have never looked through Glenda's belongings."

"That room you were searching was Glenda's, then after she died it was my parent's room," Gala said. "My father died years ago, but mother only died last year; I guess I just wasn't ready to go through their things yet."

"I grabbed everything from that room so I could look at them again; you did not lose your memories."

"Thank you," said Gala smiling. "The King and Queen of Wetpr are wonderful people; I think I will be very happy living at the castle."

"I am sure you will."

"I would not say anything to them but I worry though," Gala said seriously. "I cannot believe King Roch will let Vitomas go so easily; just because of his ego and pride alone."

"I know. This is not close to being over."

"Last night Nikki told your mother that the reason they have not been joining us at lunch is because they are trying to have a baby," Claudius said as he and Stephan rode to Mathas' for the morning meeting. "Your mother is thrilled at the idea of having two babies in the castle."

"Ingr told me too that they want a baby," Stephan said. "And I thought Ingr and I got into a relationship fast. I will admit I am a little surprised."

"I'm really not," Claudius said. "When I first met Thaos he struck me as being a little lost and alone. The life he lived before was too dangerous for him to form relationships of any kind. We gave Thaos a second chance and he has made the choice to change his life. He seems to be doing everything possible to make that happen. Mathas said he is performing well in his position as a captain. Honestly I am proud of the boy."

"Well it is about time you got here," Mathas said with a broad smile as Claudius and Stephan entered his study.

"We aren't late," Stephan said as he noticed Matthew was smiling also.

Mathas handed each man a small glass of whiskey. "Isn't it a little early in the day to start drinking?" Claudius asked.

"Nonsense," Mathas said. "We are just having a toast to celebrate."

Stephan already figured out the reason for the toast when his father asked, "And to what do we celebrate?"

"Claudius, you are not going to be the only grandfather here," Mathas said as he held up his glass. "Angelina is pregnant and we couldn't be happier."

"What?" screamed Roch as he threw his glass of whiskey against the wall.

"I am sorry My Lord," apologized Mandrake.

"Alright Mandrake, explain this to me one more time," growled Roch as he poured himself another drink.

"This morning while on patrol I led the men through Cana and past the healer's house," said Mandrake. "We stopped and I went inside and it appears to be empty."

"Yes, yes, I got that part," yelled Roch with annoyance.

"When I came back to garrison I was talking with some of the other soldiers and was told that two days ago an older man and his wife were seen moving into the healer's house," Mandrake continued. "The soldiers spoke with the man and did not feel there was anything unusual going on, but a short time later they were attacked by a flock of Enrops."

"My men were attached by birds?" screamed Roch.

"Yes My Lord and a few of them are still being treated," Cerephus said.

Roch was visibly angry, "Cerephus do you believe this bird attack is related to the healer's house being emptied?"

"I do not know My Lord; we are telling you what happened."

"Do you think the healer was there or are you saying that man and his wife stole her things?"

"We are merely relating two strange occurrences," replied Cerephus. "A couple says they are moving in but the house is now empty and moments after speaking with the couple our soldiers are attacked by a flock of birds."

"Let me think about this," said Roch. "Did anyone get the name of the man they spoke to?"

"No My Lord."

Simon was setting up the campsite, as Raul prepared dinner. "If we are lucky General Simmons will have all the materials we need, so we can get started as soon as we get there," Simon said.

"Well, he certainly has had enough time to start working on the weapons," Raul said as he put a couple of steaks into a pan. "If he has done nothing, we will have to hold him accountable."

"He is a good man, I would expect he is not waiting for us to come and hold his hand on this mission," Simon said as he spread out their bedrolls. "I just want to shorten this trip and go home." Simon paused for a few minutes then said, "If the baby is a girl, Annabelle and I are going to name her Arianna, after Mother."

"Annabelle is just convinced the baby is a girl. I think it is just wishful thinking on her part," then Simon paused again. "You should have seen the look on Annabelle's face when I told her I might not be back before the baby came. And now in her last letter she says that either she miscalculated how far along she is or we might be having twins again."

"What! Why does she think that?" Raul asked.

"Well Annabelle says she is getting really big for someone who is supposed to be only six months pregnant. I would love to have twins again but I don't want her to go through that by herself," Simon said sadly.

Raul did not say anything for a while. He handed Simon a plate of food. "Vitomas kept crying when I told her about this mission; I still feel guilty." Raul took a seat near the fire. "We will hold off Samuel's christening until we are all home; perhaps it will be a double christening," Raul said feigning a smile.

"Damn that Roch," Simon said angrily. "I just worry what might happen while we are gone."

"I know."

"My Lords, come you have to see this," said a soldier as he walked up to Raul and Simon.

"What is it Denks?" asked Simon

"Well, I am not really sure; you just need to see it," replied Denks. "I was gathering firewood when I saw it," Denks added as he took them about three hundred yards south of the campsite. They were walking through a field of high grasses when they suddenly entered a small clearing.

"What do you make of that?" Denks asked.

Both Simon and Raul squatted down as they looked at a large design made on the ground. There was a large outer circle outlined with bones. In the center of the circle was a small fire pit. A circle of bones also surrounded the fire pit. There were three human skulls in the pit, lying on top of ashes.

"These are blood stains," said Raul. "The ashes are cold, but I don't think this has been here long; no animals have disturbed the bones."

"From these tracks it looks like eight, maybe nine Hutas were here," Simon said.

"Hutas, what do you think they were doing?" asked Denks.

"They worship demons, I will bet this is some kind of altar," said Raul.

"Demons!" yelled Denks.

Simon was following the foot tracks as Raul destroyed the altar. "It looks like they came from the south, the direction of the Caves of Muldun; had their ceremony then returned," said Simon.

"They've come pretty far into our kingdom again," said Raul.

"Maybe they were looking for someone to sacrifice," said Simon as he looked at the skulls in the fire pit.

"Or maybe they are just warming up for another attack," Raul said.

Raul and Simon awoke to one of the soldiers yelling 'Hutas'. When Simon opened his eyes he saw the blade of an axe coming towards his eyes. He quickly rolled to the right and jumped to his feet. As Simon faced the Huta he could see that Raul was fighting with another warrior. The Huta swung at Simon with his axe. Simon jumped backwards as the axe sped past his stomach. The Huta lunged at Simon with the axe raised. As the Huta was coming towards him; Simon did a forward roll; putting him behind the Huta. As Simon came out of the roll he grabbed the knife that he kept in a sheath in his right boot.

The Huta quickly turned and lunged at Simon again. As the Huta tried to lower his axe on Simon's head; Simon blocked the Huta's arm, with his left forearm, and simultaneously thrust his knife into the Huta's stomach.

Simon withdrew the knife and stabbed the Huta again and again. The Huta fell to the ground bleeding. Simon heard Raul yell his name and when he looked up Raul tossed Simon's sword to him. Simon pulled the sword from its sheath and thrust it through the heart of the Huta. Simon and Raul ran to the other soldiers. But they found that the battle was over by time they had killed their attackers.

"My Lord, we counted eight, they are all dead," reported Crater.

"And our men?" asked Raul.

"None dead, a few with injuries; I will get more information and get back to you My Lord," said Crater as he turned and walked away.

"That is insane that eight Hutas would attack a group as large as ours; they had to know they would lose," said Simon.

"Something is not right here," Raul said. "Simon have the men examine the bodies of the Hutas. Maybe this was some kind of message."

Simon had his men carry the bodies of the dead Hutas to one spot and lay them next to each other. Raul and Simon carefully examined each body, while they sent men outside of the perimeter of their campsites to look for anything that was unusual.

"They decorate their clothing with the bones of their victims," Simon explained to the troops who were standing around the dead bodies. "From the looks of these men, they were experienced warriors; which makes you wonder why they launched this suicide attack."

"Did anyone see the Hutas trying to take anything?" Raul asked as he looked at a bone necklace adorning the neck of one of the warriors.

"No My Lord," said Crater, "But all the bodies were close to your campsite; which means they walked past some of our men without touching them."

"They sent some of their best warriors after us," Simon said to Raul. "Someone must want us badly."

"I am glad to see you have returned," Sudfad said. "I was beginning to think you would miss Petra's birthday celebration."

"It did take longer than I had planned and there was still one shed I did not get a chance to search. I told Gala to pack up her belongings; which I am glad I did because we found some interesting things," said the Sanuri as he took a seat in the study.

"We were interrupted by some of Roch's men, so we just started putting things into the boca without searching them; perhaps we will find more." The Sanuri unfolded the six drawings and arranged them on the table. "I found these hidden in Glenda's Bible."

Sudfad walked over to the table and stared at the drawings, "Who do you think they are?" Sudfad asked.

"I believe Glenda thought that Sharonne was a demon so I think she hid these drawings in the Bible because she believed they would be protected," said the Sanuri. "I think she is trying to tell us who his visitors were." The Sanuri placed a key on the table. "This fell out of the back of a picture that Gala removed from the wall."

"Do you know what it goes to?" asked Sudfad.

"Not yet," replied the Sanuri. "But I have something here I hope gives us some information." The Sanuri put a box on the table. "Gala moved a large cupboard and found it concealed a door in the wall of the kitchen. The door led to a typical storage cellar. Gala pointed out that there was no reason for that cupboard to be placed in front of the cellar door as there was plenty of room in the kitchen. So we spent a great deal of time searching in that area and I found this box hidden inside the wall."

"This looks similar to the box of Glenda's that holds the diary," said Sudfad as he picked up the box.

"I know," said the Sanuri. "I was waiting until we were together to open it."

Simon and Raul reached Fort Nir late into the evening. Commanding General Simmons had prepared a welcome feast for the men from Wetpr.

"Your troops will be shown to their quarters first," Simmons said pleasantly. "Then they have a fine feast waiting for them."

"We have a few with minor wounds, do you have a physician?" Simon asked.

"But of course, we will have them looked at," Simmons said. "I will take you to your quarters, I have two large rooms for you but I apologize they are not close to each other."

"Would it be possible to put us both into the same room?" Raul asked. "We have much work to do."

"But of course," said Simmons skeptically. "My Lords you seem different since the last time we spoke; is something wrong?"

Both Raul and Simon were convinced there was at least one spy in their military; since only the commanding generals of each fort had received the details of their routes, no one was above suspicion.

Simon smiled, "We have changed Simmons, we both left pregnant wives and babies at home; we don't want to drag this trip out any more than we have to."

"I understand. Why don't you come into my office for a drink while I have new quarters arranged for you?"

Simon had been stationed under Simmons's command when he was a young lieutenant. Simon liked and admired General Simmons; now Simon hoped Simmons was not their traitor. As the three generals enjoyed their glasses of whiskey, Raul and Simon had many questions for General Simmons.

"I have known you two since you were boys," Simmons said. "Your father and I are friends. These are not the type of questions you ask in casual conversation."

"You must obviously suspect a traitor since the Hutas seem to know your routes. I would not expect less of you. If there is a traitor at this fort I know nothing of it; everything here is open to your inspection."

Sudfad carefully examined the old box before lifting the lid. He did not find anything on the outside of the box that he suspected to be a message. A musty smell filled his nostrils as the lid was rising. Sudfad took out a small handkerchief and unfolded it. The handkerchief was made out of fine quality linen, decorated with lace and a monogram was embroidered in one of the corners. "I think these stains are blood," said Sudfad as he handed the handkerchief to the Sanuri.

The Sanuri studied the monogram which was written in an old language that combined letters and pictures. "This monogram is from the monastery at Malga," said the Sanuri as he tried to read the rest of the lettering. "There is a large letter 'H', surrounded by an ornate scroll that appears to lead into a letter 'L'. The Sanuri suddenly put the handkerchief on the table and shook his head.

"What is it?" asked Sudfad.

"Many generations ago the highest order of priesthood, often bestowed on the man in charge of a monastery was the title Holy Lord."

"So the person we suspected might have been a priest, may actually have been the head of the monastery?" Sudfad asked in disbelief. "Was this during Sharonne's time?"

"It was in place long before Sharonne became King; I do not really remember when the change in official titles took place. But it would make sense that someone at that level would be aware of the possibility of the holy vault."

"I cannot understand how someone at that level of holiness could be involved with Sharonne."

"It may be worse than an involvement with Sharonne. But if in fact the Holy Lord of that time had turned to darkness, he certainly would not have been the first; absolute power and greed have been the downfall of man since the beginning of time."

Raul and Simon entered their new quarters. "This room is so large it must be a meeting room of some kind," Simon said as they looked around. Two beds, two dressers a large table and six chairs filled the room. There were maps displayed on the walls. Two doors led to the outside and there were four windows.

"I wonder how many people know that we have changed quarters," Raul said more to himself.

"Do you suspect Simmons?" Simon asked.

"Right now I suspect everyone. And I have been overwhelmed with the feeling that we are not seeing something that is right before our eyes." Because of their suspicions of a traitor, Raul had asked that more Enrops join them on their mission. No sooner had they entered their new quarters than four Enrops landed on each windowsill.

"My name is Cacu," said one of the Enrops. "I am leading this flock and we have a letter for you."

Raul took the letter as Simon walked up to Cacu. "Cacu can your species see demons?" Simon asked.

"We can see true demons but we cannot distinguish between normal humans and humans who are turning into demons or humans who are filled with darkness."

"Have you seen any demons here?"

"No but it is night and most of the people are in buildings," the Enrop replied. "But we did find demon essence at the altar you destroyed."

"Please watch the troops that are riding with us and let us know if you see anything suspicious," Raul said. "The traitor might be one of our own men."

"We will stand guard over your quarters," Cacu said and left the windowsill.

Simon poured a couple of glasses of whiskey as Raul opened the letter. "This is from both of the girls to the two of us," Raul said as he sat down at the table.

"Why don't you just read it out loud then?"

A smile came across Raul's face. "Well it looks like we are both going to be fathers of daughters. The girls said they hope we aren't mad but they asked the Sanuri about the sex of the babies."

"Isn't it strange how they seemed to know they were going to have girls?" Simon asked as he too sat down at the table.

"Vitomas wants to name the baby after Laurel, she wants to call her Ariel."

"That's a nice name," Simon commented as he took a sip of his whiskey.

Raul grinned, "I think Annabelle would like you to read some of this yourself." He read in silence for a moment then a serious look took over his face. "Vitomas said she has been having the same dream over and over. She sees us sleeping in a military building and red snakes are slithering across the floor towards us. She asked the Sanuri about the dreams and he told her to tell us about them."

As the Sanuri looked at the handkerchief, Sudfad pulled a lock of curly red hair out of the box. The hair was fastened together with a piece of yarn. "Why do you think this is in here?" asked Sudfad as he held up the hair so the Sanuri could see it.

"Sharonne and his brother both had red curly hair," said the Sanuri as he looked at the lock. "This is not child's hair."

"From reading Glenda's diary she sounded like an intelligent and perceptive woman; if she hid this in a wall; she must have had a good reason."

"If that is Sharonne's hair I wonder how she got it."

Sudfad pulled a golden chain containing a locket out of the box. Inside of the locket was a lock of fine reddish hair. Sudfad handed it to the Sanuri. "This is fine baby's hair. Glenda said that baby Micha died and then mysteriously came to life an hour later," said the Sanuri with frustration. "I do not know. She is trying to tell us something,"

"There is just a piece of paper left," said Sudfad. He unfolded it, "All it says is the number thirteen."

"Gala thank you for coming. I apologize for disturbing you at this late hour," said Sudfad. "We thought you should see the contents of the box the Sanuri found in your cellar." Sudfad handed Gala the opened box. First she took out the handkerchief and unfolded it.

"I do not know this monogram," said Gala. "But these look like blood stains." Next Gala picked up the lock of red curly hair but after just a moment she quickly threw it on the table and jumped out of her seat saying, "The Great Ruler be with us."

"Gala, there is also baby hair in that locket, what does it mean?" asked the Sanuri.

"You believe Glenda put these things into the wall?" Gala asked.

"The box is similar to the one you gave us and that monogram is old," said Sudfad.

"If Glenda packed those items that means that hair is several generations old; human hair does not live that long. Look at that hair it is as healthy as if you just cut it from someone," Gala continued. "It has long been believed that some of the living parts of demons will exist long after a human's would have rotted away."

"You are right," the Sanuri said. "I should have remembered that. Both the baby and adult hair are in excellent condition. That means Micha had some demon in him also."

"Do you think that is why Glenda put the handkerchief with blood stains in the box?" asked Sudfad.

"I would have no way of telling if there was still life in those bloodstains," said Gala. "What probably happened is she picked it up while she was tending to someone."

"There is just one more thing," said Sudfad as he pulled the last slip of paper out of the box. "Does the number thirteen mean anything to you?"

"No My Lord," said Gala. "I shudder to think those things were even in my house."

"Cerephus get Erebus down here now," growled Roch.

"Is there something wrong My Lord?"

"He has been here for weeks and shown me nothing," Roch said angrily. "All he does is ask me for more samples. I don't trust him and I am not going to pay him to sit on his butt. Either he gets me a demon or he is out of here."

"My Lord, I have been keeping an eye on him for you and I know that he has been working," Cerephus said. "But..."

"But what? Spit it out Cerephus," Roch's voice was growing louder as he yelled.

"He has had some unexpected complications."

"Like what?" Roch shrieked.

"My Lord, Erebus is much older than he looks and he has been a sorcerer his entire life. He has performed hundreds, probably thousands of spells but since he has been here, strange things are happening."

Roch sat back in his chair and stared at Cerephus, "What sort of strange things?"

"He is receiving threats from the dark worlds every time he seeks information about you."

"And you believe him?"

"I didn't at first, but I decided to watch him perform the spells and it is true."

"Tell me of these things."

"Sometimes great clouds of smoke with appear and voices will scream out of them; telling Erebus to leave this castle or to stop asking about you. And sometimes messages written in blood will appear on the walls giving him the same messages." As Cerephus and Roch talked, Sophie set the table in the war room with their lunch. Cerephus noticed that she seemed to be listening intently to their conversation.

"And you have witnessed this?"

"Yes, My Lord and I did not expect it to be true."

"Who does he think is sending the messages?"

"He thinks they are coming from a dark lord or a demon."

"You do realize, now you have made it public that Petra is your adopted son," said the Sanuri as he and Sudfad walked through the courtyard which was filled with people celebrating Petra's tenth birthday.

"Yes, I had thought about that but both Renya and I have agreed we are not going to spend our lives fearing shadows."

"Well he certainly seems to be enjoying himself," the Sanuri said as he watched Petra playing a game with a group of children. "He is very happy here."

"And we love him as our own," Sudfad said warmly. "It is strange how things have changed. For a while our castle seemed so empty and now it is filled with family and friends and babies and I love it," Sudfad said with a smile.

"I think we have enough to send a message to the Sanuri," said Padre Thomas. "We can send him more information later."

"I agree, this does not look good," said Padre Bartholomew as he finished writing the letter.

"I do not want anyone to see us calling the Enrops," Padre Thomas said softy. "I hate this, not being able to trust anyone."

The two old priests left the Hall of Antiquities and walked the entire length of the monastery. They left the old buildings through a back door and walked into the gardens. "Let's get past those trees," said Padre Thomas fearfully. They walked into a grove of pine trees and stopped, both of them prayed simultaneously for The Great Ruler to send Enrops. Almost twenty minutes later the sky filled with the large black birds; a few landed while the others soared through the air.

"Thank you for coming," said Padre Bartholomew as he walked up to the closest bird. "Please take this to the Sanuri, it is very import."

The Enrop grabbed the letter with his beak and flew off. The two priests watched the birds until they flew out of sight. "Come we must finish reading those scrolls," said Padre Thomas as the two turned back towards the buildings of the monastery.

"What do you think they are up to?" asked one of the figures who had been watching the priests from a window in the monastery.

"I do not know," said the second voice. "But Meekos was right, they bear watching.

Long after the festivities had ended and quiet had been somewhat restored to the castle; the Sanuri found Petra in his room. Petra's bedroom was filled with piles of birthday presents and he was sitting in the middle of the floor playing with one of his gifts. Petra got a bright smile on his face when he saw the Sanuri.

"Sanuri look, can you believe this?" Petra asked happily.

"I know," said the Sanuri. "You have had quite a day." The Sanuri walked into the room and sat on Petra's bed. "I have something for you." Petra stood up and walked over to the Sanuri.

"I will have to admit I really did not know what to get you that you were not already receiving as a gift. So I am going to give you this." The Sanuri pulled a thickly braided silver chain from his pocket. The pendent consisted of a huge roughly cut crystal surrounded by silver.

"A necklace," said Petra with disappointment.

"This is not just a necklace; place the crystal into your hand and close it. Now call my name like you need to find me."

Petra began to call "Sanuri, Sanuri." Then he looked down at his hand, Petra's eyes growing wide with amazement.

"What do you feel?"

"My hand is really warm."

"Now open your fist."

"It changed color, it is purple now," gasped Petra.

"This is a crystal from the Ice Caves of Mordv. If you ever need me, do what you just did and no matter where I am I will hear you."

"Thank you Sanuri," said Petra and hugged him.

Simon suddenly sat up in his bed at Fort Nir. He sat there for a moment remembering what he had just dreamed. "Raul, Raul."

"What is it?" asked Raul as he jumped out of bed. "Is there an attack?"

"No," said Simon as he sat down at the table in their room. "I had a dream."

Raul stared at his brother, then started laughing loudly, "You wake me up in the middle of the night because you had a bad dream," laughed Raul. "What are we kids again?"

"This was not a regular dream, I think it was some kind of message." Raul put his pants on and sat down at the table with Simon.

"In my dream I saw you and me sleeping near a campfire, then a lion walked into our camp and stood over both of us. I woke up but you remained sleeping. I got up and followed The Lion. We walked for a long time through a dark forest; then he led me into a cave or a mine I do not know. We walked in this cave for what seemed like a very long time; then we heard voices."

"The tunnel we were walking in opened to a large chamber that had many tunnels leading into it. There were five men wearing priest's robes with the hoods pulled up. These men were in the middle of the chamber and they were surrounded by hordes of Rogetts. One of the men was holding a golden chalice and they were all chanting in a language I had never heard," Simon said as he poured himself a glass of water.

"The Lion looked to the far right of the chamber; when I tried to see what he was looking at I saw another man dressed in a priest's robe who was holding a long staff. The top of the staff was carved into a striking snake. When this man saw The Lion looking at him he disappeared into one of the tunnels. The Lion turned to me and said, "When you see his face, you will know it."

"I cannot find it," said Padre Thomas.

"What are you looking for?" asked Padre Bartholomew.

"That scroll about The Chalice of Ascension; I was reading it yesterday and I put it on this shelf."

"Let me help you look."

After an hour had passed; Padre Thomas was getting quite frustrated. "How could it have disappeared?" he asked more to himself than to Padre Bartholomew.

"I just checked the list of missing items and that scroll is not listed."

"Padre Bartholomew; that means whoever is taking these items is still in the monastery."

"No, nothing looked familiar in the dream but it was very detailed; almost like I was really there," said Simon.

470

"I think we need to get a message to Father and the Sanuri," said Raul as he lit more candles. Raul handed Simon some paper and a pen.

"The Sanuri said The Lion protected you before; but did you ever have any dreams of it," asked Simon as he started to write a letter to Sudfad.

Raul sat down next to Simon, "You know, now that you mention it I did; but at the time I did not think anything of it," said Raul in astonishment. "When I traveled I remember seeing the face of a lion in my mind several times, usually just before I went to sleep." Raul was quiet for a moment. "Simon, I had forgotten but I had a dream about finding those scrolls in that cave in Puntd long before I ended up there."

"Well that explains why you didn't get this dream," said Simon with a grin. "You always forget them."

"My Lord," called Marie as she knocked on the door to Sudfad's study. "There are Enrops in the front yard and they have a message for the Sanuri."

Sudfad walked out of the front door and down the stairs to the courtyard. He could see that one of the birds carried a letter. A bird approached him saying, "We have a message for the Sanuri from the priests at Malga, they said it was important."

"Shall I take it?" asked Sudfad.

"We should deliver it to the Sanuri."

"Wait here," said Sudfad and he turned and walked back into the castle. Ten minutes later the Sanuri walked outside and retrieved the letter.

The Sanuri walked into Sudfad's study. "Want to read it together?" asked the Sanuri as he sat down. "This letter is from Padre Bartholomew and Padre Thomas. "They say that the priests have not yet completed the inventory of the Hall of Antiquities but from their research they feel they should notify me now of some of the missing items."

"The Chalice of Ascension is missing," the Sanuri put down the letter and looked at Sudfad. "This is not good, the chalice holds great power."

The Sanuri resumed reading the letter. "They say all the scrolls and texts that have information about The Abyss are missing as well as many other items. The Diamond of Cazo is gone and so is The Seal of Natun. They are researching to find out what holy items will unlock the powers of the chalice and will contact me later with more information." The Sanuri handed the letter to Sudfad to read.

Sudfad read the letter, "Alright, so tell me what all of this really means."

"Think of the Hall of Antiquities as a considerably larger version of the holy vault. Its access is limited to only certain priests, those with higher standing. Other priests need special permission to enter the hall. It is in an obscure area in the monastery. The only entrance is through two huge doors that have seven locks each and no two locks take the same key," explained the Sanuri. "That is usually were I spend most of my time when I am visiting that monastery. While I was being tested Padre Bartholomew was attached in there; he never saw his attacker."

"So you think a priest of a high order is involved with the missing objects?"

"During my tests I wanted to believe that the men I saw wearing priests robes were impostors. But the more I learn, the more I believe there must be real priests who have sold their souls to darkness. And yes, I now think at least one priest of a high order must be involved. Sudfad, most priests outside of the monastery at Malga are unaware of the existence of the Hall of Antiquities.

"Doesn't all this just make the case stronger against those three high priests, Meekos, Pravis and Tenebrae?" Sudfad asked with disgust.

"While I would agree with you; these old bones are telling me there is much more to all of this."

"And your friends are they in danger?"

472

"The Great Ruler is watching over them."

"What are the objects they spoke of?"

"The Hall of Antiquities is hundreds of years old and so large, that once items are put in there; the world forgets they ever existed," explained the Sanuri. "During my years I had often wondered why The Great Ruler had us build the secret vault under this castle when He had the Hall of Antiquities at the monastery at Malga. Now I understand; He knew that monastery would not be able to protect those items from the darkness that ever seeks them."

"The Chalice of Ascension was used in only the holiest ceremonies of old. This chalice would be set on an altar as a symbol that The Great Ruler Himself was taking part in the ceremonies. It is solid gold and adorned with precious jewels; but it is much more than a beautiful ceremonial cup. It possesses great power itself and when used in conjunction with certain other holy objects the power can be intensified incredibly."

"So those priests are trying to figure out what pieces are needed for certain ceremonies and what pieces are missing from the hall?" Sudfad asked.

Their three weeks at Fort Nir passed by quickly and uneventfully for Simon and Raul as they worked late into every evening to build the weapons they had designed. Commanding General Simmons worked on battle strategies that included the use of the weapons and covered attacks by multiple enemies.

"Well, tomorrow we test your weapons," Simmons said over dinner. "If they work as you say, I will have many others built."

"Good, you may need them," Raul said. "But be mindful, we have not found our spy yet; so you will want to trust the construction of the weapons to men you have faith in."

"And you will leave after the weapons are tested?" Simmons asked.

"We haven't determined when we will leave," Simon said. "We don't want you notifying General Kretcher that we are on our way to Fort Polta."

473

"I understand. Considering the circumstances I would feel better if you took some of my men with you also," Simmons said.

Later that night, Raul and Simon checked on the progress of their weapons before retiring to bed. When they entered their quarters they found an Enrop sitting on the table with a letter from the Sanuri.

"Raul, the Sanuri thinks my dream was a clue to the whereabouts of the missing Chalice of Ascension. He wants us to tell him of any other dreams we have about it or any information we hear about it."

"What is The Chalice of Ascension and where is it missing from?" asked Raul as he poured two glasses of whiskey.

"It is missing from the monastery at Malga and it has many powers, is all he says." Simon handed Raul the letter so he could read it himself. "So do you want to take Simmons up on his offer of providing more men for us?" Simon asked as he took off his boots.

"We probably should," Raul said as he put the letter on the table. "But I am still not sure I trust him."

"Well I do," Simon said. "And I am exhausted." He swallowed his drink and lay down on his bed. Raul sat up a few more minutes then retired to his bed also. Both men fell asleep quickly. Neither of them heard the approaching storm.

Lightening filled the sky as strong gusts of wind blew over small trees around the fort. The earth shook from the thunder and the Princes slept. Raul tossed and turned as he kept hearing Vitomas' voice screaming in his head, "Raul wake up, wake up now!" Suddenly Raul had a vision of Vitomas as clear as if he was home; she was standing over his bed wearing a pink nightgown. Vitomas was shaking Raul and screaming for him to wake up.

"There are snakes coming for you," Vitomas screamed so loudly in the vision that Raul sat up in bed. His heart was racing and he was sweating. Raul grabbed a knife that was lying on the small table next to his bed. He could feel movement at the foot end of the bed.

Lightning struck again and lit up their room, in that split second Raul threw his knife and hit a large red snake that was slithering towards him.

"Simon," Raul yelled. "There are snakes in here." Raul quickly lit the candle that was on the table next to his bed. Simon did not move. "Simon," Raul said again as he looked at the floor surrounding his bed. Simon did not answer. Fear filled Raul's heart as he grabbed his sword and ran to Simon's bed. A large red snake was coiled on Simon's chest ready to strike. Quickly Raul swung his sword cutting the head off from the snake. Simon jumped out of bed and grabbed his sword. "Are you alright?" Raul asked as he was searching the room for more snakes.

"Yes, but I wouldn't have been if you wouldn't have woken up."

Raul and Simon only found the two snakes, which they threw on the floor, near the door. Neither of them wanted to go back to bed. Simon listened unbelievingly as Raul told him about his dream.

"Annabelle wake up," Vitomas said as she shook her friend.

Annabelle jumped up, "What is it, what is wrong?"

"Come into the kitchen so we don't wake the children," Vitomas said as tears ran down her face.

Vitomas lit a candle and both women sat down at the kitchen table. "Vitomas why are crying? What is wrong?"

Vitomas told Annabelle about her dream, "It wasn't like any dream I have ever had before," she cried. "It was like I was really there."

"I think you need to tell this to the Sanuri," Annabelle said. "I will stay with the babies." Vitomas put on a robe over her pink nightgown and walked to the Sanuri's chambers.

Chapter XXX
Death Walks

As soon as the weapons were tested, Raul, Simon and their men left Fort Nir. They did not take Simmons up on his offer of providing them with more men because the snake attack increased their suspicions of him. Raul and Simon decided to change their route again, and take a very long way to Fort Polta, which was northwest of Fort Nir. They left Fort Nir, traveling south; they crossed the River Neior and made camp on the river's western shore.

Raul and Simon planned to continue southward until they reached the border of the Kingdoms of Wetpr and Stordt. This route would take them just north of the Forest of Bach and the Rodite Forest and north of the Caves of Muldun. They planned on turning north when they reached the River Cheban and traveling north until they reached Fort Polta.

Unlike the previous night, the skies were calm and the air motionless. The screams of Gants on the hunt pierced the night air even though the creatures were several miles away. "Have you ever seen a Gant?" Simon asked as they sat by their campfire.

"No and from those sounds I don't want to."

They heard the sounds of flapping wings just moments before several Enrops landed in their campsite. One of the birds was carrying a small envelope which it handed to Raul. Simon watched Raul's face as he read the letter. "What is it, what is wrong?" Simon asked.

Without speaking Raul handed Simon the letter from Vitomas. In it she explained in detail the nightmare she had about the snakes in their room.

"How can this be explained?" Simon asked. "You both had the exact same dream."

"Yes and a dream which saved our lives."

476

Raul, Simon and their troops reached the border of the Kingdoms of Wetpr and Stordt just before noon on the third day after they left Fort Nir. There were no walls separating the kingdoms but a physical border of foothills. The Kingdom of Wetpr started at the base of the foothills that housed the Caves of Muldun on the Stordt side. Raul and Simon led their men westward, parallel to the border. One of the scouts rode up to Raul. "My Lord we found some dead Hutas up ahead."

"What did they die of?" asked Simon.

"We could not tell," responded the soldier.

"This could be a trap," said Simon.

"I will take half of the men and proceed ahead," said Raul. "Give us a head start; if we engage the Hutas you attack from the rear."

Raul led his troops forward. The land on the Wetpr side of the border was open and flat; Raul knew if an attack came it would be from the foothills. Almost twenty minutes later they came upon the bodies of four dead Huta warriors lying at the base of a foothill, just on the Wetpr side of the border. Raul did not stop his troops but kept moving forward. An arrow flew past Raul's ear; simultaneously he heard a battle cry and the Hutas were upon them.

The Hutas came out of the foothills on horseback swinging battle axes and throwing spears. With sword drawn, Raul led his troops into the oncoming Hutas. As Raul was riding forward, he thrust his sword into the stomach of a Huta riding on his left side; while evading a spear thrust from a Huta on his right. Raul quickly turned his horse and hit the Huta wielding the spear, across the lower back with his sword. The Huta fell to the ground.

Raul saw another Huta on foot fighting with one of his soldiers who was on the ground. Raul rode past the Huta cutting his head off with one powerful swing of his sword. Raul rode forward stabbing another Huta; suddenly Raul looked up because he saw movement. A man in a priest's robe with the hood up was standing on the top of a foothill watching the battle. Suddenly the priest was gone; Raul turned and saw Simon leading his troops onto the battlefield.

Raul charged at a Huta on horseback. The Huta swung his battle axe cutting Raul's left upper arm. Raul quickly turned and stabbed the Huta in the back as he was riding past him. Raul looked through the fighting throng of men until he found Simon who was on the ground battling with three Huta warriors.

Raul charged in Simon's direction. Raul grabbed a spear that was sticking out of the ground and thrust it through the body of one of the Hutas fighting with Simon; then Raul jumped off from his horse and stabbed another Huta with his sword. Simon cut the throat of the third Huta. Raul and Simon stood side by side for a moment, swords drawn accessing the status of the battle.

A Huta charged his horse at Simon. But before the Huta could stab him with a spear; Simon jumped up grabbing the shaft of the spear and the warrior's forearm. Simon pulled the warrior off from his horse and threw him to the ground. Simon kicked the Huta in the head before thrusting the spear through the warrior's heart.

There was only one wave of attack by the Hutas who were outnumbered by the soldiers of Wetpr. Raul and Simon walked through the battlefield. All the Hutas were dead, four of the soldiers were dead and many wounded.

"I saw a man wearing a priest's robe standing up there," said Raul pointing to the top of one of the foothills.

"Did you see his face?" asked Simon.

"No his hood was pulled up," said Raul. "You were right Brother, there is more to this."

"You need to get something on that arm," Simon said as he looked at the blood running from Raul's wound.

Raul looked at a cut on Simon's left cheek and started to laugh, "Annabelle is going to be so upset that your pretty face is damaged."

Raul and Simon buried their dead but they left the bodies of the Hutas to rot in the sun. The belongings of the dead soldiers were carefully packed for their families. Raul spoke over the graves, then the troops mounted and they moved westward.

"I sent a message to Father," Simon said. "It certainly is nice now that the Enrops help us. It would be too dangerous to send a soldier."

They tripled the number of scouts but without need; the men of Wetpr rode until dusk without seeing any sign of Hutas. "I had hoped to be farther from the caves by nightfall," Raul said as he unsaddled his horse.

"I know, no one is getting much sleep tonight," replied Simon. "If the demons can control the Hutas and the Rogetts; I wonder if they can control the Gants."

Simon's words rang true; none of the men from Wetpr slept that night. The screams of the Gants once again filled the night air; but occasionally they would hear something else scream.

"That sounded like a human," Simon said as he and Raul sat around their campfire.

"If we are lucky maybe the Gants are killing the Hutas," Raul said as he gazed into the fire. "Simon I have been thinking. Someone is trying to kill the two of us; do you think it is because we are strengthening the kingdom for attack or because we are Keepers of the Scrolls?"

"You forgot the obvious," Simon said. "It could be Roch trying to take our wives again."

"Well I have been thinking about that," Raul said. "If it is Roch, he knows we are far from home; why hasn't he attacked Salar? Roch does not hide in the shadows he likes to make his presence known. We have not seen any signs of Taperian soldiers."

"So you don't think Roch is behind these attacks?"

"No," Raul said. "He hates us too much to let someone else kill us. He would want us taken alive so he could torture and kill us himself."

"I haven't met him but from what I have heard about him; I think you are right."

"I suspect more and more we are being attacked because we are Keepers of the Scrolls; which means we should warn Matthew. If he hasn't told Angelina yet, he should. "Raul said as he took a paper and pen from his saddlebags. They wrote a message for Matthew and a second one for Sudfad. Raul and Simon gave their messages to two Enrops that disappeared into the night sky with others of their flock.

The Sanuri shot up to a sitting position in his bed. "What was it I was dreaming?" he thought. His heart was pounding; the Sanuri tried to calm his mind so he could recapture the images of his dream. Once he realized the meaning of his nightmare, the Sanuri jumped out of bed and ran out of his room.

The next morning Raul and Simon led their men westward. They were traveling at the base of the foot hills. As they were riding through a narrow passageway of rock the earth suddenly started to shake. "Avalanche!" screamed a soldier as tons of rocks hurled down upon them.

Raul and Simon let their horses lunge forward. The dust and debris was blinding. The roar of the avalanche drowned out all other sounds. When the dust started to settle, Raul and Simon were still on their horses but they were separated from their men by a wall of rock. Both Raul and Simon started yelling to their men as they did not know if any of them had survived the landslide.

Suddenly an axe flew past Simon's head. He stopped his horse as twenty Huta warriors charged at them from different directions. Both Raul and Simon pulled their swords and battled with the savages. Raul was the first to be dragged off from his horse; Raul landed on his feet and was able to put enough distance between him and his attackers that he could swing his sword.

Simon felt a blinding pain then nausea; he could feel himself falling from his horse. "Simon!" screamed Raul when he saw his brother fall. But in that second that Raul looked at Simon, he did not see the fist coming at his head. Raul felt like he was in a dream, he could feel blows to his body but they seemed surreal.

The last thing Raul remembered was seeing Vitomas' face and having an overwhelming feeling of regret.

A searing pain jolted Simon into consciousness. He could not open his left eye; what he could see with his right eye was unfocused and hazy.

"Please do not move, your injuries are most serious," said a soothing female voice. "I have given you some medicine to kill the pain. I am sorry I had to pour it down your throat because you were unconscious."

Simon looked to his right and saw a beautiful woman sitting on the bed next to him. She had long curly blonde hair and was wearing a white dress and a belt that looked like spun gold. "Please be still I am sewing the wound in your side," she said.

"Am I dead?" Simon asked groggily.

"No," laughed the woman, "But you were barely alive when we got to you."

"Raul," yelled Simon as he tried to get up.

"Your brother is in a bed just a few feet from you, he is alive; but you both have many injuries," the woman said. "If he is Raul then you must be Simon?"

"Yes," replied Simon. As his eye was coming into focus Simon was staring at the woman.

"What, have you never seen a woman warrior before?"

"I have never seen a woman with wings before; do you really have wings?"

The woman stopped sewing his wound and looked at Simon, "I am Ibula from the tribe of Rualas, we all have wings. The Sanuri sent us to help you and your brother and I am so sorry we did not arrive sooner. But we have brought you to our home in the Ice Caves; you are safe here and will heal."

"Is he awake?" a deep male voice asked.

"Simon this is my husband Thedes, he has brought some more medicine for you and your brother."

Simon turned to look to his left and stared at Thedes. "You are Shettee I thought the Hutas wiped out your race."

"They almost did, but the Sanuri sent the Rualas to save us, just as he sent them to save you," said Thedes. "I am putting some medicine on your wounds to numb them while my wife works on them."

"I would really like some water," Simon said as he winced in pain.

"Thedes will you help him raise up?" asked Ibula as she held a cup of water to Simon's lips.

"Where did you say we were?" Simon asked.

"You are in the Ice Caves of Mordv," replied Thedes.

"I have heard of them but I thought they were only a legend."

"I thought the same thing until Ibula flew me here."

"Is that how we got here?"

"Yes," said Thedes. "The Sanuri sent Enrops to us with a message to meet with you in your kingdom. He also sent Enrops to you with a message. The Enrops that were sent to you saw the Hutas and flew to us to help. We were already on our way but not close enough. We killed the Hutas and brought you here. The Enrops are here also."

"You can fly also?" asked Simon with amazement.

"No," laughed Thedes. "But my wife is strong enough to carry me when she flies."

"That is amazing; you are my size and from what I can see she looks much smaller," said Simon as he tried to focus his eye on Ibula.

"She is considerably smaller but she is strong and an amazing warrior," Thedes said with pride. "We did not have female warriors in my tribe."

482

"We don't either," said Simon. "My wife is also small and I taught her how to fight with a sword; I really did not think she would ever use it. Then one day some men tried to kidnap her and Raul's wife and she killed two of them."

"You taught your wife well, you should be proud," replied Thedes. "Tell me are your wounds starting to feel numb?"

"Yes."

"The Sanuri saved my race from extinction also and brought us here to make new lives," said Ibula. "The caves are rich with plants and animals of every kind; we are fortunate to have so many plants to make medicines from."

"You have all that in these caves?" Simon asked with astonishment.

"When you and your brother are well I will take you through these caves and I am sure you will react as I did," said Thedes. "The beauty is beyond belief."

"I know you cannot see very well but there are huge crystal pillars throughout the caves that provide us with light and a healing energy," Ibula said. "Simon I want you to follow my directions. There is an arrowhead lodged in your right shoulder; Thedes will turn you and hold you on your side, please try not to move."

"We have a friend who is a healer," said Simon. "She makes powerful medicines; perhaps you could tell her how you made this medicine that numbs the pain."

"Does she grow her own plants?" Ibula asked.

"Yes."

"I will send her some plants, and perhaps we will meet someday," said Ibula. "Thedes hang on to him tightly."

Simon could feel something poking in his shoulder but he felt little pain. "Are you cutting it out now?"

"Yes."

"This medicine is amazing," said Simon. "And thank you both for all you have done."

"I will never turn down a chance to fight Hutas," Thedes said with a laugh.

"Thedes were you one of the warriors who were leading all of the women and children out of Xepoltr?" Simon asked. "The Sanuri told us about your narrow escape but he did not tell us about the Rualas or what happened to your people."

"Yes, when my country was overtaken, six of us were ordered to take the women and children to the monastery at Avaide and to wait for other warriors," explained Thedes. "The priests took us in and they treated us well. The Hutas heard we were at the monastery; some priests helped us to escape."

"Later we heard that the Hutas butchered all of the priests who stayed behind and then destroyed the monastery. I am still filled with anger every time I think of it. But some of the priests who helped us are here now in these caves; they came later because the Hutas were hunting them. The priests feared they put everyone in danger who gave them sanctuary; they are safe here."

"My parents adopted a boy last year, his name is Petra. When he was nine he rode to the monastery to warn all of you about the Hutas. After the priests helped your people to escape the Hutas came to the monastery. While the priests were being tortured and killed, little Petra was able to help one of the wounded priests to escape," said Simon proudly.

"So you are telling me that a boy who is now part of your family saved us from the Hutas?" asked Thedes in amazement.

"I suspect The Great Ruler has brought us together," Ibula said with a smile. "The Sanuri has taught us that there are no coincidences."

"This Petra will be a great warrior," said Thedes. "You say he was an orphan?"

"While he was riding to the monastery the Hutas killed his family."

"They are a race that is fueled by hatred for all who are different from them," said Ibula. "Sometimes I do not know whether I should hate them or pity them."

"She may pity them for their ignorance but she fights them on the battlefield," Thedes said.

"Thedes I probably should not ask this while Ibula is doing surgery on me," Simon said smiling as he was starting to feel almost drunk from the pain medicines. "How do you feel having your wife on the battlefield with you?"

"Simon, this has been quite the subject in our home," said Thedes with a laugh. "You are a warrior and I will bet you were raised like I was; that women are in the home with the children and it is your duty to protect them and care for them, am I right?"

"Yes," said Simon. "My wife Annabelle and Raul's wife Vitomas are wonderful wives and mothers yet they want to learn how to fight and ride and well, Raul and I do not always know what to do." Thedes laughed loudly.

"Honey you are making him move," Ibula scolded.

"Isn't it funny how we are all different tribes yet our lives are the same," said Thedes. "Ibula do you want to tell him about us?"

"Thedes is a wonderful husband now but when I first met him I thought he was the most ignorant and pigheaded man I had ever met," said Ibula. "My people were not warriors before; we were farmers and herders. The Hutas almost annihilated my entire race. The Sanuri saved us and brought us to these wonderful caves to live here if we chose. My tribe vowed that never again would we be prey to demons and every child regardless of sex is taught at an early age to be a warrior; and it serves us well."

"My wife will give birth soon and the Sanuri says the baby is a girl; she will be my first daughter; I do not know how I would feel teaching her to be a warrior," said Simon.

"Well, Simon then you are just as ignorant and pigheaded as my husband."

"Thedes, Ibula reminds me an awful lot of my wife," Simon said grinning. Thedes laughed loudly again.

"Thedes stop moving him," Ibula scolded again. "Why do I have a feeling you two are going to be great friends?"

"Do you have children?" Simon asked.

"No not yet, we have been together less than one year," Thedes explained. "We are the first of our two tribes to marry, as you can see we look very different; so our children will be starting a new race," said Thedes. "And yes Simon my sons and daughters will learn to be warriors when they are old enough."

"I never gave you an answer about Ibula being a warrior. You can see for yourself how beautiful she is. When I first saw her, I could not believe such a creature existed. It wasn't long before I fell in love with her and asked her to marry me." Simon was looking at Thedes face as he was talking. Thedes smiled and winked at Simon.

"I told Ibula that if she was going to be my wife I would forbid her from being a warrior," Thedes said with a grin. "She told me that a warrior is always a warrior and I either accepted her the way she was or I could find another wife." Simon and Thedes both laughed loudly.

"It is a good thing I got that arrowhead out before you told him that story," said Ibula.

"Simon, the first time I saw her fight I could not believe my eyes because of the way she fought. I tried to stay close to her to watch over her," said Thedes with a laugh. "I was so busy watching her that I got injured."

"Tell him the rest of that story dear," Ibula said sweetly.

"My wife killed two Hutas to save my life," Thedes said. "I still worry about her but I would fight alongside of her in any battle." Thedes leaned forward and kissed Ibula on the cheek.

"Raul and I live with our families in different wings of our father's castle," said Simon. "When Raul and I return home will you bring your family and visit us? Our family would love you and you will be shocked at how much alike we all are."

Thedes and Ibula looked at each other and smiled. "We would like that, we have never visited anyone outside of the caves," said Thedes.

"You probably know our father is the King of Wetpr, we have plenty of room and can take you through the kingdom if you would like," offered Simon. "Did you know the Sanuri stays with us often?"

"The Sanuri," exclaimed Ibula. "He stays with your family?"

"Yes, he has his own chambers in the castle."

"Oh Simon we would be honored to come," said Ibula excitedly.

"We need to speak to the King and only the King," the Enrop said to one of the castle guards. Sudfad walked to the front courtyard to get the message.

"This message is better said in private," said the Enrop. Sudfad led the three birds into his office. "Your sons were attacked by a group of Hutas yesterday," said the bird.

"What?" yelled Sudfad. "Are they alive?'

"The Rualas saved them, but they have many serious injuries. The Rualas have taken them to the Ice Caves to heal, they will be safe there."

"Can you tell me what happened?" asked Sudfad as he collapsed in his chair.

"The Sanuri sent some Enrops to the Rualas with a message to meet your sons. He sent three other Enrops with a message for Raul and Simon, those birds saw the Hutas attack and turned and brought the Rualas to the scene of the battle. Your sons were greatly outnumbered and ambushed. Your sons have not read the letters you sent yesterday. And I am to tell you that they are at the home of Thedes and Ibula. From what I saw they are being well cared for."

Sudfad looked dazed as the bird spoke. "I am sorry to bring you such news," the Enrop said.

"No, I thank you," Sudfad said in a whisper. "Will my sons live?"

"That is a question for the Sanuri."

"And the men they led?"

"They are all dead."

"I have always done as you asked me," said the Sanuri with frustration. "But why am I at this castle doing nothing when so many others need my help?"

"You are so involved with this family that you cannot see?" asked The Lion.

"See what?"

"Your very presence here is the only thing that is protecting them right now."

"So then the threats come from darkness, because Sudfad's army can protect them from ordinary men."

"They come from both," said The Lion. "This family has many enemies they would not recognize. There are some who believe this family stands in the way of their plans and they are correct."

"Is it because they are the Keepers of the Scrolls?"

"There are some who suspect; but in this time, darkness has gathered to bring to fruition plans long in the process. And the dark ones will kill anyone they suspect might interfere with their plans. That includes you my friend."

"Might I ask a favor?" asked the Sanuri. "Would you protect this family just long enough for me to transport my essence to the Ice Caves to help heal the boys?"

"Your friends will be calling you in just a moment," said The Lion. "And yes, I will protect them but you must go now." With these words The Lion was gone.

"Sanuri, Sanuri," called Marie.

The Sanuri stepped into the hallway, "What is it Marie?"

"The Queen would like you to come quickly, when they told the girls the news Annabelle went into labor and it is not time yet."

Simon heard his brother moaning. "Raul are you awake?" he called over to the next bed. "Raul."

"Simon is that you?" asked Raul as he tried to raise his head but fell back down on the bed. "Where are we?"

"You will never believe this," Simon said. "The Sanuri sent Ruala warriors to save us and they flew us to the Ice Caves of Mordv."

"I did not think the Ice Caves really existed," Raul said groggily.

"Look around Brother because that is where we are," replied Simon.

"What do you mean they flew us?"

"All the Rualas have wings, they look like regular people with wings; wait until you see them," said Simon. "When I saw Ibula I thought I was dead and that she was an Angel."

"Who is Ibula?"

"We are in the home of Ibula and her husband Thedes," said Simon. "Thedes is a Shettee; I have never spoken to a Shettee before either."

"I thought they were all killed," Raul said.

"They told me that the Sanuri saved both the Rualas and the Shettees from annihilation and brought them here to live," said Simon. "You will like Ibula and Thedes; I have invited their family to visit us when we return home." Raul started to laugh, then winced in pain.

"Someone is coming," Simon said.

"They are in here," said Ibula as she and Thedes quickly walked the Sanuri to the beds of Raul and Simon.

489

"Sanuri is that you?" asked Raul. "You look like a dream."

"I have transported my essence here to see you," said the Sanuri seriously as he looked at their broken bodies. "Raul and Simon I need you to listen to me. I am going to give you of my life force to help you heal. You may not remember this but Ibula and Thedes will tell you later. Right now I need both of you to lie very still."

"I don't think that will be a problem," said Simon with a little laugh. "I don't think either of us can move."

The Sanuri stood between the two beds; his image grew until he could reach his arms to both of the injured men. He placed one hand on the head of each man and prayed. Ibula and Thedes watched in amazement as the image of the Sanuri changed, he grew lighter and lighter until the image of his body was no longer apparent and all they saw was light, a strong white light. The Sanuri stayed in this form for many minutes. When he was done, he turned to Ibula and Thedes.

"They will live and heal but it will take some time," said the Sanuri. "Thank you for what you have done and you and your family will be richly blessed." The Sanuri prepared to leave, then as an afterthought he walked back to Ibula and handed her a small envelope. "When Simon wakes tell him the news of his condition caused his wife to go into labor but they have a healthy baby girl, he will be pleased. If Raul asks, his pregnant wife is distraught but fine."

"You have been asleep for two days," Ibula said while sitting down on the bed next to Raul. As she checked his bandages Raul stared at her.

"Let me guess," said Ibula with a smile. "You have never seen a woman with wings before?"

"That is true," said Raul. "But Simon did tell me about your wings, he just did not tell me how much you resemble my wife."

"I have a message for you from the Sanuri," Ibula said soothingly. "Your wife is pregnant, she is distraught after hearing about what has happened to you but she is otherwise fine."

"Thank you, and Simon's wife?"

"The Sanuri said she went into labor when she was told about what happened to you but the baby girl was born healthy and the mother is alright."

"Good, this entire mission Simon was worried that something would happen to Annabelle when she had the baby."

"You sound like good husbands," said Ibula as she changed one of Raul's bandages.

"This mission is the first time Simon and I have left our wives and babies; it has been difficult for all of us," Raul said sadly.

"I see," said Ibula with a smile. "Have you been gone from home long?"

"Several months; before we were married Simon and I would not have thought anything of being gone that length of time," Raul tried to say with a smile. "Now it seems like an eternity."

"You will be happy then to find out how you have been blessed," Ibula said smiling.

"What do you mean?"

"Both you and Simon had such serious injuries that we could not save you," Ibula said with tears in her eyes. "The Sanuri came and gave you some of his own life force to save both of you. It was incredible to watch. And now you are healing just fine."

"The Sanuri was here?"

Chapter XXXI
The Ice Caves of Mordv

"You are awake Simon," said Ibula. "I will get you something to eat."

Simon tried to look around the room but his movements were limited. He still could not see out of his left eye and the sight in his right eye was blurry. Simon touched his head, "Are these all stitches," he asked groggily.

"Yes and do not pull at them," said Ibula as she took his hand from his head. "I have something for you." Ibula placed a small envelope into his hand. "The Sanuri told me to give this to you. Simon, your wife went into labor when she heard about what happened to you; you now have a baby daughter."

"How are they doing?"

"They are both fine."

"How do you know this?" asked Simon as he tried to sit up.

"The Sanuri came and gave some of his own life force to you and Raul so you would live and heal; that was three days ago," Ibula said smiling. "You have been asleep since."

"The Sanuri was here?" repeated Simon. "And Raul?"

"He woke up yesterday; but you both have a lot of healing to do."

"Ibula would you open the envelope?"

Ibula took the envelope and pulled out a tiny lock of dark hair. "Simon it is a lock of hair."

Simon smiled, "It must be the baby's; what color is it?"

"It is dark."

"We have twin sons who look exactly like me; my wife is tiny with dark curly hair," said Simon smiling. "I hope Arianna looks like her."

Ibula smiled, "Arianna that is a pretty name."

"Ibula where are my clothes?"

"They are folded here, near the bed."

"Would you look in the pants pockets? Our wives gave us lockets with their hair and the baby's hair." As Ibula looked, Simon said. "I really hope we still have them."

"I found it Simon."

"Ibula would you put the baby's hair in there?" Ibula added Arianna's hair to the locket and handed the locket to Simon. "Thank you," Simon said, "Would you mind checking Raul's clothes for his?"

Ibula found Raul's locket in a shirt pocket. She walked over to the sleeping man and placed the locket in the palm of his hand and closed his fingers around it. As Ibula was walking out of the room, Thedes appeared in the doorway.

"How are they?" he asked.

"Simon is awake and I am getting him some food," said Ibula as she put her hand on her husband's arm. "You were right Thedes, these are good men."

"We need to get a list of the names of all the priests who are assigned here," said Padre Thomas.

"And what will we do with that?" asked Padre Bartholomew.

"First we can try to determine if there is someone posing as a priest who is not on that list. And second if the culprit is a priest, perhaps we can determine who we are dealing with."

"The Great Ruler forgive me for saying this," said Padre Bartholomew. "Perhaps we should also get the names of the priests assigned here in the past; if darkness really is working here we may find the same name on more than one list."

In the days that followed the Sanuri's visit to the Ice Caves, Ibula rarely left Raul and Simon alone. Although she had faith that the Sanuri's essence would heal her patients, the severity of their wounds concerned both her and Thedes. Both Raul and Simon had been hacked repeatedly with the axes of the Hutas; in addition they had knife wounds, arrow wounds and broken bones from punches and kicks. Simon had been cut in the head with an axe that affected his eye sight. Ibula had stitched her patients together the best she could; but at times they resembled sewn up dolls instead of men.

Never before had Ibula heard of the Sanuri giving his essence to save another being. She knew there had to be something special about Raul and Simon that the Sanuri would make such a sacrifice. At first Ibula was taking care of Raul and Simon as a favor for the Sanuri but as she and Thedes got to know their guests they grew very attached to them.

After arriving at the Ice Caves, the Rualas had little contact with the world below; for the Ice Caves provided them with all they needed and wanted. Their tribe had become quite isolated until the Sanuri asked them to help the Shettees. Now these two tribes peacefully blended into a new culture that shared traditions and ideas.

Ibula would find herself feeling guilty at times as she cared for Simon and Raul. Living so long away from humans she had allowed herself to only remember the darkness in them. Ibula now realized she had demonized the entire race based on the hatred and actions of a few. Now as she cared for these two humans, two men so much like her husband, Ibula realized she had allowed darkness to limit her sight.

"Papa, Papa," screamed Petra as he ran into Sudfad and Renya's bedroom. "There is something wrong with the Sanuri. I think he is dead."

Both Sudfad and Renya jumped out of bed and ran to the Sanuri's chambers. "Marie get Gala," Sudfad yelled as they ran past her. When they entered the Sanuri's bedroom they found him lying on top of the bed coverings, fully clothed. His breathing was shallow and his skin looked exceptionally pale.

"Sudfad, do my eyes betray me or does he look like he is, I don't know, fading in and out of his body?" asked Renya.

"Honey I do see it too and I have no idea what is happening to him."

"Where is he?" gasped Gala as she ran into the Sanuri's chambers.

"We are back here," called Sudfad.

Gala had been feeding some of the Enrops when Marie came to get her. The Enrops followed Gala to the Sanuri's bedside. "I have never seen anything like this," said Gala as she was checking the Sanuri's life signs. Something is very wrong here but..." Gala hesitated.

"But what?" Sudfad asked with great concern.

"But whatever is happening to him is not of this world."

The Enrop called Nica walked up to the Sanuri and stared at him for several moments. Then the bird turned to Sudfad. "The Great Ruler has blessed the Rualas with great medicines and healing practices, I will fly to the Ice Caves for help."

Padre Thomas and Padre Bartholomew worked long into the night, in the Hall of Records. "I cannot believe we do not have a better way of keeping records of the priests at this monastery," said Padre Bartholomew with frustration.

"Perhaps after we figure out who is stealing the holy items; we should consider reorganizing this area," said Padre Thomas with a laugh.

"I think you are right old friend, I think you are right," said Padre Bartholomew as he picked up a pile of papers and scrolls from the floor.

"Let's try it this way, you call off names and I will write them down under the appropriate years."

Suddenly the door opened. Both Padres Thomas and Bartholomew were startled. "Oh it is you," said Padre Bartholomew.

"What are you two doing?" asked High Priest Meekos.

"Going crazy," said Padre Thomas with a laugh. "Padre Bartholomew and I were talking about priests we knew in common and well, one thing led to another and we were trying to figure out when some of us served together."

"If we weren't so old, we would be able to remember," said Padre Bartholomew laughing. "We thought we could just come in here and find some lists; have you seen what a mess this place is, you cannot find anything."

"So we decided to clean this area up; you might say it is a test of patience," said Padre Thomas.

"Leave it to you two," said Meekos with a feigned laugh. "It is late, you will never get this mess cleaned up tonight." Meekos turned and walked out of the room, shutting the door behind him.

"Have you found Meekos' name yet?" asked Padre Thomas in a whisper.

"No," said Padre Bartholomew as he grabbed another stack of papers.

"My Lord, the Enrop brought a man, I mean I think he is a man, he looks like an Angel," Marie whispered.

"Please Marie show them in," said Sudfad as he stood up to greet their guests.

Marie escorted Nica and a large man with long white hair and white wings into the parlor. The man was dressed in all white clothing with a belt made of spun gold and golden sandals. Renya gasped when she saw him.

"Thank you for coming," said Sudfad as he walked towards the man with his hand extended. "I am King Sudfad of Wetpr and this is my wife Queen Renya."

"I am Mateo, I am the Chief Healer of my tribe; I am honored to help," said Mateo. "Please show me to the Sanuri." Sudfad started to escort Mateo from the room; when Mateo suddenly turned and handed an envelope to Renya. He nodded when she took it then turned and followed Sudfad.

Renya looked at the envelope; in a woman's handwriting were the words *to the family of Raul and Simon.* "Marie would you please get the girls, then prepare a room for our guest."

"Forgive me for staring," Gala said. "But I have never seen a man with wings before."

Mateo smiled, "You are the healer?"

"Yes my name is Gala."

"Raul and Simon have spoken of you; they said you can make some very powerful medicines," said Mateo as he pulled the blankets off from the Sanuri.

"I am so glad you are here, I do not know what else to do," Gala said with tears in her eyes.

"Sudfad, I do not mean to be abrupt but please leave us; Gala and I have much to do," said Mateo earnestly.

Sudfad returned to the parlor to find that Vitomas and Annabelle had joined Renya. "It is a letter to the family, I thought we should all be together when it is opened," said Renya as tears ran down her cheeks.

"Honey do you want me to read it?" asked Sudfad as he took the letter from Renya's hand and proceeded to read it out loud.

My name is Ibula of the Tribe Rualas.

The Sanuri sent many of us to meet with Raul and Simon. If you have not already heard, when we arrived they were being attacked by many Hutas. We killed the Hutas and brought Raul and Simon to the Ice Caves of Mordv. My husband Thedes and I have taken your sons into our home and we are caring for them. We barely reached them in time and even the healing powers of the caves were of little help.

The Sanuri came and gave them some of his own life force; it was an amazing thing to watch. They will live and heal, but it will be some time before they can return home.

Sudfad stopped reading because the women were crying so loudly. After a few moments he continued.

Your husbands are good men and when they are awake they speak always of their wives and families. I put Arianna's hair in Simon's locket, because he is not yet capable of seeing it. Your husbands and my husband are quickly becoming friends and when they can walk, Thedes will show them the secrets of the caves.

Do not worry they will be healed. If you want to send some small mementos with Mateo I am sure it will lift the spirits of your husbands.

Ibula warrior princess and wife of Thedes.

Sudfad put his arm around Renya and motioned for Vitomas and Annabelle to come to him also; the family huddled together for several minutes before Renya spoke. "Sudfad did you know the Sanuri went to the ice caves?"

"No."

"They cannot walk and Simon cannot see," Annabelle sobbed. "They must be in awful shape."

"I wish we could go to them," said Vitomas tearfully.

"Honey, the Ice Caves are far from here," Sudfad said. "This woman who wrote the letter sounds very caring, why don't you do as she suggested and get something to send back with Mateo, I do not know how long he will be here." Both Annabelle and Vitomas quickly left the parlor. "Renya you could send something along too," said Sudfad then he kissed his wife and hugged her tightly.

The next morning Mateo and Gala walked out of the Sanuri's chambers. Renya was in the hallway walking towards them. "How is he?" she asked.

"He will be fine," replied Mateo wearily.

"You both look exhausted. Please have some breakfast, I will show you to the dining room." Renya turned around and opened the first door on her left, exposing a large finely decorated room. "Mateo this is your chambers."

"Thank you for your kindness but I believe I am too tired to eat now," replied Mateo.

"I too am incredibly exhausted, I need a bath and some sleep," said Gala. "The Sanuri is sleeping and may be for some time; we will return."

"I know you are both exhausted but may I ask what is wrong with him?" asked Renya.

Gala looked at Mateo and said, "Perhaps you can explain it better."

"Think of your body as a container that holds a limited amount of life force or energy," explained Mateo. "The Sanuri must have used a great deal of his life force to heal your sons; before the life force could be replenished something attacked him in his weakened state."

"What attacked him?" Renya gasped.

"All of darkness would destroy the Sanuri if it could," Mateo said. "I am sure curses or spells are constantly being done to destroy him but his normal strength repels such things."

"Will he die?" asked Renya with tears in her eyes.

"Mateo is a wonderful healer," said Gala as she looked at him with admiration. "We have been praying to The Great Ruler to use us to help the Sanuri."

"I do not understand; are you using your life force to heal the Sanuri?"

"Yes but there is much more to it, that is why Gala and I are so exhausted," said Mateo.

"Mateo, the Sanuri is very dear to this family, if you need others to give him life force you will have many volunteers," Renya said.

Padre Bartholomew and Padre Thomas left the Hall of Records just before sunrise. "I might be too tired to eat," said Padre Bartholomew wearily as the two men walked towards the dining hall.

"I too am exhausted," said Padre Thomas. "And perhaps the fatigue is playing games with my mind but I feel like we are being watched."

"Well the only good thing. If the culprit wants to steal from the Hall of Records, he will never find what he is looking for." Both priests broke into a loud crazy laughter that only exhaustion can bring.

"I am more concerned about someone taking our notes," whispered Padre Thomas as they entered the dining hall.

"Look how many tables are filled at this early hour," commented Padre Bartholomew. The two priests piled various foods on their plates and chose a table far from where the other priests were eating. Both Padres Thomas and Bartholomew found themselves surveying the room as they ate. "I don't like the feeling that we cannot trust anyone, especially in a building dedicated to The Great Ruler," Padre Bartholomew said sadly.

"Meekos is at a table near the window, I do not know the priests who are with him."

"Are you finished eating?" Padre Bartholomew asked after a few minutes.

"Yes."

"Then follow my lead," said Padre Bartholomew as he stood up and walked over to the table Meekos was sitting at.

"Your Excellency we should have taken your advice," said Padre Bartholomew to Meekos. "We worked all night trying to organize the Hall of Records with little success."

"Yes," said Padre Thomas laughing, "It is the first time my friend here ever thought he was too tired to eat." Both Padre Bartholomew and Padre Thomas laughed at this comment.

"Would you care to join us?" asked Meekos with a smile.

"Well, just for a moment, we need to get some sleep," said Padre Bartholomew as he and Padre Thomas took seats at the table.

"Are you new here?" asked Padre Thomas as he looked at the three other priests seated at the table with Meekos. "I am Padre Thomas and this is Padre Bartholomew," said Thomas as he stood again and extended his hand to the priest nearest him.

The priest shook Padre Thomas's hand and said, "I am Padre Doros, my brothers here are Padre Paullo and Padre Sirius; we are just visiting our old friend High Priest Meekos."

"It is very nice to meet you," said Padre Thomas.

"Where are you from?" asked Padre Bartholomew.

"They are from the monastery at Rubar in the Kingdom of Ryed," responded Meekos.

"You have traveled a great distance," said Padre Thomas. "Have you heard of many Rogett attacks; I am sure his Excellency told you of the horrific attack at Afax."

"Only rumors of attacks," answered Padre Doros. "This is the first place we have been where there are actual witnesses; we thought they were just wild stories."

"Will you be staying long?" asked Padre Bartholomew.

"We do not know yet," replied Padre Doros.

"Well I hope we can talk again, I must apologize but I need to get some sleep," said Padre Bartholomew with a smile as he and Padre Thomas rose from their seats.

"Those two are up to something," said Meekos as he watched Padre Thomas and Padre Bartholomew walk out of the dining hall. "I just don't know what it is."

"Those two old men are of no threat to us," laughed Doros.

"That is true," replied Meekos. "But they are friends with the Sanuri."

"Well, perhaps we can use that to our advantage," Doros said.

"How are our patients?" Mateo asked as he entered the home of Ibula and Thedes.

"They are greatly improving but not yet able to walk," Thedes said. "Would you like to see them?"

"Mateo can you tell us of the Sanuri?" asked Ibula with great concern in her voice.

"I thought perhaps I could speak with both of you and your patients at the same time," Mateo said.

Ibula led Mateo into the room where Raul and Simon stayed. "They are sleeping," she said.

"I would wake them Ibula," Mateo said.

Ibula softly shook Raul then Simon until they woke up. Thedes helped both men to sit up in their beds. "This is Mateo the Chief Healer of our tribe and this is Prince Simon and Prince Raul," Thedes said.

"Thedes is there a table here where I can lay down this blanket?" asked Mateo. Thedes brought a small table into the bed chamber from another room.

"I have information for all of you," Mateo said. "Many days ago your father King Sudfad requested my presence to help heal the Sanuri."

"You know our father?" Raul asked in astonishment.

"Not then, the Enrops told him of me."

"When I reached your home I found the Sanuri near death."

502

Ibula gasped loudly and began to cry when she heard this statement. Thedes put his arm around Ibula's shoulder. "My child do not cry, he will be alright," said Mateo with a benevolent smile. "The Sanuri had used so much of his life source to heal Raul and Simon that he was in a weakened condition and something attacked him."

"What do you mean, something attacked him?" asked Simon.

"The Sanuri has many powerful enemies, I would guess that a demon or dark lord put a spell or curse on him," Mateo explained. "But even in his weakened condition the Sanuri is so much stronger than mere mortals that whoever attacked him must have been very powerful."

"Is it possible that whoever was behind the attacks against us would know the Sanuri would heal us and weaken himself?" Raul asked.

"That is a very interesting question," Mateo said thoughtfully. "Anything is possible. Gala, your healer and I worked with The Great Ruler to restore the Sanuri's health. He is still a little weak but will be just fine. I was impressed with your healer; before my arrival she had actually guessed what the Sanuri needed she just did not know how to provide it." Mateo turned to Ibula. "She has sent us some of her plants and medicines and I promised we would do the same."

"We have asked Thedes and Ibula to bring their family to visit us, once we have returned home," Simon said.

Mateo looked at Thedes and Ibula and said, "I think you would enjoy the visit, King Sudfad and Queen Renya and their family are most gracious and generous people. I very much enjoyed meeting them and I may return for a visit also," he said smiling. Mateo pulled two envelopes out of his robe; he handed one each to Raul and Simon. "Simon I have seen your new baby daughter and she is very beautiful," said Mateo. "She has dark hair and large brown eyes."

"She must look like Annabelle," Simon said with a warm smile.

"All of your family are doing well, other than being overwhelmed with worry for both of you," Mateo said as he pulled a third envelope out of his pocket and handed it to Ibula; she took the envelope with a look of surprise. Ibula opened the letter and decided to read it out loud.

Dear Ibula,

Words cannot express how much we appreciated the letter you sent to us. You and Thedes sound like very compassionate people and we owe you everything for taking care of our husbands/sons. Please accept these gifts as just a small token of our undying appreciation and we hope one day to meet the people who saved Raul's and Simon's lives.

King Sudfad, Queen Renya, Vitomas and Annabelle.

Mateo slipped his hand inside of the blanket and pulled out a beautiful package which he handed to Ibula. "They did ask me for advice," Mateo said with a warm smile. "I hope you like them."

Raul and Simon smiled as they watched Ibula open the package. "Thedes," exclaimed Ibula as she took an elegant golden necklace out of the box. The golden chain held twenty small tear drop diamonds. As Thedes clasped the necklace around Ibula's neck she said with astonishment, "And there are matching earrings and a bracelet. Oh I cannot take such extravagant gifts."

"Yes you can," said Simon. "We owe you more than that."

"And now Thedes," said Mateo. "King Sudfad sent this to you from his own collection." Mateo unfolded the blanket revealing a beautiful sheath adorned with gold and jewels. Thedes pulled the sword out of the sheath and examined it. "This is an excellent sword and well balanced," Thedes said appreciatively.

"And now for you," said Mateo as he turned and looked at Simon and Raul. "Your wives very much want to come here to be with you but your father wisely advised against it because of the children. By the way Raul," Mateo said with a wink. "Have you noticed how much your wife and Ibula resemble each other?"

Raul smiled as Ibula said, "They keep telling me that, is it really true?"

"When you come to visit and meet Vitomas you both will think you are looking into a mirror," Raul said. Ibula gave Thedes a look of disbelief.

"They did not know what to send on such short notice," continued Mateo as he handed each prince a small package.

"Simon it is our family rings and it looks like Samuel's and Arianna's stones have been added," Raul said. "Our wives designed these rings; there is a stone for every member of our family," Raul said with pride. "Please hand me Simon's letter and I will read it to him."

"Simon would you like me to help you put your ring on?" Ibula asked.

"Yes, this is so difficult having to have others do everything for me," said Simon.

"You will be well and strong soon," Thedes said with reassurance.

"Raul I am sure Vitomas wrote this in her letter but she is healthy and hoping you make it home in time for the birth of your daughter," Mateo said.

"Thank you for all of this," said Raul.

"Oh I am not done," Mateo said and started laughing as he pulled three brightly colored pieces of paper from a pocket of his robe. "Apparently this is the first art work of your sons. Their names are written at the bottom of each page." Mateo handed the three paintings to Raul who started to laugh.

"Simon I will have to say our boys are equally talented."

"I am so glad to see you awake and eating," Sudfad said. "Gala has barely left your side and your friend Mateo was here for several days."

"How did you know to bring Mateo here?" asked the Sanuri.

"Nica told me."

505

"Thank you dear friend for all you have done," said the Sanuri as he sipped some coffee.

"Ibula sent our family a wonderful letter about our sons and asked that we send mementos back with Mateo to lift their spirits," Sudfad said. "We also sent gifts for Ibula and her husband for we can never repay them for what they have done. Ibula said the boys are becoming close friends with her husband Thedes and Mateo said Thedes was a Shettee. It has been years since I looked upon a Shettee, I have to admit I did not know exactly what they were when I first saw them."

The Sanuri smiled, "Like the Rualas the Shettees are an ancient race, once said to be part human and part lion, they are fierce warriors. The Great Ruler allowed me to save the last of both of these races from the hatred of the Hutas. I took them all to the Ice Caves of Mordv so they would be protected as they healed; I am very pleased to tell you that these two tribes have found ways to live together peacefully. I am not surprised that Thedes, Raul and Simon are becoming friends, other than their physical differences they are very similar in character."

"I found Mateo a very interesting person, he is welcomed back here anytime," Sudfad said. "He and Gala worked well together and shared their knowledge of healing."

"He is a very wise man; I am not surprised either, that the two of you would become friends," the Sanuri continued. "Did he tell you that Ibula and Vitomas look remarkably alike?"

"Yes, why do you mention it?"

"Sudfad, I have learned in all my years of working for The Great Ruler that there are no coincidences; I find it interesting."

"You think there is some significance?" Sudfad asked.

"I think there is significance in everything, I just do not always know what it is," replied the Sanuri with a weak laugh.

"Mateo said something attacked you while you were weakened after healing the boys," Sudfad said as he sat down in a chair next to the Sanuri's bed. "Is it possible that the attack on Raul and Simon was directly connected to the attack on you?"

"That I have been thinking about greatly."

"Today we see if you can walk," announced Ibula as she marched into the bedroom chambers of Raul and Simon. "Thedes are you coming?" she called. "Raul you will go first." Ibula helped Raul to sit up and to turn so his feet were dangling from the side of the bed. Thedes stood next to Raul and started to lift him from his left side as Ibula quickly removed the covers and started to lift Raul from his right side.

"Ibula, I am naked," said Raul.

"And Raul who do you think took your clothes off from you," replied Ibula. "Now tell us if you think you might pass out."

Thedes laughed and said to Raul, "Do not even try to win this one."

After some dizziness passed, Raul was able to walk the length of the room and back with Ibula's and Thedes' assistance. They sat him up in a chair and Ibula handed Thedes some clothing. "Thedes would you help him put on his pants?" she asked sweetly. "Now Simon it is your turn."

"Thedes I want my pants before your wife touches me," said Simon laughingly.

"Matthew will be here in a minute," Angelina said as she sat down at the dinner table. "An Enrop just brought him a letter."

"Well while we wait dear," Rosa said. "Would you like to go shopping tomorrow? I thought we could start looking for things for the baby."

Angelina laughed, "I would love to but we do have a long time yet."

"I know dear but I am too excited to wait."

"Son what is it?" asked Mathas when he saw the look on Matthew's face as he entered the dining room. Matthew sat down at the table and handed the letter to his father.

As Mathas read the letter to himself, Matthew told Rosa and Angelina what it said. "Raul and Simon were attacked by a large group of Hutas. The Sanuri sent Ruala warriors to help them. The Rualas took Raul and Simon to the Ice Caves of Mordv to heal but their wounds were so serious that the Sanuri gave them his own life force to save them; then the Sanuri almost died."

"What!" gasped Angelina.

"You will need to read the letter yourself because Vitomas wrote much more details. Raul and Simon will live now but they will need a long time to heal," Matthew explained. "And when Annabelle heard the news she went into labor early but she and the baby are doing well. She had a little girl."

"Matthew do you want to go to Wetpr?" Angelina asked as she saw the worry and sadness in his face.

Erebus agonized for days about what to do with the information that Sophie had told him about the Insidiae and Roch. Erebus did not want to put Sophie in danger by exposing her secrets. Yet, Roch was such an explosive and violent man that Erebus knew he had to tell Roch something or everyone's lives at the castle could possibly be put in danger. In addition Erebus had to find a way to tell Cerephus some of the information without incriminating Sophie.

Erebus had asked for a meeting with Roch and Cerephus. As Erebus was entering the war room he saw Roch pick up a chair and smash it against the wall. Then Roch threw the broken chair on the floor and started to kick the wooden pieces. "Roch that is enough," Erebus said sternly. "Stop the childish temper tantrum we have important things to discuss." Cerephus now entered the room.

Roch threw his glass of whiskey against the wall. The broken glass just added to a pile of broken glass that was building up on the floor. "I will not have you speak to me like that!" yelled Roch.

"Do you or do you not want me to help you?" yelled Erebus.

Roch stared at Erebus then sat down in the chair behind his desk. Roch remained silent for a few minutes like a child pouting. "Go ahead talk!" Roch yelled with a sneer.

"You told me that Demetries said you were born of darkness, did he tell you want he meant by that?"

"No," Roch replied. "But he told me that several times."

"Did you try to find out what he meant?"

"No, he was always talking in riddles, which I found frustrating."

"I have been searching through ancient texts; and by the way if you want me to help you it would benefit you to start compiling a library here," Erebus said with disdain. "From what I have found; it appears that phrase has significant meaning."

"What are you talking about?" growled Roch.

"From earliest times that phrase means you were literally created by darkness or demons. Now I know you are a man who doesn't bother to question anything," Erebus said sarcastically. "But demons are not in the habit of creating humans, they attack them, conquer them and seduce them but demons do not have the power to create them."

"So what are you saying?" Cerephus asked.

"Well demons don't do anything unless it somehow benefits them. So the question is why would they go to all of the work to create you Roch?" Erebus asked. Both Roch and Cerephus stared at Erebus without speaking so Erebus continued. "You are the second son of the second son of the second son, are you not?"

"I have no idea what you are talking about," yelled Roch with frustration.

"I will save you the trouble of trying to figure it out yourself," Erebus said sarcastically. "I have been researching your family tree. You are the second son of a second son of a second son. There is a legend that several generations ago, one of your grandfathers sold his soul to darkness for power and wealth," explained Erebus.

"The price he had to pay for such a contract was heavy. He killed six of his own sons to provide a vessel for darkness to insert a seed that would be passed down from generation to generation until the appointed time. The seed was passed through only the second sons of second sons."

Roch looked shocked as Erebus spoke. "Did you say vessel of darkness?"

"Yes, have you heard that phrase before?" Erebus asked.

"Yes, Demetries said I was a vessel of darkness."

"I think Demetries was trying to warn you but you are always so arrogant you do not listen to anyone. Roch you have to start taking this seriously. Something is very wrong here and I don't think you are the one in control of what is happening to you."

"That is what he said," Roch said in almost a whisper.

"What who said?"

"Demetries, several times he told me I was a piece on a game board; a game that was being played by very powerful beings."

"Well we all know it is better to be the player than the piece. I am trying to find out who the players are and what the game is. And every time I attempt to find out I am threatened. Roch I need you to tell me everything you can remember that Demetries said to you."

Thedes, it is amazing how fast we are healing," said Simon.

"You still have a long way to go but between the healing powers of the crystals and the Sanuri's life force you will be strong and whole again," Thedes replied. "I wonder if having the Sanuri's life force flowing through your veins will change you at all."

"I did not even think about that," said Raul. "But I am amazed at looking at Simon; where Ibula reattached his scalp and ear it almost looks normal."

"Thanks," laughed Simon.

"Simon I mean it doesn't even look like you are going to have scars," Raul said. "Thedes how can that be?"

"The crystals, I do not understand how they work," said Thedes. "But I have had wounds that healed without scars. When you are strong enough I will take you through the caves, I want to see your faces," added Thedes with a grin.

"What do you mean?" asked Simon.

"You and I are both from the world below, where caves are dark stone enclosures," said Thedes. "This place is like traveling from kingdom to kingdom, the beauty is incredible and some of the caves could house a city. There are forests and waterfalls, animals of all types. When my people first arrived here we did not know if we would stay, all of us are still here."

Padre Bartholomew slept for five hours then got up and knocked on the door of Padre Thomas' room. Padre Thomas did not answer so Padre Bartholomew opened the door and saw the elderly priest lying in bed. Fear gripped the heart of Padre Bartholomew as he ran to the bedside of his friend and shook him.

"What?" yelled Padre Thomas as he jumped up in bed.

"Thank The Great Ruler, I thought you were dead. I have been knocking on your door and calling your name."

"Quickly check for our notes, if I could sleep through you banging on the door I may have slept through an intruder," said Padre Thomas as he got out of bed.

Padre Bartholomew lifted a floor board under the small pine desk in Padre Thomas' room and pulled out the papers. "They are here," he said. "Now let us go to the Hall of Records."

When they entered the Hall of Records, they saw the room did not look as they had left it six hours earlier. "Someone has been in here," said Padre Thomas.

"Look at this mess. Fortunately they did not find our notes."

"But that means they will continue to look, we might have to find another hiding place," said Padre Thomas. The two priests worked in the Hall of Records until dinner time, ate a meal in the dining hall and then returned to the Hall of Records.

"It is interesting that we have not found anything with Meekos name," said Padre Thomas.

"I was thinking we should send a letter to the high priest in Ryed and ask if those three men we met were really priests there."

"The problem with that is, if that high priest is involved with our culprits; then they will know we suspect them."

"They tore this room up while we were sleeping; we are already under suspicion," replied Padre Bartholomew. The priests worked until almost dawn.

"Look at this," said Padre Thomas as he pulled an old scroll from underneath a pile of papers. "This is a list of priests in attendance at this monastery three hundred and sixty two years ago. It lists a Marcus Meekos as a high priest at that time."

"Let me see that. Well, we found at least one of them; we need to get this to the Sanuri as quickly as possible."

Padre Thomas wrapped the notes around the small scroll and covered them with cloth. "Quickly, let's get to the woods," he said.

A full moon lit their path as the two old priests hurried to the back of the gardens and into the trees. They both closed their eyes and prayed to The Great Ruler to send the Enrops. Within moments birds landed around them. Padre Thomas walked up to one of the birds and handed it the package. "Please get this to the Sanuri as quickly as possible, it is very important, and thank you very much."

"Before we leave you should know there are three men behind you, they will be upon you soon," said one of the Enrops. "If you go along the stream they will not see you."

The two frightened priests walked as quickly as they could. The route they were now taking was a longer path back to the buildings. "Please Great Ruler protect us," prayed Padre Bartholomew as they walked. Suddenly from behind them, the priests heard a lion roar, and they ran the rest of the way to the buildings.

The following morning Thedes burst into the room of Raul and Simon. "So today you take your first walk outside of this room," Thedes said excitedly as he was eager to share the treasures of the Ice Caves with his new friends.

"Thedes do not take them too far remember they have to return," Ibula said smiling.

"Yes dear," replied Thedes as he winked at Raul and Simon.

"I will admit I am looking forward to this," said Simon as he got dressed.

Raul took Ibula's hand and kissed it and said, "Thank you My Lady." Ibula blushed but did not say anything. The three men walked out of the home and into a beautiful forest.

"Thedes you are right, I have never seen a cave that looked like this before," said Simon as he enjoyed the warmth of the sun on his face.

"Is it the crystals that bring the sunlight in?" Raul asked.

"Yes and the crystals also generate light themselves," replied Thedes. "Tell me when you are getting tired," Thedes added as he led Raul and Simon down a worn path.

"Where are we going?" Simon asked.

"First I am taking you to meet some of the others in an area where we gather; I think you would call it a market," Thedes replied.

As the men walked down the path they saw many homes that looked like large cottages; similar to the home of Thedes and Ibula. The homes were made of wood and stone; most had beautiful gardens that contained both vegetables and flowers. Birds were singing loudly.

"This is truly a beautiful place," Raul said in awe.

"I have many places to show you that are much more beautiful than this; but they are too far away for your first walk," said Thedes. "When the Shettees first came here we did not trust the Rualas and had no intention of staying in the caves."

"I can see why you would stay," Simon said.

"Thedes how exactly did you come here?" Raul asked.

"You already know that there was myself and five other warriors leading hundreds of women and children from the death camps of the Hutas. Once the priests at Avaide heard that the Hutas knew they were hiding us; they helped us escape the monastery grounds through a series of very long tunnels. You have children; you know they cannot travel quickly. We made camp the first night and while I was on guard duty, Ibula came to me and said the Sanuri had sent her people to save us."

"Ibula came to you?" asked Raul.

Thedes smiled, "Actually she was able to come up on me from behind and grab me; you can imagine my surprise when I turned and saw such a creature of beauty. She told me that the Hutas had killed the priests at the monastery and were but a few hours away from our camp. She asked me to let them help us; when I agreed, suddenly hundreds of Rualas appeared from behind the trees. Here we were surrounded and I never heard them."

"The Rualas are worthy warriors. They carried all of us to these caves. Then they shared everything they had with us. The Shettee women and children were so grateful and happy but us warriors were convinced it was some kind of a trap. We had never heard of the Sanuri much less believed he would help us without a price to be paid. Well we were very wrong. Our lives have changed completely since we have been here. This is a place of great happiness and peace."

"Do you ever leave these caves?" Raul asked.

"I have only left them to do battle when the Sanuri calls upon us," Thedes said.

"Does he call you often?" Simon asked in amazement.

"No but when he does we all volunteer because they are usually great battles."

Chapter XXXII
Marriage

As they lay next to each other, catching their breath; the haze of love making still overwhelming them both, Thaos turned to Nikki and asked, "Will you marry me?"

Nikki rolled onto her side so she could face Thaos, hesitating for a moment she replied, "Yes but can we wait?"

Thaos stared at Nikki for the look of fear that he saw on her face was quite unexpected. "Nikki why do you look scared? Aren't you happy with me?"

Nikki reached over and grasped his hand. "Thaos you make me very happy and I love you; it's just that I feel like my head is spinning because everything is moving so fast. I don't think I expected my entire life to change so quickly."

"We have talked about this before and you didn't look scared, what else is there?" She did not answer Thaos. "Nikki" he said in a scolding tone. "Talk to me."

"Thaos I grew up in a village where everyone knew each other and I liked that. Now I find that I have fallen in love with a man I know almost nothing about and that scares me sometimes. I feel like you don't trust me enough to tell me things and how can we have a marriage if you don't trust me?"

"Maybe I am afraid that if I tell you about my past you won't want to be with me anymore," Thaos said solemnly.

"Thaos if Juleta didn't scare me away, what in your past could? If you are afraid to tell me that you have killed men; I too have killed men and demons in battle." Thaos did not respond. "Thaos I know you are a kind and generous man and a brave warrior you can't change that by telling me about yourself."

"If I start to tell you tonight will you go with me to buy rings tomorrow?"

Nikki laughed, "Yes, you always end up getting what you want."

When Padre Thomas opened the door to his room, he saw his belongings had been thrown around. He called to Padre Bartholomew, who was still in the hallway. "We should see if anything is missing," said Padre Bartholomew as they entered the room.

After he closed the door Padre Thomas said, "The only thing of value here were the notes and we just sent them off."

"I would say someone is getting awfully nervous about our research. We must be on to something very important." The two priests straightened the room up then they both walked down to Padre Bartholomew's room. When they opened the door they saw that room had been searched also.

As Padre Thomas was picking books up from the floor he found a swatch of crimson colored cloth. "Is this yours?" he asked as he showed the material to Padre Bartholomew.

"No," said Padre Bartholomew as he put the swatch into his pocket. "I will be honest, I am not sure if we should continue our research."

"Tonight we will both pray for guidance," said Padre Thomas. "And we will see what tomorrow brings."

That night Thaos was quiet during dinner. As Nikki and Thaos were walking back to their chambers from the family dining room Nikki asked, "Are you mad at me?"

"No, why would you think I am mad at you?"

"Because you are so quiet," Nikki said as she tried to read the look on Thaos face. "Thaos is it that you don't want to tell me about your past?"

"Yes."

"What could be that horrible?"

"Nikki I was not always the man you know me to be now; it is going to be difficult for me to tell you some things."

"Then perhaps you just tell me a little at a time."

517

"I want you to promise that you won't leave me."

"I won't leave you, I promise," Nikki said as she took Thaos' hand and squeezed it tightly.

When Matthew and Angelina arrived at Sudfad's castle it was late at night. They had not sent word that they were coming. The castle guards recognized Matthew and let them enter the castle through their private quarters. Mathas refused to let Matthew and Angelina make the trip alone; he sent a company of soldiers to accompany them. As Angelina unpacked their things, Matthew made arrangements for quarters for the soldiers of Lentz.

"I love this home," Angelina said as they both got into bed. "We have had such wonderful memories here."

"I'm glad you were willing to come here on such short notice," Matthew said as Angelina snuggled in his arm. "Angelina we should talk."

"You mean about the inheritance?" Angelina asked. "I have already been thinking about that."

"What have you been thinking?"

"I really like Vitomas and Annabelle, they are like sisters to me but to share my husband with them; I really don't know how that will work out."

"Before I met you I thought I was prepared to inherit them if Raul and Simon were killed; but now I don't know what to think," Matthew said and kissed Angelina on the forehead. "Truly dear I don't know how we would work this all out."

Angelina pushed herself up on one arm and looked at Matthew, "You almost sound afraid, are you?"

"I think overwhelmed would better describe it. But I guess I am afraid too because I don't want to do anything that will jeopardize our marriage, you mean so much to me Angelina."

A big smile overtook Angelina's face, "Or perhaps my Prince; you are scared thinking how you are going to satisfy three young wives," she said and giggled. Matthew started to tickle Angelina and soon their play turned into passion.

Nikki cried as Thaos told her about the lives and deaths of his family. Thaos' family and his village had been massacred; at the age of nine he had no one and nowhere to go. Thaos told Nikki how he walked the many miles to the monastery at Leven. Although the priests did give him some food they would not let him take shelter there, as the monastery was already filled with victims from Huta attacks. Thaos walked alone to the City of Port Friada.

"At nine you can imagine how scared I was alone in the dark. I had never been away from my family before and my father was a farmer he did not teach me the skills I needed to survive in the wilderness. I got so hungry I thought I would die. And I vowed to myself that I would never go hungry like that again; so I started stealing food wherever I could find it. One day I came upon an old farmhouse that was partially burned. I ran inside and started taking food from the shelves. And that is when I saw them."

"Saw who?" Nikki asked as she held his hand.

"The farmer and his wife and their two daughters; they had all been raped and killed by the Hutas like my family. I didn't bury them; I should have. But instead I took all of their food and anything they had of value and I hid in the woods."

"Thaos you were but a boy; you could have done nothing else," Nikki said softly. "With the Hutas on the warpath, did you ever run into any?"

"The first Huta I saw was dead; it looked like a bear had killed him. I took all of his weapons and his shield. I started to walk away, then I went back to his body and stabbed him over and over again with his own knife."

Thaos and Nikki talked long into the night; this first night was particularly difficult for him as Thaos had never spoken of these things to anyone before. Emotionally drained they both fell asleep quickly. Nikki dreamt about the lost and frightened boy who was trying to evade the Hutas in the woodlands of Ganz.

The next night, after they finished dinner, Thaos and Nikki sat together on the sofa in their parlor. "Honestly I don't remember where I left off, last night," Thaos said as he poured himself a glass of whiskey.

"You had just arrived at Port Friada," Nikki said.

"Well, to show you how foolish and naïve I was I thought people would help me there. I was better off in the woods. I had no place to stay so I slept on the streets. I met other boys and girls who were homeless and sleeping on the streets also. Soon we formed a kind of family. There were fourteen of us to begin with; ten boys and four girls, some of the children were very young. We went to the churches and the schools but no one would help us. Sometimes people would give us food but most of the time they would yell at us to leave."

"There was a boy named Derek, he was a little older than me and he was one of the leaders of our group. He tried to take care of everyone. His father had died in an accident and his mother threw him out of the house when she got a new boyfriend. Derek is the one who taught me how to hunt and track. I was the only one with weapons because I had the ones I had taken from that dead Huta. Derek and I would spend hours in the woods hunting for food to feed all of us."

Thaos stopped talking for a few minutes. He stood up and walked over to a small table and poured a glass of wine which he gave to Nikki. "This may be another long night," Thaos said as he took his seat on the sofa. "Have you ever been to Port Friada?" he asked her.

"No," Nikki whispered.

"As you might guess it is a sea port, a rather large port actually. One day Derek and I were hunting and as we were returning to the city some of the other boys came running up to us, crying. It turns out some sailors stole the girls."

"We looked all over for them but never found them. Some of the boys saw the girls being dragged away, but they didn't know which ship the sailors were from. Of course being as young as we were, we didn't realize what those sailors were going to do to those little girls."

"How old were they?" Nikki asked in a hoarse whisper.

"Between ten and six."

"And no one would help you?"

"No," Thaos said angrily. "We even went to the soldiers, who were supposed to be protecting the city and they wouldn't even listen to us."

Simon and Raul looked forward to their morning walks with Thedes. Every day they went a little farther. Both men were still very weak and would sleep upon their return to Thedes' home.

"This morning I have a treat for you," Thedes said. "We are going canoeing. Another of the Shettee warriors will join us because I don't think either of you are up to paddling yet. And Ibula even packed us a lunch."

"We have been taking walks for the last two weeks and haven't seen any water," Raul said.

"The river we are going to is too far for you to walk," Thedes said. "Naal is getting a small boca; he will be here soon."

"You have horses in the caves?" Simon asked with amazement.

"We have everything in these caves," Thedes said. "The Ice Caves are like a world above a world."

Padre Thomas awoke well into the afternoon. As soon as he sat up he surveyed his room to determine if anyone had entered while he was sleeping. After dressing he walked down the hall and knocked on Padre Bartholomew's door.

"You look awful," remarked Padre Thomas. "Are you sick?"

"I did not get much sleep," said Padre Bartholomew who looked both ways down the hallway before closing his door. "Tell me did you have any unusual dreams last night?"

"Not that I remember; I slept well, which, now that you say it is unusual considering the night we had."

"Did you pray for guidance?"

"Yes."

"So did I and I believe we have our answer," replied Padre Bartholomew as he finished dressing. "All night long it was as if my sleep was plagued by a single voice."

"Did you recognize the voice?"

"No, but it kept repeating one word, 'Continue'."

"Do you think we should go back to the Hall of Records first or the Hall of Antiquities?" asked Padre Thomas.

"The voice did not say this; but I just feel we have much more to find in the Hall of Records."

"Very well, let us get a bite of food and return to work."

There were very few men in the dining hall when the two priests arrived. "I wonder if there is any food left," said Padre Bartholomew as they both grabbed plates. The two priests took a table near one of the large windows. "Brother, what do you make of that?" asked Padre Bartholomew as he pointed out the window at a large crowd near the gardens. Padre Thomas and Padre Bartholomew both looked at each other and without speaking a word, they both stood up and walked outside.

"What is going on?" Padre Thomas asked a priest in the crowd.

"Some of the priests tending to the gardens found three bodies," replied the priest.

Padre Thomas and Padre Bartholomew worked their way through the crowd; when they got to the front of the crowd they saw Meekos and four other priests standing over the bodies of three men. Padre Bartholomew walked up to the bodies. "By The Great Ruler what has happened here?"

Meekos shot a cold glance at Padre Bartholomew, while one of the other priests explained that he came upon the bodies while weeding the garden.

"How were they killed?" asked Padre Bartholomew as he looked down at three faces that he recognized.

"We have not found any wounds and look at their faces," said one of the priests. "It is as if they were scared to death."

"Do you need any assistance?" asked Padre Bartholomew.

"No," growled Meekos.

Padre Bartholomew turned and walked quickly back to the building with Padre Thomas at his side. "Those men were the priests sitting with Meekos yesterday," said Padre Bartholomew. "No wounds, they may have been scared to death."

"And it sounds like we may have been saved," said Padre Thomas as they walked towards the Hall of Records.

"You are sure they are expecting us?" Ingr asked as she and Stephan walked hand in hand to the quarters of Thaos and Nikki.

"Yes, Thaos invited us over," Stephan said. "Why did you ask it like that?"

Ingr got a coy smile on her face and said, "Because when Thaos is home they spend a lot of time trying to make a baby." Stephan laughed loudly at her comment. "Stephan I know we have a lot of time yet but have you given any thought to the baby's name? Should we name him after your father?"

Stephan squeezed Ingr's hand, "He would like that but I think it would be too confusing calling the baby Claudius; Father has two middle names Marcus and Titus."

Ingr was quiet for a few moments as she played the name combinations in her head. "How does Marcus Stephan sound to you?"

"Perfect," Stephan said as he leaned down and kissed Ingr on the lips. They were standing outside of the door to Thaos' chambers. Suddenly they heard Nikki laughing and squealing.

"I told you," Ingr said. "I think we should go."

"No, I told Thaos we would come," said Stephan as he knocked on the heavy wooden door.

"Thaos put me down before you answer that door," Nikki yelled twice as Thaos walked towards the door with Nikki draped over his right shoulder.

Thaos ignored Nikki's requests and opened the door; both Stephan and Ingr started to laugh. "Honey I forgot to tell you that Stephan and Ingr were coming over," Thaos said kiddingly.

"Thaos," Nikki said in a scolding tone. "Put me down I am starting to get dizzy."

Thaos moved to the side so Stephan and Ingr could enter the parlor, then he set Nikki on her feet and held her for a moment until she steadied herself. "You are awful," Nikki said to Thaos then she turned to Ingr. "I am so glad you came, Mother made you some things for the baby." As Nikki left the room to retrieve the items, Thaos poured two glasses of whiskey for Stephan and himself. "Ingr what would you like?"

"Just water please," Ingr said as she and Stephan sat next to each other on a large sofa. Stephan put his arm around Ingr's shoulders and said to Thaos, "She has been getting sick a lot because of the baby." Nikki walked into the parlor with a basket full of baby clothes which she handed to Ingr.

"Look at these, aren't they cute," Ingr cooed as she held up a couple of outfits. "Stephan don't you think they are cute?"

"I can't imagine little Marcus is going to be that small," Stephan said as a joke then he looked at Thaos and Nikki. "We decided on Marcus Stephan for a name," Stephan said with obvious pride.

"Oh I like that name," Nikki said then she turned to Ingr. "Do you recognize the material?"

"Yes, it's what we bought," Ingr turned to Stephan and said, "Thaos gives money to Nikki's mother but she never buys anything for herself; so Nikki and I got her a lot of sewing things and a dress. It was the first time Gladys ever had a dress that she did not make."

Stephan stared at Ingr as she talked, then he looked at Thaos and back at Ingr. "Ingr I never thought, how is your mother doing since Thaddies is gone?" Ingr looked at Stephan but did not answer. "Perhaps we should visit her tomorrow," Stephan said. He felt guilty and embarrassed that he had not given a thought to her family.

"I would like that," Ingr said and kissed Stephan on the cheek.

"Well, we have a couple of announcements," Thaos said with a smile. "Nikki and I are getting married, she finally said yes."

"Finally? How long have we known each other?" Nikki asked and laughed. Stephan shook Thaos' hand and Ingr hugged Nikki.

"Have you told mother yet?" Stephan asked.

"No you two are the first," Thaos said. "Why?"

"You saw how she was for our wedding; I will bet you a bottle of whiskey she is the same for yours. It's your wedding so don't be afraid to tell her that," Stephan said.

"What are you talking about?" Nikki asked.

"Mother was so excited she just went ahead and planned everything; Ingr and I were hardly involved; which was alright for me but I think Ingr would have liked to have said more."

"No, I was happy with everything Bella planned; it is just whenever I think of that day I remember that I almost lost you," Ingr said sadly. Stephan hugged her.

Nikki looked at Thaos and said, "If Bella wants to plan everything that would be alright with me."

"Well, I am glad to hear you say that because Stephan and I have some news for the two of you," Thaos said.

"As you know Mother and Father were going to build a home for Ingr and me in the castle. They will also be building a home for you, Nikki and Thaos," Stephan said.

"What!" gasped Nikki.

"But according to Father the plans that Bella has for our homes are going to take some time to build, so they are currently designing us nicer quarters to live in until our homes are completed. Father said they were going to keep it a surprise but he thought we might want some say in the matter. Both the homes and the new quarters will have extra bedrooms, nurseries and kitchens. So you girls should talk to Mother tomorrow and tell her what you want."

"Marie, could you set two more plates?" Matthew asked as he and Angelina walked into the dining room; surprising Sudfad's family as they ate breakfast. After they hugged everyone at the table, Matthew and Angelina sat down. "We left right after Matthew read the letter," Angelina said as Annabelle handed her baby Arianna.

"How are they?" Matthew asked. "From your letter it sounded like they almost died."

"They would have, had not the Sanuri given them his own life force," Sudfad said. "Then something attacked him when he was still weak. The chief of the Ruala healers came here and he and Gala saved the Sanuri." Sudfad saw the looks on the faces of Vitomas and Annabelle; Sudfad looked back at Matthew and said, "I can tell you more about it later."

"He doesn't want to tell you how badly Raul and Simon were hurt in front of us because we always cry," Vitomas said. "I am afraid we haven't handled this very well."

"The worst part is that we are so far away from them and can't take care of them," Annabelle said with tears in her eyes. "See I start to cry every time I think about them." Angelina was sitting next to Annabelle and put her arm around her.

"So Matthew tell us how are you feeling? You look wonderful," Renya said.

Before Matthew could speak Angelina said, "It was awful, he and Stephan almost died. The Sanuri helped them also."

Matthew smiled as he watched Angelina holding Arianna. "Stephan and I are both healing just fine and both of us are going to be fathers soon."

As the family was congratulating Matthew and Angelina, Petra and the Sanuri walked into the dining room. "Sanuri are you sure you should be up?" Renya asked with concern.

"I am feeling fine my dear. Besides Petra wants me to take a walk with him after breakfast," the Sanuri said as he took a seat at the table. He stared at Angelina then looked at Matthew and said, "It is time."

"I know," Matthew replied.

"Demetries always talked in riddles and it annoyed me greatly," Roch said to Erebus as he slurred his speech.

"I know you have told me that but what exactly did he say?" Erebus asked again with frustration. This was the third day that Erebus tried to get Roch to tell him what Demetries had said to him. Roch's drunkenness was greatly affecting his ability to stay focused on any subject.

"He kept telling me I was born of darkness and I was a pawn and a vessel and that was about it. I already told you this," Roch said with annoyance and he poured himself another drink. "He kept asking me questions like you do, about where I came from blah, blah, blah."

"He did?" asked Erebus. "That is curious. I will bet he was trying to find out how much you knew. What was your deal with him?"

Roch glared at Erebus for several moments before answering, "How do you know I made a deal with him?"

Erebus gave Roch a condescending look, "Because he was a demon. Do you think he wanted to be near you because he enjoyed your personality?"

"That is enough!" Yelled Roch.

"Roch, I believe it is crucial to your welfare to determine why this demon suddenly came into your life. Now can you explain that to me?" Erebus shouted.

In Roch's drunken state he tried to remember if Demetries had told him anything that would explain why the demon came into his life. After a few minutes Roch replied, "I do not have an answer for you but I agree that would be worth knowing. Demetries said he wanted me to retrieve holy objects for him. He said that some of them were protected with forces that would not allow a demon to take them from the places they were hidden; so he wanted me to get them."

"And what did he ask you to get?"

"The Scroll of Imari. I had already tried to obtain it once and was planning a second attempt."

"And what was Demetries going to do for you?"

"I don't think that is any of your business," Roch spat.

"Perhaps you are right but it might be important."

"He was going to help me attack Wetpr and take my Queen back."

"Tell me about the Queen you said was taken from you. If you want her so badly why don't you have her back?"

Roch stared angrily at Erebus, "I do not need to tell you this."

"That is true but then you brought me here to help you."

"Demetries took over the body of a man named Jonas, after he was killed by Hutas; an attack that Demetries set up," Roch said. "I was badly hurt in that battle as was the man I thought was Jonas. When we finally got back home, Vitomas was gone. We believed she had been taken."

528

"So what did you do?"

"I had my men look for her for a while, then I went to the Caves of Muldun to try and get The Scroll of Imari; later Demetries told me she had married Raul, Prince of Wetpr."

"Did you look for her?"

Roch gritted his teeth. "No," he said angrily.

"So your greed was more important than your feelings for this woman," Erebus said. "Tell me do you really want her back or do you just want to take her away from Prince Raul?" Roch did not answer.

"You know it has been four nights now that I have been telling you about my life and it isn't getting any easier," Thaos said with a sad smile.

"Thaos don't you feel any better just telling someone about this?" Nikki asked.

"Not really, it is like I am living it all over again."

"I am sorry to put you through this."

"No, you were right; you deserve to know the man you are marrying. Do you remember where I left off?"

"Yes, one of the boys went into a tavern to ask for work and the bartender threw him out and broke his arm."

"Actually that was when things got a lot worse. That bartender ended up telling some men that there was a group of homeless boys in the city. One of those men was named Kagen. He looked like a kindly father but he was a monster. By the end of that week he had found all of us. He offered us work and a place to stay. We were so happy; we thought luck was finally on our side. He said he had a ranch just outside of the city. I should have known something was wrong when he took my weapons away," Thaos said angrily.

"Turns out the ranch was nothing more than a prison. He put us into cages and made us fight for our meals. Men would come out and bet on the fights. When one of the boys would get hurt Kagen wouldn't give him medical attention. If the boy died, he would just replace him with another homeless child."

"Is that how you got all of the scars on your back?" Nikki asked with horror.

"No, he would whip me when I would refuse to fight someone. I wouldn't fight Derek and some of the younger boys. He had a lot more boys captive then just our group. He had some girls too, but he would sell them for sex to the men that came to his ranch."

"How long were you there?" Nikki asked with tears in her eyes.

"I think almost a year before Derek and I escaped; we ran and never looked back."

"Did you leave the others behind?"

"Everyone from our group was either dead or had been sold. Derek and I were the only two left. We both became vicious fighters to survive. We left the Kingdom of Ganz as fast as we could. Neither Derek or I really had any skills besides hunting and fighting. We would get odd jobs here and there. But we never really stayed any one place too long. We started stealing a lot to get by. At first it was food, then before we knew it we were robbing business and gold mines. When we got older and bigger we would take on fighting jobs."

"What do you mean?"

"Mostly for sport at first. But then Derek and I got such reputations that people started to seek us out to do their dirty work for them." Thaos took a drink of his whiskey.

"What ever happened to Derek?"

To Nikki's surprise, Thaos got tears in his eyes and had to compose himself for a few moments before he spoke. "He and I rode together for twelve years. He was the only family I had," Thaos laughed.

530

"We had some wild times and some hard times. Derek was the toughest man I had ever met. There wasn't a fight he couldn't win." Thaos stopped talking as he fought back the tears. "One night I walked into this little cabin that he and I had been staying in and I found him hanging from the rafters. After I cut him down I just held him for a long time and cried; a grown man and I just cried."

"Who killed him?" Nikki asked as she wiped the tears from her cheeks.

"He killed himself."

"What? How do you know this?"

"Because he left me a note. He said he could fight everything except the voices in his head. I am not really sure what he meant by voices in his head. I know he was really lonely; hell we both were; that's why we clung to each other so." Thaos had to stop talking for a few minutes then he turned to Nikki. "He never asked me for help. I don't know what demons he was fighting inside but I would have helped him," Thaos said and started to cry.

"I am very pleased with your progress," said Ibula as she was examining Raul's wounds. "Your bones seem to be mending nicely."

"Getting out of bed and taking those long walks with Thedes, has helped greatly," said Simon as he was getting dressed.

"Tell me Simon," asked Ibula. "How is your vision?"

"It is remarkable," said Simon gratefully. "I can see clearly out of both eyes now."

"Has Thedes told you of his plans for tomorrow?" asked Ibula.

"No," replied Raul.

"Since you are warriors, he is anxious to test your fighting skills," said Ibula. "Although I understand this, I told him what I will tell you; although the scars are healing on the outside I do not know how quickly your wounds are healing on the inside. If you reinjure yourselves it is that much longer before you can return home to your families."

"So you would not have us fight at all?" asked Raul.

"I want you to go slowly and carefully," said Ibula. "Thedes is correct you do need to build up your strength. I do not know you on the battlefield but my husband gets a bit over zealous," she said with a laugh. "I believe he is going to show you how to use an ancient Shettee weapon."

"I would like that," said Simon.

"My husband feels a strong kinship to the two of you," said Ibula. "I must tell you he does not choose his friends easily."

"And we feel the same with him," said Raul. "I had never met a Shettee before this; I am amazed at how much we are alike."

"I had not either," said Ibula. "Until the Sanuri sent us to help them. Thedes was different then. He was always angry and never trusted anyone; he kept thinking my people would try to attack or enslave them."

Simon smiled, "Let me guess, did falling in love with you change him?"

"That and a lot of hard work," laughed Ibula.

Late that night, Cerephus walked to the far north side of the castle and entered Erebus' work room. Cerephus did not want Roch to know that he was visiting Erebus.

"I was beginning to wonder when I would see you again," Erebus said as he poured two glasses of whiskey.

"I don't want Roch to get suspicious of the amount of time we spend together."

"Like that old drunk could remember anything," Erebus said smugly. "I am about ready to give him a potion just so he will answer my damn questions. I am actually starting to wonder if it is just the whiskey affecting his brain."

"That's why I am here, how much of that crap that you are telling Roch is actually true. I will tell you that he believes every word you say."

"Don't you?"

"See the way you just said that I don't know if you are kidding or not. I will tell you I don't want to believe what you are saying."

"Cerephus there is some truth in what I told him. There is an old prophecy about the second son of the second son of the second son being an unholy vessel," said Erebus. "And look at him; he certainly does not look human anymore."

"Or smell human, every time I walk into that room I almost puke," said Cerephus with disgust.

"What I told him about being watched by the Holy Ruler is true, only a messenger of the Holy Ruler could do something like that; expose Roch's true nature," said Erebus. "Fortunately I did bring some of my scrolls and books with me. We need to find out the purpose of his being a vessel of darkness."

"You mean he might be?" asked Cerephus with surprise.

"You heard him yourself. He said Demetries called him a vessel of darkness. That is not a common term, my friend. Cerephus there is more going on here than you realize and I want to figure it out before we proceed with our plans."

"You need to be careful Erebus, no one speaks to Roch like you do, he will try to kill you one of these days," warned Cerephus.

"I expect he will," Erebus said with a grin. "And I have a few tricks up my sleeve. But I fear the demons more than I do Roch. Demons cannot create life. Something went to a great deal of trouble to turn Roch into a vessel for darkness, if that story is true. If we kill him before we find out what is happening to him we may have the wrath of very powerful demons upon us."

Erebus knew he needed more time to figure out what they all should do about Roch and the Insidiae. Erebus didn't want to lie to Cerephus but he did not want to tell him the truth yet either; because everyone who knew the truth was in danger.

"I have never seen anything like this," said Simon as he balanced the Shettee weapon in his hands. "What kind of metal is this made out of it is so light and balanced?"

"It is a Gafet," said Thedes with pride as he could see both Raul and Simon were impressed with the weapon. "It is forged from Taluth a metal I thought was only found in the Rosu Mountains; the mountain range that runs along the southern borders of the Kingdoms of Xepoltr and Marba. But I was extremely pleased to find Taluth; here in the Safer mountains."

"My brethren and I have been teaching the Rualas how to make these weapons. Our ancestors used to worship the sun, moon and stars and designed this weapon after these gods thinking it would give them great strength in battle. As you can see the outside of the weapon resembles a crescent moon. The three blades at each end are stars and the long protruding blade in the center represents the rays of the sun."

"These hand holds along the back are such that no matter how you hold the weapon it is balanced," said Raul with surprise.

"Those weapons are my gifts to you," said Thedes. "I will teach you how to use them while you are here."

Padre Bartholomew and Padre Thomas worked all day and long into the night in the Hall of Records without finding any information they felt was significant. "This is getting very discouraging," Padre Bartholomew said wearily.

"I know," replied Padre Thomas. "But I am still writing everything down because you never know when it may be important."

"You know Meekos will find someone else to come after us."

"After I got to my room last night I thought about some of the stories the Sanuri had told us that included a holy messenger taking the form of a lion," said Padre Thomas. I think The Great Ruler wants us to find this information and He is protecting us."

"I do not think I told you but when Petra pulled me from among the dead bodies at Avaide, a Huta warrior followed us into the forest; the roar of a lion scared him away and saved our lives," said Padre Bartholomew. "Then later when Petra, Archetenus, the Sanuri and I were hiding in a cave; we heard many lions roaring during the night and when we woke the ground outside of the cave was littered with the bodies of dead demons."

"I was so frightened when I heard that lion roar I never thought it might be there to protect us. I guess we all have lessons to learn."

Matthew, Angelina, Sudfad and the Sanuri spent an entire day in Sudfad's study as the Sanuri explained the responsibilities of the Keepers of the Scrolls to Angelina. As was her nature, Angelina asked many questions during the session.

"I am sorry that I kept this from you," Matthew said as he held her hand.

"Do not be angry with Matthew," Sudfad said. "No one is allowed to talk about this until the Sanuri tells them it is the appropriate time. One of the reason's Matthew brought you here before your marriage was to have the Sanuri meet you; to ensure you were the wife The Great Ruler meant for Matthew to take."

"I am not angry about any of this," Angelina said. "I am just amazed that you can keep such a secret. So Mathas and Rosa do not know?"

"No," Matthew said. "And it was very difficult for me not to tell you. But every time someone is told it increases the chance that the secret will be discovered; besides putting others in danger."

"Sanuri I will take the oath to uphold the responsibilities of this great honor; my only concern is that I have never kept a secret from my father. You know both Sorren and Mathas would be worthy allies in this battle against darkness," Angelina said.

"Angelina I agree with you," the Sanuri replied. "And there may be a time when I can tell them about the Keepers of the Scrolls but now is not that time."

Chapter XXXIII
Celebrations

"Father said the weapons we designed have been built and put into place at all of the forts and various locations along the borders," Raul said as he was reading a letter from Sudfad to Simon. "Here is a map of the locations of the weapons," Raul handed a hand drawn map to his brother.

"I will never take my eyesight for granted again," Simon said as he read the small print on the map. "You know the one thing that scared me before we really started healing; was that I might never be able to see Annabelle and the children again."

"We both have been greatly blessed," Raul said. "A few months ago we almost died, now Ibula says we may be able to go home in a few weeks." Raul picked the letter back up. "Father is talking about us coming home. He says that he understands that we want to surprise our wives but he suggests we tell them when we are coming because it will keep them occupied and distracted from their worry." Raul looked over at Simon, "What do you think?"

Simon thought about the question for a few moments before answering, "Actually I think Father is right. But you know Mother and the girls will throw a huge celebration for us."

"Well, perhaps that would be the perfect time to have Thedes and Ibula and some of the others visit the family. They have to take us home anyways; we should have them stay for a few weeks."

"We have all been talking about having our soldiers and the Ruala and Shettee warriors teach each other fighting styles, we might as well bring them all home," Simon said. "Let's find Thedes and Ibula and talk with them before we say anything to the girls."

"Here are a couple of more paintings to add to our collection, Raul said as he handed two sheets of paper to Simon, who smiled when he saw the childish scribbling of his sons. "I can't believe we have been gone over four months; I wonder if they will recognize us when we get home."

The Sanuri took the small scroll and the notes that Padres Thomas and Bartholomew had sent to him and walked into Sudfad's office. "Are you busy now or do you want to look at these items together?" the Sanuri asked.

Sudfad looked up from a pile of papers, "Please take a seat; I will be done in a few minutes."

The Sanuri started to read the notes while he was waiting for Sudfad to finish his paperwork. The Sanuri became disturbed that Padre Bartholomew and Padre Thomas appeared to be in danger. Then the Sanuri read the scroll about High Priest Meekos. "Meekos would have four diamonds in his ring," the Sanuri thought and the idea that Meekos could have been the murderer in the visions that the Sanuri saw during his tests; brought sadness to his heart.

King Sudfad finished signing a small stack of papers, then pushed them to the side of his desk. "My friends at the monastery sent these," said the Sanuri as he handed the notes to Sudfad. "One of the Enrops told me that three men were following my friends when they met with the Enrops. Then as you can see in the notes their rooms have been searched as well as the Hall of Records, where they are doing research. They are putting themselves at great risk to provide me with information."

Sudfad was listening to the Sanuri as he was reading the notes. "Your friends think they are getting close to finding something important and feel someone is trying to stop them," Sudfad said as he put one of the pages of notes on his desk.

"The Hall of Records should contain all of the written documentation about the monastery, who served there, events, every type of record," the Sanuri continued. "It is unheard of that such a hall would be in the disarray they have found it; unless someone was trying to hide something."

"Or perhaps someone tore it up searching for something they did not find."

"You are right, I wonder what is in there that is so important," the Sanuri said thoughtfully.

"This scroll talks about a high priest named Marcus Meekos, who has been a high priest at the Monastery at Malga for three hundred and sixty two years," said the Sanuri as he handed the scroll to Sudfad.

"But how can that be?" Sudfad asked in amazement.

"There are only two ways to have such a long life," said the Sanuri. "You choose to serve The Great Ruler or you serve the darkness."

"That means he was a high priest when Sharonne was King," Sudfad said. Sudfad paused in thought for a few moments then continued. "From the information your friends have gathered and the information we got from Juleta we all suspect Meekos and two other high priests of being members of the Insidiae and possibly dark lords; that much I know but I am still confused about some of this. First explain to me the relationships between Meekos and these two other high priests and I am sorry I can't remember the name of the third man."

"Tenebrae is the name of the third high priest. Meekos is the most senior and most powerful of the three within the Church itself; he is the Excellency of the monastery at Malga," the Sanuri explained. "Padre Thomas and Padre Bartholomew say these three high priests are inseparable." The Sanuri paused for a moment. "I know where you are going with your line of questioning Sudfad. You are wondering how men who hold such high positions of power and authority within the Church could possibly be dark lords and why no one has exposed them."

"Well yes, and I am wondering a great deal more than that. I am horrified by all of this," Sudfad said angrily. "It makes me question my faith in the Church."

"Sudfad, the Church is an institution made by men to worship The Great Ruler. Do not confuse the Church with The Great Ruler. Men are flawed and seduced by darkness, whatever they create has the possibility to be just as fragile as humanity. Within the Church these high priests have the same powers and authority as kings. One must have great proof to bring charges of allegiance with darkness upon them."

"Well your friends seem to be finding proof, I cannot believe others could not," Sudfad snapped.

"Sudfad do you remember how difficult it was for me to believe that Sporos had defiled his covenant with The Great Ruler and turned to darkness. Sometimes we just do not want to see the truth that is before our eyes."

"Sanuri, first I want you to know that I am not angry with you, I am just angry about this entire situation with the Church. Your feelings and defense of Sporos were understandable, but when you learned the truth you stopped him. These three high priests have been allowed to defile the name of The Great Ruler and to endanger people's lives. I cannot understand how men who have sworn a covenant with The Great Ruler can justify their inactions!"

"Fear always plays a great part," the Sanuri said sadly. "And there are many who uphold the man-made institutions over the wishes and teachings of The Great Ruler."

"Sanuri why doesn't The Great Ruler allow us to go to the monastery at Malga and stop these men?" Sudfad asked with frustration.

"Well, you can't go into the Kingdom of Puntd and take over their monastery, even if King Tobias is your brother-in-law; it will be considered an act of war," the Sanuri explained. "And what proof of wrong doing do you actually have for Tobias at this point? The Lion wants the Patronus to investigate these high priests. I have been sending High Priest Raphael the information that we receive; he is a good man and will stop this darkness."

"I certainly hope so," said Sudfad with disgust. Then as an afterthought he added. "Tell High Priest Raphael that if he needs anything to contact me; he will have my full support." Sudfad leaned back in his chair and looked at the Sanuri. "Now that you are getting on your feet; do you have any thoughts on where we should look for The Chalice of Ascension?"

"I have spent many hours mediating of late and The Great Ruler has not sent me any information about it," the Sanuri said. "I keep getting images of a group of thirteen, well-dressed men, who I do not recognize."

"That piece of paper in Glenda's box had the number thirteen written on it."

"I know, and I saw that number during my tests but I have not figured out the exact meaning yet."

"Sanuri before you got sick you were telling me about some of the other objects that were missing from the Hall of Antiquities."

"The Diamond of Cazo," explained the Sanuri. "Is said to have come from Mount Petrov, near the Ice Caves of Mordv. It is said to be as old as time itself in this world."

"How is it valuable?" asked Sudfad, not waiting for the Sanuri to finish speaking.

"It can call forth the powers of the center of this world."

"I do not understand what that means."

"You have been through storms of such great force that they topple over trees and destroy buildings, have you not?"

"Yes."

"Think of forces ten times, one hundred times perhaps even more powerful."

"Why would The Great Ruler create such a thing?" asked Sudfad with astonishment.

"Because as with all of the gifts; there will be a time when the world of man needs them," replied the Sanuri. "Those who strive to rise above the darkness of their natures; could use all of these gifts for great good in this world; as always it is a choice."

"I do not know if men will ever be ready for these gifts," Sudfad said sadly.

"The Seal of Natun is actually a key that if used properly can open doors to worlds unknown."

"There are other worlds?"

"What world do you think The Great Ruler lives in or The Abyss exists in?"

Sudfad leaned back into his chair and looked at the Sanuri. "How many other worlds are there?"

The Sanuri gave Sudfad a benevolent smile, "My dear friend, you are not yet ready for the answer to that question."

"Father, Angelina and I would just as soon not have it at all," Matthew said, then stopped talking as Claudius, Stephan and Thaos walked into Mathas' study for the morning meeting. This was the first time that Thaos had been asked to join them.

"Welcome back," Stephan said to Matthew. "When did you return?"

"We got back late last night," Matthew replied. "Stephan I was just talking to Father about the big wedding ceremony that we have to have for the kingdom. Do you still want to take part in it?"

"No," said Stephan as he poured himself a cup of coffee. "Ingr can't think about our first wedding without crying. And with all of our wives pregnant I think it is too dangerous."

Matthew looked at Thaos. "Is Nikki pregnant too?" Thaos nodded and smiled.

"I still think we owe it to the peoples of this kingdom," Mathas said.

"Father, I wanted Raul and Simon to stand up in the wedding; they haven't even returned home yet from the Ice Caves. And when they do, we don't know what shape they will be in. I would rather us postpone it for a year or have some other kind of celebration for the kingdom."

"Mathas, Ingr is sick all of the time now and it sounds like Nikki isn't much better. I don't know about Angelina but I don't think the girls are up to this now," Stephan said.

"Claudius what do you think?" Mathas asked.

"Well I agree with all of you. Mathas it is too soon to put all of our children through such an ordeal again, especially in the shape the girls are in."

542

"But you are right also; we should have some sort of celebration for the kingdom. I think that if we put these public weddings off another year, we will just keep putting them off."

"So what are you thinking about for another celebration?" asked Mathas.

"I was thinking of some kind of carnival with weapons competitions," Matthew said. "When we announce the carnival we can say it is being held to celebrate the weddings."

"Mathas you know we have to let our wives get involved with some of the planning for such an event or we will never hear the last of it," said Claudius.

Mathas turned to Fahron, "You have been unusually quiet, what is your opinion on all of this?"

"Personally I don't want to get involved," Fahron said with a deep laugh. "I do like the carnival idea and Isadore will want to be involved also."

"Alright then," said Mathas. "We will have a carnival for the kingdom." Then he turned to Thaos, "When are you and Nikki getting married?"

"When the Sanuri is well enough to come here."

Three more days, the two old priests worked in the Hall of Records. Exhausted they sat on the floor and compared notes.

"Although Meekos has been assigned to this monastery for over three hundred years; his name is written in very few places," said Padre Thomas. "Which I find unusual since he has been a high priest all of that time."

"I have been reviewing documentation of social events," said Padre Bartholomew. "And have found the name Meekos mentioned with High Priest Tenebrae and a High Priest Pravis."

"So Pravis and Tenebrae are as old as Meekos?" Padre Thomas asked with astonishment. "Padre Bartholomew the Sanuri once told me there are only two ways a man can have incredibly long life. They can surrender to The Great Ruler and be blessed as the Sanuri is or they sell their souls to darkness. We know that those three high priests wear a ring similar to that of the Insidiae. Now to know they are all hundreds of years old, well, I believe we found our terrorists. We must get this information to the Sanuri at once."

Both Padre Thomas and Padre Bartholomew started to collect all of their notes and writing instruments when they heard such a loud noise that they both jumped. "What was that?" whispered Padre Thomas as he slowly crept towards the window. He stood up and opened the shutters; looking into the darkness he could not see anything. Suddenly he heard wings flapping and a raven flew through the open window and into the Hall of Records.

"What is the meaning of this?" asked Padre Thomas as he and Padre Bartholomew watched the bird circle around the room. Suddenly Padre Bartholomew bowed his head in prayer. Within moments a strong gust of wind came through the open window and threw the raven against the wall breaking its neck. Padre Bartholomew picked the bird up and threw it out of the window then closed the shutters.

"What just happened?" asked Padre Thomas.

"As soon as I realized that bird was a raven, I prayed to The Great Ruler to protect us," replied Padre Bartholomew.

"Do you think the high priests are using ravens to spy on us?" Padre Thomas asked fearfully.

"What are those screams?" asked Erebus as he and Cerephus walked through the castle grounds.

"King Roch has a fresh supply of women," Cerephus sneered. "He will be busy for a while; when the screams stop we will know he is returning to the war room."

"Doesn't he ever leave the castle?"

"Would you if you looked like he does?" Cerephus asked sarcastically. "Besides Roch told me that riding greatly increases the pains in his bones."

"What was Roch like before the affliction?"

"He is always drunk now and never leaves the castle. Before, his mind was always busy planning a treasure hunt or an attack. He used to love to conspire against others and would spend hours devising the worse possible tortures for them."

"Are you sure all of these changes are because of the affliction the holy messenger brought upon him?"

"I don't understand what you are asking," Cerephus said.

"If he is a vessel for darkness he has some type of purpose. What if the life he was leading was in conflict with that purpose; perhaps the demons that created him wanted him stopped or at least slowed down."

"I still don't understand."

"You and Roch both have told me that he has almost been killed several times in the last couple of years. What if the demons were afraid he was going to get himself killed before the appointed time? That could be a reason that Demetries might want to distract him," said Erebus. "I mean they sure aren't coming to his help now with this affliction."

"Let me think about this, it is an interesting notion," Cerephus said thoughtfully.

"There are two great mysteries here that we should try to solve for our own safety," Erebus said. "First what do the demons want with Roch and second why did the holy messenger kill Demetries and not Roch?" Erebus was slowly providing Cerephus with information about Roch; while trying to make it sound as if the information was the result of his research and spells. Erebus was trying desperately to protect Sophie because she had already put her life in danger telling Erebus about the Insidiae and Roch being the Vessel of Darkness.

545

Sophie started to spend the night in Erebus' chambers on a regular basis. He knew she was extremely distressed because she had not heard from her brother for several months and because she feared that Roch might not be able to fulfill his role as the Vessel for Omnibus because of the affliction. Erebus and Sophie were now combining their resources to finding a way to get Sophie out of her contracts with the demon Omnibus and the Insidiae.

"By The Great Ruler look at this!" exclaimed Padre Bartholomew.

"What is it?" asked Padre Thomas as he came running from the far back of the Hall of Records.

"I found these behind this book shelf," said Padre Bartholomew as he blew the dust off six large framed paintings. He lined the paintings up side by side against the wall.

"They are all portraits of high priests," said Padre Thomas as he was inspecting them.

"Yes and look at this one. It is Meekos and look at the signature and the date."

"That painting is over three hundred years old and it looks exactly like him today," said Padre Thomas in astonishment.

"I think we should find out who these other priests are. Well, they all appear to be painted by different men from the signatures," Padre Bartholomew said as he squinted to read the small writing.

"Is there anything on the backs?" asked Padre Thomas as he started to turn the paintings around. "Padre Bartholomew," whispered Padre Thomas. "Look." Padre Thomas found an envelope tucked under the framing in the back of one of the portraits. The envelope was yellowed with age. Padre Thomas opened the envelope and Padre Bartholomew stood close to him so they could both read the words in silence.

On this my one hundred and eighty first year as serving as senior high priest at the Monastery at Malga, in the Kingdom of Puntd I sit in my office in fear. My heart is breaking from the darkness I have seen. I pray day and night that The Great Ruler will forgive me and give me guidance. In all my years I never thought I would see the face of darkness in the hallowed halls of this monastery; it is as if we let a demon into heaven itself.

The cancer is growing quickly and I do not know how to stop it. I suspect I will be killed soon as High Priest Timothy, High Priest Vincent and High Priest Samuel have all recently died of unusual deaths. The men who are taking their places do not pray to The Great Ruler and are emissaries of the very darkness that plagues mankind. High Priest Meekos travels often to the castle of the dark Lord Sporos in the Kingdom of Marba and to the Kingdom of Stordt to convene with King Sharonne, a man with an evil reputation.

There have been many killings in the villages and people disappear from their homes; the villagers are terrified and speak of monsters; I do not know if they are related to the monsters that roam inside these halls. In this envelope is a key to the safe in my study. I pray that a man serving the light finds it; for he will know what to do with the information I have hidden.

I beg your forgiveness for I could not stop the dark cloud that is filling this monastery.

High Priest Alexei Petlov

"We need to figure out which room was his study," said Padre Thomas.

"So what do you think?" Simon asked Thedes and Ibula.

"Father said he would like Mateo to come also, apparently the two of them got along quite well," Raul said as he held a letter from Sudfad.

Ibula looked at Thedes who nodded, "We would love to come," she said. "As for the others, I think we should have you address Manu and the Grand Council."

"Who is Manu?" Raul asked.

"He is the King of the Rualas and the Chief of our Grand Council, which is our governing body…" Ibula said but was interrupted by Thedes.

"Manu is also Ibula's father," Thedes interjected. "My wife is modest."

"The Council is made up of both Rualas and Shettees," Ibula continued. "Thedes is on the Grand Council and he could get you an audience."

Simon chuckled, "That sounds pretty formal for an invitation to a celebration."

"My people have had little contact with the world below," Ibula said. "Not only would different species be intermingling but you are suggesting our warriors should train together."

"So you don't think they would accept our invitation?" Simon asked.

"Ibula and I think they need to meet the two of you. And we will tell them of your relationship with the Sanuri," Thedes said. "For myself I very much like the idea."

"Mother is demanding that we get a count of those who want to attend so she can make preparations," Raul said with a grin.

"Of course," said Ibula. "And I am sure she will want to know how many children and babies are coming also. I will take care of that."

"Erebus is here to see you My Lord," said Cerephus.

"Show him in."

Roch poured three glasses of whiskey and handed Cerephus and Erebus each one. "Would I insult you if I declined?" asked Erebus. "I usually do not drink this early in the morning."

"It is your choice," said Roch with a shrug of his shoulders.

"I performed a spell using your blood and hair to try and find out more about your condition," Erebus said. Roch did not answer but stared at Erebus. "I am not sure how to explain what happened, so allow me a moment" said Erebus. "I am going to give you a very simple explanation of the spell. When done properly I combine certain ingredients in a bowl then ask the forces of nature to reveal certain secrets to me, then I see images in the bowl of ingredients."

"And," said Roch with annoyance.

"When I added your blood and hair to the ingredients in the bowl I saw the image of the face of the demon Sporos screaming angrily, then the bowl became very hot in my hand and started on fire," Erebus explained. "I have never heard of something like this happening before to any sorcerer."

"So what does it mean?" asked Roch.

"I was hoping you could tell me," said Erebus. "What is your relationship with Sporos?"

"I have heard of Sporos but I didn't know if what I heard was just stories. I heard he was a priest that turned into a demon."

"What you heard was true. Sporos is a very powerful demon; so powerful that the Sanuri fought him and had Sporos imprisoned in The Great Abyss to protect this world from him."

"I have never met Sporos but I did meet an image of the Sanuri one night," said Roch with a drunken laugh.

"What do you mean you met an image of the Sanuri?"

"He appeared in my room one night, screaming at me for sending demons to him and telling me to change my ways."

"And what else happened?"

"The Sanuri threw me around a little. It was that damn lion that did this to me," said Roch as he was referring to his affliction.

"You really have no idea who any of these figures are, do you?" asked Erebus with amazement. "Are you really that self-absorbed?"

549

"I am not paying you to insult me," screamed Roch. "So tell me what all this means."

"You told me before that the demon Demetries said you were a pawn in a game where the players are more powerful than you can imagine," said Erebus. "Well, you are meeting some of the players."

Roch sat in silence for several minutes thinking about Erebus' words. "Tell me what this image of Sporos looked like."

"He has the face of a man, who is bald except for a long thin ponytail down the back of his head. He wears two golden hoop earrings in each ear. He has an intensity and evil about him that even you could appreciate."

"I too have seen that image," Roch gasped.

"Tell me everything because it is important," Erebus said earnestly.

"I started seeing that image in my campfires as I was returning home after losing all of my men in the first attempt to steal The Scroll of Imari. Sometimes I would hear my voice being called and when I would look upon the fire I would see that face screaming with rage. At first I thought I was dreaming it all," Roch said hesitantly. "But then I started seeing it all of the time."

Both Cerephus and Erebus stared at Roch as it was the first time either of them had seen Roch look fearful.

Two nights later Raul and Simon were escorted to the Great Hall of Light in the Ice Caves of Mordv. They sat at a long table with Ibula as the rituals of calling a meeting to order were performed. Thedes sat among the leaders of the tribe at the front of the room, facing all those in attendance.

When the required rituals were completed Thedes stood up and addressed the large crowd. He told them of the Sanuri requesting some of their warriors to assist Raul and Simon. Thedes told of the battle with the Hutas and he told of all the events that had occurred since Raul and Simon had been brought to the caves.

When Thedes finished speaking, Mateo stood up. Mateo was also a member of the Grand Council. Mateo told the audience of the Sanuri's sacrifice to help Raul and Simon heal and the grave attacks he suffered afterwards. Mateo described his trip to King Sudfad's castle and his interaction with the humans there.

After Mateo finished speaking, Ibula stood up and walked in front of the room. Ibula explained Raul's and Simon's request that members of their tribes come to visit the Kingdom of Wetpr and train with their warriors. Ibula explained that the family of King Sudfad is so grateful that Raul and Simon are alive that they are hosting grand celebrations. When Ibula finished speaking she returned to the table with Raul and Simon. "You two should go up there next," she said.

"Why are there such elaborate explanation's for a social invitation?" Simon asked.

"Because like humans, our tribes fear what they do not understand."

As the Royal Family of Wetpr and the Sanuri were taking their seats at the breakfast table; Renya hurried into the dining room filled with exhilaration. "Marie," Renya called. "You have to be here too." Renya took her seat near Sudfad and handed him a letter she had been carrying. As soon as Marie entered the room, Renya announced. "I got a letter from Ibula. She anticipates that the boys will be well enough to travel home in three weeks." Everyone at the table broke into smiles at the news; then both Vitomas and Annabelle started to cry.

Renya stopped talking while she too wiped the tears from her eyes. "Ibula does caution us that Raul and Simon are so driven to get well that they do not always listen to their bodies and are actually weaker than they would have one think."

"Ibula said that so many of the Rualas and Shettees want to come for the celebrations that she wants to know how many we can accommodate." Renya now started to laugh as she was filled with joy. "Ibula said that Raul and Simon are just like Thedes and never think of the work involved or the details of planning such an event; so she will work with us to make sure things go smoothly."

"That means we have three weeks to plan the celebrations," Renya said excitedly then she turned to Sudfad, "I don't know if we will have enough rooms for everyone."

"My dear we have rooms in this castle that we have never used," Sudfad said with a laugh then he turned to the Sanuri. "How large are the tribes of Rualas and Shettees?"

"Together there are several thousand," the Sanuri said. "But they are true warriors; they do not need elaborate quarters. If so many come that there are not enough rooms, I would suggest having some of them stay in the barracks you have for the soldiers."

Renya stood up and started to walk out of the dining room. "Where are you going?" Sudfad asked. "You haven't eaten your breakfast yet."

"Sudfad there is too much work to do. I don't have time to eat."

Chapter XXXIV
Clues

"Two days and we have not found one word about room assignments for anyone," said Padre Thomas with frustration. "All of that information should be kept here."

"Perhaps we should be looking for charts," offered Padre Bartholomew wishfully.

"Padre Bartholomew, think of all of the time you and I have spent in this hall cleaning and organizing things," said Padre Thomas with irritation. "And look at what is left." Padre Thomas pointed to the half of the huge room that was still in disarray.

"And look at all we have discovered," said Padre Bartholomew. "Perhaps we should take a break and get something to eat."

"You are right I could use a break. I think I am just getting tired."

"Let's take a walk outside first, it is such a beautiful day."

"All those stacks and stacks of papers in the Hall of Records, yet we have found little of significance about the history of this monastery."

"My brother, I am beginning to think things have been stolen from the Hall of Records just as they were stolen from the Hall of Antiquities," said Padre Bartholomew. "I wonder if all of these missing items are being kept someplace in the monastery?" The two priests walked through the gardens and entered the main building of the monastery through a front door.

"Look," said Padre Thomas. "I so rarely enter through this door that I forgot about the maps." He said as he pointed to a huge map displayed on the left wall of the entrance. The two priests walked closer to the map.

"This map is fifty years old," said Padre Bartholomew as he was reading the print at the very bottom of the map.

"This shows all of the buildings and everyone's rooms. And look, someone is adding new information, because your name and room is written in a different color of ink."

"We need to find out more about these maps," said Padre Bartholomew as they walked towards the dining hall.

"Lords of darkness reveal to me the answers I seek," chanted Erebus then he poured a few drops of Roch's blood into the boiling mixture. As soon as the blood came into contact with the boiling liquid; great plumes of smoke filled the air. More and more smoke billowed out of the pot; changing colors of purple, blue, red and black.

Suddenly a great wind engulfed the inside of Erebus' work room. Books blew open, chairs toppled over; Erebus' hair and clothing blew back hard against his body. Erebus suddenly felt intense pain in his hands, when he looked at them it appeared that the tips of all of his fingers had been cut off and blood was pouring onto the floor. Erebus suddenly felt like he was choking and he grabbed at his throat. Just as Erebus thought he was about to lose consciousness he heard a voice.

"Who are you to interfere?" the voice echoed and echoed.

Erebus no longer felt like he was choking. "I want to make sure we do not interfere with your plans that is why I call upon you," Erebus called into the smoke.

"Explain," echoed the voice.

"Cerephus has asked me to help him rob Roch of his kingdom and his wealth," Erebus called. "As soon as I saw Roch, I knew there was more going on here, although I do not know what. I do not want to incur the wrath of the dark lords."

"You are wise," echoed the voice. And the room suddenly cleared of smoke and became still.

Erebus looked around the room then called out, "I still do not have any answers."

Suddenly the boiling pot started to shake and to rise in the air; then as if an invisible hand threw it; all of the liquid in the pot sailed across the room and hit the wall. The liquid clung to the wall without falling. Erebus walked up to the wall and saw the word WAIT appear in the liquid.

Once Padre Bartholomew and Padre Thomas entered the dining hall it did not take them long to find out who was responsible for making the maps of the monastery. As soon as they learned a name and a room number, both priests quickly ate and left the dining hall.

"Padre Dominick we are working on a history of the monastery and are looking for old maps like the one displayed at the front door," Padre Thomas said. "We were told you have created the maps for a long time."

"You are working on a history of the monastery?" asked Padre Dominick. "Why?"

"As you know Padre Bartholomew is new here and I was trying to explain the history but there were many things I could not remember. So I took him to the Hall of Records and found it in great disarray; we could find little information there," said Padre Thomas. "So we decided to put together a history."

"The Hall of Records was in disarray; why what do you mean?" Padre Dominick asked.

"Everything was off from the shelves and appeared to have been thrown around the room," replied Padre Bartholomew.

"Well, I will tell you that I go to the Hall of Records often and have always found it neat and orderly," said Padre Dominick angrily. "If it is as you say then someone did that recently."

"When was the last time you were in there?" asked Padre Bartholomew.

"I can't remember exactly maybe four or five weeks ago," Padre Dominick replied.

Padre Thomas and Padre Bartholomew looked at each other as Dominick's words confirmed their suspicions. Both Padre Thomas and Padre Bartholomew believed that someone was trying to remove information before they found it.

"It is beyond me why someone would try to destroy the Hall of Records," Padre Thomas said. "But Padre Bartholomew and I have been cleaning up the mess and trying to restore the hall to its original condition."

"Good," said Padre Dominick. "Now you want maps, you said?"

"Yes, Padre Dominick," replied Padre Thomas.

"I have been charged with making them since I was a very young priest and I have saved everything; come we will need to go to the basement." Padre Thomas helped Padre Dominick out of his chair and the three priests walked into the hallway.

"I am sorry I walk so slowly these days," Padre Dominick said as he struggled walking with his cane.

"Padre Dominick do you mind me asking but how long have you served at this monastery," asked Padre Bartholomew.

"I started to study to become a priest when I was twelve and I studied at this very monastery," said Padre Dominick. "I became a full priest at the age of twenty one and I am now ninety three years old."

"So you have been at this monastery since you were twelve?" asked Padre Thomas.

"I suppose you have seen many changes in all of those years," said Padre Bartholomew. "Do you need help down these stairs?"

"No, I will just go slow; but thank you for the offer," replied Padre Dominick. "I have seen many changes and some not for the better."

"I was thinking that perhaps we could talk with you to get information for the history we want to put together," added Padre Bartholomew.

"I certainly would be happy to speak with you but we already have a history of this monastery; I know because I wrote it."

Padre Thomas looked at Padre Bartholomew with excitement. "And you have a copy of this history?" Padre Thomas asked Padre Dominick.

"Of course," said Padre Dominick. "There are torches on the walls to the right of this door." Padre Bartholomew lit two torches and gave one to Padre Thomas. The three priests walked through a doorway and into an underground chamber of the monastery.

"I have never been here before," exclaimed Padre Thomas.

"There are underground chambers that go the entire length of the monastery but most have forgotten they exist," replied Padre Dominick. The three priests walked through a series of hallways that contained doors. Finally Dominick stopped before one door. "Hold the torch so I can see the door number," he said. Padre Thomas lifted his torch and they saw the number thirteen painted above the door. "This is the room," said Dominick as he pulled a large keychain from the pocket of his robe. He unlocked the door and the three priests entered a small storage room.

"This is where I have always stored the materials that I work on; I would suggest you find a storage room for anything you are working on," continued Padre Dominick. "What with so many people walking the halls of this monastery, things tend to get lost. All of the old maps are rolled up in the back left corner and these other shelves contain copies of projects I have worked on over the years. I always make copies of my work because I found that things would disappear, it was very odd."

"What kinds of things would disappear?" asked Padre Bartholomew.

"That is what I found odd; they were nothing of value, lists of room assignments, service dates, deaths of priests, you know the ordinary records a monastery would keep," said Padre Dominick as he walked towards a set of heavy wooden shelves and looked inside a couple of wooden boxes. "Here could one of you take this?" he asked. Padre Thomas lifted a medium size box from the shelf.

557

"This is quite heavy, what is in here?" Padre Thomas asked as he carried the box to a small table in the room.

"A very large book," said Padre Dominick with pride. "That is the history I compiled, of course I completed that twenty years ago; but those other boxes contain copies of information that needs to be added."

Padre Thomas could feel his heart leap in his chest as he lifted a large manuscript from the box. The manuscript was covered in a thick coat of dust. "Padre Dominick would you give us the honor of allowing us to read this manuscript and if you like we could help you enter the newer information," Padre Thomas said with excitement.

"Of course," replied Padre Dominick with a broad smile. "I am glad someone is interested in my work and my eyes are failing, I would appreciate the help."

"Padre Dominick it would be our pleasure to help you," said Padre Bartholomew. "Can the information on the maps be found in that manuscript?"

"Yes, I even drew smaller maps."

Padre Thomas blew the dust off from the manuscript and tried to conceal it in the cloth of his robes.

"Why don't you take the key if you are going to help me," said Padre Dominick as he handed the key to Padre Bartholomew. "Those stairs are difficult for me to walk, so I rarely come down here anymore."

"Erebus, I am telling you that something is watching us," Sophie said.

"Many beings are watching all of us at any time," Erebus said as he handed Sophie a glass of wine.

"Maybe watching us isn't the word I am looking for," Sophie explained as Erebus sat down next to her on the sofa in his chambers.

"First, I still haven't heard from Meekos. I started to keep count and I have sent him twenty seven messages telling him about Roch's encounter with the holy emissary. I have not heard one word. Meekos and I have always written to each other at least every other week. I am wondering if something has happened to him. Either that, or something is intercepting our messages. And now something is blocking my spells too."

"What do you mean?" asked Erebus with concern.

"I have done several spells trying to locate Meekos and well, the first spell I did I used a pendulum and it exploded. Then I tried to contact someone on the other side to tell me if Meekos was alright. I have done this type of spell hundreds of times but yesterday instead of receiving information all I heard was blood curdling screams."

"And today..." Sophie suddenly looked fearful and took a sip of her wine before completing her sentence. "And today Erebus, I was in the kitchen cooking when I heard a loud commotion in the pantry. I entered the panty and found pots and pans thrown around the floor, then I looked up and written on the wall was a message, it appeared to be written in blood."

"Sophie tell me, what did the message say?"

"It said *Run the shadows are coming*."

"Look at this book," said Padre Thomas in awe. "The art work and detail are amazing."

"I was serious when I told Padre Dominick that I would like to help him with adding the new information; that is, when our investigation is over," Padre Bartholomew said.

"I agree, look his information dates back to the time this monastery was built," said Padre Thomas. "I fear we will have to find a better hiding place for this book; it is too large for my hole in the floor boards."

The two priests read long into the night; copying information of importance into their notes. "What was that?" asked Padre Thomas as he awoke still sitting in his chair by the small table in his room.

"What?" asked Padre Bartholomew groggily as he raised his head from the table. "We must have fallen asleep."

"Listen," whispered Padre Thomas. They could hear voices and movement in the hallway. Padre Thomas listened at the door before he opened it. "Why, whatever is going on?" asked Padre Thomas to the three priests he saw in the hall.

"Padre Thomas, we are making notifications," said one of the priests.

"Notifications of what?" Padre Thomas asked.

"It is Padre Dominick; his body was just found in one of the gardens."

"What would he be doing in the gardens at this time of night?" Padre Bartholomew asked as he walked into the hallway.

"We do not know how long he has been there," one of the priests replied.

"How did he die?" asked Padre Thomas.

"I am sorry I cannot tell you that either; please excuse us we have many notifications to make," said the young priest as they continued down the hallway. Padre Thomas nervously looked both ways down the hallway before closing the door to his room.

"Did you hear what they said?" Padre Thomas asked Padre Bartholomew?"

"Yes and we need to find out how he died."

"We cannot leave this book unattended," said Padre Thomas. "I feel awful; I hope he was not killed because we talked to him."

"I think we better get through this book as quickly as we can and get the information to the Sanuri before something happens to us," Padre Bartholomew said as he sat back down at the table.

560

"Sophie do you know what that message means?" Erebus asked.

"I have no idea," Sophie replied. "But I will admit it frightened me."

"Sophie, I want you to leave Roch's castle. I don't like the things that have been happening here."

"Erebus, I can't leave yet and besides I am not leaving you behind again," Sophie said as she squeezed his hand.

"Why can't you leave now?"

"Not with all of this going on with Roch."

"Sophie I have a castle in Ryed, near the Sea of Talmont, go there and wait for me."

"Erebus why would you not be leaving with me?"

Erebus looked at Sophie for several moments before he spoke. "Sophie while you have been honest with me I have withheld some things from you. Cerephus and I have been friends for a long time. I came here to help him overthrow Roch and to take over the kingdom. I am sorry I did not tell you before."

"What!" gasped Sophie. "Cerephus seems so loyal to Roch."

"It is but a ruse," Erebus said. "But after what you have told me about Roch, we cannot kill him without bringing the wrath of the Old Ones upon us. I have been trying to figure out how I can warn Cerephus without exposing you." Sophie glared angrily at Erebus. "Sophie, I lost you once, I will not lose you again but this is a dangerous life you lead, owing debts to Omnibus and the Insidiae. If Cerephus and I take over the kingdom perhaps we could pay off some of your debts."

561

"Look at this," said Padre Bartholomew as he was reading the book that contained the history of the monastery. "Meekos was a high priest when he arrived at the monastery three hundred and sixty two years ago. Then a few pages later, is the first of several entries about diabolical occurrences in the villages and on the monastery grounds that seem to have started the same year that Meekos arrived here."

"What kind of occurrences?"

"I have not found much detail except for the terms unholy altars and sacrifices," replied Padre Bartholomew. "But here is an entry from High Priest Vincent, we read about him in the letter, he makes reference to fears that a group of men are involved in the unholy acts and he refers to them as the Insidiae-the conspirators."

"You and I know that Meekos, Tenebrae and Pravis are the terrorists but we cannot accuse priests of such high standing without proof. We have to find something that directly ties them to the unholy acts," said Padre Thomas.

"I know but they have done a good job of covering their tracks," Padre Bartholomew said then returned to reading the text from the book. "High Priest Vincent goes on to say, there are suspicions that some of the Insidiae have formed unholy alliances with the dark lords. And there are fears that this group is raising a private army."

"I wonder if those men who followed us in the garden were part of that private army," said Padre Thomas as he was writing the information into their notes.

"Thank The Great Ruler," said Padre Bartholomew, as he continued to read from the book. "According to these charts Petlov's chambers were on the second floor in the south wing; that is nowhere near Meekos' chambers."

"Write down the directions in case the room numbers have changed. I do not want to leave this book until we have read it completely, or we may never see it again."

"I agree."

Padre Thomas stood up and walked over to the door, "I hear voices." He opened the door and saw several priests in the hallway. "I am not feeling well, so I do not want to come near you," Padre Thomas said loudly. "But do you know under what circumstances Padre Dominick died?"

One of the priests turned and walked towards Thomas, "There are no wounds, nor marks on his body; it may have been his heart."

"Thank you, you are very kind," said Padre Thomas as he closed the door.

"Do you think it was his heart?" asked Padre Bartholomew.

"It is difficult to know, he was ninety three years old," said Padre Thomas. "I think we need to search his storage room later."

"Cerephus," Erebus called as he knocked on the door to the General's cottage just before sun up.

"Come in quickly," said Cerephus as he looked outside to see if anyone saw Erebus at his door.

"I am sorry to disturb you at this time of the morning," Erebus said as he sat down at the kitchen table. "But I found the answer to our questions. And you are not going to like it."

Cerephus poured two cups of coffee and joined Erebus at the table. "I have been studying ancient texts and well, I will try to make this simple. Roch is the Vessel of Darkness," Erebus said solemnly. "Roch was basically created by a group of dark lords to be the container, so to speak, for the demon Omnibus. These dark lords are trying to help that demon escape his prison in The Abyss."

"Nothing has ever escaped The Abyss," Erebus continued. "If these dark lords can get Omnibus out, only his essence will come to this world and that is why they need a vessel to put it in. Omnibus is an ancient demon who threatened many worlds, which is why The Great Ruler imprisoned him. If he escapes The Abyss he will destroy everything he touches."

Cerephus stared at Erebus for several moments. "And you are sure of this?"

"I will bet my life on it," replied Erebus seriously.

"I don't understand when you said Roch was created," Cerephus said.

"I will admit I don't fully understand it either, but the dark lords believed that they needed a man of great darkness to be the Vessel or they feared the Vessel would not be able to contain the demon's essence."

"So should we kill Roch now?" Cerephus asked.

"I am still doing research. If we foil Omnibus' escape we will bring the wrath of many upon us."

"Erebus, I have to think," Cerephus said seriously as he filled both of their cups with coffee again. "If he becomes a demon he will be too powerful for us to fight won't he?"

"Oh yes."

"If he becomes a demon do you think he will still want his kingdom and riches?"

"It is hard to tell," Erebus said. "But I would guess that he would."

"So there has to be a point during this transformation process when he is weak and we can kill him?"

"And bring the wrath of demons and dark lords upon us," Erebus said again nervously.

"If we allow Roch to live he will become a dangerous demon, now he is nothing but a feeble drunk," Cerephus said more to himself than to Erebus. "I think the time to kill him is now."

"Cerephus!" yelled Erebus. "Once again I remind you that if we foil the plans for the transformation that we will be punished by demons and dark lords."

Cerephus was thoughtful for a few moments. "Is there a way we can kill Roch and make it appear that we were not responsible for his death?"

"Do you think anyone saw us?" asked Padre Bartholomew as he and Padre Thomas walked through the monastery gardens.

"I think we are always being watched," replied Padre Thomas. "I hope the Sanuri can use the information that we sent to him. We have found clues but nothing strong enough to topple Meekos from his throne of power."

"We should get some sleep now and look for Petlov's study after the other priests retire."

"Look," said Padre Thomas as he pointed to a wooden fence that surrounded one of the vegetable gardens. The priests watched as two, then six, then a dozen ravens landed on the fence.

"There are many more over here," said Padre Bartholomew as he pointed to their right. The two men started to run towards the buildings. The ravens flew around them. Meekos watched from his window and laughed.

"Are you alright?" asked Padre Bartholomew as he and Padre Thomas ran inside of the monastery.

"Yes and I will bet Meekos was watching us," replied Padre Thomas with indignation.

"You don't think those ravens could stop the Enrops from delivering our letter, do you?"

"I hope not. Let's go to the dining hall, we both could use some food and perhaps we will find out more about the death of Padre Dominick."

"Do you want to look for Petlov's study tonight or search in Dominick's storage room?" Padre Bartholomew whispered as they entered the dining hall. Many of the tables in the dining hall were filled. The two priests took their food over to the table they usually saw Meekos sit at. Padre Thomas sat down. "What are you doing?" whispered Padre Bartholomew.

"It is a small gesture but I want to show Meekos that we are not afraid of him."

"Very well," said Padre Bartholomew as he took a seat. Padre Bartholomew caught the eye of a priest at the next table and asked. "Do you know when the funeral is?"

"Traditionally we wait a week and hold daily prayer meetings. The first meeting will be tomorrow at one o'clock," replied the priest. "Were you friends with Padre Dominick?"

"Yes," replied Padre Thomas.

"I have been tasked with sending his belongings to his family; but I found out that he has no family," said the priest. "Perhaps you would like to have something to remember him by."

"That is very thoughtful," replied Padre Thomas. "We would."

"After we have finished eating, I could take you to his room," said the priest. "I have the key."

"I am new here, what is your name?" asked Padre Bartholomew.

"I am Padre Xavier."

"My Lord, My Lord come quickly screamed Sophie as Cerephus was walking towards Roch's war room for breakfast.

"What is it Sophie?"

"It's King Roch, there is something wrong with him," Sophie grabbed Cerephus' hand and dragged him into the war room. When they entered the room, they saw Roch slumped over his desk. Cerephus ran up to the King and saw that Roch was still breathing. Cerephus was fearful because he didn't know if Roch was transforming into a demon. "Sophie have one of the men get the Court Physician and have someone get Erebus."

When Cerephus was alone with Roch he shook him but Roch did not respond. Cerephus had never gotten use to the smell of death that Roch emitted, but now the smell seemed stronger.

"What is it?" Erebus asked as he ran into the war room, he too was afraid that Roch might be transforming. Erebus stopped when he saw Roch.

"He is breathing but not conscious," Cerephus said.

"Perhaps he is just drunk," Erebus said.

"I don't think so," said Cerephus "Look, it is as if his skin is changing before my eyes."

"I really have not packed up many of his things," said Padre Xavier. "Feel free to look around and take anything you want."

"What will you do with his belongings," asked Padre Bartholomew.

"I will find out who else he was friends with and tell them they can take what they want and I suppose what is left will go into a storage room," replied Padre Xavier. "It is sad that such a dedicated servant of The Great Ruler had no one." Padre Xavier closed the door leaving Padre Bartholomew and Padre Thomas in the room.

"This is really sad," said Padre Bartholomew. "Now I am determined to finish his projects for him."

"Perhaps he has some names of friends written down that we could contact," offered Padre Thomas as he was looking through a desk.

"Look," said Padre Bartholomew. "He was a painter; look at all of these beautiful paintings and drawings." Padre Bartholomew proceeded to carry paintings out of a closet and display them against the furniture. "I think we should display these paintings in the hallways of the monastery."

"I am taking some of his books and I found a list with names, I will write to these people and tell them of Padre Dominick's death.

"I am taking this notebook of drawings and some of these paintings," said Padre Bartholomew. "I will tell Padre Xavier that we might want to get back into this room."

The Court Physician walked out of Roch's bedroom, where the King had been taken. "He did wake up but he is a sleep again," the physician said. "I have never seen anything like this. I really don't know what is wrong with him."

"Will he live?" Sophie asked with concern.

"I wish I could answer that question," the physician said. "Sophie why don't you fix him some broth and tea and see if he will take it the next time he wakes." Sophie turned and walked to the kitchen leaving the physician with Cerephus and Erebus.

"Is there anything you can tell us that you didn't want to say in

front of Sophie?" Cerephus asked.

"Well, he did say he was in great pain and it was a different kind of pain than he is used to experiencing."

"What do you think that means?" Erebus asked the physician.

"I am being as honest with you as I can, I really don't know what it means. I gave him something for the pain; the bottle is next to his bed," the physician said and walked away.

"Have you found his treasure yet?" Erebus asked in a whisper.

"No but I have a plan," Cerephus said.

Chapter XXXV
A World of Nightmares

"Sudfad, I will be taking leave soon."

"Sanuri I am glad to see you up and about but are you sure you are strong enough to travel?" Sudfad asked.

"Last night I had a vision. The time is drawing near for the Vessel of Darkness to unleash its madness upon the world. I am to retrieve The Chalice of Ascension that was stolen from the monastery at Malga; for the dark lords desire its powers to help them with their unholy plans."

"And you know where the chalice is?"

"I was shown a series of caves I believe to be in Ryed."

"Take a company of my men with you."

"Thank you dear friend but I have never traveled with an army; The Great Ruler is sending me on this mission, He will watch over me," said the Sanuri. "And in my absence The Lion will watch over your family here."

"When will you leave?"

"Tomorrow morning. I have some things to prepare first. I will return for the boys' homecoming."

The journey from Salar to the Kingdom of Ryed would take the Sanuri several weeks; he prayed for guidance and he prayed for speed. The Sanuri was heading to the very northern tip of Ryed where he knew a series of caves existed.

The Sanuri thought about the notes and manuscripts that Padre Thomas and Padre Bartholomew had sent to him and about the tests he had taken, the visions he had seen and the information that the ancient healer Glenda had revealed. The Sanuri felt frustrated; he was staring at pieces of a puzzle but he could not see how they were taking form.

He had traveled before with less information and The Great Ruler had always provided him with exactly what he needed when the time was right. The Sanuri had faith that The Great Ruler would lead him to the chalice. As he drove the long journey, the Sanuri thought over and over about all of the information he had received, "Are all of these clues leading to the Insidiae?" he wondered. "Or are there more threats?" He also thought about the words of The Lion, that the Sanuri was too close to Sudfad's family to see some things clearly.

"Am I putting them in danger, by being their friend? I have been traveling most of my long life," thought the Sanuri. "I do admit I like feeling like I have a family and a home; is my own weakness blinding me to my duties?" All of these thoughts greatly troubled him. He traveled the first three days with only short breaks for the horses. By the fourth day fatigue overtook him and the Sanuri made an early camp so he could sleep.

The Sanuri's slumber was disturbed by the sound of his horses. They sounded agitated and afraid. He lay on the ground listening to the sounds of the night. All the Sanuri heard was his horses so he slowly rose from the ground. No sooner did he stand up when an arrow flew past his head and lodged in the side of the boca. The Sanuri quickly grabbed his staff and took cover underneath the boca.

One, two more arrows made thuds as they lodged into the side of the boca. The Sanuri stared into the darkness trying to locate the position of his attacker. Suddenly an arm appeared from behind a tree, the skin shown in the moonlight. As the arrow was launched the Sanuri slightly raised his palm causing the arrow to turn around in its course and to lodge in the person who shot it. The Sanuri heard a scream then silence. He continued to lay under the boca, listening.

The Sanuri suddenly felt a burning pain in the calf of his left leg; turning he saw the hilt of a Huta knife protruding from his leg. As soon as the Sanuri turned to look at his leg, a Huta warrior grabbed his ankles and was pulling the Sanuri from underneath the boca.

The Sanuri began to mumble and the earth started to shake violently causing the Huta nearest him to fall upon his back. The ground came alive around the Huta; as if unseen hands were pulling the warrior into the ground. Screaming; the Huta sank into the earth.

Soon the Sanuri heard another scream and yet another; then there was silence. The Sanuri crawled out from beneath the boca and pulled the knife out of his leg. He covered the bleeding wound with both of his hands and began to pray. Slowly the blood stopped gushing from the wound and through his interlocked fingers. After a few minutes there was no more blood.

Pulling his medical bag from the boca, the Sanuri bound his wound then walked into the forest. In the moonlight he could see four areas where the earth had been disturbed, "One of them must not have screamed," he thought. The Sanuri saw a trail of blood from the tree where he had seen the arm but the ground was not disturbed. He followed the blood trail and saw that it led away from his camp. "It is not like a Huta to run away," thought the Sanuri. "He must be delivering a message to his masters."

The Sanuri could not return to sleep so he decided to resume his travels. Travelling was slower at night but the horses seemed to enjoy the cool air. He was entering the Gant territories, travelling just north of the Rodite Forest. The Sanuri could hear the giant beasts screaming as they hunted their prey. "Long has it been since I have seen one of those creatures," he thought.

The Sanuri drove his team of horses through the streets of Utha. Nothing appeared to be moving in this tiny village. The Sanuri did not want to cross the tributaries of the River Neior at night so he pulled his boca to the side of a street and decided to sleep. But sleep did not come easily. He tried to rest in the front seat of his boca, a thing he had done many times before. But this night he felt anxious, a feeling the Sanuri was not accustomed to.

The Sanuri tied his team of horses to a hitching post and decided to take a walk through the village and to the river's shore. Utha was a fishing village that was built on the shoreline of the River Neior.

The Sanuri could hear the night birds singing and could feel the cool damp wind against his face as he got closer to the water. The Sanuri always enjoyed being near water and walked along the river's edge. He could hear fish splashing again and again.

The Sanuri was feeling very relaxed and decided to return to his boca, when he heard a loud splash, too big for a fish. The Sanuri turned and stared into the blackness of the river. He heard a voice calling for help and saw a hand protruding from the dark waters. The Sanuri jumped into the cold river, pulling the body to shore. He dragged the man out of the cold river waters and laid him on the ground. The man coughed several times and spit water out of his mouth before he was able to speak.
"Thank you."

"We need to get you in some blankets, can you walk?" asked the Sanuri.

"I think so."

"My boca is just down the street," the Sanuri said as he helped the man to his feet. "Come." They walked quickly to the boca. "Here," said the Sanuri as he handed the man several blankets. "You need to get out of those wet clothes. After the man had wrapped the blankets around him, the Sanuri said, "Get in, I will drive to the edge of the village so I can make a fire."

The Sanuri set the man before the fire and started a pot of coffee. "So tell me how did you end up in the river, I did not see any boats on the water?"

"You are most kind, My Lord," replied the man. "But I fear you will be bringing trouble upon yourself by helping me; you should just leave me here."

"I do not plan on leaving you here, so let's start again; what is your name?"

"I am Temark. I am from the Village of Neva in the Kingdom of Stordt."

"Temark, I am called Sanuri; what are you doing so far from home?"

"They came for us in the middle of the night; they come for us every night," Temark said fearfully.

"Who comes for you?"

"The priests, or at least we thought they were priests," said Temark. "They wear the robes. At first my village welcomed them and brought them into our homes so that King Roch's men would not find them; as the King has killed all of the holy men in our kingdom."

"Drink this," said the Sanuri as he handed Temark a hot cup of coffee. "Please go on."

"Soon people started disappearing from our village; we do not know if they have been killed or enslaved," Temark continued. "Then some of the villagers saw it was the priests who were taking our people. Two nights ago the priests came for me and my neighbors. I ran and have been following the river north ever since."

"How did you end up in the river?"

"I heard the Gants screaming and was afraid, so I pushed a log into the water and I have been paddling upstream; I fell off from the log."

"Well then, it is most fortunate that I happened to be taking a walk along the shore," said the Sanuri. "Tell me more about these priests."

"There were five of them, men who wore the robes of priests," said Temark. "They came to our village weeks ago and asked us for food and shelter. Of course we would help them. Soon after their arrival entire families would go missing from their homes during the night. Finally some villagers saw the priests dragging a man from his home."

"What did these men look like?"

"We rarely saw their faces as they always kept their hoods pulled up over their heads."

"Did they tell you their names or say why they came to your village?"

"If they did; I do not know of it."

"You say they are still there?"

"They were when I left."

"Temark we will return to your village in the morning."

"But what are you going to do?" asked Temark fearfully. "You are only one."

The Sanuri smiled, "I have long ago learned that The Great Ruler always takes me where I need to go; not necessarily where I expect to go."

"My Lord are you saying The Great Ruler sent you?" asked Temark with surprise.

"I do not believe that our meeting was a coincidence," replied the Sanuri. "I believe that The Great Ruler will use me to help your people."

The Sanuri and Temark traveled the entire next day and well into the night. "My home is over there," said Temark as he pointed to a modest dwelling in the darkness. The Sanuri entered the home first, through the back door with Temark walking fearfully behind him.

"Shall I light a candle My Lord?" asked Temark.

"Wait," whispered the Sanuri as he listened to a sound he heard ever so slightly. "Temark do not move; we are not alone."

Temark stood motionless; the pounding of his own heart was all that he could hear. The end of the Sanuri's staff began to glow and soon the soft light illuminated the entire dwelling. The Sanuri immediately looked at the floor expecting to see snakes for his senses told him they were close at hand. The Sanuri did not see any snakes or any other living creatures.

"Temark can you tell me if anything seems to have been moved or is missing?"

"My Lord from what I can see everything seems to be in its place," replied Temark fearfully.

"You said the priests came for you, how do you know they were coming for you?"

"I heard a noise and saw the five priests outside; two were walking towards my neighbors' front door and two were walking towards my front door. I ran out the back door and just kept running," Temark explained.

"Something is not right here," said the Sanuri. "I can feel it." The home was but one room decorated sparsely with furniture. The Sanuri walked through the home looking in and behind things. Finally he opened the front door.

"What is that?" gasped Temark.

The Sanuri walked closer to the door. He saw that an image of a coiled red snake with green eyes and a yellow tongue had been drawn on the outside of the front door. The Sanuri recognized this as the same symbol he had seen drawn on Archetenus' saddlebags, so many months earlier. A cold and evil energy was emitted from the drawing; as the Sanuri studied it he realized the drawing was moving.

The Sanuri stared at the image of the snake then he realized it appeared to be breathing. He saw its yellow tongue flickering, then the tail moved. Temark walked closer to the door to look at the image.

"What sort of dark magic is this?" asked Temark almost in tears.

"This particular image of the red snake is the Mark of Satan," explained the Sanuri. "I have seen this image drawn before as a warning that a curse had been placed upon that person. But never before have I seen the image come to life like this."

"I have been cursed?" gasped Temark.

The Sanuri did not answer immediately as he was inspecting the image. "Temark do you have a cellar?"

"Yes My Lord."

"Go and hide in the cellar until I tell you it is safe to come out."

"But why My Lord?"

"I do not think this image is a warning or a curse," said the Sanuri. "I think it is a messenger and I believe we will have company soon."

Temark reluctantly climbed the wooden ladder down into his cellar. As afraid as Temark was for his own life, he did not want to leave the Sanuri to battle the priests alone. Temark lit a candle and inspected the cellar; when he realized that nothing was out of the ordinary he blew the flame out so it would not be seen by unwelcomed visitors.

After Temark closed the cellar door behind him, the Sanuri put the palm of his hand against the breathing snake that had been affixed to the door. Instantly the snake, the Mark of Satan, began to wither and collapse from the Sanuri's touch. There was a puff of smoke and the evil talisman was gone.

The Sanuri waited until the snake had sent out its message before he destroyed it. Knowing it would be easier if the men dressed as priests came looking for him. The Sanuri turned and walked out of the back door of the house and into the darkness of the night.

The Sanuri's wait was not long; as he watched the five ominous figures appear in the darkness; they moved stealthily towards the front door of Temark's home. As all five of the men stepped onto the front porch of the house, the Sanuri's voice rang out, "Oh harbingers of death what is your purpose here?" Each of the five men quickly turned around but could not see the man behind the voice.

"Show your faces; only true cowards hide from the light," called out the Sanuri as he walked out of his concealment in the tree line and into an open area facing the five men. The five men ran towards the Sanuri without making a sound. The Sanuri thrust the end of his staff into the stomach of the first assailant to reach him; as the man doubled over in pain the Sanuri administered another blow to the back of the man's head with the staff.

The second assailant grabbed the Sanuri from behind with both of his arms. The Sanuri thrust his head backwards violently hitting the man in the forehead. As the man let go of his hold, the Sanuri quickly spun around and thrust the end of his staff into the man's throat, killing him instantly.

The Sanuri felt a searing pain in his left upper arm as he spun around to face the next attacker. Blood ran from the Sanuri's knife wound as he blocked another blow aimed at his head. All of his attackers wielded unique crescent shaped knives. The Sanuri grabbed one of the men by the throat but instead of a man's voice he heard a demon scream as its' throat began to wither and to dissolve into ashes. The two remaining assailants stopped momentarily when they saw what was happening to their companion.

The Sanuri faced them as the remains of the third assailant dissolved into a pile of ashes on the ground. A bright light started to surround the Sanuri, a light of such purity and intensity that the two remaining men were blinded and fell to their knees. "Tell me what you have done with the people of this village," demanded the Sanuri. The men did not speak. "Tell me where they are," demanded the Sanuri again.

One of the men started to laugh, softly at first then it gained in volume and depth. "Your old friend Sporos says hello," said the man sarcastically.

The Sanuri took two steps forward and placed the palm of his left hand on the top of the head of the man who had laughed. Still holding his staff in his right hand; the Sanuri pointed it at the second man who was kneeling on the ground. "Again, tell me what you have done with the villagers."

Steam started to rise from the man's head as the darkness of the demon dissolved under the Sanuri's touch. When the man screamed in pain the Sanuri removed his hand and pulled the priest's hood back exposing the face of the being. "You are Beltrad," spat the Sanuri with disgust as he looked upon the hideous contortion. "You are the species the demons designed to clean up after them; like a stable boy you sweep up their feces."

As the Sanuri spoke to the first creature he saw the second creature move in the corner of his eye. The Sanuri turned only his head and stared at the Beltrad; the force of the Sanuri's gaze caused the creature to sit back down on the ground. "Now I command you creatures of darkness; tell me what you have done with the villagers," the Sanuri said with authority.

Unable to defy the command of a messenger of The Great Ruler, the creature whose face was exposed began to spit and gurgle as he tried to resist speaking. The Sanuri watched as the creature appeared to choke on the lies he intended to tell, but the Sanuri's command would allow nothing but the truth.

The Beltrad coughed and spit up a bile that appeared like tar. The Sanuri recognized this substance as the rancid filth that covered the floors of many of the dark underworlds. Finally the creature could no longer resist the command and said in a barely audible voice, "They are being kept in the caves near the River Nebu."

"No," screamed the second Beltrad. As the Sanuri looked at him this creature could feel a tightening around his throat.

"Are they alive?" demanded the Sanuri.

"Yes," choked out the first Beltrad.

"Why have you taken them?" asked the Sanuri sternly.

"The Vessel will need to feed when he starts to transform."

"Are you referring to King Roch?"

The Beltrad collapsed onto the ground choking as he tried to resist answering the question. The creature started to vomit the tar-like substance as he fought against answering. "Yes," spat the creature.

"What is Roch a vessel for?"

"The ascension of Omnibus" said the first Beltrad as he grasped his throat with both hands and squirmed on the ground.

"Omnibus," repeated the Sanuri in disbelief. "He is a darkness from the ancient times; imprisoned in the great vastness of Solv, he has no power here."

"He had great power once and will again," choked out the first Beltrad with a laugh.

"When is this transformation to take place?"

"We do not know," replied the Beltrad.

"How is this transformation taking place?"

Once again the first Beltrad fought aggressively against answering. As the Sanuri watched this creature writhe on the ground, he turned to the second Beltrad which he had silenced. "I command you to tell me by what means King Roch is the Vessel for Omnibus." The second Beltrad too started to choke on his deceitful answers.

The first Beltrad finally spoke, "The Insidiae came to be as soon as darkness was called into this world. They are the conspirators, the opposition."

"They are the opposition to what?"

"To The Great Ruler, of course," spat the second Beltrad.

"How did the Insidiae come about?"

"They are the first of creation to call darkness to this world," the first Beltrad tried to say with a sneer.

"Who is in the Insidiae?"

"They are many, as grains of sand on a beach, we do not know them all," replied the first Beltrad.

"Who do you get your orders from?"

"The high priests at the monastery at Malga," the second Beltrad said as he choked upon his hellish bile.

"Their names, tell me their names."

Both of the Beltrads fought against answering the command, "Meekos, Pravis and Tenebrae," spat the first Beltrad in anguish.

"The caves you speak of; are they near Roch's castle; are they the caves the demon Demetries used?"

Both of the unholy creatures rolled around on the ground as they tried not to answer the question. "Yes," cried out the second Beltrad. The light surrounding the Sanuri grew in intensity. The creatures of darkness could not withstand the light and dissolved into puddles of the hellish bile they were made from.

The Sanuri left his boca a distance from the caves so as not to be detected. He moved quietly through the forest; listening for sounds of disruption. The Sanuri was almost to the entrance of the cave that Demetries had used; when the Sanuri felt that he was being watched. He quickly hid behind a large boulder and surveyed the area. The Sanuri did not hear or see anything unusual.

Suddenly he had a vision, as if he was looking through another creature's eyes and saw himself behind the boulder. The Sanuri looked up and saw four ravens circling overhead. He started to chant as he watched the ravens. Soon a gust of wind of great intensity hurled the demonic birds from the area.

The blackness of the night; concealed the Sanuri as he slowly made his way towards the cave's entrance. An unsettling feeling filled the Sanuri when he saw that there were no guards anywhere in sight. He entered the threshold of the dark cave and leaned against one of the cold walls. The Sanuri made his way down the long and narrow corridor by using the wall as a guide. He could hear the slithering of snakes as he made his way through the darkness.

Finally the Sanuri saw light flickering from a side chamber. The Sanuri peeked into the chamber and saw a massive altar standing against the far wall. There was a large fire burning in a pit in the center of the room and numerous lit candles set about. Clay bowls of blood and human body parts were placed in a circular design around the altar. The chamber was filled with snakes of every variety, but the Sanuri saw no other living creatures.

The Sanuri stepped back into the darkness of the corridor and leaned against the cold wall. "Something does not seem right here," he thought as he listened for any sounds. "The inhabitants of an entire village are supposed to be held hostage here and yet there is almost complete silence." The Sanuri now wondered how long the ravens had been watching him. He turned and walked back into the lit chamber. He stood against the wall looking at all of the snakes that seemed oblivious to his presence. A smile came across his face when the Sanuri saw what he had been looking for.

Curled up behind the altar was a large red snake watching him. As the Sanuri crossed the chamber towards the altar, snakes of every sort moved out of his way. He deliberately moved some of the bowls that surrounded the altar so that by breaking the circle he would disrupt whatever power they were to bring forth. The Sanuri reached for the snake, which coiled back then lunged at him. The Sanuri caught the snake as it flew towards him. He grabbed it behind the head with his left hand as he held the staff in his right hand.

The eight foot snake started to wrap itself around the Sanuri's torso. The muscular body of the beast slowly tighten its hold on the Sanuri, squeezing the air from his lungs. He maintained his grasp on the snake's neck as it continued to lunge at his face with its long protruding fangs.

The Sanuri heard movement, he quickly looked towards the doorway to the chamber and did not see anyone; then instinctively he looked at the floor. All the snakes in the chamber were now moving towards him; a large snake started to wrap itself around the Sanuri's ankles.

Suddenly a loud and ominous voice thundered through the chamber. "Old friend you cannot defeat me," the voice yelled, then it started to laugh, a loud and maniacal laugh that echoed through the stone chamber. "How can this be?" thought the Sanuri as he recognized the voice of Sporos. Realizing that the voice was meant to distract him; the Sanuri returned his attention to the snakes.

The Sanuri pointed the staff, which he still grasped in his right hand, at the snakes coiling around his feet and legs. A high frequency sound started to emit from the staff. The sound became louder and louder and as it increased in volume the snakes shrank away from it. The creatures slithered away from the Sanuri and out of the chamber, dispersing themselves in far regions of the caves.

The red snake, the handmaiden of Satan himself; still maintained its hold on the Sanuri's body. The Sanuri stared into the eyes of the beast. His look penetrated the eyes and brain of the snake as the Sanuri sought to discover the source of the malevolence. As the Sanuri stared through the creature his energy was being transported through time and space. And then the Sanuri saw it; a death mask; a hideous, contorted face of evil.

The Sanuri stared at the being so deformed by its hatred and rage. "You are not Sporos, what do you call yourself?" demanded the Sanuri.

"You do not recognize me?" laughed the being. "You have seen my face before; in the eyes of men. You have felt my presence in your world. And yet you do not know me?"

"I command you to tell me who you are?" ordered the Sanuri as he squeezed the neck of the great snake.

The being began to shake as its face contorted. "I am Omnibus" screamed the being. "I created nightmares. I am the darkness that terrifies demons and sorcerers. I came to your world when the Insidiae cried into the vastness and I changed mankind forever."

"If you are so powerful then why have you been imprisoned in Solv since time untold?" asked the Sanuri sarcastically.

Omnibus screamed with rage; then he laughed. The maniacal laughter echoed in the stone cavern; which soon began to shake from the powerful vibrations of the demon's voice.

"I know of your plans to use Roch as a vessel for your ascension," said the Sanuri mockingly. "You have no power in this world demon and you never will."

Consumed with rage, Omnibus bellowed loudly. The red snake loosened its grip on the Sanuri and began to flail wildly in the air. As Omnibus' rage grew in intensity the snake thrashed and whirled harder and harder until it flew out of the Sanuri's grasp. The snake flew through the air in convulsions finally landing against the unholy altar. The snake hit the altar with such supernatural force that the altar crumbled and fell to the ground; exposing a thick wooden door in the wall of the chamber.

The Sanuri picked up the broken body of the red snake and looked into its eyes. The snake was dead, severing his connection with Omnibus. The Sanuri threw the snake on the ground and kicked over the remaining bowls of blood that survived the destruction of the altar. He walked over to the wooden door and tried to open it. Although the Sanuri could find no physical lock on the door it did not budge. The Sanuri carefully examined the door a second time, then tried to push it open but once again without success.

"The lock must be of dark magic," thought the Sanuri. He started to chant, focusing his energy on the lock. As the Sanuri chanted he could feel the door resist the energy he was projecting at it. The Sanuri continued to chant for about twenty minutes, then tried the door again; but it still would not open. The Sanuri picked up his staff and pointed it at the door, but the power of the staff could not open the magical lock. He was looking around the chamber for an axe when he heard a voice.

"Did you consider asking for help?" asked The Lion as it entered the unholy chamber. The Sanuri smiled when he saw his old friend.

"I did not want to bother you."

"Bother me!" exclaimed The Lion. "It is not dark magic that is preventing you from opening that door, it is me."

"But why?" asked the Sanuri with astonishment.

"Because you are not yet ready to face the evil you will find behind that door," The Lion said. "I will walk with you."

The heavy wooden door opened before The Lion and the Sanuri. The Lion crossed the threshold first. Putrid air filled the nostrils of the Sanuri when he entered the dark corridor that lay behind the door. The two beings walked in silence. Soon they found an ancient stone staircase that descended into great darkness. The winding steps were narrow and wet. The Sanuri wondered how the steps could be wet as he slowly walked down them.

The air was dank and became heavier as they descended into the darkness. After what seemed like a very long time to the Sanuri, he heard moaning. The moaning sounded pitiful and frail to the Sanuri, his heart went out to the crying being. The Lion stopped suddenly. The stairs ended at a small landing, which opened to four separate corridors. The Sanuri followed The Lion as it entered the second corridor. The smell of decaying flesh filled the air and the moaning grew louder.

The Lion stopped. The Sanuri could see little in the thick darkness. Suddenly the corridor and the chamber they were facing were filled with light. Tears filled the eyes of the Sanuri as he looked at the scene before them.

"These are the people you have been seeking," said The Lion as he entered the chamber. The Sanuri looked at dozens of men, women and children who were shackled to the walls with thick and heavy chains. All of the people looked as if they were dying. The people covered their eyes from the intensity of the light that The Lion cast.

"What has happened to these people?" asked the Sanuri.

"The Beltrad are gathering food for Omnibus. He will be weak after the transformation and will need to eat," said The Lion. Suddenly The Lion let out a thunderous roar and the heavy metal shackles fell off from each of the prisoners. "Do not be afraid," said The Lion. "Help each other up. Follow this staircase; you will come out in a large chamber. Walk through the chamber and turn left, follow that corridor to freedom." The Lion turned around walking back towards the landing with the Sanuri following him.

"But those people are too weak to make it back to their villages," the Sanuri said.

584

"They will be healed when they step into the light of day," The Lion replied and stopped before the third chamber which was closed off by a thick wooden door. The Sanuri started to walk forward but The Lion stopped him as the wooden door opened before them. The Sanuri saw a group of thirteen Beltrad with their backs to the door. The Beltrad were focused on the four people they had chained to the walls of the chamber.

"You have company," said the Sanuri.

The Beltrad turned around, still holding the instruments of torture in their hands that they had been using on the four victims. The Beltrad charged at The Lion and the Sanuri. The Sanuri lunged forward to do battle with the screaming demons; but by time the Sanuri reached his adversaries all that was left were thirteen small dead red snakes lying on the ground. The Sanuri hurried over to the people who were chained to the wall.

"They are still alive," said The Lion, as the chains fell from the wrists of the victims. All four of the people collapsed onto the ground. "Touch each of them with your staff," commanded The Lion. As the Sanuri touched them, the people were healed.

"Go now and help the others out of these horrendous caves," said The Lion. The four people thanked The Lion profusely and ran to the stairs to help the other prisoners out. The Lion turned around and walked back towards the landing.

The Lion and the Sanuri walked in silence towards the fourth door. The smell of rotting flesh filled their nostrils long before they reached the entrance. "There are many different kinds of hells in these worlds; you do realize we are walking through one now," The Lion said somberly. The door opened and light filled the chamber exposing piles of dead bodies heaped upon each other. The corpses were in varying degrees of decomposition.

"Are these prisoners who died in here?" asked the Sanuri sadly.

"No," replied The Lion. "These poor souls were murdered by their friends and families."

"I do not understand."

"For sport the Beltrad will sometimes give the villagers choices; kill someone else or be taken by the Beltrad. The demons enjoy the torment this inflicts upon people. Often times the Beltrad will specify the person to be killed," explained The Lion. "So although the person who did the killing lives, they are now destroyed because of their deeds."

"Why are these bodies stored here?"

"The same as the other victims, food for the Vessel and Omnibus."

"Didn't any of the villagers rise up against the Beltrad?"

"In most cases the villagers could have stopped all of this but they were crippled by their fears," said The Lion as he started walking towards the landing.

The Lion walked back to the landing and stood in front of the first door which he had originally walked passed. The Sanuri joined him within moments. Neither of the beings spoke as the door to the chamber opened and it was filled with light. Two Beltrad ran towards them with curved knives in their hands. Before the Beltrads could reach The Lion and the Sanuri they dissolved into puddles of hellish muck on the floor of the cavern.

The chamber was filled with snakes of every sort which slithered quickly across the floor as if sensing there were powerful intruders. Across the chamber there was another unholy altar with what appeared to be a large tank placed in front of it.

"What is that?" asked the Sanuri as he pointed towards the tank.

"That is where Roch's body will be placed for the transformation. The Insidiae planned to pour the blood of the victims, we just released, over his body. Look behind the altar, you will find The Chalice of Ascension in a small wooden box," said The Lion.

"But I thought the chalice was in a cave in Ryed," said the Sanuri with astonishment.

"You had a vision but you did not ask for clarification; you will know better next time," replied The Lion. The snakes moved from the Sanuri's path as he walked across the floor of the stone chamber. He looked behind the altar and found a wooden box. The Sanuri opened the box and found the holy treasure wrapped in linen. He inspected the chalice. "It appears to be undamaged," he said as he walked back towards The Lion. "I don't understand why you would allow the filth of hell to touch such a holy relic."

The Lion smiled benevolently. "We allowed them to bring some holiness into this hell world. Don't you think that would have an effect on the darkness?"

"I didn't think of it like that," said the Sanuri. "Does this mean that the transformation has been stopped?"

"Come," said The Lion as he turned to ascend the stone staircase. "Omnibus is already in a sort of state of transformation. There is a strong connection between the demon and Roch; as well as those who have sold their souls to be pawns in this most unholy plan. The energies needed for this feat have already been put into motion and we will let that play out."

"Why?" asked the Sanuri in disbelief.

"As always the people involved still have choices to make and we never give up hope that they will make the right choices," The Lion said. "And there are things now in motion that are beyond even your understanding my friend."

"There is a question that has vexed me for some time," said the Sanuri as he and The Lion walked up the stone steps in the hellish caverns.

"Ask your question but I think you already know the answer," responded The Lion.

"I know there is much I do not understand," said the Sanuri. "But truly why has Roch been allowed to live?"

"As much of a monster as he is, he does have a role that must be played out," The Lion continued. "The people of this world have free choice. Some of them chose to bring this horrible darkness onto their kind. We need someone from this world to take the stand against this darkness and to tell Omnibus he is not wanted here. It will take only one voice to stop the darkness," said The Lion. "There will be a time when humans realize the power they have to destroy the demons they call to."

Chapter XXXVI
Politicians and Kings

Fahron, his wife Isadore and their three children Timothy, Chaez and Tabeth were having dinner together and as most evenings Timothy and his father were arguing. Timothy was born the same year as Matthew; both of them were a year younger than Stephan. Although the three boys were almost raised together as children; Timothy never fit in with Matthew and Stephan.

Timothy was not a warrior or a man of integrity for that matter. Timothy enjoyed his father's wealth which he tried to use as a status symbol of his own self-importance. Timothy had always been jealous of the bond between Matthew and Stephan; a bond he continually tried to break during his years.

Timothy did not take after his father in any way. Fahron was a good man who had worked his way up the ranks of the Lentz Military until he became one of the ruling men

of that kingdom. Fahron was a brave and battle savvy warrior who was extremely loyal to King Mathas. Timothy's arrogance and laziness embarrassed Fahron but it was Timothy's ethics that really brought his father shame. Fahron never felt that he could speak out against Juleta for he feared his own son would one day bring dishonor to their family.

"I just can't believe it," yelled Timothy. "The King is allowing that criminal to attend the morning staff meetings."

"And why does this bother you?" Fahron asked.

"Father, I have never been included in those meetings."

"And why would you?" Fahron asked. "In the short time that Thaos has been here he has done more to protect and serve this kingdom than you have your entire life. He has earned his right to attend those meetings."

"I have done my part."

"How? Spending every night in taverns trying to impress people with the money that I have earned is not admired by anyone."

"Well I have plans," Timothy said trying to impress his father. Fahron ate his dinner without responding to Timothy. "Well Father, don't you want to know what my plans are?"

"Timothy you always talk big about plans yet you have never done a hard day's work in your life."

"I plan to ask Mathas if I can be an ambassador," Timothy said with arrogance. "I want to be a politician."

"I will admit you have the character of a politician," Fahron said sarcastically. "But I have to warn you that Mathas has found little use for politicians."

"Mathew and Angelina want you and Nikki to come," Stephan said as he, Claudius and Thaos rode to the King's castle for their morning meeting.

"I don't think that would be a good idea," Thaos said. "I don't think Raul and Simon would be happy to have me in their home."

"Well, Bella and I are going," Claudius announced. "I have never met King Sudfad but I have heard good things and would like to meet him."

"Sorren and his family are going," Stephan said trying to persuade Thaos to go to Wetpr with them for Raul's and Simon's homecoming celebrations. "There will be a lot of people you know. And Matthew and Angelina have a home there, we can stay with them."

Thaos started laughing. "Why are you trying so hard to talk me into going?"

"I stayed there for six weeks when Matthew got married and had a great time. And according to Matthew the Ruala and Shettee warriors who saved Raul and Simon are coming also. And all the warriors there are going to share their fighting styles. I have never met Rualas or Shettees before."

"Now you may have changed my mind," Thaos said with a grin.

When Claudius, Stephan and Thaos walked into Mathas' study they found the King talking with Fahron and Timothy. "Thaos this is my son Timothy," Fahron said.

Thaos extended his hand but Timothy would not take it; he just glared at Thaos. "Have I ever done anything to offend you?" Thaos asked coldly.

Stephan did not like Timothy and now was angered by his rude behavior towards Thaos. "Thaos don't let him bother you; he is not a warrior and doesn't know how to act around one," Stephan said sharply.

"How dare you speak to me like that," Timothy said with indignation.

Stephan smiled, "If you want me to take back my words I will gladly step outside with you."

Timothy looked around the room expecting Fahron or Mathas to stand up for him, when neither of the men said anything, Timothy said hauntingly, "I came here because I have business with the King."

"No you don't," Mathas said with disgust. "Your behavior tells me everything I need to know about you." Mathas turned to Fahron. "My friend I am sorry."

"Don't be," Fahron said. "I would not have given him that position either. I don't know where I went wrong with that boy."

"This is not over," Timothy yelled and stormed out of the study.

"Mathas I believe my oldest child has crippled me as Juleta did you. I think it is time for me to disinherit him and force him into the world; perhaps he will finally learn how to be a man."

Mathas waited for Claudius, Stephan and Thaos to pour themselves coffee and to take seats before he started the meeting. "Timothy was asking Mathas if he could be an ambassador for the kingdom," Fahron said as he sipped his coffee.

"Do you have ambassadors?" Thaos asked.

"No," Claudius replied. "Fahron may I speak freely?"

"Of course, my friend."

"I understand your feelings about your son; but look at what happened when Mathas disinherited Juleta. If you have Timothy in the house at least you can watch him."

"I hear your words but my son would live off my money without ever doing a day's work. I hope it is not too late to teach him some lessons," Fahron said sadly.

Matthew was standing in the doorway of the study listening to the conversation. "Claudius I do not believe Timothy has it in him to be as dangerous as Juleta. I think he is too afraid and would prefer others to do his dirty work. If he has no money, well..."

"My dear, you know the boys are going to want to spend some time with their families first," Sudfad said as he looked over Renya's shoulder at the lists she was preparing for the celebrations.

"I know dear, that is why I am planning a lot of activities to keep everyone busy until Raul and Simon want to join their guests. We will have games and competitions held in different locations as well as a variety of musicians playing around the grounds. I won't have the ball until their second night home. I wrote to Matthew and asked that he and Angelina come early to help us with the preparations.

Sudfad smiled as he listened to the excitement in Renya's voice. "Where is everyone, it is so quiet around here?" he asked.

"Laurel, Vitomas and Annabelle are preparing guest rooms. Alexander is building a stage and Marie is bringing her entire family in to help with preparations and serving. And Petra and Kyra are playing in the back," Renya looked up from her lists and started to laugh. "I was watching Petra and Kyra and I think she has a crush on him but Petra is oblivious of it."

Two nights later Fahron and Timothy were having another quarrel during dinner. "I want to go," Timothy said loudly.

"Timothy do not yell at the dinner table," Isadore scolded.

Timothy said, "I could ask Matthew."

"Matthew did invite the family," Fahron said. "But we are staying behind to govern the kingdom so Claudius and Mathas can go. We will go if there is another invitation. Matthew and Angelina left for Wetpr yesterday. They are going early to help with the preparations."

"Well, I shouldn't be punished because you will be working," Timothy said with a cocky tone of voice.

"Timothy I have had enough of your self-absorbed attitude. You are an embarrassment to this family. If you do anything in Wetpr that brings dishonor on this family, I will disinherit you and ban you from the kingdom," Fahron yelled angrily.

Although Sudfad's castle was filled with chaos as the Royal Family prepared for the homecoming celebrations for Raul and Simon; time seemed to stand still for Vitomas and Annabelle. The anticipation of being reunited with their husbands filled them both with such excited energy that neither of them could sleep.

Matthew and Angelina arrived at their home in Wetpr three days after Renya had asked for their help. The Prince and Princess of Lentz worked daily from sun up to nightfall with preparations for the celebrations. Both Matthew and Angelina were organizing many of the competitions and races that would be held for the entertainment of the guests.

Matthew worked with the soldiers of Wetpr on formations and marches that they would perform while Angelina helped Annabelle and Vitomas with the many invitations. Renya was directing all of the activities and every other day would give the women long shopping lists of items she needed them to purchase. As gifts to Laurel, Vitomas, Annabelle and Angelina; Renya had dressmakers design and sew gowns for them to wear for the dances that were planned.

Time too seemed to stand still for Simon and Raul, as they were anxious to return home to their families. Both men worked hard trying to get their bodies back into shape before returning home. But every day Simon and Raul were painfully reminded just how weak they still were, as great fatigue frequently overtook them both.

Like Renya, Ibula was a born leader. Now that Raul and Simon did not need her constant attention; Ibula took over all the aspects of preparing her peoples for their trip to the world below. Ibula was looking forward to meeting Renya, a woman she was starting to feel a kinship with, as they sent almost daily correspondence to each other in the planning of the ceremonies. Ibula and Thedes were impressed when Renya asked them for recipes of their delicacies and information about their traditions.

At Renya's request, Thedes and Ibula sent her details of competitions and games their tribes held. "Your mother says that your cousin Matthew is organizing all of the competitions and wants diagrams of things we need built." Ibula said as she served Raul, Simon and Thedes breakfast. "She is making us feel very welcomed."

"Wait until you meet her," Raul said warmly. "Mother has this quality of making everyone feel like one of her children. I think you will like her."

"I like her already. You know we write to each other every day," Ibula said as she put two large platters of meat on the table.

"I am making your father a Gafet," Thedes said. "Do you think he will use it?"

"I can tell you he will want to learn how to use it," Simon said. "Father is still quite the warrior.

"They're coming, they're coming," screamed Petra with excitement as he ran into the castle, "Papa they're coming."

Sudfad, Renya and Marie were the first people to run out to the front lawn, as Petra was running through the castle alerting the rest of the family and guests. "Why, I have never seen such a thing," gasped Marie as they saw the sky darken with the bodies of hundreds of Ruala and Shettee warriors.

Renya started to cry as she watched a sight that was inconceivable to her. "They are up so high," Renya whispered. Sudfad put his arm around her as they all stared at the sky.

"Where are they?" called Annabelle as she and Vitomas ran out to the front lawn. Marie pointed to the sky and the two young princesses were speechless. Matthew, Angelina and most of the visiting members of the Nordes Tribe were the next to run out to the front lawn; they were followed by the ruling families of Lentz, soon the front courtyard was filled with family and friends. Although the group was large, it was uniquely quiet, as the people watched the unbelievable.

The two Ruala warriors who carried Raul and Simon landed first, followed by Ibula, who was carrying Thedes. Manu the King of the Rualas and Mateo the Chief of the Healers landed simultaneously. Vitomas and Annabelle ran to their husbands, flying into their arms. The crowd started to clap as they watched the Princes of Wetpr embrace their wives.

The emotions of the moment overruled all else as tears flowed freely at the homecoming of the Princes. All of the Ruala warriors landed as Raul and Simon hugged and kissed their crying wives. Raul tapped Simon on the shoulder, "We need to make some introductions," Raul said. And with that gesture, worlds started to collide as the beings of three different species met on this festive occasion.

After embracing her sons, Renya sought out Ibula and these two women of different worlds embraced; starting a relationship that would change their lives. "My dear, it is so good to finally meet you," Renya said as she squeezed Ibula's hands. "Raul said you looked like Vitomas but I never imagined how much. Have you met her yet?"

"No," Ibula said. "I couldn't see her face when she was hugging Raul."

Renya took Ibula's hand and walked over to Raul and Vitomas. "Vitomas," Renya said. Vitomas turned and she and Ibula stared at each other in disbelief for a moment before speaking.

"I told you two, it would be like looking in a mirror," Raul said with a grin.

"Thank you," Vitomas said and hugged Ibula tightly. Simon walked over with Annabelle, who he introduced to Ibula. Annabelle was crying so hard she couldn't speak, so she just hugged Ibula.

Almost an hour passed as introductions were made and people mingled together. The members of the Ruala and Shettee tribes were just as excited and curious to meet the guests at the castle as the humans were to meet these beings of two ancient civilizations. A trumpet blew and a soldier announced, "The King will speak."

Sudfad and Renya now stood on the top of the staircase leading into the castle. "My family and I want to thank all of you for being part of this celebration. At this time we would like you to come into the Great Hall in the castle for food and refreshments and we will start taking you to your rooms." As the crowd followed Sudfad and Renya into the Great Hall, Raul, Vitomas, Simon and Annabelle walked to the playroom where the nurses were tending to the children.

"I hope they recognize us," Simon said as he and Annabelle walked with their arms around each other.

"Wait until you see them," Vitomas said as she was wiping tears from her face. "All the boys are running around like little wild men."

"You go in first," Annabelle said as they reached the door to the playroom. When Simon and Raul walked into the room, Abigail was helping the boys paint pictures, the children were sitting with their backs to the door. "Your papas are here," Abigail said with a warm smile.

When the boys turned around they started squealing and running. Alexander and Anthony ran to Simon, Little Sudfad ran to Raul, but Samuel seem confused and looked at both Simon and Raul. "Come here son," Raul said and picked him up. Annabelle and Vitomas stood in the doorway crying as they watched the tearful reunion between their husbands and their sons.

Annabelle left the playroom, returning a few minutes later holding Arianna. Annabelle walked up to Simon, "Meet your daughter." Simon was holding both of his sons and his eyes were filled with tears so he could not see the baby very well for the first moment. Simon put Anthony and Alexander down and held his baby daughter for the first time. "Raul, look how beautiful she is," Simon said and kissed the baby on the forehead. Raul turned, and Annabelle could see that he too was crying. "You are going to have to beat the boys away from that one," Raul kidded.

"Let's all of us go to the west wing, now," Vitomas said. As they walked the short distance from the playroom she continued. "Sudfad and Renya are not expecting us to take part in any of the ceremonies today or tonight, this is our time to be alone."

"Simon, I stayed here with Vitomas the entire time you were gone, so we thought we could just all spend this day and maybe tonight together in the west wing," Annabelle said.

"That's alright with me, if it's alright with Raul," said Simon.

"Of course," Raul said then smiled as they entered the living quarters. There were pictures and little signs from the children displayed all around the parlor. There were wrapped gift boxes piled on every table and trays of food. "Marie made some special things for your homecoming. Apparently she used to make you fudge when you were boys, well you each have a pan of fudge now," Annabelle said smiling. "Simon, the children and I have been staying in that room," Annabelle said as she pointed to the bedroom closest to Raul's and Vitomas'.

"Now you two just sit down," Vitomas said. She poured two glasses of whiskey and handed one to each man as Annabelle filled plates for each of them.

"Please tell me all of these gifts aren't for us," Raul said laughing.

"We might have gotten a little carried away," Annabelle said as she set a plate of food next to each of the men. "We missed you so much; it made us feel better to buy you things."

"I think you made the shopkeepers feel better too," Simon joked as he looked at all of the boxes.

"Honey let me hold Arianna while you open gifts," Annabelle said as she took the baby from Simon.

"You have to open these first," Vitomas said as she handed Raul and Simon each a beautifully wrapped gift. Both gifts were identical in size and shape. Raul and Simon tore the paper off from their presents. The two men sat in silence as they paged through the homemade books.

"We didn't want you to miss the boys growing up, so we made these daily diaries of the children," Vitomas said warmly.

Raul was becoming emotional as he read the pages, the words were written as if the children were speaking. The books contained drawings, paintings and baby teeth as well as swatches of their hair.

Simon was the first to speak and he was having difficulty getting the words out. "These are wonderful, thank you so much."

"These are the best gifts you could have given us," Raul said as he grasped Vitomas' hand.

The two couples spent the rest of the day playing with their children, opening gifts and enjoying each other's company. Overwhelmed by their emotions, their words could not convey the happiness they were all sharing this day. "We have another surprise for you, after we put the babies down," Annabelle said as she was clearing the dinner dishes from the table.

"Oh yeah," Simon said with a smile.

"Your mother took us shopping a lot while you were gone," Vitomas said with a grin. "One day we asked her what she thought you two would like for gifts," Vitomas started to laugh and looked at Annabelle who finished the story.

"Renya took us to a store where she buys all of her nightgowns, the ones she wears for your father," Annabelle said. "You should see the sexy things she wears."

"I don't want to think about that," Simon said with a grin.

"She bought us some nightgowns," Annabelle said and she and Vitomas both started to laugh. "Renya said, 'Girls my boys will appreciate these; a lot more than those daggers and swords you are buying for them.'"

"Mother knows us too well," Raul said and laughed.

The next morning Raul, Simon and their families joined their guests in the Great Hall as breakfast was being served to all. After greeting their parents, Raul and Simon sat with Ibula and Thedes. "Sorry we abandoned you," Simon apologized.

"Simon, we all understood that you and Raul needed time with your families," Ibula said. "We have been having fun; there was a horse race yesterday and some competitions and a dance last night. Apparently the Grand Ball is tonight."

"Tell them the rest," Thedes said as he carved a large steak.

Ibula laughed, "Thedes hasn't stopped eating since we got here. Our chambers are wonderful; I mean they are suitable for royalty. Last night when we went to our bedroom we found all sorts of beautifully wrapped gifts from your parents, your wives and your children. It was so sweet."

"After breakfast we want you to spend some time with us and our families," Raul said.

"Here, I grabbed a couple of these for you," Thedes said as he handed Raul and Simon each a piece of paper. "We weren't sure if you had seen them."

"No we haven't," said Simon as he read the lists of activities that were being held over the next two weeks.

"I will say Mother has outdone herself this time," Raul said with a laugh.

"Now I know you two are going to enter some of those competitions but remember you aren't as strong as you think you are," Ibula warned.

Thedes started to laugh, "Honey you are talking to them like they're your husbands too."

The Grand Ball started with a great deal of pomp and ceremony. The guests were treated to an impressive formal marching display with weapons, performed by members of the military. This was followed by a group of dancers wearing exotic costumes. Next the guests were entertained by jugglers and acrobats.

There were several long tables put together in the front of the Great Hall. The families of both King Sudfad and King Mathas were seated at these tables with Sudfad and Renya in the center. Also seated were Sorren and his family as well as Claudius and his family; both of these men felt honored to be seated at the head table. Manu, the King of the Rualas and his wife Delilia, Mateo, Ibula and Thedes were also seated at the head table. Thaos and Nikki sat at another long table with members of the Nordes Tribe.

Timothy, Fahron's son attended the ceremony although none of the other guests from Lentz wanted him there. Mathas talked Matthew and Angelina into permitting Timothy to stay at their home with the rest of the guests from their kingdom. Unbeknown to Timothy, Matthew had asked Sudfad not to honor Timothy by assigning him a seat at the head table.

Timothy had not stopped drinking since his arrival at Sudfad's castle. He planned to ask Sudfad for a job as an ambassador after the ceremonies subsided. Timothy was very social and started conversations with many of the guests, although his bragging and illusions of self-importance did not impress this gathering of warriors.

As the acrobats were leaving the stage, a trumpet blew and a soldier announced, "The King will speak." Both Sudfad and Renya walked to the center of the stage and stood together hand in hand. "They are so handsome," Ibula whispered to Thedes as she admired Sudfad in his dress uniform and Renya in a black silk and lace dress.

"There will be one more act before dinner is served," Sudfad said. "But first my beautiful wife and I want to thank all of you for helping us celebrate the homecoming of our two sons."

"These last few months have been some of the most painful in our lives; knowing that our sons were near death and there was nothing we could do to help them. For those of you who may not know the story, Raul and Simon were securing our borders from attack and inspecting every fort in the kingdom."

"They had been attacked by Hutas several times during their mission but on one occasion a great number of Hutas separated our sons from the rest of the soldiers and attacked them. Thank The Great Ruler that the Sanuri had a vision and sent Enrops to the Ice Caves of Mordv to ask some of the Ruala and Shettee warriors to help our sons."

"Many warriors answered this call and they were led by Thedes, leader of the Shettees and his beautiful wife Ibula, a warrior princess of the Rualas. Raul and Simon were all but dead when the Rualas and Shettees found them and killed the Hutas. Thedes and Ibula took our sons into their home and cared for them as if they were family."

"It was the letters that Ibula sent to us, that kept this family going as we waited, feeling so helpless to do anything for our beloved sons." Sudfad turned to the head table. "Thedes and Ibula would you please come up here." Both Thedes and Ibula were shocked and embarrassed to be called in front of such a large crowd. As they stood up Raul said to Thedes, "When you go up there face the King and Queen then bow on one knee." Thedes was about to ask Raul a question when Ibula pulled him towards the center of the stage.

Thedes and Ibula did as Raul had instructed them; as soon as they were on one knee, Sudfad pulled out his sword. "How do you repay someone for saving the lives of your children?" Sudfad asked as he looked at the audience. "There truly is nothing we can give these two warriors that would equal the gifts they have given us."

"As Renya and I tried to figure out the perfect gifts, the letters we started to receive from our sons; opened our eyes." Sudfad now looked at Thedes and spoke as he touched each of Thedes' shoulders with the blade of his sword. "From this day forward, Thedes leader of the Shettee Tribe you are adopted as a member of the Royal Family of Wetpr with the privileges that come along with such a title."

Sudfad then walked up to Ibula and said, "Ibula warrior princess of the Ruala Tribe from this day forward you are adopted as a member of the Royal Family of Wetpr with the privileges that come along with such a title. Please both of you stand." Renya handed both Ibula and Thedes a scroll containing the King's signature that they were adopted members of the family. Then Sudfad handed them each a pouch of gold coins and Renya handed both of them a small box.

"Open them," Renya said smiling.

"Your family rings," Ibula said with astonishment.

"You should recognize your stones in them," Sudfad said with a smile, "Now turn and face our guests."

Both Thedes and Ibula were overwhelmed and stunned not only by the generous gifts of the King and Queen but the standing ovation they received from the audience in the Great Hall.

"I'm going to feed Arianna," Annabelle said and kissed Simon on the cheek. Annabelle got up from the table and walked through the crowded ballroom. She glided past the dance floor in a dark blue silk gown with tiny straps. Her beauty caught the eye of darkness. Annabelle left the Great Hall and walked down the long hallway towards the east wing.

Annabelle was humming to herself. She still felt like she was floating from Simon's return home. Suddenly a sharp pain shot through Annabelle's head as Timothy grabbed her and threw her up against the stone wall. "Well pretty lady," Timothy said as he tore the right strap off from Annabelle's dress and tried to kiss her.

"Let go of me," yelled Annabelle as she was hitting Timothy with her right hand and pulling his hair with her left. "Let go!"

Timothy seemed oblivious to Annabelle's attempts to escape as he tried to tear her dress off from her body. Annabelle could hear her dress ripping and could feel his hands on her. Timothy's hot breath filled her nostrils with the smell of cigarettes and whiskey. Annabelle tried to kick Timothy when suddenly he seemed to fly through the air releasing his hold on her.

Thaos had grabbed Timothy by the back of his shirt and thrown him against the opposite wall in the hallway. Timothy turned and tried to run towards the ballroom but Thaos chased him and grabbed Timothy by the back of the neck.

Thaos spun Timothy around so they were facing each other before he punched Timothy in the stomach with his left fist. Thaos' right handed punch to Timothy's jaw was so powerful that Timothy flew out of the hallway and landed on a small table, causing the table to collapse and people to scream. Annabelle followed the two men down the hallway and now stood behind Thaos as a crowd gathered.

"Annabelle," yelled Simon fearfully as he pushed people out of his way. "Are you alright?" Simon asked as Annabelle flew into his arms.

"Yes, that man attacked me and Thaos stopped him," Annabelle said in a quivering voice. Simon let go of Annabelle and walked up to Thaos. Simon did not speak; he only nodded to Thaos who was standing over Timothy. Simon looked down at Timothy who was still lying on the floor rubbing his bloody mouth. The anger was surging through Simon as he looked at Timothy but Simon was also aware of the many guests who were crowding around them.

"Take him to the dungeons," Simon gave the order to several soldiers who had run up to them. "I will deal with him later." As two soldiers pulled Timothy to his feet, Simon asked, "You are a guest in our home, who are you?"

The whiskey that filled Timothy's veins gave him a false sense of bravado. "I am Timothy son of Fahron," he said in a loud and condescending tone.

Simon did not know who Fahron was so he looked at Thaos and asked, "Do you know him?"

"Yes, his father is a good man, unlike his son."

"What would you know of good men?" Timothy asked with a sneer.

"I know good men don't try to rape women."

Simon was turning towards Annabelle when Timothy started to speak again. "I saw the way she looked at me..." Before Timothy could finish the sentence Simon turned and punched him in the face. "Let him go," Simon ordered the soldiers as he grabbed Timothy and punched him again. Rage blinded Simon as he kept beating Timothy even after Timothy lost consciousness.

"What is going on here?" yelled Sudfad as he and Mathas pushed their way through the crowd. Each King grabbed one of Simon's arms and pulled him off from Timothy. Both Timothy and Simon were covered in blood, but it was Timothy's blood that Simon was wearing.

"He tried to rape Annabelle," Simon was so angry he could barely say the words.

Sudfad turned and looked at Annabelle; he became enraged when he saw Annabelle's torn dress. "Annabelle what happened?"

"I was going home to feed Arianna and this man grabbed me and threw me up against the wall," she hesitated for a moment. "He kept touching me and tearing my dress." Simon turned and put his arm around Annabelle as she spoke. "Thaos stopped him and saved me," Annabelle said.

Mathas looked at Thaos and asked, "What happened?"

"I was getting Nikki some water and Annabelle walked past me. I saw Timothy watching her, then he threw his cigarette down and started after her. I didn't like the look in his eyes so I followed them."

Sudfad turned to the two soldiers, "Take him to the dungeons and have the physician look at him. And I mean the physician not Gala I don't want him near any women." Then Sudfad turned to Simon, "Son take your wife home; he is mine now."

Simon and Annabelle turned to walk down the hallway; they stopped and Simon said, "Thaos come with us."

When the three were out of sight, Sudfad turned to Mathas, "Do you know this man?"

"Yes, he is the son of Fahron."

"Your friend Fahron," Sudfad said with astonishment.

"What are you going to do with Timothy?" Mathas asked.

"I will have him put to death."

"I ask you to spare his life, for his father's sake only," Mathas said sincerely. "But he must pay for his deeds, whatever else you do with him is up to you."

Simon, Annabelle and Thaos walked in silence to the east wing as the impact of the attack struck both Annabelle and Simon. As they entered their home Annabelle said, "Honey let me tend to your knuckles."

"Why don't you feed the baby first," Simon said as they walked into the kitchen. "Thaos and I are going to talk." No sooner had Annabelle left the kitchen when Alexander and Anthony ran up to Simon and Thaos. Each man picked up one of the boys. "These are my sons," Simon said with pride.

"How can you tell them apart?" Thaos asked with a laugh.

"It's hard," Simon said and grinned. "We dress them in different colors to help. The one in the green pants is Anthony and this is Alexander."

"Honey, Alexander is wearing green," Annabelle called from the bedroom.

Simon laughed at his wife's comment; as he carried two glasses to the table, putting one in front of Thaos. Since Simon was holding Anthony, he had to make a second trip to the cupboard to get the bottle of whiskey. Simon poured them each a drink.

"My Lord are the children bothering you?" asked Abigail as she came out of the children's playroom.

"No, that's alright."

"My Lord you are covered in blood are you alright?"

"Yes, Annabelle and I will still need you to watch the children; we will be returning to the ball."

Abigail left the room and Simon turned to Thaos. "Thank you for what you have done. Is there a way I can repay you?"

"Simon do not insult me; I am just glad that I saw him going after her."

Simon and Thaos sat across from each other at the kitchen table and stared at each other, as they tried to determine the other man's character. "Thaos I have heard so much about you, some of it good and some of it bad. What should I think?"

"Simon I cannot tell you what to think," Thaos said with a grin.

Simon sat back in his chair and started to smile, he was going to speak when Annabelle walked into the kitchen, still wearing the torn dress and carrying the baby. Annabelle had been listening to Simon and Thaos talk because she was afraid they would fight.

"Thaos this is our daughter Arianna," Annabelle said as she walked up to him. "Would you like to hold her?" Before Thaos could respond, Annabelle put Arianna in his arms.

"Honey he has Alexander on his lap," Simon said.

"I will take Alexander," Annabelle said with a smile as she positioned Thaos' arm under the baby's head. "Besides Thaos needs practice holding a baby because Nikki is pregnant."

Annabelle and Simon both watched Thaos as he held Arianna. "Is Nikki your wife?" Simon asked.

"Yes but we aren't officially married yet," Thaos said with a proud look. "We are expecting our first child."

After a few minutes Annabelle said, "I will take her now and let you two talk." Annabelle picked up Arianna and looked at Simon saying with conviction, "He is a good man." Then she walked out of the room.

"Was that some kind of test?" Thaos asked with a grin.

"Apparently so," Simon said and poured more whiskey into their glasses.

When Simon, Annabelle and Thaos returned to the ball they were the center of attention; a situation none of them wanted. Nikki pushed her way through the crowd until she reached Thaos.

"Are you alright?" Nikki asked as she put her arms around Thaos' waist.

"Yes," replied Thaos putting his arm around her shoulders and kissing Nikki on the forehead. Simon watched them both as he was still trying to read Thaos' character.

"Simon, this is my wife Nikki."

Simon looked at the beautiful woman dressed in a pale pink gown. "I hear you are a warrior," Simon said.

"Yes, I grew up with Angelina and Ingr."

"Well Nikki, your husband saved my wife from being raped tonight."

Nikki looked at Thaos with adoration. "Yes, he is a fine warrior," she said then Nikki looked around. "Where is Annabelle?"

Simon looked around the crowded room until he spied Annabelle who was surrounded by all of the women of the family. "She is over there," Simon replied and pointed but Nikki was too short to see Annabelle through the crowd.

"I must go speak with her," Nikki said. "Was she hurt?"

"No Thaos got there before she was injured," Simon said. "Why don't the two of you come over for drinks after the ball?"

Chapter XXXVII
Disowned

"Sophie is there any change in Roch's state?" Cerephus asked.

"No, My Lord," replied Sophie. "The physician doesn't know what to make of it."

"Sophie, I need to speak with you about some things," said Cerephus as he put his arm around her shoulders and led her over to a chair. "Please take a seat."

"Sophie you know that I am Roch's second in command."

"Yes, My Lord."

"While King Roch is ill I will need to take over his duties and I will need your help; will you help me?"

"Of course, I will do what I can."

"Sophie I am going to have to pay the soldiers and the bills and I need to know of any things Roch was working on," said Cerephus. "Will you show me where the paperwork and payroll are kept?"

"I thought he kept all of that in his desk, My Lord."

"I cannot find any of it; do you know where else he would keep these things?"

"Perhaps in that room in his chambers."

"What room are you talking about Sophie?"

"That room behind the fireplace."

"You have seen this room Sophie?"

"Yes, a long time ago; I walked into his bedroom chambers with breakfast and he was in that room," Sophie replied.

"Sophie, you have always been such a loyal servant I would like to give you a little gift," Cerephus said as he pressed five golden coins into her hand.

Sudfad and Renya were enjoying their morning coffee in the privacy of their bedroom chambers before they planned to meet their guests.

"Never in all my days have I seen so many pregnant girls in one place," Marie said as she poured more coffee into the cups of the King and Queen. "It seems like everyone is having tea and biscuits for breakfast." Marie walked across the room as she was talking. "I hope it isn't catching," Marie said seriously as she was adjusting the window drapes.

Sudfad started to choke on his coffee as he tried not to laugh out loud. Renya looked away and giggled, "Thank you Marie," she managed to say without laughing. Marie left the room and as soon as she closed the door both Sudfad and Renya broke into loud laugher. Renya started to cry from laughing so hard. A few moments later, as she wiped tears from her face, Renya said, "Sudfad have you noticed how much time Mateo and Gala have been spending together?"

Sudfad was reading some papers at the small table they shared; he spoke without looking up from his work. "They share the same interests. Gala and Ibula have been spending a lot of time together also."

"I know, it's just when I watched them dance last night, well, it seemed like there might be a spark there."

Sudfad looked at his wife and smiled, "You are always the romantic. I think you see what you want to see."

"Actually I was hoping that Gala and the Sanuri would become more than friends," Renya said. "Sometimes I feel sorry for him, he spends his life helping others and he really has no one who takes care of him."

"Honey I hope you aren't trying to push them together," Sudfad said.

"No, no just watching," Renya said with a coy smile.

"Look at his skin," said Erebus as he leaned over Roch.

"I cannot stand to be that close to him the way he smells," replied Cerephus with disdain. "Could he be dying?"

"I really don't know, he certainly looks like he could be," said Erebus as he took some of Roch's hair and skin.

"Why are you doing that?" Cerephus asked with disgust.

"I want to examine them," replied Erebus.

"You make sure he is distracted if he wakes up," whispered Cerephus. Erebus stood close to Roch's bed while Cerephus examined the wall around the fire place. Cerephus ran his hands over every inch of the wall and the stones. He moved the items on top of the mantle and examined them. Finally he found it, a button that looked like it was part of the decoration around the fireplace.

"Erebus come see," said Cerephus in awe. The entire wall which held the fireplace swung open exposing a room even larger than the bedroom chambers. The room was filled with treasures of every sort. Chests of jewels and golden coins, golden and silver items of every imagination filled the room from floor to ceiling leaving only a path to walk through.

"Now aren't you glad you listened to me?" asked Cerephus with a grin. Both men quickly got out of the room and pushed the wall back into place as they heard the physician walking into the chambers.

"We have been waiting for you," said Cerephus. "Have you determined the affliction?"

"No as I told you before, I have never seen anything like this," replied the physician.

"What is it that you have not seen before?" Erebus asked.

"As you can see for yourself he is unconscious but at times he seems to be in great pain," said the physician.

"I am sure those are things you have seen before," said Erebus.

"Yes, of course but look at this," said the physician as he led them to Roch's bed and lifted the covers. "Look at his feet." Both Erebus and Cerephus bent down and examined Roch's left foot.

"What happened to it?" asked Erebus.

"I have no idea but the other looks the same," the physician said.

"It is as if they are changing shape," Cerephus said with disbelief.

"They are changing shape, and look here," said the physician as he lifted one of Roch's eyelids. "His eyes have changed."

"They are yellow, how can that be?" asked Cerephus. "Do you think these things have anything to do with the affliction he received that affected his skin?"

"I have no idea."

"Please keep me posted on his condition," said Cerephus as he and Erebus left the chambers.

"Is he turning into a demon?" Cerephus whispered.

"I do not know," replied Erebus solemnly.

"Well, hurry up with your spells or we may never get our hands on that treasure."

On the third morning of the celebrations, as everyone was finishing their breakfast in the Great Hall Thedes stood up and approached the King and Queen; a moment later Thedes turned and addressed the crowd. "My wife and I are still reeling from the gifts that were bestowed upon us last night. Never in the history of the Shettee or Ruala peoples has there been a covenant made with humans. Because of the generous actions of King Sudfad and Queen Renya our peoples are now united."

"We brought some gifts for the Royal Family and you may be wondering why we are giving the gifts in public; please listen because there is a story to be told." Thedes nodded to Ibula who proceeded to hand small pouches to every member of Sudfad's family, including Alexander, Laurel, Matthew and Angelina.

"For those of you who do not know of the Ice Caves of Mordv they are truly a magical place. Raul and Simon can attest to the wonders that they saw there. When both of our tribes were on the verge of extinction the Sanuri saved us and took us to the Ice Caves. These caves are filled with giant crystals that reach to the sky. The Sanuri says these crystals were blessed by The Great Ruler Himself.

"Not only do these crystals provide light to the caverns but they provide a remarkable healing energy of life. For those who do not believe my words, just look at Raul and Simon; neither of them carry a scar from the serious wounds they endured. This is the powers of the crystals in our world." Thedes turned back towards the Royal Family and continued, "We have made necklaces containing pieces of the crystals for each of you; we do not know what powers they will give you in this world."

   "These are beautiful," Renya said as she stood up and showed her guests a pink gold chain with a crystal pendent.

   "Now for King Sudfad and Matthew," Thedes said, "Raul and Simon have already received their gifts." Thedes held up a Gafet. "What I hold before you is called a Gafet; it is an ancient Shettee weapon. Before we met the Sanuri our people used to worship the sun and moon and stars. The crescent shape of the back of this weapon represents the moon, these three blades at each end represent the stars and the long blade in the middle represents the rays of the sun. We make them out of a metal called Taluth which was only located in the Rosu Mountains but we have just found veins of this metal in the Safer Mountains that contain the Ice Caves."

"All Shettee warriors are trained in the use of the Gafet. In the coming days the Ruala and Shettee warriors will show you some demonstrations and teach the use of this weapon to anyone who wants to learn."

Thedes turned around and handed the Gafet he was holding to Sudfad. Ibula gave Thedes another Gafet which he handed to Matthew. The two men returned to their seats and showed their gifts to others at the head table.

"Petra would you please come up here with us?" Thedes asked. Petra looked scared but Sudfad told him to stand with Thedes.

"When the Hutas conquered my kingdom, six warriors were ordered to take all of the Shettee women and children to the monastery at Avaide. The priests there took us in and treated us well. One day this young boy left his family, never to see them again and rode to the monastery to warn us of a Huta attack. Six priests helped my people escape through a series of long tunnels, while those demons tortured and butchered the priests that stayed behind. Not only did Petra save my people but he dragged a wounded priest away from the Hutas and hid him until the Sanuri found them."

Thedes turned to Petra, "Petra I was one of the people you saved that day. And some day I would like to bring you to the Ice Caves so my people can meet the young warrior who saved their kind." Ibula handed Thedes a necklace which he put around Petra's neck, it was a leather necklace with an ornate gold pendent. "This is a Farduth it is awarded to Shettee males who have done some extraordinary feat to earn their rite of passage to becoming a warrior. Petra you are now a member of the Shettee Tribe." Petra's eyes grew wide as he looked at the designs on the pendent.

"Thank you," Petra said shyly.

"And there is one more thing," Thedes said as Ibula handed him a Gafet. "This is for you. When you are old enough I will teach you how to use it."

"This is going to take us forever doing it this way," complained Erebus.

"I do not want to wait until he turns into a demon," Cerephus said. "And we cannot let others know what we are doing."

Erebus stood at the door to Roch's bedroom chambers as Cerephus opened the door to the secret room behind the fireplace. Cerephus filled two sets of saddle bags with as many gold coins as they would hold. Cerephus grabbed four rings and put them on his fingers. He filled his pockets with jewelry made of diamonds, emeralds, rubies and sapphires; then he locked the room up.

"Come on," said Cerephus and the two men walked out of the castle. "Since I cannot get caught carrying the larger items, I plan to go into that room at least once a day."

"And if he dies, you did all of this for nothing."

"And if he turns into a demon we will never get our hands on that treasure."

"Where are you going with it?"

"I will show you," said Cerephus as they entered the stable.

The two men mounted horses and rode out of the castle gate. They rode for about a mile before Cerephus turned off from the road and entered the forest. Cerephus stopped his horse at a beautiful pool of water that was fed by a small water fall.

"Follow me," said Cerephus as he dismounted and walked behind the waterfall into a cave. "I have watched this place for a long time and have never seen anyone come here."

"You already have chests and barrels in here?"

"They are empty; I will fill them with the small loads I bring from the castle."

The Sanuri returned to the castle of Wetpr on the seventh day of the celebrations. He put The Chalice of Ascension in the holy vault then walked out of the castle to watch the various competitions being held on the castle grounds. The Sanuri could not be inconspicuous in this crowd; as soon as word of his arrival spread, all of the Rualas gathered around him.

614

Eventually the Sanuri made his way to one of the areas where Shettee warriors were training others in the use of the Gafet. He was surprised that so many people wanted to learn the use of this ancient weapon that twenty Ruala warriors were also teaching. Every teacher worked with two students at a time. Thedes was teaching Sudfad and Claudius, Potomas was training Sorren and Mathas, Iden was teaching Matthew and Stephan and Mabon was training Thaos and Ryan.

"We are learning from the best," Claudius called out to the Sanuri, referring to their Shettee teachers. Angelina, Ingr and Nikki walked up to the Sanuri. "We are so glad you can join us," Angelina said. "This has been such great fun."

"I was just told this is the seventh day of the ceremonies," the Sanuri said. "I didn't realize they were going that long."

"Renya has done such a wonderful job," said Angelina. "The celebrations will go for fourteen days and as you can see there are so many activities going on at any one time."

"Oh, look there is an opening," Nikki pointed out a Gafet teacher who no longer had a long line waiting for him. As Ingr, Nikki and Angelina ran towards the teacher; Stephan stopped training and caught up with them.

"Ingr I don't think you should do this, it is too dangerous in your condition," Stephan said.

"Has anyone been hurt during training?" Angelina asked.

"No but not everyone is pregnant," said Stephan.

"Stephan I promise we will be careful," Ingr said. "I really want to learn how to use this weapon."

Matthew and Thaos both joined the group. "Now don't tell me you are going to forbid all of us from this," Angelina said angrily.

"We just don't want you girls to get hurt," Matthew said.

"We all promised not to do anything that was too dangerous," Angelina said. "Matthew this does not seem that dangerous. We are experienced warriors and will not really stab each other."

615

Ibula could hear the anger in the voices of the three couples as she walked up to them. "Are you fighting over the training?" Ibula asked. They all looked at Ibula but no one said a word. "This has been too joyful of a celebration for anger. If you like, I will teach your wives and I will be very careful with them."

"Thaos please," begged Nikki. "It's not like we aren't used to using weapons."

"I give you my word that none of them will be injured," Ibula said persuasively.

Ingr walked up to Stephan and whispered into is ear. He started to laugh, "I will hold you to that," Stephan said then he looked at Matthew and Thaos. Reluctantly they all agreed to let their wives train.

Ibula, Angelina, Ingr and Nikki turned and walked towards a training area. "Are your husbands always so protective?" Ibula asked.

"It's because we are pregnant," Ingr said. "They mean well."

"We have all fought in battles with our husbands but as soon as each of us got pregnant, I don't know, things changed," Nikki said.

"Yes and we hate it," Angelina said then started to laugh.

Claudius pushed his chair back from the table so he could have a better view of the dancers who were entertaining the dinner guests in the Great Hall of the castle of Wetpr that evening.

"My Lord, there is a message for you," said a Wetprian soldier as he handed an envelope to Claudius.

"Thank you," Claudius said as he opened the envelope. Stephan watched the grave look that overtook Claudius' face as he read the letter.

"Father what is it?"

Claudius handed the letter to Stephan as he stood up and said, "I am going to the dungeons." Stephan quickly read the letter, then called to Matthew and the two followed Claudius. The three men walked in silence; both Stephan and Matthew could see how angry Claudius was becoming.

"Leave us," Claudius bellowed to the guard as they approached Timothy's cell.

Timothy stood up and walked to the cell door. "Well, it's about time you got me out of here," he said with an arrogant tone. Timothy was still wearing the bloody clothing he wore at the ball. His right eye was swollen shut and his face was swollen and covered with cuts and bruises.

"You arrogant piece of filth," growled Claudius. "You brought shame on all of us by your vulgar actions. King Sudfad wanted to put you to death; you do know it was his son's wife you tried to rape. Mathas asked that your life be spared for the sake of your family. I have not come sooner for fear I would kill you myself," Claudius said as he walked closer to the bars and stared at Timothy. Timothy took a couple of steps back from the cell door, fearful of Claudius' wrath.

"You will remain a prisoner here until King Sudfad decides you are no longer a danger," Claudius waved the letter in front of Timothy's face. "This is from your father. He says you have broken his heart and brought such disgrace on the family that he has disowned you. Timothy from this day forward you have no family. Fahron forbids you not only to come home but he forbids you to enter the Kingdom of Lentz. I second that and I am sure Mathas will also."

"Let me see that letter," Timothy said in disbelief.

Claudius held it up so Timothy could read it. Claudius was close to Timothy's face. "Timothy if I ever see you again I will kill you," Claudius said in a hoarse whisper. Then without turning Claudius spoke again, "Stephan, Matthew I order you to kill Timothy the next time you see him."

"With pleasure Father," Stephan said.

"Timothy," said Matthew coldly. "I am also an adopted son of King Sudfad. When I am done telling him of the kind of man you are, I am sure he will be keeping you behind bars for a very long time." The three men turned and walked out of the dungeons.

"No!" screamed Timothy and slid down the bars of the cell crying.

"I don't know why but I love it here so much," said Ingr as she lay in Stephan's arm. They were staying in the same room in Matthew's home that Stephan had stayed in on the visit when Ingr and Stephan met.

"You mean this room or Wetpr?" Stephan asked kiddingly as he was stroking her silky hair.

"Everything, the room, the castle, the kingdom; we have had such happy memories here," Ingr said and leaned over and kissed Stephan on the lips.

Stephan noticed how the rays of the morning sun seemed to make Ingr's blue eyes dance. "I just love being with you," he said and kissed her again.

"Stephan can we talk?"

"We are."

"I mean seriously."

Stephan pushed himself up on one arm and looked at Ingr. "Are you still mad at me for yesterday?"

"No, Stephan I know you mean well but I am not fragile," said Ingr. "You can't expect me to just sit around in the castle during the entire pregnancy, I will go crazy."

Stephan was silent for a few moments. "Ingr I don't expect you to sit in the castle but I don't want you training as a warrior while you are pregnant either."

"But Stephan being a warrior is all I really know," Ingr said as she ran her finger softly along the outline of his face.

"By the time we get home, the workmen should have our new living quarters almost completed," Stephan said.

"You mean our home already?"

"No, the larger living quarters that we will have while our home is being built. I will give you money and why don't you buy everything you think we will need for both these quarters and the home and also for the baby."

"So you are going to find ways to keep me distracted," Ingr said with a laugh.

"Yes I am," Stephan said with a grin and kissed Ingr on the lips.

"Actually what I wanted to talk about was your father."

"Father?"

"Claudius has been so upset over Timothy that he isn't enjoying himself. I know we planned to have something special when we told him the baby's name but perhaps we should tell him while we are here. I think it would cheer him up."

"I think you are right, we will tell him today. And he isn't the only one who is upset about Timothy. Mother hasn't said a lot but she and Isadore are so close; I can tell Mother is greatly upset also."

Later that morning, Angelina and Matthew were in their bedroom preparing to go to the Great Hall for breakfast. "Matthew I think we should stay here a few more weeks," Angelina said.

"You really like it here that much?"

"Well yes, but that is not the reason. Vitomas will be giving birth in about four weeks and she said both of her boys came early. I was thinking we should stay so I can deliver the baby."

"I think she would like that," said Matthew as he took Angelina's hand. "Let me ask Father if he needs me back sooner."

Matthew and Angelina walked out of their bedroom and heard voices coming from their kitchen. They found both of their parents, Claudius, Bella, Stephan, Ingr, Thaos and Nikki sitting around the table. "Well it's about time you two got up," said Sorren and laughed.

"We didn't realize there was a celebration going on," said Matthew as he walked over and kissed his mother on the cheek.

"We are just having a small toast," Claudius said with great pride. "Stephan and Ingr just told us the name they chose for the baby."

"Oh let's hear it," said Angelina.

"Marcus Stephan," said Claudius. "Marcus is one of my middle names."

"What is the other?" asked Thaos.

"Titus."

Thaos looked at Nikki and said, "Titus is a good name."

"I was thinking about Derek," Nikki said. Thaos bent down and kissed her.

"That would mean a lot," Thaos said warmly.

"Who is Derek?" asked Stephan.

"Someone who meant a lot to Thaos, who is dead," Nikki explained.

Thaos turned to Claudius and said sincerely, "I know we aren't family but you have changed my life Claudius. If we have a son, would it be alright to name him Titus Derek?"

Bella squeezed Claudius' hand. "Son, I just gave you a chance; you have made the changes. And yes I would be proud to have your son named after me also," Claudius said happily.

Chapter XXXVIII
Collaborators

Padre Bartholomew knocked on Padre Thomas' door. "Are you ready?" he whispered as the door opened a crack. "What do you have?"

"Extra candles and a bag, who knows what we will find," said Padre Thomas as he walked into the hallway. The two priests crept through the halls of the monastery trying not to wake the other priests. Once they made it to the second floor of the south wing, Padre Bartholomew pulled a piece of paper out of his pocket. "According to this diagram, High Priest Petlov's chambers should be the third door on the left," whispered Padre Bartholomew. "Room number nine."

Once they located the correct door, Padre Thomas tried to open the door which was locked. He pulled out several large sets of keys and tried each one in the lock, finally they heard a click. The two priests walked through the door and into the darkness of the room. They each lit candles until the room was illuminated. "These chambers have been vacant for a very long time," Padre Thomas commented when he saw the amount of undisturbed dust that covered everything. "Let's split up."

"This must have been a parlor," commented Padre Bartholomew as he walked out of the first room to the right of the entrance. A few moments later Padre Bartholomew called out, "I found his bedroom chambers."

"I am surprised no one has taken these rooms, they look very nice," said Padre Thomas. "Padre Bartholomew I found it," Padre Thomas said as he walked into a room containing a desk, a table and many chairs. Like the rest of the chambers everything in the room was covered with a thick coating of dust and spider webs. "Well, at least we can tell that no one else has been in here recently," Padre Thomas said as Padre Bartholomew joined him in the study.

They lit more candles and started to search the room for the safe. First they looked behind pictures, then they checked the walls for secret compartments.

The priests moved the furniture and looked under the rugs for a floor safe but they still did not find anything. "I will take the desk if you want to start on the book shelves," said Padre Thomas.

"I did not find the safe but I found a ledger I am taking with us," said Padre Thomas after he had searched the desk. He walked over to the wall that had several large bookshelves and proceeded to help Padre Bartholomew search.

"I found it," whispered Padre Bartholomew gleefully. Behind several large books there was a small wall safe. Padre Thomas took the key from the envelope and opened the safe. Padre Bartholomew took a large stack of papers out of the safe and put them into Padre Thomas' bag.

Meanwhile Padre Thomas found a ruby amulet on a thick silver chain in the back of the small safe. "That's it," said Padre Thomas. They locked the safe and moved everything back to the original positions and left the chambers.

"The dark lords say that the Vessel has been greatly weakened," Meekos said angrily.

"How has Roch become weakened?" Tenebrae asked. "And have you heard from Sophie yet?"

"I don't know what has happened to Roch and the fact that Sophie has not answered any of my letters concerns me considerably. We have never gone this long without communicating. It is not like her; something is gravely wrong."

"What does this mean for our plans?" Tenebrae asked.

"The resurrection of Omnibus must take place at the scheduled time," snapped Meekos. "We have put into motion forces that cannot be stopped."

"I understand that once these energies have been put into motion they cannot be stopped without severe consequences," Tenebrae said. "But if the Vessel is too weak to contain Omnibus what will happen to Omnibus? And what will happen to us?"

"We contracted with the dark lords," said Meekos. "We signed in blood to help them raise Omnibus from The Abyss; and for that we have received our desires. If there are problems we must try to remedy them."

"But we have fulfilled our parts," said Tenebrae. "Certainly the dark lords understand that."

"The dark lords are not known for their compassion," sneered Meekos. "If we fail, I fear that our contracts will come due long before we agreed."

"These papers are terrifying," said Padre Bartholomew as he read through the papers they took from the safe of High Priest Dominic Petlov. "Petlov says that High Priest Meekos asked him and several other high priests to join a secret society. Petlov says they were told the society was formed to maintain the integrity of the Church from being compromised by unscrupulous kings and wealthy land owners."

"Petlov said he and others attended several meetings of this society and became suspicious as to its real purpose. He goes on to say that there were many in attendance at these meetings and they were all asked to wear hoods to hide their true identities."

"They wore hoods," repeated Padre Thomas in disbelief.

"Petlov goes on to say that there were speakers and discussions during these meetings that revealed the identities of some of the participants, which included High Priest Meekos, King Sharonne, Padre Sporos as well as politicians and land owners such as Cedrick Teivel from the Kingdom of Ryed and Gregory Bancar from the Kingdom of Wetpr. Petlov said that although there were many in attendance there was a core group of thirteen who seemed to run the society and he was not sure of their identities."

"Petlov," continued Padre Bartholomew." Said that he and others took the oath to join the society and afterwards felt as if they had been drugged. Petlov said that he woke up on the floor of his chambers, with a bleeding wound across his wrist and no memory of what had occurred. He said that High Priests Vincent, Samuel and Timothy all related the same stories after attending the same meeting of the society."

"Do you think their blood was taken for some kind of sacrifice?" asked Padre Bartholomew as he looked up from the papers.

"I have no idea," replied Padre Thomas.

Padre Bartholomew returned to the papers. "Petlov says that shortly after this incident there was another meeting of the society and High Priest Samuel arrived early to tell Meekos he wanted to forfeit his membership. Petlov said that Samuel later stopped him, Vincent and Timothy from attending the meeting because Samuel stated that when he arrived at the meeting room there was a group of men worshiping at an altar made of bones with bowls of blood and snakes."

"Petlov says Samuel said that when he saw this he cried out with horror and several of the men turned and looked at him and one of them was High Priest Meekos. Petlov says that Samuel's body was found the next day with no apparent cause of death."

"Do you think High Priest Dominick was also killed by Meekos?" Padre Thomas asked.

"At this point I believe anything is possible," said Padre Bartholomew then he continued reading the papers. "According to this Petlov, Vincent and Timothy continued to attend meetings to find out information about the secret society. Petlov said there was much talk about raising an army which was funded with both church and private monies. Petlov said that at every meeting the attendance seemed to grow but everyone continued to wear hoods. Petlov said he tried to befriend Meekos and was allowed to attend some additional meetings."

"Petlov is asking for forgiveness from The Great Ruler over and over on this page. Oh, wait until you hear this," said Padre Bartholomew. "Petlov attended a meeting with Meekos; he said Meekos called it a special meeting. The meeting was in the forest behind the monastery. There was a great fire and men wearing masks and little else dancing around the fire and chanting in a language that Petlov did not recognize."

"Petlov said there were few in attendance and everyone was receiving either a ring or a necklace, each made of silver with a large ruby stone. Petlov said he received a necklace."

"Petlov said that suddenly more men wearing masks appeared and they were dragging people who were bound and gagged up to the fire where the dancers slit the throats of the victims. Petlov said that not only was he frozen in his spot by the horror before him but that his ruby amulet began to glow with a great light."

Padre Thomas took the necklace out of his bag and examined it. "It appears to be just regular jewelry," he commented.

Padre Bartholomew continued, "Petlov says that when he could speak again, he asked Meekos what was happening and Meekos replied it was but a small payment to the dark lords. Petlov said he was afraid to leave the meeting so he stood frozen in place. Petlov said that after the meeting he asked Meekos why he received the ruby necklace and Meekos replied that the day the Vessel of Darkness is resurrected the rubies will run as water. That is the last of his notes," said Padre Bartholomew.

"We have to get these to the Sanuri quickly; we finally have the proof we need," said Padre Thomas as he wrapped the necklace inside of the papers and put them inside of the bag. "We cannot meet the Enrops at our normal location for Meekos is watching us.

"Let us pray to The Great Ruler that He will send the Enrops to us," said Padre Bartholomew. The two men prayed and waited then prayed again. Soon they heard scratching at the only window to Padre Thomas' room. Padre Thomas opened the shutter on the window and saw several Enrops. "Please take this to the Sanuri it is very import," begged Padre Thomas as he handed the bag to one of the birds. As soon as Padre Thomas closed the shutter there was a knock at his door.

"Why, High Priest Meekos what a surprise," said Padre Thomas as he opened the door to his room. "Please come in."

Meekos entered the room and quickly surveyed it with his eyes. "Hello Padre Bartholomew, I am glad that you are here; I wanted to speak with both of you."

"Please have a seat," offered Padre Thomas.

"It has come to my attention that the two of you were friends with Padre Dominick, I realize it is short notice but I wonder if you would speak at his funeral tomorrow?" asked Meekos.

"It turns out that Dominick rather kept to himself and did not have a great many friends." Both Padre Thomas and Padre Bartholomew noticed that Meekos kept looking around the room as he spoke.

"We would be honored," said Padre Thomas.

"Padre Dominick was a great painter and has left behind many beautiful paintings, I wonder, might we hang them in the hallways of the monastery?" asked Padre Bartholomew.

"Of course, I would be interested in seeing them," said Meekos as he stood up to leave.

"Good night," said Padre Thomas as he closed the door behind Meekos and listened for his footsteps in the hallway.

"Did you see the ring?" whispered Padre Bartholomew. "He wore a silver ring with a large ruby stone."

"I saw it and did you see the way he was looking around the room?" asked Padre Thomas as soon as he was sure that Meekos was gone.

"Thank The Great Ruler we sent everything to the Sanuri," said Padre Bartholomew.

"Everything except for the historical book that Padre Dominick wrote," said Padre Thomas. "If anything happens to me the book is hidden inside of my mattress."

"I know Meekos asked us to speak at Dominick's funeral as an excuse to come into this room," said Padre Bartholomew. "But I wonder if he also wants to know how much we know about Dominick. I think we should not mention anything about his work compiling the history of this monastery."

"Perhaps you are right," said Padre Thomas. "I do not know, but I have a strange feeling something will happen at the funeral tomorrow. Maybe we should search Dominick's storage room tonight."

"Meekos may be waiting for us to leave this room."

"Yes and maybe he paid us a visit because there is still something important we have not found yet."

"Very well then," replied Padre Bartholomew and the two old priests prayed for protection then left the room.

"Should we gather the entire group?" asked High Priest Tenebrae.

"I do not want to yet," replied Meekos. "I would like to have a plan to offer when we meet with the rest."

"Demetries has been vanquished to The Abyss," said High Priest Pravis. "And the dark lords say the energy of the Vessel has greatly weakened since that time."

"Does anyone know exactly what happened to King Roch?" asked Meekos. "Demetries was our resource."

"The dark lords have said that a sorcerer named Erebus has summoned them several times to find out Roch's role as a vessel," Pravis said.

"What?" screamed Meekos. "Erebus, I know him, how has he become involved with this?" Suddenly Meekos' eyes grew wide as he thought, "Sophie."

"The dark lords said that this sorcerer and another have been planning to overthrow Roch but when the sorcerer saw Roch's condition he knew there were great magics at work," replied Pravis. "The dark lords do not care about Roch's rule over that kingdom; they are only concerned with his ability to bring forth Omnibus."

"What exactly do they mean by Roch's condition?" Meekos asked.

"I do not know."

"We need to get someone to that castle quickly," said Meekos.

"The dark lords did say that Erebus does not want to interfere with any plans they may have and offered to be of help," Pravis added.

"I will go to Roch's castle myself and determine his condition," said Meekos. "Perhaps this sorcerer can be useful to us."

"Meekos, we have all been wondering what could happen to us if the Vessel fails to resurrect Omnibus," Tenebrae said.

"Tenebrae you are making me crazy, you keep asking the same question again and again. I do not know for sure," replied Meekos. "But remember what they did to Sharonne?"

"You mean the tortures they are still inflicting on him?" asked Tenebrae.

"Yes, and remember it is our blood tied to the resurrection," Meekos said. "We will gain incredible power when he is unleashed; but I do not know if we will fall if he is vanquished. We are all concerned but we cannot let our fears get the better of us. Let me see for myself what is going on with Roch, then we will know what we are dealing with."

Padre Thomas and Padre Bartholomew walked to the basement of the monastery without seeing anyone. They listened carefully before proceeding forward to find storage room number thirteen. Padre Thomas held the torches as Padre Bartholomew unlocked the heavy door. They entered the storage room and attached the torches to the mounts on the wall.

"Where to begin," said Padre Bartholomew as he surveyed the small but crowded storage room. The two priests started to search the many boxes of papers on the shelves; next they unrolled each map of room assignments and reviewed it. They searched through boxes of art supplies and stacks of books. After three hours they decided to take a small break. "Is it possible that the historical book was the only thing of significance down here?" asked Padre Bartholomew.

"You know we do not know if Padre Dominick was asked to join that secret society or even knew of it," said Padre Thomas, who paused and searched the room with his eyes. "Where would you put something you really wanted to hide in this room?" Padre Thomas asked. The two priests looked around the room again.

"I am going to check the wall for compartments."

"I will check the floor boards."

They searched for several minutes before Padre Thomas found a loose board. "I think I found something," he said as he tried to pry the loose boards from the floor. Padre Bartholomew walked over to Padre Thomas and watched him take a small pile of papers and an object wrapped in cloth from an opening in the floor. They took the items to the table. Padre Thomas opened the cloth and found a silver necklace with a ruby amulet exactly like the one Petlov had.

Padre Bartholomew was sorting through the papers. "These are all drawings," he said. "I think Padre Dominick is showing us who was in the secret society." They looked at the pictures of naked men dancing around a fire and another of people being murdered. There was a picture of an altar made of bones with snakes and there were several pictures of men. Some of the pictures of men were portraits while others were drawings of groups. While some of the men in the pictures wore masks the majority did not.

"The only one I recognize is Meekos," said Padre Bartholomew. "We need to get these to the Sanuri tonight."

Almost two weeks had passed and there was little change to King Roch's condition. He remained unconscious, yet he often grimaced with pain. Slowly, very slowly his body appeared to be changing. Sophie was filled with anxiety because her brother Meekos had not responded to any of her letters. She had memorized all of the transcripts about the ascension of Omnibus and what was now happening to Roch was not part of the long established plans.

Sophie was now torn between her loyalty to her brother and her love for Erebus. She was gravely concerned for Erebus' safety and begged him almost daily to leave Stordt. His answer was always the same. Erebus said he would not leave without her.

"My Lord, one of the soldiers said you wanted to see me?" Sophie said as she entered the war room. Cerephus was seated behind the desk so he was facing Sophie; two men were seated so they were facing Cerephus.

629

Sophie recognized one of the men as Erebus, who quickly turned and gave Sophie a look which confused her. The second man turned around slowly and Sophie gasped as she realized it was her brother Meekos.

"Sophie, we have a guest who has traveled a long distance," Cerephus said. "Would you serve lunch for three in here?"

"Yes My Lord," stammered Sophie and quickly left the war room.

"As I was saying my name is Meekos, I am the senior high priest at the monastery at Malga." Meekos paused for a few moments as he stared boldly into Cerephus' eyes. "I also have other duties and titles which bring me to your door."

Before Meekos could continue speaking to Cerephus, Erebus interrupted him. "Cerephus, High Priest Meekos and I have known each other for many years. Do not let his robes and words fool you; Meekos is a dark lord who tried to ruin my life once. I suspect he is here because of Roch."

"Is this true?" Cerephus asked as he stared at Meekos.

Meekos laughed, "Yes every word Erebus said is true. But I am not your enemy here. In fact I may be saving your lives."

"What are you talking about?" demanded Cerephus.

"I have been told that you have been contacting the dark worlds to find out information about Roch and his destiny. I have also been told that you have stated you did not want to interfere with any plans of the dark lords; but that you were plotting to take Roch's kingdom from him," Meekos said. "Is what I have been told correct?"

Neither Cerephus nor Erebus spoke for several moments as they were trying to figure out what Meekos' intentions were. "Yes," replied Erebus suspiciously.

"Good," said Meekos with a sly smile. "Erebus I have also been told that you offered to be of service to the dark lords, is this also true?"

"Yes. Meekos get to the point."

630

"You never were a patient man, Erebus," Meekos said tauntingly. Meekos stopped talking when he saw the look of rage on Erebus' face. "We have started off on the wrong foot and it is my fault, let me start again," said Meekos apologetically.

"The two of you do not trust me and I do not trust either of you. And yes Erebus, you and I have a history that I believe brings out the worst in both of us. But it is my belief that the three of us need to work together not only to gain the things that we want but honestly to save all of our lives. I have much to explain to you but first I have some questions that must be answered immediately."

Cerephus leaned back in his chair and continued to stare suspiciously at Meekos. "Ask your questions," Cerephus said.

"I will make all of this clear to you later but the dark lords have said that Demetries has been vanquished to The Abyss and that something has happened to Roch. Tell me what has happened," Meekos said with such a look of apprehension that both Cerephus and Erebus started to think Meekos might be telling the truth.

"You knew Demetries?" Cerephus asked.

"I employed Demetries to watch Roch," Meekos replied.

"Why?" Cerephus asked.

"Roch has a destiny that how shall I say this, has been planned out for hundreds of years. The beings that I work for were starting to fear that Roch's self-destructive behavior would end his life before his destiny could be fulfilled. Demetries was a highly paid nursemaid."

Cerephus and Erebus looked at each other and smiled. "We are smiling because Erebus had guessed almost exactly what Demetries' role was here. Demetries had an unusual control over Roch," Cerephus continued. "Many, including myself would warn Roch about that demon. Whenever Demetries was losing his control of Roch, he would regain it by playing on Roch's greed."

"So you knew Demetries was a demon?" Meekos asked quizzically. "How, he was wearing the body of one of Roch's men?"

631

While Sophie had written to Meekos telling him that Demetries was no longer able to hide his true identity, Meekos did not know all of the details concerning Demetries' encounter with the Sanuri. He hoped to learn more information by feigning ignorance.

"Demetries had some kind of run-in with the Sanuri and when Demetries returned to the castle he had an affliction like Roch has now," Cerephus explained.

Meekos' eyes grew wide. "Cerephus I believe I will take that drink now. Please tell me of this affliction."

"Roch sent Jonas, that was the man who Demetries took over to find the Sanuri," Cerephus explained.

Meekos interrupted Cerephus, "Why?"

"Roch had a map that he believed he needed a holy man to translate," Cerephus said. "Demetries is gone for weeks and when he finally returns he looks like, I don't even know how to explain it without showing you Roch."

"His skin was rotting on his body and he was covered with open sores that were oozing pus," Erebus said. "He looked and smelled like a dead body, which is what Roch looks like now."

Meekos took a large gulp of his whiskey. "Please continue with your story," he said to Cerephus.

"At first Demetries says the Sanuri wouldn't let the demon take him and in a fight the Sanuri gave Demetries the affliction. But later Demetries said he led an attack on King Sudfad's castle during the weddings of the King's sons and that is why the Sanuri gave him the affliction. Before Demetries returned from Wetpr Roch said that he saw an image of the Sanuri appear in his bedroom and it yelled at Roch for sending demons to him."

"What!" Meekos yelled, then rubbed his forehead for a moment. "Demetries job was to keep Roch alive and to prevent Roch from drawing the attention of the Sanuri and other holy messengers."

"Meekos it sounds like you may not have been the only one paying Demetries," Erebus said.

632

"I know and that is of great concern to me."

"Demetries told us he was a demon and as soon as I had talked Roch into getting rid of Demetries, well that damn demon gets Roch all excited about going after The Scroll of Imari," Cerephus said. "Meekos, honestly I wondered if Demetries was trying to get Roch killed. If you were paying him to do a job, something was very wrong there."

Erebus explained, "Roch and Demetries had a plan that Demetries would control Rogetts which they would use to distract the Gants while Roch and Demetries looked for The Scroll of Imari. They took several hundred soldiers with them and were gone for weeks. Finally Roch comes back by himself and said that The Lion of The Great Ruler gave him an affliction and killed Demetries and the Rogetts."

"Apparently all the soldiers ran away in fear," as Erebus talked he watched the sweat pouring down Meekos' face. "Meekos," Erebus continued. "I am not surprised that The Lion would kill Demetries but why would he allow Roch to live? I think that might be a very important question for you and the beings you work for."

Cerephus and Erebus watched Meekos as his face became very white and he looked as if he would get sick. "Would you like some more whiskey?" Cerephus asked.

"Yes," replied Meekos in a hoarse whisper. "Then would you take me to see Roch?"

Erebus stared at Meekos. "This is truly the first you have heard of any of this?"

Meekos looked at Erebus suspiciously, "Yes, why?"

"I find it curious that the dark lords can tell you what I say during my spells yet they don't inform you that your, what should I call them, projects are not only having interactions with powerful holy messengers but Demetries is vanquished and Roch appears to be damaged. Meekos you know the underworld has to know what is going on, that is why I have been contacting them for information," Erebus said.

Meekos seemed to be overwhelmed by all he was hearing. "No, Erebus you are right in what you say." Meekos had a feeling that Erebus was trying to tell him something that he could not say in front of Cerephus.

"There is something else you should know," Erebus continued. "Some time ago, before Roch was damaged by The Lion, Roch appeared to have had an encounter with a powerful demon. Roch was alone at a campsite and basically heard a voice taunting him and laughing. Well, Roch was Roch and shot off his mouth and something grabbed Roch and held him in the air then dropped him on the ground. Roch's ankle was broken. Roch said he thought the demon was trying to prove he had more power."

"And you believed this story?" Meekos asked.

"We weren't sure what to believe but Roch seemed unnerved by it," Cerephus asked. "Erebus tell Meekos about the campfires."

"Roch hired me to find answers about reversing his affliction," Erebus said. "All my spells were blocked and I was threatened a great deal. During one of my spells, suddenly the face of Sporos appears. I could not hear what Sporos was saying but he appeared to be enraged and screaming. I questioned Roch about Sporos. Roch did not know Sporos' name but told us he had many incidents where he would see the face of Sporos in his campfires."

"Roch said that sometimes he would hear a voice call his name and then the face of Sporos appeared in the fire. Roch also told us that for years his dreams had been plagued by a lion and the face of a female seer that he once met. Cerephus and I believed these stories because it is the first time either of us had seen Roch act scared. So tell me Meekos does any of this make sense to you?"

"No, none of this makes sense to me," Meekos said as he was momentarily lost in thought. "Everything has been so carefully planned for generations and nothing that you have told me is part of the plans. Would you please take me to see Roch now?" As the three men stood up to leave the room, Sophie entered with a tray of dishes and food.

"Sophie, we are taking Meekos to see Roch," Cerephus said. "We will be back in a few moments. Just go ahead and set the table."

"Yes My Lord." As Meekos walked past Sophie she turned abruptly and bumped into him, at that moment she passed him a note. A gesture that was noticed by Erebus.

When the three men entered Roch's bedroom chambers they were all overwhelmed with the stench of death. Meekos walked up to the bed and stared at Roch in disbelief. Roch had long ago lost his resemblance to humanity. Erebus carefully watched Meekos face and saw terror in Meekos' eyes. "Meekos, Demetries kept telling Roch that he was a Vessel of Darkness."

"What!" screamed Meekos.

"It's apparent you need to find out who Demetries was really working for," Erebus said. "But that is another matter. Through my research I have discovered what that term means. So we know that whoever you work for wants Roch to be a container for the essence of a powerful demon. The reason I am telling you this is because Roch's body is changing." As Erebus said these words he pulled the blankets off from Roch. "Look at his feet. And his eyes are now yellow. Is this part of the planned transformation?"

Without answering Erebus' question, Meekos walked closer to Roch's bed and chanted a few words, suddenly smoke started to rise from Roch's skin. Meekos quickly stopped his chanting and took a couple of steps back.

"Was that supposed to happen?" Cerephus asked.

"No," replied Meekos with bewilderment as he watched the smoke dissipate. Meekos stepped next to the bed again and reached his hand forward to place it on Roch's forehead. Meekos screamed and pulled his hand back and saw that is was smoking. "What is the meaning of this?" screamed Meekos angrily. Meekos quickly spun around and faced Erebus. "Have you put a spell on him?" Meekos demanded.

"No, I have put no such spells on him," replied Erebus with irritation. "We told you he was marked by The Lion; surely you have seen this before?"

"This could be bad, very bad," said Meekos quickly. "If he has been touched with holiness, his body cannot house the essence of Omnibus."

"Omnibus!" Erebus exclaimed as he pretended this is the first time he heard this information. "That demon was vanquished to one of the prisons in The Abyss centuries ago. "You mean to tell me that the people you work for are going to help a demon escape one of The Great Ruler's prisons? To my knowledge that has never been done."

"What makes you think you can do it? And Meekos why in the world are you acting so surprised that emissaries of The Great Ruler are involved? Are you so arrogant that you think they would not notice what you are doing?" Erebus' voice kept getting louder as he talked. The anger in Erebus was not rising so much because of the situation with Roch as the pent up anger that Erebus held for Meekos was surfacing.

"You cannot speak to me like that!" Meekos snapped indignantly.

"I can speak to you anyway I want, you have put us all in great danger here," Erebus said loudly then he turned to Cerephus. "Omnibus is one of the Old Ones, which means he is one of the original demons that came to this world. The Old Ones are very powerful. From what I have read, and perhaps Meekos here can enlighten us," Erebus said sarcastically. "Omnibus was at war with other Old Ones. In his attempts to prove his powers and superiority he became such a threat to the worlds that The Great Ruler had him imprisoned to protect mankind. And Meekos and his friends want to unleash that monster on this world."

Erebus turned back to Meekos and yelled angrily, "So Meekos what do you get for sacrificing mankind? Tell me what did the demons promise you that is worth destroying this world? You disgust me! I used to think that you were such a powerful dark lord, now I realize you are just as insane as that master you serve. Do you really think that Omnibus won't destroy you too? I just can't believe your arrogance and ignorance!"

Meekos became enraged at Erebus' words and the two men started to walk towards each other; staring aggressively into the eyes of the other.

Just as Meekos started to mumble some words Cerephus bellowed out, "Stop this nonsense now! I don't know what is between you two but fighting between ourselves is not going to help anyone. So stop acting like children. You can take up your personal issues after we have figured out what to do about this business with Roch."

Both Erebus and Meekos stopped. "You are right Cerephus," Meekos said through clenched teeth.

"Now all three of us are going to the war room for lunch and start figuring out how we can all get what we want," Cerephus said with a voice of authority. When the three men exited Roch's chambers and closed the door, they did not hear the loud maniacal laughter that filled that room.

As soon as the three men entered the war room, Sophie ran in carrying a large tray of food. She quickly looked at all of their faces which were filled with tension, fear and anger. "My Lord, will your guest be spending the night?" Sophie asked. "I will prepare a room."

"We have not decided that Sophie," Cerephus said as he was oblivious to the looks that Sophie was giving to both Erebus and Meekos. "I will let you know."

"Yes My Lord," said Sophie and left the war room.

"Meekos, I have been working hard my entire life to be in a position to overthrow Roch and take the kingdom. Now when everything is in place we hear about your deal with Omnibus. I must say I am really not pleased," Cerephus said angrily.

Now it was Erebus who was trying to calm the tensions. "Meekos, we don't want to interfere with your plans so explain to us how your plans will affect ours."

Meekos was starting to relax a little. "We don't care about Roch's position or any of his holdings. Take the kingdom today for all we care."

"I will be honest with my concerns," Cerephus said gruffly. "As a man, Roch was a vicious enemy. If he returns back to his former self he will want vengeance; so it is in my best interest to kill him now."

637

"If he is supposed to turn into a powerful demon, it seems to be in my best interest to kill him now. If I allow your plans to go through and he becomes this demon or whatever, is he going to come after me for taking his kingdom?"

"So why haven't you killed him?" Meekos asked.

"Because Erebus keeps stopping me. Erebus recognized that something with powerful magics was going on here and he did not want us to bring the wrath of the dark lords upon us."

"I will tell you that you have both acted wisely," Meekos said. "If you kill Roch you will bring the wrath of not only dark lords but many powerful demons upon you. And to answer your other question, I don't know if Omnibus will want Roch's kingdom. But I now see how we can help each other. Erebus asked me what I was getting for helping Omnibus. Well, I am getting power beyond your wildest dreams. Enough power that I should be able to protect you from his wrath."

"And what do you want in exchange?" Cerephus asked.

"I want you to help me protect Roch and keep him alive until the time of the transformation," Meekos said.

"But can Roch still be used as The Vessel?" Erebus asked.

"Erebus, I don't know the answer to that question and trust me I need to find out. If we fail in this mission all of us involved will be tortured beyond belief," Meekos said.

"Meekos why would you get involved in such a thing," Erebus asked. "It seems like a suicide mission."

"For the power and so far it has been worth all that I have done," Meekos said. "I am wondering if perhaps you and I can combine our powers on some spells and perhaps find some answers. Would you be willing to help me?"

"Yes," Erebus replied suspiciously.

"I will pay both of you very well to make sure that Roch is taken care of until the time of the ascension," Meekos said.

"Cerephus since you are King now, I am sure you want the Kings' chambers; move Roch but please provide him with the same level of care that you have been. Are you willing to do this for me?"

Cerephus and Erebus looked at each other then at Meekos. "Yes," Cerephus replied.

"Cerephus I wonder if I might impose upon your hospitality for a few days," Meekos said.

"Why?" Cerephus asked suspiciously.

"I cannot give you all of the details but the people I work for had prepared a location for the transformation. I want to find this place and to ensure it is ready. Once the transformation starts, I have no idea how much time it takes to complete," Meekos said. "Do not worry I will not be a threat to anything you are doing here."

"So let me understand this," Erebus said. "You are going to leave Roch in our care. So has the transformation started? What are we supposed to do when it does? It seems like there are a lot of unanswered questions here."

"This is what I am proposing Erebus; that while I am here I will locate and do any preparations for the transformation chamber. Also, I would like to work with you on spells so that we both get answers to some of these questions. I don't know if the transformation has started and I don't know if Roch is still a suitable vessel. As you can understand I need to find the answers to these questions before I can proceed. If Roch can still be used as the Vessel and the transformation has not started, I will leave him in your hands and ask that you communicate with me through the use of ravens."

Erebus looked into Meekos' eyes then stared at the front pocket where he saw Meekos put the note from Sophie, "And you are sure these communications will reach you?" Erebus asked. Meekos glanced at his own pocket and understood there was more to Erebus' message.

"We will work out the details while I am still here," Meekos said. "So let's go over this again. I will pay you to keep Roch alive and cared for. You now have control over the kingdom."

"If Roch can still fulfill his destiny as the Vessel I will protect you from Omnibus. Do we have a deal?"

"There are still a few things that bother me," Cerephus said as he pushed his chair back from the table. "Right now might be our only chance to kill Roch. I need more assurance than your word that you will keep Omnibus at bay. Although if this demon is as powerful as you both say I don't know how you can make such an assurance. Also if there has been such careful planning for this over the centuries you must have a backup plan, what is it and how will it affect me and Erebus? And what are you going to do with Roch if he can't be the Vessel anymore? I don't want him returning to his old self."

"That last question is the easiest to answer," Meekos said. "If Roch can't be used as the Vessel, we will just kill him. He was never meant to live through the transformation. As for your question about a backup plan; Cerephus you have no reason to trust me but I have sworn blood oaths of secrecy and there are things I cannot tell you."

Meekos paused for a moment, "But also, the people I work for maintain a highly organized and extremely secretive society. Members' identities are not shared with other members and information is given only to those who need to know it. So although I have been a powerful player in trying to raise Omnibus, there are still many things that have not been revealed to me."

"I find your choice of words interesting," Erebus said.

"What do you mean?" asked Meekos.

"Demetries told Roch several times that he was a pawn in a game where the players were more powerful than Roch could ever imagine," Erebus said as he watched the look on Meekos' face.

Chapter XXXIX
Fears

"Come in," called the Sanuri as he heard a knock on the door to his chambers.

"I have not seen you at the celebrations," Sudfad said as he walked up to the desk that the Sanuri was sitting at. "Are you feeling alright?"

"Please have a seat," said the Sanuri as he motioned to a chair near the desk. "I am glad that you are here, I didn't want to bother you with a castle full of guests." The Sanuri had stacks of papers, drawings and a necklace sitting on top of the desk. "My friends in Malga sent me these things while I was gone. They have been sending me their research notes and copies of original documents, you too will have to read these when you have time."

"I have some time now," said Sudfad as he reached for a stack of papers.

"No read these first," said the Sanuri as he handed a small stack to Sudfad. "I am putting them in chronological order; it will make more sense to you that way. What I am reading in these papers breaks my heart and angers me greatly," the Sanuri said as he shook his head. All of the years I have gone to the monastery at Malga and never once did I suspect such a malignancy existed there."

"Sophie, Meekos will be staying with us for a few days," Cerephus said. "Please prepare some rooms for him."

"I have them ready," Sophie said as she stared at Meekos. "Let me know when you are ready."

"Now, would be fine," Meekos said as he stood up from the table. "By the way that was a wonderful meal."

"Also Sophie, before you leave, I will be having Roch moved out of his chambers and I will be taking over those rooms. They will need a great deal of cleaning."

"My Lord, just tell me what colors you would prefer and I will have those chambers redone for you. Might I make a suggestion about where you move Roch?" Sophie asked.

Cerephus said with a smile, "The colors would be red and dark blue. And where would you suggest we move Roch?"

"Since he requires so much care, I would suggest that we move him to one of the rooms in the central wing. That way I won't have to spend so much time from my other duties and we all can keep an eye on him."

"Sophie that is an excellent idea," Cerephus said. "I will let you choose the chambers."

Sophie and Meekos did not speak as she walked him to the southern wing of the castle. Sophie deliberately chose this remote location because she wanted to keep Meekos away from the others. Erebus' chambers were in the northern wing of the castle and Cerephus would soon be staying in the western wing. Cerephus still had no idea of Sophie's true identity which she planned to continue to keep from him. Also besides the fact that she wanted to keep Meekos and Erebus separated, Sophie was not prepared for anyone to find out that she and Erebus were having an affair.

As soon as Sophie and Meekos entered his chambers and shut the door, Sophie turned on him with an anger Meekos had never seen in his sister before.

"Meekos I have been sending you messages for weeks, telling you about Roch's condition and asking for guidance and you cannot send me one response and now you just show up here. You do know that Cerephus does not know who I am. Now dear brother before we discuss your diabolical plan that broke Erebus and me up, tell me what the hell is going on with Roch!"

"So what do you think?" Erebus asked after Meekos left the war room with Sophie. Erebus was relieved that Cerephus now knew the truth about Roch without Sophie being exposed.

"Well, I certainly don't trust him. But I think I would rather be working with him then against him. Did you believe what he was saying?"

"Cerephus I do believe him although I will bet there is much more that he has not told us. I don't think that either of us should trust him but for now it might be better to keep him close so we can see what he is up to."

"Did you see the terror in his face when he saw Roch? That was not a man acting."

"I know. I am sure the punishment for failing the dark lords and demons is what terrifies him. That is why I don't want us to be in that same position. So changing the subject," Erebus said with a smile. "As of today you are the new King of Stordt. What are your plans?"

Cerephus sat back in his chair and smiled with satisfaction; long had he worked for this moment in his life. "First I will inform the military then I will send messengers to all the towns and villages with the news."

"You should also send messengers to all of the other kings," Erebus suggested. "It never hurts to have powerful allies."

Meekos and Sophie screamed at each other for over an hour, before exhaustion calmed them both down. Sophie had always adored her older brother and the thought that he had so betrayed her by breaking up her relationship with Erebus was overwhelming for Sophie. They both sat down on the edge of the bed and did not speak for a few moments.

"So you never did explain why you have not responded to any of my messages," Sophie said with an edge still to her voice.

"Honestly Sophie I never received them and I sent you many, many letters didn't you get them?"

"No," Sophie said fearfully. "Meekos who is intercepting our letters?"

"Mother, Father," said Raul as Sudfad and Renya walked into the kitchen of Raul's and Vitomas' home. "This is a surprise."

"We haven't seen much of you or Simon since you returned," said Renya as she took a seat at the table, next to baby Samuel. "So we thought we would visit."

"Have you had breakfast yet?" Vitomas asked as she was preparing food.

"Yes," replied Sudfad.

"How about some coffee and morning cake," offered Vitomas as she was bringing two cups and a coffeepot to the table.

"I am sorry that we haven't been more active in the celebrations," Raul apologized as he was holding little Sudfad on his lap. "It's just that I want to spend time with Vitomas and the boys and I think Simon feels the same way."

"Oh, we certainly understand," said Sudfad. "We just wanted to visit. And we are going to visit Simon and Annabelle after we leave here."

"Vitomas did you make this cake?" asked Renya. "It is absolutely wonderful."

"Yes," said Vitomas proudly. "Marie was giving Annabelle and me cooking lessons while Raul and Simon were gone."

"Father was it like this for you when you would return from long campaigns?" Raul asked. "As much as I appreciate the celebrations, all I really want to do is hold my family."

Sudfad and Renya both smiled warmly. "Yes, Raul that is exactly what it was like for me," Sudfad said.

"Thank you all for coming. I am sorry to take you away from the celebrations but this is important," Sudfad said. "Please help yourselves to refreshments; we are waiting for a few more."

Claudius and Mathas could not help but notice that only the leaders were gathering in King Sudfad's dining room. "Sudfad as I look around me I see the kings and chiefs, is it alright that I told Stephan, Matthew and Thaos to join us?" asked Claudius.

"Yes, we are waiting on my sons also."

The Sanuri entered the dining room with Thedes and Ibula, her father Manu was already seated at the table. Raul, Simon, Matthew, Stephan and Thaos walked in next, they were all filthy and sweaty. "Sorry we have been fighting," Simon said with a grin. "Sorren will you pass that pitcher of lemonade I think we could use some?"

After Renya, Vitomas and Annabelle entered the dining room, Sudfad closed the doors. "This afternoon our soldiers encountered some Taperian soldiers who were heading to the castle."

Renya gasped, "Sudfad they weren't after the girls again?"

"No, they were delivering a message to me. I want you all to be aware of its contents because I don't know the effects this will have on us," Sudfad handed the letter to the Sanuri who was the closest to him. "There is a new king of the Kingdom of Stordt, a man named Cerephus," Sudfad said.

"Is Roch dead?" asked Raul.

"The letter only says that there is a new king. I asked the girls here to find out if they know this man."

Vitomas watched as the letter was being handed around the room, she suddenly felt like crying with relief at the thought that Roch might be dead. "I know him," Vitomas said. "When I left he was a general in Roch's military but he was also Roch's closest advisor. Cerephus is an evil man but he is very intelligent. If something happened to Roch I would guess that Cerephus was behind it. Actually I hope he killed Roch."

Annabelle said, "Vitomas is right he is an evil man but I don't believe he is as bad as Roch."

"I want to find out what happened to Roch," Simon said. "If he is still alive, he is still a threat to this family."

"Is this Cerephus more of a warlord than Roch was?" asked Sorren.

"Now that he is in command; who knows," said Vitomas.

The Sanuri listened to all of the comments before speaking. "I find it curious that no one has mentioned the fact that Raul would be the next in line for the throne of Stordt." The room became silent.

Meekos was consumed with rage as he searched the caverns that had been prepared for the transformation. He found no Hutas or Beltrad. He found no victims for the feeding of Omnibus. What he did find were dead snakes and piles of ash. Meekos could not contain his anger and kicked a bowl of blood that was on the floor in one of the chambers. "The Chalice of Ascension," Meekos thought. "No that cannot be gone too."

Meekos now entered the chamber that contained the large tank for Roch's body. He carefully searched the altar next to that tank where the chalice had been hidden. Meekos started to panic when he could not find the chalice. He walked over to the tank and inspected it. He saw the ancient words of the Old Ones inscribed on the outside of the stone tank. Meekos touched the stone to look for hidden compartments when he was suddenly consumed with pain. He instantly pulled his hand away. "What is going on here?" Meekos yelled out loud.

Meekos could feel his heart pounding as fear overtook him. "This is bad, this is very bad," he said out loud as he walked around the stone tank. "The transformation cannot take place here." Meekos searched all of the caverns not once but twice trying to find The Chalice of Ascension. Finally he staggered out of the caves as he now felt like he was burdened with a great weight. Meekos stood in the sunlight for a few moments as he tried to calm his emotions. Then he mounted his horse and rode back to the castle.

"Sophie," yelled Meekos as he ran into the kitchen at Roch's castle. "Have you seen it?"

"What on earth are you talking about? Seen what?" Sophie asked as she dried her hands in a towel.

"The caverns, everything is gone; I mean everything," Meekos said frantically.

"But I was just there a couple of weeks ago," Sophie said. "And the preparations were made. Are you sure you got the right caves?"

"Yes, the tank was there but it has been touched by holiness; we cannot put Roch in it. We must find another place for the ascension."

"At this late date, Meekos that is impossible," Sophie said. "The energies for the transformation have already been released."

"The Sanuri is right," said Sudfad. "Son, you will have to decide if you want to risk a war for that throne but it is rightfully yours."

"Raul that is a kingdom filled with evil men, you have been there, you know I speak the truth. If you did take the throne we would never be safe there," Vitomas said with fear in her voice. "Our children would never be safe."

"Does this Cerephus know the throne is Raul's?" Mathas asked.

"I don't know but how could he not?" asked the Sanuri.

"Then Cerephus has every reason to want Raul dead," Sorren said.

"I will have to think about this," said Raul.

"Meekos, you have to believe me that everything was in place but a few weeks ago," Sophie cried. "I saw to it myself."

"Then what has taken place here?"

"I cannot explain it," said Sophie as she looked around the large cavern that held the altar that the chalice had been hidden in. "The Sanuri must have been here."

"First we need to make the arrangements for the ascension then we will take care of the Sanuri once and for all," said Meekos angrily.

"Meekos, you have to go to the other dark lords and find a way to delay the transformation; I will find another location unless..."

647

"Unless what Sophie?"

"Unless you take him back to the monastery and keep him in those underground caverns."

Meekos was quiet for a while as he thought about Sophie's suggestion. "That is not a bad idea but how would I move him?"

"Well he is unconscious; it's not like he will fight you," Sophie said. "I mean, well, look at his condition. Buy a large boca and put a bed in the back of it. I will go with you and help take care of him. At least that way you can have more control over what is going on." Sophie paused. "Meekos know that I will help you but I am returning to Erebus, I am not going to lose him again. And if you try to interfere you will lose me forever."

"Think about it!" gasped Vitomas. "Raul I can't believe you would consider putting your family in such danger. I beg of you please do not pursue this."

"Vitomas, we could free the peoples of that kingdom," Raul said.

"Yes, but at what cost."

That evening Erebus brought Meekos to his work room so they could perform spells. "I see Sophie is keeping us as far apart as she can," Meekos said sarcastically, referring to the distance between their chambers.

"Your sister is an intelligent lady," Erebus said only half joking.

"Erebus I am going to tell you something which I shouldn't. I am telling you because it may affect Sophie's safety," Meekos said. "Today I went to the caves that had been prepared for the ascension and everything is in ruins and touched by holiness. The transformation cannot take place there. So I will be returning to Malga tomorrow to prepare another place for the transformation then I will come back and get Roch." Erebus listened to Meekos without speaking. "Erebus did you know about this?" Meekos demanded.

"No but unlike you I am not surprised. I think only a fool would underestimate The Great Ruler and His emissaries," Erebus said.

"Strange words from a sorcerer," Meekos said suspiciously.

"No Meekos," Erebus said angrily. "It is merely sizing up the other army before you go to battle. I fear for Sophie because I think you are a weak leader who is so arrogant you think you are beyond attack and that is why you are in this situation now."

"Are Raul and Vitomas coming also?" asked Thedes as he and Ibula sat next to each other on a sofa in Simon's parlor." Alexander and Anthony ran up to Thedes and Ibula, who each picked up one of the boys and held them.

"Yes, they will be here," Simon said. "At least I think they will."

"Is something wrong?" asked Ibula.

"Just tell them," Annabelle said as she carried a tray of refreshments and cake into the parlor. Thedes and Ibula looked at Annabelle then at Simon.

"They have been quarreling a great deal," Simon said. "Thedes would you prefer whiskey or lemonade?"

"Whiskey, are they fighting about him taking the throne of Stordt?" asked Thedes.

"Yes, and I agree with Vitomas," said Annabelle defiantly. "Simon you have never been there, it is an evil place, no good will come of Raul and Vitomas moving there."

"You have been there?" asked Ibula.

Annabelle looked at Simon. "You haven't told them?" Then she turned back to Thedes and Ibula. "Do you know King Roch's attachment to this family?"

"No," said Thedes as Ibula shook her head.

"Roch is Sudfad's brother. Roch murdered his own parents for the throne and tried to kill Sudfad. Roch is an evil man and a cruel dictator of his people."

"He took Vitomas and me captives when we were children. He was much worse to Vitomas; he started to rape her when she was nine; he would beat her and torture her. Roch would torture and kill people just for entertainment for his men," Annabelle said emotionally. "Roch gathered evil men to be in his service; it is a kingdom of demons. Raul does not understand what he would be up against."

As Annabelle continued to tell Thedes and Ibula about Roch and the men of Stordt, she and Simon started to argue. It seemed apparent to Thedes and Ibula that both Simon and Raul were leaning towards Raul claiming the throne, while their wives felt strongly against it. Thedes decided to change the subject to lighten up the mood.

"Well, I owe a debt of thanks to both of your families," Thedes said as he put his arm around Ibula's shoulders. "Since Ibula has been spending so much time with your children she has decided that she is ready to start a family."

"That's wonderful," said Annabelle, relieved that Thedes had changed the subject.

"There is a little more to it," said Ibula with a smile. "There are two Shettee boys that Thedes wants to adopt before we have our own baby; so we will soon have a house full."

"Simon, you and Raul met them," Thedes said. "Talmai and Cael."

"Yes," said Simon. "You brought them on a couple of our walks. They seem like fine boys."

"How old are they?" asked Annabelle.

"Talmai is eight and Cael is five," Thedes said happily. "We are going to adopt them as soon as we return home."

"Meekos has been gone for some time now," said Padre Thomas. "That concerns me greatly."

"I agree; I have a feeling that something really bad is going to happen. But perhaps my imagination is just running wild," replied Padre Bartholomew as they walked towards the Hall of Antiquities. "After finding all of this information about Meekos and the Insidiae I keep thinking about that creature Teragon that the Sanuri told us about."

Padre Thomas gave Padre Bartholomew a blank stare. "You must remember; it was well over a year ago when the Hutas stole the holy Box of Itifer. Some sort of creature was butchering Huta warriors. The Sanuri thought it might be the Centras taking revenge as they searched for the box they were supposed to guard for The Great Ruler. Remember the Sanuri and Petra and I told you about the foot prints and cave paintings we saw," said Padre Bartholomew.

"I do remember those things but I don't remember the Teragon," replied Padre Thomas.

"Months later," continued Padre Bartholomew. "The Sanuri found an ancient scroll in the Hall of Antiquities that warned that *the creation of evil begets an evil unto itself of such great proportions that the demons feed upon their own.* Then he found a picture of a creature called the Teragon which means death terror and the Sanuri believes this is the creature that is created as a consequence when beings try to create a great evil, surely you remember this?"

"Yes, my old age must be playing tricks my friend," said Padre Thomas with a laugh. "Now I remember because you and the Sanuri were looking at the picture and realized that creature could have made the footprints you saw. And you wondered what evil could be created that was so great that the Teragon would be created as a consequence." Padre Thomas suddenly stopped and turned and stared at Padre Bartholomew. Padre Thomas did not speak; his eyes grew wider as he realized his own words.

"You are thinking the same thing," said Padre Bartholomew. "The Vessel of Darkness."

"Your Eminence, the road ahead is littered with many rocks, I will try to avoid them but I am afraid the ride will be uncomfortable," the coach driver called down.

"I need to be in Malga before sundown; so don't delay," Meekos called back with frustration. He leaned back against the soft cushions of the elegant carriage and stared out of the windows. Thoughts were racing through Meekos' mind. He could feel panic rising deep within him; which he tried to control.

"Centuries of planning and now everything is unraveling," Meekos said out loud. He trusted no one but his younger sister Sophie. "She will protect Roch until the ascension," Meekos thought. "But is Roch even capable of being the Vessel anymore? That damn Lion! What has he done?"

Meekos could feel tears running down his face, tears of fear; for he was terrified of the retribution of the demons. He wiped the tears from his eyes. "This is nonsense," Meekos uttered out loud. "I can fix this." A statement he made more to reassure himself than of conviction. As Meekos was desperately trying to maintain control of his fears one question kept swirling through his head, "Why did The Lion kill Demetries and not Roch?"

During the long ride back to Malga Meekos reviewed everything he had heard and seen in his head over and over as he searched for clues. Meekos had always considered himself a meticulous man, who was rarely caught unprepared for any situation. "So how can this entire mission seem to be falling apart?" Meekos thought to himself. "Perhaps Erebus was right and I had not considered the strengths of our opponents. Perhaps I have not considered who all of our opponents are?"

As these thoughts raced through Meekos' head, something else kept bothering him also; something that haunted the corners of his mind. "What was it that I saw?" Meekos thought over and over. He was searching his memories for clarification of the shadow he saw, the shadow so fleeting and yet so ominous.

For almost one hour every day for a week, Sudfad and the Sanuri would get together to review the piles of documentation that Padres Thomas and Bartholomew sent to the Sanuri. On day five, Sudfad made an alarming discovery as he was looking at the pictures drawn by Padre Dominick. "I believe I know a couple of these men but how can that be these drawings were done decades ago?"

"The men will still look as they did the day they sold their souls to darkness," said the Sanuri. "What are their names?"

"Gregory Bancar is a wealthy landowner in Wetpr and Cedrick T. Kretcher is the Commanding General at Fort Polta."

"I have seen the name Bancar," said the Sanuri as he flipped through the papers. "Here Gregory Bancar is named as one of the Insidiae and there is a Cedrick Teivel but not a Cedrick Kretcher."

"Sanuri, Bancar was here at the castle, during the weddings. He was inside as we were being attacked," said Sudfad. "And look at this picture." Sudfad handed a drawing to the Sanuri. "The man in the middle looks exactly like General Kretcher. I will have to investigate this. If Kretcher is a member of the Insidiae then he would be our spy."

"Your Eminence it is so good to have you back," said High Priest Tenebrae as he held the carriage door open for Meekos. "I trust that your trip was successful."

"It was interesting, I will give you that," said Meekos with a sneer as he stepped out of the carriage. Then he leaned close to Tenebrae and said, "Get Pravis and come to my chambers in one hour, we have much to discuss." Meekos straightened up and spoke in a louder voice; since the two high priests were in public. "I trust things have been in order in my absence."

"Yes," replied Tenebrae as he and Meekos walked towards the main building of the monastery at Malga. "Even our pesky little priests seem to be behaving."

"What do you mean?" asked Meekos as he waved at other priests walking along the sidewalk.

"They have been spending all of their time in the Hall of Antiquities; I rarely see them out and about," Tenebrae said.

"I am not really sure that is a good thing," Meekos replied. "I would get rid of them now if it wasn't for the Sanuri. But after Omnibus is raised it will be a different story; not even the Sanuri has the power to do battle with that demon."

"So it appears that our plans are running on schedule?" asked Tenebrae tentatively.

"That is what I need to speak with you and Pravis about," said Meekos curtly. "We have to develop an alternate plan."

"High Priest Meekos, High Priest Pravis is here to see you," said the housekeeper.

"Thank you Marla, please have him join us in my study," replied Meekos. Meekos turned to Tenebrae, "There have been serious complications that I want to speak with the two of you about."

"I am sorry I am late," said Pravis as Marla closed the door to the study. Pravis walked quickly towards Meekos and Tenebrae, both of whom were seated in large leather chairs by the hearth.

"Remember that last attack on the Princes of Wetpr?" Pravis asked.

"Pravis just spit it out we are not going to play twenty questions," Meekos said irritably.

"I told you that my messengers found the Huta bodies with Ruala and Shettee arrows in them but we could not find the bodies of the Princes. Well, my spies tell me they are back in the castle at Wetpr," Pravis said.

"Are you sure of this? We thought the Gants got them." asked Tenebrae.

"Since the Enrops patrol the castle at Wetpr our ravens cannot get close but one of my men who is in Salar, delivered food to the castle," Pravis continued. "He said there are great celebrations going on with hundreds of people. He said there were even Rualas and Shettees at the castle. He said the celebrations were held because of the return of the Princes."

"Are you sure about this information?" asked Meekos with great concern.

"Yes, I trust my spy."

"This is very bad, if those groups have formed an alliance," said Meekos anxiously. "They must have been sent by the Sanuri. You do know what this means for us, don't you?"

"That the prophecy of The Seven Sons has not been broken," replied Tenebrae in a whisper.

"Not only that; but the prophecy has begun." All three men sat in silence for many minutes after Meekos made this revelation. "This is just getting worse," Meekos said with apprehension. He stood up and paced back and forth in front of the fireplace for a few moments before returning to his chair. His actions gravely concerned Pravis and Tenebrae as they were not used to seeing Meekos act worried.

"My entire trip to Stordt was a nightmare," Meekos said. "It appears that Demetries was also working for someone else besides me. I will explain more later but while Demetries and Roch were traveling to the Caves of Muldun, The Lion vanquished Demetries and put an affliction on Roch as I have never seen. He was unconscious and did not resemble a human at all. Roch's skin was rotting and he had the stench of death about him."

"Then I went to the caverns and found they had been destroyed. The Hutas, the Beltrad, the bodies and The Chalice of Ascension they are all gone. All I found were some dead snakes and piles of ash. All of the altars were destroyed except for the one that is next to the tank."

"When I touched the tank I was consumed with great pain, as if holiness had touched it. We cannot put Roch's body in there. When I had a chance to speak with Sophie, we discovered that neither of us had received the numerous letters we have been sending, so someone is intercepting them."

"Can Roch still fulfill his role as the Vessel?" Tenebrae asked with the fear rising in his voice.

"That I do not know," said Meekos. "And what worries me greatly is why did The Lion destroy Demetries and not Roch?"

"Do you think The Great Ruler suspects what we are doing?" asked Pravis.

655

"I would think He would have tried to stop us if He knew," replied Meekos. "But there is something going on because the Sanuri has been here so often of late and the prints of a lion were seen near the bodies of Doros, Paullo and Sirius."

"How will we know if Roch is too damaged to be the Vessel for Omnibus?" asked Tenebrae.

"That is exactly what I have been trying to determine since I laid eyes upon him," said Meekos. "And if he is too damaged can we replace him with another?"

"But it took generations of preparations for Roch," said Pravis. "And now the beginning of the transformation could be but months or even weeks away."

"Neither one of you are thinking," screamed Meekos. "Even if he is strong enough, there is no place prepared for the transformation. Sophie thinks we should move Roch here and have the transformation take place in the tunnels and I agree with her."

"Here!" exclaimed Pravis fearfully.

"Do you have a better idea?"

"If we fail at this mission our fates are sealed," cried Tenebrae.

"Is there a way we could contact Omnibus and tell him that the Vessel may be too damaged for the transformation?" Pravis asked.

"And have his wrath upon us," said Meekos. "I would rather seek alternatives before we contact Omnibus."

"We have talked about this before but there are other demons we can summon," Tenebrae offered. "Meekos I know you have concerns that the tribute is too costly but at this point I fear we have little choice."

"I agree with Tenebrae," Pravis said. "If this mission does not succeed we will be cast into the eternal fires of torment."

"I agree we are in a very precarious situation but I still caution that we do not want to owe debts to multiple demons; I have seen the results of such folly," said Meekos.

"There is an ancient demon, as old as time itself; perhaps he can give us the answers we seek," said Tenebrae.

"And what is he called?" asked Meekos.

"Ahriman," replied Tenebrae. "He is called Ahriman."

Pravis and Meekos looked at each other, then back at Tenebrae. "Do you know if this demon really exists or is a myth?" Meekos asked. "I have heard his name but I know of no one who has successfully summoned him."

"I do believe he exists and I have done my research," Tenebrae replied. "I have gathered all we will need to perform the ritual."

"I didn't think we would ever get that stench out of this room," Cerephus said as he handed Erebus a drink. "I have smelled bodies that have been dead for days that were not as disgusting as Roch," added Cerephus as he sat down in a large leather chair. "Why do you keep pacing like a caged animal? What is wrong with you?"

"Something is not right here," replied Erebus as he walked back and forth in front of the wall of windows in Cerephus' bedroom chambers.

"Do you mean because we have a living corpse that is turning into a demon in the castle?" Cerephus asked sarcastically.

"No," replied Erebus. "It is as if the answer is right before us and we are not seeing it. There is more to Meekos than we are aware and every fiber of my body tells me we are in great danger." Erebus stopped pacing and looked at Cerephus.

"Didn't everything just seem too easy? He doesn't care that we take over control of this large and wealthy kingdom and he is willing to pay us; just to feed Roch's body. And he didn't even tell us where or when he is moving Roch's body."

"I will admit I do not trust Meekos either but what do you suspect he is planning?"

"I do not know but I feel as if we are rats walking towards traps. Meekos has access to very strong dark magics; I am trying to think of how I can contact the underworld to get answers without alerting Meekos."

Erebus returned to his room and started pulling books off from the shelves. He took a large stack of books to his desk and started to search for answers to questions he did not yet understand. Cerephus poured himself another glass of whiskey and opened the door to the secret vault behind the fireplace in his chambers. He walked among the treasures, feeling great satisfaction that his plans had come to fruition.

Sophie was in the kitchen, preparing food for Roch. As Sophie was putting dishes on a tray, she suddenly stopped and turned towards the kitchen door. Thinking she heard voices, Sophie opened the door and walked into the stillness of the night. After a few moments Sophie returned to the kitchen, picked up Roch's tray and started the long walk to his chambers.

Roch lay fearfully; his worst nightmares coming true. He was buried alive but it was inside his dying body. Roch's brain was functioning but he could not control any part of his body. The pain was overwhelming; Roch could no longer numb himself with whiskey. But this night a new terror was consuming his being. He could hear the voices, the voices of the shadows.

Chapter XXXL
When Shadows Whisper

"My dear, you really outdid yourself this time," said Sudfad as he slid under the covers next to Renya. "But I have to admit that I am glad to have the guests gone."

"I am too," said Renya as she put down the book she was reading. "But it was a rare experience. What with meeting the Rualas and Shettees. I found it all very exciting."

"I found it incredible. Twenty years ago the Nordes Tribe would never have socialized with the ruling families of Lentz, now they are all related by blood and truly enjoy each other's company. Personally I very much like Sorren and Claudius. And as you said, not only to meet Rualas and Shettees but now to be bonded with them; never in my years did I think such things could happen."

"When Raul and Simon wrote about how much alike they were with Thedes, I rather thought they were exaggerating. Then when Ibula and I started to write to each other, I felt a real kinship towards her," Renya said. "Now we are family. Sudfad, I think all of this is actually quite miraculous. I just wish the children weren't fighting so."

"You mean Raul and Vitomas?"

"Well Simon and Annabelle are also," Renya said. "Both the girls are against Raul assuming that throne and well, I think I agree with them."

"First of all we don't know if Roch is still alive and if he is not, Raul hasn't made up his mind yet; he is considering his options."

"Sudfad, has anyone considered that this might all be some grand trick?"

"What do you mean?"

"Perhaps Roch realizes he cannot beat us if he tries to invade the kingdom so he is going to trick you and others to come to him," Renya said seriously.

"He is a cunning and evil man; I certainly would not put it past him. And speaking of evil men, what are you going to do with that beast who tried to rape Annabelle?"

"Mathas asked me not to have him put to death, for the sake of his family," said Sudfad. "Mathas never asks me for anything so I will grant his request. I have not gone to see the man for fear I would kill him with my own hands. I am going to leave him in the dungeons; for how long, I have not decided."

The screams echoed in the caverns under the monastery at Malga. Meekos supervised as each man and woman was thrown into the fiery pit. "Thirty five human sacrifices and this is just the beginning of the tribute to Ahriman," Meekos said to Pravis with annoyance.

"Better them than us," Pravis replied.

Tenebrae danced with the Hutas around the fire pit as each sacrifice was thrown to their death. Tenebrae wore a ceremonial costume of brightly colored feathers and bones. He had painted the ancient supplications to Ahriman on his body with blood taken from the people to be sacrificed.

The Huta dancers adorned themselves in the clothing they had taken off from the victims they sacrificed. Meekos and Pravis wore the robes of their priesthood. The smell of burnt flesh permeated the cavern. "I will never get use to that smell," Meekos said with disgust.

"Meekos this is the right thing to do," Pravis said. "You were right; Omnibus is in the midst of preparations for the transformation and we should not be bothering him unless we have facts."

"I still wonder if we could have found another way to get our answers; I do not like owing debts to two such powerful demons," Meekos said as he nodded his head, signaling that another person was to be thrown into the fire.

A lone Huta warrior walked up to Pravis and whispered into his ear. Pravis nodded and the Huta walked past the fire pit and into a corridor leading to the chamber. "What did he say?" asked Meekos.

"He said the livestock are ready for sacrifice," Pravis replied nonchalantly.

"This is going to be a very long night," grumbled Meekos.

"Will you stop looking at me," Timothy said with annoyance. "I hate the way you just stare." The eyes in the darkness only blinked at Timothy.

"Well, you could at least talk to me, that would be the civilized thing to do," Timothy said to his cellmate. "We might be in here a very long time; we will have to do something to endure this boredom. Why are you in here?" There was silence. "Ok then don't tell me," Timothy shouted as he stood up from his mattress and walked over to the cell door. "I just can't believe I am in here," he said sadly.

"Are you saying you are innocent?" asked the cellmate.

"No," Timothy blurted out with frustration. "I was drunk and stupid. Of all the girls at that celebration, it was the King's daughter that I jumped." Then Timothy quickly spun around and looked at his cellmate, "I will bet you anything that if it was a different girl, I wouldn't be in here because nobody would care."

"If it was the King's daughter then you are lucky to be alive."

"Lucky!" screamed Timothy. "You think this is lucky. I am going to rot in this putrid cell." Timothy pushed his head against the bars and started to cry, "I just can't believe it," he said over and over.

"You can't believe what?" asked his cellmate with annoyance.

"I can't believe I was stupid enough to get caught," Timothy yelled as he turned towards his cellmate. "Haven't you been listening to anything?"

Mathas and Claudius went to Fahron's castle the first night they returned to Lentz. The housekeeper let them in and they found Fahron and Isadore sitting in the dark, in their parlor.

"My Lord it is King Mathas and Claudius," said the housekeeper as they stood in the doorway of the parlor.

"Let me light a few candles," Fahron said as he got up from a large leather chair. "Please, please come in. Would you like a drink?"

"Yes," said Claudius.

"I will pour you all some whiskey," said Isadore. "In fact, I may have some with you." After Isadore handed each of the men a glass of whiskey, she sat down and looked at Mathas for a few moments then asked, "Is he dead?"

"No, I asked Sudfad to spare his life," Mathas said solemnly.

"What will they do with him?" Isadore asked in a strained voice.

"Sudfad will keep him locked in the dungeons, but for how long I do not know yet," Mathas looked at both of the grief strained faces of his friends. "There was so much anger at Timothy for what he did that Sudfad would not go near him, nor would he allow any of his family near Timothy for fear they would kill him. Sudfad has yet to pronounce the sentence."

"Tell us what happened, everything," Fahron said.

Claudius looked at Isadore then at Fahron, "Perhaps that is not wise, my friend."

"Mathas you had to understand the monster that Juleta became before you could let go, we need to do the same," said Isadore through her tears.

Mathas gave Claudius a reluctant look, so Claudius decided to tell the story. "From the moment we arrived in Wetpr Timothy did nothing but drink. His drunkenness and arrogance did not make him popular with the women he was trying to impress. The night of the Grand Ball Simon's wife, Annabelle, left the ballroom to go to their quarters so she could feed their young baby."

"Annabelle walked past Thaos as she was leaving the ballroom. Thaos saw Timothy watching her, when Timothy started to follow Annabelle, Thaos followed him."

"By the time Thaos caught up with them, Timothy had Annabelle against the wall of a hallway and was tearing her clothes off. Thaos pulled Timothy off from the girl and punched him twice. Soon a crowd gathered and Simon came. Now you two have to understand that Simon and Raul almost died, they were separated from their wives and children for many months, so I believe emotions were running high," Claudius paused.

"What happened?" demanded Fahron.

Mathas continued the story, "When Simon got there, Timothy was on the floor but he was alright. Simon told the guards to take Timothy to the dungeons. Well, Timothy starts running off his mouth and as he was saying that Annabelle wanted him to do it, Simon became filled with rage and beat the hell out of Timothy. If Sudfad and I hadn't pulled him off, I think Simon would have killed your son."

Both Fahron and Isadore sat in silence; after a few moments Fahron said, "If I was Simon I would have wanted to kill him too."

"I just can't believe he attacked a girl who was going home to feed her baby," Isadore said with tears running down her face.

"Fahron there is something else you should know," Claudius said. "When I got your letter I went to see Timothy. Stephan and Matthew came with me; I believe to keep me from hurting your son. Timothy showed no regret or shame for his deeds; in fact he was cocky and arrogant. He demanded to know why it was taking so long for us to get him out of the dungeons."

"I told Timothy the words of your letter but he did not believe me so I showed it to him. Fahron and Isadore you may hate me for what I am about to tell you next. King Sudfad and Queen Renya are such gracious hosts and they have a loving family. Timothy's actions brought great shame on all of us and I told him so. I told Timothy he was a dead man if I ever saw him again."

The sunrise could not be seen from the caverns below the monastery at Malga. The smell of burning flesh was overwhelming to the dancers and to the Huta warriors.

Meekos and Pravis were sickened by the smell and each took turns leaving the caverns for fresh air. Tenebrae was clearly exhausted from dancing around the fire pit for over eight hours.

"Do we even know if Ahriman will appear to us after all these sacrifices?" Meekos asked as he moved the cloth he held over his nose and mouth to block the sickening odors.

Pravis too, held a cloth over his face and when he moved it to answer; Meekos saw that Pravis was quite pale. "A demon of this magnitude chooses his own time," replied Pravis. "After all this he may not appear at all."

Another hour passed and a Huta warrior signaled to Meekos and Pravis that the last of the animals had been driven into the fire. "Finally," said Meekos. "I will be hearing those screams in my sleep." Tenebrae told the Huta dancers to leave the cavern; only Meekos, Pravis and Tenebrae were intended to see the face of Ahriman. The three high priests waited another hour with no sign of the demon.

"I do not intend to stay in this pit forever," growled Meekos. "I thought this was a waste of time." He abruptly turned and walked towards one of the corridors leading away from the cavern. Pravis and Tenebrae both looked at Meekos then at each other as they tried to decide what they should do.

"Wait," called Pravis and the two men caught up to Meekos.

The three high priests had barely taken two more steps when a dark mist appeared all around them. Soon they started to choke. "Is this smoke from the pit?" Meekos yelled. Neither Pravis nor Tenebrae answered as they were trying to catch their breath.

All three men turned quickly to go down the corridor but they found their way blocked by a Talmuth. The three men jumped back in horror at seeing the dragon-like creature suddenly appear before them. Laughter echoed through the caverns, an evil, malicious laughter.

"For men with blood on their hands you frighten easily," a taunting voice called out of the darkness.

"We have summoned Ahriman," Meekos said with authority. "Are you Ahriman?"

"I am called by many names, my little hypocrites. Who are you to call upon me?"

The three priests looked around the cavern but they could see no one, just the Talmuth that stood before one of the corridors.

"My Lord, we have called upon you because of your wisdom and strength, all we ask of you is answers," Pravis said humbly.

"You killed all those people and creatures because you are searching for answers?" Laughter echoed throughout the caverns. "You amuse me greatly."

"Why do you call us hypocrites?" demanded Meekos. "We have followed the demands for an audience with you."

"Oh, have I insulted your precious dignity?" the voice taunted. "You wear the garbs of high priests of an order that serves The Great Ruler; yet you desecrate all He stands for and you do not consider yourselves hypocrites? Are you that blind or that stupid? I do not deal with stupid people." The voice grew louder as it talked.

"We are not stupid," Pravis said humbly. "What you say is correct. Are you Ahriman?"

"I will ask the questions for now," the voice said harshly. "The one who is consumed with ego, you said you followed the demands for an audience; you are not ignorant enough to believe that you have satisfied all my demands are you?" Meekos did not answer. "Well are you?" demanded the voice.

"No," Meekos said angrily.

The voice started to laugh; the laughter grew in volume until the vibrations started to shake the cavern violently. "I love hypocrites," the voice bellowed. "Of all humans you amuse me the most, and I think the three of you actually believe your own lies about your sense of self-importance." The voice laughed again; a long maniacal laugh. After several minutes of laughter, the voice said, "I see you wear the rings of Omnibus. Does he know you are summoning me?"

"No," replied Tenebrae fearfully. "We have questions for you about how we can serve Omnibus."

"Why would you think I would want to help Omnibus?" the voice roared.

The three priests were overwhelmed with the presence of malevolence that filled the chambers. They felt as if something was pressing up against them and they were having difficulty breathing. Their bodies shook with fear.

"I am waiting for an answer, hypocrites."

"We have called upon you My Lord," Tenebrae said humbly. "Because of your reputed wisdom. We have a most unusual problem that we believe only a demon of your level can help us with. Please tell us what is your price for the answers to our questions?"

"Oh you will be paying my price for a long time, should I choose to help you," said the voice. "But you have stirred my curiosity; proceed with your questions."

"First are you Ahriman?" Meekos asked.

There was silence for a few moments then the voice said, "That is one of my names. I am called many things by the different peoples of the worlds."

"We have been members of the Insidiae for hundreds of years," Tenebrae explained. "We have worked faithfully to put into motion the energies and magics to help Omnibus escape from his prison in Solv. But now at the eleventh hour everything is unraveling and we don't know why. We call upon you to give us some direction in how we can correct what is happening."

"Have you told this to Omnibus?"

"No not yet," said Tenebrae. "We wanted to have some ways to correct the problems before we spoke with him."

"Do you mean to tell me that you fear Omnibus more than you fear me?" Ahriman asked with indignation. "I was before Omnibus and I will remain after this name is wiped out of the thoughts of men. You truly have not done your homework." The three high priests looked at each other fearfully. "Continue with your story," Ahriman demanded.

"Several generations ago a pact was made between some of the members of the Insidiae and Omnibus. Tributes were paid to set into motion a human blood line of such evil proportions that the second son of the second son of the second son would be strong enough to be a vessel for Omnibus," Tenebrae explained.

"That vessel is King Roch of the Kingdom of Stordt. We have been working faithfully to prepare a chamber and everything necessary for the transformation. But some months ago The Lion of The Great Ruler killed a demon that was watching over Roch and put an affliction upon the King."

"What sort of affliction?" Ahriman asked.

"Roch is alive but he looks and smells as if he is long dead," Meekos said. "His flesh is rotting from his body."

"And you have seen this?"

"Yes My Lord, I returned from his castle but days ago," Meekos said.

"Go on."

"Now Roch is unconscious and we do not know if it is because the transformation has started or if it is because of the affliction," Meekos continued. "And I went to the caverns that were prepared for the transformation and everything has been destroyed except for one altar and the tank. But these items appear to have been touched by holiness so they no longer can be used for the ascension. And The Chalice of Ascension was taken from us."

"I see," said Ahriman. "So what is it that you want from me?"

"How can we tell if Roch is still strong enough to be the Vessel? And if he is not, can we make him stronger or substitute another at this late hour since the energies have already been released?" asked Meekos.

"Let me think about this," Ahriman said. "Tomorrow morning return to this place with a large chest of jewels and I will give you an answer."

Roch could no longer tell if it was day or night. His eyes felt as if they had melted shut. Roch could not speak, he could not cry out. Roch lay in the silence of his prison, his heart racing; he could hear it pounding in his head. Roch tried to move his arms but they felt so heavy, too heavy for him to move. Roch could feel the panic taking control, "Stop this, get control," Roch thought to himself. "Where am I?"

Roch tied to calm himself by concentrating on the last thing he remembered before waking up in this tomb. Roch had no sense of time anymore, he felt as if he was floating in a great nothingness. "Am I dead?" the thought filled Roch with horror. Once again Roch tried to calm himself by concentrating on the last thing he could remember.

Suddenly an image appeared in his mind. Roch remembered being in his war room, he was sitting at his desk. Roch remembered standing up and walking over to the table to fill his glass with whiskey and that is when he saw them. Suddenly panic filled Roch's being again. "I remember now," he thought. "I saw the shadows, but I saw nothing that could have made those images. Then they moved."

"We're in the parlor," Bella called out as Stephan and Thaos walked in the front door of their castle.

"Have you seen the girls?" Stephan asked as he kissed his mother on the cheek.

"They are in the kitchen preparing dinner," Bella said. "And I want to talk to you both before they come out. Those two girls are so sweet and they never complain but I know they are homesick sometimes. This morning they told me that Mathas lets Angelina prepare the food of their tribe once a week and Ingr sounded so envious that I told them they could cook dinner tonight."

"They both got so excited you should have seen them," Bella said with a loving smile. "We went shopping and they took me to a market near the docks that I have never been to before. They picked out all of the food and have been cooking all day. Please, if you don't like what they make, don't hurt their feelings. And if you do like the food, Claudius I think you should let the girls cook once in a while."

"Well if it tastes half as good as it smells that won't be a problem," said Claudius as he poured them all drinks.

"And boys," Bella continued. "Both of those girls grew up poor; they don't feel comfortable with the servants and they said they want to cook for their husbands." Stephan and Thaos looked at each other and smiled at Bella's comment.

"They're home," Ingr called into the kitchen as she walked into the parlor. Ingr kissed Stephan, "Stephan we have been having so much fun."

"Good, the food smells great."

"Give us a couple of minutes," Ingr said then ran back to the kitchen.

"See what I mean," Bella said.

After a few minutes Nikki walked into the parlor and kissed Thaos before she told the family to come into the dining room.

"Girls this is beautiful," Bella said as she looked at the flowers and candles on the table. There were platters of cooked seafood, fresh bread, cheeses and fruit. Each place setting had four glasses above the plates and there were two large trays of bottles set on the table. The bottles were identical except for different colors of wax at the top of each bottle.

Claudius and Bella took their seats at the opposite ends of the long table, Stephan and Thaos took seats opposite of each other on the sides of the table. "What are all of these bottles?" Stephan asked.

"Sorren makes wonderful ale," Ingr said. "We rode to the village this morning and got some different kinds for you to try." "The yellow wax is ale with honey in it; that is my favorite." Then Ingr looked at Bella. "Bella you have to try that ale. The different dark shades of wax indicate how dark and strong the ale is."

"I didn't know Sorren made ale," said Claudius happily as he grabbed a bottle with dark wax.

"This is just the first course," Nikki said as she sat down next to Thaos. "And there are pies for dessert."

669

The first course was eaten quickly to the delight of Ingr and Nikki. They cleared the dishes and carried in platters of baked ribs with bowls of various types of sauces, yams and vegetables.

"Ingr if I had any idea you could cook like this I would have had you cooking all of the time," Stephan said as he piled more ribs onto his plate.

"Really?" Ingr asked. "Because Nikki and I would really like to cook a lot of the meals."

"Our new quarters will have nice kitchens," Stephan said. "And I can always eat, why don't you start cooking at home?" Ingr smiled then looked across the table at Thaos.

"Nikki, Ingr this is some of the best food I have ever tasted, you can cook any time," Thaos said as he looked at Nikki. "I will give you some money tomorrow so you can set up the kitchen." Nikki kissed Thaos on the cheek.

"Girls this is a truly fine meal," Claudius said. "You can prepare meals for the entire family anytime you want." Both Nikki and Ingr smiled proudly.

"Claudius wait until you see how pretty Bella looks in the dress she bought today," Ingr said.

"I think she looks sexy in it," Nikki added. Stephan's head shot up as he gave Nikki a surprised look. Nikki started to laugh, "Stephan just because she is your mother doesn't mean she can't look sexy. Wait until you see her."

Everyone at the table started to laugh. "Well, I can't wait to see you in the dress," Claudius said as he looked at Bella.

Both Claudius and Bella loved having Stephan, Ingr, Thaos and Nikki living in the castle with them. Before Stephan married, he rarely stayed home, choosing to spend his time on military maneuvers or staying with Matthew.

Although Bella and Claudius loved each other, the emptiness of the large castle was at times overwhelming, especially to Bella. Both Claudius and Bella now considered Thaos a second son. Stephan and Thaos were becoming close friends which only enhanced the relationships between the two young couples.

Ingr and Nikki had quickly worked their way into the hearts of Bella and Claudius. Bella loved them as daughters, Claudius was also very proud of them as warriors.

"I am going to pay Sorren a visit tomorrow," Claudius announced. "I want to see how he makes this ale, it is very good. If anyone wants to ride along you are welcomed."

"Have you been to our village before?" asked Nikki.

"No."

"Then Ingr and I will ride with you," Nikki said.

Ingr turned to Bella. "Why don't you come with us?"

Bella was pleased and surprised by the invitation. "I would love to," she said.

"Sorren will be proud that you are coming to visit," Ingr explained. "He will invite you to a meal, just so you know to turn him down would be considered a dishonor."

"Are there any other ways of your people we should know about?" Claudius asked. "Should we bring gifts?"

"Perhaps a bottle of whiskey for Sorren and something nice but simple for Shara," Nikki said. "Our people are poor compared to your family; to give them things that are very expensive would just accent the differences."

"Bella, one of those scarves you bought today would be a nice gift," Ingr suggested.

"I am glad you girls told us this," Bella said. "After dinner help me pick out the one you think Shara would like."

Nikki and Ingr cleared the dishes and brought four pies and a bowl of heavy cream with spices to the table. "I'll try a slice of each," Stephan said with a grin.

"I think we all will," said Claudius, who was truly enjoying the meal.

"We received a letter from the Sanuri today," Bella said. "He said he could be here in four weeks if you wanted to have your wedding then."

Thaos and Nikki looked at each other and nodded. "That would be fine Bella," Thaos said.

Bella looked at Nikki then at Ingr. "We should have you fitted for your dresses soon."

Nikki explained to Thaos, "We have been putting that off because Ingr and I didn't know how big we would be."

"You both have such little stomachs you are barely showing," Stephan said.

"But that can change any time," Ingr said with a laugh.

"So have you thought about who you want to be in the wedding?" Bella asked.

"Stephan and Ingr and Matthew and Angelina," Nikki said.

"I was thinking about Ryan too," Thaos said as he looked at Nikki. "Would you have a friend to walk down the aisle with him?"

Nikki and Ingr looked at each other and smiled. "Oh yes," Nikki said.

"How about that little brunette who was all over Thaos at our wedding?" Stephan said with a chuckle.

"No," Nikki said angrily.

Thaos started to laugh. "I don't think Ryan is ready for a girl like that."

Stephan could see that Nikki was getting angry so he decided to tease her. "What's the matter Nikki you look mad?"

"Elexas is always flirting with Thaos," Nikki said.

"Yes but Thaos doesn't do anything to encourage her," Ingr said.

"Thank you Ingr," Thaos said with a grin. Then he looked at Stephan and winked.

"Well there is more," Nikki said. "The first night that I slept with Thaos, she came to his room and..."

"And what Nikki?" Stephan asked with a grin.

"She offered to have sex with both of us," Thaos said while still grinning, then he looked at Nikki.

"What!" yelled Ingr. "Elexas wanted to have sex with Nikki too. I can't believe that."

"I didn't understand what she was talking about; Thaos had to explain it to me."

"So did she stay?" Stephan asked kiddingly as he stared at Nikki.

"No and I don't even want her at the wedding," Nikki said with a pout.

"You invited the entire village, you can't very well tell Elexas she can't come," Ingr said.

"Perhaps she will behave better at your wedding," Bella offered.

"No she won't," said Ingr. "Elexas doesn't just want Thaos she wants every man." Then Ingr looked at Stephan. "She will come after you too."

"What do you want me to do?" Stephan asked jokingly.

"What!" gasped Ingr as she quickly spun around.

"I am just kidding Honey," laughed Stephan as he put his arm around Ingr's shoulders.

"Stephan I know you had, I don't know, hundreds of girlfriends before we were married," Ingr said accusingly. "And the night we were supposed to meet you were with another woman."

Stephan was grinning as he listened to Ingr. "Well, I would not say I dated hundreds of women but I did date a lot."

673

"And you know I had no idea that Matthew was going to introduce us that night. Ingr I haven't been with another girl since I met you."

"Even when you left me?" she asked in a hoarse whisper. Ingr looked as if she was going to cry.

Now Stephan realized that Ingr was serious and had fears of him going out with other women. "Ingr I did not see any other women when we were separated," Stephan said softly.

"And we can attest to that," Claudius said as he could see Ingr was upset. "He was in such a bad humor all that time that no one wanted to be around him."

"You're my only girl," Stephan said as he leaned over and kissed Ingr.

"What are you doing?" Ingr asked as she walked out of the bedroom and saw Stephan standing at the dining room table looking at maps.

Without looking at her, Stephan said, "Just reviewing this for tomorrow's training exercises." Then he turned and looked at Ingr, who was standing beside him wearing a silk lilac nightgown.

"You look incredible," Stephan said and bent down and kissed her on the lips. One kiss grew into several as their passions were taking control. Suddenly Stephan stopped kissing Ingr and stood straight up. "Before we go to bed I want to talk about some things," Stephan said as he took Ingr's hand and walked towards the sofa.

"Is this about what I said during dinner?" Ingr asked.

"Yes."

"Are you mad?"

"Of course not, why would I be mad?" Stephan asked as they both sat on the sofa. "But it was obvious you had been thinking about those things for some time and you are still upset."

Stephan continued to hold Ingr's hand as he spoke. "Ingr when I disappeared for a while, it wasn't because of another woman or because of anything you did. I won't lie, I don't completely understand my feelings at the time but it was like I was at war with myself. I loved you and I wanted you; yet a part of me didn't want to be in love or to settle down."

Ingr did not speak but tears filled her eyes and started to run down her cheeks as she listened to him. Stephan continued, "I never thought about marrying anyone or having children before I met you and I found those thoughts scared me. I was angry and for a while I thought I was angry at you but eventually I realized I was angry at myself. And the more people told me that you were the perfect wife for me the more it scared me."

"People said that?" Ingr asked in a hoarse whisper.

"Mainly Father and Matthew but I believe Mathas thought it also."

"You sound like Nikki," Ingr said trying to force a smile.

"I think Nikki handled it much better than I did. And I am sorry that I hurt you so," Stephan said and kissed the back of Ingr's hand. "I loved my life before but I would not trade my life with you for anything." Tears were flowing down Ingr's cheeks, she wanted to speak but the words would not come.

"Ingr you make me so happy. I love you and I love our baby."

Chapter XLI
The Darkness of His Sight

"Honey please stop crying," Raul begged as he put his hand on Vitomas' shoulder. She had been lying on her side with her back to him since they got into bed. "Will you just talk to me?"

"Raul there is nothing more that I can say, you know how I feel. In my mind Stordt is hell and you are asking me to return to hell and expose our children to it," Vitomas turned and looked at Raul with eyes that were filled with tears. "Raul mark my words, if we go to Stordt we will never see our children grow to be adults."

"Honey, nothing is for sure yet," Raul said soothingly. "We don't even know if Roch is dead. If he is alive the throne is rightfully his. I am just weighing the options."

"You are doing more than weighing the options Raul, you are drawing up plans of attack," Vitomas said angrily. "Don't lie to me, I am not a fool."

"Vitomas you are right but I am drawing up plans to determine the feasibility of such a move." Vitomas sat up in bed and grabbed her stomach. "Honey are you alright?" Raul asked with concern.

"Yes, I am fine. But I am so disturbed by all of this because it is as if Roch is still tearing at our relationship and trying to destroy it. Please can't we just forget about all of this?" Vitomas asked then grabbed her stomach again as a wave of pain surged through her. "Raul, I think you should wake Angelina and Annabelle."

"Is the baby coming?" Vitomas nodded as she clenched her teeth as another wave of pain surged through her body. "But isn't it too early?" Raul asked fearfully.

"Just get Angelina."

"Will you be alright? I will be right back," Raul said nervously as he jumped out of bed and started to run out of the room.

"Raul, your pants," Vitomas called after him.

"Can I speak with you?" Thaos asked as he stood in the doorway of Claudius' study.

"Of course son; come in," said Claudius as he sat behind his desk which was covered with papers.

Thaos placed a large pouch of gold coins on the desk before taking a seat across from Claudius. "Bella will not let me pay for any of the wedding preparations," Thaos said with frustration.

Claudius started to laugh. He stood up and walked over to the table that held the bottles of whiskey and wine. He poured two glasses of whiskey then walked over to Thaos and handed him one. "Son, when you have been married as long as I have you will understand this. Bella always wanted more children. She felt like she missed out on many things, like planning weddings and preparing for grandchildren. She is so happy now; just let her do this for you and Nikki."

"Claudius I appreciate what you are saying but you both have done so much for us already and I am not your son."

"You have said that before, yet Bella and I asked you to live here as family and you and Nikki are certainly part of this family."

"And we feel the same about you which is why I don't want to take advantage of your kindness."

"Son, trust me you have brought more to us then we have given to you. Have you picked out a name if the baby is a girl?"

"No."

"Why don't you have Nikki talk with Bella? She had some names picked out if we would have had daughters. If you two like one of the names it would please her greatly."

Claudius handed the pouch back to Thaos. "We are not taking your money son." Thaos stared at Claudius for a few moments before he took the pouch. "I still don't feel right about this," Thaos said; after a pause he added. "Also, Nikki wants to ask you something but for some reason she is scared to."

"Why Thaos, Bella and I spent the entire day with the girls, we went to their village and had a wonderful time; she didn't act like she was afraid of me," Claudius said with amazement.

"No, she isn't afraid of you," Thaos explained. "Nikki was very close to her father and he died in a hunting accident. She wants to ask you if you will walk her down the aisle."

A broad smile came across Claudius' face, "You tell that little girl I would be proud to."

"This is my third child and I am just as nervous as I was with little Sudfad," Raul said as he paced back and forth in his parlor. As was the case with every new birth in the castle; the entire family, including the Sanuri gathered for the new arrival. Even Marie was up and brought refreshments to the parlor for the family.

Matthew was watching Raul pace. "You are going to wear out that rug," he said teasingly.

"Matthew you just wait, your turn is coming soon," Raul said jokingly, then he said with seriousness. "It is the most helpless feeling in the world to see your wife in that much pain and know there is nothing you can do for her."

"Simon was sitting in a chair next to Matthew. "I will tell you I was terrified that Annabelle would die giving birth to the twins. Both those babies were so big and she is such a tiny little thing. I agree with Raul, I really felt helpless."

"Now the two of you are scaring me," Matthew said.

Annabelle came out of the bedroom. "Is everything alright?" Raul asked with fear in his voice, for he had not heard a baby cry. Annabelle took Raul's hand and squeezed it. "Everything is fine, I am just getting some coffee for me and Angelina and some more water for Vitomas. Angelina doesn't expect the baby to come for a while yet, so you can go in and visit her."

Raul knocked on the door then entered the bedroom. Vitomas laughed, "Raul you look worse than I do."

He flew to Vitomas' side and kissed her. "I always worry about you so," Raul said.

"Angelina told me you had your pants on by time you got to her door," Vitomas said with a grin. Angelina laughed loudly at this comment.

Raul looked at both of the women, "Honestly I put them on outside of the bedroom door before I knocked."

"Raul!" scolded Angelina. "You mean to tell me you walked into our quarters naked. You know we don't just make love in the bedroom."

Raul laughed, "I guess it would have been a surprise for all of us."

"Wait until I tell Matthew," Angelina teased.

"Oh don't worry, Simon and I already have him nervous about your baby coming."

"Oh Raul, don't scare him any more than he already is. He is so over protective of me now that I am going crazy."

Raul and Vitomas smiled. "He really loves you," Vitomas said.

"Please tell me it will get better with the second baby," Angelina said with a smile.

Vitomas looked at Raul then at Angelina. "No Angelina it does not get better," Vitomas said and laughed.

Roch could feel his heart pounding wildly. Fear so consumed him that he felt as if his heart would explode. He tried to calm himself, he tried to yell, he tried to move his hands; he felt as if he was suspended in vast nothingness.

"Is this hell? I must have died and gone to hell," the thoughts raced through Roch's mind, over and over the same questions and that song. But Roch could not remember when he had ever heard the words to the song nor could he understand why they filled his being now.

*The terror that dwelt within him, the darkness that he called,
the monsters he created, the heavens saw him fall.*

"This seems to be taking forever," Raul said as he paced back
and forth before the bedroom door. "The last time I peeked in the
room Angelina said it would be soon. Do you think there are
problems?" Raul asked everyone in the room.

"Raul it has only been six hours, your boys each took longer
than that," Renya said soothingly. "Why are you so worried? Is
there something you haven't told us?"

Raul stopped pacing as every eye in the room was now on him.
"You know we have been arguing for days about me taking the
throne in Stordt," Raul said then paused. "We were arguing when
she started to go into labor."

"And you think that something will go wrong with the delivery
because she was upset?" Renya asked.

"Yes," Raul replied. "And I feel awful."

"But you said she was fine when you were visiting her,"
Matthew offered.

"Yes, yes, you are right. Do you think I am blowing this out of
proportion?"

"Raul, it is obvious you feel guilty about arguing and you are
always worried sick when she has a baby," Renya said. "I am sure
everything will be just fine."

Marie carried trays of breakfast foods into the parlor of the
west wing. The morning sun was climbing in the sky but not one
member of the Royal Family left the room. Simon, Matthew,
Sudfad and Alexander were playing cards, while Laurel and
Renya sewed. The Sanuri and Petra were each sleeping in
overstuffed chairs. Raul tried to play cards but could not
concentrate so he paced.

"This is his third child and look at him," Simon said to
Matthew. "Think what you will be like with your first."

Matthew laughed but before he could answer, a cry rang out. A baby's cry and everyone in the room was on their feet. For Raul the moments before Annabelle opened the door seemed like hours. "Everyone is fine," Annabelle said with an exhausted smile. "Please just give us a couple of minutes and you can come in," then she looked at Raul. "And meet your beautiful daughter." Everyone was now wide awake and filled with excitement, except for Petra who curled up in a chair and fell back to sleep.

Five minutes later Angelina opened the door and announced, "Please come in and meet Ariel Renya." Both Laurel and Renya smiled with pleasure to hear that the baby was named after both of them, a secret that both Raul and Vitomas had kept as a surprise. Raul ran up to the bedside and kissed Vitomas.

"Vitomas you look so good," Laurel said with surprise.

"It's the tonics that Angelina makes," Vitomas said. "They are wonderful."

As Vitomas put the baby into Raul's arms, Annabelle said kiddingly. "Finally a baby that looks like Vitomas."

"But I think she has Raul's aqua eyes," Vitomas said with a warm smile.

Momentarily Raul could do nothing but stare at his baby daughter. With the birth of each of his children Raul was always overwhelmed by the miracle of it all. "Raul show her to the rest of us," Simon said.

As Raul walked around the room showing the baby to the family, Annabelle said. "Simon and Raul, Vitomas and I were thinking." Both Raul and Simon turned and looked at Annabelle. "Angelina has delivered two of our babies; perhaps we should go to Lenz and help her when its time."

"We could do that," Raul said.

Simon turned to Matthew, "Would you have room for all of us?"

"You are more than welcomed," Matthew said, then added with a grin. "Maybe you can keep me sane while I wait."

The next morning Meekos, Pravis and Tenebrae had Huta warriors carry a chest of jewels to the caverns underneath the monastery. The three high priests waited in the exact same spot where they had encountered Ahriman the day before. Morning turned into afternoon and afternoon into evening. The three were fearful that if they complained Ahriman would hear them. So they sat in virtual silence for hours waiting to pay tribute to the demon.

"That is it, I am not waiting any longer," Meekos said with frustration. "I am hungry and exhausted. I am going to my chambers."

"But do you think you should leave?" Pravis asked.

"You two can stay," Meekos said as he stood up and started to walk towards one of the tunnels.

"Where are you going my little hypocrite?" Ahriman's voice rang out.

Meekos spun around angrily. "Have you been here the entire time?"

"I have just been waiting for one of you to have the nerve to call out to me. You disappointed me. You think of yourselves as such powerful men in your world and yet you do not even have the guts to ask if I am in the cavern."

"Next time we will know better," Meekos barked angrily.

Pravis jumped to his feet because he was afraid that Meekos would anger Ahriman. "My Lord we have brought you the jewels you requested."

"Open the chest so I may look upon them."

Pravis lifted the lid to the chest, exposing its contents of precious jewels.

"You did well," Ahriman said. "Now I have a few questions for you. Meekos did you touch Roch's body?"

"Why, yes and when I did my hand started on fire," Meekos said. "I thought a spell had been placed upon him so I started to say a reversal spell and Roch's skin started to smoke."

"Those reactions are from the holiness of The Lion. Even if Roch's body is strong enough for the transformation Omnibus will not be able to enter the Vessel."

"Then what shall we do?" Tenebrae asked fearfully.

"You know you must tell Omnibus."

"But he might punish us," Pravis whined.

"So is this why you came to me; for protection?"

"No, we came to you for answers as we said," Meekos stated. "We still want the transformation to take place."

"If you do not tell Omnibus and he comes in contact with Roch's body his anger will be uncontainable."

"Can we substitute another body as a vessel since the energies have already been released? Or can we rid Roch's body of The Lion's touch?" Meekos asked.

"Can we pay you to protect us?" Pravis asked.

Ahriman laughed loudly. "You have not paid me enough for all of these answers. Tomorrow night bring a large chest of gold coins here. Suddenly a great wind arose in the cavern. Dust blew violently, temporarily blinding the three priests. The wind lasted but moments and when it was gone, they discovered the chest of jewels was no longer in the cavern.

After the Huta warriors set the chest of gold coins on the ground, Pravis dismissed them. High Priests Meekos, Pravis and Tenebrae stood alone in the cavern underneath the monastery waiting for Ahriman. "Are you here?" Meekos called into the dimly lit cavern.

The Huta warriors had placed burning torches on the walls of the cavern and along the passageway that the three priests had taken. Now the flames were dancing and diminishing as if a great hand was extinguishing them one by one.

"Ahriman, do you want to play games or do you want this gold?" Meekos yelled with frustration.

All of the flames suddenly extinguished. "You will not speak to me in that manner," Ahriman's voice rang angrily through the caverns. Meekos started to choke as if a hand was closing around his throat. In the darkness Pravis and Tenebrae could hear his gurgling.

"Meekos, are you alright?" Tenebrae whispered into the darkness. Silence. "Meekos," Tenebrae whispered again.

Suddenly all of the torches were consumed with fire that shot to the ceiling. Pravis and Tenebrae stood in horror as they saw Meekos' body suspended in the air high above them. Suddenly Meekos dropped and fell to the ground with a loud thud and a scream.

"My arm, my arm, I think it is broken," Meekos wailed. Pravis and Tenebrae did not attempt to help their friend for they were afraid to move.

"Now my little hypocrites," Ahriman bellowed. "Do you understand who is in charge here? The power you have in your world is but an illusion you have created to dispel your fears. I am your fears. I am the fears of all mankind. You will not be disrespectful to me again. I am feeling generous today and will give you this one warning. For your blasphemy I will take your gold tonight. If you want the answers you seek bring another chest of gold here tomorrow night."

None of the priests moved. They were paralyzed with fear. "Well what are you waiting for?" bellowed Ahriman. "Go, leave me now."

Pravis and Tenebrae ran to Meekos and helped him to a standing position. The three High Priests ran from the demonic caverns with Ahriman's laughter bellowing behind them.

High Priests Meekos, Pravis and Tenebrae returned to the caverns under the monastery the following night. Consumed with both fear and anger, they had spent the day arguing about their need for Ahriman's help. As much as they were coming to fear Ahriman, they still feared Omnibus more.

This night they brought a larger chest of gold coins in an attempt to appease the demon. No sooner had the Huta warriors set the chest on the floor of the cavern when Ahriman spoke. "I see you are dressed differently tonight my little hypocrite," he said tauntingly.

"You mean my sling?" Meekos asked, trying to contain his anger. "You broke my arm last night."

"You are lucky that was the extent of your injuries," the demon mocked. "Open the chest so I may look upon the treasures you brought me tonight."

Tenebrae lifted the lid to the chest, exposing thousands upon thousands of gold coins. "We brought a larger chest tonight," Tenebrae said timidly.

"I see that. I will answer your questions," Ahriman said. "You asked if you could pay me to protect you. I am more powerful than Omnibus but I don't know if you are willing to pay the price I would ask. You also asked if another body could be used in place of Roch's. The answer is yes but it would not be an easy feat, since you have spent generations preparing Roch for the task and the energies have been released."

"Is there a way we can free Roch from his affliction so he is fit to be the Vessel again?" Pravis asked.

"Yes but it will take a great deal of work on your part," Ahriman replied.

"Tell us please, we will pay you any price," Pravis implored.

"If the affliction was placed upon Roch by an emissary of The Great Ruler; then only an emissary can remove it."

The three high priests were silent for several minutes as the words of the great demon shocked them to their cores.

"But, surely you don't mean we should try to get The Lion to reverse his curse upon Roch?" gasped Tenebrae.

"Is The Lion the only emissary who walks in this world?"

The song that played over and over in Roch's' head tormented him day and night. He could not stop the words from filling his mind. At one point Roch thought that he was crying but he could no longer tell because his consciousness seemed so removed from his body. "I'm not sure it is my body any longer," Roch thought as he tried unsuccessfully to move his arms and legs. "Am I going crazy?" Roch was filled with despair. "Suddenly there were new words to the song that floated through his head. *The madness that consumed him, the horror of the night, his actions brought back to him, the darkness of his sight.*

"Am I making up these horrid words?" Roch thought frantically. "What am I doing? What is that? What is that sound? What…"

"What have you done with him?" screamed Sophie as she burst into Cerephus' war room. Both Cerephus and Erebus jumped out of their chairs because of the intensity of Sophie's entrance.

"Sophie, what are you talking about?" Cerephus asked.

"Don't lie to me, I know you wanted him gone," Sophie shouted as she pointed her finger in Cerephus' face.

"Sophie, get control of yourself and tell me what is going on," Cerephus said angrily.

Sophie stopped talking and stared at Cerephus; it had not entered her mind that he might not know what happened to Roch, but now she wondered. "My Lord I am sorry for yelling at you but King Roch is gone."

"Gone!" exclaimed Erebus loudly. "Are you sure?"

"Yes I am sure," Sophie said with annoyance. "I just came from his room. His bed is empty and there is no sign of him."

Neither of the men took the time to respond to Sophie; they both ran out of the war room and up the stairs towards Roch's chambers.

High Priests Meekos, Tenebrae and Pravis sat before a fire in Meekos' study sipping on fine whiskey. The three men had been silent since they left Ahriman in the caverns under the monastery. After he finished his drink, Meekos spoke. "We are all thinking the same thing, you might as well say it out loud," he said angrily.

Pravis opened his mouth as if to speak but said nothing. "How will we ever get the Sanuri to reverse the affliction that was placed upon Roch?" Tenebrae asked.

"Well obviously he is not going to do it willingly," Meekos snapped. "We have to find a way to force him."

"But how would we force an emissary of The Great Ruler to do anything?" Tenebrae asked with fear in his voice.

"I have an idea," Pravis said softly.

"Speak up," Meekos demanded with great irritation.

"I said I have an idea," Pravis almost yelled.

"Well we are waiting," Meekos said angrily. "What is it?"

"The Sanuri is extremely attached to the Royal Family of Wetpr as well as Padre Thomas and Padre Bartholomew. I propose we use his feelings for these people to get him to help us," Pravis said.

"How?" Tenebrae asked.

"He means we kidnap someone," Meekos replied through clenched teeth.

"But what you propose Pravis?" asked Tenebrae fearfully. "That is an act against The Great Ruler."

Meekos turned to Tenebrae and stared at him as if Tenebrae was an imbecile. "Tenebrae we have committed many acts against The Great Ruler."

"Yes but this is different. It is more direct," Tenebrae said nervously.

"Who do you fear more?" Pravis asked. "The demons or The Great Ruler?"

Tenebrae looked back and forth between Meekos and Pravis, "I don't like this; I don't like this at all."

"Neither do I," Meekos said with disdain. "But we have to do something." Then he turned to Pravis. "I believe you are right. Prepare the men and leave in the morning."

"Oh this is not good," Erebus said as he walked through Roch's chambers. Cerephus was examining the windowsills and the doors.

"Unless something miraculous happened," Cerephus said sarcastically. "He was in no shape to walk out of here without help. There are no marks on the windows or doors."

"What are you looking for?" Sophie asked.

"Signs that a ladder might have been put against the window or a rope may have been used to lower him to the ground but I see nothing," Cerephus said. "If someone carried him out of here they had to be seen; I am going to call the troops," Cerephus said as he marched out of the room.

Erebus waited until Cerephus had left the room. "Sophie you really don't know what happened to Roch?"

"No," Sophie whispered. "And I will admit I am frightened.

Erebus put his arms around Sophie, "Now, you must leave. It is not safe here. You have the directions to my castle. Sophie promise me you will leave today."

"I promise but I must let Meekos know what is going on."

Erebus kissed Sophie then started to walk out of the bedroom. "Where are you going?" she asked.

"To my chambers. I have a different way of getting information."

Sophie ran to Roch's desk and scribbled a short note on a piece of stationary. She folded the paper and walked over to one of the windows and started to chant. Within moments two ravens landed on the windowsill.

"Take this to Meekos," Sophie said as she put the note in the beak of one of the birds.

Never in his life had Roch felt such terror. Helpless as he was, Roch could not defend himself or even see who was carrying him. He did not understand in what manner that he was moving; but moving he was. Roch felt suddenly very cold, a damp cold that seeped through his being and made his bones ache. Always a fighter, Roch tried frantically to move every part of his body. But his spirit seemed to be locked in his tomb of flesh.

"It's stopped," Roch thought as he realized he was no longer moving. Roch felt a coldness underneath him as if he was lying on snow. He strained his ears to hear the voices of his captors. Then the sound he heard so filled him with fright that he thought he would lose consciousness. Roch fought to stay alert as he listened to the whispering of shadows that now consumed him.

No sooner had the two ravens taken Sophie's note and left the windowsill of the castle; when the skies grew dark. Sophie leaned out the open window, "Why there wasn't a cloud in the sky a moment ago," she said out loud to herself. A wind of such intensity suddenly came up that Sophie jumped back into the room; fearing the wind would take her.

Sophie nervously paced back and forth in what had been Roch's chambers. "I have to get control of myself," she thought. "I have to get control." Sophie thought about going to the caverns where the transformation was to take place but as she listened to the storm raging she decided to wait.

"Who could have taken him?" Sophie found herself repeating. Suddenly she stopped pacing and took a couple of deep breaths. Sophie patted both sides of her head to make sure her gray hair was still tightly pulled back. Then she systematically started to tear Roch's chambers apart; looking for clues.

Sophie was filled with both fear and frustration; it had been days and still no word from Meekos. Sophie had not been able to sleep or to eat since Roch disappeared. This morning as she paced back and forth in her room Sophie realized things could not go on any longer the way they had. Sophie decided to take matters into her own hands. She packed a small bag of objects and food and rode to the caverns. It took her several days to rebuild the unholy altar which had been destroyed in the first cavern. After the structure was complete Sophie rode into Taperia and bought a crate of live willimonns.

Sophie returned to the caverns and using a ceremonial knife she cut the throats of each of these small animals and poured their blood into wooden bowls. Sophie painted the symbols of the Old Ones on the altar and on herself in the blood of the willimonns. Sophie gathered wood and built a huge fire in the pit that was in the middle of the cavern, then she removed all of her clothing and finished painting her body with demonic symbols.

Naked, the old woman danced around the fire chanting; she danced before the altar reciting her unholy mantras until she had put herself into a trance. Sophie danced for hours, singing the praises of demons of old. When exhaustion overtook her, Sophie lay down near the fire and fell into a deep sleep. As the flames died and the wood turned into ash, the cavern began to fill with every manner of snake.

Suddenly Sophie could not breathe, her eyes quickly opened as she gasped for air. When Sophie awoke she found herself staring into the green eyes of a huge red snake that had wrapped around her body and was choking the life out of her. "My Lord why do you attack me?" Sophie barely could utter.

The Satanic snake flicked its yellow tongue wildly, exposing long sinister fangs. "Why do you call me to this place which has been contaminated by holiness?" the snake bellowed.

The snake loosened its hold on Sophie so she could speak. "I am sorry My Lord but these are the chambers that were prepared for the ascension of Omnibus. And now the Vessel is missing. Can you help me find the Vessel?"

The snake released its hold on the old woman. "The Vessel is safe for now," the snake said.

"What do you mean?" Sophie asked. "Please tell me where he is?"

"You are not ready to go where he dwells."

"But what about the ascension? Will it yet take place?"

The snake did not answer Sophie's questions. "The Old Ones are greatly disturbed with the actions of the humans involved in all of this. In your ignorance and arrogance you have called to worlds that should never be disturbed. You have awaken the eyes of many not only in the underworlds but in the worlds above. For this you will all be punished severely."

"But is there nothing we can do to make amends?"

The snake started to laugh, a loud malicious laugh that echoed throughout the caverns. "Amends!" yelled the snake. "The old witch wants to make amends."

"Yes My Lord," Sophie said humbly.

"What are you prepared to do?"

Sophie felt bruised and battered as she stumbled out of the caverns and into the morning light. Numbed by fear and fatigue she returned to the castle. Without speaking to anyone Sophie went to her quarters and packed all of her belongings; then she asked one of the castle guards to ride to Taperia and to hire a carriage and driver for her. Sophie returned to her room, bathed and put on her finest dress and jewels then she walked down the stairs to the war room.

"Cerephus I need to speak with you," Sophie said this with confidence for she no longer filled the role of servant.

Cerephus looked up from the papers he was reading at his desk. He was surprised by both Sophie's appearance and demeanor. "Sophie you look so different," Cerephus said as he stood up. "What is going on?"

"I would like a glass of whiskey," Sophie said as she sat down in an overstuffed chair.

As Cerephus was pouring her whiskey, Erebus entered the room. "Good, I am glad that both of you are here," Sophie said as she took the glass from Cerephus. "I will be leaving for Malga as soon as my carriage arrives. I have made arrangements for Martha to take over my duties. She has a reputation among the soldiers as a fine cook. She is already in the kitchen working."

"Why are you leaving?" Erebus asked, as he was still playing his role for Cerephus.

"It is time," was all Sophie said.

"Sophie you are acting so strangely are you alright?" Cerephus asked.

"I am fine," she responded abruptly.

"Well, at least let me pay you your wages," Cerephus said as he took a small bag of gold coins out of a desk drawer and handed them to Sophie. "If we should find out any news about Roch, how can we contact you?"

"I will be staying with my brother Meekos at the monastery for a while," Sophie said and stood up. "Erebus would you be kind enough to help me with my bags?" Sophie asked and left the room.

"Her brother is Meekos!" Cerephus said in disbelief.

When Erebus returned to the war room, after helping Sophie load the carriage, Cerephus stared at him. "You knew she was Meekos' sister, why didn't you tell me?"

"Cerephus I never betrayed you or our purpose here. When Sophie and I were very young we fell in love and planned to marry. But Meekos broke us up by telling us each lies."

"Imagine my surprise when I find her here. Cerephus just so you know, Sophie is really a woman of great wealth and a powerful witch. She would not tell me what was going on here, she just kept warning me to leave."

"It turns out that she works for the same people as Meekos and breaking the code of silence is punishable by death. At this point I don't know any more about what is going on than you do. Which is why I told her to leave, for her own safety. After her visit with Meekos, Sophie is going to wait for me at my castle. Cerephus I lost her once I will not lose her again. But I will not abandon you either. I have already contacted a powerful sorcerer from Ryed. His name is Malus. I am hoping that by combining our powers we can be more successful getting information."

"Father have you decided what you are going to do with that piece of filth who attacked Annabelle?" Simon asked.

"Honestly I was waiting until we all settled down, then I wanted to talk with you boys about him." Sudfad said. "Mathas never asks me for anything but he asked me to spare the man's life for the sake of his family. And I told him I would do so and I want you two to honor my wishes."

"We understand," Raul said. "Matthew also told us about the man's family."

"Matthew also told us how arrogant Timothy was when Claudius spoke with him," Simon said. "According to Matthew, he and Stephan went with Claudius just to keep Claudius from killing Timothy. And every word that was coming out of Timothy's mouth was just making Claudius angrier."

"That I did not know," Sudfad said thoughtfully. "So Simon, what do you want to do?"

"I want to kill him!"

"Well you came damn close, so that should appease you some," Sudfad said.

"Then Timothy can just rot in the dungeons," Simon said angrily.

Chapter XLII
Sons

"Bella wherever did you find such beautiful material?" Ingr asked as she and Nikki looked at bolts of fine silk that the seamstresses were placing on the table.

"I bought it when we were in Salar," Bella said. "Renya took us to some of her favorite stores."

"It is the color of a peach," Nikki said in awe. "I have never seen material this color before.

"I thought it would look beautiful on both Angelina and Ingr for their bridesmaid dresses," Bella said. "Do you like it?"

"Oh yes," Nikki said softly.

As the seamstresses put more bolts of material on the two large tables that had been placed in what Bella referred to as the 'fitting room', Bella pointed out specific bolts. "That color is just a little darker and I am having dresses made up for me and your mother with that. And there are four different laces over there that you can choose from for your wedding dress."

Nikki was very quiet as she ran her fingers over the beautiful laces. "Bella I don't know what to say. You are so kind to us," Nikki said haltingly as tears ran down her face.

"As far as Claudius and I are concerned you and Thaos are part of our family now," Bella said with a warm smile.

Nikki walked up to Bella and hugged her. "Thank you for everything," Nikki whispered.

"It gives me great pleasure to do this," Bella said. Then she hesitated until the seamstresses walked out leaving just her, Nikki and Ingr in the fitting room. "I am going to tell you a family secret. Claudius and I both wanted many children. I got pregnant again when Stephan was about two years old. Those were days of great conflicts for our kingdom. We were being attacked by those awful creatures from across the Sea of Grevtd."

"In those days Claudius and Fahron did not have the large castles that we live in now so they sent soldiers to take their families to Mathas' castle for safety. We were traveling quickly to the King's castle and the small boca that Stephan and I were riding in overturned and we rolled down a rocky hill. As you can imagine I held onto Stephan tightly trying to shield him and thank The Great Ruler he only received a few scrapes and bruises. But I broke my left leg and two ribs. Two days later I lost the baby and I was never able to get pregnant after that."

Ingr walked up to Bella and put her arms around her. "Does Stephan know this?" Ingr asked.

"No, I never had the heart to tell him," Bella said sadly.

"Why is it a secret?" Nikki asked.

"Claudius and I don't talk about it. He has always been filled with guilt because he thinks that if he would have been here he could have prevented the accident."

Matthew and Angelina left the castle in Wetpr three days after the birth of baby Ariel. Accompanied by a company of soldiers, the couple was anxious to return home. They made camp late the first night of their journey. As was their habit, Matthew and Angelina set up their camp separately from that of the soldiers.

"You can make anything smell good," Matthew said as he put an armload of wood near the fire.

"Marie sent some wonderful things along," Angelina said as she was preparing their dinner. "Matthew as soon as we get back I am going to Claudius' castle to help prepare for Nikki's wedding. And you need to be fitted for another dress uniform, since yours was destroyed at Stephan's wedding." Angelina said as she walked up to Matthew and handed him a plate of food.

Matthew didn't say anything. "Are you afraid Thaos' and Nikki's wedding will be attacked too?" Angelina asked as she sat near her husband.

"Oh trust me, we are making arrangements for a possible attack," Matthew said. "It won't be a blood bath like last time."

"Then what is it Matthew? You are so quiet."

"Ever since we left Sudfad's castle I feel like we are being watched," Matthew said quietly. "The hair on the back of my neck is standing on end."

Angelina stared at Matthew for a few moments then she put her plate on the ground and pulled two small items from the pocket of her leather skirt and handed them to him. "What are these?" he asked as he looked at two identical objects that were made of small bones with jute woven around them. Both objects had designs painted on the jute.

"I don't know," Angelina said. "But I found them hanging in trees along our route."

"Sanuri how long do you plan to spend in Lentz?" Renya asked as the Royal Family was eating dinner.

"So far I was just planning on conducting the wedding," he replied. "Why?"

"We have three grandbabies who need to be christened," Renya said with a proud smile. "I have started the preparations, I just need to set a date."

"Are you going to have the christenings open to the kingdom?" the Sanuri asked.

"Yes," Sudfad replied. "I will have soldiers in place if something happens. Are you concerned?"

"I understand your reasoning and I think it wise for the most part," the Sanuri said. "But by announcing the births you are telling everyone that the children exist." Both Vitomas and Annabelle looked at each other nervously.

"Sanuri do you know of a threat against our children?" Annabelle asked with apprehension.

"Not directly," he replied. "But it is something you should take under consideration."

"I don't like this," Matthew said as he examined the two objects that Angelina handed to him. "Something is not right here." Matthew stood up. "Come."

"Where are we going?" Angelina asked with surprise.

"I am going to double the guards and I don't want to leave you here."

"Matthew you will only be gone a couple of minutes," Angelina said with annoyance. "I am a warrior too, I will be fine."

"Angelina."

"Matthew go; I still have food cooking on the fire."

Matthew stared at Angelina for a few moments then turned and left their campsite. A savvy warrior, Angelina listened intently to the sounds of the night as she finished preparing food. The night was quiet, too quiet. Angelina had been so busy talking with Matthew before, that she did not realize how silent the forest was. She stood up and walked over to her saddle, which was lying on the ground. Angelina picked up her bow and quiver of arrows and brought them closer to the campfire.

Angelina felt like she was being watched so she continued her duties around the camp nonchalantly; all the while vigilant for the sounds of intruders. Suddenly two birds flew out of the brush as if they were startled. Instinctively Angelina grabbed her bow and arrows and jumped behind a large oak tree that was to the right of the campfire.

As Angelina strained to listen for even the faintest sound; she heard something. "What is that?" thought Angelina as she tried to recognize the muffled sounds she was hearing. Finally she realized what it was. Angelina moved stealthily from tree to tree working her way towards the area the birds had escaped from.

Cautiously Angelina crept up on the sound. Silently she pulled an arrow from her quiver and placed it on the bowstring. The sound was intermittent as Angelina approached it. She was now behind the last tree that was closest to the sound.

Whatever was making the sound was lying in some low brush. Angelina pulled the bowstring back but did not yet release the arrow. She was well aware that she could be walking into a trap; all of her senses were heightened as she walked forward into the brush.

Angelina moved through some large fern leaves. "By The Great Ruler," she said out loud when she saw a small boy covered in blood lying in his own vomit. "Matthew, Matthew," Angelina yelled as she put her arrow back into the quiver and picked up the child.

Matthew drew his sword and ran as fast as he could when he heard Angelina yelling, the three soldiers he had been talking to ran with him. Within moments they entered the campsite, prepared to do battle.

"Angelina," Matthew gasped fearfully as he saw her walking towards him. "Is that a child?"

"Yes and he is covered in blood and burning up with fever. Please put another blanket down by the fire. I found him in the bushes."

Matthew ordered his men to search the area as he put a blanket near the fire. "Go with your men," Angelina said. "There may be others hurt out there. I will tend to him." Matthew grabbed his sword and disappeared into the forest as Angelina washed the bloody child looking for his injuries. She grabbed some of her herbs and tonics from her saddle bags and quickly made some medicines for the boy.

Matthew and his men returned to the campfire about twenty minutes later. "It is too dark to see; we will look again in the morning," Matthew said as he kneeled beside Angelina.

"The blood is not his," she said with relief. "His family must be out there. He has scratches on him from the brush but nothing more."

Matthew looked down at the boy who he guessed was about two years old. The child had brown curly hair and normally fair skin but now his face was red from fever. "What is wrong with him?"

"I don't know," Angelina said with concern. "But he may have been out there for a while because the blood that covered him was long dried."

The next morning Matthew rolled over and realized that Angelina was not lying next to him. "Did you get any sleep?" Matthew asked as he saw Angelina sitting next to the fire holding the boy.

"No but his fever broke and I was able to get some water and broth down him. Do you want some breakfast before you look for his family?"

"No," Matthew said as he was preparing to leave. "I will eat when we return." He kissed Angelina on the forehead and saddled his horse as the first rays of light were breaking through the early morning sky.

Almost two hours passed before Matthew and four soldiers returned to the campsite. The soldiers did not speak as they rode past Angelina towards their own campsite. Matthew was quiet as he unsaddled his horse. Angelina poured a cup of coffee and handed it to Matthew as he kneeled down beside her.

"Here," Matthew said as he handed Angelina a small pile of clothing. "I think the boy's name is Jacob because that name is embroidered on several things."

"Matthew what did you find?" Angelina asked soberly.

"Almost a mile west we found a small cabin and the bodies of a man and a woman," Matthew said as he looked at the boy sleeping peacefully on a blanket. "The bodies were torn apart beyond belief. The boy must have been in the cabin because we saw his footprints in the blood. How he was spared I cannot say."

"Matthew are you telling me this baby walked a mile to our campsite?"

"The bodies looked as if they had been dead for a couple of days. I don't understand how this child could have survived for two days in this wilderness."

"Matthew, this is a miracle. The boy was meant to come to us; there is no logical explanation."

Matthew hesitated before he spoke again. "I have no idea who or what killed his parents. The only footprints we saw were his."

"Meekos has barely been seen since he returned to the monastery," Padre Bartholomew whispered as he and Padre Thomas sat in the dining hall. The attention of the old priests was suddenly focused on a group of men who entered the large room. Seven men wearing the robes of the high priests of the monastery at Philiste, in the Kingdom of Wetpr stood in the doorway looking over the tables of priests who were eating their lunch.

"I have never seen robes like those before," Padre Bartholomew whispered. "What do the green bands on their arms mean?"

"I have never seen them either, only heard about them," Padre Thomas said as he watched the men walking through the dining room. "They are the Patronus."

"The Patronus!" exclaimed Padre Bartholomew. "The Enforcers?"

"Well, they are supposed to be protectors of the Church," said Padre Thomas. "But their reputations make everyone fearful."

"Maybe they are here to look into Meekos," Padre Bartholomew said enthusiastically.

"Or maybe not," said Padre Thomas solemnly as two of the Patronus stopped at their table.

"Are you Padre Thomas and Padre Bartholomew?" one of the high priests asked stoically.

"Yes we are," Padre Bartholomew responded as he tried to read the faces of the high priests.

"We need you to come with us," the same high priest said.

"Why?" Padre Thomas asked.

"That will be revealed to you momentarily," the high priest responded.

Both Padre Thomas and Padre Bartholomew felt fearful as the seven high priests escorted them from the dining hall. The two priests were afraid that the Patronus were working for High Priest Meekos; in which case they knew they could be in great danger. The nine men walked in silence down a long winding hallway. The walk seemed very long to Padres Thomas and Bartholomew who were contemplating their next actions.

The high priests stopped in front of a door in one of the lower levels of the monastery. One of the priests knocked on the door. Padre Thomas and Padre Bartholomew could hear the loud metallic sounds of locks being opened. They entered a large chamber that contained a long table and many chairs.

There were at least fourteen more members of the Patronus sitting in the room. No one spoke until the door was closed and locked again. One of the high priests stood up and said, "Please take a seat," as he waved his arm towards two empty chairs at the table. "Please tell us your names," the high priest requested.

"I am Padre Thomas and this is Padre Bartholomew and what is the meaning of this?"

Without answering his question the high priest continued, "Are you friends of the Sanuri?"

"Yes," replied both of the priests without hesitation.

The high priest leaned across the table and handed each priest a small scroll. Padre Thomas and Padre Bartholomew unrolled the scrolls; relief flooded their bodies as they read the words of the Sanuri.

"Thank The Great Ruler," Padre Bartholomew exclaimed. "We were afraid you were some of Meekos' men.

"I am Raphael," continued the high priest. "I am a commander in the Patronus. The Sanuri, himself, has sent us here to investigate the darkness that has been called upon this monastery. He has shared with us the notes and documents that you have sent to him. I fear that the evil here is greater than even you suspected."

"How can we be of help?" Padre Thomas asked.

High Priest Raphael smiled, "You are brave men but the Sanuri has ordered us to get you out of here."

"But where will we go?" Padre Bartholomew asked.

"Initially you will go to the castle of King Sudfad, after that it is up to you."

"Your Excellency, I have been at this monastery for two decades and just recently we have discovered rooms that I did not know existed. Please let us take you through the monastery and give you our keys before we go," said Padre Thomas.

"I have many men searching the monastery as we speak but I will take you up on your offer. Understand that I personally gave my word to the Sanuri that I would let no harm come to you so my men will remain with you."

There was a knock on the door, six more members of the Patronus entered the room and walked up to High Priest Raphael. Padre Bartholomew and Padre Thomas sat in silence as Raphael read the documents that were handed to him.

"I am not surprised," Raphael said out loud. "Then he looked across the table at Padre Bartholomew and Padre Thomas. "My men just finished doing an inventory of the holy vault and there are chests upon chests of gold coins and jewels that are unaccounted for."

"Does Meekos know you are here?" Padre Thomas asked.

"His housekeeper said that he, Pravis and Tenebrae left two days ago. She did not know where they were headed."

"Gone," said Padre Bartholomew with surprise. "He just returned a few days ago after a long trip."

"Your Excellency, High Priest Meekos is a very dangerous man; please do not underestimate him," Padre Thomas said. "How many men do you have with you?"

"Over three hundred."

"Three hundred!" exclaimed Padre Bartholomew. "Are you expecting to do battle?"

"I am expecting just about anything at this point," replied High Priest Raphael with the confidence of a military commander. "Depending on our findings we may be moving all the objects in the Hall of Antiquities as well as other priests besides you. Some of my men will take you to your rooms, please pack your things and be prepared to leave at any time."

"What is this?" asked Rosa as she and Mathas watched Matthew and Angelina walk into the dining room; while the King and Queen were eating their breakfast. Angelina was carrying Jacob and walked up to Rosa so she could hold the boy. "What a darling!" exclaimed Rosa as she held the smiling boy on her lap.

"Angelina found him near our campsite three days ago," Matthew explained as he sat down at the table. "He was covered in blood and very sick. I took some men and we found a cabin about a mile west of our campsite. There were bodies of a man and woman in the cabin, they had been torn apart. And we saw the boy's footprints in the blood on the floor but no other prints."

"Did you find out who the people were?" Mathas asked.

"No, we didn't find anything with their names on it, just some of the child's clothes with 'Jacob' sewn on them," Matthew paused. "You know come to think of it; we found very few belongings in that cabin. Either they were stolen or those people didn't live there."

"Were you still in Wetpr?" Mathas asked.

"Yes," Matthew replied. "I already sent a message to Sudfad."

"So this boy is an orphan?" Rosa asked as Angelina picked Jacob up. Angelina carried the boy to her chair at the table. When Jacob saw Matthew he put his arms out for Matthew to take him. Mathas watched as Matthew set Jacob on his lap and fed him.

"What are you going to do with the boy?" Mathas asked.

Angelina and Matthew looked at each other. "We haven't really talked about it," Angelina said.

"He looks like he is pretty attached to the two of you," Mathas said. "Are you sure you want to put him in an orphanage?"

"Orphanage!" Angelina gasped loudly. "Matthew we can't put him in an orphanage."

Matthew smiled warmly, "Do you want to adopt him?"

"Matthew I told you before, I think we were meant to find him. I would love to adopt him but what do you think?" Angelina asked hesitantly; fearful that he would say no.

Matthew looked at Angelina then at his parents then at Jacob. "I have become pretty attached to the little fella. Yes, we'll adopt him." Angelina smiled sweetly and leaned over and kissed Matthew on the cheek.

"Jacob, meet your new grandparents," Matthew said as he looked at the joyful smiles on Mathas' and Rosa's faces.

"Father, we were just at the cabin that Matthew wrote about," Raul said as he and Simon took seats in Sudfad's study. "Matthew and his men buried the bodies but the cabin is filled with blood and the way it was splattered on the walls and ceiling, those people must have had a horrible death."

"While you were gone, an Enrop brought another letter from Matthew," Sudfad said as he handed it to Raul. "He says he later realized there were almost no belongings in the cabin except for some of the child's clothing; which he took." Sudfad leaned back in his chair and smiled. "And he says that he and Angelina adopted the boy they found."

"Father it is true there was little in the cabin but Raul and I studied the blood patterns on the wall. The patterns outlined objects, so we believe there were at least a couple of chests in the room," Simon said as Raul handed him the letter.

"So they might have been travelers?" Sudfad asked.

"That cabin looked like an old hunting cabin that had been abandoned for some time," Raul said. "Perhaps they took shelter there. We did not find horses or a boca. But the ground was very hard and greatly disturbed so it was difficult to determine prints."

"What do you mean, greatly disturbed?" asked Sudfad.

"We found the prints of Matthew and his men, but it looks like before they came someone had taken brush and wiped away any prints," Simon said.

"That certainly doesn't sound like Hutas," said Sudfad thoughtfully. "Besides they would have killed the child."

"Father where is the object that Matthew talks about in his letter?" asked Raul.

"I gave it to Gala to research. The Sanuri has already left for Lentz because Claudius and Bella asked him to come early," Sudfad said.

"We dispatched four platoons to check on the welfare of people in that area," Simon said. "Hopefully there aren't any other attacks."

"Excellent idea boys," Sudfad said. "If there are no other attacks perhaps this was specifically targeted at those people."

"Whoever attacked them had to be covered in blood, you should have seen that room," Raul added.

"It makes you wonder how the child survived," Sudfad said.

"Perhaps they knew someone was after them so they hid the boy," said Simon.

"Well, look at this little warrior," said Sorren joyfully as he held Jacob over his head. "Mathas when your men came out and told us you and Rosa had a surprise for us, we never imagined a grandson."

"Rosa has invited the families of Claudius and Fahron over also; but we thought you two should meet Jacob first."

"We wondered where you two had disappeared to," Sorren said as Rosa and Shara entered the room. Shara walked up to Sorren and took Jacob from his arms. "We were just deciding what we need to make for this little one," Shara said as she looked adorningly at Jacob.

"Shara and I are going shopping tomorrow," Rosa said to Mathas.

"Get whatever you two want and put it on our account, I will pay the bills later," Mathas said.

Rosa laughed and said to Shara, "He never likes me carrying money, he is always afraid I might get robbed."

"You will have an escort with you?" asked Sorren.

"Of course, that is why I think this is funny," replied Rosa happily.

"You know this boy is big boned and has the same color of hair as Matthew; he could pass for Matthew's blood child," Shara said.

"Yes, we had noticed that too," Mathas said. "Where are Matthew and Angelina?"

"Honey I told them to get some sleep," Rosa said. "Jacob was so sick that they stayed up every night with him. I told them we would take care of the boy. Besides, I want them awake for our dinner tonight."

"Since we are all here now, I will tell you how Angelina found the boy and what happened to his parents," Mathas said somberly.

Stephan entered the chambers of Thaos and Nikki in the early morning hours. He took a seat in the parlor as he could hear them in the bedroom. Waiting until the sounds of love making had subsided; he called out, "You have company out here." Laughter came from the bedroom as Nikki and Thaos got dressed. Never wanting to miss a chance to tease Nikki; Stephan waited until she appeared in the doorway then asked, "Nikki do you always scream like that?"

Nikki blushed deeply. "Stephan!" she said in a huff. "That's embarrassing." Then she walked into the kitchen.

When Thaos stopped laughing he asked, "What are you doing here so early?"

Stephan glanced in the kitchen to see if Nikki was listening. "Something has come up that you should know about."

"Let's go into the study," Thaos said as he led the way.

After Thaos closed the door, Stephan started to explain. "Yesterday Mother sent me into Langer to order a variety of things for your wedding. Almost every place I went, someone told me that a man has been asking about you. Most of the people said this man looked dangerous and that is why they wanted us to know about him."

"Did anyone get his name?"

"Lazo."

"Was he alone?"

"From what I have heard he seemed to be," Stephan said. "Do you know him?"

"Yes, he was one of Juleta's men. The last I heard she was trying to have us both killed."

"Why?"

"Because we laughed at her," Thaos said smiling. "I thought he was dead or at least a long ways from here."

Nikki knocked on the door before she opened it. She handed a large cup of steaming coffee to each man. "I don't know what the two of you are whispering about but remember we are getting married next week and I need both of you in one piece."

Stephan started laughing, "Now what makes you think we are going to get into trouble?"

Nikki looked at both of them and smiled, "Stephan do you want to stay for breakfast?"

"Sure, thanks."

After Nikki left the room and closed the door, Stephan asked, "What are you thinking about doing?"

"I am going into Langer and find him; trust me, he is not the kind of man we want to show up here with our families."

"I thought you would say that," Stephan said with a grin. "Want some company?"

After breakfast Thaos and Stephan rode into Langer. Both of the men were vigilant for any signs of spies or attack. Langer was a bustling port city. Most of the taverns and some of the restaurants were open all night. Even though the sun was barely up, people filled the streets. "Knowing Lazo we should start looking in the taverns," Thaos said grimly.

Their hunt was not long, for they found Lazo in the third tavern they entered; a small noisy smoke filled place called the Broken Horse. Lazo was sitting in a corner table so he could watch the door; he smiled when he saw Thaos and nodded.

"Well I see the witch didn't kill ya," Lazo said with a laugh as Thaos and Stephan sat down at the table. Lazo was eating a plate of runny eggs and drinking whiskey. "Want some breakfast?"

"No, we already ate," Thaos said as he stared at Lazo. Stephan was watching the other men in the room. "I thought you were dead," Thaos said.

"Damn near, that witch was setting me up in a trap so I took off," Lazo said angrily. "Then she sent demons after me. I kept fighting demons until I was taken in by the priests at the monastery in Leven."

"You hid in a monastery?" Thaos asked in disbelief.

"Wasn't so much hiding as I almost died on their doorstep and they pulled me behind the walls," Lazo said with a laugh. "I have never been much for priests but those guys really fixed me up. I left them a big donation. I told them about the demons and they were going to fight them, can you believe that?"

Lazo started laughing at the thought. "But the demons didn't attack the monastery."

"Stiller and Larson are dead," Thaos said. "I found the bodies. Looks like she tortured them before they were strung up."

"Those fools they should have left too," Lazo said with a bit of sadness in his voice. "The reason I've been looking for ya is to find out what the hell happened to the witch. Is she still after us? I spied on her castle and it's destroyed, couldn't believe my eyes. What could have done that?"

Both Stephan and Thaos smiled. "She kidnapped her little sister and was going to sacrifice the child to a demon, so I told Stephan here and long story short, we led an attack on the castle."

"What the hell did ya use to knock down the walls?" Lazo asked with amazement.

"We had a very powerful holy man with us and he brought some of his friends, between them and Juleta's demons they demolished the place."

"Well is she dead?"

"The holy man sent her to hell."

"Damn fine place for her, that's where she should have been all along," Lazo said with a grin. "I'll be sleeping better now."

"Don't get too comfortable," Stephan warned. "Turns out she may have put a bounty on us."

"What sort of bounty?"

"Something for demons, don't know if you are included on the kill list," Stephan said with a smirk.

Lazo stared at Stephan then started to grin, "Now things are making sense, you're the one she was so in love with aren't you?" Stephan nodded. "Well damn smart of ya not to get involved," Lazo said.

"What do you mean things are starting to make sense?" asked Thaos.

"I heard you found yourself a beautiful lady and you're getting married," Lazo said. "Would she have dark hair by any chance?"

Thaos stared at Lazo warily, then slowly answered, "Yes."

"Now don't give me that evil look Thaos," Lazo said. "I am no threat to you. But when I saw how damaged Juleta's castle was I thought I would have myself a look around. I found these lined up side by side on what was left of a table in the parlor."

As Lazo talked he turned around to his saddle bags that were hanging over the back of his chair. Lazo pulled out a bundle that was wrapped in burlap and hand it to Thaos. "It's obvious one of these is ya and that doll with the long dark hair was next to it. Now that I've seen Stephan he's there too and that blonde doll was next to his."

Thaos placed the bundle on the table and unfolded the material. Both he and Stephan stared at the contents without speaking. "I figure they are some kind of dolls to put hexes on people so I grabbed them. Do ya know who they all are?"

Stephan and Thaos sorted through the dolls and laid them on the table by the families they represented. Although the small dolls were crudely fashioned their likenesses to Juleta's family and Claudius' family were remarkable. "Someone other than Juleta had to have made these," Thaos said as he held up a doll that looked like Nikki.

"There's even one here of the Sanuri," Stephan said.

"So ya recognize them all?" Lazo asked.

"Yes," Thaos replied.

"Well it's not exactly a wedding present, but I would watch my back if I were ya boys," said Lazo.

"Sanuri we are honored as always," Claudius said as he welcomed the holy man into his castle. "Jackson, tend to the Sanuri's horses," Claudius said to one of the soldiers standing outside the front door. "Your timing is perfect; we were just sitting down to dinner, come," Claudius said as he led the Sanuri to the dining room. Bella was adding another place setting at the table when they entered the room.

"You have a houseful," the Sanuri said with a smile as he saw that Matthew, Angelina and Jacob had joined the rest of Claudius' family for the evening meal. "Who is the little one?" the Sanuri asked as he sat down at the table.

"His name is Jacob," Matthew said. "Angelina found him on our way home. He was covered in blood and very sick. Some of my men and I found the bodies of his parents, at least we think they were his parents, they had been torn apart. We've adopted the boy."

"We were hoping you would find time to christen him while you are here," Angelina said.

"Of course," the Sanuri said as he stared at the toddler. "You know it was no coincidence that you found him. You were meant to find him."

"That is what I thought," Angelina said smiling. "But do you know why?"

"Not yet," said the Sanuri as he continued to stare at the boy.

The next few days were filled with chaos as Claudius' family prepared for the wedding of Thaos and Nikki. Although Thaos and Nikki would have preferred a simple wedding; Bella planned a wedding befitting the ruling family of Lentz.

Thaos and Stephan gave the dolls that were found in Juleta's castle to the Sanuri. Mathas, Claudius and Matthew were shown the dolls. None of the men wanted to tell their wives about the evil objects. The Sanuri christened Jacob at a small ceremony in the castle of King Mathas; just hours before the wedding ball that was scheduled the night before the nuptials. Claudius and Bella were as happy and proud as if Thaos was their son.

The wedding ball lasted long into the night. And as with Stephan's wedding ceremony both Thaos and Nikki joked that they did not know many of their guests.

Nikki's mother Gladys and Nikki's brothers and sisters had been guests at the castle for a week prior to the wedding. While Gladys worried constantly that her children would harm something in the castle, Claudius and Bella enjoyed the presence of the children.

Bella had gowns made for Nikki and Ingr for the ball and both women stunned the crowd. Ingr wore a light blue gown with tiny silver straps and Nikki wore a dark blue strapless gown. Both Stephan and Thaos were in the Great Hall when their brides made their entrance at the ball and both men stood in adoration.

Many members of the Nordes Tribe were in attendance including Elexas, who as predicted flirted with both Thaos and Stephan; neither man wanted to anger their wives so they introduced Ryan to Elexas to distract her. Ryan was a handsome man of eighteen; while he was not built like a fighter he was muscular. Elexas took Ryan's arm and did not let go of him during the entire ball.

"I told him to yell if he needed help," Thaos said to Stephan and both men laughed.

"We wanted Ryan to meet Sonja," Ingr said to Stephan and Thaos when she and Nikki realized their husbands had matched Ryan up with Elexas.

"Well introduce them," Stephan said.

"Sonja is almost as shy as Ryan she is no match for Elexas," Nikki said as she watched Elexas flirting with Ryan.

"Introduce them and let Ryan choose who he wants to be with," Stephan said and laughed.

Nikki walked away from the group and returned moments later with a pretty girl with long brown hair. After Nikki and Ingr introduced Sonja to their husbands they escorted Sonja across the dance floor and introduced her to Ryan.

"Nikki, Ingr you both look so nice," Elexas said sweetly as the women joined her and Ryan.

"We just wanted Ryan to meet Sonja," Nikki said as she glared at Elexas. "Sonja will be walking down the aisle with Ryan in the morning."

Ryan was both flattered and overwhelmed by Elexas' attention to him. He felt uncomfortable with all four women staring at him and wasn't sure of what he should be saying or doing. "Ryan why don't you ask Sonja to dance," Ingr suggested and smiled as Elexas gave Ingr a disapproving look.

Both Thaos and Stephan laughed as they saw the look on Elexas' face as Ryan and Sonja walked onto the dance floor. When Nikki and Ingr joined their husbands Thaos said, "I hope Sonja is a warrior too because Elexas looks like she could kill."

Claudius had soldiers stationed inside and outside of the castle to prevent the horror that had occurred at Stephan and Ingr's wedding. Many of the guests stayed the night at the castle, as the wedding was to take place in the early hours of the morning. Both Nikki and Thaos wanted a sunrise wedding.

The Sanuri and the wedding party were to stand on a stone patio that Bella had constructed for the ceremony. The patio was surrounded by flowering trees that gave a great fragrance to the morning air. Baskets of flowers were being arranged on the patio as the Sanuri was setting up the altar.

The Sanuri too, was taking precautions after seeing the unholy dolls. He had flocks of Enrops and Hengers standing watch over the castle. Harps and violins played as the guests filled the rows upon rows of chairs that had been set up around the patio. Thaos, Stephan, Matthew and Ryan stood before the altar, all wearing the dress uniforms of the Lentz Military.

Ingr was the first bridesmaid to walk down the aisle wearing an elegant peach colored silk dress that was form fitting with off the shoulder straps. Angelina followed Ingr and when Jacob saw Angelina he squealed and tried to jump off from Mathas' lap to run to her. Sonja carried a basket of long stemmed roses which she handed out to the families of the wedding party, as was the tradition of the Nordes Tribe.

Stephan and Matthew stared at their beautiful wives. Ryan was shy around women and admired Sonja when she was not aware of it. Thaos caught his breath as he watched Claudius escorting Nikki down the aisle; all eyes were on the beautiful young bride who was dressed in a simple but elegant off the shoulder dress. Nikki wore her hair down with a long veil and the pearl necklace and earrings that Thaos had given to her earlier that morning.

The Sanuri was not the only one who watched the sky as the wedding ceremony was performed. Many at attendance were alert for attack as Thaos and Nikki kissed as man and wife in front of their guests. Thaos felt a great relief when everyone had returned to the Great Hall without any sign of trouble. Thaos took Nikki by the hand and the two danced on the dance floor, although there was no music playing that anyone other than Thaos and Nikki could hear. The guests smiled as they watched the young couple.

Sudfad and Renya sat at the dining table, waiting for the rest of the family to join them for breakfast. The King and Queen looked towards the door when they heard angry voices in the hallway.

"Annabelle that is it!" Simon said as he carried his sons into the dining room. "We aren't going to talk about it anymore." Annabelle was going to speak until she saw Renya and Sudfad looking at them. Annabelle held Arianna as she silently took her seat at the table.

"It's insane that you two are even arguing with us about this," Raul said as he entered the dining room carrying little Sudfad and Samuel. Vitomas stared angrily at Raul as he put the boys into their chairs. Vitomas was holding Ariel, who suddenly started to cry; so Vitomas walked into the hallway with the baby.

Raul looked at his father and mother and said with annoyance. "The girls are mad at us because we are hiring housekeepers."

"We don't need them," Vitomas called out from the hallway.

"Honey both of you girls have your hands full with the children, besides your princesses," Raul replied. "Tell me what princesses you know who do all of their own housework?"

"Angelina," Annabelle replied.

Raul looked at Simon and shook his head, "We just can't win with these two."

Sudfad and Renya smiled as they watched the two young couples. "Where's Petra?" Sudfad asked.

"He is playing with Kyra in the back," Renya replied.

"My Lord! My Lord!" Marie was screaming frantically as she ran down the hallway.

"What has happened?" gasped Vitomas when she saw Marie and Kyra who was covered in dirt and blood.

"My Lord!" Marie cried again as she ran up to Sudfad who had now jumped out of his chair. "Tell them what happened." Marie said as she pushed Kyra towards the King.

"Some men just stole Petra," Kyra said as she was crying. "I tried to stop them but I couldn't."

Simon and Raul had already run out of the castle before Kyra finished speaking. "Kyra how many men were there?" Sudfad asked.

"Five that I could see, they were dressed in black and had hoods over their faces." Tears were flowing down Kyra's cheeks as she spoke.

"Kyra except for that cut on your mouth, this blood doesn't look like it came from you," Sudfad said as he held Kyra's hands. "Tell me where the blood came from."

"The man who grabbed Petra, I bit him real hard on his wrist."

He never heard the bullet

He never saw the stone

He never heard his soul die

He never made it home

Walking With Angels © 2009

By

Sandra J Year man

Glossary of Characters

Aaryan: a male Grand Master of the Insidiae

Abaddon: an ancient demon/one of the Old Ones

Abella: daughter of Prince Lakin and Princess Zada/Ruala

Abigail: sister of Marie/ nurse for grandchildren of King Sudfad

Adi: son of Elen and Batya/ Ruala

Adrone: youngest son of Joshua and Iris/younger brother of Vivian/Clan of Gesmal

Adwell: Prince/ son of King Zachariah and Queen Noella of New Samona/husband of Nada/father of Misha/ Adwell was killed in battle leaving Nada to raise ten children/Ruala/

Ael: an ancient demon/ one of the Old Ones

Ahriman: an ancient demon/ one of the Old Ones

Akasha: former king of Ryed/grandfather of Nehmota

Alexander: former servant of King Roch's parents/ father of Annabelle

Alexander: one of the twin sons of Simon and Annabelle

Alexandras: King of Wetpr/brother of Jaretta/uncle of Sudfad and Roch

Alexas Rose: daughter of Matthew and Angelina

Alexis: son of Usman, the leader of the Valdore Tribe

Alice: and her husband find Jorge near death in Nora

Ana: Princess/daughter of Zeman and Oda/niece of King Manu of New Samona/Ruala

Anda: one of Chief Romogi's three wives/Huta

Andres: Princess of Ryed/daughter of Oren and Astrel/ has twin sister Jorga

Andrew: jeweler in Salar

717

Andrus: father of Rabi/Ruala

Angelina: daughter of Sorren, Chief of the Nordes Tribe/female warrior

Annabar: daughter of King Sharonne

Annabelle: handmaid and best friend to Queen Vitomas of the Kingdom of Stordt

Anthony: one of the twin sons of Simon and Annabelle

Arca: Enrop leader who protects King Mathas' family

Archetenus The Brave: Captain in the Taperian Army

Arianna: daughter of Simon and Annabelle

Ariel: daughter of Raul and Vitomas

Armstrong: soldier and scout in the army of Wetpr

Arthur Marcus: father of Hannah

Asher: male Ruala warrior

Asmodeus: an ancient demon/ one of the Old Ones

Astrel: former princess of Ryed/daughter of Akasha and Norah

Atomos: Elder of the Centras and Keeper of the Box of Itifer

Augustus Endleson: a wealthy businessman who owned part of the City of Nora

Baal: an ancient demon/ one of the Old Ones

Babu: Enrop

Bac: male Ruala warrior

Bachnenus: warrior guarding refugees/Shettee

Bali: Enrop leader of the flock that does battle at Juleta's castle

Balin: Prince of Norkv/son of Thaddius and Omara/grandson of Benjeman and Esther

Banacus: General in the army of King Tobias of Puntd

Banaka: a female Grand Master of the Insidiae

Barak: Prince of Norkv/grandson of Benjeman and Esther

Barak: Prince/son of King Neputa and Queen Tiara/Shettee

Barid: Prince of Ogg

Barid: Prince of Ryed/son of Nehmota and Vasart

Bastra: Huta captain

Batya: wife of Elen/Ruala

Beatrice Endleson: wife of Augustus

Becca: Princess of Norkv/daughter of Thaddius and Omara/granddaughter of Benjeman and Esther

Behtay: Princess/daughter of Segal and Cahina/niece of King Manu of New Samona/Ruala

Bekka: female Ruala warrior

Bella: wife of Claudius and mother of Stephan

Benedict: Prince of Norkv/son of Benjeman and Esther

Benjeman: vicious rebel leader who overthrew the government of Samona

Bentra: an ancient demon/ one of the Old Ones

Berta: Queen of Stordt/wife of Micha/grandmother of Roch and Sudfad

Bertha: an elderly woman from Nora

Betty: a woman from Nora

Betu: male Ruala warrior

Black Jack: a regular patron at the Ghost Ship Tavern in Port Friada

Brik: son of Prince Lakin and Princess Zada /Ruala

Brina: Princess of Norkv/daughter of Valor and Cai/granddaughter of Benjeman and Esther

Cabal: son of Karzman and Nadia

Cacu: Enrop leader that joined Raul and Simon on a mission

Cade: son of King Pergo and Queen Vinus/ Kingdom of Gandt

Cadi: daughter of Prince Hadar and Princess Paj/ granddaughter of Manu/Ruala

Cael: Shettee boy who is adopted by Thedes and Ibula

Cahina: Princess/ married to Segal son of King Zachariah and Queen Noella of New Samona/Ruala

Cai: Princess of Norkv/wife of Valor who was the son of Benjeman and Esther

Calen: male Ruala warrior/cousin of Luca/son of Maxwell and Emeral/

Calla: female Ruala warrior

Calvin: a desk clerk at The Captain's Retreat Hotel in Port Friada

Campbell: one of the spies at the Castle at Wetpr

Canton: Cisero's second in command

Cara: Princess of Ogg

Carlsman: a Lieutenant in the Army of Lentz

Carson Dormors: a wealthy landowner in the Kingdom of Ganz

Carston: member of the governing body of Nora

Casey: male Ruala warrior/father of Melanie/husband of Tasha

Cassandra: daughter of King Friada and Queen Marla of the Kingdom of Ganz

Cassandra: female Ruala warrior

Cedrick Teivel: a ruthless, powerful man in the Kingdom of Ryed

Celo: Prince of Ryed/son of Oren and Astrel

Cere: daughter of Tristt/Shettee

Cerephus: General in the Taperian Army

Cerey: orphan girl/sister of Nicholas

Ceria: Princess/daughter of Gunnel and Uma/niece of King Manu of New Samona/ sister of Elan/Ruala

Chaez: son of Fahron

Chaladrone: an ancient demon/ one of the Old Ones

Chalta: daughter of King Pergo and Queen Vinus/ Kingdom of Gandt

Chance: works with the Patronus

Charlene: a woman from Nora

Charles: hired farmhand of Arthur Marcus

Chief Romogi: leader of the Hutas/ Kingdom of Marba

Christopher: six year old boy who Luca saves from the Hutas/brother of Lila

Ciao: female Ruala warrior

Cisero: a member of the Insidiae

Clair: a woman from Nora

Claudius: General in the Army of Lentz

Cleo: a man who works for Cicero/a vessel

Cobren: Prince of Norkv/son of Grace and Makalo/Grandson of Benjeman and Esther

Compro: Taperian soldier injured at Wall of Dorath

Corwin: son of King Fahra and Queen Sitha of Zorta

Crater: a soldier in the army of Wetpr

Crispus: a guard at King Roch's castle

Dack: male Ruala warrior

Dacron: former prince of Ryed/is murdered by his younger brother Nehmota for the throne

Dael: an ancient demon/ one of the Old Ones

Dagon: a male Ruala warrior

Dagor: son of King Fahra and Queen Sitha of Zorta

Dai: son of Gael, grandson of Manu/Ruala

Damas: an ancient demon/ one of the Old Ones

Danar: a man created to be a vessel for demons

Daniel: an emissary of The Great Ruler who takes on the disguise of a human man

Danilla: mother of King Mathas

Darius: Prince of Samona/son of Thomas and Rewel/brother of Varden

Delilah: wife of Dieter

Delilia: Queen of New Samona/mother of Ibula, Lakin, Gael and Hadar/ wife of King Manu/Ruala

Demanko: a demon

Demetries: a demon

Denise Froush: wife of Martin who is a wealthy ship builder in Port Friada

Denks: a soldier in the army of Wetpr

Denton: one of the spies at the Castle in Wetpr

Derek: friend of Thaos

Derlock: Huta warrior

Dieter: member of the Insidiae

Dion: Princess of Samona/wife of Yorggi who was the son of Thomas and Rewel/brother of Varden

Dixon: a Taperian soldier

Dominic Petlov: was the senior High Priest at the monastery at Malga before he was murdered

Dorme: Prince of Ogg

Doros: works for High Priest Meekos

Douma: King of Ogg

Duncan: Chief of the Clan of Gesmal in Ryed/ husband of Liza

Duran: father of Nikki/Nordes Tribe

Edith: wife of Lloyd a banker in Nora

Elan: male Ruala warrior/son of Gunnel and Uma/

Eldridge: works with the Patronus

Elen: son of Andrus and Naomi/ brother of Rabi/ Ruala

Elexas: a female Nordes warrior

Elsa: female Ruala warrior/mother of Mia/wife of Tyron

Emeral: mother of Calen/Ruala

Emeric: a male Grand Master of the Insidiae

Emmet: worker for Gabriel

Emon: a male Grand Master of the Insidiae

Erebus: sorcerer from Ryed

Esser: Prince/son of Segal and Cahina/nephew of King Manu of New Samona/Ruala

Esteban: a member of the Insidiae

Esther: Queen of New Norkv/wife of rebel leader Benjeman

Fabron: Prince of Ogg

Fadil: a male Grand Master of the Insidiae

Fahra: King of Zorta

Fahron: General in the Army of Lentz

Fala: female Ruala warrior

Farnsworth: General in charge of building Fort Serpha in Wetpr

Fatima: Prince of Ryed/ son of Oren and Astrel

Fatronas: an ancient demon/one of the Old Ones

Fengu: Enrop leader who helps Gabriel and his group against Omnibus

Ferguson: a Sergeant in the Army of Lentz

Fraisier: a businessman and member of the Insidiae in Nora

Friada: King of the Kingdom of Ganz

Gabriella: sister of Marie/nurse to grandchildren of King Sudfad

Gad: male Ruala warrior

Gael: Prince/son of King Manu and Queen Delilia/Ruala

Gala: a healer from the Kingdom of Stordt

Galen: male Nordes warrior

Geoff: Prince of Lentz/son of Princess Isabella and Captain Josef

Geoff: Prince of Norkv/son of Benedict and Sasaha/grandson of Benjeman and Esther

George: an advisor for King Fahra of Zorta

George: middle son of Chief Duncan and Liza of the Clan of Gesmal in Ryed

Gita: wife of Hadi/ Ruala

Gladys: member of Nordes Tribe/ mother of Nikki

Glenda: great, great, great grandmother of Gala/ a healer from the Kingdom of Stordt

Grace: Princess of New Norkv/daughter of Benjeman and Esther

Gracie: cook for the Arthur Marcus family

Grady: worker for Gabriel

Great Ruler: God

Gregory Bancar: a wealthy landowner in the Kingdom of Wetpr and member of the Insidiae

Gunnel: Prince/ son of King Zachariah and Queen Noella of New Samona/husband of Uma/father of Elan/Ruala

Hadar: Prince/son of King Manu and Queen Delilia/Ruala

Hadi: son of Andrus and Naomi/brother of Rabi/Ruala

Hadu: female Ruala warrior

Hamon: one of the members of the Nordes Tribe who was injured in an attack at Snakes Crossing

Hamond: General of the Taperian Army who declares himself king

Hanger: one of the spies at the Castle at Wetpr

Hannah: physician in Nora/ Roch murdered her sister

Harold: owner of the general store in Nora

Harriet Marcus: mother of Hannah and Laurabelle/wife of Arthur

Hatus: General in the Army of Lentz/on loan to Sudfad

Hector: fighter hired by Juleta

Hector: Prince of Samona/son of Varden

Henry: and his wife Alice find Jorge in Nora

Henry: husband of Noreen/father of Jacob

Hermanas: second in command to Archetenus at Wall of Dorath

High Priest Aaron: member of the Patronus

High Priest Amos: a member of the Patronus

High Priest Barnabas: most Senior High Priest of the monastery at Leven

High Priest Caleb: member of the Patronus

High Priest Ephraim: a member of the Patronus

High Priest Gabriel: member of the Patronus/demon hunter

High Priest Gideon: a member of the Patronus

High Priest Gregory: member of the Patronus

High Priest Joseph: member of the Patronus, in charge of the Cicero Headquarters

High Priest Josiah: member of the Patronus

High Priest Meekos: priest at the monastery at Malga

High Priest Nicholas: most Senior High Priest of the monastery at Philiste and most Senior High Priest of the Patronus

High Priest Paulas: member of the Patronus

High Priest Phanuel: member of the Patronus

High Priest Philetus: member of the Patronus in charge of Malga Headquarters

High Priest Pravis: priest at the monastery at Malga

High Priest Raphael: a leader of the Patronus

High Priest Rueben: member of the Patronus in charge of Nora Headquarters

High Priest Silas: a member of the Patronus

High Priest Tenebrae: priest at the monastery at Malga

High Priest Timothy: was murdered by Meekos, Pravis and Tenebrae

High Priest Tyrus: a member of the Patronus

High Priest Uriel: member of the Patronus

High Priest Vincent: assigned to the monastery at Malga before he was murdered

High Priest Zophar: priest at monastery at Malga/ trained as a healer

Hores: son of Chief Romogi and Anda, Kingdom of Marba/Huta

Horta: Prince/son of Gunnel and Uma/nephew of King Manu of New Samona/brother of Elan/Ruala

Hunter: Prince of Samona/son of Varden

Ian: husband of Mia/ brother-in-law of Calen/ Ruala

Ibula: warrior princess and healer of the Ruala Tribe/daughter of King Manu and Queen Delilia/

Iden: warrior guarding refugees/Shettee

Igor: brother of King Sharonne

Imad: a male Grand Master of the Insidiae

Ina: daughter of Mia and Ian/ Ruala

Ingr: female warrior of Nordes Tribe

Inon: one of Cisero's men/a vessel

Ipos: an ancient demon/ one of the Old Ones

Iris: mother of Vivian/wife of Joshua/Clan of Gesmal in Ryed

Irit: daughter of Hadi and Gita/ Ruala

Isabella: Princes of Lentz, sister of Mathas, Renya and Tasha, married to Captain Josef

Isadore: wife of Fahron

Isla: female warrior of Nordes Tribe

Isla: daughter of Prince Lakin and Princess Zada/Ruala

Ivan: youngest son of Chief Duncan and Liza of the Clan of Gesmal in Ryed

Jace: husband of Oda/ brother-in-law of Calen/Ruala

Jack: member of governing body of Nora

Jackson: a private in the Army of Lentz

Jacob: boy who Angelina found in the woods

Jacot: son of Prince Lakin and Princess Zada/ grandson of King Manu/Ruala

Jaden: Sergeant in the Army of Lentz

Jago: son of Elen and Batya/ Ruala

Jake: works for Talverson Transport Company in Port Friada

Jakiv: Prince/son of Segal and Cahina/nephew of King Manu of New Samona/Ruala

Jama: Enrop leader who protects Chief Sorren's family

James: Taperian soldier

Janja: Princess/daughter of Gunnel and Uma/niece of King Manu of New Samona/ sister of Elan/Ruala

Jared: hired fighter

Jaretta: King of Stordt/husband of Queen Lillian/ father of Roch and Sudfad

Jarrod: works for Pravis/leads attack on castle in Wetpr

Jasper: Prince of Lentz/son of Princess Isabella and Captain Josef

Jatu: Enrop leader who protects Fahron's family

Jeb: friend of Thaos

Jeb: one of Cisero's men

Jela: Queen of Samona/wife of Varden

Jeremy: cousin of Andrew the jeweler in Salar

Jerik: a male Grand Master of the Insidiae

Jess: a soldier of Wetpr

Jillian: Queen of Ogg/wife of King Douma

Jinn: an ancient demon/ one of the Old Ones

Joao: male Ruala warrior

Jonas: Captain in the Taperian Army

Jorga: Princess of Ryed/daughter of Oren and Astrel/ has twin sister Andres

Jorge: a cook who is kidnapped from Endleson Hotel in Nora

Josef: Captain in the Lentz military/ married to Princess Isabella, sister of King Mathas

Joshua: father of Vivian/husband of Iris/Clan of Gesmal in Ryed

Juleta: cousin to Raul and Simon/daughter and oldest child of King Mathas and Queen Rosa

Kadin: a member of Valdore Tribe

Kagen: a man who kidnaps and exploits children

Karta: male Ruala warrior

Karzman: leader of Kozach Tribe/ stepfather of Michael

Kasper: Prince/son of Zeman and Oda/nephew of King Manu of New Samona/Ruala

Kata: Princess/daughter of Gunnel and Uma/niece of King Manu of New Samona/ sister of Elan/Ruala

Khryriss: an ancient demon/ one of the Old Ones

Kiana: Princess/daughter of Gunnel and Uma/niece of King Manu of New Samona/ sister of Elan/Ruala

Klass: Lieutenant in the Wetprian Army

Koby: male Ruala warrior

Koh: son of Prince Gael and Princess Mada/grandson of King Manu/Ruala

Kora: Princess/ married to Raphael son of King Zachariah and Queen Noella of New Samona/ mother of Luca/ Raphael and Kora were killed in battle when Luca was a small boy/Ruala

Korth: son of Tristt/Shettee

Kraus: hired fighter and intended vessel, works for Dieter

Kretcher: Commanding General of Fort Polta in Wetpr

Krister: Princess of Samoan/daughter of Thomas and Rewel

Kyra: young sister of Marie/ friend of Petra

Laban: Prince of Samona/son of Yorggi and Dion/grandson of Thomas and Rewel

Lael: daughter of Nina and Rhea/ Ruala

Lakin: Prince/son of King Manu and Queen Delilia/husband of Zada/Ruala

Lala: Princess/daughter of Adwell and Nada/niece of King Manu of New Samona/ sister of Misha/Ruala

Lana: female warrior of the Nordes Tribe

Lana: Princess/daughter of Segal and Cahina/niece of King Manu of New Samona/Ruala

Lani: daughter of Mia and Ian/Ruala

Lara: one of Usman's wives

Larson: a fighter hired by Juleta

Laurabelle: Hannah's sister who was murdered by Roch

Laurel: Annabelle's mother and former servant of King Roch's parents

Lazo: fighter hired by Juleta

Lea: Princess/daughter of Adwell and Nada/niece of King Manu of New Samona/ sister of Misha/Ruala

Leo: Prince of Samona/son of Darius and Rebek/grandson of Thomas and Rewel

Lila: seventeen year old girl who Luca saves from the Hutas/sister of Christopher

Lilian: female warrior of the Nordes Tribe

Lillian: Queen of Stordt/wife of Jaretta/ mother of Roch and Sudfad

Lily: daughter of Calen and Natasha/Ruala and human

Liza: wife of Duncan the Chief of the Clan of Gesmal in Ryed

Lloyd: banker in Nora

Loftus: Commanding General of Fort Styls

Loni: daughter of King Friada and Queen Marla of the Kingdom of Ganz

Louie: works for Talverson Transport Company in Port Friada

Luca: male Ruala warrior

Lucifer: an ancient demon/ one of the Old Ones

Luque: Prince/son of Segal and Cahina/nephew of King Manu of New Samona/Ruala

Mab: a female Grand Master of the Insidiae

Mabon: warrior guarding refugees/Shettee

Mada: Princess /wife of Prince Gael/Ruala

Madam Bular: owner of a dress shop in Port Friada

Maggie: elderly store owner in Salar

Mahon: son of King Neputa

Makalo: Prince of Norkv/husband of Grace who was the daughter of Benjeman and Esther

Malana: daughter of King Neputa

Mali: Princess of Norkv/daughter of Makalo and Grace/granddaughter of Benjeman and Esther

Maligma: an ancient demon/ one of the Old Ones

Malik: member of the Insidiae

Malus: sorcerer from Ryed

Mandrake: Taperian soldier

Manu: King of New Samona/The Chief of the Grand Council made up of Rualas and Shettees/ father of Ibula, Lakin, Gael and Hadar/husband of Delilia

Marcia: friend of Hannah's/ Roch's men murdered her family

Marcus Stephan: son of Stephan and Ingr

Margarit: daughter of King Mathas and Queen Rosa of the Kingdom of Lentz/ cousin of Raul and Simon

Margolia: girl from Nora who was sacrificed to a demon

Marie: a cook for King Sudfad and Queen Renya

Markus: a soldier in the Army of Wetpr

Marla: High Priest Meekos' housekeeper

Marla: Queen of the Kingdom of Ganz

Martha: a cook for Cerephus

Martin Froush: wealthy ship builder in Port Friada/husband of Denise

Mary: Jared's young wife who was brutally murdered by Hutas

Mata: Igor's wife

Mateo: Chief Healer of the Ruala Tribe

Mathas: King of Lentz/ brother to Queen Renya

Matilda: one of Usman's wives

Matthew: son of King Mathas and Queen Rosa of the Kingdom of Lentz/ cousin of Raul and Simon

Maxwell: father of Calen/ Ruala

Maxwell: infant son of Nina and Rhea/grandson of elder Maxwell/Ruala

Melanie: female Ruala warrior/daughter of Casey and Tasha

Melina: mother of Thaos

Melinda: grandmother of Misha

Mia: daughter of Maxwell and Emeral/ Ruala

Mia: female Ruala warrior/daughter of Tyron and Elsa

Mica: Princess of Norkv/daughter of Benedict and Sasaha/granddaughter of Benjeman and Esther

Micha: oldest son of Joshua and Iris/older brother of Vivian/Clan of Gesmal

Micha: son of King Sharonne/ grandfather of Sudfad and Roch

Michael: ancient king of Wetpr/father of Queen Sumona

Miranda: emissary of The Great Ruler who takes on the disguise of a human seer

Miriam: a friend of Hannah's/works at Endleson Hotel in Nora

Misha: male Ruala warrior/lieutenant

Molach: a member of the Insidiae

Moloch: an ancient demon/one of the Old Ones

Morris: member of governing body of Nora

Myla: wife of the owner of the Dragons Inn in Salar

Naal: warrior guarding refugees/Shettee

Nabi: male Ruala warrior

Nada: Princess/ married to Adwell son of King Zachariah and Queen Noella of New Samona/ mother of Misha/ Adwell was killed in battle leaving Nada to raise ten children/Ruala

Nadia: wife of Karzman

Naomi: mother of Rabi/ Ruala

Napo: Enrop leader who protects Claudius' family

Natasha: sister of High Priest Gabriel

Nathaniel: Sorren's oldest son/ Nordes Tribe

Nebula: son of Chief Romogi and Anda/ Kingdom of Marba/Huta

Nehmota: King of Ryed

Neputa: leader of the Shettee Tribe when it was conquered by the Hutas

Nestor: a demon that specializes in procuring things for a price

Nica: Enrop leader who protects Sudfad's family

Nicholas: orphan boy /brother of Cerey

Nicolas: Prince of Puntd/son of King Tobias and Queen Tasha

Nieatzae: an ancient demon/ one of the Old Ones

Nikki: female warrior of Nordes Tribe

Nina: daughter of Maxwell and Emeral/Ruala

Nina: youngest daughter of Karzman and Nadia

Nita: Princess/daughter of Adwell and Nada/niece of King Manu of New Samona/ sister of Misha/has twin brother Waed/Ruala

Nobel: former prince of Ryed/son of Akasha and Norah/father of Nehmota

Noella: the first Queen of New Samona/wife of King Zachariah/mother of seven sons/Ruala

Norah: former queen of Ryed/grandmother of Nehmota

Noreen: mother of Jacob/ wife of Henry

Norris: hired fighter and intended vessel, works for Dieter

Nyla: oldest daughter of Karzman and Nadia

Oda: daughter of Maxwell and Emeral/ Ruala

Oda: Princess/ married to Zeman son of King Zachariah and Queen Noella of New Samona/Ruala

Odam: male Ruala warrior

Odell: one of the spies at the Castle at Wetpr

Omar: Prince/son of Zeman and Oda/nephew of King Manu of New Samona/Ruala

Omara: Queen of Norkv/wife of Thaddius who was son of Benjeman and Esther

Omnibus: an ancient demon/ one of the Old Ones

Omoria: former queen of Ryed/wife of Nobel/mother of Nehmota

Opago: an ancient demon/ one of the Old Ones

Oren: former prince of Gandt who marries princess Astrel of Ryed

Ottillia: Princess of Lenz/daughter of Princess Isabella and Captain Josef

Padre Augustus: a member of the Patronus

Padre Bartholomew: survives the massacre at the monastery at Avaide

Padre Cornelius: a member of the Patronus

Padre Darius: a member of the Patronus

Padre Dibon: a priest at the monastery at Malga

Padre Dominick: priest at monastery at Malga

Padre Edgar: member of the Patronus

Padre Edward: a member of the Patronus

Padre Francis: priest at monastery at Malga

Padre Joram: member of the Patronus

Padre Lucas: a member of the Patronus

Padre Octavos: runs orphanage in Salar

Padre Philip: a member of the Patronus

Padre Philip: a priest at the monastery at Malga

Padre Simpson: priest at the monastery at Malga

Padre Sorben: a member of the Patronus

Padre Stephens: priest at monastery at Malga

Padre Thomas: priest at the monastery at Malga

Padre Tobias: a member of the Patronus

Padre Xavier: priest at monastery at Malga

Paj: Princess/wife of Prince Hadar/Ruala

Pata: daughter of Chief Romogi and Trina/Huta

Paul: third son of Joshua and Iris/younger brother of Vivian/Clan of Gesmal

Paulas: Sergeant under Archetenus in Taperian Army

Paulas: a man who works for Cicero/a vessel

Paullo: works for High Priest Meekos

Pearl: eldest daughter of King Tobias and Queen Tasha of Puntd

Pergo: King of the Kingdom of Gandt

Peter: Sorren's second son/Nordes Tribe

Peters: member of the governing body of Nora

Petorus: an ancient demon/one of the Old Ones

Petra: peasant boy from Ort who saves Padre Bartholomew

Philip: Prince of Puntd/ son of King Tobias and Queen Tasha

Phillip: Court Physician to the Royal Family of Wetpr

Polgate: one of the men who kidnapped Petra

Potomas: warrior guarding refugees/Shettee

Powell: a lieutenant in the Military of Lentz/stationed at Fahron's castle

Prescott: a hired killer

Rabi: male Ruala warrior

Radnor: a male Grand Master of the Insidiae

Rael: Prince of old Samona/husband of Krister who was the daughter of Thomas and Rewel

Rahi: a female Grand Master of the Insidiae

Rakio: Prince/son of Adwell and Nada/nephew of King Manu of New Samona/brother of Misha/Ruala

Rako: a male Ruala warrior

Raphael: Prince/ son of King Zachariah and Queen Noella of New Samona/husband of Kora/Ruala/father of Luca/ Raphael and Kora were killed in battle when Luca was a small boy/Ruala

Ratri: male Ruala warrior

Raul: Prince/son of King Sudfad and Queen Renya of the Kingdom of Wetpr

Raum: an ancient demon/ one of the Old Ones

Rebek: Princess of Samona/wife of Darius, who was the son of Thomas and Rewel

Renya: Queen of Wetpr/ wife of Sudfad

Rewel: Queen of Samona/wife of Thomas/mother of Varden

Rex: a notorious pick pocket in Port Friada

Rhea: husband of Nina/ brother-in-law of Calen/ Ruala

Riftca: male Ruala warrior

Roch: King of the Kingdom of Stordt/brother of King Sudfad

Rogers: one of the men who kidnapped Petra

Rolif: son of Chief Romogi and Silva/ Kingdom of Marba/Huta

Romale: member of the Insidiae

Romos: an elder of the Centras

Rosa: Queen of Lentz/wife of King Mathas

Rosalie: a dressmaker in Nora/wife of Peters

Ryan: grandson of Jeb/friend of Thaos

Sabot: member of the Insidiae

Sahil: a male Ruala warrior

Samara: wife of Tristt/Shettee

Samat: son of Chief Romogi and Silva/ Kingdom of Marba/Huta

Samos: Prince of Norkv/son of Thaddius

Sampson: oldest son of Chief Duncan and Liza of the Clan of Gesmal in Ryed

Sampson: Sergeant in the Taperian Army

Samuel: a high priest at the monastery at Malga who was murdered

Samuel: Prince of the original Samona/grandson of Thomas and Rewel

Samuel: second son of Raul and Vitomas

Sanuri: a holy man/emissary of The Great Ruler/warrior

Sar: an Enrop

Sar: male Ruala warrior

Sara: daughter of Usman

Sarah: baby granddaughter of Mathas and Rosa

Sarah: housekeeper for Claudius and Bella

Saran: daughter of Karzman and Nadia

Sasaha: Princess of the original Samona/granddaughter of Thomas and Rewel

Sasha: female warrior of the Nordes Tribe/wife of Galen

Satan: an ancient demon/ one of the Old Ones

Saunders: a Taperian soldier

Schroeder: man who works for Insidiae leader Dieter

Segal: Prince/ son of King Zachariah and Queen Noella of New Samona/husband of Cahina/Ruala

Seguna: former princess of Ryed/daughter of Akasha and Norah/ committed suicide

Selen: house keeper for Juleta

Shara: wife of Sorren/Nordes Tribe

Sharonne: King of Stordt; great, great, grandfather of King Roch and King Sudfad

Shon: son of King Fahra and Queen Sitha

Shone: Princess/daughter of Zeman and Oda/niece of King Manu of New Samona/Ruala

Sicily Bella: daughter of Stephan and Ingr

Sila: Princess of Ogg

Silva: one of Chief Romogi's three wives/Huta

Simmons: Commanding General of Fort Nir

Simon: adopted son of King Sudfad and Queen Renya of the Kingdom of Wetpr

Sinclair: King of Lentz/father of King Mathas

Sirius: works for High Priest Meekos

Sitha: Queen of Zorta

Smoking Joe: a regular patron at the Ghost Ship Tavern

Sonja: female warrior of the Nordes Tribe

Sophie: cook and servant of King Roch

Sorren: leader of the Nordes Tribe

Sporos: priest turned demon

Stephan: Captain in Army of Lentz/son of Claudius and Bella

Stiller: a fighter hired by Juleta

Stolas: an ancient demon/one of the Old Ones

Stone: hired fighter and intended vessel, works for Dieter

Sudfad: King of the Kingdom of Wetpr and brother to King Roch of Stordt

Sudfad: little Sudfad is grandson of King Sudfad

Sumona: Queen of Wetpr/wife of Alexandras/aunt of Roch and Sudfad

Syrius: a Bakken hired by Juleta

Tabeth: daughter of Fahron

Tabith: son of Tristt/Shettee

Tabitha: Princess of Lentz/daughter of Princess Isabella and Captain Josef of Lentz

Tadeo: Prince/son of Adwell and Nada/nephew of King Manu of New Samona/brother of Misha/Ruala

Tafer: a warlord who drove the Hutas out of the Kingdom of Norkv after years of wars and rebellions

Tahira: Princess of Samona/granddaughter of Thomas and Rewel

Tahira: a female Grand Master of the Insidiae

Tal: son of Oda and Jace/ Ruala

Talmai: Shettee boy who Thedes and Ibula adopt

Tambor: male Ruala warrior

Tamour: General in the Army of Lentz/on loan to Sudfad

Tanner: a Sergeant in the Army of Lentz

Tapster: a demon who works for Meekos

Tarig: a lieutenant in the Huta army

Tarin: son of King Neputa and Queen Tiara/Shettee

Taron: Prince/son of Adwell and Nada/nephew of King Manu of New Samona/brother of Misha/Ruala

Tasha: Queen of Puntd/ married to Tobias/ sister of Renya and Mathas

Tasha: female Ruala warrior/mother of Melanie/wife of Casey

Tate: a Lieutenant in the Wetprian Army

Tavin: son of Prince Lakin and Princess Zada/Ruala

Tega: housekeeper for the cabins of the captains of the Taperian Army

Tegman: soldier of Wetpr

Temark: villager of Neva

Thadddius: Prince of the new Kingdom of Norkv/son of Benjeman

Thaddies: member of Nordes Tribe/ father of Ingr

Thanatoes: an ancient demon/ one of the Old Ones

Thaos: a hired fighter

Thatcher: Prince/son of Zeman and Oda/nephew of King Manu of New Samona/Ruala

Thatus: Taperian soldier

The Lion: emissary of The Great Ruler who takes on the appearance of a lion when he is in the world of man

Thedes: warrior guarding refugees/Shettee

Thomas: King of the original Kingdom of Samona/father of Varden

Thomas: second son of Joshua and Iris/older brother of Vivian/Clan of Gesmal

Thomas: the young husband of Zoya who was murdered in Taperia

Thompson: Wetprian soldier

Thronson: one of Meekos hired killers

Tiara: Queen of Shettee Tribe when it was conquered by Hutas/wife of Neputa

Timothy: son of Fahron

Tito: member of Valdore Tribe

Titus Derek: son of Thaos and Nikki

Titus: a lieutenant in the Taperian Army

Tobart: a member of the Nordes Tribe

Tobias: King of Puntd.

Tomas: works for High Priest Pravis

Tome: a businessman and member of the Insidiae in Nora

741

Tomi: son of Usman the leader of the Valdore Tribe

Toomback: Huta warrior

Torance: father of Thaos

Torin: oldest son of Karzman and Nadia

Tratz: one of the men who kidnapped Petra

Travor: Taperian warrior who was injured at the Wall of Dorath

Tresdore: son of King Sharonne

Trevor: Prince/son of Zeman and Oda/nephew of King Manu of New Samona/Ruala

Tria: daughter of Oda and Jace/Ruala

Trina: one of Chief Romogi's three wives/Huta

Trina: Princess/daughter of Zeman and Oda/niece of King Manu of New Samona/Ruala

Trist: a male Ruala warrior

Tristt the Horrible: Shettee warrior

Tye: Prince of Norkv/son of Princess Grace and Prince Makalo

Tyron: male Ruala warrior/father of Mia/husband of Elsa

Tyson: Wetprian soldier

Ulger: a demon

Uma: Princess/ married to Gunnel son of King Zachariah and Queen Noella of New Samona/mother of Elan/Ruala

Umar: Prince/son of Adwell and Nada/nephew of King Manu of New Samona/brother of Misha/Ruala

Uri: son of Nina and Rhea/ Ruala

Usman: leader of the Valdore Tribe

Valor: Prince of the new Kingdom of Norkv/son of Benjeman and Esther

Vandrew: Petra's male tutor

Vania: Princess of Samona/daughter of Yorggi and Dion/granddaughter of Thomas and Rewel

Varden: last king of Samona/he and his family were murdered by rebels

Vardin: one of the men who kidnapped Petra

Vasart: Queen of Ryed/ wife of Nehmota

Vinca: Queen of Stordt, wife of Sharonne

Vincent: Prince of Ryed/son of Nehmota and Vasart

Vinus: Queen of the Kingdom of Gandt

Vitomas: Queen of Stordt

Vivian: a demon hunter from the Clan of Gesmal

Voltar: Prince of Samona/son of Darius and Rebek/grandson of Thomas and Rewel/later becomes King of Wetpr

Waed: Prince/son of Adwell and Nada/nephew of King Manu of New Samona/brother of Misha/has twin sister Nita/Ruala

Wallis: member of governing body of Nora

Wilard: Captain at Fort Polta

Willis: son of King Pergo and Queen Vinus/ Kingdom of Gandt

Xeni: a female Grand Master of the Insidiae

Yara: daughter of Nina and Rhea/Ruala

Yorggi: Prince of Samona/son of Thomas and Rewel/brother of Varden

Yori: son of Usman the leader of the Valdore Tribe

Yuri: Prince/son of Adwell and Nada/nephew of King Manu of New Samona/brother of Misha/Ruala

Zac: one of the men who kidnapped Petra

743

Zachariah: first King of New Samona/husband of Queen Noella/father of seven sons/Ruala

Zada: Princess/wife of Prince Lakin/Ruala

Zadok: a male Grand Master of the Insidiae

Zede: an ancient demon/ one of the Old Ones

Zehmann: an ancient demon/ one of the Old Ones

Zeman: Prince/ son of King Zachariah and Queen Noella of New Samona/husband of Oda/Ruala

Zorda: Taperian soldier injured in battle at the Wall of Dorath

Zoya: a seer from Taperia

Glossary of Terms

Aboultis: the calling cards of demons

Abyss: a vast void used to imprison demons

Acura: the whispering shadows/are in the inner circle of demons that directly serve the Old Ones

Amark: ancient language of The Great Ruler

Amulth: means filth in the language of demons/these monsters are made out of the waste of tortured souls from the hell dimensions

Anewa: one of seven continents in the World of Nunc

Aplewort: an herb when mixed with water purges poisons from a body

Asherane: ancient tribe that lived in the northern regions of the Kingdom of Lentz

Astras: the ancient underground city of the Centras

Beltrad: a species of lower level demons

Blood rings: Large red rubies set in silver with markings of the Old Ones

Boca: a covered wagon pulled by horses

Box of Itifer: a gift to the world of man from The Great Ruler; this gift affects the balance of creation

Bozie: a game of skill played by the Nordes Tribe

Cava plant: a poisonous plant that grows freely near bodies of water

Centras: ancient race of creatures who have the responsibility of protecting the Holy Box of Itifer

Chalice of Ascension: a gift from The Great Ruler, this gift contains unimaginable powers

Cicero College: in Wetpr, outside of Salar, where Raul, Simon and Hannah attended college

Clan of Gesmal: a tribe of demon hunters who live in the southern region of the Kingdom of Ryed

745

Crystal pillars: in the Ice Caves of Mordv/are blessed by The Great Ruler and filled with spiritual life force

Czarsta: one of seven continents in the World of Nunc

Demalogs: an inferior species of demons

Demosa: a slow acting poison from the cava plant

Diamond of Cazo: a gift from The Great Ruler, this gift can unleash powers from the center of the world

Durisks: large demonic birds/their elongated beaks contain rows of fangs

Engas: a wild cat that inhabits the Vandrew Mountains

Engor: a small pack animal that lives in trees

Enrop: a large species of bird that can speak many human languages

Farduth: a Shettee necklace that symbolizes a male has completed his rite of passage to become a warrior

Gafet: an ancient Shettee weapon

Gants: large apelike creatures/Watchers of the Caves of Muldun

Gate of Isula: the only opening in the great Wall of Dorath

Gefrey Games: games of sport where men fight each other and great beasts to the death

Grand Masters: the first people to call to the demons and invite them into this world

Great Ruler: God

Hall of Antiquities: a giant hall located in the monastery at Malga/ a sanctuary for holy items and manuscripts

Hall of Light: the Great Hall in the Ice Caves of Mordv

Hengers: giant blue eagles/ birds of war

Highland Pass: the only passage through the Rosu Mountain Range

Holy Scrolls: gifts given to each kingdom by The Great Ruler, these gifts contain powers, wisdom and immortality

Holy Vault: a secret vault under the King's study in the castle in Wetpr designed to protect holy objects

Horn of Asher: a horn used by the Patronus warrior priests to signal each other

Horn of Cass: a horn used by the Wetprian soldiers to signal each other

Horn of Cornwell: a horn used by Dieter's men to signal each other

Horn of Eel: a horn used by the Ruala warriors to communicate with each other

Horn of Esker: a horn used by the Valdore Tribe to communicate with each other

Horn of Ire: a horn carried by the Taperian soldiers to communicate with each other

Horn of Shana: a horn carried by the soldiers of Lentz to communicate with each other

Horn of Tula: a horn used by the members of the Nordes Tribe for communication

Horn of Vamont: a horn used by the Kozach Tribe for communication

Horn of Xepoltr: a horn used by the Shettee warriors to communicate

Huta: a race of humans that is driven by hatred and ideas of racial superiority who live in the Kingdom of Marba

Insidiae: means conspirators/a highly organized secret group of humans who have sold their souls to demons

Jacar: giant leech-like creatures

Jacept Plant: a plant that a powerful poison is made from

Kafer: a small crescent shaped knife carried by the Beltrad

Keepers of the Scrolls: the Royal Family of the Kingdom of Wetpr entered into a covenant with The Great Ruler to protect his gifts until a time when they can be safely given back to the world of man

Kozach: a tribe that lives in the far north central regions of the Kingdom of Wetpr

Lamsman: an ankle bracelet worn by Venatores/stones in the bracelet signify great feats they had to accomplish to become a demon hunter

Linges plant: a plant that grows in damp, swampy regions in Opots/the white berries are used to make the drug Melanwhop

Mark of Satan: a coiled red snake with green eyes and a yellow tongue

Matu potage: a food staple of the Shettee Tribe

Mayka: one of seven continents in the World of Nunc

Melanwhop: a drug made from the linges plant, causes lethargy and apathy

Mordov: the special place in hell for hypocrites

Motfer: the land of the dead

Nefandus: a secret sect within the Insidiae

Nordes: a tribe of fiercely trained warriors who live in the northern region of the Kingdom of Lentz

Nunc: the world where this story takes place

Old Ones: the original demons that came to the World of Nunc

Opatu bread: a food staple of the Shettee Tribe

Opots: one of seven continents in the World of Nunc/the continent where this story takes place

Oran: a tobisk that is filled with a mixture of ramni oil, buruto powder and meno salts, designed to explode on impact

Patronus: an elite group of men who serve as the protectors of the church

Porto: one of seven continents in the World of Nunc

Prostras: an ancient tribe that once inhabited the Ice Caves of Mordv

Raftifa: ancient bat-like creatures that devour human flesh

Ravens: messengers used by the dark lords

Recupero: a sect within the Insidiae that worships the demon Omnibus

Rogetts: a tribe of humans that have digressed into murderous mutant monsters

Rualas: an ancient tribe of warriors said to be half human and half bird

Salszar: one of seven continents in the World of Nunc

Salts of Envoy: a sleeping potion

Scio: a crystal ball

Scroll of Imari: a gift of The Great Ruler, a scroll that unleashes the power of the Box of Itifer

Seal of Natun: a gift from the Holy Ruler that can open doors to other worlds

Serpents of Satan: can only be called forth by dark lords and demons, large red snakes with green eyes and yellow tongues

Seven Sons Prophesy: an ancient prophesy about seven sons who stand up against the demons and dark lords

Shesone: an ancient fighting style of the Shettee Tribe

Shettee: an ancient tribe of warriors said to be half human and half lion

Solv: a specific prison within the Abyss

Song of the Second Son: an ancient prophesy about an evil that is passed between second sons of a family resulting in a monster that brings terror and darkness to the world of man

Sundra Templer: a gift from The Great Ruler that was stolen by dark lords/an orb with extraordinary powers that can be used in multiple ways such as transporting humans through other worlds

Tabutu: an ancient form of fighting developed by the Asherane Tribe of the Kingdom of Lentz

Talisman: an object with magical or supernatural meaning

Talmuth: giant red dragon-like creatures

Tangers: large wild, grazing animals that travel in herds

Tansof: one of seven continents in the World of Nunc

Telgras: a hell beast that looks like it is half wolf and half panther

Teragon: death terror/a monster created as a result of diabolical acts

Terbot bear: a bear that roams in the northern regions of the Continent of Opots

Tervator: fourteen foot monster that walks like a man with long dark hair over its entire body and bull-like horns protruding from its head

Texts of Semalia: ancient texts about demonic language and rituals

The Celebration of Days: an annual celebration of the Centras

The Hall of Understanding: the building in Astras where the history of the Centras is documented in drawings

The Hunters: another name for the Shettee Tribe

The Lion: a very powerful messenger of The Great Ruler assumes the form of a lion when he walks in the worlds of man

The thirteenth color: not seen in the world of man it is the color of horror/hell

Timbar: ghost dragons/ demons that can fly

Tinchure water: an herbal pain remedy used by the Nordes Tribe

Tincture of the Redeti Plant: Hutas dip the tips of their weapons in this insect infested liquid. The insects lay eggs inside of the victim. When the eggs are mature and hatch, two inch worm-like creatures are produced and will eat the organs of the victim causing a long and painful death

Tobisks: sphere shaped objects, metal and hollow inside that are designed to be launched from a Trebuchet

Trebuchets: wooden machines used to catapult objects

Tygrus: a ship that docked in Port Friada

Unholy altar: altar used to worship demons

Valdees: the tribe that lives in the underwater Kingdom of Ogg

Valdore: a tribe of merciless separatists who live in the extreme northern regions of the Kingdom of Lentz

Venator: means hunter in the old language

Venom of the Atha serpent: one of the poisons that Hutas put on their arrows

Vessel of Darkness: a human created from darkness to hold the essence of a powerful demon

Wall of Dorath: a giant wall that separates the Kingdoms of Norkv and Xepoltr from the Kingdom of Marba

Willimonns: small furry creatures that are hunted for food and sport

Xelope: the oneness of spirit with all that lives

Zendoti: demons that are distinguished by the geometrically shaped tuffs of hair that protrude from their heads

Glossary of Maps

The maps are displayed in order of relevance

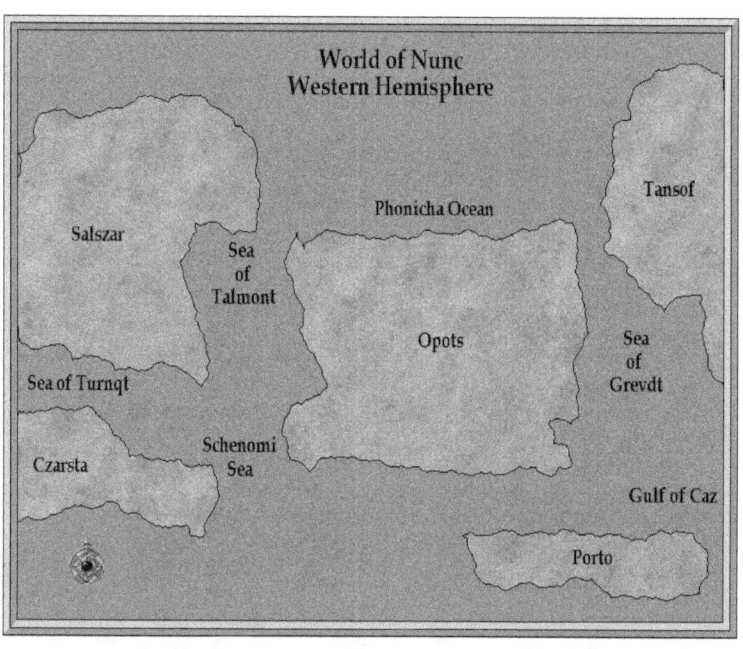

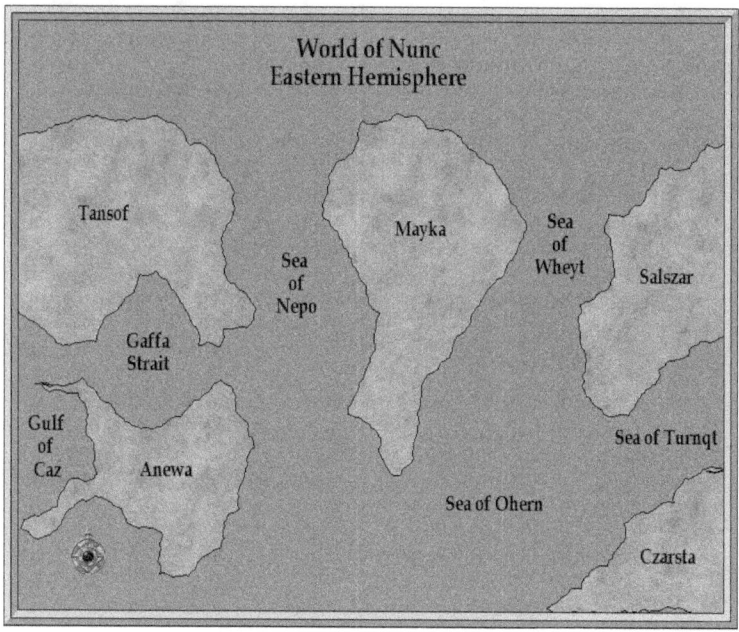

Continent of Opots

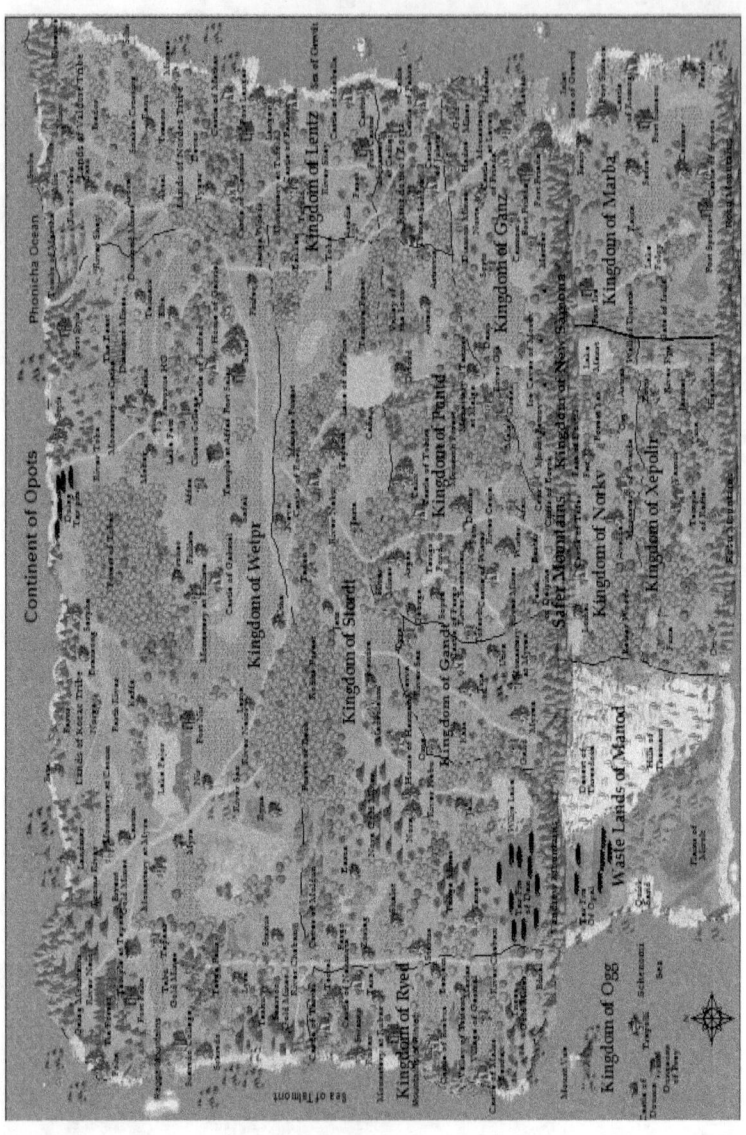

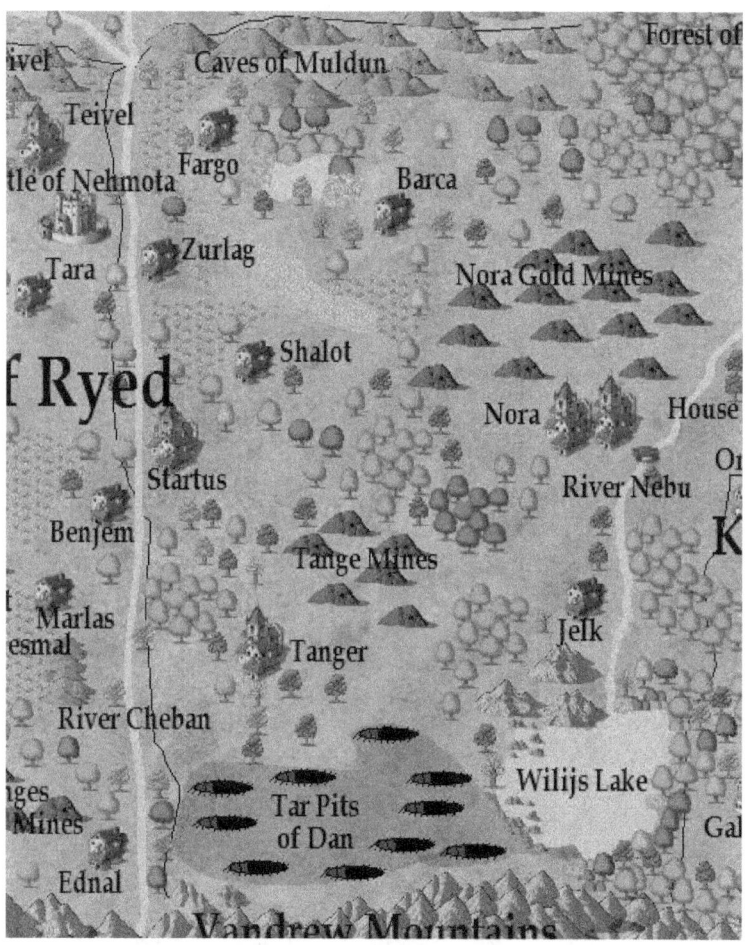

Northern Stordt

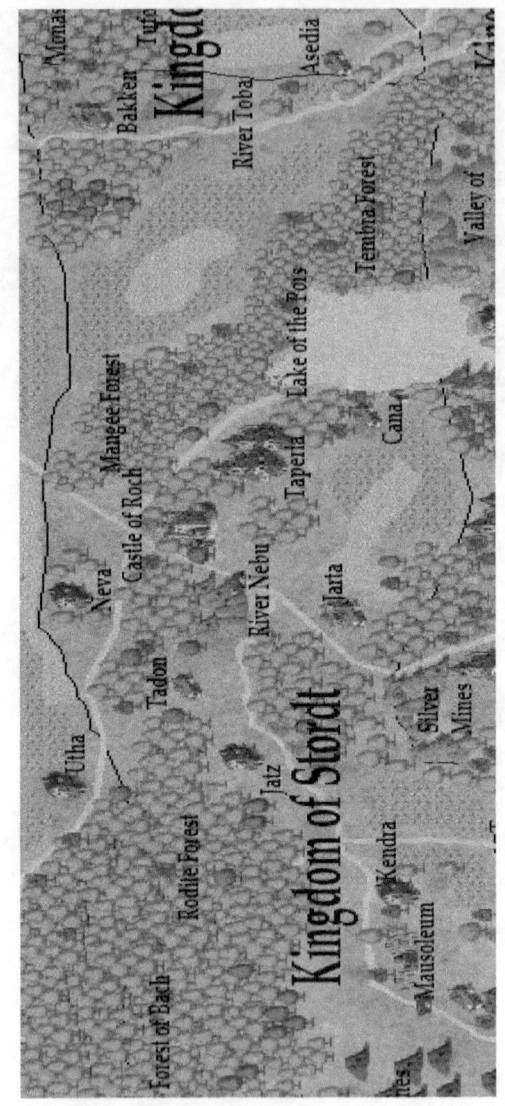

Western Wetpr

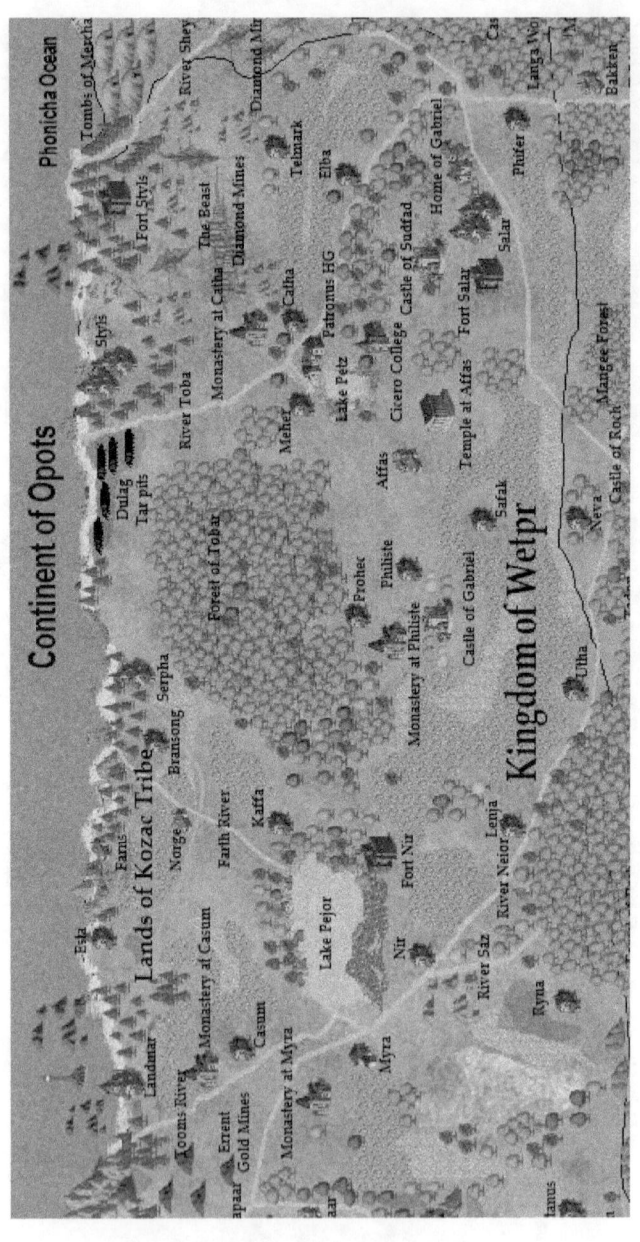

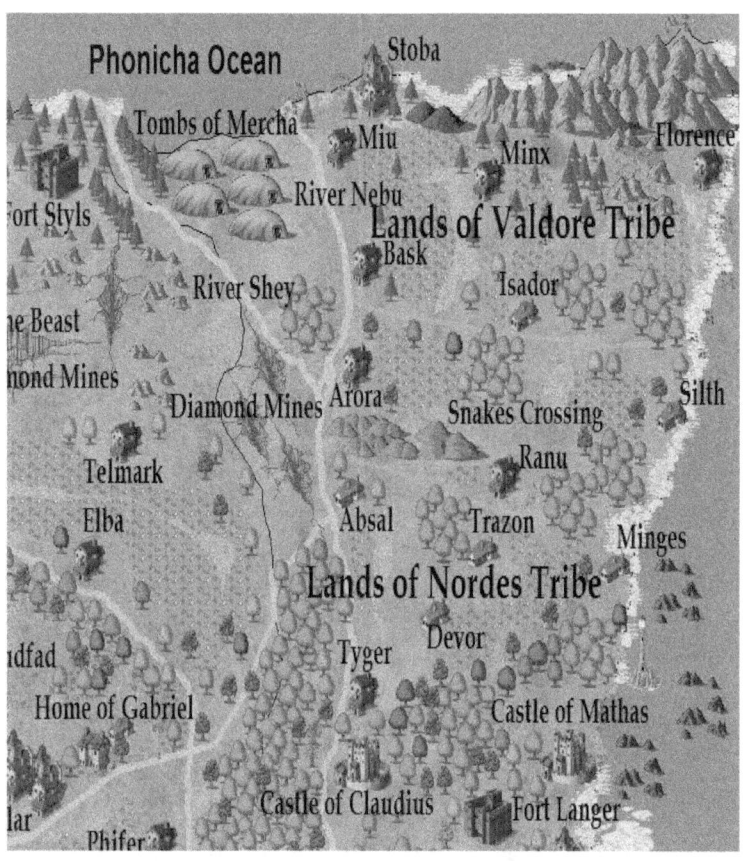

Marba

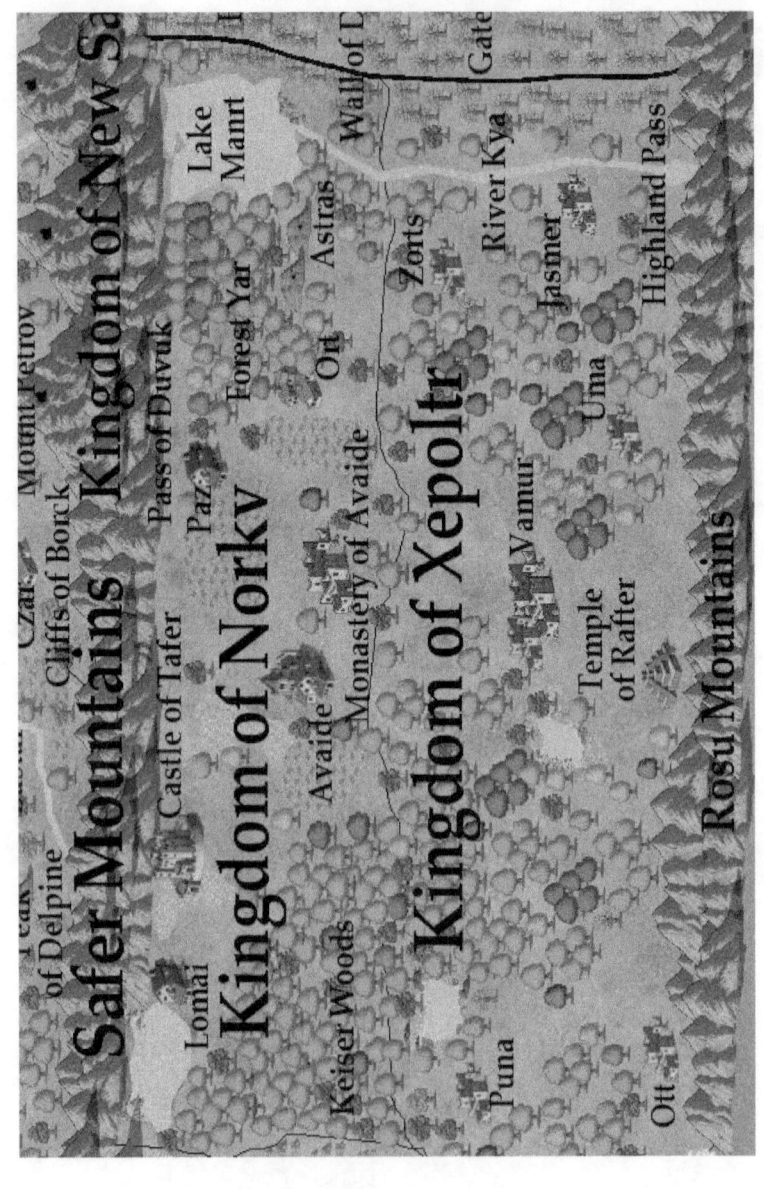

Waste Lands of Manod

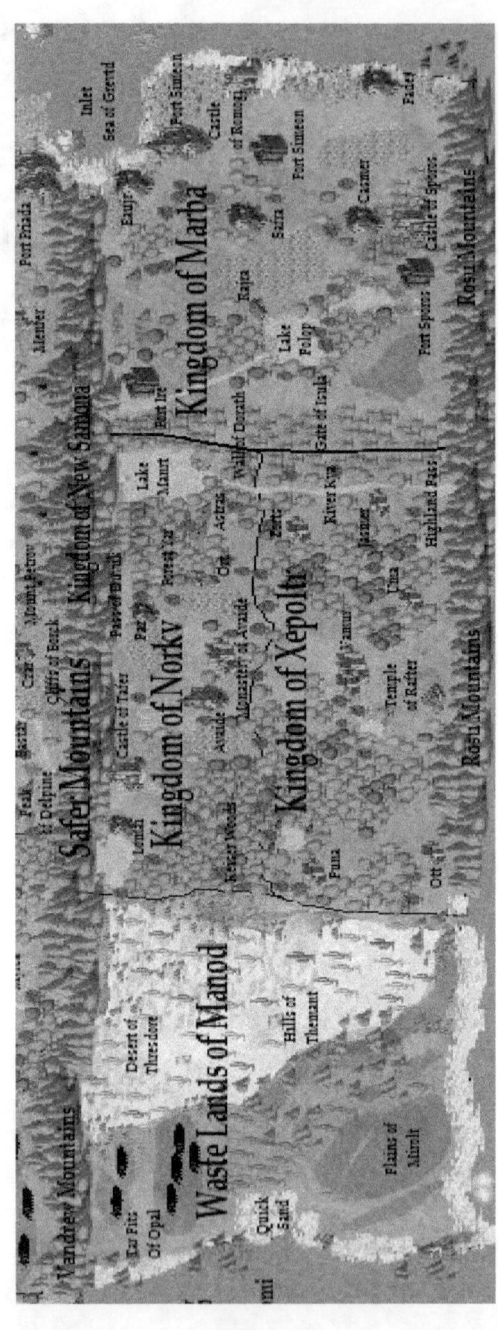

www.ingramcontent.com/pod-product-compliance
Lightning Source LLC
Chambersburg PA
CBHW070532030726
47505CB00001B/16